DOUGLAS TERMAN
SHELL GAME

"A HIGH-VOLTAGE THRILLER.... READERS
WILL BE LEFT WONDERING JUST HOW
MUCH OF *SHELL GAME* IS FICTION AND
HOW MUCH IS FACT ... A SHATTERING DE-
NOUEMENT."

—*Washington Times*

"Memorable aviation writing... Terman is a fine
writer, and his Cuban scenes are excellent.... In no
time we are immersed in a breathlessly exciting chase
sequence ... HIGH-VOLTAGE."

—*Cleveland Plain Dealer*

"[Terman] is especially good in portraying the com-
plexities of the shadowy world of the intelligence op-
erative, whether CIA or KGB, and obviously writes
from personal acquaintance with the weapons systems and advanced technology of the nuclear age."

—*Washington Post*

"A COMMANDO-STYLE THRILLER.... FANS
OF HIGH-CALIBER DRAMA ... WILL FIND
REWARDS APLENTY HERE...."

—*Publishers Weekly*

Books by Douglas Terman

First Strike
Free Flight
Shell Game

Published by POCKET BOOKS

DOUGLAS TERMAN

PUBLISHED BY POCKET BOOKS NEW YORK

All of the characters in this book (other than those normally residents of the USSR and the Republic of Cuba) are fictitious and any resemblance to actual persons living or dead is therefore coincidental. For clarity, the missiles referred to in this book are designated by their NATO code names, rather than the Soviet terminology.

POCKET BOOKS, a division of Simon & Schuster, Inc.
1230 Avenue of the Americas, New York, N.Y. 10020

Copyright © 1985 by Douglas Terman
Cover artwork copyright © 1986 Dan Osyczka
Map by Jeanyee Wong

Published by arrangement with the author
Library of Congress Catalog Card Number: 84-17889

ISBN 0-671-53291-X

First Pocket Books mass-market printing March, 1986

10 9 8 7 6 5 4 3 2 1

POCKET and colophon are registered trademarks of Simon & Schuster, Inc.

Printed in the U.S.A.

ACKNOWLEDGMENTS

To Commander Harold Feeney,
United States Naval Intelligence, Ret.
To Oscar Dalam and his box of tricks
To Jeanne Bernkopf and Ann Patty
for their clarity and insight
And to my good friend and not-so-secret agent,
Al Zuckerman

Dedicated to a someday free Cuba
and to those who lived and died for that dream:
Quijote, Pecos, Sea Fury, Rebeca,
Tony, Mononín, Waldo, and Pete

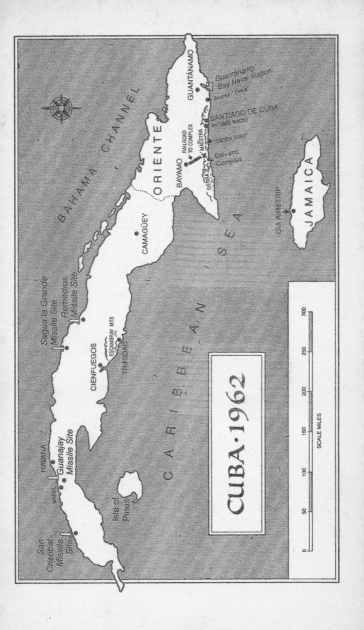

CUBA·1962

CHAPTER

1

Oriente Province, Cuba,
August 30, 1962

He was running badly, his mind out of touch with the rhythm of his body. The shock of each stride was transmitted up through bone, through joint, through muscle—the accumulative pain tearing at the fabric of his lungs. His heart, trapped within the cage of his chest, hammered in agony. They were behind him, gaining ground, and Brocassie knew he could not last much longer.

He glanced up, trying to divert his mind from the endless strip of flinty ground beneath his pounding feet. The horizon, far, unobtainable, was like an image thrown by a defective movie projector, a vision of sun and sky and earth blurred with each pounding impact of his stride, as if the mechanism had lost its ability to synchronize.

Goddamn amateur, he swore to himself, for he realized that he had begun to match the sucking of his lungs to the beat of his legs, something that his father had always warned against—the mark of a runner who has reverted to thoughtless automation rather than retaining the discipline of the mind.

Brocassie purposely broke his breathing away from the rhythm of his stride, inhaling more deeply, holding his breath and expelling it from his lungs in explosions. He changed pace slightly, slowing and lengthening his stride, eating up ground on the level crest of a ridge, then leaning forward, increasing his gait, shortening his stride as he scrambled down an embankment, through a dry, rutted stream bed and then up a steep slope to the next ridge. The glare from the setting sun reduced his vision to a looping blur of crimson, making it impossible to avoid the branches of desert scrub which whipped against his legs and lower body. Occasionally, he could catch glimpses of the sea which lay beyond the arid foothills of the Sierra, but it was too far, he knew. Perhaps too far ever to reach.

"Another ... minute," he gasped aloud. Just one more minute and then another and perhaps another. But not more than that. For distance was no longer the deciding factor. Now it was a race between him and the men behind him to darkness. And darkness might mean survival.

The rucksack cut into the flesh of his shoulders, and it beat its own flopping cadence against his back. To have dropped it, back when the patrol had first spotted him, might have been a temporary salvation, perhaps improving his speed and endurance to a point where he could outdistance the patrol until darkness had come. And then he would have cut back and to the west, resting, while they overran his position. But the load was necessary to see him through the desert and down to the coast, a matter of two days in a hostile environment. Without the food and water, he might die and then they would have won by default. Eventually, some patrol would find him, desiccated, his eyes gone to the birds, and they would display photos of him—another failed enemy of the revolution. Another gangster—a *mercenario* paid for by the imperialists. He had seen the photos pinned to a billboard outside a store in El Corojo—grainy shots of men warped in death, their shirts stained black with dried blood, and beneath the photos, a sloppy cartoon of an Uncle Sam in striped trousers, black coat and top hat, paying dollars to men with piglike faces.

The vehicle was still back there and gaining. He knew that without turning. For the only sounds now were those of his own body's efforts and of the roaring of their engine. Beyond that, there was nothing, as if God had vacuumed up all other sounds of the universe. There was no wind, only the faint cooling of air pushed aside by his own body.

They were good, he thought. Not city boys unused to the bush. More likely, men drawn from the surrounding mountains. They were not expert with the four-wheel drive, but they had used the contours of the terrain to their advantage and had kept the pace up, almost as if they were enjoying a hunt, tiring out the game, setting it up for a final kill. There had been no wild firing by them when they were still at a great distance, just the one warning shot. Their rough brand of professionalism would impel them to bear down on him, slowly closing the gap. There would be one clean shot, at most two. A third would be unthinkable, too amateurish for men like these.

It had been a fine balance, he realized. A man on foot, running directly across the high desert, pitted against the four-wheel drive which had to slow to prevent overheating or damage to the tires. The vehicle was forced to take the longer path, skirting the ravines and flinty outcrops. Once he had looked back, when they were still over a mile away, and they had stopped to add water to the radiator. But patience in a hunt is everything, Brocassie knew. And eventually, the dumb strength of a diesel engine would outlast a runner's heart and will.

He looked up again. The sun seemed to be bouncing on the horizon, squashing into a flattened ball of incandescent heat, going a darker red like a near-molten cannonball, slowly cooling. There was a chance now and he concentrated hard to clear his mind of fear.

The men in the vehicle were very good. He had already acknowledged that. But so was the runner. As he watched in his mind, the runner swept a stalk of barren grape weed from between two rocks, never altering his pace or rhythm. He bruised the weed in the palm of his hand so that it became a ball, and then took it on his tongue, causing the saliva to flow, easing the rawness in his throat. His father had shown him that—the proper plants, not the moist ones, because they gave their little burst of sweetness, clotting the mouth when the moisture was gone. Take the bitter ones, his father had said, the acid ones. They were the stimulators of flow, like citrus, and they lasted. For one more minute. Just one more.

Detached, Brocassie could hear himself gasping, but it was a controlled explosion of breath with a smooth, steady intake, as if his lungs could reduce each molecule of oxygen to its separate atoms, and then split those to gain the energy of the individual particles.

Finally, the sun was gone, down to the belly of the earth. Twilight would last no more than a few more minutes, and he knew that he would last at least that long. Ninety strides a minute, he calculated. And started to count them out.

They would be worried now, he thought. Tempted to take a shot before they lost him in darkness. Now was the critical time, and again he concentrated on his body, trying to extract the most from it. Lungs and breathing. Try to keep their rhythm separate from that of his legs. Elbows in, forearm cocked, just a light tension in the wrists, fists closed but not clenched.

From behind him, he heard the howl of the four-wheel drive's engine gearing down for the loose sand on the grade he had just breasted. Two hundred yards behind him, he thought. No more.

Now, if ever, they would try for a shot. The light was decaying but he was still silhouetted against the skyline. He picked up the pace, overreaching his reserves. By shifting his weight forward, he lengthened his stride, ready to sprint and weave if they fired. But there was very little left to draw on.

That the patrol had even spotted him had been a fluke of bad luck. Brocassie had first seen them at a distance of over two miles in the late afternoon. At that time, he had already committed himself to the desert, moving down from the rocky uplands, following the slope of the escarpment, his cover thinning from stunted pines and bush to desert plants and scrub. At first sight of them, he had thrown himself down on the dirt and waited, but a telltale cloud of dust from his own passage hung in the thin crystal air like a banner of betrayal. The vehicle had paused for a long time and then had altered its direction toward him, crawling down the eroded slopes toward the intermediate coastal plain. It was then they had fired just one warning shot.

Brocassie had first crouched and assessed the distance they would have to close to be within accurate rifle range, and then had turned west toward the remaining ridge of rumpled foothills, which, when breasted, would fold down to the sea. The sun was low and he had estimated no more than an hour to sundown. Add to that ten minutes of tropical twilight and then blackness and no moon until late into the morning hours. Standing up, Brocassie had begun to run in a smooth gait toward the sun, looking back only often enough to judge the rate of closure.

At first, the patrol had closed rapidly. Perhaps there was a road which he could not see from his lower elevation, but after a while, the vehicle paralleled him, drawing no closer. Eventually, he turned again and saw them descending a steep grade. From there on in, it was more of an equal contest. Twice he had seen them stopped, perhaps stuck or changing a tire. He had no doubt that the tires would be in poor condition, as most tires were these days in Cuba. No more replacements from Goodyear or Firestone. Brocassie had heard that all the tires in Cuba were being recapped, sometimes three and four times before they finally gave out. Fabricio, the night before he had been swallowed by napalm, had joked with him over a campfire that it was probably the same way with condoms.

During one of the vehicle's pauses, Brocassie had stopped to drink what little remained of his next-to-last bottle of water. Across the distance, he studied the men and the vehicle with the small binoculars. No whip antenna so there would be no radio, no air strike. The vehicle was not a jeep but a short-frame Land Rover, probably liberated from the sugar mills or nickel mines. Some sort of indistinct logo was stenciled on the hood but he couldn't make out what it was.

While one of the men worked on a tire, the other stood up in the vehicle and uncased a pair of binoculars and the pursued and the pursuer studied each other across two miles of desert.

The pursuer was an older man, mid-fifties and deeply

tanned with tabs of an NCO on his collar. As Brocassie watched, the NCO lowered his binoculars and cased them, then said something to the other man who had just stood up, wiping his hands on his pants. Then looking back, the NCO lifted his weapon. The sun glinted on a sporting rifle with telescopic sights and Brocassie could see the man smile, his white teeth distinct against the dark tan of his face. It was then that Brocassie realized that there would be no prisoner taken.

As he watched them, knowing that when he moved they would move too, Brocassie hyperventilated and concentrated on his heartbeat, willing it to slow, imagining his arteries expanding and his lungs swelling. He saw them start first, a sort of violation of the unspoken rules which they had established. The dirt spurted under the Rover's wheels and the vehicle wheeled directly toward him. Brocassie dropped the binoculars, no longer wanting their weight. But he turned to his pursuers and stood upright for a few more seconds as a gesture of defiance and then made a fist with his third finger extended, scything it upward toward the sun. Then he turned southwest again, pounding out the miles.

About half an hour before sundown, Brocassie had thought he had lost. The vehicle had been close enough for him to hear the grinding of the Land Rover's gears. He glanced back and saw the vehicle closing rapidly over a patch of baked ground, probably less than three hundred yards distant. He was only minutes from death. Adrenaline flooded his veins. Sprinting, Brocassie pounded over fifty yards to a shallow *arroyo,* and then hunching, scuttled back to the right to intersect the path of the vehicle. He flopped down and dug the container of plastic explosive from his pack, forming a crude sphere the size of a plum from the C-4. Into this, he inserted a three-second squib. Panting heavily, he waited, watching from the base of scrub bush that edged the lip of the *arroyo.*

As he watched, the vehicle veered through ninety degrees, turning away from him, the patrol obviously thinking that he had moved south in the ravine rather than north. Brocassie carefully eased the pencil fuse from the ball of explosive, gently inserted it into his breast pocket, then returned the explosive to his backpack. Running in a crouch, he retraced his last few steps and headed north along the gut of the *arroyo*. He had gained not only thirty seconds of rest but over five hundred yards in distance before they sighted him again.

Now the sun was gone and with it, the remaining twilight. In the dome above him, only some very high cirrus glowed in magenta going to purple and then he could see the first planets in the east. He acknowledged only now that he might make it—lose them in the darkness and ...

The miniature shock wave of a high-velocity bullet snapped past him, followed by the report. Brocassie took three strides, allowing the man to sight his rifle again and then pivoting on his right foot, veered hard to the left. Two more shots whined in the dirt behind him.

Almost without realizing what he was doing, Brocassie screamed a cry of defiance, a long shrill sound, brought up from the stomach, forced through the throat and trilled off the tongue. It was a cry that he had only heard about in legends, but it was there, buried in his genes; the battle yell of the Cree warriors who charged the enemy in the first shock of battle. The sound was terrifying and he knew, instinctively, that it both gave him renewed courage and immobilized the will of the enemy. Without looking back, he knew that the patrol would hesitate, listening to the primitive shriek of defiance, now unsure of who was the hunted and who was the hunter. As the adrenaline hammered through his veins, he felt renewed, immortal. His lungs rejoiced in the cooling air, his legs reached across continents.

He veered hard right and then immediately left. A burst of automatic fire flamed out in the darkness, the patrol now panicked at losing what they had counted as an easy kill.

A sharper crack; this time the bullet ricocheting and tumbling, leaving a whirring sound like a pheasant rising. The weapon would be the older man's, a high-velocity hunting rifle.

Brocassie cut hard to his right and sprinted for two hundred paces and then crouched, gasping. He could no longer see the outline of the vehicle but he could still hear the low growl of the engine and the whine of its gears as it crept forward.

Bent almost double, he scuttled again in the general direction of the coast.

From behind him, the automatic weapon coughed again in short bursts, tracers streaming in flattened arches to his left. He dropped, face downward in the dirt, banging his chin heavily against spalls of rock. The bursts continued, slowly traversing toward him, but he doubted that they had seen him. More likely trying for a lucky hit in the darkness.

Not good, he thought, because at some point luck crossed over a line from low possibility to high probability. It depended on how much ammunition they could waste. He toyed with the idea of setting a timed explosion of twenty seconds and using those few seconds to reverse back toward the foothills. But he discarded it quickly. It would give them a general starting point and put them between him and the coast and the game would be played again on perhaps less equal terms. And besides that, he knew that he had less than two hundred grams of explosive left and he couldn't waste it. Better to hold his position and wait. If they moved away from him, even toward the coast, he would move also, but on a diverging course.

It was totally dark now. Although his eyes were exceptional in darkness, he could not see the vehicle, and sound traveling over rough ground was deceptive. Looking up, he saw the constellations and picked out Scorpio and then Aquarius. Swinging his vision north, he picked up Schedar and Cassiopeia low on the northern horizon. Using their outrigger stars, he looked farther north for Polaris but it was hidden by the massif of the Sierra. It was close enough. With his back to the hidden star, he crawled due south.

Twin shafts of light sprang from the darkness. Brocassie flattened his body against the earth, cursing under his breath. Slowly rolling over, keeping his body flat, he turned his face toward the vehicle. The lights swept in a slow circle as the four-wheel drive swept through a full 360 degrees. Still guessing, he thought. And with each turn, he would sprint while the lights were turned away from him.

A third shaft of light lanced into the night, independent of the headlights. Brocassie ground his teeth, damning his own stupidity. It should have been obvious to him that they would have a handheld searchlight and it was now clear what they planned to do. The patrol would move outward in ever-expanding circles, the headlights sweeping the ground in front and the searchlight quartering the area behind the vehicle. When they spotted him—and eventually they were bound to—he would have to run. He would be sightless, stumbling over the rough ground, and they would only have to follow and eventually cut him down with a burst of fire.

Brocassie drew in a long breath and slowly expelled it. He felt very tired now, his energy gone and with it most of the hope of survival. Five days of dodging militia and FAR patrols, from the crest of the Sierra Maestra down almost to the coast. Almost.

There was only the C-4 plastic explosive now, and not much of that. With a minimum of movement, he unbuckled the straps of his backpack and drew it down beside his face. Working by feel, he divided the explosive into two flattened shapes and then, using his fingers, sought the sharp spalls of rocks which littered the ground. He made a small pile of these and inserted them, one by one, into the perimeter of the squashed spheres. From his shirt, he withdrew two of the three-second squibs and inserted them in the center of the crude grenades, then laid them out separately within easy reach. Beyond this, he had no other weapon except the knife strapped to his leg. He had discarded the M-1 carbine two days ago, its firing pin broken.

He unbuckled the snap and loosened the blade in its sheath. His father would have known the prayers that a Cree warrior offered to his gods before the battle, but the old man was a continent away, his bones gone to dust.

The vehicle was through its second circle. Given that each circle would take longer as the diameter increased, Brocassie calculated that it would be another eight to ten minutes before they would be close enough. And with luck, they would shift their circles south, in the direction they knew he was heading. Brocassie fitted himself lower into the shallow depression and turned his face upward toward the night sky, watching the Great Bear slowly rotate westward. He carefully fingered the ring which hung from the sweat-stained rawhide thong around his neck and tried to remember what she had been like when he had seen her for the last time, more than two years ago, for that was the only strength he could draw on.

The sloop rolled slowly in the beam swell with only the low spit of sand protecting the anchorage. The beach lay a hundred yards inshore and from there, the mass of jungle swept up into the black void of the mountains beyond.

"Me estás bromeando—you're teasing me. How can you know the names of so many stars?" She had asked this, drawing back her long, black hair, the strands still wet from the sea. An oil lamp sputtered in the cockpit and its dim, flickering glow illuminated her profile.

"My father," he replied. He reached over and lay his hand across her back and felt her flesh raise in goose pimples in response to his touch. "Just a few years before he died," he continued softly, ". . . when I was—oh, I guess about thirteen—he told me about them; made me memorize them. Not the names that you know them by but what the Cree called them. He used to say that our dead lived among the stars and that each represented a fallen warrior and that we had to honor them by knowing their names. Not exactly scientific theory, is it?" He breathed deeply, smelling the wind, looking along the dark sea's horizon to the south for lights, but there were none.

Brocassie rolled from his stomach over onto his back so that he could look up into her face. The warmth of her body felt like sunlight falling on his skin and the slow undulation of her breathing seemed to be part of his own breath. She kept silent, watching the black mass of hills rising up from the sea toward the Escambray Mountains, with the loom of lights from Trinidad de Cuba illuminating the cloud base to the north. He took her hand in his, gripping it, and she squeezed back.

"Later on," he continued, "when I was in the Colorado School of Mines, I found a nautical almanac and did a cross-reference. Most of the stars as they're named now are from the Arabic, Greek or Latin. But a lot of others are just numbers and letters, as if modern astronomers ran out of patience." He paused, looking up at the pinpoints of light flickering in the infinity of blackness. "He said—my father said—that each star was a fallen warrior of the Cree nation, and that they guarded the night against the coming of the strongest of stars, the morning star, the sun."

"Was the sun an enemy of the night?" She leaned back against the lifelines, her breasts slick and still wet in the light of the stars. Just after sunset she had stripped off her shorts and shirt and, in one fluid motion, cleared the lifelines, briefly arching her back, and then cut the black water, almost without sound. Brocassie had followed. They had paddled around the sloop, alternately hanging onto the anchor line, then racing each other to the dinghy and back. Things moved in the depths, leaving streaks of phosphorescence, but it seemed to both of them that they were immortal. Only reluctantly had they come up the swimming ladder and sprawled on the still-warm teak deck.

"Dawn was not bad," he finally answered. "Only it marked the separation of the day from the night." He pulled his hand back through his hair and looked up again at the five warriors which stood guard at the western gates of night. "My father said that dawn is the beginning and end of separate things; perhaps like now with us." He touched his forehead to hers and laughed softly, as if it were something that was not important, but he wanted her to understand.

She lay back on the deck, her eyes pinpoints of reflected starlight, and then placed her hands on his shoulders, drawing him down. "I'm not laughing," she said softly, almost shyly, ". . . not laughing, Brocassie. I want you within me. Something, here, now, that we'll both have forever—under the light of your stars."

They made love slowly and carefully, as if they were eating for the first time in many days—wanting to gorge themselves and yet cautiously holding back, tasting each bite, letting the flavor fill them.

At first, he felt her hands moving along his back, stroking his shoulders, not insistent but pleasurable. But then, gradually, her movements became more restless, and her hands were no longer careful and her nails bit into his flesh. In the back of his mind, he could hear the wind singing in the rigging. From aloft, a halyard slatted gently against the mast—almost in meter with their lovemaking—but that faded from his consciousness and his world was bound by only the two of them. It lasted a long time and he heard her catch her breath and hold it and then call his name in one long, soft cry. And it was then that he felt himself tumbling over the edge into space, blackness and streaks of brilliance wheeling in his vision as he fell.

They dozed under starlight and awoke again as Arcturus climbed to its zenith. Alicia was beside him, the blanket pulled over both of them, their faces open to the night sky. "How much longer do we have?" she asked.

"An hour or so before first light."

"So little time?" She rolled over against him, molding the softness of her shape against the hardness of his. He could feel the moistness of her lips on his back and the vibrations of her voice echoed within his chest.

"You can't go back," he heard himself say. It had been something they had both avoided discussing since they had anchored, but during dinner he had seen her tap the barograph and check the fuel gauge.

"I have to. You know that we can't alter it. My father is under constant surveillance by Batista's security police. They'll notice that I'm gone in another few days and they'll throw him in prison on some kind of conspiracy charge or whatever they can trump up. He'd be dead in a week without me to care for him." She touched his face, running her finger along the ridge of his nose. "You'd go back if it was your father, wouldn't you?"

She had gone right to his core. There was no argument. He hesitated and then nodded. "It will be over soon," he said finally. "Batista's finished. He's like a machine, still functioning but with the bearings worn out. Three months, maybe less. Castro and Maroto and Raúl will win because the people are with them. I'll be there in Havana a week after we've won. And then I'll liberate the best goddamn case of champagne that I can scrounge and we'll get a room in the Trocadero, overlooking the harbor, and we'll drink and hiccup bubbles until the sun comes up. And then, Alicia Helvia, I'll go down on callused knees and ask you to be my love for as long as our lives may last."

12

She put her arms around him, her face on his chest, tears streaming from her face. "Ask me—now," she whispered, her voice breaking. "Here—now!"

He lifted her face to his. "I want you forever, Alicia. God, how I want and need you." He buried his face in her hair, kissing her, and he heard her reply, just a whisper: "Then I'm yours and you're mine, George Brocassie of the Western plains and the warrior stars. For as long as we live and longer—forever."

Just before dawn, they made love again, less demanding, more gently, but with a sense of being and wholeness which overwhelmed him. *Forever* he kept repeating over and over in his mind.

They slept again and he awoke first, the pale cream of dawn filling the sky to the east above the Sierra. She had brought him this far, from Havana, over the northern tip of Cuba down the south coast in her father's little sloop, and now she had to return. Her father had something clawing at his guts and she had to go back. Chronic indigestion, her father had told Brocassie, but she knew that it was cancer.

Brocassie pulled his things together, stuffing them into the rucksack. She was up now, into a pair of slacks and a sweater, getting the sloop ready for sea. As they had come, so would she have to return. And she would do it alone.

He paused by the rail, looking toward the jungle and the mountains of the Escambray beyond. Somewhere up there was Maroto's column and he would link up with them. But between the sea and the mountains were Batista patrols sweeping the foothills, and to Brocassie, the possibility of making the passage safely seemed as remote as a flight to the sun with wax wings.

"You've got to go," she said. She pulled a ring from her finger and gave it to him. "This was my grandmother's," she said. "Her hair is woven into the gold filigree. Bring it back to me and I'll wear it for you, Brocassie, forever."

He held her and kissed her. "It will be finished soon. If I can, somehow, I'll write." He lowered himself over the side, the rucksack held over his head as he backstroked for the shore.

"For as long as we live and longer—forever." But she had

died in a dirt pit six months later. And as his father had told him, except for legends told over the cooking fires, there truly was no forever.

The vehicle was through its third circle. Brocassie pressed himself closer against the earth, feeling chips of stone digging through the thin fabric of his fatigues, gouging at his flesh. His throat was dry and he felt his limbs stiffening.

The waiting was almost intolerable. Once, the vehicle had stopped and an area to the west of him was thoroughly swept with both the headlights and the independent spotlight. He heard one of the men hail a challenge into the dark, followed by a brief burst of fire. Brocassie cautiously looked up, hoping that the patrol would somehow be diverted in their systematic sweep and move west in mistake. It was probably an animal that they had seen. But after the pause of a minute, the relentless circling resumed. Two more circles was what he estimated. If the vehicle approached him directly rather than to one side, his chances were greatly diminished—perhaps almost nonexistent.

The next circle was imperfect, flattened as the driver swung inward toward the center of the arc. The man with the spotlight was getting impatient, sweeping it over areas too rapidly. Brocassie thought again about running, but it was too risky. His boots would stir up dust and that would be a fatal telltale. He waited patiently for the last circle.

The headlights cut swaths of light and shadow across the scrubby land, now turning toward him. A light wind from the south carried the dust of the vehicle at almost the same speed, hazing the headlights. At this distance, he could hear first the engine and then the voices, both carried on the light breeze. He waited, carefully placing the igniter between his teeth. Eight seconds now, he guessed. A breath of diesel fumes and exhaust. Six seconds. The faint reflection of dash lights illuminated the driver's face. Four seconds. He bit down hard with his molars, crushing the fuse—swung his arm back and threw, covering his head as he did.

There was a burst of automatic fire, then the plastic explosive detonating. Rock and metal whistled over his head and

14

then his body was lifting with the concussion, and he was slammed to the earth as if by a giant's hand.

The explosion had deafened him temporarily, leaving a roaring like storm surf within his head. He covered his ears but it made no difference. Brocassie tasted blood on his tongue and felt a wetness around his nostrils. Effects of concussion but no wound, he finally realized.

Less than ten yards away, the vehicle lay on its side as if it were an animal that had taken a gut shot and, unable to lie down, had rolled on its flanks, panting out its last. The engine was dead but one headlight still burned dimly. He watched for over five minutes, but there was no movement and no sound other than the creak of metal cooling and the hiss of steam from the breached radiator.

Getting up carefully, Brocassie moved away from the beam of the dying headlight. He kept low to the ground, moving as silently as he could, skirting the wrecked vehicle. Five yards short of it, he found the younger man. He must have been crouching at eye level with the windshield, because most of his face was gone. He lay crumpled on his back, head turned toward the night sky, faceless, sightless. The insects were already on him. As would be the birds just after dawn.

The NCO was pinned beneath the Land Rover, his chest crushed beneath the body of the vehicle. One arm was thrown back, the elbow twisted inward and upward, bone showing at the fracture. He was muttering something, barely audible.

Neither of the weapons was visible on the ground—probably thrown well clear. Brocassie decided that he would only be encumbered by them and stopped searching.

Brocassie sat down next to the NCO, taking a canteen of water which lay within a few feet of the man's remaining good arm. He had been clawing in the dirt, trying to reach it. His fingernails had excavated small gutters in the earth.

"The water will be no good for you," Brocassie told him in Spanish, untwisting the cap. The older man tried to raise his arm to grasp the flask but couldn't manage. Lifting the NCO's head with one hand, Brocassie used his other to pour small dribbles of water over the man's mouth.

The NCO gagged, spit out the fluid and then motioned

15

for more. Satisfied, he lay back, trying to pant but unable to take a full breath. "You were very good," he said. His speech was not peasant, nor was it educated. Brocassie guessed that the NCO had been a workingman, perhaps in the mines. "Very good for a whore's bastard son," the Cuban added.

"It might have been different," Brocassie answered, "if you had seen me earlier. As it was, it was close."

The man nodded. "Rolando—the young one—he thought . . ." He hacked and it must have been very painful because he first opened his mouth wide, his face contorted, eyes clamped shut, and then bit down on his lips. Taking the man's head between his hands, Brocassie tried to cushion his thrashing. The heaving finally subsided and Brocassie felt the neck muscles of the NCO easing beneath his fingertips.

"I'll try to tip the vehicle back off your chest," he said to the NCO. "It will hurt." The NCO nodded weakly, his eyes squeezed shut.

Afraid to rock it deeper into the man's chest, Brocassie hacked out small pits in the soil with his knife to brace his feet against, put his shoulder and back to the upright side of the chassis and slowly heaved. It seemed impossible but he sensed movement and he pressed harder, feeling the ligaments of his back and legs taut under the pressure. Suddenly, the vehicle passed its own center of gravity and rolled over, the body landing upright, rocking heavily on its worn shock absorbers like a dog shaking its coat. As a last thought, Brocassie shut off the headlight but left the dash lights on. Ironically, he noticed a St. Christopher's medal swinging from the rearview mirror.

The NCO had turned his face to one side, spitting blood. His good hand was clawing at his shirt and the wound beneath. "Something is broken inside my guts," he whispered through clenched teeth. "Morphine in the backseat chest."

Taking a small penlight from his backpack, Brocassie fumbled open the chest. There were various tools, a grease-smudged repair manual and a first aid kit. Within the kit, he found only one syrette of morphine. Removing the cap, he darted the needle into the man's thigh and squeezed the tube.

Minutes passed and gradually the man relaxed, his chest moving more slowly in a pattern of broken respiration, catching his breath as the diminishing waves of pain washed over him.

"Cigarette . . . in my pocket."

Brocassie fished the open pack from the NCO's tunic and lit it, took one short drag and placed it between the man's lips. "What's your name?"

"Griveón," the man responded. "Eduardo Griveón. Sergeant, Oriente Province Militia. I doubt that my serial number would be of interest." He half-laughed and then gagged, racking out his lungs. Brocassie squatted beside him, gritting his teeth. "I should have killed you this afternoon," Griveón finally gasped. "I could have. The rifle is a Mauser seven millimeter with eight power sights. I have shot wild pigs at four hundred meters. I could have . . ."

"Perhaps," Brocassie answered. He looked up at the night sky. Arcturus was almost obscured by the hills to the west. He turned back to the man and said, "I've got to be going. Do you have a blanket or sleeping bag? They'll find you tomorrow."

Griveón spat a little blood and licked at the dribble on the corner of his mouth. "Not tomorrow, *gusano*. The closest patrol is thirty kilometers to the east, doubled up with two other unscheduled patrols." He drew down on the cigarette, then clamped it between his teeth, still talking. "Working for the worms?" The NCO didn't say it as an obscenity.

"No," Brocassie answered. "For a free Cuba. Not for Batista, United Fruit or Coca-Cola—just for a free Cuba. You understand, Griveón? There are some who can still make that distinction."

Griveón stared up at him, hesitated and then said, "I for one can understand the difference. It's something we all wanted, wasn't it? What we pissed so much blood away for and all we did was substitute one maximum leader for another. Fidel for Batista, Khrushchev for Kennedy. All the same breed of bastard. It is the tragedy of Cuba that we never learned to do anything other than to kneel or salute." He turned his head to the side, looking up at Brocassie. "So what have you done to free Cuba today other than to blow up an old man who would much rather be sharing a bottle than fighting with you?" He made an attempt at a smile but it was

17

more of a grimace. "With the morphine, you know, it's like I had three glasses of rum. I feel clear and light, like I could fly."

Brocassie restrained an impulse to touch Griveón's face. "I was with Fabricio's column." More than that, he didn't want to say.

"Fabricio," Griveón repeated. "Very good fighter. Before he turned against the Revolution, he fought with Camilo Cienfuegos against Batista. I met Fabricio once. Bad teeth, right? Funny smile, like he was listening to you but planning to kill you if he figured you were against him. But yesterday's hero is today's traitor. Or maybe the other way around. So how is the old *pendejo*?"

"Fabricio's dead. He died two weeks ago. Plus his son, plus two cousins. Plus nine other men and a boy who never even saw a classroom. The Russian MIGs dropped napalm on us. Out of eighteen, four of us lived." Brocassie stood up, wiping the blood of the NCO on his pants. "I have to go."

Griveón made a sound in his throat, raising his head and then dropping it back on the ground. "Stay with me awhile . . . all right, like you were an old friend? Light another cigarette for me and keep the rest but stay for a minute." His voice was as lonely as a winter wind whining through leafless trees.

Brocassie bent down, felt for the NCO's pocket and fished out the pack. He lit another one, took a drag and then placed it between the man's lips. "For a while, Griveón. But not long, you understand why."

Griveón nodded but didn't answer immediately. The tip glowed as the man sucked in and then expelled the smoke. "These things kill you, they say. I smoked since I was eleven and it doesn't look like I'm going to die of cancer so I have to say that that gives me some degree of pleasure."

"You'll live."

"You could tell that to some pup in his twenties but not to an old man," Griveón answered. "I fought in Spain, understand? With the brigade, back in thirty-eight. I have a medal and a pin in my hip to prove it, but I saw too many men die and I know what tickles and what kills and what just hurts." He clamped the cigarette between his teeth, took another drag and then spat it out, exhaling slowly. "So where are you going?"

"I have something to deliver."

"Ah, secrets . . ."

Why not? Brocassie thought. It wouldn't hurt to talk about it. Griveón would be dead by dawn. "I have a roll of film. One of Fabricio's men shot it with a good camera . . . the Russian construction project in the valley north of the Sierra."

"Our pink-assed allies. Blond men with bulldozers, ferreting in the earth like moles," Griveón said. "Not for Cuban eyes, we are told. On Cuban soil, but not for Cuban eyes." He arched his neck, the pain obviously intense, and then slowly relaxed. "What's your name?"

"Brocassie."

"I heard of you but it was a long time ago. Like Willie Morgan, right?"

"Morgan was an American."

"And you're . . . ?"

"A mixture of a lot of things—Cuban, American, Cree Indian, bastard, whore's son—take your pick."

Griveón put his left hand up and took Brocassie's. His grip was surprisingly strong. "You did a filthy thing to an old man, Brocassie. I suppose that I should ask you to say something for me to a priest—buy me a hundred-peso Mass."

"I doubt that you have seen the inside of a church in the last twenty years, Griveón. But if it pleases you, I'll light a candle."

Griveón blew out heavily through his lips. "You're right about the church so save your money." He closed his eyes, moving his head a little from side to side. "We're no different, you and I. We're soldiers fighting for something that neither of us will ever be able to attain." He opened his eyes again, attempting a smile. "I knew Fabricio when he was good— Maroto as well. Had my life been just a little different, Brocassie, we would be brothers—*hermanos,* understand?"

Brocassie stood up. "I've got to go soon, Griveón. It's not more than eight hours until dawn and I've got to cover a lot of countryside."

"Not yet . . ." Griveón whispered.

"What . . . ?"

"Give me another shot of the morphine. There is a tickle in my stomach and I find it's difficult to scratch. In return, I'll

19

tell you something you should know—something between rumor and fact. Or if you like, a fairy tale."

"There isn't any more morphine."

Griveón breathed slowly in and then exhaled. "I was afraid that there wouldn't be," he finally sighed, "so I would ask you for the obvious alternative. I trust that no priest is looking over my shoulder?"

"What's the fairy tale?"

"No patience," Griveón said tiredly. "Like my son. You want the ending of a story before it can even be started. It is a condition of these impatient times. But I won't hold you up, Brocassie. Your photographs will tell nothing. I myself have studied the construction site and there is nothing to see except holes in the earth. Everything else is underground."

"I know that, Griveón. You don't have to trade information. I know what you want and I trust you."

"But," Griveón added, "there is more. It's true—what the Russians are doing, I don't know. But I do have an acquaintance, a poor excuse of a man, who works on the docks in Santiago. He told me that the Russians have used up all the cement in Cuba—over a year's stockpile—on their underground city and still they needed more—four freighter loads from Rumania. He has also seen with his own eyes thousands of steel collars, about one and a half meters in diameter, transported into the Sierra." Griveón was spewing out words now, his face bathed in beads of sweat. "They are making something evil there, Brocassie. Not for Cuba's good but for their own filthy purposes."

Brocassie put his hand on the man's shoulder. "Understand, *cabrón*, that I like your company but I have to get moving. Are you sure this is what you want?"

"You're sure there is no more morphine?"

"That was the last of the morphine."

Griveón was quiet for a time and then said, "Which is unfortunate. With another prick of that stuff, I could soar to the moon and maybe beyond." He coughed a little. "There is a Colt automatic in the map compartment. Perhaps if you trust me, you could leave it here beside me."

The Colt was where Griveón said it would be. Something that Brocassie could use, but there are priorities for everything, he thought, aren't there? Releasing the clip, he thumbed the shells out of the feed slot and placed the weapon, the empty clip and the cartridges beside Griveón's good hand.

"You're a worthless old man, Griveón, but just to grease your way through St. Peter's gate, I'll spend twenty dollars on a Mass in Miami for you if I don't first spend it on a good meal."

Griveón looked up at him in the faint starlight. "Don't waste your money, *hijo de puta*. People like us drink rum in hell together. I'll see you there."

"Make reservations."

"Brocassie . . ."

He was already standing, tightening the straps on his rucksack, his mind already focused on the coast. "Speak."

Griveón's hand reached out for the Colt. He didn't pick it up but his fingers traced along its outline and he nodded. "There is one other thing. They knew you were coming."

"Who?"

"Who knows who? Somebody higher up. I'm on the bottom of the shit heap so I do what they tell me but the orders came from Santiago. We were warned that a counterrevolutionary—someone from Fabricio's column in the Segundo Frente—would be coming down out of the Sierra, heading for the coast, except that they thought it would be more to the east of here and they weren't sure what the destination would be. Guantánamo Bay, they thought, but it sounded like a guess. Normally, there would be three patrols in this sector but the other two were moved east a day ago. Take care, Brocassie. Someone you know talked."

Only three men knew that he was leaving and those were men he trusted absolutely. And besides, it didn't alter things anyway because he was already committed. He stood up and looked to the east. If he kept to a steady jog, he would be on the coast by dawn. As an afterthought, he went over to the Rover and jerked the medallion from its chain and placed it alongside of the Colt.

"If it means anything, Griveón," he said, hunkering down beside the man, "I'm sorry that it had to be this way."

Griveón nodded, looking up. "You were good and I was careless. That simple. You might have a glass or two on my account if you can remember Sergeant Griveón from Camagüey."

Standing up, Brocassie hitched the straps of his rucksack tighter. *"¡Qué Diós te bendiga!* Griveón—may God protect you."

Griveón grunted. "That would be a nice storybook ending but I doubt that he'd put up with me." He lifted his hand slightly. *"¡Adiós! amigo."*

Brocassie started south, not looking back. Before he had run much more than half a mile, he heard one shot.

CHAPTER

2

Brocassie stood on the edge of wind-eroded hills, looking out over the Caribbean Sea toward the south. The absolutes of night and blackness had given way to a variable pale-cream light. Wind-bent trees, brush and outcroppings of rock now had definition. He turned and looked to the north and the mountains from where he had come. The summit of Pico Turquino, over five thousand feet above the sea, caught the first light of the sun, flaming into reds and roses, then slowly mutating into the monochromes of ordinary daylight. It was over so quickly—the instant, spontaneous combustion that was dawn. But to Brocassie, it was the endless renewal that his father had talked of, until there was a day when there would be no dawn for any man.

Looking to the east, Brocassie caught the first hard edge of the sun bulging up through the horizon. He slid the battered sunglasses over his eyes and watched as the ball rose higher, distended and distorted through the refraction of the atmosphere. It was chrome and yellow and hot-white all in one. Like looking into the crucible of creation, he thought. As the old ones had said.

Sinking into a crouch, Brocassie stared south as the sea lit up. Moments before it had been the uniform color of lead, heaving in great sullen swells. But now, caught in the flat trajectory of the morning light, the sea took on definition—corrugations of blue-black, transparent toward their crests with a thin capping of white. And between the crests, in the slick green silk of the troughs, the darkness of endless depths.

It was still very cool, the scent of piñon pine was resinous and thick on the morning wind and the sparse grass still saturated with dew. But he knew that in another hour the sun's heat would bake the cliffs and the temperature would be unendurable without some sort of shelter.

Brocassie sank down to his knees, legs folded beneath him, and threw his shoulders back, arms rigidly behind him, bracing his body. He closed his eyes and waited for some minutes, feeling the heat of the sun on his face, and then he prayed first for Griveón, because he had fought well and faced death without cowardice. No Mass for Griveón, with candles and sprinkled water; Brocassie knew that the old man would not have wanted his name spoken in the sterile confines of a church. The words of the chant were blurring in his mind because of fatigue, but next he prayed to his namesake, and to the others who guarded him, for patience and for strength. He ended the prayer with a long, thin wail, the Song of Morning Light, and then threw his forehead down against the earth to acknowledge his humility and to listen for the hooves of the Dappled Death Mare, but she was not within the distance of his hearing and for that, he was thankful.

He stood up and edged toward the falloff of the cliff. Brocassie looked down on the thin ribbon of asphalt that was the coastal road which served the small fishing villages to the west of Santiago de Cuba. There was no traffic as yet and he had expected none until after nine, when the bus that serviced Corral de Río and Pilón lumbered through. Taking a red handkerchief from his rucksack, he tied it first to a branch stripped of needles and then planted it just on the crest. Fifty yards below, from the roadway, it would not be readily visible unless one knew where to look and was watching carefully. Joaquín was to be on that bus, each morning for three successive days and this was the third. Keep faith, he said to the wind.

For the next twenty minutes, Brocassie worked, stripping four larger branches of piñon pine and setting them up into two inverted vees. Spanning the apexes with light Dacron rope, he pegged the ends down into the hard earth. Over this, he stretched a mottled ground cloth and used shorter pieces of line to attach the cloth to the branches, forming a crude tent. Then he broke off fingers of pine to cover it with, giving him protection from the sun and from the casual observation of aircraft patrolling the coast. He was sure, after walking around the perimeter of his camp, that there was nothing to be seen from the air that would give away his position.

Crawling into the tent, he peeled off his fatigues, undershirt and shorts and then, using his knife, scraped the sweat from his body, starting with his face and working downward. There was just a quarter of his canteen left and he drank most of it but used the remainder to moisten his body.

Now cooled, he lay on the dirt, his fatigues a pillow, and thought of how it would be to bathe and to drink and to eat.

He finished what little remained of his rations—three sticks of beef jerky and a half a bar of dehydrated cheese. He would have liked coffee but there was no more water and fatigue was fluttering his mind.

He woke in the very late afternoon, stiff in his joints and with his tongue swollen. Impossible to tell whether Joaquín had been on the bus or seen the handkerchief. Maroto's instructions to Brocassie had been to intersect the coastal road between August 26 and September 1, approximately six miles west of the turnoff to Barrancas. He was reasonably sure he was within two miles of the pickup point. And if Joaquín did not show up as scheduled, then it was going to be a real bastard of a situation. He was cut off from the mountains, from the sanctuary of the guerrilla strongholds. And if there was no contact with Joaquín, his only option would be to hoof it along the barren coastal road until he found a village. Food was not the immediate problem, but water was. And in a village, there would be curiosity and Brocassie had no papers.

He crawled out of the tent, stretching, and looked down on the deserted asphalt strip which perched between cliffs and a hundred-yard falloff to the broken surf. It was a wild, desolate place. He could remember one other April when he and Alicia had driven down this same coastal road to go spear fishing in the Caleta los Tunalitos, the bay just to the east of Pilón. She had had her father's MGTC—a little English two-seater sports car with huge wire wheels and a fold-down windshield. It had rained, and the top had been so rotten from four years in the tropics that it had first leaked and then torn away in the wind, strips of canvas snapping like a string of firecrackers exploding. At first she swore, and then stopping by the side of the road, folded the top back down into the trunk. Then laughing, they took off again, driving very fast because she had a theory that if you did, the rain would never penetrate the cockpit. He remembered distinctly, her thin cotton shirt and brassiere, soaked through to the skin, her black hair in strands, whipping in the wind.

One memory of her triggered another and yet another. He pulled a dog-eared photograph of her from the waterproof pouch in his backpack and stared at it. She was sitting there, with the owner of a little *cantina* which they had liked, a kitten held to her neck. She was half-smiling, and it seemed that the camera had intruded on something very private that she was thinking. The kitten had been a gift of the owner and she had loved it, although she had always said that she hated cats. The light of the flashbulb had caught the reflection both of her eyes and the cat's, and he thought of the similarity between the two of them. He put the photo away and then looked back out over the sea, his eyes unfocused.

Like a wave breaking into surf, more memories of her engulfed him. Scenes of her walking in heels and a tight skirt down the Paseo del Prado, Brocassie just four strides behind, unwilling to call to her at first, because she was so sure of herself that she was not aware of her power and beauty. Men had watched her but had said nothing, perhaps intimidated. A bootblack—a thin, olive-skinned boy in his twenties with stiff patent leather hair—started to whistle and then stopped as she swept by. It was as if he had seen the Madonna dressed in gauze.

Other scenes came to him but he pushed them away. Finished, he thought. She *was* and I *am*. In a way, it seemed to him that he had forgotten the point of what he was doing. Except that he was exceptionally good at his trade and he kept going because that was what kept him going. But Fabricio was dead and the counterrevolution was dying. He had this one last thing to do—to get the film out of Cuba—and then he would go back to the mountains of Utah and try to forget her and all the rest of it.

He heard the sound of an engine, far off in the distance. Two or three miles out to sea, he saw a motor torpedo boat bucking the swell, heading east toward Santiago de Cuba. Coastal patrol; one of the Soviet-type MTB-41s. Fabricio had told him that the Russians were beefing up the coastal patrols but only in the vicinity of Havana and Cienfuegos. One further complication, he thought. Flat out, the MTB would probably be able to do forty knots, although in smooth water. Call it twenty knots in an open sea, but with the advantage of radar. Brocassie sighed, watching it run east until it was out of sight.

Sun about an hour from setting, he guessed. He stripped the ground tarp from the makeshift frame of branches and, shaking it out, folded it carefully and packed it in his rucksack. Then he scattered the branches of piñon pine and swept the area with the last branch, leaving almost no sign that he had been there.

Moving along the crest of the ridge, he worked east until he came to a ravine, heavily eroded but offering the protection of a place to descend without exposure to someone driving on the coastal road. It was dangerous going and Brocassie took his time, working down in the loose rubble and soft earth until he was on the highway. His hands stung from rubbing against the sharp stones and he felt the prickle of nettles stinging his legs.

Crossing the road, he worked his way downward again over a face of rotten rock which sloped steeply to the beach.

From the color of the water and the caldron of boiling surf, it looked as if the beach dropped off very quickly into deep water. It was strewn with boulders which had fallen from the face of the cliff, and the shoreline was a conglomerate of shattered stone and broken coral.

Brocassie first stripped limpets which clung to the surf-pounded boulders, depositing over twenty of them in his rucksack. He then shucked off his clothes and dove in a flat arc into the sea. He swam, pummeled by the breaking waves, for about ten minutes. It was not a substitute for fresh water but it relieved the dehydration of his skin and eased the tightness in his muscles. Just about sundown, he stumbled back through the surf and lay on top of a boulder, soaking in the last heat of the sun. As he lay there, he pried the meat from half the limpets and ate them one by one, saving the balance for later. They were tough but there was moisture in them and they eased his thirst. He hoped like hell that Joaquín would think to bring a beer or a flask of water. That is—if Joaquín came.

He dressed again in the fatigues, laced up his boots and hitched on the pack. Picking his way up the slope and onto the roadway, he walked east until he found a culvert and swung down into its dark shade. Another hour to wait he guessed, and he spent the time not thinking but shelling the remaining limpets of their meat. He wondered whether they had yet found Griveón and the wrecked Land Rover. We're all a bunch of dumb bastards, he thought. All of us. The endless fighting for independence, control and power. And what has been gained? Broken lives, broken bodies, a broken nation. Not even his own.

The sun had gone down and the air was cooling. Twice, Brocassie had heard trucks grinding down the coastal road, heavily laden and moving at low speed. Supply trucks, not troop transports, he guessed. About an hour after darkness, he heard a lighter vehicle, probably a jeep, sing past at high speed. He caught the faint sound of a man whistling, but it was blown away in the wind of the vehicle's passage.

Another quarter of an hour and still nothing, and then he heard another vehicle—this time crawling along in low gear, occasionally stopping. Three honks on its horn and then it moved again, edging up the road to repeat the sequence. Brocassie let the vehicle pass over the culvert and then scrambled up the embankment.

It was a light truck, one taillight burned out on the passenger side, as Maroto said it would be. He pulled the remaining sphere of plastic explosive from his backpack, inserted a three-second squib and then hailed the truck.

"Hey—headed for Bayamita?" he shouted.

A thin nervous voice came back, "Farther. Much farther."

The man had given the correct response which still meant nothing.

Brocassie crossed to the far side of the road and moved up toward the truck, keeping low. He could see the man in the gleam of the headlights, the engine compartment opened.

"You there?" the man called.

"I have a grenade," Brocassie answered. "Drop any weapon you might have in front of the headlights. Everything including a knife. Then shag your ass around to the back and open the tailgate of the truck. I want to see what's in there. Then get back into the headlights. *Move it!*"

"No weapons," the figure yelled back. He moved out of the cast of the headlights and not only dropped the tailgate but opened both doors of the cab, flicking on the interior light, then walked around into the headlights again.

"Joaquín is dead," the man called. "I'm his friend. And if you want to get out of here, make up your mind soon. I passed a four-truck militia convoy about six miles back. They were stopping for a piss call but they can't be too far behind us."

Brocassie moved closer to the truck. "Move farther away from the truck but stay in the headlights where I can see you."

The man hesitantly backed away, his arms half raised. Brocassie ran toward the truck. The bed was empty as was the cab. He jumped in, searching quickly under the seat and in the glove compartment. No weapons.

"Let's go," he yelled.

The man came trotting back and swung up into the cab. He started the engine and dropped the gearshift lever into low, accelerating up through gears until the truck was swaying with speed, the engine straining.

"Put some distance between us and the convoy," he said over the noise of the engine. "My name is Sergio—Joaquín's friend. I worked in the Frente with him a couple of years ago."

His features were indistinct in the half-light of the dash panel, but Brocassie could make out the outline of his face: thin, pinched-in cheeks, heavily pockmarked, with a hawkish nose. Sergio's eyes were close set and protruded and what little hair he had was heavily plastered with a greasy hairdressing which had an overwhelming stink to it. Sergio withdrew a thin cigar and lit it with a match scratched against the dashboard.

"Cigar?" Sergio asked, withdrawing another one from his shirt pocket, his eyes still on the road.

"No cigar," Brocassie answered. "You have anything to drink?" Brocassie's throat was raw and his mouth felt like dried leather.

"Nothing," Sergio answered. "She didn't say that I should bring anything. Maybe you wanted a cuba libre?" He giggled at his own inept joke.

The truck leaned precariously through a turn, the wheels scraping onto the rutted shoulder. Sergio manhandled the wheel, bouncing back onto the asphalt.

"Slow this damn thing down!" Brocassie shouted. "What's the rush?"

Shrugging, Sergio backed off the accelerator but only marginally. "I've got to get this thing back to Santiago before midnight. I have a deal with a guy. There are some tires up in La Plata which a buddy of his is smuggling in from Jamaica. So I get twelve tires and he gives me two for my trouble. Perfect cover for picking you up. But there isn't much time to screw around with."

"Joaquín . . . ?"

"Dead, as I told you," Sergio replied without any emotion. "He was off with two of his 'boys' transferring munitions up into the Sierra for Maroto's column. He ran into a roadblock and there was a shoot-up. Somehow, the munitions went up and Joaquín with them. There was nothing left of any of them."

"You don't seem to be grieving." Brocassie glanced over at the man.

"Sure I am," he shot back. "But he pushed both his luck and his patron saint's once too often."

"How did you know about me?"

Sergio flicked the cigar out the vent window. "Joaquín's wife. She worked with him on everything. As far as I know, Maroto had radioed the *friends* in Miami. They got a message through to Joaquín that he was responsible to pick you up. Joaquín was dead but she knew all the details of the pickup schedule."

"What was in it for you?"

"Two hundred American a day. Plus a watch that he had." He wiped his mouth with the back of his hand. "I get you to the coast down by Chivirico by ten—at the latest, eleven. From there on in, it's her problem."

It didn't fit together exactly. True, Joaquín was a "mule," responsible for bringing in supplies from delivery boats, and trucking them into the Sierra. But if he had gotten caught in a roadblock, the DGI—Castro's Internal Security Force— would have surely questioned his wife and probably sacked the restaurant for evidence.

"What about the DGI?" he asked.

"What about them?" Sergio responded, irritated.

"Didn't they question Joaquín's wife?"

Sergio lifted his shoulders, hunched them forward and let them drop, all in slow motion—a gesture which eloquently combined disdain, disinterest and dismissal. "Yes, they came," he finally said. "Poked around. Asked questions, and found nothing. Joaquín had a reputation for conspiracy. He openly criticized the government. But then again, he openly criticized Batista. And even if *Nuestro Señor en pañales* were to arrive in a golden chariot and take over the government, Joaquín would have criticized him as well and probably plotted to overthrow the Second Coming." He took another cigar from his pocket, chomped on the end and then spit it out through the window. He turned to Brocassie, his mouth tight, and said, "The DGI knew he was small fish."

"Where do you stand, Sergio?"

Sergio gave a short, bitter laugh. "Where do I stand? Shit—I stand in line like everyone else. For meat, for bread, for eggs. Even to take a piss. I say *que jodan* the revolution and the counterrevolution as well. I repair electrical appliances, see? I do my job well, I get paid OK and I drink a little and most of all, I don't get involved, because once you start getting involved, you make enemies and that's a good way to get your face blown away."

"So you're doing this strictly for money?"

Smiling, Sergio nodded. "Why not for money? So this one last time—a favor to the wife of a dead friend. But not again. You can blow the whole island up for all I care, but for me, I want to live a long time and when I die, I hope that it happens in my own house with a *ramera bien nalgona* resting between my legs."

Brocassie was tired, desperately tired. Nearly three years in the mountains of Cuba, first fighting Batista and then, after the Revolution was betrayed, fighting Castro. Alicia was dead, Fabricio was dead and so were over thirty men whom he had fought with. Only Maroto still fighting and how much longer could he last? What had they gained for all the deaths, and what point was there in it? He was sick of it: of leeches on his skin and wet clothes and the monotonous diet of rice and beans. For the last year, both ammunition and weapons had been in short supply and the counterrevolutionary forces were no longer on the offensive. Now, it was just a matter of survival. For him, it was over and he wanted just to go home and walk in the high desert of Utah, watch snow blanket the earth with silence and try to forget.

Try to forget, but he knew that he wouldn't, couldn't. For all his life he would remember the day that Fabricio's column had been caught out in the open. From under a low cloud deck, MIGs had come in and he heard the whine of their engines only seconds before the napalm had turned the clearing into a blast furnace. In those few seconds, he had turned and seen the shining silver tanks tumbling downward and knew what they were because he had seen them in Korea. He had enough time to scream a warning to the rest of them and then he ran. The jellied gasoline had burned for over half an hour, and the men who had been caught within the flaming perimeter were nothing but charred lumps of blackened meat and carbonized bone. Brocassie had led the survivors higher in the Sierra Maestra, linking up with Maroto's column.

The opportunity to get out had come unexpectedly. One of Fabricio's men had shot a roll of 35mm film through a telephoto lens a week earlier and Maroto wanted the film to get out to the CIA in Miami, hand-delivered. Maroto wasn't sure what the film represented, but he knew that in order to get more arms and ammunition, he had to have something that would (as he explained to Brocassie), "get their bowels in motion."

Brocassie was the natural choice. Part American with a degree. He could convince them. Maroto gave Brocassie a "shopping list" including mortars, SMGs and ammunition. In their last moments together, before Brocassie had started down from the high Sierra, Maroto had told him, "You've done enough. It's not your fight. Go back to your country and stay there, but, if you will, remember us. We'll fight on until we win or until we're dead." It was a typical Maroto quote for the history books.

The coastal road occasionally dipped down to sea level, skirting the beach, and then would rise again and run along the cliffs overlooking the sea. There was just the sliver of a moon lighting the sea and a faint wash of starlight reflected back from the smoothly heaving swells. Sergio had slowed a little, driving more carefully. As they came around a curve, Brocassie saw a couple of small shacks jammed together, as if leaning on each other for mutual support. A kerosene light shone through one window.

"Corral del Río," Sergio commented. He slowed further, and as he did, his lights picked up a dozen more houses, a concrete bar. The *cantina* was still open, with men sitting on the stone curb, drinking, smoking and, by their hand gestures, arguing.

Sergio shifted down and swung to the far side of the roadway, half a block down from the *cantina*.

"What the hell are you doing?" Brocassie snapped.

"One minute. I'll get some beers. Maybe a couple of *medias noches* if they have them to take out." His voice had a hurt tone to it. "I mean—you said you were thirsty and a little hot pork and cheese sandwich would go down well, huh?"

"What about the convoy behind us?" His stomach was already rumbling at the thought of food and saliva gushed into his mouth.

Sergio shrugged, withdrawing the keys from the ignition. "One minute is all that I'll take. That convoy is going half the speed we're making."

Dammit. This was stupid but he was starved and dehydrated. "Do it fast!" He grabbed Sergio's arm, squeezing it hard. "I *mean* fast."

Tumbling out of the cab, Sergio slammed the door behind him. Brocassie slumped down in the seat and angled the rearview mirror to watch the thin Cuban's progress. A few men on the curb looked up and Brocassie could see them exchanging small hand gestures of casual greeting. Sergio disappeared through the doorway.

It was hard to realize, he thought, but it's almost over. Sergio was to drop him off on the coast and from there a fisherman would take him to Jamaica. A flight to Miami and then it would be finished. He knew that he would gorge himself on meat and get too drunk and then he would head back toward Utah, savoring the drive through the rich plains of the country, anticipating that one moment when he would climb over a rise and see the Rockies shining white in the sunlight. But he also knew that with some kind of peace would also come the long hours of the night when he would remember her. In the Sierra, he had been too close to death to think of her often, but alone and safe it would be different.

He knew now that he had stayed in Cuba for these last two years, not for the counterrevolution but only because of her death. He had talked, like the rest of the counterrevolutionaries, of finally overthrowing Castro and reclaiming a free Cuba, but the Bay of Pigs had killed the dream. Kennedy, at the last moment, had pulled back from his commitment like a frightened dog fleeing a loud noise. Still, Brocassie had fought on, but only because he was fighting for a cause she had died for, no longer questioning the rationality of it.

Brocassie could remember every detail that the *carbonero* had told to Fabricio.

The *carbonero*, a sun-blackened man of over seventy, tended his charcoal ovens in the swampy area of Playa Larga. On an afternoon in December of 1960, he had seen a military six-by-six truck pull into a marshy clearing. As he had described it, eight guards, an officer and seven prisoners had left the truck. The prisoners were two women and five men, all naked, bound to one another and blindfolded. Three of the men were then separated and their blindfolds removed. It was for them to dig the grave—a pit measuring three yards square, two yards deep. Without boots and just using their bare feet on the hard edges of the shovels, the prisoners had taken five hours to complete the pit to the officer's liking. During this time, each guard was given, in turn, the women who were tied like animals to banyan trees. They were forced to take the men, one after the other, kneeling over on hands and knees. The *carbonero* had said that he had watched this happen until he could watch no more, and he had hunched down in the bush and vomited. But all through the afternoon, he had heard the women weeping and crying out and the Fidelistas laughing and the sound of men drinking and throwing the empty bottles on the rocks.

In the early evening, he had said, the soldiers turned on the headlights of the truck and roped the prisoners back together in a chain. Goading the prisoners toward the pit with their rifle butts, the old man said that it was like a scene out of hell, with the damned driven to the pit before the devil's fork. The prisoners were pushed forward in a stumbling, shuffling mass, three guards behind them. There, first one man and then another, had stumbled over the mounds of fresh earth and fallen headlong into the pit, dragging the rest of the prisoners with them. The old man said that it was a mass of confusion coupled with curses and screams of pain. One man had started to sing something, defiantly, until the guards pelted him with clods of dirt and then he fell silent, along with the others. At that point, the *carbonero* said hoarsely, all of the prisoners had at first fallen silent and although he could not see them, he could hear very distinctly, carried on the light evening wind which blew in from the sea, a prayer of contrition.

It was then that the guards and the officer had withdrawn back to about fifty feet beyond the pit. Then they had used grenades. The old man said that there had been eight explosions. Four guards had returned to the edge of the pit, handkerchiefs tied over their mouths, and had filled in the red-stained dirt which lay in heaps at the side of the pit.

Fabricio and Brocassie knew that seven or eight counterrevolutionaries had been taken at a roadblock a few weeks before. They were from a separate group, operating farther to the west, near Trinidad, and no one knew details. But a week later, the official government newspaper had published a list of names of "terrorists, working under CIA control" who had been captured, tried and executed. Her name was among those on the list.

Brocassie's life had stopped that day, and from there on in, he knew that he talked and moved and fought only because his body refused to die.

He glanced in the rearview mirror again. Sergio was taking his time and Brocassie now began to wonder about the wisdom of stopping for the beer.

No keys in the ignition. He had not noticed Sergio take them, but then again, he had not been that concerned. Another spare set under the seat? He had already swept that area for weapons but he tried again, guessing perhaps that the owner would have tied a spare key there with a bit of string. He felt first under the passenger seat and his fingers touched only the coldness of metal seat coils and jute stuffing. Under the driver's seat, it was different. No key, but his hand traced over the polished leather of a holster and then, the cool, knurled grip of an automatic. It had been jammed up under the springs, wedged between two coils.

The grip parted from the holster easily. He could not tell the make exactly but feeling the shape of the barrel, he guessed a Luger. Not evidence. It was not a standard DGI issue; in fact, he thought, he had never seen one in Cuba. First ejecting the clip, he then worked the action. There was a round in the chamber. He reloaded this into the clip, inserted the clip and then rechambered a shell. Flicking the safety on, he dropped the weapon into the right thigh pocket of his fatigues.

It was possible, he thought, that Sergio had just brought the weapon as insurance against the liabilities of the unknown. Then again . . .

Sergio reemerged from the *cantina*, bottles and a bag held against his breast. He said something to the men at the curb and one man spat in the dust of the street. Another laughed and then they returned to their drinking and arguing.

Sergio dumped the bottles on the seat through the open driver's window and then got in, pushing two bottles toward Brocassie.

"Opener?" Brocassie asked.

Sergio produced one from his shirt pocket and between them, they opened two bottles. Brocassie took a long pull, feeling the cool liquid fill his throat. He nodded back at Sergio. "Let's go."

Sergio drove carefully out of the village, slowly working up through the gears.

"Took longer than I thought," Sergio said between sips. "The old man that owns the place was playing canasta. Had to bribe him before he finally took care of me, then rambled on about how Hemingway used to drop in. Even had a photo of him on the wall."

"Like every other bar in Cuba," Brocassie answered, his head turned aside, watching the edge of the road. They were slightly inland now, the sea hidden by groves of manchineel. They were more than three miles from the town and there were no headlights as yet behind them.

"Stop the truck here," Brocassie ordered. He felt down to his thigh, his fingers curling around the grip of the Luger. "Now back up." The Luger came up smoothly, the safety audibly clicking off.

Sergio made an incomplete motion toward the seat, groping for the automatic, but he stopped in the reflexive action.

"Hey," he said smiling, "I brought that thing in case of trouble. Who knows . . . ?" He made a shrug of his shoulders, his teeth parted, still smiling.

Pointing with the Luger, Brocassie motioned him to back up. "Reverse into the manchineel. Get as far back as the truck will go. Far enough back not to be seen from the highway."

Sergio was starting to say something and Brocassie brought the barrel of the automatic down hard on Sergio's kneecap. "Now!"

The Cuban clutched in pain at his kneecap, howling a

blasphemy at Brocassie. Step number one, Brocassie knew, was to show that violence was thinkable. Step number two, which was rarely necessary, was to show that violence was even inevitable.

"This is small-caliber stuff, Sergio. With a bullet in your guts, you'd probably last the whole night. Now back it up."

Grunting with pain, Sergio reversed back off the road, gunning the engine in the soft earth.

"Back farther!" Brocassie saw the long-hanging branches whip past, felt the vibration of the wheels spinning, heard small shrubs fracturing under the chassis, as the truck ground into the darkness. It finally stalled against a manchineel sapling. He reached over and switched out the lights, then took the ignition key.

Sergio huddled over against the door, his knee drawn up, massaging it with his hands.

"Who did you call in there?"

"By the Holy Mother . . . no one. I swear . . ."

"What's holy to you, Sergio? Money, life or immortality?"

Sergio started to display an unexpected resilience. "There was no phone! How could I call anyone. Didn't you notice that the place has no electricity, no overhead poles—all the lighting was by kerosene. Even the fucking refrigerator was butane-powered. With any eyes, you'd have seen."

Brocassie slumped back in the seat, relaxing. He hadn't noticed but it was probably true. No power poles, then probably no telephone lines. The coastal road was a backwater, a place of no commercial importance.

"It may be," he finally answered. "We'll wait for a half hour and then head back toward Santiago."

"The tires!"

"Some other night, Sergio. Tell your friend that you had engine troubles. Give him a broken fan belt. That's your problem. Mine is getting down to the coast and getting off the island. And that's what you're being paid for."

"I can't . . ." Sergio started to object.

Headlights first illuminated the tops of the trees and then Brocassie could see them—four sets, moving slowly. The first truck to pass was a troop transport, the cargo area covered over with laced-down canvas. Illuminated by the headlights of the following truck, Brocassie could see tightly packed troops in the back of the first vehicle. The next two trucks were monstrous flatbeds. The last truck was another troop transport. All four were marked with the Cuban star. Long after they had disappeared down the coastal road, the stench of diesel exhaust remained. Brocassie realized that he had been holding his breath. He exhaled and turned to Sergio.

"That was no ordinary troop convoy."

Sergio sucked in his cheeks and then sniffed. "One truck looks like another to me."

"What kind of uniforms were the troops wearing when you saw them?"

"How should I know? It was dark. It was like I said. Couple of men by the side of the road, pissing in the ditch. Another bunch, standing around, smoking."

"You notice anything odd about those trucks? Have you ever seen flatbeds that size in Cuba?"

The Cuban gave an explosive laugh. "You're the great Yankee spy. I would think you would be very much of an expert on such things." He reached over for the ignition keys.

"Not yet," Brocassie said. "Just keep your hands in your pants pockets. We'll wait another fifteen minutes."

Sergio made a noise in his throat, as if he had run out of patience. "What for? The convoy is past. Are you frightened?" He laughed, but to Brocassie, it sounded forced.

"We sit and we wait," Brocassie repeated. Something in Sergio's voice, he thought, something in his increasing nervousness which he was trying to overlay with casualness.

Fifteen minutes passed. Sergio was nervous, but it was probably just that he valued his own hide and wanted to deliver Brocassie to the coast and get back into Santiago before midnight. Two minutes more, his mind said.

He had started to count in his mind and had gotten to fifty seconds when he saw three headlights traveling in the same direction as the convoy but moving very fast. He watched them for a few seconds and decided that the leader was a motorcycle and the vehicle behind it a car. His attention was on the road but his peripheral vision picked up a movement in the near-darkness of the truck's cab: Sergio's hand moving carefully toward the headlight switch. Brocassie had kept the Luger in his right hand, the safety on. In one quick motion, he slammed his body sideways against Sergio, pinning him against the truck door. He rammed the Luger into Sergio's stomach.

"Move and you'll die, you pimp!" He shoved the barrel deeper into the flab of Sergio's gut.

The motorcycle and car roared by. Brocassie could see that the car was a pale blue Olds 88. The same cars used by the SIM, Batista's secret police, had been confiscated for use by the DGI because the Oldsmobiles had been heavily modified both in handling and performance, making them the fastest vehicles in Cuba.

"How did you get hold of them?" He pushed the automatic even deeper and Sergio winced with pain.

"No—please!" he said in a high cracked voice. "I didn't contact anyone."

"You were reaching for the headlight!"

"I wasn't reaching for anything. My knee still hurts. For the sake of God, can't you move that pistol away from my gut?"

Backing off, Brocassie moved away from the Cuban, keeping the barrel trained on his chest. "That was a DGI car and you know it," Brocassie said through clenched teeth.

"Let's understand one another," he finally said. "You tell me straight off whether you're taking me to some sort of ambush. If you are, I'll tie you up and leave you here and you'll probably live. But if we get to the coast and the DGI is waiting, you'll be the first one to go. Now what do you say, Sergio. Live now or die later?"

The Cuban gave a forced laugh, relaxing. "You mind if I have a cigar before you pull out the blindfold?" He lit one with shaking fingers.

"You think about it, *hombre.* If I had tried to pull on the headlights you would have shot me, correct? So it would not even be logical for me to try. As to the DGI vehicles—if anything, they were probably trying to catch up with the convoy for only God knows whatever reason."

"Maybe it's like you say. But then again, maybe you found a way to reach the DGI back there in the village."

Sergio lifted his hands, rolling the palms slowly upward. *"¿Por qué, carajo?* The stop was of our mutual planning." He was calmer now, visibly relaxing. "Look—I'll take you to the coast. Joaquín's wife has made the arrangement for the boat. If there is a trap there, you shoot me. But I don't care to sit here in the brush with ants crawling over my testicles all night." He put out his hand for the ignition keys.

They drove east now, backtracking down the coastal highway. Passing through Corral del Río, the scene was exactly as it had been nearly an hour earlier. Same men, same argument, a boy in his teens looking into a darkened shop window.

Brocassie opened the second bottle of beer and chewed off the end of the sandwich. Could be that it was all coincidence. Perhaps, really, that his own nerves were to the point of breaking. Just get out of this thing. Completely. Back to Utah. There was always a job for a man who knew explosives, although, he regretted with a half-smile, one did not list under "job expertise" the blowing up of bridges, of railroad tracks or of deep-water piers.

"Exactly where do we meet Joaquín's wife?" He glanced at Sergio.

"A fishing village across the bay from Santiago de Cuba—a small shit hole called Antonio Maceo. I am to drop you off in front of a garage. It is owned by a cousin of Joaquín. Joaquín's wife, Juana, will meet you there."

"How much farther?" he asked.

"Ten, maybe fifteen miles."

Brocassie thought about it for a while. There was still the possibility that Sergio was setting him up. Perhaps, he thought, it was prudent to take out an insurance policy.

"How's the time? When was she expecting us?"

Glancing down at his watch Sergio grunted, "We're going to be more than an hour early. And you can tell her for me that I want an additional two hundred. I'm going to get hell because I didn't produce any tires and that means another trip tomorrow night to pick them up. Which means that I'll be charged rental for the truck tonight, plus the extra time and effort. You tell her that."

"I think perhaps you're going to tell her in person."

Sergio turned to him, his mouth set in a hard line. He looked back again at the road, keeping silent for a while, tapping his finger against the steering wheel in agitation.

"I'm not stopping," he finally said, "except to drop you off. It's a little village. A truck stopped in front of a garage which is closed is going to rouse someone's interest. And I'm not getting paid to take any more chances than I already am."

"I think that you don't have a great deal of choice, do you?" Brocassie lifted the Luger from his pocket.

Sergio exploded. "I run up and down the coast for three days in that damn, stinking bus, looking for your flag. You think people don't notice something like that? You can get out of here, but I stay behind, and if something goes wrong, it's me who ends up against the wall."

"I feel great sympathy for you," Brocassie answered. "And even greater sympathy if something goes wrong because it's going to be you who steps out into the street and it's going to be me who's driving off in this truck. Pull it over to the side." He motioned with the Luger.

Sergio slowed the truck, pulling it off the asphalt onto the shoulder.

"Now out," Brocassie ordered. He still wasn't sure but Sergio's reaction would betray him if there was any sort of a setup. "Strip!"

Standing in the roadway, the Cuban seemed to have shrunk. He started to take a step forward toward the truck and Brocassie brought the weapon up, holding it level on Sergio's chest.

"Strip, I said," Brocassie repeated.

Muttering under his breath, Sergio loosened his belt and let his pants drop down into the dirt. He kicked them away and stood there, legs thin and white in the gleam of the lights. Then he unbuttoned his sports shirt and threw it toward Brocassie.

He looks about as lethal as a ten-year-old, he thought. Sergio had the beginnings of a pot despite his thin body and he was all but hairless. He had virtually no hips and his underpants sagged over his buttocks. He stood in the harsh beams of the headlights, his arms up around his chest, hugging himself against an imagined cold.

Brocassie stripped off his fatigues and threw them to the Cuban. "Pull these on and then lie down in the dirt, face-down."

"You're going to kill me!" Sergio screamed, unable to control the fear in his voice. "I've helped you and now you're going to give me a bullet!"

Christ, but he looks pathetic, Brocassie thought. But the suspicion had been growing in his mind that Sergio was some-how playing a double game—either forced into it or, more likely, free-lancing for Cuban intelligence. The story about Joaquín's home not having been ransacked by the DGI had to be bullshit. Plus the DGI cruiser going like the clappers of hell in the same direction that Sergio had wanted to head and now the drop-off in Antonio Maceo. Why would Joaquín's wife pick a place in the middle of a town, even a small one? The country of the south coast abounded with back roads and hid-den coves. The whole setup smelled bad and was going more rancid by the minute.

"Shoot you?" he finally said. "No, Sergio, if I shot you, the DGI would still be after me and what they need is a body to satisfy their records. Let's say that in the morning someone sees the wreckage of a pickup truck down in the surf—driver still in the cab but badly mutilated from the crash. The barra-cuda and the crabs will probably have had breakfast by then and not much will remain to identify him except a pair of fa-tigues and a rucksack. I think that the chances are that they'll think that body is mine, don't you?"

"You . . ." Sergio was groping for words, his mouth open-ing and closing like a stranded fish.

Brocassie lifted the Luger with his right hand, slapping the butt with his other, as if ensuring that the clip was well seated. "They'll be looking for you, but if they don't find your body, they'll assume that you were with me but somehow got out of the cab in the surf and tried to make it to shore. Tried, Sergio, but didn't make it. 'Sharks,' someone will say and someone else will nod. They'll look up and down the coast, but after a couple of hours, they'll give up looking."

Brocassie slipped into Sergio's clothing, the pants too short, the shirt tight against his chest. Unable to button it, he let it hang loose. "Get in the truck, passenger side with your hands laced behind your neck."

Sergio was shaking now. He crawled in, Brocassie covering him with the Luger.

"Let me give you my opinion, Sergio. I think you sold out Joaquín. And then I think you offered to go in his place to pick me up. How much are they paying you, or is it just that you get some cheap tin metal for being a hero of the Revolution?"

Lunging across the cab at him, the Cuban was surprisingly fast. Grunting, he flung a series of thrusts into Brocassie's side, using his fists and elbows. He was frantic, clawing, his hands and fingernails now flailing at Brocassie's eyes.

Brocassie fought back, fending off the blows, but knowing that he either had to kill him or hammer him senseless in a very short time. Sergio had cracked but not in the way that Brocassie had expected. Not the defiant denial of a guiltless man who had risked his life nor the crumbling resolve of a traitor facing death but rather this—a man with his back to the wall, fighting with what skill he had.

Stiffening the fingers of his left hand into a wedge, Brocassie feinted with his right toward Sergio's face. The Cuban's hands flew up to defend himself and Brocassie rammed his left hand into Sergio's solar plexus. Sergio doubled forward, his breath expelled in a sharp whoosh, and then Brocassie brought his right hand down hard just below the ear. The Cuban screamed just once. Brocassie brought his hand down again, this time farther back on the neck with even greater force, and Sergio collapsed, his limbs twitching in an unconscious spasm. Lifting him back upright, Brocassie felt for the beat of the Cuban's heart. Rapid, but strong.

He drove with the lights out, keeping his speed low, looking for a drop-off to the surf below. There was a low guard fence of wooden posts and cable strung between, but it had not been repaired in some time. Rockfalls and erosion had washed away the fence in some places and before he had gone a mile, Brocassie found a suitable spot. It was on a curve, with only a couple of yards of loose dirt and gravel between the asphalt and the falloff. The posts had broken away and drooped ineffectually over the edge, retained only by the still-attached cable. Getting out, Brocassie walked to the edge. A few tufts of grass held the soil on the lip of the falloff, but beyond that, the ground fell away in a steep slope with surf crashing on rocks over a hundred yards below.

Brocassie got back into the truck and edged it forward until the front wheels were inches from the edge. Then he pulled Sergio from the passenger seat into the driver's seat. From his backpack, he took some of the tent line. Shoving the Cuban's hands past the spokes of the steering wheel, he tied them together on the other side. There was a bit of the sandwich left and he sat on the running board, eating, as he waited for Sergio to return to consciousness. If there were headlights on the road coming from either direction, he would have to push the truck over, and Sergio with it, but it would be a waste, because, he felt, under these circumstances, Sergio would talk his bloody head off.

After five minutes, the Cuban began to grunt and moan. Brocassie stood up next to the Cuban. He had removed the backpack and he had the Luger tucked into his waistband.

"Let me tell you of a television game that used to be played in the States, Sergio," he said softly, his lips next to Sergio's ear.

Sergio opened his eyes wide. He first looked at Brocassie and then out at the ocean before him. He tried to withdraw his hands from the steering wheel but realizing how close the truck was to the falloff, he stopped his movements.

"Cut my hands loose," he said hoarsely. "I can tell you . . ."

"Tell me what?"

Sergio clamped down on his jaw muscles. "I can tell you that I am only doing what the woman said to do. If you don't believe me, take the truck and leave me here. But you can't do this . . . this *thing*!"

"The game," Brocassie said to him softly, "is called Truth or Consequences. I ask you some questions and you tell me no lies. That's how you stay in the game. But if you lie, and I think I will have to be the judge of that, then you pay the consequence. The consequence, of course, is that you have to learn how to swim with a truck tied to you."

Sergio spat out an obscenity. He struggled and then suddenly quit as Brocassie's hand felt for the parking brake.

"That's better, Sergio," Brocassie said. "Just calm down and pay attention to my questions, but remember that we might not have enough time to play the game out to its conclusions." He glanced back down the highway. "If headlights appear from either direction, then the game is over. I would have to release the parking brake and wish you a fond ¡adiós! Then I would scuff out the marks of the tires and lie down in the ditch on the opposite side of the road and feel very guilty." He reached up to the dashboard and took two cigars which remained. "Very good cigars, Sergio. But they don't taste too good when they get wet."

"The DGI is waiting for you at the tire place, with a backup force in Antonio Maceo," Sergio said in a rush. "But I swear before God Himself that I had—that I have no choice. They took Joaquín over two weeks ago—not only him but also his wife. A DGI lieutenant took me to the barracks in Palma Soriano to identify them." Sergio paused, looking back over his shoulder toward the east as if he expected headlights. Sergio's face was wild now, sweat beading his forehead, running down into his eyes. He ducked his face against his shoulder, trying to wipe it away.

"What did she and Joaquín tell them?"

Throwing his head from side to side, Sergio was shouting, completely out of control. *"MY GOD, EVERYTHING!* The DGI worked on both of them for two days straight. There wasn't anything left of their bodies, except their faces. And this little boy lieutenant took me into a room and showed me the pipes and the drains in the floors and hoses that wash the blood away and he said that I could very quickly start paying off my debts in purgatory with Joaquín and his wife if I wished it."

"Then why didn't they come and get me on the coast?"

"Man—they wanted whoever it was coming down out of the mountains alive. They planned to wring you dry and then trap the counterrevolutionary guerrillas. But they thought that if you knew you were about to be captured, you might take one of those pills or get killed when they were trying to capture you. This way, they figured to get you alive and in one piece when you were with me in Pilón, humping tires into the truck."

It all made sense except one thing, Brocassie thought. He could see how Sergio could be forced into this thing, but the DGI would never issue him a Luger. What in hell for? The DGI wanted him alive. On a hunch, Brocassie leaned down and reached under the driver's seat, feeling for the holster. He finally felt the hard, smooth leather and he tugged at it, pulling it free from the seat's supporting coils. Just as the holster came free, Sergio's foot snapped off the floor, grazing Brocassie's head. He stumbled backward, off balance, tripping over his own feet and knowing that the cliff's edge was only a breath away. He landed heavily on his back, his head over the edge. Brocassie froze and then could feel the earth crumbling under his body, breaking away. He could see Sergio sawing frantically at the rope against the spokes of the wheel and now there was no doubt in his mind. Cautiously moving his arm, he reached for the knife strapped to his leg and slammed the blade into the dirt, driving it in to the hilt. Using this as an anchor, Brocassie inched back over the edge, slowly gaining ground. A large chunk of earth broke away beneath him and at the last moment, he heaved desperately against the knife and then used the momentum to roll inward from the cliff's edge. He lay there panting for long seconds and then stood up, drawing the Luger. He placed it against Sergio's ribs and thumbed off the safety. "Relax, Sergio. One more movement and you're going over the side. Put your foot on the brake." Sergio moved his foot to the brake and then Brocassie released the parking brake lever. "If you try to kick me, you might just lose control of the brake and I think you should consider just what your priorities are. You all calmed down now?" Sergio made a sound in his throat, as if he could not speak, and then nodded.

Retrieving the holster from the ground, Brocassie flicked on the parking lights and studied the holster in the dim glow. The identification was stamped neatly into the leather on the interior side of the holster:

SHELL GAME

Capt. Sergio Piedra, DGI
Counterintelligence Operations
Oriente Province
Serial No. 353112

Brocassie shoved the holster beneath his belt, smashed in the glowing brake light with the butt of the Luger and then went back to the opened door and flicked off the dash lights. "Our game resumes, Captain Piedra, but it's a little more serious now. You haven't played well so far. I should terminate the game right now with your consequence, but you can live a little bit longer if you start telling the truth."

Sergio swallowed noisily in the darkness. He was staring out over the sea. Carefully, he bent forward, resting his forehead on the steering wheel. "All right," he finally said. "The truth. I swear on the cross . . ."

"Spare me the bullshit. Are Joaquín and his wife alive?"

"No. What I told you about their arrest and interrogation was true. I didn't have anything to do with it. I didn't know about the interrogation until it was over."

"Explain."

"I work as officer in charge of electronics counterintelligence, directly under the *comandante* of Oriente Province. We had radio directional finders set up—new stuff that the Russians gave us—and we knew of at least four stations operating either in Santiago or in the Sierra. We monitored a transmission out of the Sierra that we knew had to be Maroto but we could never pinpoint the damn thing. Two days later, we intercepted an incoming message from the CIA station in Coral Gables, Florida, but instead of Maroto responding, this station in Santiago did. We got a fix on it and passed it to the Palma Soriano station because they were the closest. Joaquín and his wife were picked up within fifteen minutes. I phoned the lieutenant in charge to hold them for questioning and that I would be down in two days. You know the procedure—two days of softening up so that the prisoner is receptive to questioning. But instead the lieutenant started right in on them on orders of someone higher up. The *comandante* would never allow stuff like that, but he's out of the country and . . ."

"Exactly what did Joaquín and his wife spill?"

48

"That someone from Maroto's or Fabricio's column was trying to get out of Cuba with some film. Joaquín had the dates and the passwords."

"So there are DGI waiting for me?"

Piedra nodded. "I told you the truth, understand?"

"You've told me three different versions of the truth, pimp." Brocassie grabbed Sergio's wrist, checking his watch. Time running out. "OK," he said. "I want a few names. The man who ordered the interrogation."

"*I . . . don't . . . know!*"

"The little-boy lieutenant?"

"Lieutenant José Caballero."

"Lieutenant José Caballero is a dead man," Brocassie said softly. "And the name of the *comandante*?"

"Álvarez. Julio Álvarez."

The name hit him like a jolt of high voltage. He had known that Julio had gone into the 26th of July Movement after he got out of Havana and that he had fought with Raúl Castro's column and was in on the taking of the Leoncio Vidal Barracks in Santa Clara, but he had heard rumors that Álvarez had gotten out of Cuba when the Revolution was over. He willed his breathing to slow. It was a common enough name. "Describe Álvarez to me."

"Thin, dark skin, very widely spaced eyes. He speaks English without an accent and he's said to have immigrated to Cuba back in the fifties, although that's just rumor. He never talks of it, if he did."

"Does Álvarez have a degree in law?"

Sergio frowned. "I think . . . I don't know. He is well educated. Fidel and Raúl occasionally get drunk with him, and when Fidel is tight, he calls him 'Doctor.' "

Which fitted, Brocassie thought. In Latin countries, a lawyer was sometimes called "Doctor." "Where does Álvarez live, Sergio?"

"On the coast east of Santiago. A *finca* in the country on Road Eighty-seven—a place that an American who worked for the Bacardi family owned before the Revolution. Álvarez lives there with his whore."

Not like Julio, Brocassie thought. Julio went in for stylish women with good backgrounds like Alicia, not *putas*.

"You said he was out of the country. Where?"

"Moscow. Some kind of KGB-sponsored counterintelligence training. He's due back soon."

I ought to kill this little bastard, Brocassie thought, but he realized that he couldn't. Too much death already. He looked at Sergio and saw, even in the dim light, fear pinching the man's face.

"I've told you everything. Let me live," the Cuban whispered in a dry voice.

Brocassie reached into the cab and pulled on the parking brake and then walked around and climbed into the passenger's seat. He took out his knife and held it, feeling the edge with his thumb and then reached over and cut the knots of the rope which bound Piedra to the wheel. "Start the engine and then back up carefully. Then head for Antonio Maceo—*slowly*. You'll live if you do what you're told."

The Cuban's hands were shaking but he got the engine started and in gear, backing out onto the coastal road. He headed east.

"How far?" Brocassie asked. The headlights bore tunnels of brilliance in the blackness.

"Another fifteen minutes."

Neither spoke for several minutes, Brocassie thinking of Comandante Álvarez. A common name, but still his curiosity kept gnawing. "Álvarez," he asked carefully, "does he have an old leg wound?"

Sergio glanced at him from the corner of his eyes and then stared back at the road. "I don't know. He limps sometimes but he never mentioned a wound."

He wouldn't, Brocassie thought. Not if it was his stepbrother, Julio Álvarez, because that wound had bought him the Silver Star in Korea. "Which leg?"

Sergio didn't hesitate. "The left one. He rubs it a lot when the weather's damp."

A minute ticked by on the dash clock. It had to be him, Brocassie thought. "What's he like, the *comandante*?"

Sergio breathed deeply, compressing his lips. "He drinks a lot. I don't care for him. I could do his job twice as well in half the time." He glanced sideways again. "Speaking professionally, I mean."

Brocassie ignored the implications. "I mean his personal life."

Relaxing, Sergio babbled on. He talked about the *finca* and how the *comandante* would invite a few of his officers over for a Sunday of pigeon shooting and drinking and then a dinner which the *comandante* would prepare himself.

"You said he had a *puta.*"

"Álvarez never allows her to come down when the men are there. I met her only once when I had to deliver some papers to the *comandante* and he wasn't there. She's a beautiful bitch. I can't understand why he keeps her hidden." Sergio turned toward Brocassie. "You've heard of Álvarez."

"I've heard of him," Brocassie answered. So Julio had finally made it, he thought. The big time, *the deep end of the pool*, as Álvarez had always called the high-risk aspect of success. And it made sense because Julio was clever, intelligent and he was a good fighter. Sergio was saying something and Brocassie snapped out of his past. "What were you saying?"

"Just that his whore is a woman of good family. I could see it in her features."

"What's her name?"

"Alicia," Sergio responded.

His fingers tightened involuntarily on the trigger of the Luger. He stared without seeing into the night, his peripheral vision catching the blur of trees as they whipped past in the darkness. "Say her name again," he said slowly.

"Alicia. I don't know her family name."

He realized that he was holding his breath. He slowly relaxed the pressure on the trigger. "There was a famous whore in Santiago who called herself 'Alicia,' " he lied, not wanting to hear Piedra's reply. "She had a . . . she had a chipped front tooth."

"The same bitch, then," Sergio laughed. "She would be two handfuls with those pointy tits and that round little ass."

Anger, relief, disbelief, exhilaration, all tumbling in his mind like a gyroscope gone wild. But it couldn't be, and his mind wouldn't accept the idea that she lived when he had borne her death for these last two years. A signpost was illuminated in the headlights and then whipped by into blackness: ANTONIO MACEO-3 KILÓMETROS. "Stop!" he shouted.

Startled, Sergio slammed to a halt, the brakes locked, the smell of burned rubber and exhaust fumes flooding the cab.

Brocassie raised the Luger, pointing it at Sergio's chest. "Tell me the absolute truth or you'll die in ten seconds. Describe everything you know about this woman."

Sergio held his hands out as if he could stop the bullet. "Hey! I told you. She is like I said, a woman of black hair, very long. Very fine features, Spanish, you understand. Her tooth is chipped and she's not as tall as I am."

"Are there cats? Did she have cats?" Brocassie was shouting at him.

Sergio was beginning to panic. "Cats? *CATS*? How in hell would I know?" He lowered his hands to the wheel and was silent and then turned back. Then finally, "Yes. I remember now. There was a cat. She was holding it. I remember it now because it only had three legs."

It was as if a great wind had swept through his mind. He almost lost the grip on the automatic. She was alive and he wanted to weep or shout but he couldn't. He exhaled, staring ahead, and lowered the Luger. "Get moving. Keep the speed down and stop when you get to the outskirts of Antonio Maceo. Describe what the place is like."

Sergio ground the gears as he dropped the clutch in. The old truck shuddered and slowly gained speed. "Fishing village. Typical *pueblecito* with one paved street and a square. Wood shacks and tin roofs. I was to drop you off in the square next to the garage and then drive on. Once I was clear, they'd switch the spotlights on and rush you."

"What about the fishing boat that was going to take me offshore?"

Sergio shrugged, not answering. They were just coming out of a curve and below them were a few scattered lights which roughly defined the streets of Antonio Maceo. The village was wedged between high inland cliffs and a broad beach. The surf line shone faintly in the splintered moonlight. "Pull over and stop."

Slowing, Sergio pulled off on the gravel shoulder.

"Headlights off, leave the parking lights on." The DGI, he guessed, would still be waiting at the tire pickup point; Antonio Maceo was the backup ambush. He and Piedra were probably an hour, maybe two, ahead of schedule and it was unlikely that they would be expected this soon. He studied the village below for movement but it was lifeless, like a stage set.

Pulling the remains of the nylon cord from his backpack, he tossed it into Sergio's lap. "Tie a slip knot, put it over your right wrist and then pull it tight." Sergio fumbled in the pale wash of the dash lights, complying. "All right, Captain, now put both your hands behind your back, your right wrist over your left."

The Cuban hesitated and Brocassie caught just the faint distortion on Sergio's lips, as if his face had involuntarily betrayed a decision. Brocassie slipped the knife from its sheath and pressed the point into Sergio's side. "Don't think," he whispered. "Not about going for the horn or shouting or trying to overpower me because you'll bleed a bucket of blood before you can even squeak and you don't know what it's like to have a knife sawing through your intestines."

The Cuban slowly overlaid his wrists, Brocassie whipping the line around and around, then knotting it with half hitches. Brocassie leaned back in the seat, feeling the pounding of his heart vibrate through his body.

"Very good," he said. "You're halfway home, Sergio." He reached up with the butt of the Luger and crushed the overhead light fixture, then pulled his backpack from the luggage rack in back. From the canvas, he extracted a matchbox and opened it, pulling out two thin tubes of silver. "You understand what these are?" He held them in front of Sergio's face.

"Detonators." Sergio was breathing heavily through his nostrils.

"Correct. Contact fuses and they're old—unstable, understand?" From the back flap pocket on the rucksack, Brocassie withdrew the plastic explosive. He cut it in half with his knife and held up one of the pieces. "C-4," he said. "About an ounce." He inserted one of the detonators into the plastic. "Now here's the situation, Captain Sergio Piedra. We are both going to get out of the truck and then I'm going to turn you loose. You are going to walk very slowly and very carefully down into the square. It's my guess that you'll require about twenty minutes and that will give me some time to do some traveling." He reached over and opened the passenger door. "Now get out."

He followed Sergio through the door, dropping lightly onto the asphalt. Down below, the village was still, unnaturally so. It occurred to him that there was not even the barking of a dog or the occasional sound of a vehicle moving.

"I can almost hear you thinking," he whispered into Sergio's ear, "but don't. You're not going to shout and you're not going to run. Just a calm, steady pace, befitting an officer's dignity." He leaned back into the cab and using the knife, slit the upholstery, taking out a handful of the foam rubber stuffing. Next, he removed his shirt and tore off a long strip.

"Say 'ahhh,' " Brocassie whispered. Sergio slowly opened his mouth, reluctantly, as a child would do with a dentist hovering over him. Brocassie jammed the foam rubber in and then wrapped the strip of cloth around his head.

He molded the C-4, flattening it, and set it on top of Sergio's head. "Like a woman carrying laundry, understand? Keep your head up and walk slowly. Because if that explosive drops on the road, you'll blow your balls off from the toenails up. Take it easy. You're a pimp, not a hero." He turned Sergio toward the village. "One more thing. If you make it, I want you to deliver a message to Comandante Álvarez. Can you remember?"

Sergio made a muffled sound, his body absolutely rigid. In the dim light, Brocassie could see the man's eyes bulging.

"Tell Álvarez and his"—he couldn't bring himself to call her a whore—"and his woman that I'm coming back. Tell them that I give my word on that." He put his hand against Sergio's back and applied a little pressure. "Enjoy your stroll, Piedra."

The Cuban shuffled forward, moving as if he were an old man with a diseased prostate, the steps mincing and unsure. Brocassie watched him until he faded into the blackness.

He took the last chunk of plastic explosive and imbedded the remaining contact fuse in it and then, opening the hood, placed the C-4 on the edge of the air cleaner. Using the point of his knife, he jabbed into the bottom of the radiator until a thin trickle of water began to spray his wrist. Five, ten, twenty minutes. He couldn't begin to estimate how long the water would take to drain out, but eventually the engine would run red hot, and in its death throes, it would begin to shudder like an animal in seizure, and the plastic would fall, impacting on the detonator. It was a diversion and a poor one at that, but there wasn't much else to work with.

He lowered the hood carefully and paused, looking again toward the village. Nothing moving, except a few streetlights swaying in the wind. He then ran, back along the road, away from the village. With over two hundred yards separating him from the truck, he paused again at the edge of the embankment which sloped down to the beach and took a final glance toward the village. No movement except a glint of polished metal or the reflection from glass. Binoculars? Or just the glint of an insulator on the crosstrees of a power pole?

Carefully, he edged down the rock-strewn embankment until his feet crunched in pebbles and sand.

His eyes had adapted to the blackness and he could now define the topography of the beach. It was a crescent of sand, perhaps half a mile long and no more than fifty yards in width. To the west, toward the village, was a small breakwater which protected half a dozen small fishing boats. Beyond that, the pewter glint of dying breakers, spending themselves on the shoreline.

He moved west, away from the town, skirting along the base of the embankment, following it to where it terminated in steep cliffs which abutted the sea.

Once, he heard the crunch of sand under boots and he froze, watching the silhouette of a man with a carbine slung over his shoulder pass between him and the sea. He waited for more than two minutes and saw the silhouette pass back toward the village. One man, he thought. There would be more but it was probable that they would be stationed back toward the village, placed along the beach to prevent any attempt to escape by sea.

Five minutes passed, he guessed. He moved more quickly now, running in a crouch along the base of the embankment, feeling brush whip at his legs, smelling the strong taste of the sea. It was farther than he had thought it would be, but slowly, the embankment merged into cliffs and the cliffs with the sea.

"Manuel?"

The voice was a stage whisper. He couldn't see the man but he sensed that he had to be the outermost perimeter guard. It was a shit duty and probably the man was no more than a corporal.

In a normal voice, Brocassie answered, "No. This is Captain Piedra. The exercise is terminated. The man didn't show up as expected."

"Lieutenant Ferrer . . ."

"What about Ferrer?"

"Where is he? I report to him."

Brocassie was moving closer, walking slowly but confidently, homing in on the man's voice. "Ferrer is conferring with a KGB lieutenant. They seem to have some interest in this affair. Let's get moving."

He could now see the vague outline of the man as he moved toward him. "You have a match?" he asked. He was within five feet of the man and he paused, hands on his hips. "I said, do you have a match?" he repeated, putting the right amount of indisputable authority into his voice.

The man grunted something and slung his rifle over his shoulder, his hands working into his fatigues.

Brocassie put one of Sergio's cigars in his mouth and walked toward the guard.

The man had the matches in his hand and he lit one, cupping it from the wind. The light flared briefly and the man started to say something when Brocassie hit him on the temple with the butt of the Luger. In that one brief second's flare of light he had the impression of a plain, moonlike face under a peaked forage cap—a boy no older than his late teens. The boy's legs folded and he went down with nothing more than a sigh, Brocassie catching him and then lowering him gently into the sand.

He wanted to tie the kid up but there wasn't time. He took the carbine and removed the clip, working the action to make sure that there were no shells left in the chamber, and then he started for the beach, keeping low in an easy jog.

Little time left, he thought. The kid would be out for a

long time but he didn't know whether the other guard got that far west on the beach. It would make sense that they checked in with each other, and if that were the case, then he had no time left at all.

Suddenly he was in wet sand with foam rushing over his insteps. He shrugged off his boots, threw the Luger away and waded out until the water was up to his chest. He swam straight out to sea for a hundred strokes and then turned, paralleling the beach, heading for the breakwater. Twice he rested, lying on his back, paddling water, trying to see any movement inshore or on the road. He thought that he could still see the parking lights of the truck. Had the damn engine seized and the explosive not gone off? Damn. He had needed something as a diversion and the engine should have seized by now.

The breakwater was nothing more than rock rip-rap, piled loosely into a mounded wall of debris, but it was sufficient to protect the fishing fleet in the normal summer winds. Treading water, he studied the breakwater and the small wharf beyond but he could see no movement. They would probably have overlapping patrols farther inland, between the village and the sea.

He started to swim again, moving in among the bobbing shapes. They were mainly powered vessels, twenty-five feet or so in length, with a single small deckhouse, the type of launch that a man and a boy would spend a day at sea in, long-lining while drifting with the current, working for bottom fish.

Brocassie checked the wind. It was offshore and the boats tugged at their mooring lines, their topsides reflecting back the sound of the light chop. Toward dawn, the wind would begin to die, to be replaced by a few hours of calm and then an onshore wind would set in by midmorning. Between now and then, he had six hours or less of a favorable wind and wanted to make the most of it.

A bit farther inshore, he found what he was looking for: an open sailing skiff with a sprintsail rig and oars, about twenty feet long. It was one of the breed of traditional Caribbean small boats, doubled-ended, buoyant and seaworthy, and able to sail handily in appalling conditions. The mooring line was of thick nylon, covered with stringy moss at the waterline.

Brocassie drew himself down the line, hand over hand, until he felt where the nylon terminated in a thimble which was shackled to rusty links of chain. It would be easy to cut the line with his knife, but he wanted to make it appear that the skiff had broken loose of its own accord or the neglect of the owner. It seemed likely that the DGI would first assume that he had moved back into the mountains, and he needed as much time as possible before they started searching the offshore waters. The boat would be missed by its owner in the morning but there would be the element of doubt. At best, it was a poor gamble, but six hours at five knots of speed would put him thirty miles offshore and in international waters, if that meant anything to the DGI.

It took two more dives to unwind the safety wire and then two more to unscrew the clevis pin from the shackle. He finally rose to the surface, gasping, the temperature of the water now beginning to stiffen his muscles.

The skiff at first drifted slowly to seaward, but then some perverse eddy of current dragged it in toward the breakwater. Brocassie hung on the mooring line, his head just above water, willing the damn boat to clear the rip-rap, but with a temperament of its own, it moved in closer and closer. The rocks loomed above him and his feet touched bottom. He tried to shove away from the breakwater and as he thrust his feet against the rocks, needles of intense white-hot pain speared into the flesh of his bare feet. Involuntarily, he cried out, the sound escaping his lips before he could control it, and he bit at his arm, trying to muffle the sound.

"*¡Quién anda por ahí!*" There was the distinct click of a cartridge being chambered—the sound stark and metallic in the stillness of the night. It was a guard, and Brocassie knew that to make any further sound was to die.

The man was erect now, his weapon traversing the arc in front of him. "Who goes?" he challenged again, and then he started to move seaward along the broken surface of the breakwater.

The light came first and then the distant, muffled explosion, rumbling off the cliffs and echoing in multiple reverberations. There was a secondary *crump* and flare of light and then the shrill of a siren. The guard hesitated and then stood upright, his body now in full profile, looking toward the burning truck which flamed like a bonfire in the road above the village.

The sudden glare of a flashlight illuminated the base of the breakwater and slowly traversed back and forth, sweeping farther in each direction. Brocassie took three deep breaths, holding the third one, and propelled himself downward, breaststroking into the blackness, landward, away from the breakwater. He went deeper and deeper, surprised at the depth of the anchorage, and his ears were howling now and he had no sense of direction.

Unconsciously, he realized that he was counting. *Thirty-four, thirty-five, thirty-six.* His extended hands touched sand and slimy weed and he grasped at the stuff, holding himself on the bottom. *Forty-seven, forty-eight, forty-nine.* Heart thudding in the cage of his ribs, his lungs on fire and bursting. *Fifty-nine, sixty, sixty-one.* He couldn't hold his breath any longer and he pushed off the bottom with his hands, allowing himself to drift upward. It seemed an eternity and he almost panicked, believing that, somehow, he was still only inches from the bottom in some strange state of neutral buoyancy, but then he broke the surface.

The guard was in the skiff, shining his flashlight along the interior of the vessel, probably looking for the mark of wet feet on the floorboards. Brocassie treaded water, more than eighty feet away, trying to keep his movements to a minimum. He felt exhausted and the pain in his feet was intense. He now realized that he had pushed off from rocks infested with sea urchins and that the spines of the urchins would fester within a day and from there on out, without antibiotics or a means of extracting them, it would be a race with gangrene.

At last the man moved to the bow of the vessel and pulled in the mooring line. He examined the thimble and threw the slime-covered nylon up onto the rocks of the jetty and scrambled out of the skiff. "Fucking *pescadores,*" he swore. He hitched the line twice around a protruding rock and sighed, unzipped his pants and urinated.

Brocassie was desperately cold, even though the water was tepid. His reserves were gone and it seemed to him as if his limbs were leaden weights with no ability to support him. How much longer? he wondered.

Looking toward the land, he could see that the truck was still blazing, yellow sheets of flame roiling up from the carcass of the vehicle. Lights were moving in the street now, bobbing beams of flashlights and vehicles with spotlights stabbing up at the cliffs above the village.

Two sharp shrills of a whistle lanced the night and then the guard on the jetty zipped up his pants, slung his rifle up higher on his shoulder and started picking his way carefully over the rocks of the jetty toward the shore.

Brocassie gave it another two minutes and then stroked slowly to the skiff. He pulled himself up over the gunnel of the skiff, grunting at the pain when his feet touched the floorboards. His father would have told him that pain was a stimulus, but he was past that now.

He flipped the mooring line several times until it came loose and pushed off the jetty with one of the oars. Once clear, he set both oars in their tholes and stroked slowly, keeping his back hunched down. He would be down-moon, nearly invisible in the starlight but still within the range of spotlights if they decided to sweep the bay.

As he stroked he could see individual lights of vehicles illuminating the gutted truck. Then he saw more flashlights sweeping the hillside leading to the beach and he knew that it would not be long before they would find his tracks in the sand.

Could they organize chase boats? Probably ... undoubtedly. They would rouse fishermen and there would be delays but they would surely come. With an offshore wind, he had six hours until dawn when the aircraft would start searching. He knew that he was cutting it fine.

He was well beyond the breakwater now and he stood up, tears involuntarily flooding his eyes from the pain of the needles in his feet, but he raised the mast and bent on the sail.

Looking back to the north, he used Polaris as his guide and steered, keeping the point of light in his wake. The skiff came alive as he got out from beneath the lee of the land, a bow wave now breaking the sea into streaks of phosphorescence. He steered carefully, the land behind him falling away.

Jamaica, he thought. Ninety miles—fifteen to twenty hours away. He settled down onto the floorboards, shivering, the tiller under his arm, and he tried to concentrate on the idea that Alicia was alive and he'd come back to her. Come back, regardless of what she was and what she had done.

CHAPTER

3

She slowly came awake in the early dawn to the distant sound of roosters crowing. For a few moments, she lay there, listening to the beat of her own heart. Finally Alicia Helvia studied the ceiling, gazing at the familiar patterns of cracks in the plaster—like a road map of her life, radiating out in erratic directions with no purpose or pattern. Gradually, she began to be aware of the sounds and smells which drifted up from the kitchen. The old woman with the sharp tongue, thick hands and potbelly would be making breakfast now, knifing thick slabs of pig shank into sizzling fat, cracking eggs, frying them in holes stamped out of bread slices.

The old woman, Marta, had been taken in by Julio after the Revolution. Her son, Alberto, a scrawny kid under Julio's command, had been killed in a raid on an army *cuartel* in Sagua de Tánamo in the last days of the fight against Batista's forces. The boy had been one of the first over the wall in the final rush and he had taken two bullets in his chest. Julio rarely showed emotion, but when he had first told Alicia about it, his eyes had been clamped shut, tears wetting his face. He had turned away from her, ashamed.

"It was the final assault and he was carrying the satchel charges to blow the gates. He was a kid," Julio said, over and over again. "Just a fucking kid with a runny nose who believed I was God." Julio had found the boy's mother and given her the job of running the household. She had not cared much for the boy according to the gardener, but she kept his photo in the kitchen on top of the refrigerator as a constant reminder to Comandante Álvarez as to her reason for being there, and despite her slovenliness and bad temper, her entrenchment was now unquestioned.

From the sound of rattling crockery and conversation, Alicia knew that the men were being fed. When Julio had first left for Moscow, the old woman had demanded that Alicia join them in eating because she said that Cuba was now a place where the only ones who had privilege were those who worked for the Revolution—not those who had opposed it. "There are excellent jobs in the cane fields," Alicia retorted, "for those wishing to truly help the Revolution." From then on, the subject was closed and a fragile truce arrived at, whereby Alicia made her own breakfast and lunch and ate dinner alone in the dining room but from the food that the woman had prepared.

It was not that she disliked the woman or even the gardener. But the three guards were all cast from the same clay—rough, crude types who seemed to delight in mental explorations of her anatomy whenever Julio wasn't around. She was prohibited from leaving the grounds of the old estate without one of the guards with her, and even then, could go only as far as Berraco, a small nearby village set in the coastal range some fifteen miles to the east of Santiago. When Julio was around, he sometimes took her driving along the coast and twice now, within the last year, to Santiago, but beyond that, she was a prisoner in the house.

She got up and padded to the window. The wind was raking through the palms which ringed the estate, producing a soft rasping which would never let up until the alternating calms and storms of the hurricane season. The still-low sun shot shafts of light across the lawn, catching small prisms of violet and blue and red from the dew and two cats, Mookem Flower and her offspring, mauled each other in mock combat, tumbling and rolling in the wet grass. It was a wonderful old place, originally built by the Bacardi rum people, a south-coast retreat constructed in the 1800s from quarried rock and plastered, Spanish style. It was a place to dream in and to listen to one's own mind, except that she could not leave. Perhaps better than a prison and infinitely better than the blood-soaked ground of the Isle of Pines, but still, in its own way, a kind of slow, comfortable death.

She turned from the window, drawing off her nightgown, and sat down at her dressing table. For fifteen minutes, she stroked through her long hair, which hung to her waist. Normally, she tried to avoid looking too closely in the mirror, for the scar was still a welt of bright pink tissue which spanned from her left breast to the base of her rib cage. Álvarez had discussed it with the few competent doctors left in Cuba but they knew nothing of cosmetic surgery so he had finally told her that in a year or so, if Raúl Castro gave his permission, he might take her to East Germany where there were plastic surgeons. But she had become used to it, and now she was no longer really conscious of it.

Julio had been gone over a month now. He hadn't talked much about it before leaving—only that he and seven other officers in the DGI were to receive training in Russia. Until his departure for the Soviet Union, he had been head of the task force formed to destroy the counterrevolutionary forces in Oriente Province, but he had also talked about the possibility of an even more responsible command in Havana within two years. In a way, she would hate to leave the peace of this place, but then again . . . Havana, and perhaps a bit more freedom. With time, memories would die, records would be lost and Julio would become more powerful. He had promised her that, eventually, there would be no danger of conviction for her work against the Revolution.

Finally, she stood up, pulled on a pair of nylon underpants and cotton duck trousers. She had lost weight, largely because she would only eat by herself. Exercise had been a problem but she had bribed the guards into building a crude backboard in a grassy area off to the side of the garage, where she could spend an hour a day slamming tennis balls against the rough, wooden barrier. She had only two balls left. Both had the life knocked out of them, but Julio had promised to bring two or three cans if he could find them. From Russia? she wondered, where the elastic in underpants stretched out of shape after a few washings.

She pulled out an old bra, one of three remaining. It was from Hungary, built from roughly finished cotton and fitted with nursing flaps—the only bras available for purchase in Cuba within the last year. The cups seemed to indicate that women in Hungary had breasts shaped like tea saucers, slightly oblate and very flattened. She pulled the thing on, crushing her breasts into the fabric cups. She would save the others, both American and five years old, for when he came home. But until then, she thought, tightening the straps, this bra would give the guards nothing to build their sexual fantasies on.

She pulled on a man's blue shirt, knotting it at her waist. Julio had promised to bring her some clothes and underthings as most of what she had was pre-Revolution, but she doubted that he would remember. Instead, he would probably come home loaded down with duty-free liquor, East German high fidelity components and black lace panties which were more air than fabric. He had a thing about black lace, and loved to see her in it, but she would gladly trade a drawer full of that fluffy nylon for three decent pairs of cotton briefs. She smiled, amused, because in a way, he was still a small boy, fascinated with toys and fantasies, and she found that easy to love.

She hesitated, her mind trying to define *love*. *Love?* What was *love*? One single word in a dictionary of thousands of words to describe the greatest spectrum of feelings in one's experience. Love for Brocassie had been one thing, like a wildfire crowning a stand of dry timber; hot flying embers, enveloping heat and whirlwinds driven before the flames. And still there, even after his death, smoldering, never to die completely.

But love for Julio Álvarez was quite something different. Caring for him when he was sick or discouraged, thankful for his protection, obligated for his generosity, dutiful to fulfill his need for sexual release, a certain binding to him by chance or fate, but *love*? Not love as she had known it with Brocassie, but by some definition, still love. Perhaps the clever Chinese, with their idiograms, had a hundred different brush strokes to differentiate between the many meanings of love.

His photo was on her night table and, reluctantly, she picked it up and stared down at the dark face and brilliant smile of Julio Álvarez. She had taken that photo back in the spring of '58, when the world was more predictable. Julio was sitting cross-legged on the hood of his Jaguar, his body erect and proud, like a self-indulgent monarch holding court.

Havana had been his kingdom, and the beautiful women within his subjects. The fathers of those women despised him, their mothers wrung their hands at the thought of broken hearts and hymens, but the daughters loved it all—his body, his money, his power.

All of them except Alicia Helvia. She was, of course, flattered that Julio had singled her out, mounting an all-out attack on her heart and her supposed virginity. But she kept him at arm's length, rejecting all but the most simple and inexpensive presents, and made a point of turning down his invitations to country weekends with nonexistent friends at nonexistent *fincas*.

For a while, back in the late part of '58, she began to believe she was in love with Julio. He slowly settled down, became more serious and less demanding, dutifully read serious books so that he could match her far-ranging interests—even talked of buying a beach house in Bacuranao. For a while, she had considered him as a mate, for she knew that it would come to the point where he would propose and she had to know her own mind. Although he didn't come from one of the old accepted families, he excited her with his charm and brilliance and his future was assured. He had started to go out of his way to cultivate her father and meet her friends. His drinking tapered back to a few daiquiris a day and he made a point of stopping to admire handsome children playing in the parks. And as the days and weeks and months went by, she knew that she would have to give him an answer and she thought it would be yes.

And then there was Brocassie.

She had met Julio one rainy August afternoon at his favorite watering hole, the Floridita Bar on Avenida Monserrate. Immediately, she sensed a suppressed excitement about him. He had three daiquiris and only picked at his lobster Mariposa, rambling on about inconsequential happenings. He went through half a pack of cigarettes during the luncheon, nervously flicking the ashes on the floor despite the icy glare of the patron.

"Something's eating at you," she finally said.

"My brother is coming down to Cuba. I invited him. Sent him the tickets and a thousand bucks. He's arriving on Pan Am this afternoon."

"You never said that you had a brother!"

Álvarez leaned back in his chair, avoiding her eyes. He glanced at his watch and then back to her. There was something uneasy in his manner, she thought—almost apprehension.

"He isn't my brother," he answered angrily. "His father and mine were partners in the mines. Had been for fifteen years. A team, understand. They would only work together. Brocassie . . . my brother . . ." His voice trailed off. He wadded up his napkin and threw it on the table. "I've made a goddamn stupid mistake. I should have never asked him down."

"But you called him your brother."

"Partly because that's what most people thought we were, partly because we grew up together. His mother was Mexican, an illegal. She died when he was very young. So his father used to board him out with my mother in the winters when my father and his went off to the mines." He shook his head. "When Brocassie was thirteen or so—just a couple of years younger than me, his father died. My parents took him in, no questions asked, never a thought about the cost although we had bugger-all for money. Then my father died in a cave-in and my mother raised both of us until he finished high school and went off to the university on a scholarship."

She reached across the table, laying her hand on his. "Tell me about him."

Self-consciously, Julio withdrew his hand and signaled

for another drink. He turned back to her. "What's to tell? He's part Mexican, part Cree Indian—a *mestizo*. It was dumb of me to ask him. He won't fit in with our friends. He speaks Spanish all right, but he's got two left feet and his idea of a conversation is keeping his mouth shut and watching your eyes. It used to give me the creeps."

"Did you and Brocassie get along together?"

"It was OK."

"That doesn't tell me much, Julio."

Álvarez made a face. "We lived together in the same house, we went to school together, swiped apples together, kicked the asses off the local hoods together, went climbing in the mountains together, but we never really were close and yet in some ways we were. Like a fence was between us but the gate was there, unlocked, waiting for either one of us to push it open."

She forced a smile. "It sounds like the love-hate thing that most brothers have. Absolutely normal."

He shook his head. "No, not normal. Something that was always beyond reach. I couldn't understand him, what made him tick. He had some kind of fucked-up relationship with himself—being part Indian, understand? Read this old journal of his grandfather's, ran miles and miles by himself, prayed to Indian gods—for Christ's sake, prayed!"

"You sent him the tickets and money. You must have some love for him."

He looked down to the tablecloth, drawing circles on it with his fingernail. He didn't speak for a long time, then looked up at her, his face softened.

"Yes, I had—I have—love for him. It's a hard thing to say, Alicia. When you're a man, it's difficult to say that. But yes, I love the bastard. He's brave like I never was, strong when I was weak, willing to give when I wouldn't bend. I love him, babe, but I also fear him. Almost everything I've done in life has been a means of proving to him that I'm worthy of being his brother. It's a shitty thing to live with—something that I may not ever be able to overcome. I asked him to come down because I wanted to prove that I was—am—something."

Her heart collapsed. She put her hand out again, taking

his, holding on hard to it. In that one moment, he had opened his soul, and sympathy for him suddenly overwhelmed her. She couldn't express it but she squeezed his hand. "Let's go meet your brother, Julio."

The flight was late. Most of the passengers had gotten off but Brocassie finally shambled down the ramp. He was tall, all angles, his face hard planes and yet in some odd way, graceful. His clothes were cheap and ill-fitting and he carried just one bag—a fiberboard suitcase. But she saw something about him—a dignity or perhaps even a nobility that seemed to set him apart from those around him. Julio was suddenly transformed into an excited boy, waving, laughing, shouting.

The three of them met at customs. Julio personally called over the chief of customs, demanding that the bag be cleared through immediately, then signaled the porter by waving a handful of pesos.

Smiling, Brocassie took her hand and held it, as if he were trying to read her soul, and she felt a wave of weakness pass through her. He smiled and said softly with precise, accentless Spanish, "I've waited a long time to meet you, Alicia."

It was something that anyone would have said but it was the way he said it. As if he really had been waiting for years, knowing that they'd meet. All the training and conditioning which represented her background went tumbling end over end into space. There was something about him, a kind of electromagnetic force, which polarized her. It was her most vivid impression of Brocassie. He had stood there in the filtered sunlight of the reception area, towering over her, his face a copper tan, his nose so large and broken that it set his eyes deeper into the shadows, but as their eyes met and their hands touched, it seemed as if all movement in her world had ceased.

So long ago, she thought. Four years ago and yet it was a lifetime. Faces in her memory, so many of them gone—to other countries, to the mountains, to the lists of "missing" and to unmarked graves, all enemies of the Revolution, so said the Maximum Leader.

In April, more than a year ago, Álvarez had told her, after the Bay of Pigs, that Brocassie had died on the beach and had been buried in a mass grave. Eventually, the bodies had been exhumed and Julio had identified Brocassie's and reburied it, but Julio would not tell her the place of the grave.

When Julio had told her about Brocassie, she had sat there on the couch, listening to his words, her mind numb. She knew what he was saying was a lie because she could still feel the warmth of the ring she had given him there on her finger, as strong as the first day she had given it to Brocassie, and she knew that he would wear it as long as he lived. Finally, she had gotten up and walked calmly out of the house, not knowing where she was going or why, her mind evacuated of all thought. Even now, she could not remember what she had done except for the scar beneath her breast and what the doctor had told her. She had gone to the tool shed and the gardener had found her there, kneeling on the dirt floor, weeping hysterically and trying to force the broad-bladed cutting shears into her heart.

For three days she had lain in bed, dumbly trying to resolve the warmth on her finger and the pain in her chest. The wound was a surface laceration because the blade of the shears could not penetrate the gap between her ribs, but she knew that the real pain was much deeper—somewhere inside—and that could not be sutured, sprinkled with sulfa powder, bandaged and, finally, healed. That deeper pain was a wound that would remain forever.

On the fourth day, she got up, dressed and scrubbed the floors of the house. Julio pleaded with her to quit but she had ignored him until, finally, in the evening, exhausted, she had said to him, "I loved him, you know—more than you can understand. He will always be with me." She slowly climbed the stairs and lay down on the bed and tried to cry once more, but couldn't. Everything had gone out of her and there was no emotion left to draw on, and that, she knew, was what death really meant.

Julio had gotten very drunk that night and she had found him slumped over the kitchen table the following morning, a photograph of the three of them taken back in '58 still clutched in his fingers. She had woken him gently and helped him up the stairs to the bedroom. For another three days, he wouldn't speak to her and wandered around the *finca*, chain-smoking and drinking heavily in the evening, alone on the veranda. He never mentioned Brocassie's name again, but he had the photograph framed in silver and it rested on the library mantelpiece as a kind of shrine, a remembrance to both of them for different reasons.

Now, a year later, she had finally reconciled herself to the fact that Brocassie was dead and she knew that some part of her life had expired. She supposed that anything she felt toward Julio was more an acceptance than love. She was there for him—for being with him when he wanted her company and for withdrawing when he did not. When he thought of it, he was kind to her, paying her small compliments or bringing her gifts. But she felt, most of the time, that she was a pet—there to amuse, to be shown off to his intimate friends during rare dinner parties or *borracheras,* but for the most part, to remain silent, awaiting his orders. Still, without his protection, she would be dead, and there was no sense in screaming out her revolt. If she married him—and what other alternative was there?—she would have his children and that would be her compensation. But she knew, no matter what he said, that the firstborn son would be called Brocassie.

She was still holding Julio's photo and she put it down, very carefully, as if she were afraid that she would drop it. Her hands were shaking and then her whole body, and she slumped down on the bed, racked with sobbing, but she bit her lip so that those down below in the kitchen wouldn't hear. She wept for a long time, but gradually stopped, finding nothing left and hating herself for the weakness of memory. Brocassie was gone. Past. There was only the present and the future. Julio Álvarez was the means of her survival, and she was a survivor.

She got up and looked at the blotched redness of her face, then gave the mirror a tentative smile. She made the bed and cleaned up the bathroom. Her two-piece bikini, still damp from yesterday's swim in the pond, hung in the bathroom. Taking it from the shower curtain rod, she folded it over the windowsill to catch the morning sun. Finally, as she did each morning when Julio was not there—almost a ritual—she reached into her wardrobe, pushing up against the paneling of dark, dry mahogany. A board in the back gave way easily, allowing her fingers access to the dusty interior space. The compartment was small, the size of a small book, but it was large enough for the 9mm Beretta.

The automatic was a tiny thing, slab-sided and chromed, its bore the size of her little finger. Three months ago, she had seen it lying on the garage workbench, field-stripped into parts for cleaning. On a stupid impulse, she had taken a pin and a small angular piece which was part of the trigger mechanism and hidden it. Like a kid who has stolen an apple from a fruit stand, she walked away, waiting for a hand to grab her shoulder, but nothing had happened. Later in the day, she had seen Rafael, the oldest of the guards, groveling on the dirty concrete, obviously agitated. Rafael questioned the other two guards, the gardener and the driver. *Nada.*

It was a weapon that Rafael had taken from the dead body of a Batista NCO and kept for its uniqueness. But because of its uniqueness, it was improbable that there would be spare parts available. The remaining parts of the weapon lay on the workbench for another week and finally, Rafael had discarded them into the trash bin. Alicia scavenged through the trash bin the next day and smuggled the parts back to her room. She had always been clever with her hands and she had had weapons training with the Frente but still it had taken her four or five hours to fit the little pieces together.

Ammunition had been no problem. Julio carried a Czech Lastoy and shot regularly, sometimes three boxes of cartridges a week, on the pistol range he had hacked out of the brush behind the tool shed. She took only a few cartridges at a time and he never seemed to miss them. So she had a weapon. For what, she wasn't sure. She had been a guerrilla in the Sierra, and when you have been a guerrilla, not having a weapon is the same as being naked. She had no idea of what use she would put the weapon to, but it was a primitive kind of security. She had no valid papers or passport, no money, and surely no safe way out of Cuba, but the weapon in itself was a kind of reassurance that she was not powerless. As long as Julio was here to protect her, she wouldn't worry, but there might be a time in the future when she would be on her own and she thought of the weapon as a kind of ultimate passport.

Downstairs, the house echoed of emptiness, the scuffing of her sandals the only sound in the long corridors. Marta was gone, off marketing for the day. Through the front windows, Alicia could see two of the guards sitting under the shade of a palm tree, laughing and smoking and playing dominoes. She went into the kitchen and found half a pot of coffee still warm on the woodburning range, poured herself a cup and sat down at the long table. She felt tired, out of sorts. There was a twinge in her abdomen, as if her period were coming on. Today or tomorrow would be about right, and that would mean that she would be through with it before Julio came back. Somehow, suddenly, she acknowledged that she had missed him.

Feeling almost light-headed, she poured another cup of coffee and lit a cigarette. Beyond the kitchen window, the day was bursting with white-hot sunlight, vapor rising from the garden, wind swaying the flowers, and it seemed that, somehow, everything was behind her. Guilt and pain and the emotional privation that went with all of it were gone and she felt that she must refill herself with some kind of love if she was to continue. Unconsciously, she touched her ring finger: the sensation of warmth was not there for the first time that she could remember.

She dipped her finger in the saucer, wetting the tip with the overflow of coffee, and drew the profile of a child's face on the tabletop. The crude caricature was pudgy and round and smiling, and she recognized her final acceptance that she would have Julio's children, and the past would finally be buried along with the dead. The future was in her body and Julio's, and now she desperately wanted him back. He would be a good father, a tolerable husband, in the Latin sense of the word, and she wheeled her mind forward to blurred images of children in bright-colored clothes, the comfort of small lips against her nipples and the warmth that children would finally give her barren life.

Sweet Jesus, she thought, laughing out loud. Julio's not even home and I've married him, gotten pregnant and had two children. She laughed again. No . . . three or four at least. A boy first, and two girls and another boy. And I will get a big dog for the children to grow up with—something that has huge paws and a shaggy coat and a tongue to lick dirty faces. The thought sobered her momentarily. Children and a husband would be the final door closing. She would be here in Cuba for the rest of her life and the thought appalled her. But she recognized that it was easier to plan one's life within the framework provided than to speculate on unrealizable alternatives. And in the end, Castro would die, and the old desire of independence would arise again within the Cuban people. Of that she was sure. Perhaps her sons would have to fight for that independence, as she had.

She refilled her coffee cup, and moved to the screen door which overlooked the yard. The two guards on duty were passing a bottle of white rum between them, as they would until they were both semidrunk—a state which they managed to maintain through the late afternoon until the third guard came on for night duty. Bastards, she thought. Shiftless bastards of Havana *putas*—no good for anything, other than to carry a gun, drink themselves into a coma and whore away their lives. It was their kind who were always available to whoever would pay. She knew one had been in Batista's SIM and had easily made the transition when he saw that Castro would win. Why in hell, she wondered, had the Cuban people never learned—one dictator after another and always foreign interests to prop up the regime? And the Church—delicately wringing its hands, consoling the poor and growing fatter on the feast of spoils.

The wind gusted, its breath suddenly chilling her. Out to sea, she watched a rain squall momentarily obliterate the horizon as it swept west. She was fascinated and appalled by the violence of the squall; somehow, a tiny microcosm of Cuba. No subtlety to the land or the weather or the people or the politics.

In the early days of the Revolution, she had paid no attention to the fighting in the distant mountains. Her days with Julio and Brocassie overwhelmed all other concerns in that fall of 1958.

People talked guardedly and there was always a group in the far corner of a cocktail party who spoke in whispers about their nonexistent conspiracies against Batista. Like wing-tipped shoes and canasta, the Revolution was in vogue. But the papers were derisive. Castro was a clown, fighting forces thousands of times greater in size and equipped with the best arms the United States had to offer. It seemed to her that Castro was nothing more than a phantom, thrashing about in the mountains of the Sierra Maestra on some quixotic crusade.

But then, gradually, she began to understand that even her own father was involved. He had always been addicted to the intrigues of thirty years in politics and now, there were telephone calls at night, sums of money which disappeared from his account and sometimes unexplained absences. One morning she had questioned him and he had thrown down his napkin, knocking over his orange juice, and stared at her, unbelievingly. "If you cannot understand the principles in question, and what is being fought for," he shouted, "then silence your tongue!"

And she had. The pleasurable events of her life whirled on, like the colors of a pinwheel, each contributing beauty, excitement and distraction, moving so quickly that she never could distinguish one from another. Picnics with Julio and Brocassie, a trip to Camagüey, an afternoon spent sailing, a charity ball . . .

At 4:20 P.M. on the first Friday in November of 1958, the pinwheel stopped turning.

Alicia had just finished washing her hair. She wrapped a towel around her head and then sat down at her dressing table, buffing her nails. Julio was to pick her up at eight and they would drive in his Mark VII Jaguar to the Casino Capri for the opening of the Black Silk Tie, a by-invitation-only gaming room for stateside high rollers. Three chartered airliners were bringing in the crowd who would attend the opening, the ceremonies presided over by George Raft, the American actor. Johnny Weissmuller would be there, as would Juan Fangio, the Argentine race-car driver. Julio had promised that it would be a gala affair with a big band, two Hollywood leading ladies and enough champagne to drown Havana. It wasn't something that she really wanted to do, but Julio was the lawyer who represented the casino's owners and he told her that he could not refuse the invitation. And she could not refuse his.

Things had been going rapidly downhill between them. Julio had hinted at a spring wedding, had showed her a solitaire in Preston's window and yet she could not find the strength to reply or refuse. There would be no spring wedding, she knew. Not to Julio Álvarez. And now, almost every time that they met, there had been fights between them, and always, always, it came back to Brocassie.

She knew that she couldn't change the course of the careening relationship. She loved Brocassie, only Brocassie, and yet, even when they were alone, there was some code of honor she had to hold on to. By unspoken mutual consent, they didn't touch, didn't speak of the future, except that she *knew* there would be one. With him.

So much had changed in so little time and her emotions were in pieces, like the fragments of a mirror, each reflecting its own image. Brocassie was running out of money and Julio would not lend him any. As crazy as she knew her decision was, she was determined to follow Brocassie back to the United States.

She had just picked up the bottle of nail polish and started to apply the lacquer when the telephone beside her bed rang.

"*Diga,*" she said into the mouthpiece, irritated.

"It's me." The voice was Brocassie's; he was breathing heavily as if he were winded. "I need your help."

"What . . . ?"

"Not over the phone, Alicia. I don't have much time. Julio's been shot. He needs a doctor—one that won't talk and I don't have the damndest idea of where I can find one I can trust."

"Where are you?" She was already shaking out her hair, dropping her robe, pulling jeans and a sweater out of her drawer.

"On Calle Twenty-six around back of the ESSO station."

"Don't move. Keep him warm. I'll be there in five minutes." Without waiting for his answer she hung up, then dialed a doctor who had a small, private clinic in the Puentes Grandes section of Havana. He listed himself as a pediatrician, but he was known to the wealthy women of Havana as a doctor who performed clean, competent, illegal abortions. Assuming, of course, that a generous cash contribution was made to his clinic to "further research." The good doctor answered on the second ring. No, he was not interested. The news was already on the radio. He knew Julio, knew his connections and it was something that he wanted to stay out of.

Alicia mentioned the names of three men in government whose wives had had abortions in the kind doctor's clinic. The abortions, she said, were not paid for by those well-respected men, and would this cause the kind doctor to reconsider?

The kind doctor swore at her, pleaded with her and finally angrily consented.

She finished dressing, ran down and opened her father's safe and took all the loose cash that he had. Scrawling a note on his desk top blotter, she was in her MG and slewing out of the gravel driveway within another thirty seconds. She made it to the service station in under three minutes.

Brocassie had Julio's Jaguar hidden in the palmettos of an overgrown lot behind the gasoline station.

She pulled her MG up next to the Jaguar as Brocassie opened the back door of the Jag. Julio was stretched out, unconscious, his pants leg saturated with blood. A tourniquet, fashioned from a belt and letter opener, was already in place.

Brocassie was sweating, his shirt soaking. He ran over to her car, wiping the blood from his hands with a rag. "They shot him in the leg. He's lost a lot of blood. The owner of the station has a De Soto station wagon. He knows the score but he'll rent it for fifty bucks and then call it in as stolen two hours from now."

"Why? The Jaguar is faster."

Agitated, violently shaking his head, Brocassie snapped back, "No, they'll be looking for it all over Havana. We've got to switch cars. I'll explain later."

In two minutes, they were headed east toward Puentes Grandes. Julio was covered with an old tarp, his beathing shallow and rapid. There was only one roadblock but they were waved through with a smart salute without having to stop.

"How did it happen?" she asked, her heart cold.

Rubbing the sweat from his face with the back of his hand, Brocassie stared straight ahead. "He didn't tell you about the casino, did he?"

"He told me that he only worked occasionally on their legal problems. He had other clients as well."

He shook his head. "It wasn't that way. The Syndicate that owns the Casino Capri is Miami-based. They needed a sharp lawyer with local connections, one who spoke English and knew the score—a lawyer that they could buy. They set up Julio's practice, made it look separate from the casino operation—respectable—then provided him with all the clients that he wanted. But his main job was in greasing palms in the Batista government. He was also in charge of all accounting. About a year ago, he started to cook the books—skimming profits in a way that the government auditors wouldn't catch onto. But he took it one step further—he started to skim profits for his own account. He kept telling me that he wanted to marry you and give you the very best. Didn't you ever wonder where all the money was coming from? Even established lawyers in Havana don't make that kind of money."

She put her face in her hands. "Oh, my God. He did it because of me?" She turned to the backseat, touching Julio's unconscious face. "How did you find out?"

"It came out a little at a time over the last couple of months. When he's drunk, he talks. He was probably trying to impress me, attempting to justify what he was doing, pushing the idea that you were his woman and that he was the only one of the two of us that could provide properly for you."

"You argued with him and you shot him for that!"

"Christ *no*. This afternoon, I was reading in my room at his apartment, the door closed. I heard the buzzer ring but Julio got to the hallway first. I didn't pay much attention but then there was some arguing and the sounds of a struggle. I cracked the door open and there were two heavies, working him over with the muzzle of a pistol. They probably had no idea that I was living there. My room connected with Julio's through the patio. He kept an old service thirty-eight revolver in his nightstand drawer, something that he had hung onto since Korea. I grabbed it and barged into the living room. The guy with the gun turned on me and I shot him. The other one had Julio by the neck and he shoved him at me and then fired twice. He missed me but got Julio in the leg. I had a clean shot and nailed him. Within a minute, the telephone was ringing and the neighbors were shouting. I grabbed his keys to the car, put him over my shoulder and ran like hell."

Her mind was blank, no solutions except the obvious. "We'll get Julio to this doctor but you have to turn yourself in. It was self-defense."

An Oldsmobile of the SIM howled by them in the opposite direction, the siren screaming.

He studied it in the rearview mirror and shook his head. "Can't be that way. The Syndicate is too heavily involved with Batista. Payoffs, corruption of high officials, mob influence. They would never allow it to come to trial. I'm a murderer as far as they're concerned and you're an accessory. We've got to protect Julio and then get the hell out of this country."

And she now understood that what he said was true. Somehow, a border had been crossed and the barrier closed behind her.

Twenty minutes later, her hair still damp, her clothes stained with Julio's blood, she had him in the doctor's operating room. It was obvious that Julio would not move for several weeks, but he was safe. She gave the doctor two thousand American, with the promise that Julio would be able to cover the rest, and left with Brocassie. It took three hours, two bus rides, a taxi and walking the final half mile, but they made it to the Havana Yacht Club undetected. The first evening editions were already on the streets with Álvarez's blurred photo captioned, ¡Asesino!

They had to swim to her father's yacht after sundown, because there was no way that they could walk through the polished halls of the yacht club, tip the steward and call the launch. They pulled themselves aboard and then waited until after midnight to slip the mooring and drift out of the channel with just the lightest of wind filling the mainsail.

It was then that she realized that something had changed within her. The pressure, the excitement, was almost unbearable, like the growing prelude to an orgasm, and she knew, now, without hesitation, that she too had suddenly, irrevocably changed.

At first she lay a course for the Straits of Florida, hoping to make Key West, but the wind, once clear of the land, was growing stronger and the seas beginning to overrun themselves, breaking in cascades of white water. The small sloop shipped two huge combers in succession, burying its fine bow and reluctantly rising to meet the next, and she knew that they would never last another hour, so she jibed over and ran parallel to the coast of Cuba, skirting reefs, the rain stinging her face.

By dawn, they were well west of Havana, still skirting the northern shore of Cuba. He had made coffee for both of them and then taken over the helm. The rain was tapering off but the wind, backing toward the north, had strengthened and was pressing them down toward the reefs.

She did not feel so defiant now, her eyes burning from salt, her body cold.

"You'll be missed," he said.

"I don't think so. My father will understand. I left a note for him. If they report his sloop missing, he'll guess what we've done and deny anything until he hears from me." She said it confidently, but she wasn't.

He nodded but she saw disbelief in his eyes. "We can clear the reefs and Cape Guahahacaribes. Drop me ashore in the bay and then turn around. You can be back in Havana in twenty-four hours."

She knew from the rumors that Maroto had a band of guerrillas in the Escambray Mountains fighting against Batista's army. Her father was an old friend of Maroto; she had seen Maroto's nephew twice in the last month in her father's study. That was where he had been sending the money, she suddenly realized. Surely, Maroto would honor his debts by taking care of Brocassie. Hard to tell, but she thought it was the only possibility.

"There's a cove to the west of Trinidad de Cuba that my father took me to in this same yacht when I was much younger—fifteen or so—and I remember that place very well because I dreamed that a wild young Indian came swimming out to the yacht and crawled aboard. In my dream, I could see him, outlined against the sky as he lowered himself through the hatch, and then, all wet and smelling of the sea, he came into my bunk and took me."

Brocassie gave her one of his rare smiles, laughed, and she echoed him, knowing that he would never believe what she had said, but the dream had been real and this was the fulfillment. Someday, she might convince him that she had really remembered the dream and that she had not conjured it out of the gossamer of pubescent fantasies. But for now, it was enough that he had agreed.

For the rest of that day, they beat along the north coast of Cuba, the sail hard as sheet steel under the driving strain of the wind, but by that nightfall, they weathered the cape and headed west. Twice, they saw the lights of ships on the horizon, moving between the mainland and Isle of Pines, but the small wooden yacht would present a poor radar return and they were both so tired, they no longer cared.

Both she and Brocassie knew that she could not stay with him. Her father was barely able to get around, but he was like a Roman candle burning itself out in one final blaze of glory—expanding his law business, ranting in the Senate against the corruption of Batista and, clandestinely, involving himself in the intrigue of the Revolution. The old man had cancer and they both knew it, and she had no choice but to go back and care for him.

Leaving Brocassie in that quiet cove under the lee of the Escambray had been the hardest thing she had ever done. But it seemed that Batista would fall within months and in the meanwhile, Brocassie would be safe with Maroto. It had taken her three days to sail up the south coast of Cuba and then to beat the final 120 miles against the trade winds to the shelter of Havana. In that eternity, she had learned to sleep in snatches of no more than half an hour at a time. Her hands toughened and her skin, which she had always protected from the sun, browned to a deep mahogany. She lost seven pounds and felt better, physically, than she ever had before. When she brought the sloop into the yacht club, she noticed eyes following her, and at first she was terrified that she would be reported, but then a fat little television actor walked up to her and kissed her fingertips, very gently, very warmly. "You shame us all," he

whispered, gave her a moist kiss on the cheek and then walked
away.

No one, then or later, asked her questions, and she realized that she was a heroine of the Revolution in some minor,
offhand way. The slicks of the yacht club let it be known that
she had been on the South Coast, running guns to the revolutionaries and *that,* she soon found out, was the newest vogue,
surpassing intrigues, whether real or imagined.

As soon as she could reach a pay phone, she called the
good doctor. He answered, his voice flat, hostile.

"He is well. *He* is not receiving visitors. *You* must not ever
come here," and slammed down the phone.

In the final month of 1958, both her father and Batista
grew weaker. Her father had multiple myeloma and it was in-
curable. Batista also had a terminal disease—defeat—the
army losing one outpost after another to the forces of Castro
and the Segundo Frente. But Batista outlasted her father. She
put him in his grave in a private ceremony and then, cleaning
out what remained of his bank account, headed south for the
Escambray and Brocassie.

She never saw him again. Brocassie had joined up with
Maroto, but as the final stages of the fight against Batista had
accelerated in intensity, Maroto had broken from his second-
in-command, Fabricio, to form a two-pronged pincer on the
plains south of Sancti Spíritus. The attack had failed and Fabricio's column had withdrawn eastward, toward the Sierra
Maestra, his force cut by hit-and-run firefights to less than half
of its original strength.

Through the fall and winter of 1958, Alicia acted as courier for Maroto. In her MG, she ran back and forth between
the Escambray and Havana, ferrying arms, explosives and
money. Batista roadblocks came to know her and let her
through with almost cursory examination because she took
care to wear tight-fitting shirts and to carry a cooler full of
Cristal Polar beer on the passenger seat, which she carefully
doled out at each roadblock. She casually let it be known that
there was an army major in Trinidad de Cuba who would be
greatly aggravated if she was late for her weekly visit. Ah—
knowing smiles, the occasional wink and then a quick wave
through the barricades.

During all of this time, she heard nothing from Brocassie or Álvarez, Maroto was out of contact with Fabricio, and the only news was third hand—*bolas,* rumors, scraps to chew on but with no substance.

In early January of 1959, Batista finally fled. The American government had withdrawn its support, looking for a more acceptable successor, and Batista thought early retirement was advisable. He left, and what remained of the government crumbled. Cuba went wild in an orgasm of joy. Castro's 26th of July Movement and the Segundo Frente each moved to take over the reins of power, but Castro was much faster. He had the foreign press and the radios in his pocket. He bathed in adulation but he swore that he wanted no position of power. A moderate government, basically anti-Communist, was installed, but within weeks that was dissolved. Castro, the concerned citizen, went on TV and harangued the people of Cuba.

"There is no reason for a constitution," he bellowed into the microphones, "because our Revolution is moving too fast and it is the people who are in control—the people who are dictating the course of our history. And we want no part of a previous class mentality."

Castro installed himself as the will of the people, swept away judicial law and declared that those who opposed him were counterrevolutionary worms. One war ended and another began, this one much bloodier, yet almost unknown beyond the shores of Cuba.

Alicia made two final trips to Havana for munitions and money. The roadblocks were no longer manned by Batistianos but rather by the *barbudos*—the bearded ones—some no older than thirteen but much tougher and suspicious of anyone who looked as if they were from the upper classes. "People's Tribunals" were already condemning those with obvious wealth to labor camps or death, in the same mindless craving for justice that reigned during the French Revolution.

She was stopped at a roadblock by a boy, carrying a submachine gun, just eight miles north of her cutoff to the Escambray and the safety of Maroto's perimeter guards. She saw him walking toward her and she knew that he would be like all the rest. She undid one more button on her shirt and pulled it tight under her belt, making her breasts more prominent. There were five bottles of beer left in the cooler and she wasn't nervous, even though there were twenty yards of primacord explosive in the trunk and a suitcase filled with grenades strapped onto the luggage rack.

"You are going where, *compañera*?" he asked politely. His face was pockmarked with acne and his beard was like down. He wore a beret and kid's rubber sneakers, and for all the world, he was no more threatening than the boy who had tended her father's garden. Until she looked into his eyes and saw that they were cold and very old.

"To my uncle's place in Trinidad," she answered. "He is a member of the local Revolutionary Council."

The kid smiled. "That is truly wonderful, because my brother heads the Revolutionary Council." He lowered his carbine toward her navel.

She reached into the cooler and brought out two bottles of beer, opened them and gave one to him, drinking from the other.

"You are a liar," she said, her voice calm.

"As are you," the kid replied, toasting her and drinking from the moisture-hazed bottle. "You are Alicia Helvia. I have an excellent photograph of you sent out by the counterintelligence. It says that you are a whore of Maroto's, known to be running munitions between Havana and the Escambray."

For the first time in her life, she knew real fear—the spike of terror that started in her gut and penetrated all the way to her bowels. Involuntarily, her bladder voided and she snatched her sweater from the passenger seat, threw it over her thighs and felt the shame of warm fluid saturating the seat beneath her.

"Don't move and keep your hands on the sill of the door where I can see them." He moved behind her and she heard him untying the suitcase on the luggage rack. He lowered it to the ground and then reached into the trunk and withdrew the shopping bag that held the primacord.

"Is this all that you're carrying?"

She nodded weakly, the stink of her urine strong in the small cockpit of the MG.

He came back to her, holding the weapon negligently, its barrel pointed just above her head, but with his finger on the trigger. "I knew about you when you fought against Batista. You were on the right side, but it is now the wrong side." He shrugged and then smiled. "It is a family feud between men, you understand? I would advise you not to be involved. Your face is beautiful and it should remain so." He stepped back, drew himself up and saluted. *"¡Adiós! compañera."*

She smiled thinly and dropped the MG into gear, accelerating slowly, not knowing whether her brains would be shattered within seconds. She shifted to second and third and then, only then, looked back in the rearview mirror. The kid was still standing in the dust, smiling.

From then on, she stayed with Maroto's guerrilla commandos, fighting against the increasingly effective sweeps by Castro forces, working as a paramedic, feeding shells to mortars in the incessant firefights and sharing in the cooking of what little food they were able to gather or buy. She, like any other fighter, went through the standard small-arms course, learned to set trip wires, stood guard and kept moving. In two years of fighting, she could never remember sleeping in one place more than three days on end. Eventually, because the radio operator died of gangrene, she became Maroto's radio operator and encoder. Her perspective of the extent of resistance to Castro expanded, and she realized that there were as many as twenty thousand guerrillas, all Cuban but with fractional political goals, fighting Castro—The Horse. But because they were not unified and had no supply of arms, their numbers dwindled and, one by one, their transmitters went off the air.

It was during this time that she met Willie Morgan, an American mercenary who had joined Maroto's group early in fifty-nine. He had just come back from the Sierra Maestra on a liaison trip and he told her that he had seen Brocassie and that he was alive and well. He brought a letter. She snatched the mildewed envelope from his hand, realizing as she ran toward the dugout pit covered by a tarpaulin that was her home for fourteen hours, that she had not thanked him, but she knew that he would understand.

The letter was brief; the ink smeared by sweat or rain.

I have so little time to tell you that I love you, always will. Morgan must leave within a few minutes and it's only now that I know that you are with Maroto. So Willie brings this message of love to you from me.

Keep well and safe, and remember that we will be together soon. I wear your ring around my neck on an old shoelace, waiting only to return it to its rightful owner.

The offer of champagne still stands. Forever.

My love, Brocassie.

She read and reread the letter, the paper limp in her sweating hands, the ink blurring from the drops of condensation which fell from the tarpaulin, mixed with her own tears of joy and relief. That night she got drunk on the rum that she had hoarded from the weekly ration, and she fell asleep, clutching the bottle, dreaming that it was champagne, drunk on a balcony of the Trocadero with him.

For the next two months, things were quiet, and then Maroto got word of a major thrust by Castro's FAR into the Escambray. It was to be the last fight, as far as The Horse was concerned, and he would clean the bastard counterrevolutionaries out in one massive sweep. For eleven days, Maroto's forces fought and ran, ambushed and then withdrew, losing one man for every five of the FAR, but still bleeding away men and arms that could not be easily replaced. And then the rains came and the mountains turned into a morass of mud and body-sucking humidity, and both sides pulled back, too exhausted to fight on.

In those eleven days, Morgan had fought off a column of fifty FAR and in so doing, had bagged a truckload of Russian mortars, two thousand rounds and a pile of papers, none important. But among them was a recent copy of the FAR newspaper, the *Verde Olivo*. More than just a rag, it was a slick, professional paper, filled with propaganda and exhortations of *¡Patria o Muerte!* The columns were saturated with stories about the imminent invasion by the Americans, photographs of the CIA training bases in Guatemala and even of aircraft being prepared by the CIA for the assault.

Alicia read through the copy, sitting in the shade of dense

brush, mosquitoes humming in the still afternoon. On the last page, a photo caught her eye. It was Julio, bearded, much thinner, and with a carbine slung over his shoulder and a canteen on his hip. Next to him stood the *Caballón,* the Maximum Leader, Fidel Castro, their arms twined around each other's shoulders, the ever-present unlit cigar grinding in Fidel's mouth. The caption under the grainy photo read, "Comandante Julio Álvarez, head of DGI counterintelligence in the Eastern Provinces, with Fidel, planning defense of Oriente against the Yankee adventurists' invasion." Nothing else, but now she knew that Julio had somehow made it to Oriente Province and had survived the last, fierce year in the drive against Batista. She held the paper closer, trying to see his face more clearly, but it was just a mass of shaded dots. There was no substance to him now, either in the grainy photograph or in her memory, and yet she somehow, abstractly wished him well. She balled the newspaper and threw it onto the smoldering fire and watched it burst into flames. Odd, she thought, that he was now the enemy.

Her capture had been in the fall of 1960. She had gone down into the foothills with fifteen other guerrillas from Maroto's group to help transport supplies and arms back up to the main encampment. A truck was going to rendezvous with them at the end of a logging road, as it had three times before. The arms had come from Miami, paid for with the contributions of the exile Cuban community, then air-dropped into the mangrove swamps on the north coast near Carahatas. Moroto's cousin, Pepe, transported them south, one-third of the shipment per trip, so that if he was caught in a roadblock, not everything would be lost. Pepe was grossly overweight and he had always joked that if he was captured, they would have to cut through two hundred pounds of rum-deadened fat to reach his nerves. Apparently, the DGI had a sharp enough knife, for when the truck flashed its lights in the coded sequence, four of Alicia's group had walked into the open field and had instantly died in a slashing cross fire from automatic weapons. Six magnesium flares arced up, trailing sparks and bursting into chrysanthemums of brilliant white over the killing ground. She knew then that it was all over.

For another two hours, the small group fought on against

the FAR but it was obvious that the escape route behind them was sealed off. The FAR kept them pinned down, firing over them, waiting for dawn and an easy capture.

Before dawn, Raúl, Maroto's nephew who led the group, tried to make a breakout. Of the original fifteen, six survived, most of them wounded. At dawn, they raised a bloodstained white shirt on a stick.

Four hours later, she was thrown into a DGI cell. At first they used a woman interrogator who argued reasonably and interminably that Fidel was the savior of Cuba, and that all Cubans should band together and support him. The guerrilla leaders who fought against him were paid dupes of the CIA. During all of this, Alicia had nodded occasionally and asked how Fidel would correct this injustice or that. The woman would smile, look it up in her book and then give the stock answers—usually just the phrase, "Fidel will know how to handle that when the time comes." Alicia played out the charade for two days, praying that Maroto would have time to clear out of the main encampment and fall back to a stronghold higher in the Escambray.

At last, the DGI woman interrogator had lost patience, demanding to know passwords, the route to Maroto's camp and the strength of his forces.

Alicia, waiting for this one moment, smiled sweetly, and said, "Fuck you and your brand of revolution, and fuck Fidel in that place where the sun never shines." With insane fury, the woman had struck her across the face with a briefcase and kicked her repeatedly in the stomach. Alicia lost consciousness and when she came to, she realized that she was dead, even though she still breathed.

They came the next morning—two men in civilian clothes. At first they were polite—the Spanish propensity to exude courtesy toward women. "Why, please . . . ?" they prefaced their questions. She laughed at them and called them *deshuevados* and *maricones*, the ultimate Cuban insult. They left, furious, and within minutes, an old NCO with a veined face and carefully groomed fingernails took her to a basement cell. He had a little wooden box and he explained to her how he personally had taken a magneto from a Harley-Davidson motorcycle and had fitted it inside with the shaft protruding and then had attached the handle from a car window—a Buick convertible's, he said with a boy's shy smile on his old face. He showed her the wires leading from the box with the little clips. It was a very technical explanation and he seemed to be very proud of his device. He demonstrated on a light bulb, making it flicker, and it had made no sense to her. The thing that terrified her was that the man was detached—completely remote from what he was doing—as if she were some kind of animal to be experimented on. He bound her carefully into a chair which was bolted to the cement floor and thoughtfully placed a block of rubber between her teeth. He then stripped off her blouse and bra, lovingly rubbed salve over her breasts and, with calm precision, attached the alligator clips to her nipples. And then gave the handle a few quick experimental cranks. Lightning bolted through her body. She bit down on the rubber, her body contorting in spasms, but she somehow choked back her agony. This time, frustrated at his failure, he ground the handle furiously. She couldn't contain the scream, and she fainted.

In the end, after two days and twenty-two hours, she told them everything. She couldn't walk to the courtyard where sentences were handed down, so a lieutenant of the DGI came to her cell and read, rapid fire, a sentence of execution. A clipboard was pushed into her hand and she was told to sign. She hesitated and then the lieutenant snatched the clipboard from her hand and signed her name on the line. "Nothing important," he said, his voice bored with what was obviously a routine procedure. "It is a waiver of appeal to the sentence, but the appeals court is suspended anyway." He threw her a sloppy salute and left.

Alvarez came on the third morning. For a minute, he had stood outside her cell, his lips set in a tight line, speechlessly watching her. Then walked away. Ten minutes later, he was back with a blanket which he wrapped her in, and then led her down a corridor into a back alleyway where his Oldsmobile was idling. He pushed her down onto the floor of the backseat and went back into the building. Finally, he emerged and took the wheel, heading east for Santiago at high speed. He didn't speak for over an hour except to tell her to keep quiet and stay on the floor. He went through two checkpoints, his siren wailing, his identification papers flashed casually at the militiamen. He was recognized, of course. The *comandante* was well known and one checkpoint radioed ahead to the next, smoothing his passage.

Finally, they were past Santiago, on the coastal road, only a few miles from his *finca.* He slowed and pulled over to the grass that bordered the road. He lit a cigarette with shaking hands, turned to her and said, "I could be shot for what I've done to save you, Alicia. I paid that bastard of a lieutenant over three thousand pesos to do a switch, and although I never believed in what the priests crammed down our throats when we were young, I know fucking well that I'll burn in hell because I've committed another woman to death to take your place. She was about your age and height and I substituted your papers and some of your personal effects for hers. She was just a simple, ignorant whore who's going to die for you in two days and God help me." He flicked the cigarette out the window, slammed the transmission into gear and pulled back onto the highway, heading east.

For two days, she alternately cried and prayed, and then Álvarez received a telephone call, turned to her, his face pale, and said, "It's over. We'll not talk about this again. *Ever.*"

She took the empty coffee cup to the kitchen and washed it under the hand pump, then went to the kitchen window which overlooked the garden and the lime tree grove beyond. Miguel was working up the rows of melons, watering each one in turn, his back bent to the hot morning sun.

He had on a pair of outsized pants, cut off at the knees and held up by a length of manila rope. Other than that, he was naked, his back a rich chocolate brown, glistening with sweat, his bare feet almost indistinguishable from the cocoacolored loam of the earth.

He had shown up at the *finca* less than two weeks ago, begging for food. Not more than fifteen, she had guessed, as she watched him motion toward his stomach and then toward the garden as Marta towered over him, her hands on her hips. Marta had shoved him away, propelling him toward the road when Alicia had intervened.

It was not much of an interview. The boy was dressed in

rags and he carried a battered, cardboard suitcase. He wore sandals shod with crudely cut out tire treads. It pained her to look at him—dirt caked on his skin, ulcerated sores on his face and neck, his hair matted. She had told Marta to get back into the kitchen and make the boy some rice and beans. Finally, she had motioned the boy to sit down on the bench under the banyan tree, where it was cool.

"What's your name, *jovencito*?"

The boy remained mute, his eyes lowered. He opened his suitcase and produced a pad of paper and a stick of charcoal. He wrote, "Miguel" and handed her the pad.

"Can you speak?" she asked, suddenly feeling a hard band around her heart.

He shook his head.

"Parents . . . relatives?"

He shook his head, took the pad from her and then wrote, *"Nadie—Desaparecieron."*

She brushed the hair back from her forehead, avoiding his eyes. So he didn't have parents—disappeared. How many people in Cuba, she wondered, could be described by that epitaph—*Desaparecieron*? "What do you want?" she finally asked.

The boy tentatively started to smile but it was as if such a thing was an impossibility and he drew in a long breath and then exhaled, took up the pad again and wrote, "Food, bed and work." He pointed toward the garden.

She didn't know how Julio would react, or whether he would even notice. She withheld her decision while he ate, watching him from the window of the kitchen as he crammed the food into his mouth like an animal. When he was done, the boy looked around him and then licked the plate and his fingertips. She moved away from the window, burying her face in her hands and wept.

Marta maintained a sullen silence, unwilling to become involved, so Alicia had the gardener make room for the boy in the loft over the garage. He was not to eat in the house but Marta condescended to prepare him a bucket of food twice daily which he picked up after the normal meals were finished. His food was scraps and leftovers, filled out with rice, but the small, tin bucket was always returned to the porch scoured out with sand, empty and shining clean. In less than a week, the garden flourished, each plant tended with care, the weeds picked and the earth moist with water. Miguel visibly began to gain weight.

Alicia had climbed the ladder to the loft just once, while Miguel worked in the garden. The canvas cot was neatly made, the floor swept and the few pathetic things that he owned were laid out in neat precision. There were no photographs, no letters, no sign that Miguel had ever lived in anything except the limbo of a scavenger's existence. Except for one thing. Above his cot was a torn and yellowed print of Martí, the Cuban martyr-poet, inscribed by hand with the legend, *"No me pongan a lo obscuro a morir como un traidor"* . . . Do not place me in the darkness, to die like a traitor. She touched the print with her fingertips, as if it would give to her the answer of the boy's past, but it was, as her father had often said, like trying to touch the sun to determine the nature of heat. There was no answer—only a question.

She looked again toward the garden and saw Miguel kneeling, picking bugs from each plant, crushing them between his fingertips. She started to turn away and caught the glint of sunlight on metal from farther down the long drive which led up to the *finca*. As she watched, a blue Oldsmobile climbed the driveway, trailing dust behind it. It had two antennae mounted on the rear bumper, both whipping in lazy arcs. Mounted through the roof was a powerful chrome spotlight. Her heart beat faster and she realized that her hands were clutching the sash of the window, her fingers bloodless with the pressure that they unconsciously exerted.

There were two men in the car, both wearing civilian clothes and mirrored sunglasses. The driver remained behind and the man in the passenger side got out and walked slowly to the entranceway, limping a little. He rapped on the door, waited just a brief second and rapped again, impatiently.

Alicia thought for a second that Marta would answer it but then realized that she had not returned from marketing. The man looked vaguely familiar although she couldn't place him. He stank of DGI, she knew that much—the same kind of car that Julio used. There was no point in waiting. If they took

92

her, she couldn't prevent that, but it was more likely that the man was looking for Julio. She calmed herself, raised her head and opened the door.

The man was thin with pockmarked cheeks and receding hair. He wore a linen jacket and pants which were rumpled, as if he had been driving for a long time in the heat. Showing his teeth, he removed his sunglasses in the shade of the entranceway. "Señorita Helvia?" He touched his forehead with two fingers in a casual salute. "I am Captain Sergio Piedra of the DGI. I work with the *comandante*. May I come in?"

She opened the door and showed him into the library. "Coffee?" she offered, keeping her voice calm.

He sat down and looked at her and she had the feeling that he was looking through her, his eyes focused on some far imagined point. Then he smiled. "Scotch, if you please, with ice and a twist of lemon. It has been a very difficult night and a longer day is still ahead of me." He smiled at her again but it was artificial, held for just an instant and flicked off.

In the kitchen, she poured him a very large drink, added ice and poured herself a glass of wine. Through the screen doorway, she could see the other man with sunglasses talking to the guards who were now standing at rigid attention. She closed her fist, knuckles white, afraid and yet unable to establish what was wrong. That's what he wants you to feel, she told herself. Fear, uncertainty. But because I am Álvarez's woman, I am protected. He promised me that. But in her mind, it was hollow reassurance. She composed herself and returned to the library.

The only sound in the room was the ticking of the mantel clock and she wondered how it could possibly cover the concussions of her heart.

Piedra took the glass and held it, looking at her dispassionately as if he were inspecting meat displayed in a butcher's showcase.

"We have met before, *socially*," he began. There was a slight emphasis on the word,

She smiled, forcing it. "Of course. A dinner party late last ..."

"... November," he completed the sentence smoothly.

93

"Of course," she said. "It is kind of you to stop by but the *comandante* will not be back for some days. I can take a message, of course."

Piedra sipped noisily at his Scotch. "The message is not from me but from another man, and I think it is for both *you* and the *comandante*."

Mookem Flower the Younger stalked in, swaying her tail in delicate brushstrokes. She veered toward Piedra, brushing against his pants leg. He looked down and picked up the cat with his hand, holding the animal as if he were grasping the handle of a suitcase; his hand tight around the cat's gut. The animal yowled, clawing at the air, and Piedra dropped it, wiping his hand on the upholstery of the chair.

"Cats are difficult animals, don't you agree?" The fluorescent smile again. "Independent, which is an admirable trait in the right circumstances, but flawed by their lack of loyalty. It makes for a difficult personality in both animals or their masters, as the case applies." He sipped at his Scotch again, his eyes on hers.

"There are things that I must attend to, Captain. Is there something specific that I can help you with?"

"My apologies," he said. "I don't want to detain you, of course, but there are a few questions." He withdrew a cigar from his shirt pocket and waved it vaguely in the air. "You don't object?" and not waiting for her reply, lit it with a silver lighter. He inhaled deeply and blew the smoke out in a thin stream, the blue haze rolling up through a shaft of sunlight which lay in the space between them.

"Last night," he started, obviously enjoying the sanctity of his position, "I apprehended a man who is an enemy of the state. A criminal, you understand?"

She sipped at the wine, keeping her face bland, but wanting to scream with the insanity of tension Piedra was creating. *Damn* the man. He had something but he was stringing her out, watching for weakness.

"I am sure that the *comandante* will be pleased with your work. He's always spoken highly of you, but I doubt that I can do anything to assist you."

"Difficult to say. This man was a counterrevolutionary who has been operating in the Sierra Maestra with the other terrorists up there. Under interrogation, there was something that he said that made me uneasy. He indicated that he knew both you and the *comandante*. Improbable, of course, but I have to check on these things, you understand."

"You have him in custody, then?"

Piedra dropped his cigar into a flower vase and then turned back to her. "No, unfortunately, there were men whom I had positioned with explicit instructions as to the final phases of the capture. They bungled and the man escaped in a small fishing boat. We now have several aircraft searching for him and it will only be a matter of a few hours before we find him."

"Then all your questions will be answered." She bent down and Mookem Flower II padded over to her, arching her back in anticipation of being stroked. Piedra was fishing, she thought, and all he's got is an empty hook. She began to feel the tension ease out of her body.

Piedra nodded. "Undoubtedly. He cannot be more than twenty miles offshore although there is the matter of low clouds moving in over the sea which hampers us. But there is still the question of his acquaintance with you and the *comandante*."

"Those questions will be better addressed to the *comandante*," she flared. "Both he and I have had many mutual friends from before the Revolution. Not all of them chose the correct direction, as you can understand."

Piedra withdrew a sheath of papers from his jacket, exposing for a brief instant his shoulder holster. "Yes—understandable. But you realize that as an officer in the DGI, I must follow these connections to their source. Therefore, knowing that the *comandante* would hardly object, I took the liberty of searching his personal safe for relevant files. There was a metal box marked with his name among other official documents. Lacking a key, I forced it open." He smiled wanly, tapping the folder.

Glancing back to his lap, Piedra shuffled through the papers with infuriating slowness and then glanced up, as if trying to read her expression. "I had not realized it before, Señorita Helvia, but it appears that you were in some trouble. There was not much to go on but I made some telephone calls and it was confirmed that you had once been ... ah ... associated with Maroto. Very unlikely, of course, but could this have any basis of truth?"

"I have nothing to say, Captain. I think you are dealing in hearsay, not facts." Her stomach was rolling over, the taste of bile in her throat. She realized that she was clutching her wineglass with a grip intense enough to shatter it and she had to will herself to relax her grip.

He raised his thin eyebrows, the expression of piety and expiation on his face. "But that is the past and I am only interested in the present and the future. I think that the *comandante* is seriously considering my promotion to major. Perhaps, although I can only guess at his thoughts, a position of much greater authority and trust." He stood up slowly, straightening the creases in his pants. "Very pleasant," he said, "but there is work to do."

He walked over to the mantel, picked up the silver-framed photo and studied it, a wistful smile on his face. "This man," he said softly, turning the frame toward her, "told me last night that he would come back to Cuba just to see you again." He raised his eyebrows again, smiling. "Such an odd name, don't you think, 'Brocassie'?"

CHAPTER

4

Moscow, September 4, 1962

She was from Aguascalientes, Mexico, a not-yet-woman, no-longer-child. Her twenty-one-year-old body was shaped with a tropical richness beyond her years, and yet her face had the sensuality of late adolescence: sweetly provocative but still innocent.

Julio Álvarez watched her moving around the matchbox-sized kitchen of his apartment. She was humming a bolero, not quite identifiable. She had a good voice and the song, like the dinner that she was making, was Latin. He filled his glass with Haitian rum—God knows how the KGB commissary officer had gotten it—and turned to the window overlooking the street.

It was only early September but already there had been heavy snows followed by subzero temperatures. There were piles of gritty ice in the streets that been compacted by the plows and were now intractable as granite, and he wanted to get the hell out of Russia and smell real flowers and wet earth and hear Cuban kids chattering in rapid-fire gutter Spanish as they played in the streets. He turned back toward the kitchen and watched the woman, suddenly thinking of Alicia. And then he pushed her image from his mind. Alicia was permanent—this was transient, and he would not confuse the two of them.

Consuelo Martín was one of the thousands of romantics who had gravitated toward revolution as a means of righting the sins of entrenched governments. Governments, which, themselves, were violent revolutionaries in their younger years, before they learned the pleasure of fine cognac, big limousines and Swiss bank accounts.

Moscow obligingly supplied advanced degrees in terrorism under the guise of "cultural exchanges" and "scholarships of friendship." Consuelo was in her second year at Patrice Lumumba University majoring in the finer points of making gasoline bombs and running underground printing presses. Violence, Julio thought, seemed to attract people of her disposition like a flame attracts moths. He knew from experience that she would be the perfect martyr for the revolution. There would be a photograph someday in a Mexican newspaper, grainy and distorted, and it would show her supple body contorted in death, and then in weeks there would be posters that the underground would plaster to the walls and her name would be added to the honor roll of those who died for La Causa.

Weeks before, Álvarez had made a comment to his KGB counterpart about the possibility of meeting a woman. Two days later, the KGB major had dropped her dossier off at Álvarez's apartment. The major, Rublev, had described her as a "safe screw." Which probably said less for her state of physical hygiene than it did for her reliable political outlook.

It had all been neatly arranged. A small reception for Spanish-speaking visitors at the Ministry of Culture. Introductions by the major, a few drinks, and in less than an hour, she had suggested that they go back to his apartment. It had gone as smoothly as if she had followed an organizational manual. She later told him that he had been the seventh in two years but that she had demanded of her KGB controller that she would not be "friends" with anyone under the rank of colonel, and that her "friends" must be Latins and if at all possible, handsome. As far as she was concerned, it was a match made in a Soviet bureaucratic heaven.

As if she felt his eyes watching her, she glanced toward him, wiping her hands on a towel, and picked up a glass of wine. She was smiling, relaxed, just a little tipsy. She came over to him, tucking her head beneath his chin and licked his throat. "How much longer will you be here?" she whispered.

He shrugged. "A week, maybe less." He had not particularly wanted to make the trip to the Soviet Union, but the KGB had requested him by name, along with seven other officers of the DGI. The reason given had been "special liaison and counterintelligence training." But it was a particularly sensitive time for him. There was too much going on in Oriente Province and he didn't like leaving the search efforts to weed the counterrevolutionaries from the Sierra Maestra in the hands of subordinates, particularly Captain Piedra. If Piedra made a botch of it, it would still reflect back on him, and if Piedra had success, only he would get the credit—a case of "damned if you do and damned if you don't."

"You're thinking again, *Comandante,*" she said, her voice mildly reproving.

"Sorry . . ."

She smiled and ducked out of his arms, went to the record player and set the needle down on an old 78 that she had brought with her. The music was scratchy and thin but the sound of the bolero transported him out of the dirty barren grayness of Moscow snow and concrete, back to an open dance floor of the Havana Yacht Club.

It had been a garden party, given by some not-quite-prominent, not-yet-powerful flunky of Batista's, back in the spring of fifty-seven. It was the first time that he had seen Alicia and he had been stunned by her beauty. The bolero was playing: primitive yet sophisticated, pure yet powerfully sexual, and she *was* the inner heart and personification of the bolero. Unlike the other women who were there— creamed and lacquered, dressed in splashy rayons and silks, hair cropped short and varnished to the latest American fashion—Alicia's black hair cascaded down a graceful cream-white neck, flowed over her shoulders and down to the small of her back. She wore no jewelry except a long strand of pearls which spilled down over her breasts. Her dress was a simple indigo sheath of velvet which molded to her body, accentuating but not overstating the full lushness of her body.

Álvarez had a woman on his arm, a singer from Colombia who was in vogue but he was no longer aware of her.

As he stared, Alicia had turned slightly toward him, a champagne glass in her hand, held lightly against her cheek, and she had laughed liquidly and the sound cut through him, chilling and yet burning. Álvarez dropped the singer's arm and walked toward her, brushing aside dancers. She had been escorted by a young army lieutenant but Álvarez had ignored the man's proffered hand and had drawn her smoothly onto the dance floor. He could never reconstruct that night, how he had danced with her, what they had said, but when the dance was over, he had paid the band two hundred pesos to keep playing and the two of them had danced until the sun pinked the puffy turrets of cumulus which floated like popcorn castles over the Caribbean to the east of Havana.

He had kissed her that morning, held her and told her that he loved her with his whole being and that she would marry him and she had laughed and said no and yet there had to be a promise in that laughter and he could still hear it, buried in the sound of the bolero.

The Mexican woman was in his arms, moving against him, and he started to drift through the steps, beginning to enjoy the sensuality of the rhythm and the hard spheres of her breasts against his chest. But in his mind, he was with Alicia, whirling past muted globes of rice-paper lanterns, faces beyond them just pale blurs.

"Who are you dancing with?" the Mexican woman asked softly. She started humming again, and he could feel the vibrations of her humming as she pressed against her.

"With a Mexican woman of great charm and beauty, Consuelo." He held her a little tighter and did a fancy step, bending her backward in a classical Valentino dip.

"How grand." She giggled a little. "And who do you love?"

"I love you, of course."

She laughed but it was a gentle laugh, not cynical. She gave a quick shake of her head. "No, Julio, I think you love the woman whose photo is in your suitcase. I studied her while you were in the bath. But I also know that you love me—or shall we say, love to love me."

"That too."

She moved her hips against him and worked her hands down into the small of his back, searching for bare skin under the tunic. "The *arroz con pollo* will be another forty minutes," she whispered. "Perhaps you show me how well you love to love me. We will both make believe that I am the woman in that photograph." She moved the needle on the arm into the first grooves of the record and then drew him down to the carpet. By the time they had finished their lovemaking, the record had replayed four times.

"You are a very good lover, Julio," she breathed in his ear.

"And you are as fine and talented a woman as I have ever made love to. I didn't know that such things could be done."

She giggled and snuggled closer against him. "What is her name?" She poked him in the ribs. "Really, I'm not jealous. I like her photograph. She looks like a woman with manners. Breeding, you understand. The Spanish influence in her cheekbones, the thin nose, the pointy little breasts."

He smiled inwardly. Pointy, yes. Little, no. Alicia had the body of a madonna, small but proportioned in three-quarter size. He rested his head against Consuelo's body and drifted off, listening to the scratchy strains of the phonograph record.

She rubbed his forehead, stretching his skin taut between her fingertips and then drawing it back together, over and over again. His mind was drifting again, totally relaxed.

She was saying something and he pulled his mind back, trying to seem interested.

"Someone was asking me a lot of questions about you."

"Who was asking questions about me?" He suddenly felt cold, as if there were a strong draft of frigid air blowing over him.

"I was called down to the administrative offices two days ago. There was a woman waiting for me—not in uniform, but with the look like she had worn one since she was born. You understand, Julio? Hard eyes, hair pulled back in a bun and a tight mouth. She took me to a car, unmarked but a Chaika sedan with a driver in plain clothes. She would say nothing. I kept asking her where we were going and why, and it was like she was deaf. We drove out the Ring Road and then took the turnoff on the Enthusiasts Highway. Finally, there was this garage set back in from the road and we turned in there. It looked like a garage from the outside, but inside it was empty and clean as a scrubbed operating room. The woman took me to an office off to the side and then waited in the car. I was terrified, Julio."

He was wide awake now. "Go on—what happened?"

"There was this man—early fifties or maybe older, except that he had almost no lines to his face. Overly long white hair, and with a face like an Englishman, you understand. Pale blue eyes, a thin mouth and a chin that simply melted away into his neck. He could have been a bookkeeper except when you saw his hands. I think that he could have crushed bricks with those hands and I remember staring at them, fascinated.

"He didn't say anything for a long time. Just looked at me like you would look at a tropical fish in an aquarium, and then he would glance through this folder he was holding, flipping the pages. After about five minutes, he looked up at me, as if I had just walked in the door and he was embarrassed that he hadn't risen to greet me. He smiled and then took my hand very gently and held it, not like he was going to shake it or kiss it, but as if he were trying to sense something through contact with my skin. He stared at me with this smile on his face and I wanted to pull my hand away and I tried, but it was like my hand was locked in ice. It couldn't move, and yet it wasn't as if he were gripping me with any pressure. It was just this terrible, irresistible force that I couldn't pull myself away from."

"What did he want?"

"He asked me about you. About everything. About sex, and how you shaved, and what foods you liked. It was crazy, like he was trying to get inside you through me."

He could feel the wind blowing harder now, chilling not only his skin but deep down into his organs. "So what do you think he wanted?"

She got up on her knees and stretched over to the sofa where her purse was. She pulled out an envelope and handed it to him. "He said it was an invitation, not a command, but that he wanted to meet you. In the same place—the garage. There's a map drawn on the envelope and I can help you if you don't know that section of Moscow."

He opened the envelope with his fingernail and pulled out the note.

On Friday, at 1300, you will find a dark green Siat-124 parked in a space reserved for the Assistant Research Librarian at the Foreign Literature Lending Library on Ulyanovskaya Street 1. The vehicle will be unlocked and the keys will be beneath the passenger seat. (Windshield wipers, should it be snowing, are in the glove compartment.) I invite you to join me for lunch at the garage, the address of which is on the front of the envelope. I look forward to a long and mutually profitable discussion.

There was no signature.

She sighed. "I wanted to throw it away. I wasn't going to tell you about it."

He put his arm around her neck and drew her face to his. He could smell the musk of both fear and arousal on her. "We will forget about this conversation, all right? There are better things to do."

Friday was fair but bitterly cold, the sky a brittle pale blue with a hatchwork of cirrus overlying the sun. He dressed in mufti and walked the nine blocks from his apartment, watching for a tail but there was none.

The car was exactly as described, the engine still warm. It had no official markings or plates, and yet, it had the sterility of official ownership. The cigarette tray was clean, the seats recently vacuumed and he could find no trace of human ownership beneath the seats—no ticket stubs, no receipts, not even a burned-out match.

He drove north on the Dimitrov Highway, intersecting the Moscow Ring Road, and then east, past Lianozovo, past Yurlovo and finally down to Ivanovskoye, turning through the maze onto the Enthusiasts Highway. Just past the Izmailovo Recreation Park, he started to slow, looking for the brick garage. He finally saw it, set very far back off a snow-packed road. He pulled through the turnoff, and then drew up before the overhead door.

Immediately, it raised and he drove inside. It was as she had described, surgically clean, with not a trace of grease on the floor. He shut down the engine and waited, not yet willing to leave the security of the car. There was no one around but he could hear, from somewhere deeper in the building, the sound of a radio program playing Stravinsky's *Firebird*.

He waited for another few minutes, smoking a cigarette, and then reluctantly got out. If he was going to play this game, he would play it without showing fear or hesitation.

"I'm pleased you came," the voice said in precise, accentless Spanish. Álvarez looked up and saw the man that Consuelo had described, leaning against a railing on a balcony which overlooked the garage. "I have a lunch prepared. Please come up."

Álvarez met him at the top of the flight of stairs and followed him down a slim corridor. At the end of the corridor, the man pushed open a heavy door and stood aside, motioning him in.

The room was totally at odds with the rest of the building—blue-slate shag rug of very good quality, modern chrome furniture, upholstered in pigskin, and a fireplace which radiated heat into the room. The paneling was a rich hardwood, possibly walnut.

The man turned to face him, offering his hand, the smile on his face correct but without warmth. There was a vaguely plastic quality about the man's skin—too smooth and perfect to be real. The eyes were a watery blue, like spring twilight, and he was balding.

Julio took his hand and felt the restrained strength in the man's grip. "Normally, I know the name of my host."

"For now, just call me 'Roy.'" He fetched a decanter of clear liquid from the mantel of the fireplace and poured out two glasses. "Vodka—a very good brand that we don't export. We call it Zveroboy, which means 'animal killer.' Ice?"

"No ice, if you please."

"No, I thought not." He lifted his glass and touched the rim of Álvarez's. "To friendship, *compañero.*"

Álvarez sat down carefully in a chair by the fireplace, his drink still in his hand. KGB, Álvarez thought, or possibly Internal Security. "Suppose that you explain," he said.

Roy smiled, showing very good teeth, the gums pink and firm, the enamel almost artificially white. "Yes, I suppose that I should but let's first eat and then we will talk and I will not play games with you." He walked to an adjoining door, knocked on it with his knuckles and then sat down by the fire in a matching chair, facing Álvarez.

Two men came in, one carrying a small wooden folding table, and the other rolling in a cart of food. Within seconds, they had left, eyes never raised above waist-level.

The meal was a well-marbled roast beef, baked potato with sour cream and a green salad.

"Your favorite meal, I believe. The salad dressing is an approximation of blue cheese—impossible to get, I'm afraid, here in the Soviet Union. But the beef is English, rare, as you like it, so I'm told. And I have Polish ice cream if you should desire a dessert. Not exactly Sealtest, but then again, not bad."

The thought occurred to Álvarez that the food could be drugged. "You should know, Roy, that I left your invitation in a safe place."

Roy cut through the slab of beef, forked down the bite and then leaned back against the leather, chewing. He held eye contact for a long while, not saying anything, just methodically chewing, as if he were counting before swallowing.

From his jacket pocket, Roy withdrew a piece of paper. "My invitation—at least the invitation you say that you received—was under a molding behind your bed. Very destructive, Julio. Prying out the moldings of state property."

I have to call his bluff, Álvarez thought. Now or never. He laid down the silverware and then slowly stood up. "Thanks for your hospitality, whoever the hell you are, but I think I should be going. It's been very entertaining, but for all I know, you're in the black market or dealing in illegal currency. I'm afraid that I'm not interested in either. If you don't mind, I'll use your telephone."

"How rude, *Comandante!*" Roy leaned back. "And who would you call?"

"The KGB First Chief Directorate, Eleventh Department."

"Then sit back and finish your lunch. Your beef will be cold if you don't eat it soon. General Suslev and I are passing acquaintances, and I think he would recommend my company." He lifted his glass ceremoniously. "You can't just eat and then run, Julio. No wonder you Americans have such bad stomachs."

Álvarez felt a rush of blood to his head. So the bastard knew, he thought. He tried to keep his expression placid.

Roy, completely at ease, remained silent through the rest of the meal.

Eating carefully without haste, Álvarez attempted to keep his body language relaxed. He glanced up only once and found Roy studying him—just as she had described—as though he were some exotic tropical fish, trapped behind glass.

As if he had been reading Álvarez's mind, Roy leaned back and relaxed, smiling. "You're obviously wondering why you're here?" He pulled out a pipe, stuffed it with tobacco and flamed a match into the bowl, making little sucking sounds. He whipped the match out and tossed it into the fireplace. "This is a sensitive and very private matter. If you had reacted in some hostile manner and reported this to the police, you would have been arrested and deported and there would be no connection to me. I think you can understand the necessity of security from my standpoint, can't you?"

Álvarez shrugged. "I can accept that on face value for the time being. Why not get to the point?"

Roy fingered the bowl of his pipe. "So what do you think of your Russian trip?"

"I've learned a few things. It's been helpful."

"But of course you want to get back to Cuba."

"The prospect appeals to me greatly."

". . . Born where and when?"

Álvarez didn't answer.

"Dillon, Montana, 1926, as I recall." He leaned back, puffing on the pipe, his eyes on the ceiling. "Law degree and some service in Korea, I believe. Silver Star, if that has any meaning. Immigrated to Cuba in 1956. But our dossier that we have compiled on your life doesn't really indicate why. Tell me."

Julio sighed. "First of all, Fidel knows all of this. He and only two other men in Cuba know the full details of my background, but the curious thing is, Roy, the records reflect that I was born in 1925. I simply made a mistake when I filled out background information for Cuban naturalization. So how is it that you know my correct birth year?"

"Go on with the answer to my question. I don't think you would be so stupid as to believe we wouldn't do our homework well."

"I got a law degree at the University of Montana. But I'm Hispanic—what some people in the States call a 'greaser.' I didn't fit in with the average law firm's concept of an associate, let alone a partner. They want lily-white Anglos who don't wear crucifixes under their T-shirts. You understand?"

"Not in the context of a classless society like the Soviet Union's but go on." His smile was more a smirk.

Julio let it slide past him. "So I did some legal work for immigrant Mexicans but you might as well have called it charity because they couldn't pay and I couldn't eat their thanks. But I still had one option open to me if I wanted to practice law. Understand, my father was a Cuban. Came up illegally about 1905 to work in the silver mines. So I immigrated to Cuba because my father had relatives there—people who were doing well, running a trucking service that hauled food to the various army posts in Cuba. My relatives had paid off all the right Batista underlings and had the business locked up. So I went down there and worked with them, took additional courses at the University of Havana, and got my Cuban law degree down there. For your records, I'm a Cuban citizen now."

"And then?"

"In the fall of fifty-eight, I joined Castro's Twenty-sixth of July Movement and fought with him in the Sierra Maestra, until we defeated Batista."

"But you've omitted the most interesting part, Julio. The time between your arrival in Cuba and when you joined Castro. Correct me if I've forgotten anything." He knocked the ashes out of his pipe and then stuck it back into his mouth, sucking on it. He turned over a page in a thick folder, running his finger down the lines of type and then looked back up. "You did a bit of gambling at the old Casino Capri. Run by a Sicilian syndicate out of Miami. You became friends with some of these men and they eventually approached you to work for them. Why?"

"Batista had his own set of auditors. They checked the books of the casino and took the payoffs based on the house take. Mangionni, the principal owner, had tried to bribe the lead auditor but he wouldn't play ball. But I knew the auditor personally. We occasionally did some deep-sea fishing, drank together, that sort of thing. So Mangionni figured that I could do it if anyone could."

"You were successful, it would seem."

"It was because I knew something about the auditor that Mangionni didn't. This poor, pathetic little prick of an accountant was sleeping with the mistress of a general in Batista's army. He was so full of himself that he couldn't contain it and he spilled his sexual exploits all over me in the locker room. So I had him over the barrel. He had to let Mangionni report a smaller take if he wanted to keep his balls from being cut off by a dull bayonet."

"And Mangionni kept you on as a troubleshooter?"

"Just routine legal work at first, but then I started to work as a go-between for him on other stuff. Payoffs to people in the government, bribes to the police. And then Mangionni set up a couple of whorehouses and he needed someone with the right connections to see that the proper wheels were greased."

Roy stood up and refilled the glasses with vodka. "By this time, you had started to skim off profits . . . skim . . . is that the right word, like cream from the top of a bottle of milk?"

Álvarez was growing tired of this. "Look, Roy, where is all of this leading? You seem to know exactly what happened."

Roy swirled the vodka around in the glass and then drank it down in curious little sips, then belched politely. "Written reports do not convey the meaning, you understand. So please be patient with me, Julio."

"All right. At first I was skimming off a thousand, sometimes two thousand a week. I bought a Jaguar sedan, an apartment, all the right stuff. But it was getting to me. If you want a real reason, it was a woman by the name of Jacinta. Turning points in your life are sometimes only small hinges on which doors to the future either open or slam shut. Jacinta was my hinge."

"Explain."

"Mangionni was having trouble with some of the whores in the Red Rooster—a place he owned in the old quarter. Nothing serious. Just that they were begging for tips, hassling the customers. There was a complaint from the U.S. Navy that some of their sailors on shore leave were getting their wallets emptied while they were sleeping it off. I was supposed to go down and push some of the girls around. I didn't like it but it had to be done. I kicked a couple of them in the ass and there was no problem except when it came to Jacinta. I walked in on her and found that she had three kids squirreled away in a closet—one of them hers but the other two just newborns whom she had picked up out of the alleyway where they had been abandoned. Beside supporting her family of six, she was taking care of these kids, not one of them older than seven months, and all she got was the equivalent of forty cents for each trick she turned. I checked her chit sheet. She was turning twenty and thirty tricks a day, just to feed those people of hers plus the kids. She had every kind of VD that you could name and she bled all the time—the same way that you or I would have bleeding hands if we worked at hard manual labor ten hours a day. I listened to her that night, began to understand her pain and the pain of people like her and what a filthy system Batista was running, and that it had to, was going to, stop somewhere. Castro was up in the Sierra Maestra by then, as was Maroto and some of the other groups fighting in the Escambray. I began to move some of the money that I was skimming off through couriers to support the Revolution."

Roy smiled sweetly. "So you have the heart of the true social reformer—the pure revolutionary?"

Shrugging, Álvarez was silent for a minute. "That was a part of it," he finally said. "No one could be exposed to that degree of corruption and not want changes. But I'm not going to kid you or myself. There was another very good reason. Batista was going to fall. A year, two, maybe as much as three, but the whores would tell me that even the soldiers who came down to get laid would say that when it came to fighting, they would side with the Revolution. Like they say, the winds of change were blowing. It seemed to me that if I wanted to hold onto what I had in Cuba, it would be smart to be on the winning side. The new government, whether it was to be Castro, Maroto or whomever, would probably reward the sources of money that had kept them going. And I had a degree in law. You might say that I was simply paying insurance premiums to retain some job security."

Roy grunted in satisfaction. "Candid." He stood up, walked to the window and looked out. He turned back. "What about your . . . ah . . . falling out with the Syndicate?"

"You have it there in your files."

"Not much of it." His face clouded. ". . . In your own words, what happened?"

"Mangionni somehow found out about the skim. He sent two of his thugs to rough me up, maybe kill me. I never found out exactly. Both of them were amateurs. They played around at first. I was able to get a revolver that I had hidden under a chair cushion. There was a fight. I killed both of them but in the firefight, got my leg shot up. I made it to a doctor who was a friend of mine. He had a clinic on the outskirts of Havana." It was close enough to the truth, Álvarez thought. If Brocassie hadn't fucked it up, he thought, I never would have even been wounded. He remembered how Brocassie had hesitated that fatal split second, as if the hood were going to try to negotiate a surrender. Goddamn amateurs, all of them!

Roy nodded, not commenting. He seemed mentally to turn a page. "So you finally joined Castro? Why not Maroto instead?"

"By the time my leg was healed, things had quieted down. The doctor's son drove me to Santiago de Cuba. Practically everyone in the city was for Castro. I joined his forces because it looked like it would be his faction of the Revolution that would be able to seize power. The foreign press was already talking about him as a real comer. As I said, I like to go with winners."

"And it would seem that you made the right choice, Julio.

You've done very well in these past three years." He rapped his pipe against the bricks of the hearth, as if closing that part of the conversation.

"Reasonably well," Álvarez responded. Damn well, he thought.

"I would say that you are extremely modest, Julio. I understand that you are thought of highly by Fidel. But I also understand from our sources that you will probably not rise much higher—certainly not to a position in Havana."

He felt his guts tighten, his breathing suddenly quicken, but he forced himself to relax, keeping his face expressionless. "I fought in the Sierra for a year with Fidel. I'm the most capable *comandante* he's got in counterintelligence."

"Undoubtedly true. But you are still a foreigner—an American at that. Some advisers to Fidel have expressed doubt that you can ever be entirely trusted. In Oriente, you are simply squashing counterrevolutionaries and the results can be measured by dead bodies. But in Havana, there would be more latitude to play at intrigue. You should note that even Ché Guevara is slowly being eased out by Fidel. Consider that Ché fought with Fidel from the very beginning of the Revolution, but he *is* an Argentine and therefore not admitted to the innermost band of brothers."

"You're sure of this?"

"Very. There is a tape recording of a telephone conversation that I may let you listen to at some future date—assuming, of course, that we can achieve a true appreciation of each other's objectives."

"Presuming that you define these objectives?"

Pursing his lips, Roy examined his glass, thinking. He seemed to come to a conclusion and looked up. "Yes, to a limited degree. But first of all, I would express the obvious. What we discuss here today is only between us. It concerns a very sensitive political matter, the knowledge of which is restricted to a very few people who hold real power within the Soviet Union. I will not insult you by describing what measures we would take to punish you should you commit the indiscretion of discussing this meeting."

"Consuelo knows about it."

"Consuelo will say nothing. You are not to approach her

again, for any reason. Nor will she approach you. Understood?"

Álvarez nodded. He could feel sweat matting his shirt beneath his armpits. This thing had gone too far. "One question," he said. "Do I understand that I can walk out of that door now, keep my mouth closed and that would be the end of it?"

Roy fluttered his hands in a gesture of reassurance. "Of course. Nothing has been said of importance, has it? But if you serve my interests, then I would suggest that you might find yourself as the assistant minister of defense of Cuba within three years. I believe that there could also be a discretionary account of money available to you in the currency of your choice and in the bank of your choosing. My friends who know about such things suggest deutsche marks in Liechtenstein."

"And what's the downside risk?"

Roy frowned, slightly puzzled, and then smiled. "Very expressive." He closed his hands together, making a steeple with his fingers. "The downside risk would be if Fidel found out that you were working for us. He might be displeased, but you have to understand that such a situation would be more injurious to the Soviet Union than to you. You would merely be shot but we would lose billions of rubles of investment in our only base in the Western Hemisphere." He flashed a sardonic smile. "I'm talking about the more historical perspective, you understand. And I assure you that if we did learn that Fidel was becoming suspicious, we would bring you back to Russia and award you with citizenship, a very comfortable life-style and, if you chose, interesting work with the firm which pays my wages."

"The KGB?"

Roy withdrew a plastic identity card and handed it across. A slightly younger man with more hair but the same drilling eyes, the same slick skin, stared back at Álvarez. The photograph was identified as Colonel Dimitri Mikhailovich Roychenko, First Chief Directorate, Technical Services.

Álvarez handed back the card. "Roychenko? Your name has come up in Cuba."

"I would expect that it has. I am responsible for the security and operations of all Soviet installations in Cuba, specifically for the one in Oriente."

"The underground complex? The rumor is that it's some kind of communications facility. Even I'm not allowed within the fence."

Roychenko stood up, got another log and heaved it into the fire and then turned back to Álvarez. "You are free to go, you know. It's your choice. But I would suggest that you consider it carefully. Nothing is going to be decided today. There is still a long way to go in my examination of your capabilities and in your consideration of the benefits. But in the end, it will be your choice."

"I'll stay in for another round."

"Ah, like poker. I'm familiar with the game because I once had a posting to England during World War Two. Grand country, generous people, although they're a bit too trusting." He leaned back in his chair. "Let me deal out some of the cards so you can look at them. In the Soviet Union today, there are two elements of power—those who presently set policy, and those who wish to pursue a more aggressive course.

"The new policy that we wish to pursue," Roychenko continued, "will cause NATO and more particularly, the United States, to slowly hemorrhage out its economic life's blood, its will and its credibility as the champion of freedom. The process will take ten, fifteen years or even more, but it will be achieved."

"Berlin?"

"Things like Berlin but on a grander scale. We have picked two countries, oceans apart, to launch this conflict from. In Asia, Vietnam and in the Western Hemisphere, Cuba."

"Christ! It wouldn't work. Cuba's right on the doorstep of the United States. The Bay of Pigs was a defensive action but for us to launch offensive wars would be impossible. They'd squash us."

Shaking his head, Roychenko continued. "No—you will not be fighting a war with the Americans on Cuban soil. We know that you couldn't win, and we are not in a position to assist you in the event the Americans invaded. The logistics are impossible. But we do have other plans which will achieve the same effect. At this point, I don't think that I need go further in discussing Soviet policy. The balance of the conversation will be, in general, what we would ask of you." He made motions with his hands, as if he were shuffling a deck. "Perhaps you would like to see three more cards? This, of course, requires a raise in the stakes."

Álvarez knew that he should walk away from the table, but the stakes were high and he wanted to play the hand out. "I'm still in, Roychenko."

"The first card—we have an underground complex in Cuba that even Fidel does not know the full purpose of. This knowledge must be kept from him for several months and the only way that we can do this is to have a trusted officer, such as yourself, tell him only what we want him to know. In the spirit of cooperation, we will suggest to Fidel that we turn over certain aspects of the security arrangements of this project to you as his trusted representative. Because of your familiarity with Oriente Province and counterintelligence, you would be his—and our—logical choice. Another card?"

He hesitated for an instant and then nodded. "Yes."

"The second card. We want to know everything that is going on in Cuba. The definition of an ally is someone whom we can trust eighty percent of the time and spy on for the other twenty percent. You are highly placed. You will hear things that we won't. You are our twenty percent margin."

"And the last card?"

Roychenko glanced at his watch. "The last card comes later, after you have decided to pick up the first two and fit them into your hand. I think that we both want to consider the stakes and perhaps either you or I will fold." He stood up, not offering his hand. "A driver will take you back to the library whenever you're ready. I'll contact you within forty-eight hours for your decision." He turned and left through the rear door and Álvarez sat for a long time, just watching the fire, his mind tumbling.

CHAPTER

5

Kapustin Yar, USSR, September 4, 1962

At midnight the day after the meeting, Roychenko had called.

"You've thought about my offer, Julio?" He didn't identify himself but Álvarez knew who it was immediately.

"I've thought about it." He had thought about nothing else, weighing the risks, the potential rewards. The stakes were too high not to stay in the game. "I've decided that I want to see the last card."

The receiver echoed with silence for a few seconds and then Roychenko answered, "You understand that once you place your bet, you're committed?"

"That's the way the game is played where I come from, my friend."

There was a click on the line. Another pause. "There will be a car waiting for you at the library—the same place as before. Drive to the garage. I'll meet you there. I'd strongly suggest that you make sure our meeting is private. Wear your

Class A uniform, medals and bring an overnight bag." The connection went dead.

Two hours later, Álvarez boarded an Antonov 12PB which had no markings. VIP express, Álvarez thought, lushly upholstered in leather with widely spaced seating and a built-in bar. Roychenko, uncommunicative, retired to a private compartment. There were no other passengers; only two stewards in plain clothes. They made no offer to serve him. He slept fitfully.

The plane flew southeast through thunderstorms, finally breaking out into clear sky shortly before dawn.

At 5:30 A.M., Roychenko shook his shoulder and handed him coffee. "We land in ten minutes at Kapustin Yar, our cosmodrome. As senior Cuban officer, you are on an official inspection tour. You will meet Yuri Gagarin, the first man into space. He is also the president of the Soviet-Cuban Friendship Society. There will be cinephotographers. Shake Gagarin's hand and say something clever. That is all that will be required."

"Why?"

"There are too many people in Moscow who are interested in what we are doing. Understand that there are two major factions contesting leadership in the Soviet Union right now. The principal players concerned with your involvement find a facility totally controlled by the Red Army much more conducive to security. Khrushchev still has his followers and he's not without power."

Because of a faulty connection in the microphone, Álvarez gave his speech a second time for the cameras. Gagarin, smiling while the cameras ground through rolls of film, walked away once it was finished without even a backward glance. So much, Álvarez thought, for "My Cuban friend who is bonded to the Socialist peoples of the world in political brotherhood."

The chopper touched down. A KGB captain saluted and led them to a security checkpoint.

Roychenko moved him through the formalities, photographs, fingerprinting and signatures in the logbooks. Two

KGB lieutenants escorted them through an access door and down a corridor, turning them over to an interior guard.

They swept down a carpeted corridor and into a conference room. The lieutenants saluted and closed the door behind him.

Álvarez felt a thin film of sweat forming on his back, despite the air conditioning. Roychenko was much more formal now, the veneer of friendship peeled away.

Roychenko motioned him to sit down but remained standing. "We have come a long way, *Comandante*. Things will move very quickly now, but first I need your firm decision." His eyes were brilliant blue pricks of light.

"First some questions and conditions," Álvarez said, keeping his voice level.

Roychenko raised his eyebrows slightly. "And what would those be?"

"One—I want no pay—no secret numbered accounts."

Roychenko smiled again and nodded. "That option will remain open to you, should you change your mind. What else?"

"Your assurance that what I do for the Soviet Union, and the KGB in particular, will not jeopardize the Cuban Revolution."

"Commendable. Yes—I can assure you of that. Not only assure but guarantee that your work will enhance the survival of your revolution. And . . . ?"

"I agree with the essentials of the concept that you have explained to me—to withhold information from Fidel concerning Soviet activities in Cuba, and to keep the KGB apprised of events in Cuba which you might not otherwise be aware of, but I draw the line in any plot to assassinate Fidel. I want no part or knowledge of such a plan. And finally"— he paused, trying to frame the vision that he had into words —"when Fidel is gone, there's going to be one hell of a power struggle and it may require Soviet intervention to control the outcome. I'll need your backing to take command —through Raúl or directly, it doesn't matter. And in return, I will support whatever the Soviet Union requires of me, but I want the necessary degree of autonomy to run the country my own way and I want economic support to accomplish the task."

Roychenko clapped his hands together, lightly, as if he were politely applauding a string quartet. "Excellent, Julio. Really excellent. That was exactly what I was looking for. Ambition for its own sake, loyalty to the Soviet Union and yet a measurable degree of honor. I think we have judged you well." He sat down on a table and leaned back, his hands laced together over his knee. "All conditions agreed to. And before we continue, I have only one condition which you must agree to."

"That being?"

"Absolute, unquestioned loyalty to the Soviet Union in the application of our policies. You must realize that you are crossing a threshold and once you have crossed, there is no going back. Do I have that oath of loyalty?"

"Agreed. If what you ask me to do does not violate the boundaries that I've laid out, then you can rely on me to carry out your orders."

Roychenko nodded his head, stood up and walked over to a television monitor. He switched it on and stood there, waiting for the image to appear. "One of our miracles, Álvarez. What we are going to see is a television image generated in Moscow—the Lubyanka Prison to be specific. Not transmitted by buried cable but relayed by one of our Cosmos satellites. As you will see, the picture quality is excellent."

The image expanded from a bar of light, growing vertically until it filled the screen. It was a sterile room, devoid of furniture, except for a wooden bench and a door. The floor appeared to be concrete with a central drain in the center of the room. Near the door stood an armed guard, a woman in the dull twill of KGB Internal Security. She was dumpy but not fat. Álvarez reflected that the woman probably juggled cinder blocks as a hobby. There was another woman in the room. She sat on the bench, a bundle of belongings beside her on the floor. Álvarez could not see her face—only her back— but she had the slouch of a defeated person. There was an unreal quality about the video display that Álvarez couldn't immediately fathom. It was as if he were looking into a department store window, watching plaster mannequins, frozen in artificial and static poses. "Impressive," he said.

Picking up a pointer, Roychenko tapped the screen, indicating the woman on the bench. "This is not pleasant, Álvarez. But it is necessary. The woman you see here is not an enemy of the state. It is doubly unfortunate, because she actually is a dedicated Communist. Her only crime is that she knows too much."

Álvarez felt a hard knot of pain forming in his gut as he began to recognize the profile of the woman. He looked at Roychenko, his expression barely under control. "What bearing does this have on our conversations?"

"A great deal," Roychenko answered, staring at the video monitor. "A very great deal. The woman represents a threat to the Soviet Union and to you. She knows of our involvement and if she was to divulge that to *anyone,* our relationship would be compromised. And you must admit, *Comandante,* the situation will tax your fidelity to us."

"What are you going to do?"

"Not what I am going to do," Roychenko replied, ". . . what *you* are going to do." He speared the phosphor image of Consuelo with his pointer. "In two minutes, she will be free to walk out of that room, through a security checkpoint and onto Dzerzhinsky Square. Her exit visa is stamped and she has a ticket to Mexico City. She is a free woman, to leave the Union of Soviet Socialist Republics, as she desires."

"But there is a condition?"

The Russian colonel dipped his head in acknowledgment. "If she does, then our operation is subject to compromise—worse yet, exposure. Dangerous for you, untenable for my associates. So within the next two minutes you must decide. It is for you to give the order."

The acid eating at the walls of his stomach was now palpable agony. "Decide what?"

"Decide whether she leaves the room or whether she dies immediately. If you allow her to leave by default, our relationship is terminated." He glanced at his watch. "One minute, fifty seconds remaining, Julio."

"What is it that you want me to do?"

Reaching up, Roychenko flicked a switch. A red light glowed above the video monitor and looking up, Álvarez realized that Roychenko had switched on a small television camera which was suspended from the ceiling. As he watched, the lens rotated, focusing on him. "Call the woman. Tell her to approach the television monitor where she will be able to see you, face-to-face. You will then tell her that she is to be executed as a security risk to the state. You will then order the guard to carry out the sentence. The guard will kill her cleanly with a bullet to the head. Believe me, she will feel no pain."

"JESUS CHRIST!"

"I doubt that he can intercede, Julio. One minute and twenty seconds remaining."

Time seemed to contract and then expand. He felt light-headed and nauseous. "Consuelo . . . ?" he heard himself call.

The woman on the bench turned around, startled, and then slowly stood up, picking up her pathetic bundle. Her eyes were bruised and her face had a gaunt appearance, but it was her, unmistakably her.

"Ye . . . yes?"

"Move over to the television set."

She walked hesitantly, pulling her belongings behind her. The sound of the bundle dragging on the concrete floor was plainly audible. As she came closer, her eyes opened wider. "Julio? Where are you?"

"Fifty seconds," Roychenko breathed.

He knew that he couldn't do it. In the background, the woman guard was moving toward the camera. Her hand lowered to her waist and unbuttoned the flap of her holster. In one clean movement, she withdrew a small automatic and held it at port arms, the barrel pointed toward the ceiling.

"Julio—where are you? My flight is leaving at three in the morning. We could have a few hours together." She gave a warped smile and Álvarez suddenly realized that two of her front teeth were missing.

"Forty seconds, Julio." Roychenko's voice was remote and mechanical.

The woman guard was behind her now, only a foot or so away. Her eyeglasses flashed in the light of the overhead fluorescent lamps.

His heart was hammering, his blood pounding in his brain, his whole body flushed with a heat which seemed to emanate from his gut. He cleared his throat and then whispered, "You are a security risk to . . ." His mouth dried, the moisture was gone from his tongue. He wheeled on Roychenko. "You sadistic *prick*. Put her in a cell! There's no fucking necessity to kill her!"

Looking down at his watch, Roychenko marginally lifted his shoulders and then relaxed them. "There are only two options, Julio. Choose one. There are eighteen seconds remaining."

He turned back to the screen. He could see in her eyes that she suddenly had realized that she was not really free to leave. She sank down on her knees and then collapsed sideways, as if she had no body strength left, but her eyes were still staring up at him, wide but without tears. Only a kind of horror.

"Nine seconds, Julio. Think carefully. Is it the life of a slut or your future and Cuba's?"

He was dizzy, nerves jangling. He breathed in and out three times and then whispered, "Consuelo . . . Consuelo . . . I'm . . . Christ—I'm sorry." Then, "Execute her." Instead of turning away, he forced himself to watch.

She had laid her head on the concrete, closing her eyes. Her arms were crossed across her chest and she hugged herself, her trembling visible. The guard placed the pistol to Consuelo's forehead and then looked up at the camera.

"She's waiting," Roychenko said calmly. "The guard didn't hear you."

"*DO IT!*" Julio screamed.

Clinically, the guard nodded, looked down to ensure that the position of the muzzle was placed so that there would be no mistake, and then squeezed the trigger. The snap of the firing pin falling into an empty chamber echoed electronically across twelve hundred miles of space.

He felt himself reeling backward. His legs buckled against a table, and he sank down on the cool linoleum. His hands were shaking and as if in sympathy, his whole body began to vibrate. He looked back up at the screen and she was rising from the concrete, smiling. She slipped her fingers into her mouth and withdrew a small, black device. Suddenly, her teeth were all there and she was laughing. She blew him an elaborate kiss. "That was a shitty trick to pull on you, Julio," she said. She withdrew some clips and then flounced her hair, letting it fall from a bun into a cascade of black velvet. "But we both work in our own ways for the world revolution." She blew him another kiss. "Sometime again, lover. We'll make it last for days."

Roychenko reached up and switched off the set. He walked to the far corner of the room, withdrew a bottle from a cabinet and then returned, setting it next to Álvarez's hand. "Very fine old brandy," he said softly, and took Álvarez's shoulder in his grasp, the pressure painful. "We had to know the limits of your loyalty, you understand?" He turned, paused and looked back. "I'll be back shortly. You might like a minute alone." He walked to the door, opened it and then pulled it closed behind him. Álvarez sat on the floor, the bottle untouched, staring at the blank face of the television, seeing in it the distorted reflection of his own face, moonlike and dumb.

In less than ten minutes Roychenko reentered the room with another man.

"Sit down." The man walked to the front of the conference room in easy strides. He was deeply tanned, full gray eyes set widely apart over prominent cheekbones. He wore general's tabs on the uniform of the KGB, medals cascading over his chest. Álvarez rose to attention but the general gestured for him to remain seated.

For a long time, the general stood facing him, his eyes unblinking and then he said, "My name is Anatoli Ivanovich Lazarev. I am with the First Chief Directorate, head of the Illegals Section. I have been chosen to direct your efforts although Colonel Roychenko will be your controller." He fished down into his tunic and pulled out a pair of glasses, then paused to read from a paper. He then looked back up at Álvarez, peering over the rims of his glasses.

"Colonel Roychenko feels confident that you will serve our interests well.

"I have thought a great deal about your involvement,"

Lazarev continued. "There is the natural temptation to limit your access to our plans—to use you, as it were—to carry out specific orders and nothing more. Based on your previous life in Cuba, your involvement with the casino and your affiliation with Fidel, it has been suggested that your psychology is that of a mercenary. Ideology does not motivate you—but power does." He lifted his eyebrows. "Correct?"

"Close enough," Álvarez responded. And that's what turns you and Roychenko on as well, he thought.

"Professor Lunts, a noted psychologist in our service, has reviewed your dossier and found something in your personality which I find both useful and disturbing: a propensity for danger."

"I like challenge."

"Some would call that a death wish."

"And some would call it calculated risk taking. Great enough reward coupled with reasonable risk and I'll take it." Álvarez leaned back in his chair.

He felt tense and he realized that Lazarev would push him, try to upset his emotional equilibrium, and he was prepared for that.

Lazarev turned aside, saying something to Roychenko in a whisper. Roychenko nodded, stood up and left the room. Lazarev got up and locked the door. He turned back to Álvarez.

"We are arranging a small demonstration which we feel you will benefit from, but before that I have some things which I wish to speak to you about in absolute privacy. The information that I'm about to give you is known to only a few men, and most of them know only small pieces of it, not enough to form a complete picture."

Álvarez lifted his eyes to meet Lazarev's. He felt a hardening in his stomach. Lazarev's eyes held the stare and a ripple of tension passed between the two of them.

"Nikita Khrushchev is finished," Lazarev said softly. "He is a peasant and his policies of reform and devotion to consumer goods production have stifled the development of the global military capability that we seek. Consequently, the decision has been made to replace him."

"With whom?"

"Leonid Ilyich Brezhnev," Lazarev replied. "He is a full member of the Politburo and is much more disposed to the needs of the Soviet military than Khrushchev, our Ukrainian clown. Perhaps of significance, Comrade Brezhnev has headed the development of the Soviet Union's rocket program."

Brezhnev's name was only vaguely familiar to Álvarez—a face on the parapets of the Kremlin Wall, caught by a telephoto lens. "How soon will Brezhnev take over?"

"Within a year if events go as we have planned them. Khrushchev will have the option of retiring gracefully or being forcibly expelled from the leadership in the spring of 1963. If he plays out the game that certain of the top leaders of the KGB and Politburo have devised, he can sign his name to his memoirs, have a pleasant dacha and lead a gentle life for a year or two and then, when the world has forgotten about him, die painlessly. He already has cancer of the liver and he will welcome the relief he's offered. But if he chooses to oppose us, his life will end much sooner from a very painful but unspecified disease. We refer to it as 'terminal displeasure.' "

Álvarez felt the pressure building up within him. What Lazarev was saying was deadly dangerous—information that Álvarez did not want to possess.

"Why are you telling me this?"

"The rationale," Lazarev answered, "is to impress upon you that your job in Cuba will entail a great deal more than tattling on the inner working of Fidel's government. You have a very specific task, *Comandante,* a task which the future leadership of the Soviet government views as critical. And the entire point of telling you this very sensitive information is to make you aware that you are not working for the Soviet Union or for Nikita Khrushchev." Lazarev tapped his own chest. "You are working for me, Álvarez. And I work for Yuri Andropov, head of the KGB and *he* works for Leonid Ilyich Brezhnev. In a critical situation, you may possibly receive orders from Moscow which will conflict with mine. I want no mistake about this. You will follow *my* orders."

Álvarez felt sweat saturating his back and armpits. Somehow, he had been caught in the vise of a power struggle. "Roychenko," he asked. "Where does he stand in this?"

"With me, of course. This is no feeble palace coup attempt. It reaches through the upper echelons of the Red Army, the Long Range Rocket Forces, the Red Banner Fleet, the KGB and four of the members of the Politburo. But you see, Julio, you are, oddly enough, a focal point, if you will—not a major component but a critical one. I am the trigger mechanism. Andropov is the barrel and Brezhnev decides when we must fire."

"Specifics . . . ?"

"Not quite yet, Álvarez. I first want to know whether you can accept the terms of your own involvement."

Lazarev spoke as if there were options but there were not. If he hesitated, he was a dead man because now he possessed too much knowledge. Lazarev was studying him with squinting eyes, as if trying to probe visually beneath his skin to the inner workings of his own mind.

"I have no problems with my involvement. I've given you and Roychenko that assurance already," he said, keeping his tone level and confident. Agree now, he thought, but decide later. He held Lazarev's stare and finally the Russian's face relaxed and he nodded to himself.

"Yes, I believe you will be loyal. I don't like to make threats, so I won't. You understand, of course, that you are expendable—as I am as well, should this thing go wrong." He suddenly leaned back, stretching his arms, flexing his hands, smiling. "Heavy work, isn't it? The plotting of downfalls, the security of nations." He leaned forward again. "Tell me, Julio, tell me honestly, what is your image of the Soviet bear?"

"Powerful . . ."

"But not that powerful. Be honest with me, friend."

Friend, my ass, he thought. But he shrugged gently. "Powerful but not that powerful as you say. A bit heavy-handed. A nation, as far as the West is concerned, to contend with but not yet one to really fear."

"Soviet rockets—what is your perception of them?"

He held his reply for a second too long and saw the look in Lazarev's eyes and then replied. "I was going to say 'powerful' again but we both know differently. Obsolete, cumbersome, unreliable."

Nodding, Lazarev smiled. "And Soviet intentions internationally?"

This was leading nowhere, Álvarez thought. A blind alley. He shrugged. "Eastern Europe. You have your sphere of satellites. Perhaps some influence in the Middle East. 'Wars of liberation' in various Southeast Asian countries, but on the whole, merely annoying to the West."

"You are refreshing, Álvarez," Lazarev said smiling, his voice mild. "Very, very few of my contemporaries would have the courage to voice such opinion, although we all know it's true. We are a second-class power with no direction but that will change." Without warning, Lazarev smashed his fists against the table, sending a shock wave of sound rattling around the room. "We will change that, *Comandante,* but it will take time. The Soviet Union is arming for a specific task. We need a whole generation of men and money and dedication, and in the meanwhile, the West has to be bled with a series of little wars conducted by our satellite states. Not on one or two fronts but on many—Southeast Asia, Latin America, the Middle East and Southern Africa. Over a period of time, the West will grow tired of endless contests, whether won or lost, which produce no change in political alignments. Those who pay taxes will rebel and those who have to fight the wars will revolt. Eventually, the Western nations will grow weary and divided and they will fall far behind us, both in armaments and in political will."

"And what will the Soviet Union do then?"

"What Lenin promised. We will fight one last great battle and we will win. The entire planet will ultimately be under Soviet rule: one flag, one language, one wholly integrated economy with common purpose."

My God, Álvarez thought, this sounded like a replay of a 1930s newsreel, except that Lazarev was no crazy little runt from Austria and what he was saying was a reflection of the planning of the top echelon of the Soviet Union's military.

He kept his voice expressionless. "What part does Cuba play—do I play?"

Now calm, Lazarev fished out a pipe and lit it with a battered brass lighter.

"Cuba," he started, "is our most important project, because it represents the first Marxist state in the Western Hemisphere. From there, we can confront the Americans on their own doorstep. And from Cuba, we can penetrate all of Latin America. Cuba will become an armed fortress, impregnable and equipped with the best arms that the Soviet Union can build. We will supply what is required for you to fight the wars that we direct."

"And what's in it for Cuba?"

"*When* the Soviet Union brings the world under one rule, there will be a small, select group of most favored nations, Cuba included. Cuba would naturally be the seat of government of the Western Hemisphere, understandably directed by leadership from Moscow."

He was astounded, almost incredulous. "You can't be serious!"

Lazarev shook his head. "But I am. Cuba is geographically positioned at the center of the axis of the American continents. It is an island, therefore not vulnerable to civil unrest from the countries which it would administer. Similar to England, if you like, when she owned an empire."

Álvarez leaned back in his chair. "It will take one hell of a long time for the Soviet Union to gain this advantage."

"True. It's a twenty-five-year plan. There may be alterations, of course, a year or so earlier or later, depending largely on the ability of the West to accommodate to our challenge for global leadership, but in the end we will win, not through political power but through military strength. To this end, the Soviet Union will commit, on the average, twenty-two percent of its gross national product over the next quarter century, starting the day that Leonid Ilyich Brezhnev assumes leadership of the Politburo."

Silence fell between them, only the hum of the air conditioning audible in the background. Sweet Jesus, Álvarez thought. One-fifth of a nation's wealth poured into a military machine constructed to be used twenty-five years hence. The automobiles that the Russians made weren't even on a par with those the United States built in the thirties, and he had seen state-produced watches that gained three minutes on the hour because of an engineering miscalculation in the number of teeth in the cogwheel. It seemed incredible that central planning could respond to the magnitude of such a task based on current Soviet technology.

Finally, Lazarev broke the silence. "You don't believe we can do it, do you? A backward nation, only forty years old, with peasant leadership and a severe lack of technological skills."

"The thought occurred to me."

Smiling, Lazarev bowed his head in acknowledgment. "I can understand why, but all of that will change—is changing already. Today's demonstration will show you the leading edge of Soviet applied science."

"And what is this demonstration?"

Lazarev ignored the question. He rapped his pipe against the heel of his boot and stuffed it again. Methodically, he applied a match, working the flame around to ignite the tobacco evenly. With some satisfaction, he finally leaned back in his chair. "What's your opinion of the prospects of Kennedy invading Cuba?"

"Almost inevitable. The Bay of Pigs hurt him politically and he's under a great deal of pressure with the November elections coming on. He's gearing up for it now. But given enough Soviet arms and training, we can repel them. We need coastal defense weapons, surface-to-air missiles and fighter interceptors. We learned from the Bay of Pigs that you have to control the skies over the beaches if you're going to push the invaders back into the sea."

"So let us assume that it is ninety miles to Cuba from the Florida coast and eight thousand miles from Russian ports, do you feel that the Soviet Union could sustain shipments in a protracted war, let alone not be drawn into the fighting?"

Álvarez pulled a cigarette from a mashed pack in his jacket pocket and lit it. "If you don't support us," he answered, "Cuba would be overwhelmed within three months."

"Three weeks," Lazarev corrected. "That is the maximum that we think Cuba could hold out without direct Soviet intervention, and that, my friend, is something that we must avoid. Based on our intelligence estimates, Cuba is only a few months away from an American invasion and this time I doubt that Kennedy will employ a ragtag army of Cuban counterrevolutionaries. He'll use five divisions of marines, an entire invasion fleet and the total capability of the American Air Force."

Julio tapped the cigarette ash onto the floor. He looked

back at Lazarev, watching his eyes, the movements of his hands, the subtle body language, trying to judge what the man was thinking. Lazarev's eyes finally met his and in them was some sort of suppressed amusement. The mouth might not betray but the eyes did—something that Álvarez had learned a long time ago. "Indirectly, you're saying that, somehow, the Soviet Union is going to be able to forestall or eliminate the threat of an American invasion. And I have some part in that plan. That's why I'm here—the specific project you referred to."

"We have devised an elegant plan—the ultimate means to defend Cuba: the introduction of Soviet-crewed, nuclear ballistic missiles in Cuba, targeted on the United States." He was smiling broadly now.

The concept was numbing, Álvarez thought, a surge of panic sweeping through him. A direct challenge to the Monroe Doctrine, surely something that would accelerate Kennedy's invasion timetable. "He'll flatten Cuba!"

Lazarev calmly picked a shred of food from between his front teeth, examined it distastefully and flicked it away. "We think not. Eisenhower might have, Truman surely would have, but not this man. He styles himself a diplomat, not a warrior. He will negotiate. We've studied very carefully the men around him: Schlesinger, Stevenson, McNamara and Rusk, as well as the president's own brother. We are quite certain that they will apply pressure in slow and measured stages, seeking an accommodation."

"But the missiles . . . ?"

"Sixty of one of the older types called the S-4 Sandal. Not terribly threatening strategically because their range is only in the neighborhood of eighteen hundred kilometers—a thousand some odd miles—not even enough to threaten Washington or Chicago. The Sandals are liquid fueled, and fired from launchers which we will set up in open fields on the northwestern rim of Cuba. Were we to attempt to fire them, the fuel and prelaunch preparations take nearly two hours. The Americans will be watching them with satellites, with spy planes, from submarines and through Cubans in the pay of the CIA. The missiles are not a real threat because they are exposed and cumbersome, but it is the very fact that they are *there* in Cuba that makes them valuable as negotiating chips. It is the perception of threat and its political ramifications that Kennedy will fear. If he were to attack, such a decision would be very damaging to him both domestically and internationally. But oddly enough, so would his decision not to attack. There are many Americans who smart from the embarrassment of the Bay of Pigs fiasco."

"OK," Álvarez conceded. "But Kennedy doesn't have to mount an invasion. Jet fighter bombers could take off from bases in southern Florida and smash the missiles before they could even be erected, let alone fired. The missiles are a hollow threat."

"But that's the point, isn't it?" Lazarev retorted. "The Sandals are a *perceived* threat, not a real one. Their very vulnerability will allow Kennedy to go slowly, to negotiate. The missiles will be manned by Russian troops. To destroy the Sandals would cause many Russian deaths and *that* Kennedy would not do because it would force us to retaliate." He stood up and flicked a switch. A projection screen unrolled from a fixture on the ceiling. He turned off all but a few of the lights, then thumbed a remote control recessed into the desk. A hard beam of light, a click and then a map of Europe filled the screen.

"These are things which Kennedy will give us in return for the removal of the Sandal missiles from Cuba. One—removal of American Thor and Jupiter missiles in Europe," Lazarev lectured. He tapped the pointer on the screen. "Sixty in England, thirty in Italy and fifteen in Turkey—all with a range of fifteen hundred miles, each with a one-megaton nuclear warhead." He switched slides. "Two—Berlin," he said, his voice hard. "We want Berlin and we will take it by making a separate peace treaty with the East Germans. What we will require of Kennedy is a private assurance that the United States will not try to intervene." He turned to Álvarez, his body spotlighted in the beam of the projector. "And third—we will obtain Kennedy's pledge that no American invasion of Cuba will ever take place and that he will suppress the guerrilla raids that the CIA is presently supporting—the so-called Operation Mongoose."

"But why would Kennedy buy such a lopsided deal?"

Lazarev stuck his hand in his pocket, jingling keys. "Because he is an astute politician. And he wants to be reelected by the greatest majority in American history." He nodded to himself. "Certainly, he will initially impose some sort of sanction against Cuba—perhaps a blockade—and he will certainly put his nuclear forces on alert as will we. Very quickly, the entire world will realize that it is on the threshold of nuclear war, but in private, negotiations toward an equitable settlement will continue. After all, what is Kennedy to do? Subject the world to a nuclear war over a little piece of real estate in the Caribbean? Our missiles in Cuba will be exactly the same kind of threat to the United States as the American missiles in Europe are to the Soviet Union. And the positive side is that we will assure him that, if he accepts our conditions, Chairman Khrushchev will immediately go to Radio Moscow, humbling himself before the world, admitting that the emplacement of missiles in Cuba was his own personal error, not that of the Soviet Union's, and that those missiles will be immediately removed. In the eyes of the world, Kennedy will have prevented nuclear war through firmness and mature restraint. The same will hold true on his nonaggression pledge toward Cuba. The victors, Álvarez, can always be magnanimous, but these seemingly minor issues will be buried in the euphoria of a world saved from war by a handsome young president."

"And Khrushchev?"

"We will have private discussions with the Americans, assuring them that Khrushchev *must* be replaced by more responsible leadership." He smiled. "What is your opinion of our little plan?"

My God, he thought, it was brilliant but it was also fragile—so much based on the personality of one man, John Fitzgerald Kennedy. "It might work but it's a huge risk. The real question is, what happens if it doesn't work?"

Lazarev frowned. "We have not overlooked that possibility. Kennedy could react irrationally. It is not impossible that the American military could precipitate a crisis situation on their own, forcing Kennedy to attack Cuba, and in that event, we have prepared a contingency plan."

There was a pain under his heart. His hearing, his smell, all his senses seemed to dull. "To accomplish what?"

"To win the resulting nuclear war, of course." He stripped the slides from the projector and dropped them into his briefcase. "And you are also part of that plan, Álvarez."

The Sandal missile was cradled in its transporter. It was nearly eighty feet long and over five feet in diameter, its surface skin featureless and finished in dull black matte. The three of them stood together under the harsh floodlights of the missile assembly building.

Roychenko was tour director. "This is one of the last fifteen missiles to be fabricated. Forty-five other Sandals are already on the way to Mariel, Cuba." He touched the skin of the missile, drawing his hand along the smooth surface, almost lovingly.

Not replying, Lazarev nodded. He touched the skin as well, tapping it lightly with his fist. The sound surprised Álvarez because instead of the hollow boom of sheet metal, there was a dull thud.

"They're stainless steel, aren't they?" Álvarez said. "Like American missiles."

Roychenko smiled like a cat who had just devoured the first robin of spring. "No, not steel. Fiberglass. You might say that these are highly modified Sandal missiles."

"Longer range?" Álvarez pinged his fingertips against the skin.

"No," Roychenko answered. "Shorter range. Much shorter." He took Álvarez by the elbow, guiding him past the booster section of the Sandal toward a partitioned-off section of the building. A KGB lieutenant and two Soviet marines stopped them at the entrance, checking papers. Beyond the entrance was another missile in a cradle, much shorter than the Sandal and smaller in diameter. "Our latest submarine-launched ballistic missile: the SS-N-5 Serb. Testing was completed less than eight months ago. It is now in mass production to be used aboard the nuclear Hotel class of submarine. Unfortunately, we can build missiles much more quickly than we can submarines. Consequently, we have a large surplus of the Serbs."

Walking slowly around the missile, Álvarez counted paces. Fourteen. The missile was not just a cylinder of metal with a warhead like the Sandal, but rather like a necked-down, high-velocity rifle cartridge.

"Quite graceful in its own way, don't you think?" Roychenko said from behind him. "With the warhead removed, a bit less than one-half the length of the Sandal, smaller in diameter and yet, with its solid-fuel propulsion and guidance system, it far exceeds both the range and accuracy of the Sandal. It can be launched from a submarine's tube or, for that matter, from a silo. Completely self-contained without all the cumbersome ground-support equipment required of the Sandal"—he smiled—"and much more reliable as well."

"I don't see the point . . ."

"But you will," Lazarev said softly. He led the way back out of the enclosure, across the missile assembly bay to an open cage elevator. The machine rose slowly, the electric motors whining. The cage clanked to a jerking stop. Lazarev slid open the door and led them along a short catwalk, through a door and out onto the roof.

It was dark now, the lights of Kapustin Yar angling out toward lighted launch gantries. Headlights bobbed, their beams sweeping the desert. Two helicopters with spotlights patrolled along the far-distant perimeter fence.

Lazarev remained silent for a few minutes, staring out into the night, and finally turned back to Álvarez. "I think that you understand the risks that are involved. The introduction of nuclear rockets into Cuba may produce an easy victory or it may precipitate a war. Our strategic analysts put the possibility of us having to enter into a nuclear war at less than thirty percent but it is still a significant risk and one that we must prepare ourselves for." He turned to Roychenko. "What is the present balance?"

"The Americans have sixty-seven intercontinental missiles based in the western United States and one hundred and five intermediate range missiles in Europe."

"And the strength of our rocket forces?"

"Seventy-three ICBMs in commission. Within a month, another six. And we have over two hundred shorter-range missiles targeted on Europe."

Álvarez compared the numbers in his mind and suddenly realized that the Soviets had a decided advantage.

As if Lazarev were clairvoyant, he shook his head. "Numbers do not tell the whole story, Álvarez. The missiles the Americans have in Europe can easily reach Soviet territory, as far north as Moscow and as far east as Kuybyshev. Therefore *all* their missiles are threatening to Soviet territory, while our shorter-range missiles in the Urals will only be capable of impacting on European soil and that, of course, is not of great concern to the American military. In effect, the ratio is roughly two and a half to one in favor of the Americans."

It suddenly fitted together. "By placing sixty Sandals in Cuba, you even the odds."

"Not enough," Lazarev replied. "Not nearly enough and as I've already pointed out, the Sandals' range is not sufficient to destroy much of the American nuclear capability which is centered in the western states." He shook his head. "No, we would need twice that number of missiles, designed to be more accurate and with a range of over two thousand miles. They would need to be protected in deep silos and able to launch within seconds of the launch order. But suppose, just for argument, that we could emplace over a hundred of such an advanced missile in Cuba. Then, if we chose to, we could totally eliminate almost all of the American strategic forces within eight to twelve minutes. The balance of forces would be totally reversed in our favor. The Americans would lose most of their bomber and tanker fleets, all of their ICBMs, their communications capabilities and their nuclear submarines which were in port." He rapped his pipe against the ledge of the roof. "The incredible thing is that due to their stupidity, the Americans would never know that they were under attack until our warheads were actually starting to impact on target because their highly touted Dew Line early warning radar only looks north toward the Arctic—not south toward Cuba. True, we would take losses, but *our* ICBMs would be intact, as well as our bomber fleet. If it came to war, we could, by an acceptable margin, win."

"But the purpose of this goddamn exercise was to prevent war while still securing Cuba as a Soviet base!"

"But there are also factions within factions," Lazarev shot back. "Military and political supremacy is our mutually agreed-upon goal. Brezhnev hopes to achieve that goal within a quarter of a century but others, myself included, believe that it can be obtained in a much shorter time." He paused, looking out over the plains of Kapustin Yar and then turned back to face Álvarez. "Do not make the mistake of believing that those of us in the military would, without reason, initiate a preemptive war, but my own personal analysis is that the chance of war occurring from this adventure is very high, perhaps higher than a sixty percent probability. If those of us within the military see a deterioration in political relations that we feel may cause the Americans to launch a strike, we will act first and decisively, and we—will—win."

It was suddenly obvious to Álvarez. Lazarev wasn't talking about a war which was just an improbable contingency—a one-to-three shot. He was laying down what was being planned as the main event. Lazarev wanted to precipitate a war—a war that he and Andropov were planning. He could feel the intense presence of the two men who bracketed him. They were waiting for his response, ready to calibrate his reaction in terms of total commitment. To blindly accept the contingency plan as Lazarev had outlined it would be insane. But to object violently to it would mean his own elimination. He chose the middle ground, stalling. "You couldn't get the Serbs into Cuba without the Americans finding out."

Surprisingly, Lazarev laughed. "You're right, of course. They track our ships from the time that they leave Murmansk. They take aerial photographs of everything that is unloaded at Mariel and then, within Cuba, there are thousands of men who are paid by the CIA to report on whatever is transported to military sites in the interior. We couldn't risk it, but just for the sake of argument, suppose we *could* bring in the Serbs without the Americans knowing?"

Álvarez knew that he was cornered and he composed his response to strike the exact chord between acceptance and reluctance. He took the plunge. "Then if a war is possible, we should be equipped to win it."

Lazarev remained silent for some time, sucking on the dead pipe. "Of course," he said, finality in his voice. "We would have to be equipped to win—or at least try to." He slipped the pipe in his pocket and looked back out over the plains. "I am the devil's advocate, you understand. The man charged by Brezhnev to do the alternative planning if things don't go as the politicians wish." He turned to Roychenko. "I have to go, my friend. What time do you have?"

Roychenko peeled back the cuff of his blouse. "Twenty-one thirty-three."

Lazarev nodded. "Let us say in five minutes, then. Thirty-eight after the hour."

Nodding, Roychenko embraced Lazarev, hugging him, slapping his back and then giving him a dry kiss on both cheeks. "We will not disappoint you, Anatoli Ivanovich."

Lazarev reached out, touching Álvarez's hand. "Until . . ." and not waiting for a response, walked slowly across the roof and disappeared through the door. Seconds later, Álvarez heard the rattle of the elevator cage door and the whir of the motors.

"He is brilliant, of course," Roychenko said. "A man with concepts which transcend ordinary thinking." He sighed, turning back to Álvarez. "Before you asked for specifics . . . ?"

"It would help."

"Khrushchev and Castro have signed a private protocol about the introduction of the Sandals into Cuba. It is to be a joint Cuban-Soviet command. Obviously, Castro wants final say in the use of the missiles. In other words, an order from Moscow to fire the missiles has to be seconded by Castro."

"But how could he prevent them from being fired anyway?"

"The 'two-code' system. I am given a nine-digit code by Moscow. Castro gives you a nine-digit code of his own choosing. In theory, neither of us knows the other's code. In the event that there is an order to fire that both Moscow and Havana agree upon, we will be given separate confirmation. You punch in your nine digits and I do likewise. This enables the firing circuitry."

"General Lazarev said that the Sandals would be placed on the northwestern coast of Cuba. I assume that we work out of Havana or Pinar del Río?"

"No," Roychenko answered. "Not Havana. We exercise control over the missiles from the Calvario Complex in the valley to the north of the Sierra Maestra."

Álvarez had known about it for some time. A purely Soviet operation, built by Russian construction battalions, guarded by KGB, manned by Red Army types. He had been briefed by Raúl Castro that it was a communications facility that the Soviets wanted for their submarines operating in the Atlantic Ocean and Caribbean Sea. Strictly off limits.

"Why there?"

"Because I say so," Roychenko answered, his voice flat. There was no invitation for discussion. Roychenko tapped his watch. "A quarter of a minute now." He pointed to the southwest.

Seconds ticked away. And then a brilliant burst of flame lit up the night sky, clouds of smoke illuminated by a glare from within, boiling upward. In a smear of incandescent light, a missile rose, slowly at first and then accelerating, arching up and over in a smooth parabola. The concussion of the shock wave hit him, a sound of sustained violence hammering his senses.

The flames consolidated to a pinprick of intense light, painful to his retinas, and yet he couldn't tear his eyes away. The rocket exhaust was swallowed by a cloud layer and then reemerged, blue-white hot, accelerating with an incredible rapidity. He watched it, mesmerized, until it was swallowed by the curvature of the earth.

"In nine minutes, the dummy warhead will impact two thousand miles from here, on the plains of Transbaikal, with an accuracy of under a quarter of a mile." Roychenko's voice was emotionless.

Álvarez fumbled a cigarette from the pack and lit it. "That was the Sandal." He made it a statement, not a question.

"No," Roychenko answered. "That was a Serb."

The flight back to Moscow was incredibly smooth. Roychenko had fallen asleep even before takeoff but Julio, unable to sleep, held his head to the cold Perspex of the window, watching isolated lights slide back into the extinction of the vast Russian heartland.

He recognized that he was locked into the venture and he saw no way out. But the end product was power and that was tantalizing and worth the obvious risks. The stakes had escalated much more quickly than he had anticipated, and yet he knew that he had to play out the hand for its own sake.

He suddenly sensed that Roychenko was awake, studying him. He turned. "You sleep the sleep of the innocent."

Roychenko ignored the gibe. He yawned, stretched his arms and then glanced at his watch. "We'll be on the ground in thirty minutes. You'll have tomorrow and the next day to go through the motions of finishing off your training. Two nights from now, we'll fly Aeroflot to Havana." His voice was dull, monotonal. He turned away, breathing through his mouth, already falling back into sleep.

Álvarez looked out into the night. Stars dipped on the horizon as the plane banked gently toward the north. Up ahead, individual lights merged into strings, leading to the north and beyond that, the pulsing illumination of Ryazan and beyond that, Moscow. Two days in this goddamned bitter land and then home. Alicia, he thought. Christ, he wanted her softness. To feel her hair between his fingertips and to smell the scent of her thighs and the taste of salt on her skin. Involuntarily, he hardened. He felt the need of a woman now, strongly.

He tapped Roychenko on the arm.

"What is it?"

"Consuelo. You have no objection to my seeing her?"

Roychenko sat up straight, working his shoulders, stretching the kinks out of them. He inhaled slowly and then exhaled through his nostrils as if irritated. "I thought you understood, Julio. That isn't possible."

"I don't see why—"

Roychenko interrupted him. "She *died,* Julio. She was struck by a truck as she was crossing Dzerzhinsky Square, only minutes after you talked to her." He sighed. "But perhaps it's for the best, don't you think? Women talk too much, don't they?"

CHAPTER

6

Steen, Colonel Jay Royce, Jr., U.S. Army, Retired, met Hagger at the door of the concrete block ranch house located in one of the older, decaying sections of Coral Gables. Steen had the complexion of a side of beef, fully aged, and his eyes were red-rimmed, reflecting the thirty-year-old life-style of a man who was pushing into the middle sixties. He gave Hagger a crunching handshake and then padded back into the living room, leaving wet footprints on the terrazzo floor.

The house was early Floridian tract with furniture out of a discount store. The place had probably been built and furnished for the anonymous people who drifted in and out of Florida, like De Soto, in search of wealth or immortality. Hagger had often reflected that few of them found the former and none of them the latter.

Hagger followed Steen's footprints into a living room which fronted a small screened porch—the liana room which seemed to be grafted onto every Florida house. Beyond that, dominating the fenced lawn of parched crabgrass was a swimming pool. The water had the cast of split pea soup.

"You need some chlorine in that thing," Hagger said, heaving himself into a bamboo chair with pink floral cushions.

"Not out of my pocket," Steen grunted, toweling himself off. "Agency rents these shit heaps but never provides any operating funds. No wonder we have a lousy, fucking PR image." He pointed to a wet bar which had several bottles and a bucket of ice. "Help yourself. I'm going to shower off." He disappeared toward the bedroom, trailing little dribbles of water like a naughty puppy.

Hagger poured himself a Canadian Club and ginger and then stood by the steps leading down to the pool, sipping slowly on the drink.

Steen, Hagger reflected, was pure, early American agency—nurtured in the Wild Bill Donovan school of the Last Great War, then recruited when the CIA was first formed. He kept his rank of colonel but now he was *only* agency and within spitting distance of retirement. The agency was changing, Hagger thought. Bright, young, bushy-tailed college graduates with degrees in the exotics. They wore ties and shined their shoes and had vocabularies which pivoted around words like "appraisal," "parameters" and "macroeconometrics." All wonderfully vague, coordinated by camel-producing committees and designed to leave no one at fault in case the shit flew. But not exactly like putting it on the line in plain language and over your own signature. Christ, he thought, I'm getting old—too old for this kind of game.

Hagger took a large bite out of the drink and swallowed, not looking forward to the begging that had to be done, not at all sure that Steen would go for it. Pending retirement did funny things to a man's sense of commitment.

Steen returned, now in a fluffy white bathrobe, his hair plastered back on his scalp, his face more than usually flushed from the shower.

"You're out of your territory, Hagger," Steen said. "JM Wave doesn't mix with Operation Mongoose. Run your own show, not mine."

"Something a little unusual," Hagger replied. He swallowed more of the drink, waiting for the lubrication that it would give his tongue but knowing that it wouldn't.

"We picked up a guy who came out of Cuba just three days ago. He had a roll of film."

"Feelthy peeksures, Señor Hagger?"

Hagger bit down hard, knowing that he would have to take this from Steen. It was part of the game that Steen played and they both knew who held the cards.

"Something like that. This guy was picked up on the north coast of Jamaica by local defense forces. One of our people got wind of it and soothed away all doubts of the locals by dropping two bills on the desk of the head of immigration. My guy is an American—been in Cuba for the last three years. He's worked with Fabricio and more recently with Maroto's column. Knows the Sierra Maestra like the back of his hand."

Steen walked over to the wet bar and poured some gin in his glass, then topped it up with tonic. "Trick of not getting hooked on booze, Hagger, is to make the first drink just straight mixer. Fills your stomach with gas. Then you can mix in the hard stuff on the second round. Same thing as stuffing your face with a sandwich before you go to the supermarket so you don't buy all the sweet crap that they stash on the shelves, understand?" He didn't wait for an answer. "So what about the film?"

Hagger scratched at a heat rash on his neck. "Fabricio had sent out a message, oh, about nine months ago, that Soviet construction brigades were building one hell of an underground complex in the Sierra Maestra. We got two U-2 fly-overs but they picked up nothing because it seemed that all the construction work was being done at night or under dense cloud cover. So we sea-lifted in supplies to Fabricio as usual but included a Nikon and a couple of long-range lenses, infra-red film, the whole works. One of Fabricio's men had been a commercial photographer so we figured that he would be able to handle the job. In an air strike, the photographer got cooked but the film survived. My man went through real bull-shit to bring it out."

"Photos of what?"

This is the break point, Hagger thought. Either he'll go

for it out of curiosity or he'll cut me off. He finished the remains of the drink, flicking his eyes toward Steen's, trying to fathom the man's expression, but there was nothing decipherable. He tried to make it a teaser, hoping Steen would take the bait. "Stuff like we've never seen installed before anywhere outside of the Soviet Union."

Still no real reaction from Steen. He merely stood there, clanking ice cubes in his glass, studying the ground, and then led the way toward the pool. He huffed and then sat down on the steps which led into the wading area. Hagger sat down beside him, pulling off his shoes and socks and then dangling his feet in the water.

Steen heaved a sigh as if he had heard it all before. "So what does the film show, Hagger, old buddy of mine?"

"For one thing, they show that the construction troops are Ivory-pure Red Army—Pioneer Battalion, Second Corps of Construction Engineers. The last major project that they were involved in was at Plesetek which is in the Leningrad District. Missile base of some sort. The markings on their trucks match up and two cranes that they're using have numbers which were photographed on a U-2 overflight in November of fifty-seven."

Steen blew between his lips like a winded horse. "So what's so fucking threatening about that, Hagger?"

"I sure as shit don't have a clue," he said tiredly—perhaps a bit defensively. "That's what I got to find out. The photos my asset brought out show something like work sheds—galvanized roofs set on poles but open on the sides. Under the roof is some kind of hole. Apparently, the Russians excavate only at night or only under dense cloud cover with the roofs removed. Under clear skies, they reattach the roofs and vacate the site so that from the air it's as populated as Death Valley. The area we're talking about is in a nickel mining district in the Sierra. There are tool sheds all over those hills. We compared back to old aerial survey photographs and these are new, but there are so many of the old sheds, you'd never notice unless you were looking for something."

Steen stood up and walked around the pool, looking down into the opaque depths. "Chlorine, huh?" He turned back and trod on flat feet toward the bar. He poured himself half a glass of tonic, tasted it, poured it down the drain, and filled the glass half full with straight gin. "So they dig these holes in the ground and then what?" Steen asked.

"Based on the photographs taken by Fabricio's man, they line the hole with interlocking steel collars—exactly fifty-three inches interior diameter and maybe to a depth of fifty feet. These are superaccurate estimates based on the size of known objects like truck tires, sections of galvanized sheeting, stuff like that."

Steen laid his finger alongside of his nose like an expectant St. Nicholas. "So surprise me, Hagger. What are the bastards building?"

"Fuel storage tanks maybe. That's the rumor in Cuba but I can't buy it."

"Tell me what you are buying?"

Hagger smiled inwardly. Steen was starting to make tentative passes at the bait. He eased out more line, jiggling the lure. "I think they're building silos." He stirred the water with his toe and then withdrew it. "Chlorine will do it every time. Slosh in a gallon or so—let it sit overnight and you'll be looking at a pool as transparent as the Colorado River."

"The Colorado's liquid mud."

"I was speaking in—shit—what do you call it?"

"Metaphors."

Hagger shrugged. "Whatever."

"Quit screwing around, Max! What are they going to store in your so-called silos—Romeo y Juliet cigars for the export trade?"

"Missiles."

"*MISSILES!* You're off your gourd!"

"I'm not talking about intercontinental or even intermediate range. I'm talking about stuff with a range of maybe fifty to eighty miles."

Steen looked down at the tiles lining the swimming pool. He crossed his legs and began to tap one foot to the beat of an imaginary drummer. "Keep talking," he said.

"It's the only thing that washes. Soviet construction crews with maybe two hundred KGB security patrolling the perimeter. Cuban DGI controlling everything outside the fence and the access roads beyond. DGI and FAR troops combing the mountains around for guerrillas. So it isn't just fuel tanks. Forget surface-to-air batteries. They're not fired out of fifty-foot holes in the ground. Long-range nuclear missiles? Interesting thought but even I don't think that the Soviets would have the balls to install something like that within spitting distance of the United States, and besides, nothing that they've got that I know of is that small in diameter. So it has to be short-range surface-to-surface missiles."

Steen groaned a little, heaved himself upright and then motioned toward Hagger to follow him. "Let's move into my lair. It's too open here and despite the fact that there are a couple of guards wandering around out there trying to look like gardeners, it's not secure." He thumped at his chest with both fists, a degenerating Weissmuller. "I'm sixty-three, Hagger, and I don't feel a day over eighty. Bring in the gin and I'll get more ice from the kitchen. Back bedroom, second door on the right down the hallway."

Hagger picked up the gin and found his way down a narrow hallway of stuccoed plaster, decorated with a few cheap prints of insipid doe-eyed children with gangly necks.

He found the room and seated himself in a canvas deck chair.

Steen came in behind him with a salad bowl filled with ice and two glasses. He heaved himself into the chair and poured each of them a gin. He raised his glass. "To a couple of burned-out, deskbound spooks." He swallowed noisily, set the glass down and leaned back. "So make me a proposition."

"Look, Jay," Hagger said softly, knowing that Steen had made a pass at the bait but still not taken it. "I work for you. Mongoose is a division of JM Wave. I need your support and I expect it. I want to send a team into Cuba to determine exactly what these silos are going to be used for. Maybe, if possible, take them out, using the men that I send in and Maroto's column."

"So go to Bobby Kennedy. You only work for me according to the organizational charts. And in case you've forgotten, there's a presidential directive that specifically prohibits any of us getting involved in an operation that would endanger the lives of those precious little Soviet nationals."

"I can't go to Kennedy," Hagger answered. "Fredericks is

the go-between and I've already sounded him out. I got a flat no. My only recourse is to do the job illegally and lean on you for the equipment to do it with."

"So what's the big deal?" Steen said, yawning. "You've got some holes in the ground in Oriente Province. And you want to make the holes bigger. Use your own assets or grab some of those exiled Cubans from Alpha Sixty-six. You can find them, dime a dozen on West Flagler, but leave me out of it."

"Jay," Hagger started, "we've both seen how it's been going over the last ten years. Everything is done by faceless, nameless committees, overseen by congressional subcommittees. What comes out in secret testimony is in Jack Anderson's column the next morning. Security is inversely proportional to the number of people involved and the Pigs invasion was a perfect example of that. You damn well know that when a situation goes critical, the Executive Branch always has the option of copping out and leaving the people we have to live with stranded on the beach.

"The Soviets are bringing in two, sometimes three freighters a day into Cuba. They're pouring in stuff—surface-to-air missiles, tanks, artillery and ordnance, all of first-class quality. This is no simple supply operation to a client state. They're building Cuba into a fortress, and from that fortress, the Soviets are going to launch a campaign to conquer Central and South America.

"The rumors going around," Hagger continued, "are that the Joint Chiefs are bugging Kennedy to take out Cuba before Castro has too much equipment. It's a little more serious than just tanks and artillery. Word is that Castro is getting IL-28 bombers which means that, on a one-way mission, they could hit anything as far up the East Coast as Washington and anything as far west as Dallas."

"So let's hope they go for Washington," Steen said. "Relieve freeway congestion and give the Pentagon something to justify its existence." Steen sighed and then slouched back into his chair. "I still don't know why in hell you need me to stick my neck out because of some holes in the ground."

With his fingernails, Hagger scratched at the rash. So go for it; set the hook and start reeling in the line. There was nothing to lose except everything. "Look," he said, "Kennedy ultimately, from the force of circumstances, from political pressure, from screams echoing down the halls of the Pentagon, is going to have to invade. But rather than going through the tedious process of preparation—getting adequate people on the ground in Cuba, blowing up critical installations, doing the kind of preparation that was done for the Normandy invasion—he'll dick around until the last minute and then throw everything we've got in the inventory at those beaches. You and I know that it takes months of groundwork to pull something like an invasion off and if it isn't done properly, the invasion could fall flat on its ass. And if that happened again, the United States would have about the same military credibility as Iceland."

He scratched again at his heat rash, agitated. Not going well and he was pushing hard but knew he had to push harder. "OK—bottom line. The silos are probably for FROGS."

"What's a fucking FROG?"

"Short-range missile. Maybe fifty to eighty miles in range. Conventional warhead normally, nuclear warhead possible. Sophisticated guidance. Infrared homing or homing against a radar source. The Soviets and Cubans need something which is capable of hitting ships far enough offshore that they're still out of naval gun range. Plus, from the Sierra, they could lay payloads on the runways of Guantánamo Bay. And with the site in a deep valley, equipped with surface-to-air missiles, it would be damn near impossible for us to throw in an effective air strike without it being a one-way, kiss-your-ass-good-bye mission."

Standing up, Steen stretched his arms out, flexing his fingers. "I'm an asshole Little League daddy, Hagger," he said. "The whistle blows in fifteen minutes because I've got a drive of forty minutes up to Fort Lauderdale and ump third base. You're talking about involving me in an off-the-cuff operation, totally unsanctified by the director and potentially involving the killing of Soviet nationals. I can't buy it, Max."

"*Jesus*, Steen," Hagger shouted. "Everyone—the agency, the Pentagon and the White House—is scared shitless to pull off anything which would involve the killing of Soviet troops. These wimps in the Pentagon will churn out their useless fucking plans and everyone will look the other way until it's too late. I think that what's there in the Sierra has to be taken out. *NOW!* Whatever they've got, they'll eventually protect with surface-to-air missiles and then nothing will get in. But with a team of two or three guys right now, I might have a shot at it."

"So possibly, just possibly, I could do an airdrop for you."

"They'd never get in. The Cubans have net radar and MIGs. They have radar-directed antiaircraft. A drop plane would never get within fifteen miles of Cuba. And on top of that, besides a team of two men, I want to get about five hundred pounds of arms and supplies down in one piece. The drop site is in the mountains and it's going to have to be at night. So forget airdrops."

Steen heaved a sigh. "No promises but outline it."

"I want the loan of two of your turbosupercharged Helio Courier aircraft, plus pilots, maintenance, security and support people. I want the use of the base in Jamaica. I want some of those funny little airplanes that you've got tucked away in Utah, and I want Porto."

"You think I'm going to give you all of that stuff just like that? I've got my own operations to run, Hagger. And you really think I'm going to give you Porto? What the hell am I supposed to tell him—that he and some other nerd are going to fly into the mountains of Cuba in the middle of the night, blow shit out of a heavily defended installation and get back out? That's horse hockey and we both know it." He laid back most of his gin and then slammed the glass down.

"We've both done dumber things, Jay. I need Porto because he's trained in this stuff, knows the aircraft and looks the part. He's Latin extraction as is my asset. So regardless of what happens we either win or break even. If they pull it off, great. If they get caught, we don't embarrass Washington because our operatives are pure, bona fide Cuban look-alikes without agency connection. But even if they don't blow the complex, as long as they can get close enough to really find out what kind of equipment is going in there and how it's going to be used, then we can get some support for a full, all-out effort. It would be a stunning accomplishment to top off your career, Jay."

Steen frowned. "You're talking about dumping both of these guys in the shit and hoping that they can swim. Porto is one of my best people and I owe him more than this."

"Porto is the only man who fits the bill," Hagger shot back. "The alternative is to do nothing and watch the invasion fleet get smeared in the first half hour." He saw uncertainty in Steen's eyes and he leaned back, holding his tongue.

It took five minutes and two cigarettes but Steen finally leaned forward and nodded. "You understand that this operation is going to be completely off the books. No paper, no signatures. You also understand that as your senior officer, I'm reiterating a presidential directive which states that any action involving possible hostilities with foreign nationals other than Cubans is strictly negative." He paused, beating ruffles and flourishes on his chair arm with his fingertips. "You understand also that as your superior I get the ax first if anything goes wrong, and although the sunny side of forty may be shining on your ass, it ain't on mine, sonny. One year, four months and a couple of testimonials and I'll be out. It may seem mundane to you, but I've got kids, a house frau and a bone-lazy, flatulent Airedale to support. As far as Porto is concerned, you can tell him that it's OK with me but that he'll have to make up his own mind. I'd suggest that you make him a very sweet offer out of your slush fund. He could use the money."

Steen's back was saturated with sweat, even though the room was cool. Hagger breathed deeply once and then again. "I appreciate this, Jay. It's something that has to be tried."

Steen nodded. "I seem to remember General George Armstrong Custer saying the same thing."

Brocassie had spent the afternoon pounding down the white-grained sand beach of Hammerhead Key. It was not much more than a spit of sandy land in the Florida Keys which no one in their right mind would want to own. Hagger had told him that back in the forties a couple had tried to build a fishing camp here and had gone broke within two years. For the next fifteen years, the mosquitoes, the rats and the crabs had reclaimed it.

Hammerhead Key, by its appearance, was still uninhabited unless you knew that the boathouse contained three modern high-speed launches which could cross the Straits of Florida into Cuban waters in less than four hours. The main bungalow, now Hagger's office, was a slapdash rambling structure, the clapboards warping in the sun, an air of decay about it. But on the inside, it was fitted out with air conditioning, a teletype, two high-frequency transmitters and other electronic toys which the agency had installed in their undeclared war against Cuba.

There was also a small warehouse on the west side of the island stacked with mines, explosives and automatic weapons. Lining the eastern beach were six rotting "guest cottages" for resident personnel and visitors. And in a grove of stunted pines, Brocassie had stumbled on a burial plot—all the crosses marked with numbers—for those who made it back from raids on Cuba but didn't survive their wounds.

Brocassie sprinted out the last quarter of a mile, working the soreness from his body, feeling the salt air fill his lungs. Crabs, mincing sideways, scuttled out of his way. Gulls, scavenging the foreshore, shrieked and took flight, arching out over the sea and then turning back, spiraling up in the hazy sunlight, squawking threats at the lone intruder. He alternately ran through the hard-packed sand and through wasting surf, burning energy as if it were a commodity to be only spent, never stored for another time.

Plenty of food, uninterrupted sleep in a clean bed, medical care and exercise had put his body back into shape but he felt as if his mind had died. The machine of his body was rebuilt and functioned perfectly, but there was no guidance system inside to direct it. The perfect mechanical man, he thought bitterly.

He slowed to a jog and stopped, panting heavily, then sank down in the sand, allowing his body to cool slowly in the late afternoon wind. He picked up handfuls of sand, letting the grains trickle through his fingers, forming a cone. My whole life like this, he thought, destined to be washed away by the tide and the wind in one brief instant.

All the crap about the Cree concept of universality—man harmonious with nature, his father's words—a truth that generations of his ancestors had lived by. He had embraced that belief through the years that his father still lived, held desperately to it while he lived in the Álvarez household ignoring Julio's mocking derision, seen it begin to erode in Korea and finally die on that last night in Cuba. Now it was just a mindless ritual of a withered faith, one that he could never again believe in. Because he had not lived by that truth and it had thus become a lie. It was bullshit. What universality? What harmony?

Both Korea and Cuba had been killing grounds and he had been one of the killers. Who would name a star for him because he had been a great warrior? Warriors had honor and what honor was there in lobbing 60mm mortar shells into a convoy of trucks, sniping at the enemy through telescopic sights or blowing up an old man in the Sierra with a wad of plastic explosive? What right did he have to call upon some imagined inner spiritual strength when the only thing he had tapped was his own fragile ego and the belief that he fought for the ideals of someone he had loved. And in the end, his own ego and the woman he loved had betrayed him.

He had fooled himself into believing that he was fighting for a free Cuba—for a Cuba she had died for, for a nation, like the land his ancestors had fought for—to make it free. What a goddamn mockery! He wondered whether she would laugh when Sergio Piedra delivered the message.

"Damn, damn, damn," he swore, and for the first time since he had been told of her death, he felt tears streaming down his face. He bent over, his vision blurred, watching the droplets fall, cratering the sand into minute depressions. His tears wet the sand and then, almost immediately, dried. The wind, rustling across the beach, filled the depressions, leaving nothing behind to mark his despair.

Just get the hell out, he thought. Put it all behind you—Cuba, Álvarez, Hagger and most of all Alicia.

To his right, much farther down the beach, the gulls shrieked and took flight. Brocassie turned. The woman, Miller, was walking along the sand in some sort of a caftan. The wind caught at a hood on the garment, blowing it up against the back of her head, strands of her hair streaming in the wind before her. She was quite beautiful, he thought. Perhaps, more than that because, although he knew that she received a paycheck from the agency as a psychologist in order to understand the stress that he was carrying, she had not pushed to extract it from him. In a world of enemies, one didn't need friends—only impartial neutrality.

She was only yards away now, and she lifted her hand in the peace sign. "Am I intruding?"

"Yes."

"Run everything out of your system?"

"Just trying to keep the crab population down," he replied, averting his eyes.

"Beautiful afternoon . . ."

"Is that a personal or professional assessment?"

She sank down beside him. "Both." She hesitated. "No, personal. I took the afternoon off."

A hard knot of anger balled within him but he suppressed it. She was, after all, no different than Hagger—only more subtle. He brushed aside the pile of sand, smoothing it with his fingers, then scuffing at the marks until it was just part of the sloping plane of the beach. "Tell Hagger that I don't work for him and all that I want for bringing that film out of Cuba is a Trailways bus ticket to Utah. Just be kind enough to remind him that a lot of people died to put that film on his desk."

She nodded, her eyes lowered. "Please believe that I understand your anger, even if I can't identify it. We've talked for three days and you've said nothing to help me help you."

"Don't try to analyze me, lady."

It was as if she hadn't heard him. She planted her hands behind her in the sand, leaning back, turning her face up to the dying sun. The light caught the small, fine, golden hairs of her cheeks and Brocassie found that he had to turn away. Not the same woman, not the same time nor the same place, but sitting on a beach with the smell of the foreshore in his nostrils and watching whitecaps flecking the sea was something that he would never want to share with any other woman.

"I'm sorry," he said carefully. "You and I are through talking. I respect you and I understand the pressure you're under to get me to go back into Cuba, but let's finish it."

A swell, larger than the rest, curled and broke, the prismatic effect of spray creating a multiple halo of colors along the crest. The wasted surf rolled up the beach, nearly touching them and then retreated, taking shells and weed with it, leaving the sand behind it vacant.

"That's what you want, isn't it," she finally said. "Like the sea, sweeping everything clean. No memories, no tragedy, no guilt—nothing to burden your future. But something happened in Cuba that you haven't told either to Hagger or to me," she said softly. "It's eating at you." She lowered her head, looking at him evenly. "Don't you really want to get it out of your system, once and for all?"

"You're reading too much into it. I'm an errand boy, a courier. I brought out film. I've told Hagger everything that I know which will be useful to him. Why not just give up gracefully and let me go home."

"Where is home?"

He thought first of Utah but that was a decade ago—light-years away and the image of Cuba blurred it. Kids running in the streets, singing, and the wildness of the mountains that would never be tamed or bulldozed by developers. A man, blind, strumming a guitar, recognizing you by the sound of your gait, or the smell of bread, baked in a box of crude sheet metal, fired by coconut husks. Jesus, he remembered it and the smells of Cuba overwhelmed him. Rain smell and jungle smell. The sweet scent of Havana in the early hours of dawn and the fragrance of her. Home? Neither place seemed real.

"I have none," he answered finally. "Any real home in this country that I could ever claim was liberated by the U.S. cavalry and doled out by the politicians over eighty years ago. With a great deal of generosity, they gave what was left of our nation a dried-up patch of dirt. I suppose that I can go there and collect a monthly allotment from the Bureau of Indian Affairs. Like I said, all I need is a bus ticket."

She looked at him hard. "Poor little dog soldier. All tired out. Your pony's dead and all the arrows are gone from your quiver, so go home and suck your mother's tit and wail at the moon." Her face softened and she lowered her eyes, drawing shapes in the sand with her finger, and then brushing them away. "I'm sorry. That was uncalled for." She gathered the caftan around her, hugging it close. "It's getting cold," she finally said, standing up. "I really want a shower and some clean clothes."

Dammit, he thought. He didn't need her or Hagger but he still wanted her to understand the pain *"What is it you really want?"* he shouted at her.

She backed off two paces, anger in her face. "A little civility, maybe. Perhaps your trust. Some belief that what I'm trying to do for you is based on my desire to help you to understand yourself. And more important, your willingness to appreciate that what is going on in Cuba is more than just a family dispute. You left people back there—people who will die because you're too ... too fucking selfish, too damned wrapped up in yourself to help them."

He wanted to smash her face and he found himself screaming at her. *"It's over! There's nothing left back there for me. FINISHED!"*

"Is it, Brocassie? Is it *really*? If you want money or a new gold-plated Cadillac, talk to Hagger. If you're so frightened of going back into Cuba that you're wetting your pants, then forget it. But if you're smart enough to recognize that both your problem and its solution lies in Cuba, then let's talk because I'm the shrink and I know damn well that I can help. Just make up your stubborn bloody mind." She pulled sunglasses out of the pocket of her caftan and set them firmly on her nose. She wheeled, somewhat less than grandly, stumbling a bit, and then marched away, kicking up little puffs of sand, toward the main house and Hagger.

He watched her go, a little numbed. She didn't look back and he suddenly realized that he had to exorcize the demons or be haunted by them forever.

"Hold it," he shouted after her. She slowed, hesitated and then turned toward him and he closed the distance between them, still unsure.

They sat together on the screened porch of his cottage, listening to an old recording of the Modern Jazz Quartet playing "No Sun in Venice," the thin, intricate piano chords mixed with vibes, cascading out in a minor key of eloquent desolation. When it finished, he got up and set the needle down in the same track, listening to it begin again.

"That's beautiful, almost heartbreaking," she said, barely audible. "It has some special meaning to you, doesn't it?"

"Something that a woman I know . . . knew, played one evening, just like this—warm wind, the sounds of insects and the sea rolling in on a deserted beach. She said that everything that had ever been said about love, both the joy and the sadness, was wrapped up in that piece of music." He suddenly felt stupid.

She shook her head. "Remember it for what it was. Why turn away from something that was great, even if it's somehow changed." She paused. "The woman you spoke of yesterday—Alicia. That's who you're talking about?"

"Yes." He offered no explanation or endorsement for her to pursue his thoughts.

She held the bottle of beer against her cheek, her eyes focused beyond him and then said, "Fundamental question. Hagger wants—needs—you to lead a team back into Cuba. I'm not going to play a role in that decision. It's between you and him. I'm only here to help you, and what passes between us stops here. But I have to know if you can trust me completely."

He had no illusions about her motivation but he had to get it out. "All right—nothing held back, but on the condition that you accept my decision, whatever it may be, and if I decide not to go back into Cuba, you agree that all the dossier crap that has been generated on me be burned. Nothing to haunt me, no entries in a computer—just a bus ticket and a good-bye. Deal?"

She pulled her hair back with her hands, smoothing it and nodded. "My word on it," she answered. She sipped again on her beer and then blew across the top, sounding a discordant little whistle. "So if you finally trust me, tell me more about her now, and about Julio Álvarez."

It was painful but he started, and the words spilled over the dam of his restraint. "We were all on the same side once. And then it turned out that we were on opposite sides. It's hard for anyone to understand a civil war unless they've lived through one. The enemy isn't from another country, of a different skin color or speaking another language. It's your father or a cousin or a man you knew down the street. And sometimes, it's your own brother or the woman you loved. Who you can trust today may kill you tomorrow. A civil war tears the guts out of a country and the guts out of the people that fight it, both friends and enemies, winners and losers."

"You refer to Julio as your brother but he wasn't. And yet he was. It really starts with the relationship between the two of you."

He bent down and studied his glass, lifting it and then setting it down again, overlapping and interlocking the rings of moisture from the condensation. It had been—still was, he supposed—like that. His life and Álvarez's; always overlapping but never quite matching. He touched a fingertip to the intersection of two rings and smeared the faint haze of moisture.

"Álvarez . . ." he started, "is too complex to ever understand. Brilliant, aggressive, a liar, a cheat and then he can turn around in a second and feed you the smoothest line of crap you ever heard and you're convinced, *absolutely,* that he's the greatest guy you ever met. Even as a kid, I never could decide about him. We were as close as you can be to being brothers, but Julio kept something inside him that he never exposed. And you never knew where you stood with him, or how you really felt about him. Love, hate, anger, admiration, confusion, jealousy, all of these wrapped up in one untidy package."

"For example?" she asked.

It had been in the fall of 1954. Brocassie had been shipped back from Korea in the summer and was enrolled at Colorado School of Mines, picking up his final year. Grades were all right, nothing exceptional, and he knew that he would graduate, but something had gone out of him—wonder, innocence, ambition—he couldn't tell. The spirituality of being Indian had gone out of him but he tried to regain it, going back to the high mountain valleys, listening for the sounds of his heart that he once heard.

He had sluffed off on that particular Friday, skipping classes, and drove up to St. Mary's Glacier in his old Ford pickup. He set up camp at the foot of the glacier and panned the feeder streams for gold as he had often done before.

The showings were thin flour gold, but the isolation and

work fulfilled him. He worked steadily through the midafternoon, sweating in the autumn sunlight, his bare feet in the icy water.

Just before sundown, he saw the plume of dust crawling up the canyon, trailing behind a bright red convertible. His hands clenched. He had wanted the magic of the glacier and the surrounding mountains to himself.

He cracked the cap off a Coors, slumped against a rock and waited.

It was Julio, suntanned and lean. He slammed the car door, pulled a rucksack from the backseat and labored up the slope.

He stretched out his hand, his face set in a grin. "Long time, Injun. Been hanging around any cigar stores lately?"

Brocassie grasped Julio's hand and, surprised, felt warmth flowing through him. He tightened his grip. "Long time, spick." They hugged each other, and to Brocassie, after all these years of separation, it felt as if they had never been apart.

Álvarez had brought steaks and they grilled them over an open fire, passing a bottle of Southern Comfort between them. In the high altitude of the Rockies, the sky was brilliant with stars. An occasional meteor streaked green-gold across the southern sky.

Álvarez stirred the fire with a stick. Sparks showered upward in the hot draft. "I've only been back from Korea for three weeks. They flew me home. Battlefield commission and Silver Star." He slugged down some of the amber fluid and passed it to Brocassie. "Fucked my way from San Francisco to Reno, blew my mustering-out pay on the crap table and here I am. There's a law firm in Denver that wants to interview me. I've got just enough to get there."

"How did you know I'd be here?"

Álvarez first puckered his lips and then smiled secretively. "You'd believe me if I told you that I just knew, wouldn't you?"

He shook his head. "Probably not." And yet he did.

Shrugging, Álvarez leaned forward and lit a cigarette with a burning pine branch. "We came up here before, in the summer after your freshman year. I know you like this place, all that sacred ground stuff and the thumping drums. The guy in the apartment next to yours thought you were headed for the hills. I stopped at the Blackhawk Hotel for a beer. The old lady who runs the bar said that she saw you drive through this morning. Figured that you'd be up here."

"I gave up the apartment four months ago. I live in a house trailer now, Julio, and I didn't drive through Blackhawk this time."

Álvarez's face was highlighted by the fire. He turned toward Brocassie, his expression masked in shadows. "So I lied. I drove in straight from Nevada. Just knew you'd be here. Somehow. Understand?"

Brocassie smiled in the blackness. True or false, con or reality. Impossible to tell. "I understand," he answered, not really understanding, not wanting to.

He woke at first light—a habit of Korea, when the charges by the Chinese always came, heralded by bugles, then the sound of tennis shoes pounding across the frozen mud and finally the crack of weapons. For a second, Brocassie was disoriented, his hand reaching for a nonexistent carbine and then his heart slowed. He turned toward Julio who lay there, his head propped on his elbow, an unlit cigarette in his mouth. "It's a wonder you came out of it alive, Brocassie." Álvarez crawled backward out of the tent and then started to whistle softly, clanking cookware as he prepared breakfast. Julio made eggs and sausages and boiled coffee in a pot. They ate without speaking.

Brocassie washed the pans in the stream bed, scrubbing them out with sand. He was uneasy, sensing that Julio wanted something but he couldn't even ask himself what.

When he got back to the tent, Julio had laced up his climbing boots and was strapping on crampons.

"Where you headed?"

Buckling the straps tight, Julio looked up. "With you." He pointed toward the head of the glacier. "Up there."

Brocassie shook his head. "Bad news. The ice is unstable and it's rotten. We could climb in Estes . . ."

Something flashed across Álvarez's face—anger or intolerance or something—but he suppressed it quickly and his lips transformed into a grin. "I don't have much time. Only today.

157

I want to climb and that's where." He nodded again toward the face of the glacier. "You coming with me, brother?"

The lower pitch was easy—wet granular snow mixed with ice. Runnels of meltoff had channeled deep into the glacier. Julio was climbing easily, conserving his energy, a good partner. Brocassie began to relax.

By noon, they were swapping off the lead, roped together, hacking out steps in clear ice, the pitch steeper, the wind getting up, the sky darkening. Brocassie knew the high country; there would be snow before nightfall.

"It's time to go back," he said as the two of them rested, brewing tea on a small Sterno stove. Above them, the glacier was fractured by an inclined rock pitch, black conglomerate flecked with mica and slick with ice.

Álvarez laughed. "What we've done was the preview. I came for the main feature."

"I'm going back." It would take two hours to make it down the glacier, and there were only three hours of light left.

"And I'm staying. I'm going to climb, Brocassie. With you or without you."

"That's fucking dumb, Julio! What are you proving to me or to yourself? I'm not going to . . ."

Unsnapping his carabiner, Álvarez disconnected himself from the nylon rope. He picked up his ice ax and took a handful of pitons from his rucksack.

"Like I said, Brocassie. I'm climbing. Do you have the guts to come with me or have your bowels loosened up?"

An hour later, the valley was already in shadows, the first flakes of snow beginning to sting Brocassie's face in a rising wind. They were more than halfway up the pitch, each inch won with pitons pounded into the cracks, the soles of their boots hugging fissures of nonexistent support, the rope lifeline between them always in tension. Julio was above him, on belay.

The small ledge that he was working slowly tapered off into nothing. Five feet away on the lateral was solid ledge, more than a foot wide, but between was a scalloped flute of rock, bulging out of the cliff's face. Brocassie had seen Julio deftly grab the flute and vault to the ledge but that was more than a half an hour before and now, the flute was wet with melted snow, the ledge beyond slick with the black sheen of ice.

From above, Julio's voice echoed down. "Drive a piton, Brocassie. It's an old woman's way but it's safe." His voice trailed off in a chuckle.

Screw that, Brocassie thought. The same old thing, stupid, but he knew that he was still competing. He took a deep breath, balanced on his toes and tried to overhand it, boots scrambling on the flute for temporary support and then he felt the gut sickness of his boots slipping, the momentary suspension in air, his hands windmilling, desperately trying for a handhold, and then the fall. The blur of rock rushing past, his knees and elbows and face smashing off the granite and then, finally, the lurch of the rope taking up, driving the wind out of his lungs.

Like a ball on a rubber string, he bounced, tremors vibrating the rope like a taut fiddle string, then slowly swung to rest. He reached out and touched the rock face, unbelieving that he was still alive and then his vision went dim.

Somewhere, there had been a void in time. A second, a minute or more. He opened his eyes. The light was nearly gone now and the fur of his hood was plastered with snow. He realized that, involuntarily, he had pissed in his pants.

The rope was crushing his chest. Weakly, he called twice and then again. Nothing. The cold was invading his body, his extremities numb. He called again, shouting against the wind, but there was no reply. He drifted off again into unconsciousness.

It was almost dark. Julio was beside him, slung on rappel from a separate rope. Skillfully, Julio linked him into his own harness with carabineers, working one-handed, humming. Humming! The bastard was humming!

The rappel down the face of the cliff was a nightmare. The rock face was plastered with snow and the wind was gusting hard, swinging them to and fro like weights on a pendulum.

With their combined load on the nylon rope, the fibers twisted under the strain, overstressed. And still Julio hummed.

Once they reached the glacier, Julio took the lead, working carefully down the face, retracing their steps.

They reached the glacier lake after nine and followed its shore to the camp. Julio made dinner from cans of hash and, as if by magic, produced a second bottle of Southern Comfort.

"Cheers," he said, his face ruddy in the firelight.

The snow had tapered off and then stopped. Stars flamed in the black steel bowl above them.

"Why . . . ?" Brocassie finally asked. He couldn't bring himself to thank Álvarez, couldn't face how close he had been to death.

Álvarez poked the fire with a stick, was silent for a while, and then replied. "I wanted to find out whether the risk was still worth the reward, whether I still had it."

"After Korea?" Brocassie was incredulous.

Álvarez threw the stick into the fire, angry. "There was nothing there as a reward except living through shit you couldn't even control. This was different. It was my choice, my own free will, to try that rock face—to try myself—to try you."

Brocassie, his hand shaking, hurled the bottle at his brother. In the darkness, they both heard the bottle shatter. "You asshole," he screamed, "we could have lost our balls up there."

Julio cupped his hands over his crotch and smiled. "Mine are still there, warm as toast." He stood up, hawked and spit into the night and then turned back to face his brother. "But for you, Brocassie, what you never had you can never lose." He slung on his rucksack and walked away into the blackness.

The engine ground over and then caught and for a long time, Brocassie could trace the faint taillights as they trailed down the canyon road.

She shook her head sadly. "You have anything stronger?"

"Hagger's flunkies have a sense of humor. They stocked the fridge with Russian vodka, Cuban rum and American sour mash. Do you think that's some kind of a loyalty test?"

"Bacardi?"

He poured two tumblers of rum and then handed her one.

She sat for a long time, studying her glass. "You're quite something, Brocassie. Like a man caught in a time warp between centuries and civilizations. You want love and fidelity and yet have come to fear your own vulnerability. Everything, everyone penetrates your skin." She stood up and got some ice, neatly dropping cubes, one by one, into the remains of her drink. "But you're not wrong, Brocassie. Just not in tune with what the rest of us are willing to accept as normal human behavior."

She stood up and pressed her forehead against the framework of the screening. "Why did you stay in Cuba so long? You could have gotten out anytime."

He nodded, knowing that she was right. "Something inside me," he finally answered. "I'm not sure. I had some half-assed concept that individual men can change the world for the better, and I guess . . ." He left it unfinished.

"You stayed behind, after you thought she was dead, because you had to honor her—to give her death some meaning. Wasn't that really the reason? Be honest with me, Brocassie. More important be honest with yourself."

"She was just part of it."

"Alicia?"

He nodded.

"You have a hard time saying her name, don't you?"

He hesitated. His mind tried to form her name but couldn't.

"She's living with him now. Can you handle that?"

He gripped one hand with the other, squeezing, until the pain blotted out her presence. *Get out,* his mind shouted.

There was a long silence and then she finally spoke. "It's something you have to face." She pressed her hand to the screening against which moths had collected in the darkness, frantically beating their wings. "You want to be like that?" she said evenly, drawing her nails down the mesh, throwing the insects into a frenzy. A large brown gypsy moth flung its body at the mesh, battering against an unpenetrable barrier which separated it from the heat and light.

He reached for the screen door handle but her hand fell over his, clamping down with surprising strength.

"You can go and I can't hold you back but first hear me out. Before I switched to psychology and other related black magic, I was a music major. Really bad, Brocassie. Not merely bad but awful, although I learned a lot about composition. And it stuck in my mind because it applies to an area of psychology which the books ignore. It's called *resolution*—a series of chords which beg to be finally completed to make the composition whole, and I've always thought that it's the same way with most people who have a passion. They have to play and replay those final, inconclusive series of chords and then find the right structure to finish the composition."

"You're telling me that I should go back in. To find out why she betrayed me."

"Yes. Dammit, Brocassie, you're too close to the chords to see the resolution."

"That's what you're paid to say. I told you before not to bullshit me."

She relaxed the pressure and then withdrew her hand, leaving his free. "I'm not saying it for that reason. You have to confront her to find out why she betrayed you and the ideals that you both shared. And you have to face Álvarez, because that's unfinished and you have to get him out of your system as well. And perhaps, not as obvious, you have to understand what Cuba means to all three of you. *Do it,* Brocassie, or you'll be listening all your life for those final chords and you'll never hear them."

She stood up, a little unsteady. "I've already withdrawn five hundred bucks from the slush fund, Brocassie. Hagger knows nothing about it and you have my word that you can walk out of this place and never hear from any of us again." She pulled an envelope from her purse and laid it on the table. "The supply boat goes over to the mainland at five-thirty in the morning and I've already cleared you to be on it, no questions asked. There's a bus out of Marathon at seven-twenty in the morning for Miami. It'll stop if you flag it down." She leaned over and touched her lips to his face and then opened the screen door and stepped out into the blackness. He could hear her heels crunching on the gravel, fading into the night.

He poured himself a last drink and then put the tone arm back on the MJQ record, listening to the same track again and again, trying for resolution.

Hagger rocked forward, planting his elbows on the desk, supporting his chin. "Let's dispense with the dog and pony show, Brocassie. Are you going in as the team leader and what's your price?"

"How much has Dr. Miller told you?"

"Nothing."

Incredible, he thought, that she had put honor before duty and country. She would probably catch hell for not observing priorities. "What do you want done in Cuba?"

Hagger sighed, opened his desk drawer, groped around and then extracted a cigarette. He flamed a battered Zippo, leaning down to light it, then blew the smoke toward the ceiling where it stratified in a blue fog. He phrased it like a kid in a department store telling Santa his wish list. "It's not going to be a big massive operation—just two of you going back into the Sierra by air, meeting up with Maroto and then working down the slopes to the complex. At the minimum, I want to know what kind of equipment the Soviets are installing. Telephoto shots of the stuff they're moving underground and first-hand on-the-ground intelligence. I want reports out fast, within ten days of landing. And if they're installing what I think they are, I want you to use Maroto's people to blow the complex."

The room was silent, except for the sound of a telephone which rang insistently in some office down the corridor. Hagger couldn't keep eye contact.

"I'll try," Brocassie finally answered. "No guarantees. Maroto might not be willing to help us and I couldn't blame him. I'll give it one shot and if I can't pull it off within ten days of landing in Cuba, then that's the end of it. After that, you can send in the marines or the girl scouts for all I care."

Hagger nodded. "You'll need a month's training before you go in. We'll set the date for thirty-four days from now. Salary as a contract player will be a thousand a week during training—three thousand a week while in Cuba. That's generous, I think."

"How does a gold-plated Cadillac sound? Something to run around the reservation in."

Hagger scowled, a pencil poised over a desk pad. *"What?"*

"Forget it, Max," he said. "Just a tasteless joke." He pulled a paper from his pocket and passed it across the desk.

"That's a description of some land in Utah. I want everything between the two streams, as far to the north as the tree line and as far to the south as the county road. It's now national forest land—about fifteen hundred acres. I want it transferred to the Cree nation, free and clear."

"I can't . . ."

"Yes, you can, Max. Use your considerable influence. I want to see a title deed, properly registered, all clean without conditions and an easement guaranteeing access and I want it before I go into Cuba."

"I could try . . ."

"I'm not concerned with the details, Max. Arrange it. And one final thing."

Hagger glared at him, his pencil poised. "Speak."

"When I'm ready to come out of Cuba, I want the whole thing done my way."

"Specifically?"

"No debriefings, no contact with the agency. You get a written report plus any film that I shoot and that's it. I want your word on that."

Hagger seemed relieved. He scratched with his pencil on the pad and then looked up. "No problem."

Reaching over, Brocassie grabbed the pad and turned it around, reading it. Hagger had scratched down a string of cemetery crosses. He wadded up the sheet and threw it down on Hagger's desk. The problem with making compacts with the devil was that there weren't any arbitrators.

Looking up, his face innocent, Hagger shrugged. "I heard what you said, Brocassie. I'll deliver." He extended his hand. "It's a deal?"

"Consider the fact that I'd die before I'd welch on this, Hagger. Consider also, that your commitment is reciprocal. People like me don't take kindly to broken treaties." He walked out, slamming the door behind him.

CHAPTER

7

St. George, Utah, September 10, 1962

Dawn came to the mesa, scalding the eastern horizon. Brocassie sat on a jumble of stones, breathing deeply, inhaling the still-cool air, rich with the smell of mesquite. An animal moved in the brush, scurrying for the safety of its burrow. For only a brief moment, Brocassie bent down, touching his forehead to the ground and said the prayer, more from habit than from belief. He then stood up and walked back toward his house trailer, scuffing his boots in the dust.

Belief in spirituality was dead within him, and he knew that he would probably never be able to regain it, but he still said the prayer at dawn because it somehow gave him the familiar peace that it always had. He smiled to himself. What would Gretchen Miller say about that? Opiate for the masses or would she somehow have understood? He doubted it because he now accepted the fact that she had manipulated him, however deftly. Still, he knew that he had made his own decision, knowing that he must find his own brand of resolution.

Inside the house trailer, the air was stale, the aluminum already beginning to groan as it expanded in the heat. He made coffee and returned to the stoop of crudely nailed together steps.

It was clean, barren country, and he felt the vastness of it filling his mind. It was a land which was as changing as it was changeless—sculpted by wind and heat and water—a place so vast that man could never really alter it.

More than two hundred miles to the south where the high country dipped into the desert lay the junkyard chrome and neon of Las Vegas. Hagger had pointed it out as they flew over at twenty thousand feet. From that altitude it was just a geometrical smear of glitter on the desert floor, but Brocassie found that he had to turn away from the window. It was a violation of the land that he could not explain to any man whose skin was white.

He looked to the north and could see the peaks of the Wasatch Range, freshly capped by snow, brilliant in the morning sun, and to the east and west, the great American desert. Good land, he thought. Dry, desolate and vast. But able to sustain the lives of both the hunted and the hunters—large and rich enough to provide life for thirty nations of Plains Indians through thousands of years. And it was the land that was the inheritance of my fathers, he thought. Was.

He turned and reentered the trailer. He stripped, did fifty sit-ups and then showered, trying to keep his mind blank. But he couldn't. Hagger's conversation on the Lear kept coming back.

The Lear had brought them nonstop from Opa Laka, Florida, he and Hagger the only passengers. For most of the flight, Hagger had slept, his legs stretched out and his mouth agape. He awoke after they had crossed the Mississippi, pulled a beer from the galley cooler, talked with the flight crew for a few minutes and then came aft and sat down opposite Brocassie.

"Thirty days from now, I'll brief you, just before you go into Cuba. You're the team leader, understand, but Porto has full command of flight operations."

Brocassie nodded as Hagger spoke, not really listening until Hagger said the name "Alicia."

"What did you say?" Brocassie's mind snapped on.

"The woman. Alicia Helvia. I got some more stuff in from Langely just before we took off this morning. They had two separate transcripts from eyewitnesses who knew her. One, dated in early 1960, was given to us by a man named Jesús Cardona, a civilian employed by the DGI to service their vehicles. On"—he shuffled some papers, running his finger down a page—"Sancti Spiritus, working under a truck on some kind of transmission problem. A big van came in and the DGI guards cleared all the contract mechanics out of the compound except for this guy, Cardona. Just overlooked him, probably. At any rate, they had a whole bunch of people in the van, most of them shot up. Cardona identified two of them, both people he had known in Havana before the Revolution." He showed Brocassie the sheet, pointing to her name. "Cardona says that all of the prisoners who lived through the interrogation were taken away about a week later and executed."

"How in hell could Cardona be sure?"

"Pretty sure, not positive. The prisoners had been held in a detached section of the cell blocks. Cardona knew a DGI guard who had to go into the block after the prisoners were taken away to clean them out with a steam hose. There wasn't anyone left inside, Brocassie."

He felt sweat prickling along his back and his throat was dry as old leather. "What about the other report?"

"This one's more solid. Taken in late sixty-one in Santiago de Cuba by a street photographer who used to sell us some of his stuff." He turned the facsimile photograph around and passed it to Brocassie. Álvarez was sitting in the shade, sipping some sort of drink. He wore a sport shirt, one that Brocassie recognized. Álvarez's name had been typed over the photograph and a file number attached. But to Álvarez's left, backlighted by sunlight, her lips pursed as she sucked on a straw, was Alicia. Even in the poor quality photograph, she was unmistakable. Brocassie wanted to pass it back to Hagger but he couldn't take his eyes off it. She wore a light-colored dress, cut low across her breasts, and he could see just the beginning of a smile, as if she were listening to something amusing that Álvarez was relating. Brocassie took a deep breath and passed the fax back to Hagger.

"Is that her, positively?"

Brocassie nodded, unable to speak.

Silent for a long time, Hagger finally spoke. "You sure you want to go through with this? If you've got any doubts, I want to know right now."

"No doubts, Hagger," he said softly.

Hagger leaned forward. "You're mumbling. What'd you say?"

"I SAID, 'NO FUCKING DOUBTS,' HAGGER!" He turned away and placed his cheek against the cold plastic of the window, watching green prairie give way to brown desert, crystal-glazed mountains rising like fractured glass on the far western horizon. No doubts, he repeated to himself. Not now.

They came in over the desert, descending rapidly. Up ahead, Brocassie could see truncated mesas rising in clusters from the desert floor. Utah, he thought. It was like coming home if there were such a thing.

"St. George off to the left," Hagger motioned. "Hamburger stands and gas stations, mainly. The town's run by Mormons and they don't tend to snoop." He pointed to the right. It was a mesa, heavily eroded on the edges with a single strip of black asphalt running down its length. On the edge of the strip were a few weather-beaten hangars and some shacks, but the place looked abandoned. Looking closer, Brocassie could see a single dirt road winding up from the valley floor to the plateau and a chain link fence ringing the perimeter of the mesa.

"An old auxiliary field," Hagger explained as they circled for the landing. "Used during the second war as an emergency strip for cadet training flights out of Nellis Air Force Base. I doubt that any civilians have used this place in twenty years. It's still government land and we can control the access to it."

"What's my training involve?"

Hagger smiled. The Lear's turbines were throttled back now, flaps extending. Meaty thunks and the gear was down and the Lear squeaked its tires onto the strip, rolling out easily with half the runway ahead of it.

"No time to explain," he answered. "You'll get briefed by your instructor tomorrow morning. His name is José Martínez Porto. Good man. Mother was an Irishwoman who came out as an indentured servant around the turn of the century and the father was Cuban, one of those tramp freighter captains who believed that navigation was something between black art and a religious experience. Unfortunately, he wasn't practicing either when he ran up on a shoal in the Florida Keys during the Prohibition years. After that, he settled down in Cuba. Couldn't get his master's ticket back so he seems to have devoted the rest of his life to attempting to match his intake with the output of the Bacardi rum factory. Porto did some jobs for the agency in 1960, doing clandestine flights into Cuba. There was some trouble. The plane that he was flying got banged up and some people down there took care of him but they got burned by an informer."

The turbines whined down to an idle and the copilot brushed past them, headed aft for the cabin door.

"Porto's regular agency or is he contract like me?"

"Contract only, based on the job. He's done work for us on occasion. But he knows his stuff, so trust him." Hagger stuck out his hand. "We have a deal, Brocassie. You hold up your end and I'll hold up mine."

He saw Brocassie to the door. "This is as far as I come. There's a guy in a jeep who will take you to your quarters." He motioned to a trail of dust arrowing across the mesa. "Porto will meet you at your quarters bright and early. You've got a lot of ground to cover in three weeks but I think you can handle it." He stuck out his hand again, a little awkwardly, and Brocassie shook it.

"¡Adiós!" Hagger said and withdrew back into the air-conditioned cabin of the Lear.

Brocassie had stood on the side of the runway and watched the glint of the sun on the aluminum skin of the Lear until it was lost in the distance. You've got me by the balls, Hagger, he thought, and you know it. He picked up the first faint streamers of contrails, snow white against the deep blue of space, and then hefted his duffel bag over his shoulder and trudged toward the waiting jeep.

By 6:30 A.M., Brocassie saw a jeep heading toward his house trailer, rocking from side to side over the rough terrain. He could see nothing of the man's face, just the sun reflecting off the windshield in flashes of exploding light. The jeep made a final dive into a depression and was briefly airborne, thumping down again into the dirt yard which surrounded Brocassie's trailer. The driver spun the wheel, locking the jeep into a four-wheel slide. When it had stopped, the man unfolded his body from the seat, rolled over the rim of the driver's compartment and stood in the sun, stretching. He was compact, a head shorter than Brocassie but much broader across the shoulders. His hair was a thick black mat, not combed in any particular direction, but short cropped with no regard to appearance. Sun wrinkles etched his face, radiating outward from the eyes, the furrows untanned in contrast to the rest of his skin. The nose looked as if it were made from putty, scooped up by a cosmic hand at the last minute and stuck on the face slightly lopsided. Below the nose, a black mustache perched like a furry bat on the protrusion of the lips.

Porto stuck out a thick hand. "You're Brocassie?"

Taking it, Brocassie squeezed. It was like massaging warm concrete—rough, firm, abrasive and unyielding. They shook mechanically.

"Coffee?" Brocassie turned toward the trailer.

"A cup if you've got some already made. We've got a long day ahead."

Brocassie pushed through the screen door and into the darkness of the trailer. He poured two mugs and set them down on the dinette table, sliding down opposite Porto.

"Counterrevolution makes strange bedfellows, doesn't it?" Porto said. He sipped from it, made a face and sipped again.

"Hagger didn't tell me what the training is."

Porto smiled. "No hints?"

Brocassie swilled the coffee around in the mug, watching it churn up the grounds into a muddy fluid. "I assume that we're going to parachute in."

A smile split Porto's lips, showing strong, uneven teeth. "No chute, paracommanders, hang gliders or pogo sticks. I'm teaching you to fly." He stood up and dropped his mug into the sink. "So get off your ass. Before this day is finished, you'll be dragging it behind you with both hands."

* * *

They stood in the cool shade of the hangar's interior. The hangar was a prefab from World War Two, rotting board and batten on the exterior, cranked over at a slight angle as if it would fall in the first windstorm. But inside, a new concrete floor had been poured, the walls braced up with steel shoring and the wood siding packed with insulation. It was clever, Brocassie recognized, because any pilot flying over the field would see just another abandoned strip with no signs of recent activity.

"Functional," Porto commented. "This is Steen's operation, on loan to Hagger. Not much money put into it, but it's remote and doesn't attract much attention." He moved farther into the interior, toward a canvas-draped shape.

"Let's take a look at it," he said, peeling back the canvas.

The aircraft was something out of the thirties: high-winged with a rudimentary cockpit for two, seated in tandem. It was blunt and ugly, a creation without the blessing of grace upon it. What's more, it had no engine.

Brocassie kept his thoughts to himself and stepped up to the fuselage, feeling the surface. It yielded to his touch.

"Plywood and fabric," Porto said. "The only metal parts in this thing are a few control wires and rods, the tire axle and bronze screws . . . about twenty pounds maximum."

"What the hell is it?" Brocassie moved along the wing, feeling the smooth plywood, the individual wing ribs and the fabric covering.

"Slingsby Type 42 Eagle. First built in England back in the fifties as an advanced trainer for glider pilots. Not exactly state of the art but it'll do quite well for our purposes. We'll use two of them. Me in one, you in the other. The backseats of both planes will be crammed with explosives and equipment—two hundred and fifty pounds per plane. And like I said"—he paused, turning toward Brocassie—"you're going to be flying one of them."

"You're not going to strap me into this collection of sticks. Why not a DC-3? They've been used to bring supplies into Cuba for the last three years."

"A lot of reasons, Brocassie. Hagger wants you—us—to get into the mountains with about five hundred pounds of equipment, and he wants us to get in undetected. A year ago, you could have tooled over Cuba in a transport plane and gotten away with it. But now Castro has MIG 17s and Czech pilots, SAM-3 surface-to-air missiles and a coordinated radar chain."

"So why shouldn't the Cubans detect these things?"

"Three reasons, two obvious. No engine, no heat—no heat, no infrared radiation. Consequently, infrared tracking is out. Also no engine, no noise. And visually: the two gliders we'll use will be painted dull black." He balanced his weight against the leading edge of the wing, examining it with his fingertips. "Less obvious is the fact that this thing goes slow and it has no hard metal surfaces to reflect radar. We've tried it. A good radar station can't paint this thing on their scopes at three miles, even if they know exactly where the hell it is. We've flight-planned the trip into Cuba to avoid getting closer than twenty miles to their major radar tracking stations."

"You're talking about flying into the mountains in one of *these* at night?"

"Correct," Porto answered deadpan. "Let's call it a controlled crash. We'll be down to about forty knots for landing speed. Subtract a headwind of—say—fifteen. So you'll be landing at roughly twenty-five knots. The plan is simply that you follow me. I'll use a couple of radio stations in Cuba to navigate by. If things go OK, I'll have us set up within three miles of a strip Maroto's troops will hack out of the bush. We'll be in radio contact with them through the last ten miles. When we're set up for the final approach, Maroto will use two guys with flashlights, one at each end of the strip. All you have to do is line the two lights up and start the descent. Touch down just after the first light and be sure to stop by the second one and you're home free."

"How about you?"

"I'll offset—land to one side of you about thirty seconds later. If you use up most of the strip, I'll have plenty of room."

"And if not?"

"Shit, Brocassie. You've got the mind of an old woman. If I hit you at less than twenty-five knots, you'll probably get nothing worse than a nosebleed."

Dumb, he thought. Worse than that—insane. Flying into

172

an airstrip hacked out of a mountainside in the middle of the night. Unconsciously, he shook his head.

Porto had sat down on the concrete, his mouth creased with disgust. "I told Hagger that I wasn't going to work with any pussy, let alone fly into Cuba with him. You going to try it with me or not, buddy?"

"You and Hagger are out of your minds!" Brocassie shouted. "Those mountains are sheer cliffs, with falloffs of over five hundred feet in places. And I've been up there. I've seen winds the strength of hurricanes blowing from every point on the compass. You start flying this thing into turbulence like that and you'll end up without wings." He turned toward the glider. "Wood and fabric, Porto! And no goddamn engine. So what happens if Maroto and his happy band aren't there? Do we just hitch onto a cloud and float on down to Jamaica?" He slammed his fist against the leading edge of the wing, causing the whole plane to shudder.

Porto sat on the concrete, his face in shadows, speaking very softly. "Hagger asked me to figure out a way to get the two of us plus five hundred pounds of shit into Cuba in one piece and this is the only way to do it that I know of. If I knew of a better method I would have suggested it long ago. The CIA has been getting stuff into Laos for three years now with this kind of clapped-out glider. In my books, Brocassie, I think that you've got loose bowels."

Brocassie lunged toward him as Porto was rising to his feet. Brocassie swung from the shoulder. Something moved, a flash of clothing, Porto diving inward and under the swing. Their bodies collided and then Brocassie was in the air, spinning head over ass, landing on the hard concrete. Porto was on top of him, pinning his head down, thumbs into his neck.

"Get out of it, Brocassie," Porto hissed. "If you really want to get into Cuba, buy a ticket on Cubana Air or do it my way and no questions asked."

Porto stood up slowly and backed away, still facing Brocassie. "You think about it, champ. If you want out, call Hagger, but if you've got the balls at least to try it, then I want your ass back in this hangar in one hour." He opened the door, letting the hot wind of the desert howl in, and then slammed it.

The bastard, he thought. *Fuck* Hagger and *fuck* José Martínez Porto. Let them play their own silly-assed spy games. His shoulder stung from the blow that Porto had landed and he got slowly to his feet rubbing it. His shirt was open and her ring, hanging from its leather thong, brushed his hand and almost automatically his fingers went to it, held it, felt the warmth of it. He stood there in the darkened hangar for a long time, twisting the ring in his hand, listening to the wind work under the eaves, and the hollowness of its sound, like her smile in the photograph, mocked him. All right, Porto, he thought. Beggars can't be choosers. Not this one, anyway. Not yet.

Somewhat after 2:00 P.M., Brocassie took his first flight, wedged in the forward cockpit, the sides of the cabin just touching his shoulders. Porto had already strapped him in; lap belt plus shoulder harness. Brocassie tentatively touched the control stick, trying to sense the machine's inner strengths. But it was no more alive to him than the handle of a broom.

Porto had made no comment when Brocassie turned up at one; in fact, there had been something in his eyes and just the suggestion of a smirk, otherwise hidden by the great walrus mustache. He had wordlessly gone through the preflight, herding Brocassie before him, showing the placement of safety pins, testing for control surface freedom and thumping the fabric skin of the aircraft with his fingers as if he were tuning a kettle drum.

Now, Porto was whistling, something Brocassie vaguely recognized from the *Threepenny Opera*. He looked back toward Brocassie, wiggled his mustache, and gave a thumbs up. Then turning toward the ramp, he gave an arm signal and an L-19—an aircraft Brocassie had seen used as spotter planes in Korea—taxied to a position about fifty feet in front of the Slingsby glider. Porto attached a slim towline which streamed from a fitting on the L-19 into a hook beneath the Slingsby. He then scrambled into the backseat, buckled in and slammed the canopy closed.

The towplane was kicking up dust as it taxied straight ahead, slowing as the towline tautened. The glider gave a little lurch as the line came tight.

"I'll make the takeoff and tow, sport," Porto said. "Keep

a light hand on the stick and dainty feet on the rudders. Just watch and try to feel what's happening. I'll answer questions later."

Grit and red dust whipped back from the prop wash of the L-19 as it started to accelerate, dragging the glider behind it. At first, the controls were dead, the instruments inert, but then suddenly, the thing was alive, responsive. Porto lifted her off about two feet and remained there, directly behind the L-19.

"We start flying before he does," he yelled. "Have to wait until he's airborne and then we'll move slightly above his flight path to stay out of the prop wash." He was humming again but then stopped to shout, "Still time to bail out, *hombre!*"

Shrugging, Brocassie watched the needles of the instruments quiver at their lower limits, then surge clockwise.

The runway slipped away beneath the wing and they were out past the mesa. The towplane angled into a shallow bank and Porto followed, both aircraft climbing a transparent spiral into the hard sunlight. The altimeter slowly crept to a reading of twelve thousand feet.

"We drop off here," Porto shouted. There was a mechanical snap and Brocassie saw the towrope, now released from the Slingsby, whip forward toward the towplane. Porto pulled up to the right and the towplane dived toward the left.

It was suddenly quiet, just a soft rush of wind over the fuselage and wings.

Craning his neck, Brocassie swept his eyes around the horizon. To the south, the desert rolled away to a murky rim, hazy and indistinct and yet vast. A thin ribbon of asphalt arrowed toward the rim of the earth and disappeared in the blur of distance. To the north and east, worn-down ranges of mountains prodded their broken backs into thin sunlight. He settled back against the cushions and closed his eyes, trying to implant the sense of it in his memory.

Porto shook the stick a little. "You take it, redskin. Hold it like you would a sore dick—real light and easy. No pumping up and down. Just small movements in any direction to get the feel."

"How about the rudder pedals?"

"Use 'em. Left stick, left rudder and feel for the response. You'll learn it faster from feel than if I tell you."

Trying, Brocassie felt the lightness of response, the coordination of the controls—stick and rudder. He experimented, pushing the stick forward, and watched the nose dip and airspeed start to build.

"Ease the stick back," Porto coached and he did, watching the horizon sink and sunlight fill the cockpit as he leveled off, climbed and leveled again. It was a great equation of energy, he realized, trading altitude for airspeed, banking against the soft cushion of air with rudders following the ailerons, carving through the turn. It was good—better than that—great, even, he thought, spiritual.

"Porto," Brocassie said, turning toward the aft cockpit, "I did a dumb thing in the hangar. You weren't the real reason for my anger. It's something else that I have to get out of my system."

Porto showed a full set of teeth. But he didn't offer his hand. "Just stay loose, Brocassie. We'll see how it works out." He pulled up abruptly into a steep climb, rolled to the left until the wing was vertical, paused for a second at the top of the arc and then dove. Brocassie felt his stomach sagging with the G-forces, the skin on his face pulling downward. Porto leveled off and then carefully trimmed the control so that the ship would fly nearly hands off.

"That's the end of the fancy stuff. I'm training you for one thing and one thing only—to stay about a hundred feet behind my aircraft and follow me right down to the deck on a black night. Tonight we start flying again for real. This is the last joyride. Now watch real close."

He pointed forward over Brocassie's shoulder. "There's St. George—got it?—no, more off to the left. And just about straight ahead is the mesa. You can see the black asphalt. Got it?"

Brocassie scanned and picked up the strip of black against the reddish-brown of the mesa.

"I've got it."

" 'Swonderful," Porto laughed. "OK, my friend, first of all we trim this thing out for its best glide ratio which is forty-five knots. At that speed, we lose a foot of altitude for every thirty feet we go forward. Hold that airspeed exactly and head for the strip. If you start to drift off in either direction, adjust your heading to overcompensate a little."

"What about—"

"No whats. Just do it. You'll catch the hang of it."

Brocassie slid down the long transparent slope, dropping five thousand feet in altitude until the strip was obscured beneath the Slingsby's nose.

"We're two thousand above the strip," Porto said. He took the stick and shook it lightly. "I've got it now; just watch."

He banked to the left into a spiral, sweeping down until the runway was perfectly aligned, the strip stretching out before him, the end of it less than a hundred yards distant.

"OK," Porto said. "Now the barn doors." There was a mechanical thunk and the plane slowed, starting to lose altitude rapidly.

"Look out on the wings."

Brocassie glanced out to both the left and right wings. Plates, over six feet long, were projecting out into the windstream.

"Spoilers," Porto grunted. "They're on both wings, both top and bottom. Kills the lift over the wings. I can pump them out or suck them in or anywhere in between. Kills off altitude in a hurry without increasing airspeed. Now watch closely. You've got to learn this so it's exact."

The glider was still losing altitude rapidly, the mesa rising to meet them. It looked as if Porto would land a hundred feet short of the runway, but within twenty feet of the ground, he flared, spoilers slowly retracting, the nose coming up smoothly, airspeed bleeding off. For a second, the flight of the plane seemed almost suspended and then they touched down, the wheel making contact just a few feet from the lip of the runway. Porto hammered down on the brakes and the glider rumbled to a stop after having rolled less than fifty feet.

With the frantic compulsion of a claustrophobic, Brocassie slammed open the canopy, the hot desert air hitting his face like the blast of an open hearth furnace.

"Cheated death again," said Porto, unbuckling. He pulled himself up, balanced on the edge of the canopy sill and then dropped to the asphalt. "We've got to push this sonofabitch back to the hangar. And then we can down a couple of beers." He paused just for a second. "Understand about what this kind of flying means to me, sport?"

Brocassie realized that his hands were shaking, his whole body hot with the rush of adrenaline. His flight suit was soaked with sweat and he still felt the fear of flight eating in the pit of his stomach but there was something else there now. Elation.

Black. Stars gone, obscured by the high, thin overcast which had hazed over the sky toward dusk. Below, six thousand feet down, there were pinpoints of light winking in the cooling desert air, but he could not watch them. No time for that.

Cold. Cold that seeped into the cockpit and permeated his flight suit, the double pair of thermal underwear, the sheepskin-lined flight boots, the heavy gloves. Cold that ate into his body, slowing the flow of blood to his heart and brain. Cold that fed the fear.

Most nights, there had been two flights. Tonight only one. Not graduation but more of a midsemester test. To crash and die was a failing grade, to survive, a pass.

Ahead and to port, Brocassie watched the two pinpoint lights that were set into the top panels of Porto's wing tips. Invisible from the ground and barely visible from above. He sat patiently, watching the lights grow closer, sliding into his flight path.

Overrunning, he thought. Coming in too fast. He essed the glider, slewing around with his rudders, trying to maintain the distance. The spacing between the two aircraft stabilized and Brocassie pushed the stick forward, coming down from a slightly higher altitude, picking up airspeed and then leveling off again. Porto was tucked just below his left wing tip, rock-stable, holding forty-five knots. Brocassie triggered the button on his stick and spoke. "In place." Two clicks of Porto's mike echoed in his ear.

Porto's ship started a long, slow-wheeling turn, edging back into a northerly heading. Brocassie kept with him, tucking into the trail position. The two ships, a hundred feet apart, settled into the slow glide toward earth. This was Brocassie's twelfth flight, his third solo descent with Porto leading the way. The training period was half over and Porto acknowledged that Brocassie would be ready in another five or six flights. Assuming, of course, that he didn't break his neck or bust his ass. Porto had a way with words.

The flight tonight was not back to the mesa but rather to a dirt strip cut by a bulldozer from the brush in hilly country. Porto had not told him where it was—only that it was three hundred feet long with trees at both ends of the strip. There would be two men with shielded flashlights, one at either end. Brocassie would follow Porto onto the final approach and with the flashlights aligned, fly the Slingsby to touchdown while Porto flew through a 360-degree turn and then followed him in. Simple. In theory, at least, traced in chalk against the blackboard in Porto's air-conditioned trailer. Not so simple now, Brocassie thought.

Still the fear chewed on the raw edge of his mind but he had control over it. He willed his muscles to relax and tried to whistle, but he couldn't. It'll be over in minutes, he told himself, safe on the ground, drinking from Porto's flask of brandy, laughing.

Down through seven thousand now. Warmer, if warmth was measured by decreased cold. Brocassie wiggled his toes. No feeling, as if they were amputated. He pulled a glove from his left hand and stuck the cold flesh under an armpit. There was no warmth there. He pulled the glove back on and beat his hand against his knee, trying to restore circulation.

Sinking through sixty-eight hundred feet now, the hills to the northwest of St. George rising up to meet him.

Porto went into a shallow bank to the right, steadied, then banked to the left. Brocassie followed him imperfectly, cutting the corners and starting to get too close. Although cold, he was starting to sweat. No ground lights, but he realized now that there were mountains on either side, a continuous ragged profile rising up, blacker than the void of the night sky. They were in a broad valley uninhabited and desolate. He had seen so many of them from the air, sprinkled with boulders the size of barns, with washed-out stream beds, mica particles sparkling in the sun. But now, he thought, dangerous dead ends with death in the form of a bent tree or a jagged pinnacle of rock. Not to think, he told himself. Only to fly.

Warmer now. Blood starting to move and his finger pained from the tingling that comes from restored circulation. Almost missed seeing Porto's beginning of a turn. Brocassie followed it, refining the circle both inward and outward, trying to hold station so the lights on Porto's glider were no more than the span of his hand, fingers outstretched, held at arm's length. Crude ranging device but effective.

The turn continued and Brocassie realized that Porto was over the landing strip, throwing away altitude, preparing for the setup to final. He risked a glance down but saw nothing. "First rule of flying formation," Porto had repeated again and again, "is to watch the leader. Fly on him and watch nothing else." Look away for even a second and things started to go to hell, but he had the compulsion to glance again. With land rising up beneath him he felt the puny fragility of the wood and fabric which surrounded him.

He looked up to refine his course and saw only blackness. He closed his eyes and opened them again, staring with his eyelids wide open, as if it would enable him to see better in the blackness. Nothing. He steepened his bank. There—off to the left—Porto's wing lights. Sweating now, feeling tremors in his legs, he increased his bank and rocked the plane level, skidding badly in the recovery. Porto was a good distance away— the twin lights so distant that they had nearly merged into one. Porto was turning. Turning more, in a tight circle. One circuit, and then another. Porto would be mad as hell, worried, sticking out his own neck to allow Brocassie to close in on him.

There was a click in Brocassie's earphones, then Porto's harsh voice, "You got me in sight?"

"I've got you."

"I'm out of altitude. I'll land to the left. Try not to prang into me."

Porto's flight path straightened and sunk toward the earth, still a black, invisible nothing beneath Brocassie.

With Porto's light gone, so was his orientation. He blindly kept his heading, searching for the ground lights, expecting that someone with enough sense would switch on some car headlights.

Nothing. Just blackness. Experimentally, he banked first one way and then another. Far to the left a light winked at him. He turned toward it, knowing that he was impossibly low. Easing back on the stick, he held it lightly, willing the sailplane to hang on for another quarter of a mile. Seconds passed, dark shapes whipping by beneath him, a lighter patch and then the blackness of rocks or trees below the wing. Now—there—a second light but not aligned with the first. He banked, trying to readjust his flight path. Speed dangerously low, the controls responding with a mushy feeling, the sound of wind over the wings just a soft whisper. Dreamlike, he thought. It will fly on forever, skimming. . . . There was a whipping rasp of branches slashing along the underside of the fuselage, a pause and then a grinding. The Slingsby settled in, impacting against the earth, became airborne for another second and crashed again, cartwheeling horizontally in a slow, agonizing cacophony of splintering wood and tearing fabric. He felt himself slammed first against one side of the cockpit and then the other, the straps of his harness biting into his flesh. In the blackness ahead he saw a shape filling the windshield and then he was hurled forward against the instrument panel as the ship impacted.

Porto was stretched out, feet on the table, sweat shirt stripped off. Late afternoon, with the laboring sound of the air conditioner that could not hold back the dry heat of the desert until the sun fell. A black cat, mangy, with large patches of hair missing, was settled in Porto's crotch, methodically washing at the scraggly remainder of its coat. Porto alternately stroked it and sipped at his beer. He finished one, crumpled it with his hand and popped the lid from another. His face was wet with sweat, beads of perspiration dripping off the hairs of his mustache.

Like Brocassie, he had a house trailer, but unlike Brocassie's it had a crude screened-in porch, air conditioning and a seemingly inexhaustible supply of beer.

"How's the lip, redskin?" he asked.

Brocassie traced the split on the inside of his lip with his tongue. Seven stitches. Plus a black eye and a bruised ego.

"It still works." He tried for a smile but it hurt like hell and although he hadn't mentioned it to Porto, he carried a permanent headache since the crash the night before.

"What kind of shape is my plane in?"

"What plane?" Porto laughed. "Thing was good for kindling wood. I went back this morning in the chopper and burned it."

"Burned it!"

"Had to. The damn thing was fractured in a dozen places. Some airliner flies over and spots the wreckage and next thing you know, there'd be newspapers, cops, the FAA and a delegation from the Flat Earth Society camping on our doorstep. The agency does all kinds of training here and it is rather insistent about keeping our profile slightly lower than a garter snake."

"How long will it take to get another Slingsby from England?"

"Longer than we can wait. They don't make the damn things any more. The closest thing made here in the States has metal wings and a tubular steel framework. The Cubans would see it miles away on radar."

So that's the end of it, he thought. And like Miller had said, the final resolution of it would haunt him for a lifetime— the goddamned ultimate lost chord.

He looked over at Porto and realized that the pilot had been studying him carefully, smiling.

"Fundamental question, Brocassie. Could you fly again? What's your gut say about that?"

Brocassie lifted a beer from the cooler and drank slowly. Fundamental question. Can I fly again? There was fear but there was also the ecstatic silky magic of flight, and he could juggle those two emotions. The real reason that he could handle it was because he had to. He turned back to Porto. "OK— they don't make wooden gliders anymore. So get me an American-made one."

"I told you, it's no good for the job, Brocassie. They'd have you on radar thirty miles out."

"That's my problem, isn't it? Get me the American-made one and teach me what I have to know about navigation for just that one flight. I'll go in alone. If I make it, I'll radio you and you can come in the following night."

"You're saying that you're willing to try it alone?"

"I'm going back into Cuba, Porto. With you or without you. With the sanction of Hagger or without it."

Porto raised his eyebrows. He laughed, a rumbling sound like a Caterpillar diesel coming to life. "That's what you thought, Brocassie?" He smashed the beer can down on the table, sending up a small spray of liquid and foam. "Christ sake, redskin! We've got six more Slingsbys packed in shipping containers. Surplus from the operation in Laos. We'll unpack another one for you tomorrow morning. I would have expected you to prang at least two before the end of training so you're ahead by fifty percent as of now. And the landing—not good but you got it down and you were in one piece. You and the cargo would have survived." He punched down a gulp of beer and then poured some into his cupped hand, offering it to the cat who eagerly slurped it up. He looked back up at Brocassie. "This is no dainty operation. If you pay attention and do like you're told, you won't even muss up your pubic hairs. Just stick on my tail with those lights spaced properly and we'll both live to write our memoirs."

He picked up the cat and threw it toward the wall. The cat did a neat tuck and landed on the bed, turning over on its back and then returned to Porto's lap for a second launch.

"I've got the best fuckin' aerobatic cat in Utah," he laughed, muzzling the cat with his putty-lump nose. "You're OK as a pilot, Brocassie. We'll start again, tomorrow. Same routine from here on in. Just one flight a night to a dirt strip in the mountains, each one different. Mostly, they slope uphill so you'll have to get used to that. Flare the Slingsby a lot more after you're past the first flashlight and expect the landing to be hard. If you break another ship, don't sweat it." He lifted his eyebrows again. "But try like hell not to."

"You knew that I'd want to keep going, didn't you?"

"Thought so, sport, but I wasn't sure. I do now, so let's drop it." He sprawled back in his chair and with a two-handed push shot, tossed the cat at Brocassie. It tucked its legs together, executed a perfect snap roll and rebounded from Brocassie's shoulder, landing feather-light on the window ledge.

"Learn to fly like that, Brocassie," Porto laughed, "and I won't have any bitches."

* * *

Two A.M. Stars out—a galaxy full. Porto sat next to him on the stoop of the trailer, watching meteors burn tracks across the horizon, giving them each a number, a destination.

"Whooooosh," said Porto, sounding like a drunk owl. "Number nine. Big green muthah, huh? Hope it took out LA." He mashed his palms together. "Splat. Santa Monica fried! Serve those rish bas'ards right." He giggled, his legs sprawled out on the grass, his belly shaking with laughter.

Too drunk, Brocassie realized, taking the bottle from between Porto's legs and laying back a long pull. Feel the stuff burning holes through my guts and brains. He lost the grip on the neck of the bottle and it fell to his feet in the dust.

Porto snatched it up, licked the mouth and took another drink. "Dummother. Like gold. Eighbucks a jar, Brocassie!"

"That's—all—for—me," Brocassie said in slow motion, trying to put the words together in sequence. All for me, but he didn't have the strength or the will to stand up. Kept thinking of the woman. Hard to say her name. Formed the letters in his mind like they were on a billboard. Easy . . . Alicia. Alicia in Wonderland. Remembered her, everything about her, every moment with her, only single images, but vivid ones. Like putting a nickel in the slot and cranking the handle, seeing the pictures flip by so that they had the illusion of motion. He leaned back against the steps, hands laced together behind his neck, staring blankly up at the sky.

"Sad motherfucker . . ." Porto yawned, breathing out the smell of dark rum.

"Whacha mean?"

"You. Sad motherfucker. Like mashed spuds, Brocassie. No humor atall, atall, atall."

"I'm supposed to have?"

"Sure!" Porto belched and then swallowed noisily. "Sure. Getta little joy outa life. Laugh. Pay you a quarter a laugh." He fished in his pocket and dropped coins in the dirt. "Laugh, redskin buddy pilot asshole. Good for you."

Brocassie forced himself to his feet, stood uncertainly, feeling the blood drain from his head. "See you, Porto. Have lotsa fun." He tried a tentative step but Porto grabbed his belt and pulled him down to the steps.

"Don't mean it," he said. "Don't get pissed." He paused and then laughed. "... mean ... get pissed." He passed the bottle, sticking it into Brocassie's face. "Last chance, friend. No more boozing after tonight—understand. *Mañana* we work for honor, dooooteeee and the Yankee dollar." He picked up the bottle and held it against the night sky, shaking it. His voice was suddenly sober. "Here's to our collective asses and the way that we'll bust 'em." He started to sing, offkey, about going in on a wing and a prayer.

"Why the hell are you doing this, Porto?"

"A-HA! Biggest word in the Anglo language is 'why.' Second biggest word in the Anglo language is 'money.' Lotsa money, Brocassie. Got a debt I have to pay off my back, OK. How 'bout you? Dumb to go in, Brocassie. Get your *cojones* shot off. For what?"

"I have to go back. See people I have to see to get something straight. For old times' sake."

Porto struggled into a sitting position, his arms braced behind him. He was so drunk that his hands kept slipping in the dirt and he finally gave up, falling flat on his back again, giggling. "Old times' sake? You're dumber than I thought, 'Cassie. You wanna get killed for 'old times' sake'?"

He staggered upright, teetering, pulled the cork, drank the remainder of the rum and then sent the bottle spinning into blackness. "So much for ecology," he said, turned and then stumbled up the steps of his trailer.

So much, so very much, for old times' sake, Brocassie thought, and then gently passed out in the dirt, the quilt of a whole universe of stars covering him.

185

CHAPTER

8

Havana, Cuba, September 12, 1962

They landed just after dark in a driving rainstorm. Álvarez had expected to feel some kind of elation on returning to Cuba, but he didn't. It was as if he had returned as a grown man to the town he had been raised in and found the houses smaller and shabbier, the lawns less green, the trees that he climbed as a child, only small, stunted things. He had lost something and gained something, he thought. Innocence traded for realism, perhaps. There was no way to assess the value of the exchange.

He nudged Roychenko awake and then collected his baggage. A deferential Aeroflot steward led them to the exit door.

The raindrops were huge silver bullets, briefly caught in the floodlights of the terminal, then fragmenting into liquid shrapnel against the asphalt. At the foot of the boarding ramp was a ZIL limousine and two men in unmarked gray uniforms holding umbrellas. Álvarez followed Roychenko, ignoring the umbrellas and the men who held them, climbing quickly into the backseat.

The men got in the front and one handed Roychenko a sealed manila envelope.

"Marked 'urgent' for you from Center, Comrade Colonel." The man showed his teeth in a mechanical parody of a smile. "Where do you desire to be driven?"

"The 'Library' on La Quinta Avenida for a minute. I have to read this first and possibly send some cables. You'll wait for me. Then to Mariel Harbor, if the *Omsk* is unloading."

The man in the right front seat was nodding before Roychenko finished the sentence. "She arrived eight hours ahead of schedule, just after noon today. The unloading started at seventeen hundred hours."

Roychenko motioned the driver to move and hit the switch which rolled up the interconnecting window. He leaned back, yawning. "Did you ever notice, Julio, that the concept of a classless society is a paradox. The workers just can't feel comfortable without knowing who to be humble before." He made a sound of disgust in his throat and leaned back, his eyes closed.

The limousine drove through deserted, rain-swept streets. Álvarez caught glimpses of men slouching in doorways, of women timidly peering out through windows partially shuttered. Every second streetlight was turned off, to conserve electricity, Álvarez guessed. No more neon signs or flashing lights. Havana had been a town, he thought, that only really lived after sundown. Now, it was nothing more than a shabby, tropical suburb of Moscow.

"You seem distracted, *Comandante.* No joy for the returned warrior?"

"Tired. I'll drop off at the Miramar and catch tomorrow's morning flight to Santiago."

Roychenko put his hand over Álvarez's arm. The grip was viselike yet without real pressure. Álvarez wanted to smash the hand away but he turned to Roychenko, his face immobile. "Remove your hand, please," he said evenly.

Shrugging, Roychenko released his grip. "I'm sorry, *Comandante,*" he said overly enunciating. "I must apologize for

187

my bad manners but you seem to think that our relationship is somehow altered once we're on Cuban soil. Our work tonight hasn't finished. I want you to come with me to Mariel. There are arrangements for transshipment of cargo which you will be in charge of."

"What cargo?" He was dull from the flight. He wanted a couple of drinks and then sleep. And tomorrow, he would see Alicia. My God, how he needed to see her.

"The cargo which was shipped from Kapustin Yar, Álvarez." He sounded impatient, agitated. "The first fifteen will be transported to Oriente tomorrow night by rail. You'll be in charge of security."

Álvarez's heart quickened, the easy lassitude gone. Roychenko was talking about the long-range missiles but they were intended for installation on the north coast of Cuba at San Cristóbal, Guanajay and Sagua la Grande. Oriente was four hundred miles to the east. He glanced toward the interconnecting glass partition but it was closed, protecting the passenger area from the hearing of the men in the front seat. A car sped by in the opposite direction, the glare of its headlights a dazzling blur of brilliance, briefly flooding Roychenko's face with light, throwing his features into hard relief.

As if he had read Álvarez's thoughts, Roychenko nodded. "It's safe to talk. They can't hear anything and if they did and repeated it, they would be employable only as choir boys."

"If I'm still going to play the part of a DGI *comandante* returning from training, I can't simply make my own schedule. I've got to sign in, file a report on the training and be briefed on current developments. Fidel will want me to give a full report on equipment that the KGB is going to supply as well as give me the nine-digit code. I have to—"

Roychenko cut him off. "Castro knows about the transshipment. You're in charge. I cleared this through Moscow Center who cleared it with Fidel before we left the Soviet Union. Your work for us begins now, tonight."

Álvarez leaned back against the leather seats. "Why are the missiles being shipped to Santiago?"

"Not Santiago," Roychenko replied. "To the installation in the Sierra, Julio, the Calvario Complex. We built a warehouse near the port of Mariel so that we could uncrate the mis-

siles and check them out under cover until all the launch facilities had been completed. Unfortunately, the architects and
engineers in Moscow misread the planning criteria and the
girders which were to support the roof were inadequate for the
winds which we have experienced during the hurricane season. We have therefore had to alter our plans. The complex in
the Sierra has very large underground maintenance facilities.
So we must now ship the off-loaded missiles down there, check
them out and then put them to bed until the launch facilities
up here on the west coast are ready."

"That's one hell of a lot of open country. Everyone along
the railway line is going to see what we're carrying!"

Roychenko lit his pipe and cracked a window, allowing
the smoke to siphon out. "A little more than four hundred
miles. The missiles will be in crates, covered by canvas. The
train will move only at night and will be shunted onto sidings
during the daylight hours, in the event that the Americans are
making overflights. I think that there is little to be concerned
about. Fidel has already been apprised of the change and he
has no objection. The missiles are, after all, the property of the
Soviet Union. What he has to say about how the weapons are
handled is immaterial, although we like to make him feel as if
he is a part of the decision-making process." Roychenko
slouched in the seat, kicked down a footstool with his toe and
stretched out. "He trusts you, Julio. By having *his* representative in charge of security, he feels that he can keep a finger on
what his Soviet allies are doing."

A cluster of shops whipped by in the blackness, the plate
glass of the windows taped over in a gridwork pattern. Álvarez
recognized the district and looked for the theater which he had
taken Alicia to, when they had seen *An American in Paris*.
Leslie Caron and—what was his name—Irish—yes, Kelly.
Took her to see it because Alicia was so much like Caron: the
impish compulsiveness and a lack of awareness of her own
sexuality. She had held his hand through the love scenes, and
he mentally danced with her across misty Paris bridges, by
fountains, on the tops of tables. That was before Brocassie had
come to Cuba.

"There was no design fault in the missile checkout building's roof, was there?" he heard himself saying.

Roychenko gave a mechanical laugh. "Engineers have a weakness, Julio. They believe only in numbers. Your weakness is that you're a cynic. You suspect devious workings of the Russian mind, but, in fact, there were simply a series of bureaucratic errors. You have to understand that even in the Soviet Union, we make mistakes." He laid his hand on Álvarez's knee and squeezed it gently, as if he were checking the firmness of a ripening fruit. "Patience. We'll see the missiles on flatcars by dawn and start east tomorrow night. You can sleep all the way to Guayos. By the next night, we'll be in the Sierra and you can go home to your woman." He dug into his coat pocket and withdrew an object which flashed dull silver in the glare of the passing streetlights. "For you," he said, putting the cool metal object in Álvarez's hand, "from a friend who wishes you success."

It was a chronometer, Swiss-made, massive, with luminous dials. Roychenko switched on an overhead light. "Read the inscription on the back."

Julio held it up until the engraving caught the light. "From L.I.B. with regards."

"From Brezhnev," Roychenko said very softly.

The "Library" on La Quinta Avenida had been just that—a graceful stone structure dedicated to knowledge and learning. Now it housed both Cuban counterintelligence DGI and KGB personnel.

Roychenko had gone into the "stacks," a back room which was staffed only by KGB personnel, estimating that he would require only a half an hour. Álvarez gave it ten minutes and then entered the DGI annex, flashing his identity card to the officer on duty.

"I want a phone," Álvarez said. "A secure landline. One that's not monitored."

"Mine . . ." the lieutenant replied. He pushed the telephone across the desk and smiled ingratiatingly.

"What's your name, Lieutenant?"

"Méndez," the lieutenant replied.

"Get the hell out of here, Méndez. I want some privacy."

She answered on the seventh ring, her voice drowsy with sleep. "Eight one two," she said.

"Alicia?"

"Who?"

"It's Julio. I'm in Havana."

The line was silent except for a slight buzzing.

"Do you hear me all right?"

"Yes," she answered. A pause. "I'm sorry. It's after midnight."

Her voice, now awake, was like silk. He felt a shiver pass through his hands. "I'll be back in two days, perhaps three. I've missed you, Alicia. I wanted to tell you that—that I . . ." He paused, irritated. Méndez was standing in the corridor which led to the operations room and Álvarez flashed his arm in that direction, waving the idiot away. He cupped the phone closer to his mouth. "I had to call you. I've missed you. Do you understand what I'm saying?"

Silence again. "I'm glad you're safe," she answered. Hesitation. ". . . and home."

He was lost for something to say. Having said everything to her in his mind during the long transatlantic flight, he couldn't bring it back. "You're well?" he finally managed.

"Yes," she replied. "Did . . . ?" Hesitation again.

"I can't hear you."

"Captain Piedra. There's some trouble, I think. Have you heard from him yet?"

Damn that ambitious little bastard. What was Piedra up to? He was one officer in his command that Álvarez knew he had to get rid of before too long. Maybe a candidate for crab counting on the Isle of Pines. "No," he finally answered. "I haven't heard from Piedra. I just got off the flight from Moscow."

"Julio—I thought you would have heard. He was here. At the *finca*, almost two weeks ago. He somehow got into your office safe and went through your personal files. He knows about me. There's something else as well but I can't talk about it over the telephone."

Christ! he swore under his breath. I'll hang that little prick from a meat hook. She was saying something, her voice just a hoarse whisper. Voices speaking Russian filtered down the corridor and he heard footsteps. Roychenko was coming toward him at a brisk pace.

"I've got to go," he said. "I'll call when I can. Don't worry."

Roychenko stopped in front of the desk, his eyes abnormally bright, glinting like black marbles. He motioned with his head toward the door, impatient.

"Don't worry," Julio said again into the mouthpiece but the line was silent. He hung the phone up carefully and followed Roychenko. Like a dog after my master, he thought.

The rain had tapered off to a drizzle. Roychenko was silent and withdrawn during the drive up to Mariel, his face turned toward the side window, watching the blur of the roadside beyond the wet glass.

At Mariel, there was unusual security. The entrance gate was manned by KGB in unmarked Cuban fatigues, except for flash marks on the collar of their uniforms. Despite the obvious importance of the passengers, the sergeant in command went through each of the occupant's identification.

"Comandante Álvarez?" The KGB sergeant threw the beam of his flashlight into the backseat. His Spanish was terrible, the *c* harsh, from the back of his throat.

Roychenko pushed the light away. "He's with me, Sergeant. Let's get on with it."

The guard hesitated, then stepped two paces back from the car, threw a rigid salute and waved them through the barrier.

"Once you get down to the south pier, pull over beyond the cranes," Roychenko ordered. The ZIL snaked through the shipyard, past cavernous warehouses with yawning doors, the interiors stacked with crates. The road finally opened up into a long concrete concourse which fronted the docks and the driver wheeled the ZIL into the shadows and stopped. Fifty yards beyond them, across the wet concrete dock, lay the Soviet ship, *Omsk,* bathed in mercury floodlights. She was rust streaked, her plates dented by the sea's force, but she was a powerful presence, looming over the docks like a massive cliff of steel.

"Let's take a stroll, Julio," he said, opening the door. Roychenko led Álvarez along the dock, past the stern of the ship, into the pools of darkness beyond. The smell of tar, machine oil and wet cement blended with the ammonia stench of decaying seaweed. Roychenko stopped at the edge of the wharf, overlooking the black water. He took out a handkerchief, blew his nose and then turned to Álvarez. "We have—or let me rephrase it—*you* have a serious security problem."

"What . . ." Immediately, his stomach tightened. Had Roychenko monitored his phone call?

"Captain Sergio Piedra. What is your opinion of him?"

Suddenly, the cool wetness of the night was stifling. "Mediocre," he answered noncommittally. "An ambitious hack with some political connections. Why ask?"

"There was an incident twelve nights ago. Piedra claims in his report that he's had an agent in Maroto's column for more than a year, without your knowledge, I might add, and in Piedra's own words, 'on his own initiative.' Piedra received word from his agent that Maroto had been able to obtain some important film of the Calvario Complex. What, exactly, is on that film is unknown but it could be very damaging to Soviet interests in Cuba. Piedra set up an intercept using forty DGI and KGB men."

"Where's the man being interrogated?"

"Miami, most likely," Roychenko answered. "Piedra somehow bungled the whole thing and Maroto's man got away."

"That incompetent idiot! For him to do something like that without my knowledge goes against standing orders."

Roychenko smiled vaguely in the half-light. "That part of it doesn't concern me. What does concern me is that the CIA may now be very interested in the complex." Roychenko had his hands driven down into the pockets of his raincoat, his back hunched away from the wind and drizzle.

"You've probably noticed, Álvarez," he said, turning his face away from the light, his expression hidden, "that Russians think in terms of chess moves. You don't play the game, do you?"

"I understand the moves."

"Then you understand that pawns are sacrificed in the early stages of the game to advance or position the more powerful pieces?"

"I'm familiar with the strategy."

Nodding, Roychenko looked at the *Omsk* and turned back. "In those holds are fifteen out of the total consignment of sixty Sandal missiles. Once those missiles and their support equipment are discovered by the U-2s, the Americans will make their opening moves and the game will be started. During the game, both sides will sacrifice pieces in an attempt to position themselves for the final win. Think about those missiles as pawns, Julio. We advance them across the board, only to sacrifice them in order to protect other, more valuable pieces."

"If you want to advance them so that you force a predictable American countermove then what's the problem?"

"The problem is the complex in the Sierra. *That* is one of the more valuable pieces I'm talking about. It's inevitable that the Americans will learn about its existence but it's also imperative that they do not connect that site with Soviet missile capability in Cuba. In one way or another, we must ensure that the Americans believe that the complex is a Soviet communications facility with only self-defense capability. *If* they believe that, they'll leave it alone, just as we accept the presence of their stations in Japan, Turkey and Iran."

Álvarez nodded, not fully understanding where Roychenko was leading him. "I'm tired, Roychenko. What do you want from me?"

"*If* the photographs which were smuggled out of Cuba contain details of the type of equipment being moved into the complex and construction details of work being done on the surface, the CIA may be tempted to send in an assault team to destroy it or, at least, to find out what its true function is. I don't believe it would be an assault team of any great size—more likely, a group of six to twelve men, parachuted in, who would then join up with this Maroto group that you seem to have been unable to eliminate. You are in charge of counterintelligence in the province as well as the security of the complex. Given a situation like that, how would you handle it?"

Álvarez turned away from Roychenko and paced slowly down the wet concrete of the wharf. It was suddenly clear to him that Roychenko's whole focus was not on the Sandal missiles but rather on the complex. "What's in that complex, Colonel, besides the communications facility?"

Roychenko stiffened, examining Julio's eyes. "Your curiosity sometimes exceeds reasonable discretion, *Comandante*. That is a subject for another time—a time of my choosing. However, let us assume that it is a facility which is vital to the interests of the USSR. So my focus is not in just repelling an assault force but rather in defusing any further interest in it by the CIA."

Álvarez rubbed his face, tired, tired, tired, but the idea was clear in his mind. "All right," he said at last. "It could be done but it hinges on breaking the code that Maroto and the CIA use to communicate. My experts in the DGI have been trying to crack that damn code for two years without any success so I turned over all the messages that we had intercepted to Moscow Center for computer analysis. Assuming your people have been able to break the code, we'll know where and when the assault team will land. A day or two prior to the scheduled landing, we jam Maroto's transmitter and send the CIA a message on the same frequency in Maroto's code, switching the landing site. We'll be there to pick up the assault team and we'll saturate the real landing site with DGI and militia in order to wipe out Maroto's men. We then interrogate the assault team to find out what their mission was, what the CIA suspected and, most important, how they were to get their report back out of Cuba. Presuming that we can dig the information out of them, we devise our own message—whatever we want the CIA to believe—then transmit it. Subsequently, we execute the assault team, dump their bodies on a beach, photograph them and let the militia claim that they got in a firefight with CIA saboteurs who were trying to get out of Cuba. The Cuban Ministry of Foreign Affairs could even lodge a protest in the UN. Your people could run some stuff in the European papers that you control and then drop any further reference, as if it were just another of the botched hit-and-run raids that the CIA has been instigating over the last two years. We make a few more phony transmissions from 'Maroto' and then his transmitter goes permanently off the air. The CIA will probably figure that the operation was a success but the patient died. End of American interest in the complex."

Roychenko nodded. "Good. Much better than I expected. Except for your qualifier. The Eighth Directorate of the KGB has analyzed the codes and they can't break them because they're 'book codes' based on sending the page, line and word number of each coded word from one particular book. Without knowing what book Maroto and the CIA are using, there's no way to break it."

"Perhaps Piedra can find out through his mole in Maroto's outfit. That is, assuming such a mole exists."

"The mole exists, Julio," Roychenko answered. "Of that I'm convinced. But it should be obvious that Maroto keeps the code book under his control at all times. Coding would be done exclusively either by Maroto or by his radio operator. It's obvious that Piedra is trying to undermine you on one hand and pull off an intelligence coup of his own on the other—a dangerous opponent, I think, Julio, and a clever one."

"Piedra intimates that he has recently learned of the whereabouts of a former Maroto radio operator in Cuba—a person with the knowledge of what book code Maroto used and might be still possibly using. Lazarev feels that it's worth a try, even though it bypasses you."

That hit him like a blow to the stomach; he knew that if Piedra were to replace him, either on Fidel's orders or on the KGB's, he would be professionally finished and, because he now knew highly sensitive information, probably dead. "What if I beat Piedra to it?"

Roychenko snorted softly. "I would say it's very late in the game to make a comeback. Piedra promises that he can deliver in ten days."

"Give me seven."

Roychenko nodded. "A week, *Comandante*. We are not exactly friends, but neither are we enemies. My future is tied to yours but you must understand that if it appears that you're ineffective, I would have to take steps to protect my own career." He started to walk slowly back toward the *Omsk*, as if everything had been settled. But then he paused, still in the shadows. "The man was an American—the one that Piedra intercepted. I read the report tonight and Piedra thinks that this man would logically lead the assault. Piedra has a photo-

196

graph of him taken years ago. It's a positive identification."

"Where did he get it? From Records?"

Roychenko sighed, as if he were arbitrating a dispute between two close friends. "No, Julio, from your mantelpiece."

Alicia untwisted the hair from behind her head, withdrawing the two tortoiseshell combs, letting it cascade down her back. From her dresser drawer, she took a brush and stroked firmly downward, snapping the bristles through the ends.

Álvarez, lying naked on the bed, supporting an ashtray on his stomach, watched her, admiring the rising of her breasts with each upstroke. She wore a short nightdress, something that he had purchased on the Mazilovo black market of Moscow. It was thin as smoke, a golden apricot to complement her skin, and transparent enough so that he could see the deeper shading of the aureoles of her breasts and the dark triangle of her pubis. From Sweden, the label read, and she had genuinely liked it. She said.

Time was running out. Three days of Roychenko's grace period already gone, four remaining, he thought. But only these two days alone with her before I have to drag my butt back to Mariel for the unloading and transshipment of the second load of Sandals. He was beginning to feel desperate with Piedra in the wings, waiting to take center stage. Álvarez knew that he couldn't force her to reveal the book code, even at the cost of his own career and even, perhaps, his life. In some way, a way that he hadn't yet conceived of, she would have to betray herself, and vaguely he knew that her betrayal must hinge on Brocassie.

"Eres un bonbón," he said. And she was—only a few feet away, yet so far as to be unobtainable.

Sighing, he propped himself up farther on the bed and lit a cigar. He blew the smoke toward the ceiling and watched it fan out and stratify. There was no wind; the trades had fallen to a whisper by midday and, with sunset, had stopped altogether. Night was a huge, black squatting thing, ancient smelling and oppressive.

"Did you miss me?" he asked softly, half earnest, half taunting.

"I was lonely," she answered. He caught her eyes turned toward him in the mirror. He recognized her answer as the evasion it was.

"That isn't what I asked, Alicia."

"I missed you," she said. "That's what I meant. It's just that . . ."

He inhaled the smoke from the cigar. They were a casual welcome-home gift from The Horse, with a scrawled note which read, "We are proud of your diligence," whatever the hell that meant.

"Just that . . . ?" he mimicked gently.

"It *was* Brocassie, wasn't it?"

"The description fitted but he's not positive, even with the photograph." As he said it, he realized that it sounded like the lie that it was.

"But Piedra said that the man told him that he was Brocassie. Why would anyone say that if it wasn't true?"

He snuffed the cigar, irritated. Had it been Brocassie? In the hundred-degree heat, the dead bodies of the invasion force at the Bay of Pigs had decomposed rapidly. Fidel and his retinue had been stomping around, joking, and Álvarez had been there sharing in the victory. Graves registration had laid out the personal effects and weapons of the unidentified invaders for the press, and quite by chance, he had seen the .38 lying there among the dog tags, the bloodstained letters and the cheap crucifixes.

Had it been Brocassie? Even then, he hadn't been absolutely sure. The bodies had been bulldozed into a common grave but Álvarez had frantically started to look among them. There was one, his face shot away but the right height, and the boots on the rotting corpse were Gokey brogans—the kind Brocassie had brought with him to Cuba. But the thing that convinced him was the .38. Álvarez had stolen it from the Marine Corps when he was mustered out and he had held it a thousand times. The notches on the grip were the same and so were the serial numbers. It was the .38 that Brocassie had used to save my life, he thought.

He had picked up the revolver, fingering it, turning it over and over in his hands, and he felt something welling up inside of him—something between grief and the relief that he would never have to compete with Brocassie again.

It had taken Fidel's personal intervention, but he had gotten the corpse exhumed and had laid it in a grave, overlooking Trinidad and the sea beyond. Facing east toward the rising sun as he knew Brocassie would want to have been buried. He had wept then, but inside he had gladly closed a door to the past. Except now, there was what prosecutors termed, "reasonable doubt."

"I don't know," he finally said. "You have to believe me that I thought Brocassie was dead. I didn't lie to you. There's a grave on the Melincino road to the north of Trinidad that I buried him in."

She was sitting, staring at the mirror, as if there were something beyond it that only she could see. Her right thumb and middle finger were moving in a circular motion around her left-hand ring finger.

"There was a gold ring on a thong around the throat," she said, more a statement than question.

That's where it had gone, he thought. When he had known her in Havana, she had always worn a ring—some antique that had been in her family. "No," he answered. "But something like that could have been easily lost."

She turned to him, tears forming slowly in the corners of her eyes, then trailing in streaks down her face. It was as if she didn't know or care that she was crying. "You have to warn him, Julio. You have to keep him from coming back because if he does, he'll die. And if he does, you'll be the one who is responsible for the bullet that kills him."

How could the bitch say this now, after both of them had accepted his death for over a year? They had both agreed, each for their own secret passions, to put it away, to be done with his death, and after all this goddamn time . . . Infuriated, he flung the ashtray against the wall and stormed out of the room, crashing down the stairs to the main floor. Slamming the door to his study, he locked it, grabbed a bottle of Scotch from the cabinet and dropped on the couch, his whole body shaking.

Bugger you, bitch, he swore. Why had he risked his neck

to get her out of that goddamned prison? The cunt had no sense of loyalty or honor, let alone love. All she wanted was for him to put his neck under the ax again for her bloody phantom lover.

He threw down a drink, feeling the stuff burn its way past his throat, forming a hard ball of fire in his stomach, then sipped at the bottle more slowly, his anger finally calming. He could hear her moving overhead, the floor creaking, the toilet flushing, the sound of footsteps on the stairs.

Oh, no, he thought, never again. If it was Brocassie, then bad luck, buddy. I'll blow your guts out and gladly. He drank from the bottle again. Two years with her. He had given her sanctuary in exchange for what? For this shit? What kind of insane thing had prompted him to risk for her everything that he had built up in Cuba?

She knocked softly on the door.

He ignored it, still naked, beginning to feel the damp of the night sucking away his body heat.

"Julio?" she whispered, her voice muffled by the door.

"Fuck off!"

"Let me in. I won't leave until I can talk to you."

At first he ignored her, sipping at the Johnnie Walker. And then thought, all right. She was forcing the decision on him. If she wanted Brocassie, she could have him. On a platter. And Roychenko had given him the carving knife.

She knocked again, more loudly. "Open the door, Julio."

His mind already made up, suddenly everything clicked into place. Roychenko had known from Piedra's report about Alicia's involvement with Maroto—knew that she had been his radio officer—knew that she would have had access to the code books. So bloody subtle and yet subtle like a sledgehammer. Roychenko was putting heat on him, insisting that he turn liabilities into assets, and quite suddenly, all the little pieces fitted together into a neat pattern. He took another sip of the Scotch, dazzled with the idea.

She knocked again, and he thought to himself, Why the hell not? Liabilities into assets. He got up slowly, almost wishing that she would go away, for one brief second furious that she was leading both of them into betrayal, but she rapped again, more insistent. He let her in. Sitting down, she faced him from across the room.

"Drink?" he offered. "A toast to the resurrection of my brother—your lover?" He couldn't keep the bitterness out of his voice, even though he was already playing a part.

She was calm, her voice precise. "Before you came back, I did a lot of thinking. Do you still want me as your wife?"

He avoided her eyes. "I've thought about it," he said evenly, but he knew that she would recognize his reply as a flagrant lie. There was no helping it; he wanted her, now more than ever.

She leaned back in the chair, her eyes closed, and she remained that way for a long time, and then leaned forward again. "Then somehow get a message to Brocassie. You have ways. Keep him from coming back into Cuba. That's my only condition."

"So all I have to do is to send a cable to Miami, attention of Operation Mongoose. 'Brocassie denied permission to enter Cuba, signed Álvarez.' " He shook his head. "There isn't any way, Alicia-bitch. No way." He sipped at the Scotch. "Funny thing, you know," he said. "I don't want Brocassie parachuting in here either. Forget blood ties because there aren't any. I just want to be rid of the bastard—not see him killed."

"There's a way," she said. "I know of a way, but I have to think about it." She stood up, the smoke of her nightdress an ache to him as he watched her move toward the door. She paused and turned to him, only briefly. "Except I don't know whether I'd trust you."

She pulled the door closed behind her and then he listened to her footsteps on the stairs.

Carefully, he thought. Very carefully.

For hours he thought, weighing one thing against another. The Scotch was gone and twice he went to the kitchen to make coffee, burning through eight more cigars, his mouth dry, his stomach acid, but his brain burning bright.

Finally, for an hour or more, he stood on the veranda and listened to the night sounds, waiting for the dawn, because he knew that the mind was most vulnerable then. A thick black pudding of cloud in the east turned almond and only then did he climb the stairs to their bedroom, now completely sober.

He lay down beside her, his hand on her waist, and with the other hand, stroked her neck. Her body jerked but then seemed to relax beneath his touch. He was startled at the coldness of her skin. "You're awake?" he asked.

She made a movement with her head, nodding, her face still turned away.

"Assuming that I agree with your conditions, assuming that I was willing to warn Brocassie, it's still almost impossible. For me to send a message in plain language would be an act of treason and Piedra would know about it within ten minutes."

She rolled over, turning toward him, brushing the hair from her face. "But you've thought of something?"

"It might be possible. The simplest way would be for you to get a message to Maroto for retransmission. You still must know people in the Segundo Frente who would pass the message to Maroto. In turn, he could transmit it to Florida."

She frowned, suspicious. "That would take days, perhaps a week, and I couldn't trust you not to follow the messenger." She shook her head. "I'm sorry, Julio, but I can't tempt you with that opportunity. Those people were my friends and I'd die before I betrayed them."

It had been something he had never questioned her about and she had never been willing to discuss. Her involvement with Maroto and the Segundo Frente was a no-man's-land, mutually agreed upon under the terms of an unspoken truce. He smiled to himself, because he had counted on her reaction, leaving only one other option.

"There's one other alternative. Only one." He took a strand of her hair in his hand, gently pulling it through his fingers, waiting cautiously for her reaction.

He glanced down to her face and found her eyes on his, studying him. "What is it, Julio?" she asked but there was a hard edge of distrust in her voice.

And it was her distrust that he had counted on, because in the end, she would betray herself. "We've never talked about this," he began hesitantly, "but I knew that you were a radio operator for Maroto. You probably knew his code setup and even if it's out of date, the CIA would recognize it even today. Together, we'll draft the message and encode it. As head of the DGI in Oriente, I approve twenty or thirty messages a day that are sent out to our agents in Jamaica, Puerto Rico, Mexico and Florida, all of them encoded. I could assign a message to Brocassie with a phony file and priority number, insert it in the stack of stuff to be transmitted and no one would ever question it."

She shook her head slowly. "The code that Maroto used, for all I know, might still be valid. The same principle applies, Julio. I couldn't trust you."

He lay back against the pillow, his eyes on the ceiling. "Then there is nothing left to do but wait for him to come back into Cuba." He swiveled his head toward hers. "And when that happens, I can't prevent the inevitable."

Neither of them spoke for a long while and the sounds of the house and the wind were magnified, unnaturally loud.

Then she spoke. "We will decide on the message. I will encode it but I will not give you the key to the code. Is that understood?"

He placed his face against her back and nodded, trying to convey to her his willingness to accept her conditions, yet withholding his promise.

He reached over her waist and put his hand on her breast. He squeezed it softly, teasing the nipple between his fingertips. "Blow out the lamp," he said.

She pulled away from him and blew across the top of the chimney. The room fell into blackness, the orange glow retained on his retina, fading first into blackness, then replaced by the faint, intangible light of dawn.

Beside him, he listened to her steady breathing, but he knew that it was not the prelude to sleep. She was weighing things in her mind, deciding. Give her time, he thought. In the end, she'll tell me. He pulled her closer, trying to be gentle, but the act of restraint was a psychological trigger and he felt his organ thickening, straining out from his body toward hers. He tightened his hold on her but she reached back and shoved him away.

"It's not decided yet, Julio," she said. "Give me time."

* * *

In the morning, a pelting rain sluiced through the palms and ragged clouds, torn away from the low overcast, seemed to sponge up what light was left, leaving the south coast of Cuba in a bleak twilight. Everything in the house seemed damp. The windows rattled in their sashes, lashed by the buffeting wind.

He sat across from Alicia, sipping coffee, silent. He could hear the whine of Marta's voice in her quarters, singing in accompaniment with the tinny notes of a phonograph record. The cats, both wet from an early run, lay like sodden lumps on the windowsill, watching each other with suspicion.

Álvarez got up, shut the kitchen door to the servants' quarters and then sat back down, facing her. "It's difficult to say this, Alicia, because I wasn't constructed to be the gentle lover or the perfect husband, but I've always loved you and I desire you even more now. I want children and I want you as my wife. Anything from the past, whether it had to do with the Segundo Frente or your relationship with Brocassie, I want to forget—will forget. And although Brocassie was"—he hesitated for a second—"your lover, he's still my brother. He saved my life once and I don't want him killed fighting for something that doesn't concern him."

Her face was expressionless, but he could see in her eyes the fluctuations between hope and fear, between things of the past and those of the future.

She finally spoke. "I'll give you the encoded message. But not the code."

He shook his head. "No. That's not enough. I need the code, the frequencies that Maroto would use, his whole operating procedure."

She shut her eyes and put her hands to her temples, pressing so hard that he could see white under her nails. *"You'd use it to trap Maroto,"* she answered in a raw whisper.

No lies now, he thought. Only half-truths that she needed to accept because she *had* to believe them. "Maroto's a hemorrhoid in the ass of the Revolution. He's a bandit, not a patriot. Damn well right I'll use the code to flush him out of the Sierra, but if I can, he'll be taken alive, given a show trial and then traded to the Americans. A year from now, Maroto will be sunning his skinny butt in Miami, counting the profits from whatever business the CIA will give him. Even without the code, I'll eventually get him because I have to and it won't be pretty. It's my job and there's a lot of pressure on me to clean him out. Which way do you want it?"

"There are other men with him. Men that are fighting for something they believe in—something that you believed in once, Julio—a Cuba free of foreign influence. And what do you have now?" she spat at him. "Marx instead of United Fruit, Lenin in place of Esso?"

Her voice was on the edge of hysteria and he recognized that she had passed through the barrier. It was not a matter now of "if" but of "how." Tell her what? he wondered. Tell her what she wanted to believe or already knew. " *'A free Cuba,'* " he said, keeping his voice soft, as if it shouldn't be overheard, "is the same asshole rallying cry that every would-be dictator has ever used in this country. What did those men ever do besides serve whoever filled their Swiss bank accounts? This country isn't Plato's Republic and I'm not saying it is, but Fidel will give us something better than anything we've ever had before. Not perfect but better. And he forgives, Alicia. You've seen it. Maroto and his people will be held for a while but eventually allowed to emigrate. We need live bodies to build the foundations of the Revolution. Dead bodies have a habit of becoming martyrs."

There was silence between them now. She got up and poured herself more coffee, then sat down in a chair which overlooked the grounds, stroking one of the cats. It mewed, turning on its back, stroking the air with its paws.

At last she said, "Would you give me your word that Maroto and the men in his column wouldn't be harmed?"

"It would be arranged." He paused and then said, "Yes, my personal guarantee."

"And Brocassie? How could you be sure that he would get the message—and believe it?" She got up and moved around behind him, her hands on his shoulders. "Julio—I want to believe you, so very, very much. He's gone now, for both of us. Let it remain that way. I can forget if you can and I'll keep my end of the bargain." She squeezed his shoulder blades, the pressure of her hands actually hurting him.

Standing up, he moved to the window, his face turned away from her, for he could barely suppress his elation. It had to be right the first time, he thought. He turned back to her, leaning on the windowsill, stroking one of the cats.

"We'll agree on the message and you will encode it. I'll assign the message a phony file and authorization number, then place it in the outgoing message stack for transmission."

"Somebody will question it!"

"No one will question it," he answered. "No one, because all of the hundreds of messages transmitted weekly from Oriente pass my desk for final approval and only then are they transmitted. The radio officers don't know what's contained in a message, only the frequency the message is to be sent on, the time it's to be transmitted and the actual encoded message. A lot of the messages are transmitted in the blind. There wouldn't be any problem."

"How can you be sure that it will ever get to Brocassie?"

"I can't. If the CIA wants Brocassie to come back into Cuba, they may withhold the message from him, possibly even use it to discredit me. You can imagine Fidel's reaction if he learned that I communicated directly with Mongoose." He heaved a sigh, emphasizing his own vulnerability. "I'd be shot, Alicia, and then Piedra would take my job and we both know how that would affect your future."

"But how would we ever know whether he'd received the message, let alone know whether he'll agree not to reenter Cuba?"

He gave her a slight smile. It was difficult not to overplay the scene. "I've thought of that and I think I have a solution. Assuming that he gets the message, assuming that he's even willing to reply, he can answer through a classified ad in the personal column of the *Miami Herald*. The proof that it's him will be a name that he will use in the ad which will be known only among the three of us."

He lit another cigar with a match and whipped the flame out. "Did Maroto use some initial group of letters as an identifier in his coded transmissions?"

"Five letters," she answered. "The first letter identifies the name of the book to be used in decoding, the second letter the originator of the message and the third stood for a number which was added or subtracted from the coded page number."

"And the last two letters?"

She hesitated, her eyes lowered. "It was something that was used in routing the message once the CIA received it. I'm fairly sure that's the way the system worked." She made a helpless gesture with her hands. "I suppose that the last two letters would allow the message to be directly routed to whoever was Maroto's controller—a man by the name of Hagger, I think."

She said it casually, almost too casually. He watched her eyes, her hands, her body language which might convey a lie but he wasn't sure. "You *were* the one who actually transmitted the message by Morse code?"

She nodded.

"Did you use some means of identifying yourself, such as letters at the end of the message."

She shook her head. "No. Never. There would be no reason to." She suddenly frowned. "It doesn't really matter, does it? I'll give you the five letters. What they mean is of no further concern to you."

He nodded, keeping his body calm, but within him, he felt an overpowering sense of victory. "You're right, of course. We need only send the one message, as long as you're sure that it will be properly decoded. This doesn't guarantee that they'll give it to him, but I think that the content of the message will speak for itself." She was still behind him and he couldn't help but smile. If something happened, just by chance, of course, she could not hold him responsible.

"I want to see what you're going to send out, and I want your word, Julio, that you'll send it just that way. No alterations, nothing added."

He stood up. "Give me a little time to word it," he said and walked into the library. He had already formed the message in his mind but he spent half an hour, drafting and redrafting before he had it right.

"I think this will do it," he called to her.

She read it over his shoulder.

MESSAGE TO CIA JM/WAVE OPERATIONS KEY WEST PASS TO OPERATION MONGOOSE FOR GEORGE BROCASSIE STOP PERSONAL MESSAGE IS AS FOLLOWS

SHELL GAME

PART ONE

SERGIO PIEDRA CONVINCED YOU WILL TRY TO RE ENTER
CUBA AND DGI ALERTED FOR SUCH AN ATTEMPT
STOP   JULIO WOULD NOT BE ABLE TO INTERVENE FOR OB-
VIOUS REASON WERE YOU TO BE CAUGHT STOP   BOTH OF
US BEG YOU NOT TO ATTEMPT REENTRY FOR THE SAKE OF
OUR FORMER FRIENDSHIP STOP

PART TWO

JULIO AND I MARRIED SEVEN MONTHS AGO WITH CHILD
DUE DECEMBER STOP   HOPE THAT IN SOME FUTURE TIME
WHEN RELATIONSHIP BETWEEN OUR TWO COUNTRIES
IS NORMALIZED WE CAN MEET TOGETHER AGAIN IN PEACE
STOP   JULIO HAS TRANSMITTED THIS MESSAGE AT GREAT
PERSONAL RISK STOP   PLEASE DO NOT COMPROMISE HIM
BY ALLOWING THIS INFORMATION TO BE FED BACK TO DGI
STOP

PART THREE

PLEASE CONFIRM THAT YOU HAVE RECEIVED THIS MES-
SAGE BY INSERTION OF YOUR ANSWER IN PERSONAL COL-
UMN OF MIAMI HERALD SOONEST STOP   SIGN MESSAGE
WITH NAME OF CANTINA OWNER WHO GAVE ME MOOKEM
FLOWER STOP   UNTIL THEN WE WISH YOU THE BEST AND
GOD BLESS STOP   SIGNATURE SEÑORA ALICIA RUTH HEL-
VIA DE ÁLVAREZ STOP   END MESSAGE

She stared at the message for a long time. "Is it necessary
that we lie to him about being married and having a child?"

He let the question hang between the two of them and finally answered. "He has to be convinced that coming back
would be futile. He's not planning to come back to fight
against Castro, is he? Not a chance, Alicia, he's coming back
for you."

She walked to the mantelpiece, staring at the photograph
of the three of them, fingering the silver frame. When she
turned back to him, her eyes were rimmed with wetness. "I
will encode it, Julio. I want it sent exactly as I give it to you."

He nodded. "That was agreed upon already. But I want the name of the book that's being used for the code and I want the exact construction of the identifier. That was the bargain."

Her voice had a stubborn quality to it. "Not until you bring me his printed reply from the *Miami Herald*. Only then, Julio."

He gave her a half-smile, not pressing the issue. It didn't really matter one damn bit but he knew she would expect him to pressure her for the code and the identifier construction. Which made the deception all the more believable.

He turned back to her, reached up and clasped her arm gently. "No, I'll go along with you. My curiosity is a professional compulsion. You encode the message and I'll transmit it exactly that way." He paused. "The book used for coding—do you have it?"

She shot him a blistering look. "You never give up trying, do you? Of course I don't have it. I'm going to get on the Santiago bus tomorrow morning and I don't want anyone following me because if there is, I'll know about it. No interference, Julio, and if there is, I'll never return, regardless of the consequences."

"If you're picked up, you won't have papers. I couldn't protect you."

"Then that's a risk I have to take, isn't it?"

He held up his hands in surrender. "I'm not going to interfere. I don't want Brocassie's death on my hands and I do want you—very much." Both true, he realized, except that there were other factors, such as Piedra and Roychenko and his own future; the future of Comandante Julio Álvarez. And as in all things, there were priorities.

She didn't say anything, only looked at him for a moment and then turned away, walking unsteadily toward the kitchen.

Julio glanced down at the message again. He would have to work quickly. Two women to tail her in shifts once she was in Santiago, but she would probably duck through the Old Quarter and lose them, and if she suspected, the whole operation would be blown. No, he thought, let the bitch run free. He would have four bookstores and the library of the Universidad de Oriente covered. Chances were very high that she would go to one of them. If not, then he still could cope because all that the computer-assisted code breakers under Roychenko's control would need would be the exact text and the coded message that resulted from it. It might take time to scan electronically through hundreds of thousands of books but they would have the exact correlation. It would be just a matter of time.

And then there would be a coded transmission to Rivas in Fort Lauderdale to make the insertion in the *Miami Herald*. But that could wait for a day or so.

He leaned back, stretching. He didn't want to smile but found it hard not to.

CHAPTER

9

St. Ann's Bay, Jamaica, October 13, 1962

Tree frogs peeped in the bush, their voices shrill and monotonous. The sound of them was fraying his nerves, making it almost impossible to concentrate. Brocassie stood in the doorway of the small shack, looking out into the Jamaican night, unconsciously clenching and unclenching his fists. A fitful wind blew in small gusts, and thunder rumbled in the west, backlighting the massed thunderstorms over Montego Bay. He turned and slumped down in a chair opposite Porto, trying to keep his mind free of either hope or despair, speculation or uncertainty.

Porto stabbed the remains of a wizened hunk of meat, pushed it into his mouth, clamped his teeth down and extracted the fork.

"You want the rest?" he mumbled, his mouth full, indicating the serving platter which held the remaining meat.

"All yours," Brocassie replied, leaning back in the camp chair. "I don't know what that stuff is but you can bet that the

211

SPCA would be interested in finding out." He settled into the canvas, his hands clamped behind his head, tired of waiting, worn out from frustration. Five days of waiting for the tropical depression to work its way north and still the bastard squatted stationary in the Windward Passage, pissing down on the Greater Antilles like a cow on a flat rock.

Other delays, some trivial, some intolerable. A C-47 with sun-faded paint and an obscure pea-patch airline logo from somewhere in the Bahamas (another CIA Air America operation, undoubtedly) had brought down three Slingsby sailplanes, wings and tail structures removed, all neatly crated. With Porto supervising, Brocassie and two of the mechanics had assembled the ships, only to find that the precision-machined locking pins were missing. Quick calls to Miami, Porto reading out measurements over the phone. From Miami, calls to England and then another two days until the pins arrived by BOAC. Another day, fighting Jamaican customs without importation documentation to get the pins.

The dirt airstrip was on an old plantation, set on the north coast of Jamaica. An Englishman with a splotchy red face ran the place.

Brocassie had asked Porto whether the plantation was another piece of CIA real estate.

"Steen leases it through a phony evangelical organization the agency set up for Caribbean and South American operations. We're supposed to be missionaries bent on training for a tour in the Brazilian bush. The C-47 transport, the crates of food, raggedy-ass types like us—all explained if any one in this part of the island wants to know, which I doubt. Tourists keep glued to within a fifty-foot radius of their hotels and the government doesn't want to know—not with Cuba sitting ninety miles to the north."

The airfield was not much more than a strip of red dirt, ripped out of the upland forest with gelignite and bulldozers. Less than three thousand feet long with trees at both ends, it was suitable, just barely, for the C-47 Gooney Bird to get in. Off to the side of the strip, set back under mahogany trees, was a large wooden hangar, a maintenance shack and a bunkhouse, rats, cockroaches and dirt floors included.

"More coffee, 'Cassie?"

"I'll pass. Have a hard enough time sleeping with those damn tree frogs croaking." But it had really been the night-mares which wouldn't allow him to sleep for more than a few minutes at a time. She had invariably been in them, dressed in a white gown which slowly dissolved to black, her features running together like wax melting in a fire. There had been others in the dream too, his father shriveling before his eyes, and Julio, laughing, his face blurred and distorted. He would awaken in the sodden bed, sweat streaming from his body, heart trip-hammering.

Porto grimaced between bites, forking down the remain-der of the burned meat. "Hagger's due in tomorrow," he said. "The National Hurricane Center is forecasting the depression to start moving again with a prognosis of 'severe clear' in three days. They reckon that the winds will be light easterly with good visibility all the way to Cuba. Moonrise on the sixteenth would be about three A.M. Barring any problems with Hag-ger's end of it, we'll go then."

Outside, the wind increased, rattling the galvanized steel roof, buffeting the windows. A giant pressure seemed to be weighing on him, tightening his chest. "Two days from now?"

Porto nodded. "You feel OK about going in?"

"I'll do what I agreed to. But once the job is finished, I've got personal business. Frankly, I couldn't give a shit about the complex. But it's the price I have to pay Hagger for getting back into Cuba and, more importantly, for getting back out. *You savvy, Porto?*" He suddenly realized that he was shouting.

Porto held his hands up in surrender. "All right— ll right! Easy! The Cree natives are restless tonight, aren't they?"

Brocassie slumped down into a chair, his face flushed, his heart beating rapidly. "I'll give it my best, Porto. You know that. But Hagger expects something that's damn near impossi-ble. He has no real plan or even a concept of what's in that valley. And yet he expects us to enlist Maroto and what's left of his column to mount some sort of banzai attack on it. 'Use your imagination' he says! My God, what kind of crap is that?" He examined Porto's face, looking for agreement, but it was innocent of doubt. "So how about you—any second thoughts?"

Porto turned down the wick of the Aladdin lamp, leaving his face in deep shadow.

"I've never had anything *but* second thoughts about this, Brocassie," Porto said in a tired voice. "Why do you think Hagger is using us? Because we're the best? Baloney! Hagger's using us as a pair of expendable stalking horses, to find out what the hell's in there. He's hot for 'boom and bang.' Poke a stick in the anthill to see what comes out, understand?"

"But if this is so damn important to him, why the hell is he using us?"

Porto refilled his cup and then sat back down. "Look in the mirror, Brocassie. What do you see? Half-Latin, half-Indian—a *mestizo*—like most of the population of Cuba. Me—Cuban as they come. Neither one of us has any kind of contract with Hagger. We're paid in cash. And you can bet that somewhere there are files that prove we're both Cuban citizens—me, because my old man was a citizen and you . . ." He wiped his face with his hand. "Look, Brocassie. You fought with Cuban nationals both against Batista and Castro. When you did that, you technically lost your American citizenship, because it's presumed that you've given your stand-up-in-classroom oath of allegiance to some other country. Pure and simple, Brocassie, we're on our own. If we get nailed by the DGI in Cuba no one in the State Department is going to bust their ass to bail us out."

Brocassie was surprised that Porto would lay it out, stark naked.

"Then why are you willing to go in?" he asked softly.

"For the same reason that ninety-five percent of the people on this planet do distasteful, ugly jobs ... money. *Muchísimo dinero,* Brocassie." He rubbed his fingers together. "I need it—a lot of it—and I need it fast."

"What's the money for?" He watched Porto's eyes, trying to catch lies or evasion, but all he could see was the reflected light of the lamp.

Porto sighed, sinking farther back in his chair.

"You wouldn't believe me if I told you, Brocassie, and what's it to you anyway? Accept that I've got no choice except to go into Cuba, just like you have no choice, but each for our own private reasons."

Porto was leaning over the table now, his face backlit by the lamp, his shadow a grotesque Halloween mask against the wall.

"The only help we'll get is what we provide for each other, Brocassie. We're married by circumstance, and we have to make it stick. We go in together, we do the job the best way possible, and then we get out together. If Hagger tries to fuck us, at least one of us will live to carve out his fat belly." He extended a callused hand. "We give it our best shot together or not at all. Deal?"

Brocassie hesitated, then took it and squeezed. "Deal," he echoed. But he sensed that Porto was trying to pump him up, get the juices going, like a coach at halftime when both fortune and time were running out.

The thunder sounded nearer. A few spats of rain hit the shack, ceased for a second and then resumed again in a torrential drumbeat. Cree legend, his father had told him, was that raindrops were the tears of mothers for their dead sons, slain on the battlefields of lost causes.

Porto was mopping up his plate with a slice of stale bread and he washed it down with a gulp of coffee. He leaned back, satisfied, and for a long time they both remained silent, listening to the rain.

The sound seemed to drum into his head, like some message, not quite understood, repeated over and over. Brocassie finally stood up, wanting to be alone.

"We all do things for reasons, but those reasons are seldom obvious," Porto said evenly, his voice gentle, almost with warmth. "No man, except a lunatic, ever went into combat for the sheer pleasure of it, and anyone who does it for flag and country has got to be plain stupid. We do it out of love and fear, or pride or personal gain, or just because we happen to be there and there's no one else to do it in our place. We're a combination of all those reasons, 'Cassie. And we're together and that alone is both our consolation and our strength. When we're finished with the job on the complex, I'm coming with you. We're a team going in, we're a team while we're there and we're a team coming back out. Both of us have to understand that it works that way because that's the only way that it can work."

He dipped his finger in his coffee cup and shook it solemnly in Brocassie's direction, as if he were blessing him with holy water. "And if you need divine guidance in your quest, Brother Porto stands ready to intercede on your behalf, be it with bullets, beatitudes or final benedictions. So may *pax vobiscum,* Brocassie." He stood up, belched and walked out of the shack into the rain. "Sleep well," he said over his shoulder, the screen door slamming behind him.

For a long time, Brocassie sat staring into the fluttering glow of the lamp, his eyes unfocused. Why should Porto be willing to stay with me, once the complex job was done? Hagger's brainstorm, maybe, but unlikely. If we pull it off and get the information out, Hagger will write me off as a depreciated asset. Maybe because Porto has more depth than just the transparent beer-swilling, loudmouthed, jockstrapped soldier-of-fortune role that he loved to play. There was a fragile bond between the two of them, he acknowledged. It startled him to realize suddenly that he actually cared, liked the man because he was so improbable, unpredictable. Perhaps most important, trusted him. Maybe there was something to the idea that only mutually shared danger could make men brothers.

He stood up, blew out the lamp and then headed through the night toward his own cabin. "So good night to you, Brother Porto," he said, his lips tasting the sweet rain.

At 10:23 the next morning, like an ill wind, Hagger blew in. Standing beside Porto in the shade of the trees, watching the Aztec taxi into the parking area, Brocassie could feel an uneasiness, like a disease spreading through his body. No symptom he could name, and yet he had the sense that something was very, very wrong.

The hatch opened and four young, crew-cut men, uniformly clad in severe white shirt-jacks, poplin trousers and lace-up boots, deplaned and stood milling in the heat like an expectant flock of sheep. Hagger followed them down the steps, dressed in a flower shirt and Bermuda shorts, his face streaming with sweat.

It was plain to Brocassie that Hagger was in a funk. The handshakes were perfunctory and Hagger rushed off to shower and change, leaving Porto and Brocassie speculating on what the problem was.

"Our reverend father looks troubled," Porto said, palms pressed together. He flopped his fingers over and did the "here is the church and here is the steeple—look inside and see all the people" routine.

"A bolt of lightning out of a clear blue sky is going to fry your ass someday, Porto, and I don't want to be standing within a half a mile of you when it does." Brocassie had meant it to be funny but he realized that he had a hard edge to his voice. He reached over and squeezed Porto's shoulder. "Sorry. It's just that I smell problems. We've come a long way and I don't want to see it fall apart now."

"Let's get back to the chapel," Porto said softly. "There, if the stars are properly aligned, we will learn the truth according to Father Hagger." He shuffled in the direction of the briefing shack, his hands placed together in prayer.

The two of them walked through the steaming heat, not speaking. The ground beneath Brocassie's feet burned through his thin, rubber zoris. Not good, he thought. Hagger had exuded all the confidence of a frightened child on his first day of school, and he realized that the whole operation could be on the edge of crumbling. Once you involved a lot of people, he speculated, the operation became overly complex—more chances for error. Hagger had sworn to keep it simple. But already the plantation was bulging with Mongoose operatives. Besides Porto and himself, there were two mechanics and two pilots for the towplanes, a cook/housekeeper and a communications guy who fiddled with a battery of radios and a teleprinter. Add Hagger and the four "missionaries" whose functions were still unknown. The complement was beginning to approach the proportions of a small battalion.

The weather was clearing after seven days of rain and overcast. Rents in the cloud cover revealed patches of blue and the wind was back into the east—a good sign. Entering the shack, Brocassie slumped down in a camp chair, lit a cigarette and waited uneasily for Hagger's briefing, trying to avoid speculation. But fear of failure, he realized, was a communicable disease.

217

* * *

"As the joke goes," Hagger said, "I've got some bad news and I've got some good news." He gestured with his head toward one of the "missionaries" who had come down with him on the plane. "Montgomery—give them a briefing."

Montgomery was not much more than a kid, skinny with wispy red hair, freckles splattered over his face as if he had unwittingly walked past the business end of a farting cow on a bran diet. He was wearing razor-pressed khakis and a sport shirt. Montgomery reeked faintly of ivy and clambakes.

Montgomery confirmed the impression in his first sentence with a precise, elongated Harvard accent. "Eight days ago, on the sixth, our station in Key West transmitted a message to Maroto, telling him that he was to clear out a landing site on the southern lip of Pico Turquino and expect two aircraft to land there between the nights of the fifteenth and sixteenth. We gave him all the details he'd need and requested confirmation. About fifty minutes later, he transmitted back a coded reply, confirming that he could handle it and asking for a list of various supplies to be flown in. We acknowledged and he signed off."

He shoved his hands in the pockets of his trousers as if checking to see that his balls were still in place.

"Both Maroto and our station were using a book code—*Los De Abajo* by Mariano Azuela, first paperback edition published by the Fondo De Cultura Económica in Mexico." He said it as if he had revealed the living gospel.

Hagger interrupted. "This particular book code, I want to emphasize, is less than three months old." He nodded to Montgomery again.

"Then on the eighth," Montgomery continued, "we started to receive this hash on Maroto's frequency—something like a heavy static. It fades in and out, but it's always there. Maroto has a battery-powered transmitter which is OK for field use, but it's not that powerful and the receiver is pretty minimal. We've analyzed the hash and we're damn sure that Maroto can't read what we're sending and we can't get much of what he's putting out—just little snatches but the same thing, over and over again."

"This hash as you call it," Porto interrupted, "is man-made?"

Montgomery smiled sardonically, as if the question were asinine. "Of course it's man-made. Pure and simple, we think Maroto's being jammed."

There was a silence in the room. Brocassie felt as if the temperature had climbed ten degrees. "Can you pinpoint the origin of the station?"

Montgomery nodded, as if he were pleased to be the bearer of bad news. "Santiago, plus or minus ten miles. It's a DGI operation."

Hagger stood up, pulled a paper from his attaché case and thumbtacked it to the wall. It was a message form, photo-graphically blown up to many times its normal size. "OK," Hagger said, "that was the bad news, but this is the good news." He pointed a stubby finger at the message form. "Like Montgomery says, the static is heavy, but he still has been re-ceiving a message—the same thing repeated over and over in Morse code, specifically, seven times in two days. Montgom-ery and his scout troop have electronically dug out as many letters from each transmission as possible and then overlaid them to get a complete message. This is it."

Following message received seven times over during period October 9th to 12th. Each word verified at least three times. Message text formerly valid book code Mike Oscar which was abandoned on schedule, December 1960, replaced by book code Mike Papa and ultimately by present valid book code Mike Quebec.

Felix Montgomery, cryptographer,
Communications Services Division, JM WAVE (signa-ture)

Text reads:

FMCBR:
CURRENT WORKING CODE BELIEVED TO BE COMPROMISED
DUE TO CAPTURE OF ERNESTO FRÍAS AND TWO OTHER MEN

ON RAID INTO PALMA SORIANO STOP   FRÍAS HAD WORKED AS ENCODER FOR ME AND KNEW BOOK WHICH IS BASIS OF CURRENT CODE STOP   FEEL IT BEST TO SUBSTITUTE EDITION CODE MIKE OSCAR FOR PRESENT UNTIL NEW CODE EDITION SUPPLIED.

FRÍAS ALSO KNEW DROP ZONE LOCATION STOP   FOR THIS REASON ESSENTIAL TO RELOCATE DROP ZONE TO LOCATION SOLARIO BETWEEN OCTOBER THREE AND FIVE STOP   CONFIRM ON FOUR ONE TWO FIVE KILOHERTZ USING THIS CODE TWO DAYS PRIOR TO COMMENCEMENT OF OPERATION STOP   SIGNATURE MAROTO STOP   END TRANSMISSION

Brocassie reread the message form twice and then turned to Hagger. Hagger peered back, his expression innocent of judgment. "What do you think?" Hagger asked.

"Solario is an abandoned banana plantation that both Maroto and Fabricio used back in the late part of 1960. It's OK for parachuted airdrops but you'd never get an aircraft in there." He glanced over at Porto. "You know the place?"

Porto nodded. "Yeah—so did Ché Guevara. He used it even before that as a munitions dump when he was fighting Batista. It's boxed in by cliffs on one side and mangrove swamps on the other. I wouldn't go near that place with a ten-mile pole."

"Another thing," Brocassie continued. "Maroto is educated, and his English is good but not that good. The wording of the message is too damn perfect. I doubt like hell he'd use words such as 'essential' and 'commencement of operation.' "

Hagger scratched at an insect bite, succeeding only in drawing blood. He looked at the smear on his hand and then wiped it off on his pants. "OK, I'll accept what you say, Brocassie." He turned toward Porto who was leaning against the wall, drinking a Red Stripe beer. "What's your two cents' worth?"

"There's only one explanation," Porto answered, his voice brittle. "The DGI sent this, hoping that we'd think it was from Maroto. Which means that they know we're coming." He gulped the remainder of a beer and threw the empty in a wastebasket. "Some bastard gave them the old book code and you can bet your ass that the FAR is cleaning up its antiair-craft guns right now."

Hagger nodded slowly, like a mechanical penguin. He rolled a pencil back and forth between his palms, not saying anything, letting the tension build. Finally, he looked up at Porto, his eyes hooded. "Does it occur to either of you that this is about the best thing that could have happened?" Porto started to say something but Hagger raised his hand, fending off the question, pushing on with his explanation. "So, all right—the DGI got an old code, but based on these faked messages they obviously don't know how or where or when you guys are flying in. They're fishing, trying to get some sort of response out of us. I think that the current working code is secure—otherwise, why would the DGI try to fake us out with an out-of-date code? Maroto had already confirmed the time and place of the flight in. Let's stick with that, even if we can't communicate with him. Actually, the bad news is good news. You'll fly in on the night of the sixteenth as originally planned."

Something was whispering in Brocassie's mind, very softly but insistently. He read the message again, trying to jog his memory loose. Porto was already out of his chair, heading for the door, and Hagger was beginning to pull the tacks out of the blown-up message form.

"Hang on, Hagger," he snapped. "Those first five letters—what do they mean?"

Hagger paused, his expression blank, and then turned to Montgomery. "Felix—answer the man's question."

Montgomery was mopping his face with a handkerchief and he seemed irritated. "The first five letters are what we call 'the identifier-verifier.'"

It was coming back to him now. Fabricio had mentioned it only once, but Brocassie suspected that the procedures would be the same for all the operatives in Cuba. Brocassie stood up, and traced his finger under the first in the group of letters. "This letter stands for the book title and edition to be used, right?"

Montgomery nodded.

"Second letter." Brocassie pointed to the *M*. "This identifies Maroto as the message originator, correct?"

Another nod. Hagger had gone rigid, watching them.

"Third letter. Something to do with subtracting or adding a specific number to all other numbers in the body of the coded format."

"We're getting into 'need to know' information, *sir*. The idea of the identifier-verifier is to ensure that only the originator and the recipient of the message can verify the message's authenticity. We know damn well that radio operators sometimes do the encoding, even though they're not supposed to. But only someone like Maroto or Fabricio are given specific instructions as to how the first five letters which precede the main body of the message are arrived at."

Hagger was beginning to get restless. He clicked open and closed the latches on his attaché case, repeating the action again and again. "Like Felix says, Brocassie, the first five letters don't concern you. The message is a fake anyway."

It was suddenly there in his mind, fully crystallized. He wanted to walk out, not to know, but his mind wouldn't let it rest. "The last two letters," he said. "They're the code initials of the operator. How can something like that help authenticate the message?"

Montgomery looked at Hagger for direction. There were now stains of sweat darkening the armpits of his shirt.

"Tell him," Hagger said flatly. "It doesn't matter."

Montgomery sucked on his lip for a second and shrugged. "The last two letters *are* the code initials of the operator who actually transmits the message. Each operator has a certain identifiable swing in the way that he transmits Morse code. It's called 'the fist.' To the experienced ear, the 'fist' of an operator is as identifiable as a signature or the sound of a voice. We keep code tapes of all the radio operators in the Caribbean section so that we can compare the 'fist' of the radio operator who sends the message with the initials that the message originator inserted in the first five-letter grouping."

"Would the radio operator necessarily know this?"

Montgomery shook his head. "Normally not; at least he or she shouldn't be given that information but it's possible. At any rate, if the 'fist' of the operator matches the code name of the operator in the verifier-identifier, we have a completely independent means of authenticating the transmission."

"Who was the operator then, and did the code tapes match up with the 'fist'?"

Hagger and Montgomery again exchanged glances. "No," Hagger finally responded. "They didn't match up. Like I said, the message is a fake." He tore down the blowup and stuffed it in his briefcase.

Hagger locked the hasps of his attaché case—little mechanical clicks which signaled the finality of the briefing. "Chowtime, Brocassie," he said, exhibiting a floorwalker's smile. "We brought down corn-fed Kansas steaks. Two inches thick. Paid for by our grateful and trusting taxpayers." He dropped his shoulders, as if he had been tense and was now only beginning to relax. He placed his hand on Brocassie's arm, guiding him toward the door.

"Tell Montgomery to get the hell out of here," Brocassie said. "We're not finished, Hagger."

Hagger dropped his hand, stood back, lips compressed. He thought about it and then nodded to Montgomery. "Outside; you too, Porto," he said, motioning with his head.

Brocassie let Montgomery slide past him and he didn't move, wouldn't move, so that the red-haired bastard had to slip sideways to avoid body contact. Brocassie latched the screen door, pulled the wooden door closed and locked it. With no air circulating, the temperature inside the shack seemed to soar.

Hagger was on the defensive now, behind the table, the attaché case in a hammerlock underneath his arm. "What do you want?" he said, his voice tight.

"Who was 'BR,' Hagger?"

"That's classified."

He shot out a hand, gripping Hagger's shirtfront, pulling him across the table. Hagger gasped, stumbling, the briefcase clattering to the floor.

"Get your hands off me!" he hissed. His breath smelled of peppermints and fear.

Brocassie tightened his grip, twisting the shirt into a knot, choking off Hagger's windpipe. A button popped, dropping to the table, rolling and then falling to the floor. In the enclosed space, the sound of it was enormous. Brocassie pulled Hagger closer.

"WHO?" he shouted, his spittle spattering Hagger's face.

Hagger's skin was livid, going purple, the sweat and spit combined into a sheen of greasy slickness.

"Babe Ruth," Hagger gasped, his hand pawing at Brocassie's body.

"AND WHO THE FUCK IS 'BABE RUTH'?"

Shaking his head violently, his eyes fixed on Brocassie's, Hagger clenched his teeth as if to keep from speaking. Brocassie rammed his arm forward, hurling Hagger against the wall. Hagger's breath exploded and he slumped, his feet skidding on the wooden planks, his hands clawing for support. His fingers caught the edge of the table, but instead of supporting him, he pulled it over on top of his body, the blow of the impact on his rib cage causing him to grunt.

There was a rap on the door, polite at first and then louder, insistent, and he could hear Montgomery outside, shouting for help.

Picking up the briefcase, Brocassie unlocked the hasps. From the corner of his eye, he saw Hagger's hand move, and by reflex he stomped his boot down on Hagger's hand. A .45 Colt went spinning across the planks and Hagger stared up at him, his eyes wide with terror, his mouth working but no sound coming out.

Brocassie scooped up the .45 and worked the slide. He centered Hagger's forehead in the notches of the gunsight. "Call Montgomery off," he said, zeroing in on Hagger's forehead.

The mouth continued to work but no sound came out of it.

He pushed the automatic into Hagger's gut, his finger involuntarily beginning to tighten. *"Call off your preppie asshole dog, Hagger. NOW!"* he whispered.

Hagger's eyes were saucers, the whites really a dull yellow, like rancid fat. "Get away, Montgomery!" he shouted, his voice strained into a falsetto pitch. There was some muttering outside the door, footsteps, another voice questioning, the knob of the door rattling against the lock and then silence.

Both of them were panting, listening, their eyes locked on each other. Brocassie moved the barrel lower, into Hagger's crotch. "If I pull the trigger, Max, you won't die," he whispered. "But you'll wish you did." He shoved the barrel of the gun hard into the yielding mass of flesh. "Tell me, Max, who's 'Babe Ruth'?"

Hagger surrendered. Brocassie could see it in the dilation of Hagger's pupils.

"Alicia Ruth Helvia. It doesn't mean anything, Brocassie," he said, his voice rising in pitch.

"You knew this, didn't you, Max? But you didn't want me to know because you were sure that I'd kiss that double-dealing little bitch off and that would be the end of your project in the Sierra, right?"

Hagger slowly relaxed, his body settling against the wall, all the fight gone out of him.

"Yes," he breathed, his voice just a whisper. "But how could I be sure, or for that matter, how could you be sure that it was she who gave the DGI the code and the identifier? Maroto has had six different radio operators over four years, three of them dead from air attacks, one from a pulmonary infection and the other two captured or missing. The DGI isn't stupid. They probably don't know what initials matched which operator, so they guessed, based on previous transmissions. It was coincidence, you fuckhead." His hand shaking, he pushed the automatic aside and pulled himself to his feet. In the heat and humidity of the room, he seemed to be tottering, a beaten, unstable old man.

For a long time they stared at each other, and then Hagger moved past him. "You're a poor, dumb fart, Brocassie. There's one hell of a lot more here at stake than the satisfaction of your fucking ego. If you can't stand the heat, get the hell out of the kitchen."

He lay on the red dirt of Jamaica, his head pillowed by his hands, trying to feel vibrations from the earth. There were subterranean messages there, flowing deep beneath the surface, but he could hear only the shrills of foreign tongues, babbling in pain or fear or softly mumbling repetitive chants. He strained harder, trying to shut out the sounds of the night and the jumble of other voices, listening only for her voice but it wasn't there.

Why did you try to do this to me? he whispered, his lips brushing the soil. Wasn't it enough just to be silent and passive and let something die that I thought was already dead? What is it that you want?

He listened one final time for her voice but there was nothing except the sound of his own breathing. He rolled over onto his back, exhausted, and closed his eyes, giving himself over to the night.

Porto settled down in the grass next to him, leaned back, supported by his arms, and looked up at the sky. "It's something that always staggers me," he said, his voice barely audible. "The sky. Transparent and weightless, nothing you could ever feel or touch, but it supports a bird or an insect or a plane in flight. I never really understood the goddamned physics of it and I guess I don't have to." He lit a cigarette and flicked the match away into the darkness. "You finally cured your fear of it, didn't you?"

Brocassie nodded in the darkness. "Almost. Not all of it. There was still fear but the thing that you're talking about overbalanced it."

"Only autopilots don't brown their skivvies, Brocassie. Any pilot who never admitted fear to himself is a real dipshit, and he's preordained to bore a big, smoking hole in the ground." He squashed the freshly lit cigarette into the grass, the gesture very slow and deliberate. "So it's over for you, isn't it?"

Brocassie could feel the bile in his throat and bitterness in his guts. "Yep, it's quitting time. For me, at least." He rolled over, sucking on a blade of grass, looking north toward Cuba, ninety miles over the horizon. "You'll find another sucker."

"No time left, Brocassie, and like I said before, we go in together or not at all. I could have used the money, but there's always crop-dusting rice in Mississippi and the orchards farther north in the late summer. Who knows—maybe Hagger will come up with another job for me to pillow my Social Security with. I'll get by, pal."

Something shrieked in the bush—an animal, probably—

and the silence that followed was more intense than the sound itself. Somehow, Brocassie felt that it was the same between Porto and him—the silences were more devastating than the words.

Long minutes lapsed, neither of them speaking, and then Porto broke the silence. "Hagger told me a little about her, Brocassie. Don't get pissed. I just want to understand—to hear it from you, the way it really was."

He lay on the ground, the earth damp beneath him, the scent of the endless, tropical summer, honey sweet in his nostrils. Sweet Jesus, he wanted to get out of it, to leave Cuba and her behind. He had never talked about her very much, even to Miller, but somehow he owed it to Porto although he couldn't rationalize any reason for believing that.

He started, reluctantly at first, scratching for words, because he had never said aloud before the things that he had felt about her. And about Álvarez, for he was somehow part of the whole. He held nothing back, saying exactly what he had felt, what he felt now, and he was grateful that it was dark and neither of them could see the other's face.

It took over an hour of rambling, disjointed recollection, but as he talked, he realized that there was someone else within him, detached, carefully analyzing everything he said, drawing a conclusion that wasn't obvious. He tried to ignore that voice but it was speaking in a soft but insistent tone, saying words that he was not yet, not ever, willing to hear.

When he finished, Porto kept silent for a long time, balling blades of grass between his palms, rolling them into lumps and throwing them against the backdrop of the night sky.

"You don't believe she betrayed you, any more than I do. And what did you think you'd accomplish in the first place? Ride your pinto pony into the enemy camp and snatch her up into your saddle?"

"Something like that. I had to talk to her, to understand what happened, why it turned out the way that it did. You don't give up easily on the only thing that ever made sense in your life, do you?"

"What about Álvarez?"

The question repeated itself in his mind. What about Álvarez? "I don't know," he finally answered. "What can you

227

say about someone you both love and hate. He's my brother. I guess ..." He hesitated. "I think I just wanted to say 'good-bye,' for whatever that would have been worth. I don't hold anything against him personally. Just that we made different choices."

Porto sat up, turned and faced him. "You're too close to it, Brocassie. You're swamped with personal stuff and you can't see the forest for the bears. Neither can Hagger. He believes in something else, some fucking vision of patriotism or justice or global strategy or Christ knows what, but it's fogged his glasses."

"You're trying to convince me that we should still go in!"

"Huh-uh. Forget that. The Aztec's flying back to Miami tomorrow morning and if you want a seat on it, neither Hagger nor I will stop you, but I want you to understand what happened—or at least my version of what happened. You willing?"

"Not willing, Porto, but listening," he finally answered.

"The message is a phony—we both know that. And I checked with Montgomery, perhaps twisted his arm would be a better way of expressing it. The book that the phony message was coded from was *Guerra Del Tiempo,* the book that Maroto used when Alicia worked as his radio operator. Anytime there was a change of the radio operator, a new code book was substituted. When she was captured, Maroto changed the book code as per operating procedure. My guess is that the DGI was able to originate this message because she either gave the information to Álvarez or it was forced out of her."

"It's possible." More than possible, he realized.

"Suppose," Porto continued, "that Alicia was forced into revealing the code. How or why, I haven't the slightest, but the evidence indicates that she did. But why in hell would she insert her own initials in the identifier group?" He let the question hang like a perfectly formed fruit, ripening in the sun before the harvest, allowing it to mature before it was ready for picking.

Brocassie hesitated and then tentatively reached to pluck it. "She might not have known the purpose of the identifier," he answered, doubt now in his mind.

"Doesn't hold up," Porto threw back at him. "The first

three letters were correct. And for that reason, I think she knew how the identifier group worked. It's one thing for Montgomery to believe that things work according to the book in a field operation, but I think that Maroto would have told her the whole thing if he trusted her, which I'm sure he did. *She knew!* And she used that knowledge. In my very humble opinion, she bullshitted the DGI as to the meaning of the last two letters."

He inhaled slowly, filling his lungs, and then released his breath slowly, trying to think. "Strange, then, isn't it, that her message would be designed to suck us into a trap?"

Porto was up and pacing now, lurching back and forth in the darkness. "You're as blind as Hagger, Brocassie. Forget about the text of the message. Álvarez or some other dumb shitcake drafted it. That's obvious because it's not Maroto's kind of language and the Solario location isn't suitable for a landing site. It's a crude attempt. But the point is that they had to rely on her for the identifier. The only thing that they didn't know was that her code-name initials were embedded in the format. *That* was the message, asshole? She was trying to warn you, Brocassie!"

Christ, if you're right, he thought, it would change everything, but if you're wrong . . . He knew that he couldn't deal with it while Porto hovered over him, waiting for his reaction.

Brocassie stood up. "Wait here for me," he said and then walked away into the blackness.

He wandered through the night for a long time, down rows of coffee beans, inhaling the rich smell, stopping sometimes to take a leaf and crush it between his fingers and to taste the fragrance. Hagger's idea? he wondered. Would he be desperate enough to stoop to it, and would Porto stoop further? It was something he had to know.

But the rest of it made sense in some jigsaw puzzle way and yet it didn't. He stopped once and took the ring in his hand, closing his fist around it. It was like dry ice or molten metal. But he couldn't tell which.

He came up behind Porto, silently. He put his hand on Porto's shoulder and turned him so that they were face-to-face, their eyes only inches apart. "Was this your idea or Hagger's?"

Porto delayed, staring back, unblinking. "Mine. Only mine, Injun. I told you what I think."

"Will Hagger still let me go in?"

Porto nodded. "If he doesn't, he's an idiot. Too much is on the line, Brocassie, for him to back out."

"Then I'll go. You tell him that."

"Then you believe . . . ?"

He shook his head. "I can't take anything on faith anymore. I just have to find out for myself."

CHAPTER

10

Oriente Province, Cuba,
October 15, 1962

It had drizzled all through the afternoon and into the evening, but now it had stopped, just as forecast, leaving behind a heavy ground fog which softened the hard shapes of the switchyard south of Bayamo.

Álvarez stood in the darkened vestibule of a passenger car, watching the outlines of switch towers, maintenance shops and the odd jumble of storage buildings slowly slipping by as the train gathered speed. Beneath his feet, the corrugated platform trembled and swayed and the rhythm of the wheels formed an almost hypnotic counterpoint to the muffled clanging of the locomotive's bell.

This was the third and last trip south to the complex, the final load of Sandal missiles. God, he was tired and still a lot farther to go—south across the plains, the slow ascent to Guisa and then the final, tedious crawl up to the box canyon which lay in the shadows of the Sierra Maestra. It would be nearly dawn before they would be within the security of the underground sidings of the Calvario Complex.

Seven days since he had conned her into revealing the book code and so far it had gone well. Just as he had anticipated, Alicia had bussed into Santiago and slipped into the side streets of the Old Quarter, easily losing the two women who were tailing her. He had been only vaguely worried, but that worry grew to concern and then to panic as the day progressed and no sighting had been made by the eight other DGI personnel who had staked out the library and the various bookstores throughout Santiago and its suburbs. Then, shortly after three, she surfaced at the central library of the Universidad de Oriente. Álvarez had positioned two young DGI secretaries there, both dressed as students, with instructions to observe what sections of the card file she used or what numbered aisles she entered. Alicia had browsed through numerous sections of the fictional aisles, pulling books out at random and reinserting them. Finally, when the closing bell had rung, she had hung back, waiting for the cavernous hall to empty, and at the last minute, had rapidly run down the alleyway between the *A*'s and *C*'s and plucked a volume from a lower shelf and shoved it into her leather bag. The DGI secretary nearest her couldn't identify exactly which shelf but the search had been narrowed from over three million books to less than eleven hundred.

Instead of reopening at seven, the library had been closed "for repairs." Three men Roychenko had flown in from Havana had compared, shelf by shelf, bookcase by bookcase, those volumes which were missing with the file cards of books properly checked out. In the end, they narrowed the search to eighteen stolen or missing books. Álvarez had telephoned DGI Havana with the list of titles and by the following morning, copies of them were stacked on his desk.

Alicia had returned to the *finca* by late evening as promised, the message to Brocassie encoded. He had taken it and the clear text message to the complex and turned it over to Roychenko's men and within three hours, they had broken the code.

The jamming of Maroto's frequency had already been started. Now, with the code drawn from the pages of *Guerra*

Del Tiempo by Alejo Carpentier, they slowly fabricated a counterfeit message from Maroto to Hagger. By that evening, the message was being transmitted, over and over again, as if Maroto were trying to get through the jamming. Roychenko had slapped him on the back, beaming. "General Lazarev will be more than pleased," he had said. Still, Álvarez worried about the identifier but he withheld his doubts from Roychenko. In three or four days, they would know if an assault team would make the attempt.

Álvarez doubted that Alicia would ever understand that in betraying her, he had saved her, eliminated Piedra's threat, made her future safe and his own secure.

He looked out into the night again, savoring the smell of wet earth and mahogany. What I wouldn't give for some sleep before the train grinds up through the pass near Guisa, he thought. The Segundo Frente would pick a place like that to attack if they knew what was on this train.

He pulled his hand through his hair, weary, two days now without more than a few short naps. But so far, it had gone well. Roychenko had pulled out all the stops, badgering Fidel with protestations, threats and love notes from the Soviet embassy in Havana, to provide anything Álvarez required to make the shipment more secure. Thirty Sandal intermediate-range ballistic missiles in packing cases (marked "agricultural equipment"—misspelled in Spanish), two to a flatcar, were the main load, but inserted between each flatcar was a steel-sided coal car, manned by regular Cuban Army FAR troops, armed with quad-ZSU 23mm aircraft cannon, their muzzles depressed so that they could sweep either side of the tracks. Álvarez had requisitioned eight passenger cars and filled them with DGI troops, pulled in from other provinces, armed and ready to go should they be required to fight off a determined guerrilla attack. But the security risk that worried Álvarez most was the four cars which Roychenko had inserted into the middle of the train. Two of them were passenger cars, filled with men armed with automatic weapons, wearing Cuban fatigues but with no unit flashes or badges of rank. The men were entirely Slavic, most of them blue-eyed Russians. "Elite KGB detachment," Roychenko had commented, "called the 'Hard Ones.'" Álvarez had looked into the expressionless faces of these men as they boarded the train and he decided that the name was apt.

Sandwiched between the KGB cars were two steel-shuttered boxcars. Álvarez had seen them unloaded from the *Omsk* in special cargo slings, the security so tight that even the floodlights had been turned off. They had not been on the list of cargo. Roychenko answered his questions with a terse statement. "There are nuclear warheads in those two boxcars, each of them yielding over a megaton."

Álvarez had looked back at the dangling boxcar, swaying in the beams of a dozen shielded flashlights, his extremities going cold. The boxcar was lowered gently to the switching track, Soviet crewmen maneuvering it onto the track until it settled, secure for the time being. He found that he had been holding his breath.

So ends the fairy tale, he thought, about design errors in missile assembly buildings, and last-minute arrangements to ship sixty missiles on an eight-hundred-mile round trip, simply for the stated purpose of checking them out. It was too convenient that the Calvario Complex could substitute as the maintenance facility. But he knew that Fidel would buy it because he wanted those missiles—saw them as the ultimate phallic replacement symbol of a revolution which had suffered from a premature orgasm and now was going limp. Very simply, Fidel would buy whatever the Soviets told him because he had to.

Álvarez leaned back against the wall of the vestibule, the vibrations of the car making his brain hum. Like a horse, he thought, I could sleep on my feet. Just thirty minutes would be enough. Alicia would be near waking now, the musk smell of her body blending with the scent of the earth, carried on the dawn wind through her opened bedroom windows. He loved those few moments, between sleep and waking, when he could reach out and touch her warm flesh and pull her close, and like a cat, she would curl against the contours of his body. He shook himself awake and moved to the opening, looking out into the night, willing the rush of air to keep him alert.

He sensed rather than heard someone behind him.

"That is a dangerous place to stand," Piedra said. "Very

hazardous in the darkness, one could fall and be crushed under the wheels." He brushed past Julio to the opening, one hand lightly on the iron grab rail, leaned out and thrust his head into the rushing night.

You silly bastard, Julio thought, smiling. You think I'm terrified of your knowledge about Alicia's past, that you can shove without being pushed back, like a little child who has witnessed a dirty act by his older brother and then starts to test the limits of blackmail. He relaxed, standing with his back against the vibrating steel bulkhead of the vestibule. You'll lead a sweep of the Sierra for counterrevolutionaries, Piedra, he thought. With the most incompetent patrol that I can put together. Maroto will kill you for me, with a mortar round or a high-velocity bullet. Like having a paid assassin without having to pay.

"Give me a report, Sergio," he said.

Piedra pivoted back into the vestibule, snapped on a penlight and read down the paper which was clamped on his clipboard.

"Only a few problems. Of sixty-two men, fifty-nine were awake and on station. These two," he flashed his light on two names of DGI men that Álvarez did not immediately associate with faces, "are on report. I suggest sixty days hard labor."

Álvarez pulled the sheet from the clipboard, wadded it into a ball and threw it out into the night. "You're an ass, Piedra. Those men haven't had any sleep in two days. Since Mariel, they've been standing guard at the sidings during the daylight and then standing guard at night when we're moving."

"They're scum," Piedra objected. "Uneducated peasants who don't know the meaning of duty."

"And what are you, Sergio? Something better? Officers lead, they don't drive their troops like cattle."

There was an audible hiss as Piedra sucked in air between clenched teeth. "Because you obtained the code does not mean this business between us is over, *Comandante*. There is still the future of your little *puta* to consider."

Álvarez tried to force a laugh but it caught in his throat, his anger building. "Fidel knows about her—has known for over a year. As obviously does Roychenko. Who else are you going to carry your tales to?"

Piedra took a step backward, off guard, stunned for a moment, and then said, "If the facts were discreetly placed before a People's Tribunal, Fidel would not interfere, would he? An American who poses as a Cuban, placed so highly in the DGI, harboring a convicted counterrevolutionary? Perhaps that puts another light on the matter?"

Julio felt his stomach contract, sweat suddenly flushing his neck despite the coolness of the night. The little prick had it all doped out and it was a course of action that he hadn't even thought that Piedra would have the balls to attempt. And he was probably right. Fidel wouldn't, couldn't, protect him in an open inquiry. Álvarez knew that, like anyone else, he was politically expendable. Without even thinking, he stepped sideways, blocking Sergio's path to the interior door of the car and then moved forward toward Sergio, pushing him backward toward the opening.

Caught off guard, Sergio stumbled but regained his balance, grabbing the rail with one hand, his other clawing at the flap of his holster.

"Stay back, Álvarez!" he bellowed. The Lastoy automatic was out, a black mass of oiled metal in Piedra's hand. "Those papers I took from your safe"—he thumbed back the hammer and his voice gained confidence—"those papers are in the hands of a friend. He knows what to do with them if I were—if something happened."

The lines were straight out of a Cagney movie. The idiocy of the situation somehow insanely mixed with fatigue and he involuntarily found himself laughing. "You . . ." He was unable to get the words out.

"What's so damn funny!" Piedra was furious.

"You're a whore, pretending to be a madam," Álvarez wheezed, barely under control. "You think that you can sell favors without really getting your crotch wet or the sheets dirty, but someday, Piedra, you're going to get fucked by an expert—me. *Hasta el entronque,* understand?" He backed to the compartment door and opened it, his eyes still on Piedra's. "One other thing," he said. "When you draw a Lastoy, *Captain,* be sure to work the slide so that you chamber a round."

The hammer of the Lastoy fell on an empty chamber, the sound distinct even in the noisy vestibule.

Álvarez felt his heart thudding, the moment crystallized forever in his memory. "That was a mistake, Piedra," he said softly. "You'll breathe for a while but you're a dead man."

He drank rum from a flask and pulled on his last cigar as the train rumbled through the coffee plantation, now only a half a mile from the tunnel entrance into the complex. Just after daybreak, the valley was still in shadow, but the peaks of the Sierra glinted in the morning sun. He looked up to the south where the Sierra Maestra climbed more than five thousand feet into an overhanging rock fortress, jagged battlements protruding from the flanks of the massif, alternating with rivers of scree and eroded ravines. It was the ultimate guerrilla territory, suitable once for Fidel's revolution, and now a refuge for Maroto's group. The terrain, not having a political conscience, was still just as effective a barrier. He knew, from personal experience, that one man with a telescopically sighted rifle could hold off a patrol of twenty men almost indefinitely. And that it was terrain that Brocassie, if he came . . . No, he thought, correcting himself, when he came . . . would use to maximum advantage. He looked up the slope of the mountain, his eyes traversing higher toward the peaks. The dumb bastard. He didn't want to see Brocassie killed, but he also knew that it wouldn't, couldn't, be any other way.

The train was slowing, couplings clanging together, air brakes hissing. This was the changeover point, where all the DGI troops would stagger off, only the KGB Hard Ones remaining for the last quarter mile of track which descended into the depths of the complex.

The complex had been beautifully engineered, almost undetectable from the air. The coffee plantation had been selected as the entrance to the Calvario Complex because of the large stands of mahogany trees on its northern border. From there, the land led uphill over a quarter mile onto a plain. By tunneling into the side of the upsloping hill, the Russian engineers had created a vast underground complex, layered in four levels with branches leading out to service the silos.

The complex was shaped like a cross. "The Cross at Calvary," Roychenko had named it, tracing his finger along the blueprint. He had turned to Álvarez, a look of amusement on his face. "Something, I think, to crucify the Americans with, once our nails are ready to drive. And just think, Julio—we won't even make them carry it on their backs." For Álvarez, the metaphor had been too close to the bone. For if there was a crucifixion, who then was the Judas except himself?

Behind him, there was a rap on the glass window and Lieutenant Méndez slid open the compartment door, saluted and handed Álvarez a sheath of papers.

"All accounted for," he reported, dropping his hand. His eyes were red from lack of sleep, and his face showed a stubble of two days, but he was smiling. A good man, Álvarez thought. Unlike Piedra who had sat through the Revolution, safe in a Havana lawyer's office, Méndez had fought for three long years in the Escambray with Ché. He still had the pitted scars of tropical infections which never quite healed, and two front teeth were broken at their roots, but he was a soldier's soldier.

Álvarez scribbled his signature. "OK, Méndez. Get the men off. Have them set up tents in the plantation near the river, but keep them under the trees during daylight, understand?"

Méndez nodded. "When will they be returned to their units?"

He offered Méndez his flask of rum. Méndez sniffed and took a couple of polite swallows. "They're not going back—not yet," Álvarez said, suppressing a yawn. "Give them two days of rest, no duties except general cleanup. Send a truck down to Santiago for beer and a couple hundred chickens, beef, fresh bread and vegetables."

Méndez handed back the flask, hesitated, as if waiting to be dismissed, and then paused, broken teeth exposed in a hesitant smile. "The men will want to know when they are returning to their units."

"Not for a while," Álvarez said. "They're going to get some good mountain air in a few days. Hunting wild game, Méndez."

The lieutenant raised his eyebrows. "What kind of wild game, *Comandante?*"

"A variety of American pig," Álvarez replied.

* * *

An easterly wind stirred the pants legs of his fatigues, bringing with it the smell of coffee plants, of bougainvillaea, of frangipani, of sweat.

Both sailplanes were positioned on the runway, one behind the other and a little off to the side. Sitting on the single main wheel and tail skid, the starboard wing of his aircraft was tipped over, touching the dirt. Like a tired albatross, he thought, with only one flight left in its aging body.

Brocassie shuffled his feet in impatience, checked his watch and waited. Eighteen after midnight. Porto was making a last-minute check on the weather over Cuba but without having to plot isobars, gradients and pressure systems, Brocassie knew that the weather would be fine. Clear sky and light wind. The rim of the world above the tree line to the east was still dark; moonrise not until after three. He turned and opened the canopy once more to check the lashings in the rear cockpit. Thirty pounds of C-4 plastic explosive, grenades, a miniaturized single side band transmitter, spare batteries and a sleeping bag, all lashed with light nylon line to the cockpit floor. On top of that, concentrated rations for ten days, an M-3 machine pistol, a Nikon camera, a 2000mm telephoto lens, polarizing filters and mounting tripod for the folded optics telescope that Porto carried in his ship. Other stuff—mountain tent, knife, survival gear, spare socks, lightweight binoculars—all contained under a protective netting which was tied down to the wooden ribs and longerons of the aircraft. He had weighed it all: 261 pounds.

Brocassie shivered, not from the night but from—what was it? Fear, anticipation, what? He dug his hands into his fatigues and pulled out a chocolate bar, stripped off the foil and ate the semisweet in two bites. He wanted a cigarette or a cup of coffee, just to have something for his hands to do—so he fiddled.

Plucking at the straps, he readjusted the shoulder harness which held the Colt snub nose. Felt in his fatigue pockets again for spare cartridges, inflight candy bars, sheath knife and phony Cuban papers. For the third time.

He kept turning his mind away from the thing which had plagued him since Hagger's briefing. Why and to whom had she given away the code? And was it to lure him into Cuba or to warn him off? Was there something even more subtle buried in the message? He had gone over and over the message, looking for a clue but not finding it. And Álvarez? What role was he playing? Had he forced her to give him the code or had there been some sort of quid pro quo? He squeezed his fist, the nails biting into flesh. *Damn.* He felt like an animal being whipped, too stupid to understand why, if there was a reason.

Gravel crunched behind him. Porto's voice. "You have a tight sphincter?"

"I've got a cork jammed in, if that's what you're asking."

Porto snorted. "So who doesn't?" Peeling back the sleeve of his jacket, Porto checked the time on the luminescent hands of his watch. "A few minutes left," he said casually, as if they were both waiting for a train to roll in. He sighed. "Look, Brocassie. You're good enough to make this flight if it can be made, but before we go, I want you to understand how thin our chances are. If I had any sense, I'd tell Hagger to stick it up his ass, I'd go back to Alabama and do something sane like spray fields of carrots or become a world-class alcoholic." He kicked at the dirt with his heel, making a small depression, and then reshuffled the loose earth with the side of his boots, stamping it back in place.

"What are you trying to say?"

"I didn't tell you this, Brocassie," Porto answered after a long time, his voice soft, "but it's important to me that you understand why in hell I got involved. I flew for Cubana Air in the early fifties but got canned for drinking too much. Nothing spectacular but sometimes when I showed up, all the plants in the operations shack would wilt. The management was good enough not to put it on my record." He looked down at the dirt and then up at the sky, as if he were trying to find words. "Then in fifty-seven, I had a sweet job flying twins in a little commuter airline in Georgia which was expanding like wildfire. Good bucks—not great—but enough to keep me going and then some. And the prospects looked good. But I pranged in a plane and busted up my head. Nothing serious but they sent me to a quack for an examination. The physician's accident report showed that I had been drinking and that was it. The Feds pulled my license." He grunted, something between pain and a laugh. "You understand, Brocassie, that three or four beers before noon ain't nothin' to a good ole boy like me, but they didn't see it that way. I got a call from an old friend just after they canned me and that was how I met Hagger.

"Hagger didn't care about licenses. He wanted pilots to fly crap into Cuba, three thousand bucks a round trip, as many as you could make. In those days, it was easy—a piece of cake."

Brocassie filled his lungs, then expelled it in a long, slow breath. He waited, silent.

"In February of sixty," Porto continued, "I flew in a load of food and munitions to the Uvero strip, a chicken scratch in the hills west of Santiago. It was a night landing and I ground-looped—busted up the prop and the landing gear. Cardona, who was then the agency's favorite counterrevolutionary, arranged for me to hide out with some relative of his in Santiago until the next flight in could take me back to Florida. So I stayed with this widow lady and her kid. It was funny, Brocassie. I've drifted all my life and with a face that has the appeal of a stale pork chop; I've never been able to wow the ladies, but this woman didn't give a shit. She found something worthwhile in me that I didn't know I had." He rubbed his hands together, as if he were cold, but Brocassie understood the toll that it was taking on Porto—stripping away his tough hide, showing the softness beneath.

"So you're going in just to bring her back out?"

"She's dead," Porto said flatly. "Less than a couple of hours after I snaked back out of Cuba, she was picked up by the DGI and that was the end of it. Your buddy Álvarez's people. She was found in a field, a hood over her head, her body beaten into a pulp. An example, understand, of what happens to those who support the counterrevolution." He slammed his fist into his palm, the sound an explosion of pain and anger. *"Christ Almighty!* She took care of me, no questions asked. That was all, Brocassie. She didn't give diddley squat about politics."

An aircraft engine fired, splattering the night with ragged, mechanical clatter. The mechanics would be checking out the towplanes by now; not much time left, he thought. "Then why go back in?"

"The woman had a kid. Just a kid, no more than twelve or so. A tough-skinned little bugger but sweet and soft in the core. He aped my mannerisms, listened absolutely fascinated to my bullshit, even went out and stole cigars for me. The kid called me 'uncle,' Brocassie. Loved me, and although I never told him, I loved me as well—like a son that I'll never have. So this one night, you know what he did? I was bunked out on the floor in the kitchen and the kid came to me and he said, 'My mother is very lonely and she needs you. Please go to her.' That was it—no explanations—and then he trotted off to his bedroom in the attic. I lay there for a long time, just grinding over the old gray matter, trying to figure his reason and then I finally realized—the kid loved us both—enough to share his mother's love with someone else who loved and respected her, even though there was no future for any of us together. Shit, 'Cassie, I cried for the first time in fifteen years and then, finally, I went to her bedroom and you know, the kid had left a whole huge bunch of field flowers in front of her door for me to give her."

"So you're going back in to get him?"

Porto nodded. "The last I could find out, he's in a state-run school on the Siboney road outside of Santiago. That's all I know but I'm going to find him and arrange to get him back out of Cuba. The right palms can still be greased, and for fifteen thousand, a Swiss woman Hagger knows can get him out via Mexico and then to the States. I've got a second cousin in Orlando who can raise him and maybe someday, I can be with the kid. Like taking him duck shooting in the fall and kicking his butt if he doesn't make good grades and all the other silly-assed things parents do. He'll be something—a lot more than me, Brocassie."

He crossed his arms, the set of his body challenging and determined. "And frankly, Brocassie, I want to be with that kid and love him and give him what I never had. So that's what Hagger's money is buying for me."

"And what happens if you don't make it back out of Cuba?" He had an unsettled feeling, deep inside, stronger than a premonition, and he wished that he had said nothing.

"The agency pays another twenty thousand to my beneficiary, Brocassie. So either way, the kid doesn't lose." He pulled his flight jacket up around him and zipped it. "If I don't make it and you do, I'm trusting you to make sure that Hagger coughs up the insurance. I've left my cousin's name and address in an envelope, mailed to general delivery in Provo, Utah, along with Hagger's letter of commitment. It's addressed to you." He sighed, dropping his arms, and looked down the airstrip into the darkness, and then turned back. "There's one other thing, pal. I want to see my old lady's grave. That's part of the schedule, all right?"

Brocassie nodded. Down inside all of us is a complicated mechanism that makes us run, he thought. Makes the gears turn and the escapement tick, but for most of us, it's only the clean, expressionless face that shows. "All right," he finally said. A second engine barked into life, blue flames of exhaust, feathers of fire.

Brocassie put his hands gently on Porto's shoulders. He felt the slightest ripple of tension pass through Porto's body and then nothing, as if he were a rock waiting for a millennium to pass.

The two of them stood there in the night, unmoving, until Brocassie finally dropped his arms. Almost hesitantly, Porto reached over and squeezed Brocassie's hand. "Time to go," Porto finally said. He turned away and headed for his glider.

A tug on the towline and the Slingsby lurched forward a foot or so. He could see the feathery blue of the Helio Courier's exhaust and its dim silhouette against the skyline. He had a down jacket and pants on now, sweating in the heat but knowing that above ten thousand feet it would be his only protection against the penetrating cold.

Altimeter set
Electric gyro set
Nav-com on to 123.5
Controls free
Spoilers locked
Oxygen on 100 percent, diluter demand on automatic

He nodded to himself, touched the straps to his oxygen mask and wiggled the penlight toward the dark form of a man who stood near his wing tip. The man picked up the wing tip so that it was level and, in turn, flashed a light toward the Helio Courier.

Nothing for a second and then another lurch forward, the Helio Courier starting to roll, the sound and wind from its prop blast rolling over him. The man was walking at first, then jogging, then running, keeping the wing tip level until Brocassie had sufficient airspeed to attain aileron control. The man fell away and he was level and rolling, light on the controls, the Slingsby in that little space and time between earthborn and flight. Then he lifted off.

Climbing. Watching the pinpoints of light on the tops of the Courier's wings, his only horizon. No time to check the ground beneath him, the sky, the instruments. Just keep glued on the towplane.

Up. Through eight thousand feet and slowly circling, waiting for Porto's ship and towplane to rendezvous. Second turn and then third. Slews of stars sliding across the canopy and still Brocassie concentrated on the wing lights, waiting.

He went over the checklist, committed to memory, pounded into him over the last three days. Wait until Porto and his towplane joined up at 8000, between 0130 and 35. Then climb, one towplane behind the other, in long, lazy circles to 28,000, still 80 nautical miles south of Cuba. The two towplanes would then join up, flying side by side, allowing Porto and Brocassie to spot each other.

Committed now, like a kid on a sled, thundering down a hill. What Miller had called "the final resolution." In the darkness he whispered her name, willing that, somehow, she would hear him across the miles of sea and blackness . . . and understand why he was going, even if he did not know himself.

Álvarez stood, facing the plotting board, unconsciously rubbing his fingers together to quiet the irritation of waiting. First one, then two blips, had been plotted on the board which portrayed the approaches to Cuba from the south. The blips were presently over the Jamaican north coast but their flight path seemed to be aimless—first east along the coast and then west again, going nowhere.

Roychenko, who had been bent over a desk with a Soviet communications officer, stood up, nodded and then walked back to Álvarez.

"Interesting," he said. "No flight plan on the international teletype and yet Captain Sorge reports that a return from that far a distance would indicate that the two aircraft have to be at over fourteen thousand feet of altitude and presumably still climbing."

"He has some idea of their size?" Álvarez looked back at the plotting board, the two blips swimming in small circles like fish in a garden pond.

Shaking his head, Roychenko sank down into a lounge chair. "Nothing concrete. Their speed and size of return would indicate that they are small, single-engine aircraft—certainly not capable of flying in even a minimally sized assault force." As if he had already decided, he stood up, stretched and motioned toward the corridor. "Let's move down to my private quarters. They'll send some sandwiches and if anything happens, Sorge will ring me."

Roychenko led the way, down the carpeted corridor, past a manned checkpoint to the elevators.

They descended two levels, entering another corridor. Roychenko slipped a card into a slot and the door opened.

The living quarters were sparse but well decorated.

"Home, such as it may be," Roychenko said. He poured two measures of Scotch and gave Álvarez one. "To friends," he said, smiling. They clinked and drank.

Álvarez leaned back against the soft leather, feeling the warmth of the liquor soak into his bloodstream. Roychenko's words echoed in his mind. *To friends.* He finished off the glass and lifted it for a refill. Roychenko raised his eyebrows but filled the bottom third of the glass.

"You should watch your drinking, Julio," he said with just the proper amount of concern—so finely graded that it was just short of condescension.

"I've had four hours sleep in the last three days," Julio snapped back at him. "There are forty-two Sandals in the underground siding and eighteen more in the maintenance bay upstairs, safe and sound. What else do you want?"

Roychenko smiled, raised his glass in a salute and then

sipped. "True," he responded. "You've got to be tired. You need a couple days leave. A few nights with your woman, perhaps." He coughed politely, a cheap imitation of a laugh. "Yes," he said, "some time with your woman. But then, I want you to bring her back here. You will move into one of the cottages in the plantation leading to the complex."

"Meaning what?"

Roychenko settled down into a stuffed chair, crossed his legs and leaned back. "Your duties are here. I want you available and I would think that you would want her available to you. In fact, we both have need of her services." His hands stroked the glass—huge, powerful hands, out of proportion to the size of the man. Álvarez couldn't take his eyes away from them.

"What services?" he asked, almost whispering.

Roychenko sloshed the drink in his glass, holding it to the light. "The Archimedes principle, Julio. It's called 'leverage.' *If* Operation Mongoose buys the message that we've transmitted, *if* this brother of yours parachutes in with the assault force, *if* we are able to capture him in one piece, then we will need his cooperation. Her presence would be a powerful lever."

"I don't want—"

The Russian's voice cut through his words. "What *I* want is your loyalty and obedience." His voice eased slightly but there was still a hard edge on it. "I don't think that there should be any unpleasantness," Roychenko said. He raised his eyebrows in a question. "Do you?"

Julio settled back, unable to hold eye contact. His mind was swimming, brain cells breaking down, so fucking tired that there was nothing more desirable in the world to him than just closing his eyes.

A phone buzzed. Roychenko picked it up, mumbled something, listened and then dropped the instrument into its cradle.

"That was Sorge. The radar returns disappeared over the coast of Jamaica. A false alarm, I think, and at any rate, there are three helicopter gunships patrolling the coast." He made a gesture toward the tiny bedroom. "Get some sleep. I'll lay on a helicopter for tomorrow morning so you can have a few days back at the *finca.*" He hoisted himself out of the chair and walked to the door. His hand was on the knob but he hesitated, turning back. "I want you back here in two days. With the woman."

What had he said to Piedra on the train about being a whore masquerading as a madam? He had played the same game, accepted the payment for his services, planning never to be touched and now, suddenly, he was being forced to bend over and spread his legs. Involuntarily, he laughed.

"No unpleasantness," he echoed. He looked up at the Russian for the last time, his eyelids slitted. Like watching a man through binoculars across heated ground, the image swaying and distorted in the refracted heat. "No unpleasantness," he repeated and passed out.

They had joined up and started the merry-go-round, circling up through ten and then twelve thousand feet. Oxygen system on to 100 percent, the radio hissing in his earphones. No transmission yet from Porto and he expected none. The radios had been set up with a switch which reduced output power from ten watts to a minute fraction of that so that they could communicate within a range of half a mile. Any station monitoring the frequency beyond that range would receive nothing except a faint, garbled transmission. But Porto was not one to chatter and Brocassie took his cue.

Fifteen thousand, then eighteen, with the Helio Courier sucking turbo supercharged air, climbing like an elevator.

Twenty-two, then twenty-five thousand. Small traceries of ice glazing across the canopy. He rubbed at it with a glycerin-soaked rag, as Porto had told him to do. He checked oxygen flow, watching the blinker, like lips, flutter in the indicator cage. The Helio Courier was climbing more and more slowly, the air now just scattered molecules separated like planets in a thin cosmos, but still they climbed.

Ice crystal embroidery, etching over the Perspex above him; cold eating his body's heat, soaking into his bones. Sounds of the sailplane moving under his fingertips—creaks and flutters, moans and rumbles. He looked at the instruments, scanning the panel for needles locked into normal patterns, then glanced back over his shoulder at the coastline of

Jamaica receding to the south. A rim of lights, blurred by distance and altitude, formed a silver halo around Ocho Rios then dwindled to a thin string of luminous pearls along the shore.

Twenty-eight thousand. The climb slowed on the altimeter's needle and then stopped. Out on his starboard side, he saw the other Helio Courier inch up, Porto's towship, distinguishable only by its blacker profile against the night sky.

Release in two minutes, said the voice in his earphones, disembodied and mechanical. *How's your oxygen?*

He thumbed the mike button, finding his own mouth dry as desert sand, leached out by the oxygen. "It's good. Eighteen hundred."

Roger on eighteen hundred, Porto replied. *Stand by for my countdown. Starting on five, release on my mark. My wing lights coming on NOW. You see them?*

Twin pinpricks of light winked on, each marking the outer extremity of Porto's wings, housed in fiberglass shields so that they could only be seen from the side or from above.

"Lights on," Brocassie replied. God, he thought, they're dim. He keyed the mike again. "You have the rheostat turned up?"

Maximum bright. Battery—ah—shows a full charge. Probably will seem dim until you get tucked in behind me. OK?

Brocassie could feel condensation in the mask wetting his cheeks and the salty perspiration irritated his skin. Throat dry and tongue strange, like sucking on a sponge. Taste of metal in his mouth. It was not OK. "OK," he transmitted, not trusting his voice further.

The formation of aircraft, two Helio Couriers wing tip to wing tip, two sailplanes on their three-hundred-foot leashes trailing behind, heading northward toward Cuba. Anytime now, he thought. The long transparent slide toward the Sierra.

Five . . .

Porto's voice in his ear, like an old gramophone recording.

Four . . . three . . . two . . . one . . . MARK!

He had his hand positioned on the plastic knob, the slack taken up, and then he pulled, straining his eyes to see whether the hook had released. No way of telling, but the Slingsby started to slow. For luck, he jerked the knob again and watched as the towplanes disappeared, spiraling down to warmer air and Jamaica. Porto's ship was sliding over toward him, fifty or so feet lower. Touch of the spoilers and then trim for forty-five knots. Porto's ship moving closer and then stabilizing in heading. Touch of spoiler, trim off some speed, and Brocassie found the two ships wedded together in the night sky, stabilized and gliding silently across the black, featureless sea below.

How you feeling, Brother Brocassie?

"Like a million." A million ants crawling up my spine. God, it's black out here. Quick check on oxygen, airspeed. Drifting farther away from Porto, so he trimmed forward an eighth of a turn, then watched the airspeed increase a knot. Porto had predicted that the atmosphere above six thousand would be free of turbulence but that minute mismatches in the rigging of the Slingsbys would necessitate some fine tuning. "I'm falling behind," he transmitted. "By inches."

Porto had a bag of lead shot in his cockpit, his own ship intentionally heavier than Brocassie's. By dropping handfuls of lead shot he would gradually lighten so that the speeds matched.

No problem. Dumping some shot now.

A minute passed, Brocassie not touching the trim, his fingers light on the stick. Still falling behind.

"Drop some more."

That's the last of it. If I can't match your weight, I can always shit out the window.

He would, Brocassie thought, smiling to himself. But after another two minutes, their speeds matched, Porto's ship too far ahead but neither drifting ahead nor being overrun. "Perfect."

A pause and then the hiss in his earphones, a little faint and distorted. *How far back are you?*

Guess. "Couple hundred yards."

Right. Now for the fine speed control. Porto had installed a primitive speed brake on the belly of his sailplane—nothing more than an envelope-sized flap of plywood actuated by a piece of nylon fishing line. But its drag was enough for fine speed adjustment without playing with the controls or trim.

There wasn't any apparent speed difference but gradually, the wing lights of Porto's ship spread farther apart, drawing closer.

"That's enough," Brocassie said.

There was only the hollow hiss of static. Porto's Slingsby crept closer and closer—too close.

"That's enough," Brocassie said again more loudly, worried now that his transmitter was somehow at fault.

Can't get the friggin' board up, Porto grunted into the mike. *The goddamned line is hung up on something. If I pull it harder, the line will probably break!*

There was the small controlled desperation in his voice. Brocassie glanced back at the coast of Jamaica, now only a faint loom of light, but close enough. Not now, he prayed. Not after we've come this far, tried this hard. "What happens now?"

More silence from Porto. Brocassie touched the spoilers, pulling up slightly, bleeding off speed until he was in position. Possible to do this all the way to Cuba, he thought, except that there wasn't that much margin of spare altitude to throw away. Airspeed and altitude were all that they had. And the equation of drag versus lift would finally dictate their range.

Porto finally came back. *The bastard's jammed. I'm going to put tension on the line until it breaks. It may retract far enough to reduce the drag to an acceptable point. I'm showing a sink rate of two hundred thirty right now. If I can get it pulled in far enough to reduce the sink to two hundred, we're in hog heaven.*

Brocassie glanced at his watch. Another ten or eleven minutes and they would be fully committed—far enough away so that they could not regain the coast of Jamaica, and possibly not within gliding range of the Sierra. But it was Porto's show.

"Let me know how it turns out." He hadn't meant to sound sarcastic but somehow it did. Porto didn't respond.

Five minutes elapsed. Twice, Brocassie was about to key the mike and then didn't, waiting.

Line broke, Porto said softly into the mike. *But I think it's at least partway in. I'm showing just a hair over two hundred feet per minute down. What are you reading?*

Slightly more, he thought. More like 210. To keep from

overrunning Porto's ship, he was cracking the spoilers open once a minute, pulling up slightly to bleed off airspeed and then setting back into the overrun situation.

"A little over two hundred," he finally admitted. "I'm having problems not running up your ass. What's the decision?"

Stand by, was Porto's answer. He would be hunched over the E6B calculator, penlight held between his teeth, working out a new equation of time, speed, sink and distance. The minutes were ticking by and the coast of Jamaica was now only a suggestion of light beyond the horizon. Eight minutes gone, then ten. Eleven.

It's marginal. I won't have much altitude to spare—probably less than a thousand feet. A hesitation, his mike key still down and then, *Your heading back to the field is one ninety-five magnetic. Switch to high power on your transmitter once you're over the coast and tell Hagger to turn on the field's landing lights. It'll be no sweat.*

"And where in hell are *you* going?"

Seconds ticking away, yards traveled that would have to be retraced. Porto's voice was calm, detached. *No work, no pay, buddy. Them's the rules. I think it's pretty thin but I'm willing to give it a shot. I'm going to Cuba and it's up to you to make sure that Hagger puts that check in the mail if you don't hear from me.*

Brocassie gritted his teeth. More seconds, each one 84 more feet farther to the north, 168 more he'd have to fly to return to the red Jamaican dirt and safety. *Damn* Porto. The sweat on his hands was saturating his flying gloves, soaking through, a conduit to the erosion of cold. Beneath his flight cap his scalp prickled and he found that he couldn't concentrate, his eyes aimlessly scanning the instrument panel, comprehending nothing, near the edge of panic.

The old fear. Falling, the wings folding in on themselves, ribs cracking, fabric tearing away and then his own body free of the aircraft, hurtling toward the earth, faster and faster. He had dreamed of it before: watching the earth rise toward him, first only an indistinct blur of green and brown, then individual trees and fields, growing larger and larger, wheeling through his vision as he tumbled. And the impact—one long tearing pain that never stopped until he woke, bolt upright, sweat streaming from his body, his heart hammering.

One ninety-five degrees, Porto was shouting at him. *Turn back now. That's an order.*

It was his imagination, he knew, but the ring which hung from the thong around his neck radiated heat, taking the chill from his body. His fingertips and then his face tingled and he felt warmth flowing through him.

He glanced down at his watch once and then again. Past the point of no return and he smiled, his cheeks touching the wet interior of the oxygen mask. For the first time in a very long time, he felt completely alive and whole. He keyed the mike, found no words but then laughed.

Silence, just the hiss of static in his headphones for a long minute and then the words, *You're a dumbass, Brocassie,* softened by echoing laughter.

Lift, weight, speed and drag. He touched the spoilers again, bleeding off altitude, slowing the Slingsby. Porto's wing lights slid back into the canopy, spreading farther apart, then stabilizing.

He snatched a second to glance at his watch: 2:37—half an hour until moonrise, and still thirty-five minutes to the coast and another twenty minutes to the landing site. He and Porto were more than two thousand feet lower than the flight plan had called for, and thirteen minutes behind schedule. There was no margin left to give away.

Ahead of him, he saw Porto begin a slow drifting turn to the left and he followed through ten, then fifteen degrees. He keyed the mike. "Ebb Tide One, this is Ebb Tide Two. Problems?"

Distant crashes of static and the familiar hiss of an empty channel. Then, *Refiguring our flight plan. Stand by.*

Glance at the altimeter. Down through 14,500 feet, rate 210 feet per minute of sink, based on the last hour's flight. Unconsciously, he felt himself pushing upward against the straps of his safety harness, willing the damn sailplane to rise, but as the straps bit into his shoulders, he realized that he had to relax. Gravity was gravity. Children's balls, rocks, even aircraft, might go up but eventually they came down. He willed himself to loosen up. Easy. Porto knew what he was doing and if circumstances came to it, they would land on the coast of Cuba and walk their way into the mountains. Fat chance, echoed the disbeliever within.

A click, Porto's voice, hoarse. *We're making a major alteration in heading. No way to play it safe now. We've got to chance a direct shot for Maroto's site. It's the only way that we don't end up swimming and I'm not so sure even about that.*

Which blew the navigation, Brocassie thought. Because it had all been predicated on picking up the Santiago de Cuba beacon, crossing it with a bearing from Guantánamo Bay Naval Air Station's transmitter and then, using that as a navigational fix, turning west and paralleling the coast along the crest of the Sierra, trying to pick out two pinpricks of light from the strip that Maroto had hacked out of the brush. Now, it was going to be a matter of flying blindly into the coast, hoping that their landfall would be within a quarter of a mile in accuracy after ninety miles of flight in unknown vagrant winds.

He looked down toward the void of wet blackness, knowing it could be his green liquid death. *The snotgreen sea. The scrotumtightening sea,* James Joyce had called it. He felt a chill pass up through his spine. "What are you going to use for a fix? We damn well need something. Once into the Sierra, there's nothing to fix our position."

Ahead, Porto replied. *Look on the horizon, about your eleven-thirty position.*

He had been flying Porto's lights, locked on to them as his only point of reference in a referenceless universe, but now he stared beyond Porto's glider, scanning the horizon. There was a cluster of lights, flickering.

Porto answered the question for him before he could ask it. *Coast Guard cutter Bibb. Hagger's got them on station in case we have to ditch.*

"You know their location exactly?"

Hesitation. *Not exactly. I'm going to ask for it to get an exact fix but it means that I'll have to go to high power on the transmitter.*

Unstated statement; decipher to mean that electronic ears in Cuba would hear. A gamble, but he knew that Porto had weighed all the options and this was the best one, perhaps the only one.

"Tell them to keep the cocoa warm."

Porto gave a snort.

The lights on Porto's Slingsby banked slightly to port and Brocassie followed him through the turn. The glow of the ship was now steady, already starting to slide under the nose of his aircraft as they passed overhead.

Porto's voice blasted in his ear and he reached down to reduce the volume control.

Rusty, *this is Ebb Tide One—you copy?*

Zilch.

Rusty, Rusty, Rusty—*Ebb Tide!* Porto's voice was more insistent.

The vessel was now almost beneath them, still more than two miles below.

Shit! Porto's voice, the frustration clearly evident, his unconscious keying of the mike a confirmation of it.

Ebb Tide. This is Rusty. *Go ahead.* Deep South accent, laced with the taste of grits.

Brocassie sighed.

Porto again, this time his voice old-boy laid back, as if he were chatting with a beer buddy over the back fence. *Over your station at—ah—two forty-three. Kindly give me a reading on your position.*

Wait one, Ebb Tide. Got to sharpen my pencil 'fore I can give you that.

Seconds. Then minutes. Brocassie chanced a glimpse over his shoulder through the aft canopy. The Coast Guard cutter was behind him now, sliding away. He realized that his teeth were clamped together.

A different voice. Mid-Atlantic with the taste of the Chesapeake to it. *Ebb-tide Air, this is the motor fishing vessel* Rusty. *You read us all right?*

Brocassie smiled, relieved, and then laughed. The genius of improvisation and there was some kid down there in the night, perhaps a petty officer or some savvy lieutenant who had more brains than most admirals.

Five by, Rusty, Porto answered.

The *Bibb* reeled off latitude and longitude, repeated them and then finished off the transmission with *Anything we can do for you, friend?*

Negative. We got low oil pressure on number three engine and we're diverting to Haiti. Just wanted to firm up our position. If we have any problems, we'll come back and see you. Much thanks, Rusty. You fellows keep your feet dry. This is Ebb Tide off and clear.

The *Bibb* came back, one final time. *Good flight, Ebb Tide, but be advised that there's a bogey bearing zero one five magnetic, range sixteen miles. Coastal patrol eggbeater, we think.*

Porto keyed the mike twice in acknowledgment and then switched to low power. *'Cassie—you read me?*

"I read."

Get this—write it down because we don't have much time until that bastard's in range of our radio transmissions. Heading to the site is three five seven. It's on the south side of the ridge. You know the drill.

"I'm with you."

"No, you're not! There's a chopper out there to the north. We're still over international waters but if he picks us up, he'll trail us into the coast. Forget about staying with me. Hold the heading that I gave you. If he has radar, we won't give him much of a return, but at really close range, it might be enough for him to spot us if we're flying formation. I'm jinking off to the west and once he's by, then I'll converge on your course. Give me a call on low power when you reach the coast and if you can't raise me, start calling Maroto. His call sign is Montaña. Got that?

The cockpit seemed to close in on him, the heat of the flight suit stifling, the oxygen mask choking off his breath. Ahead to the north was the blackness of Cuba. Unconsciously, he nodded. "Yes, I got it."

OK, sport, don't sweat it. Fly the heading. We'll be eating Cuban mangoes in forty minutes. Over and clear.

He wanted to say something and couldn't find words except, "Good luck." And silently added, God speed, you crazy critter.

Beneath him, he saw Porto's ship slowly slide off to the

west, the lights extinguishing. Now blackness and for a second, disorientation. He checked the gyro, then the compass, then airspeed: 357 degrees.

Until this minute, he had kept his eyes locked on the wing-tip lights of Porto's Slingsby, but now he was able to divide his attention, first scanning the instruments and then the horizon. Far ahead, he saw the profile of the Sierra Maestra, chrome-edged where the moon was rising behind it. And below and off to starboard, an indistinct blur of yellow which he knew was Santiago de Cuba. Somewhere to the east of Santiago was where she would be, and almost unconsciously he drifted that way, like steel to a magnet. "I've come back, Alicia Ruth Helvia," he whispered into the mask. "Because I had to. Can't you hear me?"

The plane shuddered slightly and the sound of air flowing over the fabric diminished, the controls going mushy.

Inattention is a pilot's terminal mental disorder. Porto's maxim. He dumped the nose a fraction, picking up airspeed, and then eased out, retrimming. His heading had drifted off over thirty degrees and he savagely racked the glider to the left, rolling out on three five seven. OK teacher, he thought. First things first. He started to work his scan, cutting the horizon into small segments, sweeping his eyes through each small arc, searching.

It was just a spark of light at first, so indistinct that he had to search again for it, not really sure that he had seen it. And then he saw it. Not really a direct flash, but more a reflected one. It was down and to his left, the distance impossible to judge but closing toward him rapidly. Again the flash and he realized that it was a rotating beacon set on the belly of an aircraft, only its reflected strobe momentarily lighting its fuselage.

Brocassie's muscles contracted, his body tautening. The Cuban chopper. It was too far out from the coastline, now over international waters but that wasn't something that would concern them. What in hell had drawn them away from the coast? He felt naked, vulnerable, all the theoretical discussions about the sailplane being invisible to radar now academic. He had seen the MIL choppers before, over the Sierra, and he knew that they were heavily armed with automatic cannons—

cannons that he had seen scythe through a mountain clearing, cutting four packhorses and two men from Maroto's column into an unrecognizable pile of bleeding red offal.

The chopper passed underneath him, how far he couldn't estimate but close enough that he could hear the distinctive whumping of the rotor blades.

His mind went wild, and he found himself gasping in the mask for oxygen, his lungs starved. He ripped the mask from his face and sucked great gulps of air, panting like a dog in heat. Jesus, he thought. Did he see me? Too damn close to be pure coincidence. The hollow of his back seemed to burn, knowing that the cannon shells would hose through the Slingsby without even losing velocity. Tracers! The cannon would use a phosphorous tracer shell every five rounds and the wood and fabric would ignite and then he would fall, his body trapped in the burning wreckage, then realized that he would never feel a thing because less than thirty inches behind him were over thirty pounds of high explosive. Instantaneously, he would be reduced to atoms, part of a beautiful expanding ball of fire in the night sky like the final agony of a meteor.

Somehow the thought calmed him. It would not be the terror of his dreams—just instant, painless death. He fought down the panic, bringing himself under control. How much time had elapsed? Seconds, minutes? He looked back over his shoulder, straining to see out of the aft canopy. Walking the rudders, he eased the glider to the left and then to the right. Nothing at first, and then looking higher, he saw the strobe, clear now, unshielded by the body of the chopper, which meant that it was climbing, still searching.

Speed! He wanted speed to get away and he pushed the stick forward, watching the needle waver from fifty knots to sixty and then to seventy. He was burning off altitude, giving away the little margin that he could spare, but there was no avenue left other than the final desperate act of escape.

The concussion of sound and the stream of fire passed under him, arcing out and then downward, separating into brilliant traces of color which died as they fell away toward the sea. He stared, fascinated, his hands frozen on the controls before the meaning impacted on him. There was no time to think, nothing to reason with. Violently, he rammed the stick farther forward, his body thrusting up against the straps, dirt and trash and bits of gravel rattling against the canopy of the glider as gravity was reversed. He was plunging toward the sea, speed building up, the aircraft now vibrating, fabric drumming, the frame groaning. Another burst flowered above him, beautiful, remote, like the spray of a watering hose, the droplets glinting of red and crimson and liquid gold, incredible brilliant greens and saffrons. Time became an eternity condensed into microseconds.

No way of knowing how far back the helicopter was but it had to be close and closing. Already he had been bracketed and the next burst would be the final killing one. He could not turn and he knew that he could not give away another inch of altitude. There was just one option and he took it.

Porto had told him how it was done more than a month ago during a lazy afternoon's bull session over a couple of beers. It had looked simple as Porto moved his hands, simulating the flight of an aircraft. Now not so simple at night with no horizon or means of judging whether the aircraft would hold together. He glanced at the panel—airspeed over 94 knots and altitude down to 8400, burning away like dry grass in a brush fire. He eased back the stick tentatively, then with more force, his body mashed down into the seat. He climbed steeply, up through the vertical, G-forces building. A sheet of flame arced just under his wing, the burst so close that it lit up the cockpit in a blaze of red light and he felt shocks rippling through the aircraft.

The sounds of the cannon shells impacting merged with the pounding of the rotors and the helicopter flashed by him, only feet below. He was up over the top of the loop, gravity inverted, hanging from his straps, completely disoriented, no reference to what was sky or sea. The instruments were a confused jumble, the dials moving so rapidly that he had no ability to correlate them and he was suddenly frantic, fighting the controls, unable to remember what he should do now. He banged one rudder pedal and then the other to the stops but there seemed to be no effect. He shoved the stick forward but the aircraft just slowed, shuddered, hanging helpless in space like a fly trapped in amber. Vibrations, a jarring series of snaps, dirt from the floor showering his face, the oxygen mask hanging from its strap, flapping against his forehead, and then the aircraft creaked and started to fall sideways, rolling off on one wing. He was headed down, stalled out, the plane spinning, centrifugal force pressing him against the side of the cockpit. Stars rotated across the canopy, tilted at an insane angle, and the noise—a thrumming of fabric and broken wood—sounded like the final death rattle. The old dream, no longer a dream, a vivid reality which blotted out everything except the overwhelming thought of death.

It was there, etched into his reflexes by Porto's training. Stick forward and then rudder opposite to the spin. The stars wheeled more slowly and stopped. Neutral rudder and pull out, *Easy, asshole,* Porto shouting in his mind. *EASY! Pull too hard and you'll tear the wings off!*

The stars no longer spun, and as he eased the stick back carefully, they dipped, drifting more slowly below the frame of his canopy. Airspeed! Down to eighty, then sixty-five, then fifty-five. He neutralized the stick and slumped back, his body trembling, his hands wet and shaking, the stink of his own fear flooding his nostrils.

Christ, he had looped it! Correction. Had taken it to the top of a loop and for some reason had stalled the aircraft upside down. The rest was a blur of sound and sensations that he knew he would never be able to put together into a coherent sequence.

But it wasn't over. Out there, beyond him, was the strobe of the chopper, sweeping first to the west and then turning back, and he knew that it was just a matter of time. He glanced down: altimeter, 6800 feet, heading, 025. He banked gently, bringing the compass sluggishly back to 357, and settled his body deeper into the seat. There was the option of flying back to the *Bibb* but he immediately rejected it. He would head for the coast because either way, the chopper would have him and he wanted, at least, to try.

The strobe was brighter now, lower and off to his left, closing, but not quite a collision course. He kept his heading, trying to avoid speculation, yet unable to do so. Death wasn't bad, he desperately tried to believe. It was just the anticipation of it that was unbearable.

Suddenly, a beam of light from the chopper speared out, scything the sky.

Brocassie saw it, knew what it was and what it meant. The chopper was no more than a mile away, pivoting in toward his flight path, climbing. The beam was brilliant, flooding the night in front of it, reaching out more than a mile.

The sound startled him, hammering in his headphones. RUSTY, *THIS IS EBB TIDE. I'M HIT. GOING DOWN.*

No answer, but suddenly there was a flash of an explosion to the west, very low on the horizon, and then another and another.

Finally, the *Bibb. Ebb Tide, this is* Rusty . . .

No response, silence mocking silence.

The spotlight extinguished and then the strobe turned away toward Santiago. It diverged from his flight path, a firefly growing more distant, until he could no longer see it.

Porto's ship had been shot down! Seconds after the flashes, he had felt the muffled shock waves and knew that he was alone. All his life he had been alone and it had never mattered, but now he understood the real meaning of the word. Alone—the hollowness in the pit of your stomach, the dryness in the back of your throat, a heaviness that could not be measured.

Sixty-three hundred feet. He rechecked the compass. Only a few degrees off but it was impossible to tell whether he was on track. He would fly out the heading, call Maroto as he passed over the coast and hope that he would still have sufficient altitude to make the landing site.

He glanced down at the variometer and found that his rate of sink had diminished to 180 feet per minute. Which gave him ten, twelve, maybe even thirteen minutes until he was down to the altitude of the landing site. But the problem was that he didn't know which way he would have to turn once he reached the coast. East or west. Fifty-fifty. He decided west, if only because it was away from Santiago, toward more sparsely settled areas.

He was down to the level of the highest mountains now, 6100 feet and sinking slowly. Below him were a few scattered lights of the coastal road, but his navigation was not good enough to identify one small village from another. The lights thinned then disappeared beneath him.

He rechecked the radio with his penlight, sure that he was on 123.5 and low power and then keyed the mike.

"*Montaña, Montaña.* Here is *Ebb Tide Two.*"

The frequency hissed, empty.

He tried again and still no response. The mountains which rose so rapidly up from the sea were getting closer. He entered a gentle bank to the left, heading west and tried again.

"*Montaña, Montaña,* here is *Ebb Tide Two.* How copy?"

Ebb-tide Two, this is One. What's your location?

It was as if he had just thrust his finger into an electric light socket, the shock reverberating through his body, his nerve endings suddenly frying.

Two, this is One. No time left. I'm down to fifty-one hundred. You see my lights?

He leaned forward, sweeping the space below him, and saw nothing except blackness. "Negative."

What's your heading?

"West!"

Watch for the flash. If you don't see it, turn through one eighty and head east. You got it?

Flash? And then he understood. Somehow, Porto had been able to cut through the webbing behind him, pull out grenades and chuck three of them out of his storm window to explode far below him over the Caribbean Sea. Christ, what a risk he had taken with three-second fuses.

GOT IT?

"YES, DAMMIT, I GOT IT!"

He scoured the horizon, afraid to blink. He counted seconds: "One thousand one, one thousand two, one thousand three, one thou . . ." Far away he saw the detonation, a brief flicker of brilliance, like lightning on the far horizon. "I SAW IT!"

Keep coming, Porto's voice rattled in his headphones. *I've got Montaña's lights in sight but it's going to be close.*

Brocassie concentrated, shutting out everything else, and for the first time ever, felt at one with the aircraft, his fingers extending out through the cables and rods, sensing the delicate whisper of wind which flowed over the control surfaces. Felt the slight flutter which he had never before sensed in the rudder pedals, the movement a subtle extension of the pressure of his feet. Flight was no longer defined by a mechanical formula, chalked on a blackboard. He *was* flight.

Turbulence. Not bad yet but increasing in the lee of the mountain, just as Porto had briefed him. He edged over toward the slope, feeling for calmer air, the dark face of the mountains closing in on him. Blurs of cliffs, rock faces, trees emerged out of the blackness. He banked slightly, paralleling them, only the span of a wing away. He followed the slope downward, along the face of the mountains, altitude evaporating.

How much farther? Two miles, three, five? Didn't dare glance at the altimeter, too close to the mountain's face. He found himself starting to overcontrol, fighting the stick. Sweat saturated him, the flying suit which he had worn as protection against the cold of high altitude now a suffocating envelope. The canopy was fogged, the warm air inside condensing on the still-cold canopy, and he used his hand, desperately wiping away the haze of moisture. Dammit! Smooth it out! He took three deep breaths, exhaled and relaxed. It was just an equation of time and distance.

Seconds passed, minutes, a lifetime.

YOU SEE THE LIGHTS?

"NEGATIVE!"

I'm over the field, Brocassie. Montaña's radio is screwed up—garbled. Here's the last grenade—pin out—dropping it!

A flash, much closer but almost on the level of his horizon. He imprinted it on his memory, altered heading just fractions and steadied out.

Trees under him now, reaching up. Distinctly, he could smell pine. Ahead, a flashlight waving madly and then the second one, but not aligned. There was no room for the textbook approach. Heart thudding, respiration high, body already bracing for the crash. He knew it was over and there was nothing left but to keep going, like a man far from shore, desperately tired but still stroking even though he knew he could never make it. He eased back on the stick, trying to gain inches of altitude, willing the damn thing to float. A muddle of bouncing lights, men scattering and then the lights disappeared behind ragged silhouettes of fir and he knew the sick feeling of the aircraft stalling, sinking, the controls buffeting. A snap, a shudder, and then the final whipping impact. He was hurled forward against the panel, feeling shock but no pain, everything in individual frames of sound and sight: vibrations, grinding, ripping, Plexiglas shattering. For an instant the aircraft hung, teetering in the branches, rockabye baby in the treetop, and then the wing spar snapped, folded upward in slow motion and then lurched downward in the final plunge. The words flashed across the screen of his mind in huge block letters insanely printed in pink.

    ... when the bough breaks, the cradle ...

CHAPTER

11

The Sierra Maestra, Cuba, October 17, 1962

He awoke, half-light and shadow falling across his face, his fatigues saturated. He was strapped to a litter and he tried to lift his head but found that he couldn't. A streak of pain shot through his body.

Overhead, all he could see were branches of trees and a pale sky, obscured by tendrils of white mist. It was cold, and drops of condensation fell from the leaves, splattering his face.

"Porto . . ."

The man in front slowed and turned his head. "Porto will be back soon, *Jefe*. He's working with Maroto to move the explosives and weapons as far up the mountain as quickly as possible while there is still time. The Russian pigass helicopters are making sweeps over the Sierra and the coast. Maroto thinks that it won't be long until they find the gliders. As for you, you're a crate of eggs that we have been instructed to move carefully, and therefore slowly. I have been told that I will lose essential glands if I treat you otherwise."

"Do you have some water?"

The kid, all of fifteen with a pinched face and a body smell that would have knocked over a locomotive, kneeled beside him, lifting his head to help him drink from a cup. Brocassie suddenly felt the overwhelming urge to urinate, and did. The wet warmth spread across his thighs.

The kid looked down, slightly embarrassed. "I wouldn't worry," he said. "You can't control your body yet. We'll give you a wipedown, powder your ass and tuck you in. There's an overhanging rock ledge up higher where we'll stop for the night. No more than another two miles."

The kid undid the flap of a satchel and pulled out a black cardboard box. From that, he withdrew a syringe and an ampoule of honey-colored fluid. "This now." Expertly, he spiked the needle through the rubber-tipped cap and withdrew fluid into the barrel of the syringe.

"Porto's all right?"

The kid expertly squirted a few droplets from the syringe, clearing any entrapped air from the barrel. "He landed two or three minutes before you. I believe that his major complaint was a chipped tooth."

The needle pricked and Brocassie felt the warmth, like a golden wave, spreading through his body, eradicating pain, constricting his vision until the light was gone.

"Sweet dreams," the kid said from a universe away.

He swam through morphine-laced dreams, the pain always there, sometimes surfacing and sometimes submerged but never entirely gone. He heard voices, the touch of a hand, the smell of men and then that slowly faded to a void, replaced by swirls of color, streams of voices. Faces, names, places, events, all blurred. He tried to separate them but the harder he tried, the faster the images moved.

He was swimming backward through time. Alicia beside him, her face too close, out of focus, words that she was saying undecipherable. Julio there too, laughing, reaching out for him; for what? Snatches of Korea—the impression of mud and filth, frozen bodies and bleak pockmarked hills. A schoolboy hockey game, cold biting wind on his face, the impact of bodies, the scream of blades cutting ice, hockey sticks whistling. Street scene with Julio running ahead of him, down an alleyway, body banging off overturned garbage cans, the stink of decay in his nose and someone behind him, shouting, gaining with each stride.

The images slowed, each flickering longer, more vivid. He smelled the sweet scent of grass, the coolness of high country night wind on his face. And heard the voice of his father.

The old man, far older physically than he should have been, sat on his mat, smoking the pipe. It was one of the two remaining from the pipe quarry of Canumpa O'ke which was south of Coteau des Prairies, still farther south of the great Winnipeg Lake of the Ouisconsion Territory. The pipe was sacred; it dated back four generations. Brocassie, only twelve summers in age, knew these things, just as he knew of the River that Lies and of the legend of Soft Dove and Ee-Kto-mee, for these things were part of his training and heritage.

His father was no more than fifty but his skin was like weathered hide, cracked from the heat of the sun and creaking with age. Now, he held the pipe carefully, using both hands. He took the smoke into his lungs and leaned back, his face thrust up at the night sky, shoulders thrown back.

In the starlight, the old man was stronger and larger than he was in the ordinary day. Now, there was no coughing and choking and his movements were constrained and graceful. The rings beneath his eyes were erased by the darkness and his profile was firm.

Beyond the mountains to the east, the horizon silvered. As Brocassie watched, a star rose, first yellow and plump like a peach in the first season of harvest, then turning fire-white. His father called the star Hanhepi-wakan but Brocassie had learned in the government school that it was a planet, the one called Venus. Within a short time, when the planet was no more than two fingers' span above the horizon, the sickle moon rose. Brocassie waited with patience.

The chant was an unfamiliar one but he knew many of the words and he slowly realized that it was a hymn of thanks, a promise of atonement and a prayer for release. The old man ended it with a beautiful, mournful sound which tapered off into silence, and seconds later echoed back from the cliffs as if in acknowledgment.

The old man listened in silence for many more minutes, breathing deeply as if winded from long exertion, then stood up, and folding his mat, trudged back to the cabin, his hand on his son's shoulder. He stopped before going in and turned to Brocassie.

"I am at peace with myself and my gods," he said simply, without preamble. "I want you to know that, regardless of what may happen. My *feenin* is strong and undisturbed." He drew Brocassie to him, touched both cheeks with his and then held him against his chest. "You are to pack now, for tomorrow you will go to live with Álvarez, the Spanish Man."

"You're going with me?" Brocassie asked. He stood as straight as he could, almost matching his father's height.

"Not this time," the old man said. "Not this time." He took his son by the arm. "This time we say good-bye. We're both grown and we understand what it means to be men of the Cree Nation. I would have wanted you to make the passage from youth to man in the proper ritual of the old ways, but that cannot be. You are enough of a man already and the gods will accept you."

Brocassie felt his throat contracting, his chest tight. "We'll be together in the spring. When you come back with the Spanish Man. Just like all the summers."

The old man moved around behind his son, holding his shoulder. "We'll discuss this no further," he said softly. "I know what is to follow and it will be that way regardless of what we would want. When the corn comes ripe, it gives up its harvest and dies. You are my son and my harvest. It is part of the cycle." He squeezed, so that Brocassie's shoulders hurt under the pressure.

His father died during the night, making no sound. On the table of the cabin was a jacket of cured deer leather, sewn together by sinews of animals and decorated with tufts of feather and small locks of hair bound with dried squirrel gut. Next to it was a knife, hand forged and chased in silver with a handle of elk horn and beside that were four golden eagle coins. A flat shape, wrapped in cracked deer hide, laced with tarred twine, completed the pile.

There was a note, awkwardly printed:

My inheritance to you is small. These are things of your grandfathers' and of mine. Keep them for your sons. My love for you has been strong and will remain so. Hold our ways, for they are the truth. But learn their ways if you are to survive. Both the gods and I will always be with you.

Brocassie purified his father's body with wet aspen leaves, placed wild sage over his body and wrapped him in a robe. He did not know the chant of the dead but he prayed silently. At sundown, he buried his father on a bluff which looked toward the west.

Porto stood over Brocassie, checking his pulse. It was past five in the morning and a cold, damp wind billowed in the nylon walls of the shelter. He opened Brocassie's lid and shone the beam of a penlight on the pupil. He nodded, then released the lid and stood upright, his frame hunched under the low pitch of the roof.

"He's all right, I think," he said, turning to Maroto.

"It was a very stupid thing that the two of you attempted, pilot," Maroto said. He scratched at his neck, an old man, tired of war and fatigue and dirty clothes. He nodded toward the drugged body. "He always had a hard head. But when he landed that contraption in the trees I believed that he had run out his days."

Porto sat down on the edge of the cot and took a sip from a bottle of beer, still wet with the moisture of the stream. "I agree—it was stupid as hell but then again, you know Hagger. He loves this kind of rah-rah-siss-boom-bang shit but you also have to admit, old man, that it was about the only way to get in quickly with a big load." He looked down at Brocassie shaking his head. "I knew how dangerous it would be and I gave Brocassie every chance to get out of it but he just kept coming on for more. He's lucky to be still kicking. As for me, I gave up keeping track of my nine lives a long time ago."

"How soon can he move on his own?"

Porto hunched his shoulders and took a final swallow from the bottle. "Another day on the stretcher, at least. He could have a concussion and I don't want to start up the bleeding. He lost a couple of pints at least but he's a tough sonofabitch. Two days from now is my guess." He glanced back at Brocassie. "Shit—those stitches look like they were put in with a meat hook. The forehead will heal but the nose should be rebroken and reset. It looks like he tried to stop some fuckin' avalanche with his face."

Maroto offered him a cigar and both of them lit up from Maroto's old brass zippo. An animal, probably wild boar, grunted and rooted in the night, trampling heavily in the brush.

"You found the traitor?" Porto finally asked.

"It is a possibility, a man called Enrico. He joined us only six months ago. He swore that he wanted to fight against Fidel, but I now know that he was a common criminal wanted by the police. He openly admits that he has a record of many convictions for theft and two for rape. He is a pig of a man but a good fighter. Only Enrico and two other men were out of the camp in the two days following Brocassie's departure with the film. Only those three would have the opportunity to make contact with the DGI. Of the two other men, one is a trusted friend of twenty years and the other is my nephew."

"What of it? Being your nephew doesn't make the kid automatically trustworthy."

"True," Maroto replied, "except that the boy's father was tortured and executed by the DGI for counterrevolutionary acts against the state. That was when Luis joined us. Of all the men in my column, he hates the Fidelistas most passionately." The old man spat on the di : floor and then wiped his mouth with his sleeve. "No, pilot," he continued, "I think it is Enrico who we must watch."

"Christ! Why don't you just sack the bastard's head with a bag of rocks?"

The tip of Maroto's cigar glowed as he inhaled. He withdrew it, tapping a nonexistent ash on the sole of his boot. "Because he has fought well. I have seen him kill militia and therefore I cannot be sure. All that I can do is watch and only when I am positive will I act."

"You have him under observation?"

Maroto nodded. "Enrico is helping to carry supplies from

your ships to the cave on the other side of the ridge. Four of my oldest men—men who have been with me now for over three years—are keeping a close watch on him." He sighed. "It is unfortunate about the radio, of course."

"What radio?"

"Before you told me tonight that Brocassie had been betrayed by someone in my column, Enrico was involved in unloading Brocassie's aircraft. He reported to me that the wonderful radio that was in Brocassie's ship was badly damaged in the crash."

"Or did he smash it?"

Drawing on the cigar, Maroto leaned back. He shrugged. "How can I be sure? Luis was tending the pack mules, helping to secure the loads of equipment. He has told me that he saw the radio drop from Enrico's hands. He thought the act deliberate, but would you kill a man based on that alone?" He left the question hanging.

"Dammit—then interrogate Enrico!"

"And if he denies everything, am I to kill him? Maim him? Tie him up and leave him for the ants? I don't have the stomach for that, pilot. I think we will learn more if we are patient. If he moves, he will not get far and then there will be proof. Until then, I'll keep a close watch on him so that he cannot do any further mischief. And in the meanwhile, we have the benefit of one more back to haul your cargo over the crest of the Sierra." He smiled. "You see—I am not impatient. These things will come out eventually and if he betrays himself by his actions, I will gut him without any remorse and a clear conscience." The old man stood up in a crouch. "Get some sleep, pilot. There will be work to do tomorrow. I want eight more miles toward the crest before sundown." He brushed aside the flap of the tent and disappeared into the night.

Porto turned back toward Brocassie. Breathing steady, the pulse strong. You're a lousy pilot, he thought, but you've got the balls of a bull. He bent down, brushing a fly away from the wound. *"Hasta luego, hermano,"* he whispered.

They lay on a blanket, overlooking the sea from a high dune, the heat of the sun baking into their bodies. There was no wind to speak of—only small vagrant gusts that stirred the slick of the Caribbean into ruffled taffeta. Sargasso weed in bright yellow clumps heaved slowly in the swell offshore and it was easy to believe that there was no land beyond the blue curvature of the sea's horizon.

She was on her stomach, the back straps of her suit undone, pale white breasts just barely visible where the fabric of the suit was unsupported. She turned her face toward him. It had a sheen of perspiration which gave her skin texture a subtle gloss. She wiped the sweat from her upper lip with the back of her hand and smiled.

"Hot, isn't it? But I love the feel of the sun on my skin. Is there any ice left?"

Brocassie rattled the foam cooler. "A bit."

"That's wonderful. Would you mind making me a rum and cola? I'll share it with you if you'd like."

Brocassie smiled and tried to laugh easily, not really sure how he should respond. She was Julio's girl and Julio always had clever answers, but Brocassie found that he was incapable of them. He pulled the bottles from a beach bag and glanced back at her and found she was studying him. Like a kid, he blushed and turned away, busying himself. She was so damn lovely, like a sculpture in a museum protected from the crowds by a velvet roped barrier, something he was compelled to touch and yet beyond reach. He fumbled open the cooler and fished out four cubes of ice, poured rum into her glass and added some of the remaining warm cola. As she put out her hand for it, her suit fell partially away from her breast and the soft, white skin with the darker aureola just hidden in the curve of the meshed fabric drew his eye but he avoided looking, shifting his gaze to the blank horizon.

"It's a little warm," he apologized. "Give it time to cool."

She held the glass against her cheek, and he could feel her eyes studying him.

"You're a strange one, but not the kind of person that I thought you would be. 'Brocassie' . . . your last name, isn't it?"

"It's my grandfather's name, an Indian name, neither first nor last. Governments and administrators don't understand that so in order not to confuse the people who keep records, I took the first name 'George.' But Brocassie is my name."

"Julio said that you were of mixed blood."

"Half-breed" or "red nigger," white men in the streets of Montana had called him when he was growing up, *mestizo* here in Cuba by the socially elite. But she hadn't said it to classify him into some imagined substandard category. There had been curiosity in her voice, without the inflection of bigotry. He turned back to her, a curious form of hunger gnawing at him.

"My mother was a Mexican immigrant without papers or a marriage license. I don't remember her well, just a warm wonderful woman with brown skin who rocked me when I hurt myself and whispered stories to me as I fell asleep. But I remember how she would endlessly draw pictures on a slate, then tell me their Spanish names and mimic the sounds they made. Creaks for a rocking chair, moos for a cow, a hiss for the wind. She died of pneumonia when I was six."

Her eyes softened. "I'm sorry." She made the minutest gesture to reach out, then drew her hand back. "Julio told me that you moved in with his family then. That's why you speak Spanish with the Cuban idiom?"

He nodded. "After her death, my father boarded me with Julio's family in the winters, then picked me up when he and Julio's father came back from the mines in the spring. I stayed with my father at his camp in Utah during the summers until he died when I was twelve. After that, I lived full time with the Álvarezes in Montana. We only spoke Cuban-Spanish, except when Julio and I were alone." He had to pause, smiling, remembering Jacinta Álvarez. "His mother thought the evils of the world were personified by Protestantism, the blasphemous English language and a diet without enough green peppers in it."

She laughed, then pulled a strand of her hair through her fingertips, twisting it, her voice now serious. "Julio never talks about his childhood. What were his parents like?"

"The Spanish Man," as his father had always called Carlos Álvarez, was a barrel of a man, drunk half the time, and sorry that he wasn't the rest. He never talked in a normal voice, only roared or whispered, according to his level of whiskey intake and the degree of resulting remorse. But he was a father to both of them, son and almost-son alike. He smashed their heads together with impartiality when they fought, pounded their backs when their grades were passing and loved them both with the gusto of a man who knew the meaning of the word and wasn't afraid to hide it.

His memory of Jacinta Álvarez was a softened blur, like the modern photograph of a person moving, taken in multiple exposures. She scrubbed, she washed, she cooked, she split wood, she knitted socks and sweaters, she cleaned, all as if she were trying to work off in advance her penance in purgatory. She went to Mass daily and twice on Sundays. She crammed the Scriptures into her sons' heads and her version of hell was a stark, mountainous region where it always snowed and the wind blew so hard that it tore the flesh from your bones. Heaven she spoke of less often, but when she did, it was a land of warmth and joy, fruit hanging from the trees for the taking, a country of lush grass and flowing streams, its coast nuzzling blue waters.

In Brocassie's senior year of high school, the Spanish Man had died in a cave-in at Leadville, and eight months later, Jacinta passed away without any sign of disease or distress. Just simply died. He and Julio had come home for the Christmas holidays, Julio in his third year of law school, Brocassie in his first at the Colorado School of Mines. She had been waiting for them, holding on.

A new hand-knitted sweater was laid out on each of their beds, along with a pocket Bible. A woman from her church was there to keep the house and cook the food. She called to them both that night, ushering them to Jacinta's room.

Brocassie remembered standing there, his hand and Julio's held by hers, as if she were trying to link them together through her own body's spirit. "It is for you both to care for each other," she said, "for now I must return to Cuba." She smiled, closed her eyes and was gone.

They buried her next to her husband in a cemetery on the top of a hill which overlooked the Rockies to the west and the plains to the south. It was the only time that he had seen his brother cry.

He took the rum and poured some into a paper cup and drank. "They were fine people," he finally answered. "They loved us both, each in their own way."

"And Julio Álvarez, his eminence. Would you be like him? He is successful, so it seems. And," she taunted him, "very wealthy."

He felt that she was playing with him. "I'm not either of those things," he answered. Why was he apologizing to her? She was Julio's and there was nothing else to consider. He took a sip from the cup. The rum was hot, with a taste of salt to it, like a wind blown in from the sea in the heat of summer. Automatically, he looked to the west along the long spit of land they called Varadero, looking for Álvarez. In a solitude of dunes and saw grass, the thin peninsula of sand extended into the Caribbean for another ten miles to the northeast, until it terminated in the cliffs of Cabo Hicacos and then fell away over tumbled rocks and sand into the Bahía de Cárdenas.

Ten minutes before, Julio had told them that he was going to run around the entire island of Cuba in less than an hour, an Olympic record, of course, although he wanted no mention of this to the slavering press, nor did he care for a golden medal. Applause from his brother and his most favored lady would be sufficient, *por favor*. He had leaped up, spurted toward the surf, thumping his chest and hollering with Tarzanlike whoops, and disappeared to the west on the hard-packed sand. He was fit, strong and tough. This particular exercise of his, Brocassie understood, was for Alicia's benefit.

"Still, he's your brother," she said. "You must know him well."

"Sometimes I think I do, most of the times not. I don't think he knows my mind either. Lack of understanding is generally a two-way street." Without meaning to, he felt embarrassed, as if he had betrayed Julio. "You understand how it was," he amended. "We lived together. Sometimes being too close is painful when there's no common ground."

"I've heard that it happens that way, but sometimes the common ground just has to be taken on faith." She rolled over, her face to the sun, the top of her suit held by one hand, her drink in the other. Her nose was fine and aquiline, casting a shadow across her cheek. Brocassie felt an immense desire to move toward her, as if, physically, there were a gravitational attraction between their bodies. He edged nearer her, excavating sand with his hand as if he were demolishing a physical barrier.

"He has his soft side, you know," she added. "Sometimes he is difficult, a little distant, but most of the time, very thoughtful. A good person in so many ways. He thinks of small things—flowers and presents for the children's birthdays of the woman who cooks for my father. He calls me in the morning when I'm grumpy and cheers me up with his stupid jokes."

She turned more toward the sun, opening her eyes. They were deep and green, with yellow flecks, like the lake at the foot of a glacier which caught the sunlit reflection of autumn trees. A secret place where you could go when you were sick to death of the dust and tired of your own company—a place where you could be alone and yet completely whole. He suddenly realized that he was staring at her and he tore his eyes away. He sipped again on the rum. Frigate birds flew in formation down the coast, skirting the tops of the dunes, then wheeled out to sea.

Her description wasn't the Álvarez Brocassie knew. Flowers and presents for kids? Thoughtful telephone calls? That was just one side of his personality, the side he exposed first. The Julio Álvarez whom he knew stroked with one hand, then gouged with the other. The unpredictability of his moods kept those around him permanently off balance. Brocassie accepted that it was some kind of a self-defense mechanism but Julio employed it like a bludgeon, never trusting, never giving an inch.

She had been saying something and he turned to her.

". . . doing in Cuba?"

"I'm sorry," he apologized. "Daydreaming."

She smiled, not offended. "I said, what are you going to do in Cuba?"

"Nothing," he heard himself say. "Nothing except sit here with you and sip rum and watch the Caribbean. I don't have much money left and I think Julio would like to see me get back to the States pretty soon. He's paying my bills."

"He said that you're a mining engineer?"

"Trying to be. There isn't much work in the mines with the depression on."

"There are mines here in Cuba. They pay well, the American firms, particularly, since you speak both languages. My father has influential friends . . ."

He could feel it coming, overwhelming him, and he felt powerless to deflect it. He reached over to her and took her in his arms and kissed her, roughly, without skill. His blood vessels were bursting, the heat in his chest spreading outward like a brush fire. Something in the back of his mind about honor but that was submerged as she moved, of her own accord, against him, her drink spilling, the top of her swimsuit falling as her breasts crushed against his chest. He could smell her skin, feel her body molding to his—her tongue touching his timidly at first and then again, as if she were the aggressor, thrusting. His hand found her breast and held it, beneath his fingertips, he felt the nipple growing, as if it had a passion of its own to fulfill.

Locked together, they fell back against the sand, and for the first time he opened his eyes and looked into hers.

"No," she whispered. And yet her arms were around his neck, drawing him down to her.

"Alicia," he said hoarsely. He felt the restrained surge of her hips against his, just a suggestion, and yet, because of her denial, all the more compelling.

"No, please . . ." She turned her face away from his, her eyes brimming with tears. "I can't. We have to stop. I'm not that kind of a woman—you're not that kind of man."

He shoved away from her, dropping his face down in the sand, his lungs heaving. He cursed himself. He had to get away from her, from Álvarez, from Cuba.

Her hand was on his shoulder, then his cheek, touching him. She drew his face around toward hers.

"I want you so very much, Brocassie. No logic to it, no reason that I can understand. I've known that from the beginning. But he's your brother and I'm his friend. There may be a time for us—not now, but someday." She took his hand and pressed it against her bare breast, then leaned toward him and kissed him gently. "And if there is, you will be mine and I will be yours," she promised, "if you want it to be."

"I do," he answered. And for the first time in his life knew that he meant it.

They lay together and talked and laughed and were serious. She poured a warm rum and cola and they shared it, then they lay down again, side by side, only their hands touching. Slowly, he drifted into a light sleep, the dull thudding of breaking waves lulling him.

She had spoken only once more as they lay together. "Everything about you is wrong, except that I know it's right. It happens that way, my mother told me, only once in a lifetime. I don't want us to lose this one chance."

He couldn't reply, couldn't find words, could only squeeze her hand.

Minutes or hours later, he felt chilled, and he opened his eyes and looked up to see Álvarez standing over them, blocking the sun. Nothing was said, nothing explained, and yet each of them knew what had happened. As if a secret treaty had been signed, old alliances had been broken and new ones made. And after that, it had never been the same between him and Julio.

He woke with the feeling of an insect biting into his skin. Opening his eyes, he saw someone standing above him.

"Lie back, Injun," Porto said quietly. "Cracked skull, a couple of bumps, but your pecker is still in one piece."

Brocassie tried to sit up but Porto gently pushed him back down onto the cot. "Save that for tomorrow. Today's your day off."

He closed his eyes again, listening to the sounds of men joking as they worked, of wind blowing through the pines, of water running in a stream close by. And smiled, sliding off again into the soft, black, familiar tunnel of darkness.

Álvarez sat on a desk, sipping coffee, watching the farce being acted out between the two men. He didn't envy Captain Valentin Dmitriyevich Maksheyeva.

"Is this the one?" Roychenko demanded of the pilot.

Captain Maksheyeva shook his head.

Roychenko flipped a page. "This one?"

Maksheyeva studied the photograph, scowling. "No, Comrade Colonel. Like it but not exactly. There was less than a second to . . ."

"But you're sure that it was a glider?"

"With your permission, comrade?" He was sweating, his forehead beaded with moisture. Maksheyeva pulled a package of cigarettes from his jacket pocket. Roychenko nodded and the young Russian pilot lit one. "It *was* a glider," Maksheyeva repeated. "We had such types in Young Pioneer training. High wing, not tapered, large bubble canopy and typically built of wood covered with fabric."

"You think you shot him down with your cannons?"

"Yes. There is no doubt. I saw the explosions as it fell."

Roychenko turned to Álvarez. "Tell our friend the results of the search."

You poor bastard, Álvarez thought, glancing first toward Maksheyeva, then scanning the message form. "No wreckage within a five-mile radius of the reported incident. Six MIL helicopter gunships from Coastal Command participated in the search from zero six hundred until ten hundred hours."

Roychenko turned to Maksheyeva. "Wood and fabric would not give off a radar return, am I correct?"

The captain nodded. "No return or very little, comrade."

"But," Roychenko injected, "wood and fabric would float, would it not?"

"I would think that . . ." Obviously, he knew he was trapped. "Yes, comrade, it would float."

Roychenko stalked the vinyl floor of the command post, pacing out four steps, wheeling, retracing his steps. "You detected the aircraft, Captain, and entered into a chase. You fired your cannons but after that, by your own report, you saw the aircraft climbing, still in one piece. Correct?"

Valentin nodded, weakly.

"So you returned for a second pass and suddenly, miles away, you saw a couple of explosions."

"Three explosions, comrade."

"So you automatically presumed that what you saw was the aircraft you had fired upon and subsequently gave up the chase?"

The pilot nodded weakly. "I assumed . . ."

Drawing up in front of Maksheyeva, Roychenko said, "I'm finished with you, Captain."

He stood up, relief on his face, and saluted. "Thank you, comrade."

Roychenko shook his head. "I mean *finished,* Captain. Report to your commander. As of now, your flight duties are terminated. A suitable assignment will be found for your talents."

"Colonel, I—"

"THERE WERE TWO AIRCRAFT, PERHAPS EVEN THREE OR FOUR. DID THAT EVER OCCUR TO YOU, CAPTAIN?" Roychenko roared. He took one step, closing the distance between their faces. He lowered his voice but each word cut like a honed blade. "You believed what you wanted to believe, you idiot. Your specific instructions were to *shadow* any aircraft penetrating Cuban airspace, not destroy it unless fired upon. Very possibly, you've ruined an operation that has cost the Soviet Union a tremendous amount of effort and money." He stepped back. "Dismissed, Captain!"

The door closed and Roychenko slumped down in his chair, his face blank of expression. He poured tea from the china pot, added lemon and leaned back, sipping it. "Maksheyeva was unforgivably stupid, of course. We can only deal with the situation as we now know it. The objective still is to capture this assault team, not kill them. Suggestions?"

"Do you know where they landed—even if the landings of the aircraft were successful?"

"No," Roychenko answered. "But given the altitude that Maksheyeva fired on them, it would have been impossible for them to have landed on the inland side of the Sierra. I think that within a day or so, we'll find the landing strip on the south slope of the Sierra. The assault team will have to make its way over the ridge of the mountains and start down toward this valley."

"And that will take them two—maybe three days. In which case, the first step will be to truck troops to the crest and seal off their escape to the coast and then begin to drive them down into the valley."

Roychenko shook his head. "We run the risk of involving the assault team in a firefight. And even if we were able to capture one of them alive, any survivors of the Maroto column that we might not capture would then advise the CIA. Thus any message that we were able to fabricate about the nature of the complex would obviously be counterfeit." He wrapped his hands around the mug and studied the contents as if he were trying to read the future in the bits of tea leaf which clung to the sides. He looked up, his decision made. "All right, Julio. Seal off the escape route and put patrols into the Sierra, but order them not to look too hard. Tell them that, if anything, we want the assault team to penetrate our patrols. If we want to capture the assault team alive, our only hope is to isolate and trap them without many of Maroto's men being involved."

Álvarez groaned inwardly. Tell that to uneducated men who would just as soon spray a hillside with machine-gun fire if a lizard rustled the leaves. Roychenko was asking the impossible. How in hell would it be possible to cut the assault team out of Maroto's column? "It's going to be difficult to get those men alive."

"But that's your job, isn't it?" Roychenko snapped back at him. "That assault team came in two days earlier than the Solario arrangement. It's obvious to me that your woman was suspicious of what you were trying to do and somehow warned them. I would suspect that the identifier format was the means that she used, despite your reassurances that you had her complete confidence—all of which leaves you in a rather precarious position as far as we are concerned."

A flush of heat spread over his face, prickled his scalp. "I can handle it," he shot back. "I only said that it would be difficult."

"More than difficult, I would think," Roychenko answered smoothly. "Because if you don't succeed in capturing the assault team, you will be in the same category as Captain Maksheyeva—a failed player in need of replacement. And your friend, Piedra, seems to be a very determined understudy."

"Piedra," he said carefully, slowly, "couldn't handle an operation like this."

"Perhaps he doesn't need a whole army," Roychenko said. "Perhaps he just needs one man—the right man." He lifted his leg so that his foot was on the seat of the chair and massaged his calf. "And the right man is the mole that Piedra has had in Maroto's column for more than a year."

Álvarez shook his head slowly in disbelief. "I don't buy that—I never have. If Piedra controls this mole, why wasn't he able to get word out that the Solario operation wasn't going to come off?"

The thick hands kept massaging, working up to his thigh. "The damnable humidity of this country affects a wound I got in the Ukraine," Roychenko said. He grimaced, working over his leg, kneading his fingers deep into his muscles. "It's an inconvenience that the cheap gold-plated medal I received for the action never seemed to have offset." He dropped his leg and then shifted in his chair, turning around to inspect Álvarez, his eyes squinting behind the frame of his glasses. "My question, as well, Julio. I asked Captain Piedra and the answer is that the mole has no access to rapid communication. What information he gets out to Piedra is by the rather quaint method of written notes left in a tin can on the edge of the Sierra road." He leaned back in the chair, ruffling his hair with his hand. "I had to laugh when he told me that. I did the same thing with a girl that I passionately loved in my schooldays." Roychenko sighed. "It seems the mole was more successful than I was. Maroto is shifting his camp more often now and he keeps his men together in one unit. There's not much chance for Piedra and his mole to keep up a lively correspondence but he feels that his man will be clever enough to improvise an excuse to leave camp and get to the message drop point."

"Meaning?" Apprehension tightened his throat.

"Meaning that I have already given Piedra instructions to attempt to contact his man. Piedra will direct his mole to volunteer as guide for the initial reconnaissance mission of the assault team. My guess is that they'll first want to observe the complex before deciding how best to attack it. If we know what area the advance party of the assault force will use as an observation post, then there will be the possibility of capturing them intact without Maroto's column being involved." He paused, examining his hands, snapping the ends of his fingernails with the nail of his thumb. He looked back up at Álvarez. "Based on my report of events which I unfortunately can't alter, I am going to be subjected to criticism by General Lazarev for your failure to extract the full code and proper identifier from your woman. And now, I have to ask myself whether I can accept responsibility for yet another failure."

A hard knot of despair lodged in Julio's solar plexus. Alicia had somehow betrayed him, just as he had tried to betray her. Funny—so goddamned funny—that she had turned his own weapon back on him.

"There's a consolation prize, however," Roychenko offered up with a benign smile. "We have a man in Jamaica—a young revolutionary of the home-grown variety. He works in the Customs Service. Several days ago, two men came to clear a package marked 'aircraft parts.' He was able to delay them, forcing them to come back the next day. While they haggled with another customs officer over documentation, our young revolutionary took their photograph with a telescopic lens. The film was airmailed to Mexico that night and sent on to Havana the following day. The photographs are poor quality but I don't think that there's any doubt as to identity."

He pulled a stack of grainy prints from a drawer in the desk and spread them out like a winning hand. Six separate shots of two men, hunched over a counter, obviously arguing with a blurred figure in the foreground. One of the men was a lumpy-faced Hispanic, replicated millions of times over in any country on the South American continent. But the other man was Brocassie. No doubt. The hawklike nose, deeply inset eyes, high cheekbones, hair sweeping back over his head in a shock of black. So he had really come back to Cuba. You stupid bugger, he swore to himself. You just couldn't stay away from her, could you?

"It's him," he acknowledged. "It's Brocassie."

"I know that," Roychenko answered sarcastically. "Piedra recognized him immediately. The other one is a Cuban exile called 'Porto.' A mercenary pilot who flew supplies into Cuba some time ago. I think we'll find that there were only two aircraft and these were the two pilots. Brocassie is the one we'll want the most. If we can get hold of him, then he'll talk because Alicia Helvia will be the lever."

"I told you once before, Roychenko. You're not dragging her into this!" he shot back.

Roychenko smiled back, his expression bland. "Julio—I

282

like you and we work well together. But this is critical. It's not just your career which is at risk, nor is it just mine. It's the whole project and the Soviet Union's future. If she has to be used, then *we* will use her. You know them both and will understand what fulcrums are the most powerful without the need of violence. A successful interrogation will be your possible redemption in the eyes of Lazarev and myself." Roychenko lifted his hand in a benign gesture. "Is it worth it to disobey my orders, Julio? I'm only asking you for your loyalty."

He felt that all his blood had drained out of him, leaving him standing and yet not really alive. Roychenko settled deeper into his chair, an inquisitive smile on his face, waiting for a reaction.

"You're right, of course," Álvarez agreed, knowing now what it meant to be a servant of the state.

CHAPTER

12

Oriente Province, Cuba,
October 18, 1962

She knelt in the rich black soil of the garden, weeding, the sun hot on her back. The cucumbers and tomatoes were ripe, ready for picking and canning, and there was no real need to rip out the weeds, but it gave her serenity: this simple physical pleasure of the body, the smells of things growing, the heat from a star a million miles away.

Five rows to the right, Miguel paralleled her, his movements unhurried yet efficient. He was humming. Pausing, she listened more carefully, the tune a children's song from a decade ago; something his mother had undoubtedly taught him, she realized, sadness suddenly engulfing her. So very much like a son she would want for her own, a boy who would surely track dirt onto clean floors and be compulsively attracted to mischief, but also a boy whom she would love and be loved by in return. For Miguel, she knew, had that capacity. She saw it in his eyes when he was near her. She saw it in the gentleness with which he played with the cats who, contrary to their normal aloof behavior, actively sought him out.

Earlier in the afternoon, she had spilled a glass of tea, irritated at her own clumsiness but not thinking much of it. Only minutes later, Miguel had brought her a fresh glass with cubes and a sprig of mint, an embarrassed half-smile formed on his lips. Laughing, she had planted a kiss on his forehead as a casual gesture of thanks, but he, in return, had clutched at her hand in return, squeezing it with all his strength. What he could not say, he still could express in every other way.

She watched him for a long time, her heart aching. Miguel was still withdrawn, unable to speak. There had been times when Alicia had talked to him and he had listened to her intently, sometimes, it seemed to her, on the edge of speaking, but each time he had opened his mouth, starting to form words, he had only been able to voice guttural sounds, his frustration mirrored in his tortured expression. In the end, he would run away from her, mortified.

As if he sensed she was watching him, he turned toward her, smiled hesitantly, then turned back to his work. Dear God, she thought. What can I do to help him? She knew that there was no easy answer—perhaps only time, love and trust. Somehow, some mechanism inside him had frozen, protecting the delicate circuits from overload. It was his hurdle and he had cleared it, but damage had been done. Textbooks would have answers but she knew that what would restore Miguel lay much closer to the heart than to the brain.

Every once in a while, she glanced at the sun. It had been high in the southeast when Julio had arrived in the khaki helicopter, the first time that she had seen him in more than a week. He was haggard, his eyes darkened with fatigue, and he had said nothing to her, only kissed her once and headed for the library. He had locked the door behind him, worked for half an hour and then she had heard his nasal breathing of deep sleep.

She gave Marta instructions to prepare a pumpkin soup and a salad of rice, beans and tomatoes. Three beers were set to frost in the ice chest. She returned to the garden, waiting.

Now, the sun was in the southwest, hanging in the haze

like a fat orange balloon. Shadows had lengthened, the wind gone quiet as it often did toward sunset. She stood up, her limbs aching, and looked toward the main house. Sunlight blared back in reflection from the glass panes and she knew it must be after five. She collected her things, threw them into a wicker basket and slowly walked toward the house.

She bathed first, working the heat and the grit from her skin. She washed her hair with what little remained of the Finnish soap that he had brought back from Russia for her. It was not good, but it was adequate, and the fruity smell pleased him. Finally, she combed out her wet hair, pulled on a white terry-cloth robe and quietly walked down the stairs to the library door.

She tried it very gently but it was locked. Putting her ear to the thin panel, she could hear him moving around, the sound of a match lighting, the wadding of a sheet of paper. She held her breath, hesitating, and knocked.

At first there was no answer, but now there was a sound of footsteps from beyond the panel. She put her lips to the door and called his name. "Julio. It's me."

"Just a minute." There was the sound of papers rustling, footsteps and then he eased open the door and let her in.

He looked even worse now. His hair was mussed from sleep, his face puffy. It was as if he had aged ten years in just the last week.

"You slept?" she heard herself ask.

He pulled his hand down over a day-old beard. "Some."

"Marta has left you lunch, or would you prefer dinner? I'll make it. We have some freshly butchered pig. I can make a salad."

He smiled but it was perfunctory, not genuine. "In a while. I've eaten nothing but stale rations for five days and a big dinner is what I really want, but first there's something that I want to discuss with you." He walked to the window and looked out across the lawn. The sun was down, almost below the horizon, the last light a scalding red, flickering like flames behind the swaying palm fronds. "Brocassie got the message. There was a classified in the *Miami Herald* yesterday. It came in by courier last night."

He went to the wall safe, something that he had installed

more than a year before, withdrew a key which hung on a chain around his neck and fitted it into the lock. From a stack of papers and bound manuals, he withdrew an entire page of newspaper and handed it to her.

The date and stylized type of the masthead were set at the top of the sheet above the streams of classified ads. One was circled with red felt-tipped pen under the "Personals":

> To Alicia and Julio. Message received. Belated congratulations on marriage. Undoubted made for each other. Surprised about kid. Didn't know Julio had it in him.
>
> Sorry that your welcome mat's not out. Will accordingly cancel visit. However, can't say the same for friends who plan long visit.
>
> By way of confirmation, man who gave you puddy cat was Ernesto. Adios, Brocassie.

She read and reread it, staring at each word as if the newsprint would re-form into some different meaning. Part of it was the phrasing. Not Brocassie's—not exactly. Too flip, too brittle. She reread it once more, some other inconsistency nagging her. Ernesto. . . .

Julio had drafted the message to Brocassie and she had altered nothing. For Brocassie to verify the message, Julio had selected the name of the *cantina* owner who had given her the cat, Mookem Flower. Something that Julio, Brocassie and she had shared as casual knowledge, too inconsequential for others to know or be concerned with. A good choice she had thought when she first had read Julio's draft. She had almost told him what Brocassie's reply would be because Julio had only known *about* the man, not really known him. Ernesto *was* his first name—that is, if you were only an occasional customer and not his friend. Or if you were checking his records.

Her father had first taken her there on her eighth birthday. And every year, until the Revolution, she had faithfully gone back for her birthday or whenever she was within twenty miles of the little run-down *barcito* which served the best *camarones al ajillo* in Cuba.

Julio had never gone there, even though she had asked

him to. It was "too dirty, too common," he said, preferring the fine cafés in Santiago or Havana, where the linen was clean and the maître d' greeted important men at the door with ruffles and flourishes.

But Brocassie had gone to the Corral with her, three times as she recalled, and because of her, Ernesto had taken Brocassie as a friend.

Ernesto loved Gary Cooper, mimicked his walk, his drawl, his gestures. He had a cowboy outfit made up including tooled boots and a belted holster in which he kept a cap pistol. Ernesto had seen all of Cooper's films ten, twelve, in some cases, twenty times over. He had a standard fan-club autographed photo of the actor framed in his office. He developed the clipped, dust-dry accent down to perfection. And he wanted his friends to call him "Coop," which they did to please him. A harmless old man, going to fat, belly bulging out over a tooled-leather belt, with a love of Gary Cooper Westerns, stray alley cats and good friends who didn't snicker at his eccentricities.

So though customers knew him only as Ernesto (and he admitted that there *was* a certain dignity in that name for a man of property), in the favored back room which he kept only for the entertainment of his friends, he was "Coop." Brocassie knew that, Julio didn't, and she had never told Julio because she knew that he would scoff at the man and his simple fascinations.

She sat down at his desk. Her hands were shaking slightly and she put them in her lap, hiding them.

"This really came from Miami?" she asked.

"I said it did," he answered, irritated. "Last night. I had it flown down by courier, for my eyes only."

He was behind her. She felt his fingers on the back of the chair, steadying himself. "It was from him. The name's right, isn't it?" There was just a shadow of doubt in his voice.

She read through the classified again. Printed in Miami, counterfeited in Havana—what did it matter? It was a fraud and Julio was a betrayer. "Yes," she replied, half-lying, half-truthful. "His name is Ernesto." She turned to him, standing up. "Tell me honestly, Julio, no lies. This came from Brocassie?"

He nodded, and she couldn't tell, one way or the other, because in the failing light, there seemed to be no depth to his eyes.

They both were silent for a long time. She went to the window, looking out at the gathering darkness but seeing only her own dim reflection. He came up from behind and slid his arm around her waist.

"That's the end of it," he said quietly. "Brocassie is out of our lives, out of Cuba. It's finished, *chirrín, chirrán*."

She shrugged. "I suppose so."

He dropped his hand and returned to the desk, briefly read through the message and then wadded it and threw it in the wastebasket. He turned back to her. "You're quiet," he said. "Is something bothering you?"

She managed a smile. "I suppose. We both were involved with him, weren't we?" She maintained the smile, freezing it on her face, walked toward him and put her arms over his shoulders. "We'll have our own life, Julio. No regrets, nothing from the past dredged up." She drew him closer and his arms wrapped around her body. *You stinking filth*, she thought. *You slime*. She turned her face up to him, inviting a kiss. His lips were dry and his breath stank. She pulled away from him. "Would you get me something—something strong, perhaps a punch? Marta has a bottle of it in the ice chest." She pressed against him again, feeling the hardness grow in his groin.

He tipped her face up to his. "You loved him, didn't you?" It was more than a question but not quite a challenge.

She parted her lips but kept her eyes closed because she knew if she opened them, she would betray herself. "Let's not bring that up. He's behind us, Julio. Someone we both knew in a different time and place. We'll both remember the good and the bad but eventually all of it will fade like any other memory. You fulfilled your end of the bargain. We're *here and now* and I want you and I want your sons and daughters." She pulled him tighter against her, moving her body against his. "Isn't that what you want?"

"God, yes," he answered. He was aroused now and he gripped her, his fingers pressing into her lower back, arching her toward his pelvis.

She withstood another kiss, faked a shudder and pressed

her hand against his chest. "A rum punch, *especialidad de la casa*. Two of them—for you and me. A drink to the past and to the future."

His face was flushed, his eyes bright. "Yes, that first." He turned for the kitchen.

She knew that she had less than two minutes. She swung open the door of the still unlocked safe and started to rifle through the stacked papers and manuals.

The top message-form was gibberish to her, in Russian she supposed, as was the next. The third sheet was a carbon copy of a supply order, written in Spanish, an incomprehensible list of items coded by numbers with Julio's writing scrawled across it, some items x-ed out.

Her heart was thudding, nerves screaming. She could hear him in the kitchen, whistling, the click of the latch of the icebox door opening.

The next two items were thin manuals sheathed in clear plastic covers with red stripes running diagonally across their covers, marked *De Sumo Secreto* in Spanish with indecipherable Russian characters underneath. Top Secret. She pulled one out, leafed rapidly through it. Nothing that she could understand, technical drawings, long cylindrical shapes with parts identified by numbers, cross-referenced to things detailed in the blueprints; interminable tables, parts breakdowns. But one diagram caught her eye on page 19. Whatever it was, it was important. She jammed the book back into the stack of papers and pulled out the next: three papers clipped together.

The first: his handwriting, the original text that was to be sent to Brocassie. Underneath that, her handwriting, the encoded message. Beneath that, yet another encoded message, his handwriting but with the same identifier that she had used.

Clink of a bottle touched to a glass, the sound of liquid pouring and then the slam of the icebox door. His footsteps in the hall, coming toward her down the corridor.

Only seconds now. She rammed the sheets back into the safe and in doing so, her hands touched a hard shape. She reached back into the recesses, feeling it, then drawing it out. *Guerra Del Tiempo* by Alejo Carpentier. Same edition but not worn like the copy she had stolen to encode the message to Brocassie and then had hidden, wrapped in plastic, beneath the garage crawl space. No, this one was pristine. No time now. She pushed the book back into the far depths of the safe and swung the door shut, wheeled and took two steps to the desk. She slumped down, her head in her hands, waiting.

She could sense the tenseness in him because he stopped whistling and hesitated in the doorway. The room was so quiet that she could hear his breathing.

"What have you been doing?" he asked.

She opened her eyes, looking toward him. "Thinking about what we'll call our firstborn son. I like the name 'Enrique,' don't you? For my father, Julio."

"Not 'Brocassie'?"

She wrinkled her forehead. "No, I told you that we have to bury the past—not perpetuate it."

She watched his eyes move to the safe and then to her. "Enrique would be good," he finally said. Slowly, the tension of his body visibly eased. He set her drink on the desk, and then, his fist wrapped around his own glass, touched it against her cheek. "To us, then." She felt his other hand in her hair, drawing it out to its full length and releasing it, like a man stroking the mane of a favorite horse. "And to my firstborn son."

She nodded, picked up her glass and drank, forcing the sweetened drink down her throat. "To your son," she echoed. She turned to him, giving him a soft kiss on his chest and then stood up, moving toward the door. "You have more to do?"

He nodded. "I'll be another hour or so. There is paperwork to catch up on."

"I'll begin dinner, then," she said. "Something to put some meat back on your bones. *Costillas de puerco con mojo, moros, plátanos,* and perhaps something special to give you strength."

He raised his eyebrows, his look quizzical. "Strength?"

She smiled, pursing her lips. "I will send Miguel down to the village. The fishermen should be back by now. I thought perhaps you would enjoy some fresh oysters with lime juice."

He burst into laughter. "I have plenty of strength for *that.* Surely you don't believe the bullshit about oysters making a man more potent?"

"Tonight would be a very good time for us to try," she answered. "The old people swear by it and I want my son to be strong like his father."

Julio shook his head in disbelief but he was grinning, his juices flowing. "All right. Have him get a dozen. No—make that two dozen and you can eat half of them so we double our chances. But don't blame me if you give birth to a whole soccer team of Álvarezes."

She turned away, unable to hide her expression any longer. She could hear him laughing again, the sound echoing down the hallway. *Rotten bastard,* she swore to herself.

She went directly to Marta's quarters and gave her instructions to start the preparation of the dinner. Marta shot back a sullen look. "For the *comandante,*" Alicia said fiercely. "Get your fat buttocks out of that chair and earn your keep!" She slammed the door and moved back to the kitchen, glanced down the corridor, then headed toward the garage.

Miguel was in the workshop, sharpening his machete. He looked up, surprised, lay the blade down and stood up, respectfully.

"Miguel, I need you to help me," she whispered. She looked back out across the lawn. One of the guards, Sánchez, was lounging in a chair, drinking a bottle of beer. "Where are the other two?"

Miguel pointed toward the bunkhouse and lay his head against his hands, miming sleep.

"Good," she whispered. "I need you to help me do something very, very important. It's dangerous and I don't want to ask you but I have no one else to turn to. I ..."

Impulsively, he grabbed her hand, but it was his eyes that conveyed his willingness to do whatever she would ask.

Oh, God, she thought. The newspaper message was a fake—she was positive of that, and her quickly formulated plan had been based on abstractions but the boy standing in front of her was flesh and blood. He's so young, he's been through so much already and yet he still has so much to live for and if they were to catch him, he'd be shot. No, it was too much to ask. She knew that she couldn't. She attempted a smile and, putting her hand under his chin, said, "Miguel, I can't ask this of you. I didn't have time to think it through."

His expression was tortured. He was shaking now, and his mouth worked, gasping like a beached fish, guttural sounds forming in his throat.

She drew the boy against her, put her arms around him and then hugged, slowly rocking him. "I love you, Miguel," she whispered in his ear. "Like you were my own. It was nothing—really nothing. A silly idea, *mi amor*."

Miguel put his arms around her, surprisingly strong, fierce and demanding. He buried his head against her breasts, his tears wet on her skin, but she suddenly recognized words, muffled and distorted, but understandable. He forced each word out, one at a time, gasping for breath between them.

"I will—will try! For you. TRY! LET—ME—TRY!"

Astonished, she held him at arm's length, looking into his face. "Oh, Miguel, oh, sweet Holy Mother!"

The boy's eyes were wide, mouth open in amazement. Tears streamed down his dusty face, his mouth working, and then he was back into her arms, words and sounds intermixed, sobbing and laughing, his body racked in a spasm of emotion.

She led him up to his room and held him for a long time, stroking his hair, rubbing his back, whispering half-words to him, rocking him against her. Slowly, very slowly, he calmed under her touch, wiped his eyes and looked at her, his face determined. "I ... will," he said, the words clear but hesitant. "You ... cannot take ... that from me."

She couldn't look at him, afraid to lose control. Knowing that he was right because she had no one else to turn to and to deny him would tear him apart. She thought it through again, each part of the idea, and then finally nodded. "Miguel, what I ask of you is dangerous but it's so very important because it involves the lives of others. I will let you help me but you must promise that if you are caught, you will tell them that I ordered you to do this for me. That is the condition. Do I have your word of honor?"

He drew himself up, pushed his thick black hair back, his shoulders squared. "Whatever it ..." He swallowed, started again. "Whatever, I will do ... will do it. For you."

She held his face between her hands. "Tonight, before moonrise ..."

* * *

Drunk, he had taken her to the bedroom, his hand locked over her wrist, and then thrown her down on the bed. It was somewhere between rough playfulness and rape, as if he had condensed all his frustration, hope, joy and hate into one physical act. He had been violent, pounding into her, yet when it was over, he had stroked her face gently with his hands, working across her forehead and temples. Her heart had finally slowed to the point that she thought it would stop. She lay there, exhausted, at first feeling the touch of his hands and when they fell away, listening to his heavy respiration, slowly modulating to a gentle snore.

She was raw inside, and she remembered the pain and his rank breath on her face as he pumped against her body, arched his back and groaned in the final spasm of orgasm. She knew that she was fertile, at least within a few days of it, and when he was asleep, she had gone to the bathroom and douched twice with vinegar and water, but she had no confidence. There were millions of women who had believed in the contraceptive powers of vinegar who learned of their own ignorance when their belly swelled. But it was the only thing that she had and she prayed that it would protect her.

Twice, she flushed the toilet, testing the depth of his sleep. Finally, she scuffed her way back to the bedroom and sat down heavily on the bed, the springs creaking.

His voice was heavy with fatigue. "What's wrong?"

"I couldn't sleep." She lay down, moving against him. Her fingers walked through the mat of hair on his chest, briefly touched the chain and key, then traced down through the growth which bisected his belly, playfully exploring the wiry bush of his pubic hairs. Gently, tantalizingly, she brushed his penis with her nails. "Do the oysters give you strength, Julio? Perhaps you're too exhausted." She stroked along the shaft, teasing it, and then cupped her hand under his testicles, pressing gently but insistently.

He groaned.

She bit at his lip, knowing that she had to exhaust him. For the first time in her life, she hated her body, the act of sex, the sweat and stench of coupling, but it was her only weapon and she used it, her body performing once more while she tried to detach her mind. Thinking of waves breaking on the beach, the wash of the sea around her body, the wind cooling her damp skin. Her fingers moved expertly, coaxing, pleading, growing more confident as he hardened. When she was sure, she lifted herself onto her knees and hands like a bitch in heat. "It will go deeper this way," she promised and then she felt his weight on her back.

The luminescent hands on the clock moved past 2:00 A.M. Julio was on his back, his mouth open, breathing heavily. She touched his chest, at first just teasing the skin then pinching it lightly between her fingernails. He grunted once and turned on his side. Gently, with infinite care, she lifted the chain and the key, her fingers trembling. Working with her nails, she unlocked the hasp, withdrew the key and substituted a key which she had secreted beneath her pillow. It was chromed brass, like the one that Julio had used on the safe, but it was smaller, a key from the padlock she kept on the liquor cabinet in an attempt to keep Marta from pilfering their supply of black-market whiskey. Gently, very gently, she lowered the key to his chest. He grunted once again and rolled over on his stomach.

In the darkness, she waited, counting slowly to fifty. Julio shifted again, this time away from her. The clock ticked out seconds, the only sound in the silent house.

Finally, she eased herself out of the bed, tiptoed to the bathroom and with infinite care, closed the door. From behind the toilet bowl, she withdrew a roll of sewing thread, knotted one end through the hole in the key and then, opening the window, she lowered it. It made a small metallic sound as it contacted the galvanized porch roof. She eased the thread more, listening to the small scraping sound the key made as it slid down the roof's corrugated channel and then the silence as it cleared the edge, hanging suspended in space. Confident now, she lowered away, slowly, trying to estimate the number of feet that she eased from the spool. She guessed three feet, then five then seven. Not enough, she thought, and eased out another foot. Nothing for seconds that dragged out to minutes. She jiggled the thread. Nothing.

Was Miguel there? Had he understood? She thought about whistling and rejected the idea. One guard would be on patrol and in the stillness, he would hear her.

She was desperate now. Somehow, she had to do something to attract Miguel's attention yet not alert the guard.

She swallowed twice, her throat dry, her palms wet, her body tense with fear. She checked to make sure that the door was completely closed, then flicked on the lights of the bathroom. On the lawn below, she could see the golden trapezoid of light. She jiggled the key again but there was no answering tug. Desperate now, she searched for a way to attract Miguel's attention. She had told him to hide in the bushes which edged the porch sometime after midnight but it was obvious that he wasn't there.

So she had to do it herself—walk through the bedroom, down the stairs and into the library, to open the safe, extract the message forms, copy each of them and replace the originals in their exact order. If Julio wakened and found her gone, he would suspect the worst. And he would come looking, first in befuddled concern, then in confirmation of her betrayal.

Suddenly from below she saw the reflected glow of a match's flare, heard a cough—the scrape of a chair being moved on the porch, the sound of hawking and spitting. Footsteps below on the wooden planks of the porch, a pause and more steps. A flashlight switched on, flaring in sweeps across the grass. The light moved into the open, jinking across the lawn. She realized that the guard had been dozing in a porch chair and had been awakened by the sound of the key scraping on the galvanized porch roof.

Without warning, her bladder seemed to be on the verge of exploding. She swept up her nightgown and sat down on the toilet, voiding in a sudden torrent. She was reaching for the paper when there was a soft rap on the door.

His voice was blurred with sleep. "You all right?"

Her heart pounded in a staccato. "Don't . . ." She felt a tug on the thread. She quickly eased out the spool, felt two light jerks and then a steady pressure. Reaching behind her, she flushed the toilet. "It was the oysters," she said weakly.

From behind the door, he grunted. She heard the sound of his feet on the floor, the creaking of the mattress and then silence.

For the first time in five years, she crossed herself, stood up, her legs shaking, washed her hands and flicked off the lights. Opening the door, she moved across the floor and sank down on the mattress. His hands found her, pulling her toward him. "The oysters have a different effect on me," he breathed into her ear, and as he moved against her, she could feel the radiant heat of his body.

She woke to sun in her eyes, panic as her hand found only fading warmth in the space next to her. She tried to focus, the fatigue of sleeplessness and sex burdening her body.

The bathroom door was closed, the shower hissing.

On his nightstand was his watch and the chain with the key. She snapped it open, removed the liquor cabinet key and slid it under the mattress. Only seconds now, if that. She ran to the bathroom door. Inside, it was a steam bath. He was humming something, his body in a dim blur beyond the partially closed pebbled glass door.

She swept the door closed, slamming it shut.

"HEY!"

"Oysters!" she said weakly. "I must have had one that was rotten."

He pushed the door open again, water streaming off his body, his skin pinked by the heat of the water.

"*PLEASE!*" she screamed, drawing up her nightgown, ramming her foot against the door, slamming it shut, then sinking down onto the toilet.

From behind the glass, he laughed. "Your idea, *¡mi corazón!*" He started to sing again and then opened the door with one hand, sticking his dripping head out, soap covering his hair and face, his eyes clamped shut. "The old people seem to understand the effects of *ostras.*" He laughed, his voice male and husky. "One more time, Alicia. Here—in the shower?" He roared with laughter. She threw the roll of toilet paper at him and he ducked, pulling the door shut once again.

He was making blubbering sounds, wallowing in the spray, braying out an obscene marching song.

Desperate, terrified, she tugged at the thread. It came easily at first and then suddenly she met resistance. *¡Que coño!* she swore under her breath. The key was there but it was caught on the lip of the galvanized roofing.

She tugged again, let out slack, jiggled and pulled again.

The sound of the shower changed; squeak of a faucet handle being turned. He gargled, taking water in his mouth and spitting it out. Seconds now.

She let out three or four feet, jerked it three times to set the key swaying and then yanked. She saw the flash of chrome arc over the edge and land on the galvanized roofing of the porch. Retrieving it quickly, she balled the line in her hands, finally feeling the cool metallic surface of the key.

"TOWEL!" he demanded, poking his head out, eyes squeezed shut, his hands groping in front of him.

She grappled a towel from the rack, shoved it into his face and with the thread and key balled in her fist, fled through the doorway, slamming it behind her.

It took her agonizing seconds to tear the key from its knotted loop and reattach it to Julio's chain, seconds more to gather in the yards of thread and shove it beneath the bed. The door flung open and he stood there naked, toweling his back.

His eyes traversed her wet footprints on the floor and the look of easy amusement faded from his face. He flicked his eyes back to her and then again to his night table, strode over and reached down for the chain.

He held it up carefully, watching the key rotate in the sunlight, the mirrored reflection of the sun arcing slowly across the whitewashed walls. With a finger, he wiped the beads of water from the surface of the key. His voice was suddenly hard. "You will never touch this again—do you understand?"

She lowered her head. "I was going to bring it to you."

He set his mouth, lips tight, then slowly relaxed, smiling. "Coffee," he said. "Make me coffee and bring it to me in the study. And some eggs."

She pulled a robe over her nightdress, brushed past him and opened the door into the hallway.

His voice rang after her, rough and commanding and yet with a ring of humor in it. "And tell that kid to bring me a dozen more oysters. Before noon!" His laugh followed her down the stairs.

She was trembling, light-headed, her hand on the banister to steady herself. But within her, the hot, bright banner of victory unfurled.

* * *

She had driven Marta out of her room, setting her to prepare coffee, fried eggs and country ham, and from there, she had moved across the lawn to the garage.

In the darkness of the garage, at first she did not see Miguel. Then he came forward, out of the shadows.

He was smiling. "I did it," he said softly. His voice was a little mechanical, as if he had to reach for each individual word, but the words were clear.

Impulsively, she drew him against her and kissed his forehead. "If nothing else, Miguel," she said, "you are forever a hero."

Looking past her shoulder, he suddenly stiffened and pulled back from her. "One of the guards . . ." he hissed. He moved to a workbench, picked up a trowel and bucket and brushed past her out into the hard morning sunlight.

A shoe grated on the concrete behind her. She turned, drawing her robe tighter around her.

"Is there a problem?" the one called Sánchez asked. A cigarette hung from his lips, the AK-47 slung negligently from his shoulder.

"A very large problem, Sánchez," she answered. "I was questioning the boy about a silver bracelet that I lost yesterday. Perhaps you found it. It *was* a gift from the *comandante*."

Sánchez scuffed one boot nervously against the other and then backed off a step. "I have seen no bracelet. I will ask the other men if you wish."

Sensing her own power to intimidate the man, she moved toward him and, predictably, he retreated another step. "It was an expensive bracelet, Sánchez. Something that could be sold for a good price. You're sure that you haven't seen it? Perhaps we should discuss this with the *comandante*. He is very concerned."

Sánchez was shaking his head, still moving away. "I know nothing." He tried a smile but it was a strained, artificial grimace. "I will ask the other men—my sacred word on it, Señorita Helvia."

She watched him walk across the lawn toward the guards' bunkhouse. Her breathing was rapid, a lump of lead in her stomach, but slowly she calmed herself. Sánchez would not be back, nor would any of the others. All of the guards were petty thieves and they would want no further contact with her on this matter. For minutes more, she watched the guards' bunkhouse and then, satisfied that no one would disturb her, she climbed the ladder to Miguel's room over the garage.

She found the sheets of tracing paper that Miguel had used neatly pressed between sheets of cardboard, stuffed under his straw-filled mattress along with the small penlight, the ball-point pen and her own stolen copy of *Guerra Del Tiempo*, encased in its waterproof wrapping, moisture and dirt still spackling the plastic cover. She settled onto his cot, examining the tracings. The first one—a book-code message, all numbers but the same identifier that she had used—FMCBR. This message was much longer. In the bottom-right-hand corner was a wobbly tracing of two concentric ovals which contained a time and date grouping—undoubtedly the stamp that a radio officer would use to indicate the time of transmission. More than twenty-four hours after she had given Julio the coded message.

The second tracing was the one from page 19 of the manual, this one done carefully and with great precision. She could imagine Miguel lying beneath Julio's desk, penlight clamped between his teeth, sweat making his fingers slippery, studiously tracing each line, knowing that at any minute the door to the library could slam open and strong hands snatch at his neck, yank him upright and beat him senseless. It had taken great courage—more than most men would have and incredible for a boy of his age.

How much time had passed? she wondered. Julio would be ready for breakfast, but she had to confirm what she already suspected.

It took her over forty minutes. Each group contained three numbers, separated by dashes. The first number, the page, the second the line number, the third the word. And from that, the identifier indicated a number to be subtracted or added to each. Complicated and because of that, almost unbreakable, but Julio had somehow done it. For the bastard he was, she had to give him credit.

Julio had exploited her and now she knew the depth of his treachery. The only thing needed to break a book code was both the clear text message and the matching encoded message. Somehow they found out what book she had stolen. Someone in the library? She had been careful, so very careful, but then she was alone and an amateur while Julio had hundreds of professionals at his disposal. She had stupidly handed him Brocassie's life, Maroto's life, and the lives of Maroto's men. She had had the first inklings when she had seen the newspaper Julio had given her but even then she was not absolutely sure. These paper tracings were the proof.

The damage had been done and there was nothing she could do to rectify it. Slowly, she lay down, burying her face in his pillow. Energy finished, no options. Brocassie would be parachuting in within two days, perhaps three at the most. Nylon chutes in the night, drifting down to be pinned like moths in a spotlight, helpless. What Julio would do then . . .

On the surface of her reasoning, she knew that she wasn't responsible, and yet, something deep-rooted within her grabbed at her heart and squeezed with unrelenting force.

There was only one thing left for her to do. She had to get word to Maroto, through the old network, whatever was left of it. And there was only one person to do it: Miguel.

From a distance, she heard her name being called. She stood up and looked out the small shutter opening, across the courtyard. Julio was on the porch, hands cupped, bellowing. *"ALICIA?"*

She scrambled down the ladder into the garage and that was where he found her.

"What in hell have you been doing?" he demanded. He was wearing his uniform, starched into hard creases, his boots glistening.

"Nothing," she answered, keeping her voice soft, compliant. "Just trying to find some radish seeds for the garden." She lifted her hands in a gesture of helplessness.

"Christ!" he swore. "You're still in your nightgown. What in shit do you think the fuckin' guards are imagining? Get the hell inside and change. Pack a bag for a week's trip. We've got a chopper coming in less than an hour."

Her heart sank. "Where are we going?"

"Pack," he demanded. "I was saving it for a surprise. You're coming with me. I've demanded that Roychenko give me a cottage close to the complex where I'm working in the

Sierra. It will be better for us. I'll be able to be home most nights. If we stay a long while, I can always send for more of your stuff."

"I want to stay here!" She was surprised at the defiance in her voice and she saw immediately that it was a mistake.

Very slowly, very distinctly, he answered, "I said *pack.*" He literally spat the words at her. "*NOW!*"

She threw things into a bag, douched again with vinegar, showered, brushed out her hair. She finally sat down on the bed, everything gone from her body. There was no feeling left. She stood up, opened the wardrobe and manipulating the secret compartment's door, withdrew the Beretta. It was cool, inviting, comforting, like an old acquaintance's handshake. She tentatively smelled the barrel, sensing the pungency of oiled metal. It would be over so quickly, she thought. So tired, so tired, and the slab of metal in her hand offered rest. She drew back the action and watched a gleaming brass cartridge slide from the clip into the chamber.

Pressure, she thought. Only a tiny amount of pressure on the trigger and it would be finished. She put the barrel up to her mouth, resting it against her teeth. Is this the way it was done? The barrel tasted of oil and bitter cold like the breath of wind in winter.

Voices in the lower hallway, footsteps on the stairs. She knew for certain that if it was Julio, she would kill him. How could he have done this thing? She lifted the gun, wrapped her other hand around it and aimed at the door, her eyes watering, her body shaking, finger tightening on the trigger.

Footsteps in the hallway but not the hard clap of army boots. She eased the safety on and quickly slid the weapon under the pillow. There was a soft rap at the door.

She opened it. Miguel stood there, worry creasing his forehead. "I have come for your bags," he whispered. "The *comandante* sent me. He was telling Marta that you're going away with him. Why?"

She pulled him in and shut the door behind her.

"There is no time left, Miguel. Do you know how to get to Santiago?"

He hesitated and then nodded. "I could . . . I can find my way."

She felt frustrated, incapable of decision, and yet she had to make one. So much at stake, so little time. There was only one option. "There is a woman in a bakery on Libertad in the Old Quarter. Her name is Felicia. Take the tracings that you made and the other paper that I have written. They are under your mattress. I will also give you a letter telling her who you are. Tell the woman everything—about me, about yourself, anything that she asks, but demand—I mean absolutely demand—that this information gets to a man by the name of Maroto. He has to be told that Solario is a trap. If he believes it, he'll have the means to do the right thing." How insane, she thought. There was not enough time and who would listen to a boy with a fantastic tale?

He stood up, his face set with determination. "I will do it. I promise that."

She rummaged in her drawer, finding only thirty-seven pesos. She thrust the bills into his hands. "It is all that I have. Can you remember the message?"

He asked her to repeat it slowly and gave it back to her, word for word. He touched his forehead. "It is here—forever."

She bent down and touched her lips to his temple. "Take my bag down first and then leave. Use the coastal bus." She kissed him again, mussed his hair with her hand and then held his head up to hers. "And when you do, go quickly. Very much depends on it, Miguel. It is all in your hands." It sounded too formal, too stilted, but how did you explain love, hope, hate, fear and betrayal in two minutes?

He took her bag, hesitated in the doorway and smiled brilliantly back at her. "Thank you for letting me do this," he said simply, evenly, very adult. "Thank you for everything." He turned, humping the bag down the corridor.

She sat back down for a few minutes, composing herself, stilling her mind. Sounds of the helicopter beating down the lawn with the pressure of its coming. Go quickly, Miguel, she said soundlessly.

CHAPTER

13

Sierra Maestra, October 19, 1962

The wind was fitful, gusting one minute, dormant the next. Rain fell in a continual drizzle and fog wrapped them in a damp gray shroud.

The four of them toiled up the col toward the ridgeline of the Sierra Maestra. Brocassie could barely make out trees which were no more than a few feet away. There was the stink of rotting vegetation and the insistent sound of the rain and machetes hacking.

He felt fatigue melting down his bones, seeping through his muscles, wearing away at what little remained of his strength. He counted the steps between each rest period even though they became fewer in number.

Through the morning, they had heard choppers beating down the ridge, but from this they were safe. The choppers could only fly above the cloud cap on the Sierra. It seemed, besides, that they were still looking on the southern slope from where they had come.

"Hanging in there?" Porto asked wearily, his chest heaving with exertion. His growth of beard was now greasy and his eyes were haunted by too little sleep. He waved his hand and the two Cuban kids stopped and sank to the ground in one easy motion. One of them lit a cigarette and the other pulled out a stick of dried beef jerky. They both were carrying pack frames loaded with over fifty pounds of gear, plus their M-2 carbines wrapped in black plastic bags to protect them against the damp. One of them carried three sticks of Russian grenades. The grenades were scuffed and smeared with mud and Brocassie speculated that the damn things would go off immediately once the handle was cocked. Dumb kids but tough as nails.

One looked back at him, made a face and gave the finger. Brocassie found himself smiling and spiked a finger back. OK little bastards, he thought. We can all play the game of war. There's no minimum on the age that you can die. He smiled briefly, thinking of the junior thugs on the streets of Denver, and how they would handle climbing through mud and fog, knowing that in the next thirty seconds, they could just as well be spitting up blood from a mortar round as breathing. Probably, these two kids could walk down Larimer Street at 2:00 A.M. and leave a trail of mangled muggers behind them without mussing a hair.

Porto sat down, his back to a tree, and lit a cigar. "My fucking kingdom for a beer," he groaned. "Climbing in mud sucks, doesn't it?" He made an attempt at a laugh. "I mean, literally." His boots, like Brocassie's, were covered with a rich, chocolate muck.

"How far to the crest?"

Porto shrugged. "When we start walking down instead of up. I figure in another hour at this pace. But I think we should hang it up for the day. You've walked about four miles, most of it straight up. I don't know what keeps your motor running." He cocked an eyebrow. "Hang it up, kid. You're wearing me out."

Brocassie leaned over and took the cigar, puffed on it and passed it back. The tobacco was stale, like breathing exhaust fumes from a diesel truck. He coughed and spat out phlegm. "Let's keep going. Make the ridge anyway. The Russians must have three or four choppers working the ridge. This cloud cap is pure bonus. We get to the ridge, rest until sundown and then start down toward Maroto's camp. We could make it by dawn?" It was a question.

Porto leaned back, his head against the trunk of the tree, his face exposed to the dripping condensation and rain. He shielded his cigar under his fatigue cap and he looked faintly ludicrous—a cold warrior who could pass for a wet tramp camped on the edge of a railroad yard, smoking a cadged butt.

"You're driving me straight into the ground," Porto said in a mock grumble. "Where'd you get the strength? It's me who should be on a stretcher." He pulled down on the cigar with a series of sucking sounds, inhaled, then blew the smoke outward in fractured rings. He nodded. "OK—you're right. We'll knock down the march to ten minutes walk, ten minutes rest. That'll still see us to the crest by early afternoon. If we can find some shelter, we'll bag in there, then cut south in the early evening until we hit the supply road over the pass that the Russians have cut. According to Maroto's sketch, we intersect the road and follow that down to the forty-one-kilometer marker and then cut north again. His sentries will pick us up about three miles in, assuming that they're not too busy screwing wild goats."

Brocassie got to his knees, used a young sapling to support him and pulled himself to his feet. He had the overpowering desire just to lie down in the mud and sleep. Unsteady, swaying, a little light-headed, he checked the compass. Due north and upslope—the same. "Let's get on with it. Like the song says, milk and honey on the other side." He started to move up the grade. He heard Porto behind him and the two kids took the point, machetes flailing at the brush.

One foot after the other, slipping on the slimy rocks, the slick red mud, using what handholds were available.

They stopped four more times before noon. Hernando, the younger kid, had developed a case of the runs and it affected his sense of manhood. He tried to make a joke of it but his face was pale and he was shivering badly with the onset of a fever.

Porto had caught up to Brocassie, breathing heavily, limping. "We're beginning to look like a lineup for the old-age home. I've got a small problem with my right foot. How you holding up?"

"Whipped," he answered. He was beginning to feel giddy, almost as if his body had become disconnected from his brain. He surrendered and sat down on a ledge of rock. "Let's take ten."

Luis and Hernando slumped down a few feet away, pulled their ponchos over their heads, used their carbines as props and imitated tents.

Porto flopped down beside Brocassie and unlaced his right combat boot, withdrawing his foot from the mud-saturated leather. His sock was wet with blood, dark where it had congealed. Stripping off his sock, he wiggled his toes in the rain. "Sweet Jesus. That feels better than a Flagler Street telephone booth handjob." He massaged his foot, then unsnapped the flaps of his backpack, jostling around inside for the aid kit.

Brocassie sat still, eyes unfocused, staring off into the fog. It seemed to him that it would be impossible to go on. How quickly the muscles decomposed. Sickness was like a foretaste of death. Two—nearly three—days behind schedule now. "Did you have any luck repairing the radio we brought in?"

"No, it's fritzed. Two of the vacuum tubes are busted and some thingies inside are leaking goo all over the circuit board."

"How about Maroto's radio?"

"Useless. Receiver works OK but the jamming is still going on. The transmitter section seems all right but it doesn't have much more power than an old peanut whistle. We're cut off, sport."

"And if we're supposed to transmit a status report to Hagger, how can we get it out?"

"Hand delivery, I guess. Either that or tape-record the report, include the films and have one of Maroto's boys run it out of the country by fishing boat."

"How about this guy Hall at Guantánamo Bay that Hagger mentioned?" Brocassie suggested. "It's only sixty miles east of here."

"Hagger's bright idea but a bad choice, according to Maroto. Castro has minefields all around the place. Maybe twenty thousand permanent troops ringing it. We'd never make it in. Nope," he shook his head, picking at the blistered flesh with his knife, "hand delivery is about all we've got to work with."

"How many days to do that?"

Porto shook his head, preoccupied with cleaning the raw flesh. "Ten, I figure. If everything goes right. Fifteen days if it doesn't." He winced as he applied the antiseptic. "Ehhhh! *SHIT*!" He waggled his foot in the air, his teeth gritted.

"Two days behind schedule right now, two or three more to get Maroto organized so that we can do a recon, four days for the recon itself then probably eight more to get the information back to Hagger. This whole thing strike you as impossible? A bunch of old men, a couple of kids and us."

Wrapping the galled flesh with a bandage, Porto shook his head. "You're like me, Brocassie. A bona fide cynic. What do you *think* Hagger expects, miracles? Huh-uh, ace. He's realistic. Hagger knows something important is going on in that complex. If it's a total Soviet operation, it's hot. There's a presidential directive that says 'hands off' on any U.S. military or agency involvement which would possibly cause Soviet casualties. So Hagger can't get backing for a flat-out military action." He waved his hands in the air like a conductor, directing a fanfare. "So *dah-dah*, he sends in a couple of expendable Cuban look-alikes—two bums without any family ties, no known addresses and no current tax returns—and he expects to see some action, enough to create a fuss. Probable results: a few killed Russians, a hole blown open in some goddamn field, a photograph or two—not a big deal, see? *BUT* he jazzes it up till it's mouth-watering and then he goes to the big bosses in the CIA and says—hey, fellows, some unauthorized action took place in Cuba—strictly without agency knowledge or approval, but lookie what they turned up and doncha think we should do something about it? Such as maybe setting up a hundred-man assault force with one of the Cuban groups in Miami or better yet, send in the Eighty-second Airborne and do the job right?" He shook his head. "We're just the stalking horses, sport. Expendable stalking horses, I might add."

"You're saying that we should forget about it—leave Hagger flat?"

Porto wiggled his toes, wincing. "Not exactly, but we're

only the preliminary match. The main event comes later." He
eased back, admiring his work, and then pulled his boot on. "I
figure that we've got an obligation to do what's possible.
Photos, we can take. Surveillance of guard schedules, patrol
routines, strengths and weaknesses of their security. If we're
really hot shit, we lob in a couple of mortar rounds and blow
up some fencing and then run like hell. You really believe that
Hagger thinks we can penetrate that fuckin' complex?"

Brocassie stared at the ground, knowing that Porto was
right. "So where do we draw the line?"

Porto stood up, kneading the stiffness from his legs.
"Prior to getting Hershey bar stains in our skivvies." He hefted
his carbine. "Once we're satisfied that we've done what's possible, we'll send Hagger a taped report and whatever photos
we can get and then head east for Santiago. From there on out,
it's our show."

From there on out, it's our show. Almost as insane as what
they were attempting to do now. Brocassie shrugged, not answering, eyes unfocused, images flopping over in his mind.
Her dark green, black, hazel, gold-flecked eyes. Hair cascading over her shoulders and back like the spring runoff from a
glacier. The small mole on the back of her neck which she
touched when she was nervous, unconsciously lifting her
breast, drawing his eyes to it. How she pursed her lips in an
impish grimace just before eating an orange, how she would
hold the cat up by the belly before her face, blowing little puffs
of breath at the animal's whiskers, the cat loving it, pawing in-
dolently at her with harmless little jabs. The memory of her
swamped his senses and none of it matched up with betrayal.
Yet he didn't know, and for the sake of the one commitment
he had ever made in his life, he had to find out.

"Yes," he finally answered Porto. "After this is done, it's
our own show, isn't it?" He heaved himself upright, his feet
feeling like wooden stumps, rooted in the earth. "But first of
all, we give Hagger his money's worth."

Porto gave him a curious look, shrugged and got to his
feet. "It's your funeral, sport—just as long as it's not mine as
well. Just understand that I don't go in for John Wayne stuff."
He shrugged into the straps of his backpack.

The four of them headed higher.

They crested the Sierra sometime after three.

The broken rubble of the crest was treacherous underfoot, and the trees had disappeared, replaced by stunted, wind-bowed scrub. Large boulders, like the teeth of an old man, protruded in a ragged line down the ridge. Brocassie thought it was the most desolate place that he had ever seen.

The four of them caught their wind, panting, and then headed down slope. They roped up, one man always on belay, edging down the steep grade. The fog was getting patchy, blue sky showing through the ragged tears, the sun a dim halo behind the muslin mist.

Porto was limping badly, lines of pain engraved on his face. And the younger kid, Hernando, no longer even had strength to drop his pants. The seat of his pants was stained through.

They found a slab of rock which had broken off, forming an open-ended windfall against the face of the mountain's slope. It gave some protection from the wind and more important, it would shield them from the view of the choppers if the fog cleared.

They made coffee and ate cans of beans, heated over a Sterno stove. Hernando was shivering, unable to keep anything down. He wrapped his tarp around himself and dug into the earth, like a wounded animal, burrowing for warmth and safety.

"He's in a bad way," Porto said softly. "I don't have anything in the aid kit to give him except Lomotil. And the poor bastard can't keep it down."

Almost indifferently, Luis spooned beans out of the can with his fingers, finished them off and shoved the empty can deeper under the rock. "He has this problem often. He will not die, but he also will not be able to move very much. Maybe by darkness or by tomorrow." He hand-rolled a cigarette expertly, lit it with a twig from the blue flame and leaned back. "We must change the plan," he said simply.

"Such as?" Porto grunted.

"Maroto's camp is difficult to find." He scratched the stick in the sand, marking the route. "But two miles in from the road at kilometer forty-one is a large outcropping of rocks they call the 'Needles.' If I find that this afternoon, then I could come back upslope from there by evening. And in the morning, we could work down toward Maroto's camp directly. It would save seven, maybe eight hours of walking. It would also allow us to avoid the patrols because they stick mostly to an area on either side of the road to avoid a bullet in the head from our snipers. They control the road but we control the Sierra." His voice had the cutting edge of pride in it—not just a kid's brag, Brocassie thought.

"What do you think?" Porto asked, turning to Brocassie.

He glanced over at the shriveled form of Hernando. The kid was sleeping now, exhausted. And Porto. He kept a good face on it but his foot was bad. You could smell the stench of corruption, even in the drafty windfall. There was risk involved but Luis was savvy, like a mountain goat with a strong sense of the territory and an even stronger sense of survival. Brocassie nodded. "Let him give it a try."

Luis took only a small rucksack with food, matches, water and ammunition. With the carbine still wrapped in plastic, he started downslope and in twenty steps, he disappeared into the fog.

"What do you really think?" Porto asked. "I mean, Maroto said that there were three men who could have turned traitor. Luis was one of them."

"But he thinks that it was Enrico, right?"

Porto nodded. "Yeah—I've seen that cat and he'd get my vote as well: a regular prick. Still . . ."

"I thought about it as well, but Luis has no means of communicating with anyone. If he's on the level, then we shorten the march tremendously. If he comes back by early evening with the shortcut all figured out, then we can trust him. If he suddenly shows up with a squad of DGI, then we've got to be prepared to fight our way out of here. We hold the high ground. They'd never make it up that slope. If we held them off and started east along the slope, we'd be moving deeper into Maroto's territory and sooner or later, we'd get support."

"So we post a watch." He heaved himself up into a sitting position, reaching for his M-3.

"No." Brocassie shook his head. "I'm wide awake. I'll take the watch until nightfall and then I'll rouse you out. Got things to think about."

"Your only fault, sport: you think too much." Porto scratched his head, raked his fingers through his beard and then lay back, clasping his hands on his chest. In thirty seconds, he was snoring.

He kept guard, squatting in the entrance of the overhang. Behind him, Porto snored and Hernando, even in his sleep, chattered with cold and fever. Brocassie closed his mind to everything except the slope below him. He swept it with the 7 x 50s, picking out details in the exposed slope where cover would be available to men trying to storm their encampment. Damn little cover, and a slope that was close to 30 percent grade. Only one gully, but that was far off to the left, maybe more than two hundred yards. He smiled finally, and then lit a cigarette. Easy to understand why Castro had used these mountains in the early stages of the Revolution—why Maroto used them now. They couldn't be taken.

Slowly he relaxed, leaning back against the rock. Flies buzzed around him, making him drowsy. An ant crawled across his pant leg, then a second and a third, inspecting crumbs. Two lizards scrambled up the rock near his head, turning bright eyes toward him, their colors melding from green to brown. He watched them, silently betting on which one would reach the top of the rock. Then he fell asleep.

He awoke just before sunset. The fog was gone and with it the dampness. The air in the valley was polished and brilliant, like a crystal glass. Just rimming the northwestern horizon was a mass of black swollen-bellied clouds; tomorrow would be overcast with rain and snapping gusts of wind. And the mud would be even worse, even more dangerous because it would retain their footprints. But that was tomorrow. Tonight was a time of peace.

He stood up in the protection of the overhanging rock and looked out over the valley. Blades of sunlight from beneath the retreating clouds on the western horizon sparked off the mica-flecked rocks on the chain of hills which lay on the opposite side of the valley, the Sierra de Micaro. And down below him, already in darkness, was the floor of the valley. Pale green lights formed rings within rings, enclosing an immense area. The perimeter lighting for the complex he thought. There were a few other scattered lights within the complex, mostly moving. Patrols, maybe. Or surface transport for the technicians. The rest of it would be underground.

His body was stiff and brittle, like a wet piece of leather which has been stretched and left to dry in the sun. Stitches in his forehead tugged at his skin and he had an insatiable urge to scratch. But it was OK. Clean, without complications. Internal workings of the brain pudding were something else, he thought. Still the persistent pounding headache and blurred vision in his left eye. Food and sleep. Clean sheets and a long soaking bath with a bottle of whiskey as a companion. All as remote as ice cream in the Gobi Desert.

He left the protection of the overhang and sat down on a rock, massaging the cramped muscles in his calves. Wonder what the old man would have thought of me working for Hagger and the rest of the fish bellies, making the world safe for HoJo's, Studebaker and Howdy-Doody. The old man probably would have told me that there was no honor in it, could almost hear his words. Men fought their own battles, not for others, and not for gain. And certainly not for the love of a woman. Any fool knew there were many women, there for the taking. Perhaps, he thought, except that the old man had never known this woman.

His eye caught a blur of movement down below him in the half-darkness. He gripped the M-3, chambered a shell and laid the sights on the moving shape. Fifty yards away and then thirty. The kid. He eased on the safety, waiting.

Luis came up the slope from the northwest, lugging his legs up the grade. He glanced up, grinned, raised his hand and kept coming. Close up, he was flushed with exertion, panting like a dog in the August heat. He dropped his rucksack and carbine next to Brocassie and hunkered down.

"How did it go?"

The kid shook his head, reached into his rucksack, pulled out a hunk of sausage, bit into it, then washed it down with water from his canteen. He lay back, his chest still heaving. When his breathing calmed he sat up and swallowed from the canteen again. "A bastard. The mountain's a bastard." He blew his nose between his fingertips and flung the snot away over his shoulder. "But I found the rocks—the 'Needles.'"

"You have a compass bearing to it?"

313

The kid stared back at him as if he were mad. "What do you think I've been doing while you've been sitting on your ass? Of course I do. Zero two three magnetic. About three miles down and to the northeast. Then east along the contour. It will save miles."

"You've done a great job. You've saved us a hell of a lot of trouble."

Luis nodded, agreeing, his face set in a self-satisfied smile. "Yeah—it was a great job. Even I would admit that. But talking about it isn't going to get Hernando and your friend into Maroto's camp. If we wait until tomorrow morning, it will be raining. Your friend's foot is not good. The grade is steep, very dangerous. We should go tonight while it is not raining and we wouldn't need to worry about the aircraft or the patrols." He pulled out the rest of the sausage and gnawed on it, taking small bites like a rodent, teasing away the skin with his teeth. And all the while, he looked out over the valley, his eyes owning all of it. King of the hill, Brocassie thought, in complete control.

The kid had a point and yet he couldn't see moving Hernando down three miles of rough slope in complete darkness. Better to wait through one whole day and try it tomorrow night. "No," he said. "We stay put for now."

The kid picked at his teeth, silent for a while. "I heard you talking earlier, when we were up near the crest. You're behind on some kind of schedule? You have to observe the Russian's base below, right—first that before any attack."

"Information is what we're after. Porto tells me that Maroto is not interested in an attack."

The kid nodded. "That was what I thought. Maroto is an old man and his guts have gone. He would not help with an attack, I think. He only wants to hang on until the Americans invade and then he will be a hero. He dreams of being the *jefe* of the government that the Americans will install. Maroto is— how do you say it—very political, understand? The rest of us just want to survive."

He looked over his shoulder to where Porto and Hernando still slept and then turned back to Brocassie, his voice just a whisper. "You know the condition of your friend's foot."

"A bad blister . . ."

"No—not just a blister. It is badly infected. He lanced it with a heated knife before we left this morning. A lot of pus and the veins running up his leg are starting to turn red. I saw with my own eyes."

"There are antibiotics in his aid kit . . ."

Luis shook his head slowly like an old man reading obituaries. "No—we used most of them on you. And he took the last of them this morning. Only Maroto has more." He stuffed his hands into his fatigue pockets. "Your friend must get to Maroto's camp soon, as must Hernando."

"That's what the hell we're trying to do!"

"*Lo que usted quiera*," he answered, drawing out the words as if he were extracting silk scarves from his sleeve, "I have a proposition. One that would accomplish much in little time, for the good of all."

"Go ahead."

"All of us will move downslope to the 'Needles' tonight. Tomorrow, at daybreak, your friend and Hernando can walk east along the slope. By nine, they'll be picked up by Maroto's pickets and by eleven, they'll be under warm blankets with hot food and medicine in their bellies. From the 'Needles,' Hernando knows the way as well as do I."

"And just what in hell do we do, Luis?" The kid was too eager, too self-assured, the whole presentation a little too slick.

"I have watched you today. You are not strong yet, but you are getting better. Still, you would need my help."

"To do what?"

"At dawn, we will leave the 'Needles' and move down into the valley. There are old nickel mines that have been abandoned for years. The openings are boarded up and overgrown with weeds and bush, impossible to find unless you know exactly where they are, even if you're within pissing distance of them. No militia patrol would ever find us, and from there, with your big telescope and camera, you could see the opening in the hillside of the Russian camp where it passes underground. I have seen trucks enter there, even freight cars. You can watch the guards, record their schedules, all those things which you talked of today to your friend."

He tried to decipher the kid's expression but in the darkness he could only see reflections of the boy's moist eyes and they gave back nothing.

"Why are you volunteering this?"

Luis hunched his shoulders. "You would not understand it. It is something that I have to do for my father. I don't wish to talk about it. The only question is, do you want to accomplish this or do you wish to waste days and days, waiting for your friend's foot to heal, and listening to Maroto's lies about how many Fidelistas he has killed?"

It made sense, a great deal of sense. He might be able to accomplish everything he and Porto had come for in just four or five days. "How far are these mines from the complex?"

"The mine that I am thinking about is on a small bluff just across the river from where the underground opening is. I would guess it to be six or seven hundred yards away."

With the telescopic lens and a tripod, he could shoot film that would be sharp enough to catch the smallest detail.

"I don't know," he hedged. "I'll talk to Porto about it."

The kid shrugged. "It is your decision, not mine."

As Brocassie stood up, the kid looked up at him and then turned his face back, withdrawn, to glare down into the darkened valley, alternately sucking bits of sausage gristle from between his teeth and spitting them out.

"I don't like it." Porto was stripping away dead flesh with the blade of his knife, as if he were peeling the skin from a catfish. The stench was as overpowering.

Brocassie swallowed noisily, his stomach on the edge of rebellion. "It's the best option we've got."

"Piss off, Brocassie! That's your style, isn't it? We've come this far together but now you want to play your own game. I'm telling you that my hoof will be OK in two, three days at the most." He winced as he patted the raw flesh with a wadded ball of gauze drenched in iodine.

"Come off it, Porto. Four or five days' minimum for your foot to heal and you need antibiotics damn quick unless you want to leave Cuba on a peg leg. I can't carry you and you've got to move tonight before that leg gets any worse. While you're laid up with Maroto, I can be down at the mine with Luis and get most of what we came after."

"Something about him . . . I don't trust that little prick."

"And he probably doesn't trust us. Let's get it over with as quickly as possible. Once the DGI finds the sailplanes, they'll start sweeping the Sierra with every man they can get. In and out and damn quick about it. Those were your words, turkey."

Porto turned to him. "You're probably right. I've got the early stages of blood poisoning—can you believe it, from just a goddamn blister. So how many days?"

"One to get down, one to get back and five there. Give me a week."

"All right. A week. Whether or not you've got enough stuff, you pull back out six days from now and no later. Agreed?"

"Agreed."

"And I want you to send Luis back up to Maroto's camp midweek with a report. Take the tape recorder. Mark the tape that you send back up just like Hagger showed us. Those are my conditions."

"You really don't trust him, do you?"

"There are only two people in the world that I trust, sport. Me and thee."

Brocassie hesitated, then nodded, knowing that it was true for him as well. He reached across the flickering Sterno flame and touched hands.

They left just after ten. The sky was still clear, starlight a ghostly pale fluorescence. Porto hung on Brocassie's shoulder for support, Hernando a dead weight on the line below them, Luis on belay. They moved downslope, over the rubble, inches at a time.

By five, in the washed-out light of a dawn not yet come, they overlooked a field of spiky monoliths, the "Needles."

Luis led the way, working laterally across the slope. There was grass now, and the dirt beneath it was firm. Every twenty paces or so, Luis would stop and the four of them would listen. Nothing, Brocassie thought, but sounds of the night, wind in the trees, a limb rubbing against another limb, forest primeval

317

stuff. He glanced down at his watch. Five-thirty. Dawn just thirty minutes away.

He moved forward past Porto to Luis. "We've got to get moving. Not that much darkness left."

The kid shrugged, obviously irritated. "We take it easy or we don't take it at all. It should be safe but I've seen cigarette butts and burned-out cooking fires here. Sometimes the patrols penetrate this far in. We're on the border between what we control and what the Fidelistas patrol. So we go slow, skirt the eastern edge of the 'Needles' and then you and I head north, Hernando and Porto toward the east."

They came to a bluff overlooking the "Needles" at dawn, a tarnished pewter glint in the eastern sky. There was the smell of rain in the air, the leaves turning their underbellies up to the rising wind.

"This is where we divide," Luis said. He gripped Hernando's arm. "Keep to this contour and head east toward the sun."

Hernando nodded. "Maroto will not like this," he said. "You know that he does not approve of independent action."

"He's an old man. He thinks like an old man, he acts like an old man. Tell him that for me." He slapped Hernando's shoulder. "Two miles, perhaps a bit more." He reached into his fatigue pocket, extracted a small wooden object and handed it to Porto. "A wooden bird call. You twist it like so." He rotated the plug and the thing chirped. "Two miles in along the contour. Then stop every quarter of a mile and use this. If you hear movement in the brush, stand up with your hands over your head, your weapons on the ground. Maroto's pickets don't take chances."

Porto hobbled over to Brocassie. "Seven days, sport. Like we agreed." He shook hands solemnly. "I mean it."

"So do I." He squeezed Porto's hand hard. "You're sure that you can make it these last couple of miles?"

"A piece of cake, Brocassie. You take care of yourself and keep that kid in sight. He spooks me, like a fifty-year-old man in the skin of a fifteen-year-old."

They separated. Brocassie watched Porto and Hernando head east, then turned north, downslope toward the valley, Luis leading.

Luis moved fast but almost noiselessly. With lighter packs and moving downgrade, they made good time.

Curiously, they heard no helicopters, no search aircraft. At times, Brocassie could see the ribbon of the Sierra road far off to the left. No traffic on it.

They stopped for a rest in the shade of a pine grove just after noon. Brocassie uncased the binoculars, sweeping the valley and what he could see of the Sierra road. He handed the glasses to Luis. "Take a look, Luis. What do you think?"

The kid made a cursory scan and handed the glasses back. "I see nothing."

"That's the point, isn't it? Yesterday, there were choppers all over the ridge. Now, nothing."

The kid shrugged. "Maybe it's a saint day." He gave a contemptuous laugh. "It is possible, I think, that they are not even sure that anyone has landed here in the Sierra."

Like hell, Brocassie thought. Like bloody hell.

Through the afternoon, they moved steadily lower. The pines had given way to mahogany stands and clumps of spiky-leaved trees covered with tiny red berries. Luis slipped through the brush almost effortlessly, like an animal would. Give him credit, Brocassie thought. The kid was at home in his element—one savvy guerrilla.

The vegetation grew sparser, mainly saw grass and a few runted trees. Here and there, there were mounds of mine tailings and rotted wooden rail ties strewn across the slope where there once had been tracks leading to the mines. Roads that had been cut into the slope were washed out and overgrown.

Luis called a halt at the edge of a small stream in the late afternoon. They refilled their canteens and doused their faces in the icy water. "Not much farther," he said, sloshing water over his matted hair. He shook his head like a wet dog. "A mile, maybe a bit more. Those bastards"—he nodded toward the valley floor—"patrol up here. Generally in squads of six men, twice a day. We'll be all right until just before sundown. They prefer not to send out patrols in the heat of the day—just in the early morning and at twilight. Never at night."

"Don't they check the mine tunnels?"

"These mines are very old, *Jefe*. Some of them built back in the 1880s. All small private holdings, never any big com-

319

pany. The rich veins of ore went very quickly, see? Not profitable. So most of the mines were just abandoned and eventually, most of the entrances collapsed. Those that were still
open were dynamited by the government back in the fifties
because three people entered a mine back about eight years
ago and the roof fell in on them." He made a face. "They were
English travel writers. If they had been Cubans, there would
have been no notice."

"How come you know so much about this area? I never
heard Maroto or Fabricio talk much about it."

"I was born and raised no more than a day's walk from
here. My father was a noncommissioned officer in Batista's
army. We lived in Ciguani where my father was stationed, a
little horse-piss town about twenty miles from here. I walked
all these hills in the summer when I was younger. No one up
here then." He bent down to take a final drink of water and
then looked up. "I know this country like most men know the
pimples on their own prick."

Charming, Brocassie thought.

They kept moving, Luis leading, picking up the pace as
the slopes gentled into the valley basin.

They crossed several streams, waded through a thicket of
marshy swamp, spiked with cattails, on through a meadow of
lush grass, waist high, all the while working northwest and
lower into the valley.

Sometime after four, the light now hard and flat, Luis
paused under the branches of a dead divi-divi tree. "It is not
far," he said.

"Which is what you said an hour ago."

The kid screwed up his face, half leering, half challenging. "We could stay here if your legs are weak. The grass is tall
enough and the tree gives us some cover. We can rest here and
then move on after dusk."

Brocassie looked around him, considering. Not much
cover. The tree was barren, its limbs rotten, the grass sparse. A
few shrubs clawed at patches of dirt on the rock-strewn hillside but it was dangerously thin cover. "Not that good. We
better keep moving."

Luis shot him a look of contempt and clambered up the
slope. He pushed back the limbs of the bushes, moved a rock

aside and then turned back to face Brocassie. "Welcome to my hole," he said, grinning, and then slithered through the small opening with the ease of a snake.

The entrance was blocked by a jumbled pile of rocks, right up to the crown of the tunnel's opening. It was little wonder that the tunnel couldn't be seen from outside the entrance and even with the rock removed, the branches of the bush outside masked the opening. Perfect. The kid knew his stuff.

He switched on his flashlight and moved deeper into the tunnel. Thirty paces and the mine shaft ended abruptly, a void gaping in the floor of the tunnel, crudely boxed with rotting timbers. With his flashlight, Brocassie examined the overhead sheave with its rusting cables which dangled down into the shaft. His light did not penetrate far and a stone kicked off the ledge rattled against the sides of the shaft—silence and rattle again and the dull reverberation of a distant splash. Not a place to sleepwalk, he thought.

He walked back, carefully, his hand trailing the overhead beams. Mines were something he knew about and this one was a deathtrap. The shorings responded to his knuckles with a soft thud. Termites and rot, he calculated, and the overhead beams bowed under enormous pressure, some of them fractured. He gently worked his way back out to the entrance.

Luis had already set up housekeeping. He had the Sterno out, boiling water, his sleeping bag arranged, food and equipment neatly stacked up on the side of the tunnel. He looked up, the Cheshire cat licking cream from its lips. "You like?"

"I like," Brocassie replied. "As long as nobody coughs."

He woke to the smell of coffee brewing, rolled over on his side and checked his watch. Ten A.M. He had slept sixteen hours. He felt stiff, but for the first time in four days no headache and no blurred vision. The stitches itched like hell but that was the process of healing, wasn't it?

Luis had broken open two cans, mixing dried eggs and canned ham in a skillet. He had a small kerosene lamp going although there was a small shaft of light which leaked in where the hole broached the rockslide at the tunnel entrance. Luis put the concoction over the fire. Brocassie lay back in his

sleeping bag. He came awake slowly, stretching his arms
above him, savoring the smell of hot food and then he froze.

"Christ," he whispered, "get those ham and eggs off the
fire! The patrols might not be able to see this place but that
smell will carry."

Unconcerned, Luis stirred the eggs. "They passed no
more than one hundred feet of here just after sunrise. They
will not patrol again before dusk. It is not something to be
concerned with."

Brocassie crawled carefully up the rockpile until he was at
the hole. Rain was falling, driven by a hard wind. Nothing
moved except the branches of trees, the muddy river which bisected the valley and a small bird which preened at its wet
feathers on a swaying limb of the divi-divi tree, not more than
five feet beyond the opening.

He squinted in the flat light, trying to make out details.
Below him, the rocky field fell away to the River Yara. And
across its broad, muddy expanse were the ruins of a plantation, set under a canopy of trees. Luis had talked about a tunnel entrance to the complex but he could see nothing other
than dense vegetation skirting the eastern edge of the plantation which rose in a shallow grade to a flat plain of scrub and
grass. He thought that he could make out the dull shape of a
chain link fence but the light was bad and the distance too far.

He crawled back down and ate breakfast. Canned and
dehydrated, it didn't matter. To his tongue, it was ambrosia.
"You're a good man," he said, finishing the plate. The kid
looked up at him for a second, embarrassed, a little puzzled.

"You think of me as a man?" There was a wary disbelief
in his expression.

"*Muy hombre,*" Brocassie said, his voice serious. "You
and Hernando carrying me, wiping my ass, keeping me warm,
going out to find the shortcut. That probably saved Porto's leg.
And then risking your neck to bring me down here." He
paused and smiled. He knew how much a boy needed to be
accepted as a man and Luis was all of that and more. "You're
a lot of man, Luis, as well as a friend. As good as they come."

Luis kept silent through the meal, eating mechanically.
Finally, he leaned back, picking at his teeth with his fingernail.

"What would they do to you if they caught you?" Luis asked.

"You mean, what would they do to *us, compadre*. I don't have to draw a picture, do I?"

The kid nodded. "I mean, they want you very badly, don't they?"

There was a catch in his throat, a certain queasiness in his gut that he couldn't quite identify. He put down his coffee. "They don't know that I'm in Cuba, Luis. Why do you think they know?"

The kid looked back at him, his face blank, and then he drooped his eyelids. "I was only guessing that they knew, Brocassie." He got up, scraped the skillet and scoured the mess kits with sand. "I think it would be good for us to leave. I have a feeling that it is not safe here."

"What kind of feeling?"

"Just a feeling," Luis answered softly, his eyes now averted. "I have done wrong to bring you down here."

Brocassie got to his feet. He lightly punched the kid's shoulder. "Don't worry about it, Luis. We'll be out of here in five days. If I couldn't see the entrance standing five feet from it, I don't think the patrols will from a hundred. We just lie low and watch. We cook in the morning after the patrols have finished and then only after dark. Don't sweat it."

The kid nodded, not answering. He lay down in his sleeping bag, turning his face away from the glare of the lantern. Strange kid, he thought. Moody, arrogant, proud, then suddenly spooked. He was a boy in transition to manhood and as it had been in Brocassie's own life, the process was abrupt and painful.

He collected the Nikon, the tripod and the 1000mm telephoto lens, then carefully crawled back up to the entrance. The hole was only slightly larger than the width of his shoulders. The branches of the scrub which blocked the opening obstructed his view; he spent a few minutes tying them back with nylon thread so that he had a clear sweep of the valley. He set up the Nikon on the tripod and attached the zoom lens to it.

Blur, focus, zoom; the image in the eyepiece refined slowly until there was a knife-edge clarity to the details in the field of view. He examined the plantation first, picking out the shape of the old main house, now gutted by fire. The rafters had fallen inward, the windows fire blackened.

He nudged the instrument again to the right. Cottages. One after the other. Those would have been for the field supervisors, the overseers, the graders.

Yards overgrown, paint blistered and stained with green mold, the appearance of abandonment. He swung the lens to the right, hesitated, and then edged it back to the left. A grove under the trees, the grass cut down. Several shapes blurred by the foliage. He fiddled with the focus, trying to clarify the image. And as he did, a figure walked through his field of view. Light brown uniform with collar flashes of red, epaulets, high jack boots, peaked officer's cap. My God, he thought—a Russian captain! Two more men swam into the lens, both in tiger-striped fatigues, lace-up boots and helmets with netting. They saluted and the officer whipped his hand up to the peak of his hat in returned salute.

Hurriedly, Brocassie bent down and advanced the lever to the first frame. He put his eye down to the viewfinder, setting the exposure.

Click. The shutter locked the image of the three men onto the film's emulsion.

The three men moved toward one of the shapes. The shorter of the two men in tiger-striped fatigues stooped down and released a line from a stake. He hauled on it and camouflage netting slowly lifted like a tent—a conjuring act which transformed foliage and bushes into an SA-3 Goa surface-to-air missile launcher. He recognized it immediately: Hagger's slide show briefing the last morning in Jamaica was aptly named, "Missiles of the Soviet Union, Current Inventory." And this had been one of them. A ZIL 157 tractor streaked in blotches of tan, green and black; the two Goa missiles bracketed side by side in the launcher frame.

Click. Frame advance. He was breathing heavily. He worked the lens around and surveyed the rest of the grove. Seven—eight— He counted twelve similar shapes. Other details emerged as he moved the lens more carefully, examining each small increment of arc. Guard shacks, well camouflaged with netting, three or four automatic weapons pits sporting

12.7mm DShK heavy machine guns, two ZSU-23-4 self-propelled antiaircraft weapons carriers covered with netting, tucked back into the gloom of overhanging trees.

Shit! They had enough firepower here to repel any kind of air strike and this was only one grove. He couldn't see deeper into the plantation because of the blocking trees but it was likely that this was just one element of many. He ran through a roll of film and then another.

He broke for a lunch of Spam. The date on the C ration was 1952, ten years old, the can rusty. Hagger didn't waste money on luxuries like food for the troops, he thought. Give this stuff to corn-fed Iowan GIs and the army would have a revolt on its hands, but as far as Hagger was probably concerned, this stuff was good enough for the boys in the Sierra. It stank but he ate it.

Afternoon. Nothing much moving, just the occasional figure trotting across the grove through the driving rain, poncho flapping in the wind. Two jeeplike vehicles grinding through axle-high mud.

No tunnel entrance that he could see. Just dense foliage at the edge of the plantation. He folded the tripod and made coffee. Perhaps Hagger was right.

Evening. The rain had tapered off to a drizzle, the light going rapidly. He reduced the shutter speed, opened the aperture and scanned the complex once more.

Near the eastern end of the plantation where before he had only seen foliage and scrub bushes, there was now a gap and behind the gap was the hard even surface of concrete. As he watched, the gap widened and he suddenly realized that he was watching a massive camouflaged roof and curtains being drawn back on rollers through a spider web network of cables. The process took over two minutes. The opening into the hillside, very much like a train tunnel but on a much larger scale, had concrete triangular walls which began at ground level and wedged upward with the grade of the hill's slope. Where the concrete walls terminated in the side of the hill, he could actually see into the tunnel's interior. He had no real estimate of the width of the tunnel until he noticed an armed guard pacing across the entrance. He marched to the far side, wheeled neatly in an about-face and started pacing back. Forty-two paces. Brocassie did some mental arithmetic. Damn close to 120 feet wide and by rough proportions, the height of the entrance would be close to 40 feet.

He shot three frames, knowing that the light was almost nonexistent, but that Hagger's people would be able to deal with the film to extract the maximum amount of detail possible.

Luis had crawled up the rockpile and squeezed in beside him, looking out the opening. "I told you, didn't I?"

He took a final look through the telephoto lens, snapped one more frame and then lay back on the rocks, turning toward Luis. "I had no idea the thing was so goddamned big. You mentioned that trucks were able to drive into the hillside and I was visualizing something the size of a large garage door, not something like that!"

"Maroto didn't believe me either," the kid said. "I told him but he laughed."

"Did he come down here to check it out?"

"Not Maroto personally, but two of his men did. They saw nothing except a few Cuban regular army troops walking around in the plantation, a gasoline truck, a motorcycle, nothing more. But they had no binoculars and besides, it would be stupid for the borscht eaters to remove the camouflage netting during the daylight hours on a clear day. Only at night, like now, would they be safe from U.S. spy planes. The men stayed until dusk and then climbed back up into the Sierra. They called me a fool and Maroto agreed with them."

No wonder Luis despised Maroto, Brocassie thought. In the Latin countries, you don't call a man a liar even if he is.

That night, they waited until after nine before cooking dinner, such as it was: Spam, canned peaches and crackers.

"Your father," Luis asked. "What was he like?"

Frozen in time, locked in another age, he thought. "He was kind, and he believed in something that he wanted me to believe in as well. I'm not sure that I do anymore, but still I loved him."

The kid nodded. "Mine too. He was a soldier in Batista's army, but he was a good man, a good father, a real friend. My mother died years ago. So my father brought me up. I was wild but he understood me, tried his best to . . ." Luis couldn't finish the sentence.

"You miss him?" Dumb question. Porto had told him that Luis's father had been tortured and executed by the Oriente Division of the DGI—Julio Álvarez commanding officer.

"He is . . ." The kid hesitated. "I love him, would do any-thing for him, Brocassie."

"Your father died, didn't he?" Perhaps he had misunder-stood Porto.

Luis nodded. "He died. As dead as you can be."

The kid rolled over in his sleeping bag, his face turned away. But then he spoke, his voice muffled. "We must get away from here. I think it is dangerous. Tomorrow, all right?"

He thought about it. Not yet. He wanted to see more, photograph the opening process of the camouflage, record on film and tape recorder what he saw. Even now, it would be enough to confirm some of Hagger's suspicions about the magnitude and importance of the complex.

"We'll talk about it in the morning," he hedged. But he knew that he would take the full five days.

The next day was a bust. Low fog hung on the floor of the valley, visibility reduced to less than a hundred yards. A patrol came through at dusk, less than a stone's throw away, plod-ding steadily, going through the motions without any real en-thusiasm. But not FAR regular army or militia. DGI, and on the point was a Slavic-featured man, no insignia on his fa-tigues. He was much more alert than the rest of the men in the squad, like a good field dog, sniffing for game, quartering the field. Once, he looked directly at the mine entrance, and Bro-cassie imagined that the man had a suppressed smile on his face. But that was the imagination of a paranoid, he thought.

They turned in early, Luis again raising the question of leaving tomorrow, Brocassie fending him off with vague an-swers. He was deep into the mother lode, mining the richest vein, and he wasn't going to be diverted until he absolutely had to pull out.

Wednesday: The depression was clearing out, no longer raining but still a solid cloud deck.

Luis was antsy, moving around the tunnel. He made

breakfast, scrubbed the mess kits with sand, stacked them, rearranged the equipment, cleaned his weapon, always in motion.

"For Christ's sake, kid—sit down. You'll drop the whole mountain on our heads!" He had said it in half-jest, half-seriousness, then immediately regretted it. Luis was not a kid, didn't want to be called one. Bad mistake, he thought.

Hunching down, Luis rolled a tailor-made and smoked it, his eyes like gunsights steadily on Brocassie. Even when Brocassie turned away, scanning the complex, he felt the eyes boring into his back.

Same routine. Men removed the camouflage netting from the antiaircraft weapons in the grove, started the engines, swiveled the barrels through their arcs then shut down, dropping the netting again. He recorded one jeep transiting the plantation at noon, then nothing more until sunset.

He was just loading another roll of film when Luis squeezed past him. He caught the kid's belt when he was halfway out the hole. "Where in hell do you think you're going, *chico*?"

The boy turned around, staring at him, his face twisted. "Out of here, man! I'm tired of the smell of our own shit and piss. I'm sick of the smell of rotting food. I'm going out!"

"The patrol . . . ?"

"The patrol will never see me, understand. I'm a *boy* and men don't see *boys. Boys* are invisible, understand? I'm getting out to get some air and don't stop me!"

Luis wasn't dumb, he acknowledged to himself. The kid knew the patrol schedule and he could easily hide until they passed. He slapped the kid on the ass. "OK, *chico*. Get it out of your system. I didn't mean anything. Keep out of sight but get back here before ten."

"*Yes, sir, three bags full, SIR,*" he shot back and scrambled through the hole.

Mistake, Brocassie told himself. Injured pride was the most painful of emotions and he wanted to call the kid back, tell him that "chico" was a state of age, not of mind. But Luis was gone, scrambling down over the slope, disappearing into the grove of divi-divi.

He bent down to the telephoto lens, watching, waiting.

328

Dusk. The camouflage rolled back like the opening of a stage production: portentous, majestic and thrilling. This time, the light was much better. He ran through a half a roll of film.

Nothing happened for over half an hour and then, from the tunnel entrance, a drab gray switching engine emerged, towing a crane on a flatcar. Not an ordinary crane but a crane of huge proportions. Once clear of the overhang of the tunnel, like a snake lifting its head to strike, the crane arm raised, its boom extending.

There were smears of bobbing light as men walked around the crane, their flashlights held with beams pointed downward. Then nothing for another quarter hour.

Brocassie didn't notice it at first. He had the lens centered on the crane but from the periphery of the lens he caught a distorted blur of movement. Swivel to the left, just a small increment of arc.

A flatcar—a crate on it—extending the full length of the bed, over eighty feet in length. Three men stood on the bed of the flatcar, the crate double their height. The flatcar slowed, ran through a switch and slid alongside of the crane on a parallel track.

He shot a frame, his heart pounding in his throat. His hands were shaking, fingers fumbling with the lens, trying to catch the image on film before it was too late.

The men moved along the edge of the flatcar, unlatching clamps. The boom of the crane descended, the cable unreeling. The side of the crate folded down and he saw the missile, supported by an elaborate cradle. Seventy, maybe eighty feet long, perfectly cylindrical, featureless, no more threatening than a length of gigantic sewer pipe except for the shrouded rocket motor and the tapered nose cone. SS-4 Sandal; Hagger's briefing. Capable of leaping continents, more powerful than ten thousand fucking locomotives. Instant death for a million people, packaged in a black mottled case of aluminum, squatting on a flatcar in a valley of the Sierra Maestra. His hand sweated, fumbling with the frame advance. *Click*.

"Brocassie!"

Luis had hissed his name, only yards away. Twilight gone, this side of the valley in darkness. He eased his head out of the hole, looking for Luis. Dumb bastard! Patrol was due thirty minutes ago, maybe less. Where were they and what in hell was Luis up to? He listened and heard nothing. "Luis," he whispered but no answer.

He pulled his body through the entrance, shoulders first, wriggling his hips behind him, feeling like a lame rabbit scrambling out of its hole.

Sergio Piedra was waiting for him, the gun barrel of an AK-47 silhouetted against the skyline.

"Welcome back to Cuba," he said easily and then smashed the barrel downward with a vengeance.

CHAPTER

14

"Stand up!" Sergio Piedra snapped.

The cell was suddenly colder, and through the opened steel door he could see dim light washing a concrete corridor. He rolled over, squinting up at Piedra who was silhouetted in the backlighting. Suddenly, a flashlight dazzled Brocassie's eyes.

"*UP!*" Piedra shrilled.

Rolling in from the corridor was the smell of disinfectant, overlaid with the acrid ammonia scent of urine and camphor. He could hear the mumble of men talking far down the hall.

Brocassie sat up on the edge of the pallet, then bent over, pulling on his cotton slippers.

"Forget the slippers. Take off your fatigues—*strip!*" Piedra waved the automatic at him, motioning him to stand.

So this was it, he thought. Interrogation. His stomach was hollow, a dull ache somewhere under his heart, his hands in-

331

voluntarily shaking. He wondered if Álvarez would have the guts to show his face. He looked up at Piedra. "I knew it was a mistake not to run you off that cliff, you prick."

Piedra kicked him in the pit of the stomach and he reeled backward, smashing his shoulder against the wall.

"I'm looking forward to this, Brocassie. Get on your feet and drop your fatigues. Let's see whether you actually have any balls, *gusano.*"

He took his time standing up, swaying in pain, breathless. He knew now that if he baited Piedra, he would have nothing left to fight with. The pain was already diminishing but he faked confusion, staggering upright, gagging, bending over double, weaving his head in disorientation.

Piedra took him savagely by the neck, his fingers squeezing into Brocassie's flesh. "Now, Brocassie, now!" he whispered. "We have a little interview planned and I don't want you to be late."

Brocassie stepped out of his fatigues, stumbling a little.

Piedra grabbed him by the arm, forcing him to bend over. "One hand in front, the other behind you. Hunch over, bastard." He jerked on Brocassie's arm, pulling him into a crouch, and then clicked handcuffs from the wrist in front, passing between Brocassie's legs to the wrist behind. He gave a hoarse laugh, punching Brocassie's back lower into a stoop. "Waddle like a duck, *hijo de puta,* if you want to keep your balls from being sawn in half." He pushed Brocassie toward the cell door, goading him from behind with the barrel of the automatic.

In that one moment, Brocassie swore to himself that he would kill Piedra with his bare hands, that he would not live out his life without that satisfaction.

Piedra kicked him from behind, his boot impacting on the base of Brocassie's spine. Falling forward, he could not protect his face and his cheek smashed on the cell's concrete floor. Brocassie was stunned and the breath went out of him as Piedra fell, dead weight, on his back. Brocassie felt a gag rammed between his lips and a gauze quickly being wrapped around his head, covering his eyes.

"My mistake, Brocassie. I forgot, didn't I? See no evil,

hear no evil, speak no evil." He pressed his body down on Brocassie's back, whispering in his ear. "When they're through, you're mine, Brocassie. I want to find out how tough you are—slowly." His hand squeezed Brocassie's buttocks, fingernails sharp into the flesh. "I do believe," he whispered, "that you are a virgin."

Piedra pressed him to his feet and guided him, his hand on Brocassie's elbow, not allowing for any hesitation.

They went down a concrete corridor, chilled by air conditioning, left, then right, a long stretch down a hallway. There was a pause when Piedra snatched up on the chain of the handcuffs, sending a bolt of tearing pain through Brocassie's genitals as the links ground into the soft tissue. He sensed it was some sort of a checkpoint—the sounds of paper shuffling and another man breathing. Then he was prodded ahead, stumbling, hunched over like an animal in chains. He wiped away everything except hate and the will to survive.

He was shoved to the left—a pause and then left again, through two sets of swinging doors. Colder. And a smell, not of disinfectant but more like a morgue—formaldehyde, carbolic acid, alcohol—things associated with dying and the examination of death.

Through another set of doors now, Piedra pushing him forward with a shove. Someone had taken up station in front of them, a man in hard leather soles whose footsteps echoed back from the walls of the corridor. There was a pause, a fumbling of keys and a door unlatching.

The handcuff on his left wrist was unlocked and he was taken by the shoulders and moved to the right. The hands turned his body around and pushed down gently. He could feel the man's breath on his face and smell a combination of tobacco and mouthwash, a hint of expensive cologne.

"It's all right," the man said antiseptically. "There's a bed behind you. Sit!"

Brocassie eased down into a sitting position, hard springs creaking beneath him. He heard the handcuff clink against metal and snap closed.

"You can sleep again," the voice said. "And then we will

talk." Brocassie was pushed down and a blanket was thrown over him. "You may remove the blindfold and the gag."

Brocassie slowly pulled off the elasticized bands with his free hand. The room was in darkness but the corridor was lit, silhouetting his attendant. The man moved away from him, toward the door. Brocassie caught one glimpse of him, just a profile. A man, slightly overweight and balding, with glasses. He was replaced by two men who entered, both in white uniforms. One carried a tray. They came across the room and stood over him.

"Roll over," one of them said in badly accented Spanish. Brocassie hesitated.

The larger one reached down and wrenched his shoulder up, forcing him to roll onto his belly. Two hands pressed into his shoulder blades. Brocassie felt the stab of a needle into his fleshless buttocks, pain growing into a hard knot of pressure as the fluid was injected. He tried to roll over but was only able to lift his head and turn it before his coordination faded and his vision blurred. His body felt as if it were falling away into a void, spiraling downward, the forms of the two men merging and fading as the light grew dimmer.

Brocassie was just below the level of consciousness, unable to rise to the surface. Thoughts raced through his mind but they were disjointed, irrational. He willed himself to concentrate on just one thing, feeling that if he could isolate one thought, he could build on it.

I am . . . He formed the words on his lips, in his mind, but could not get enough breath to say them aloud. Try again. I am, he thought. Therefore, I. . . . But that was the end of it.

He could not open his eyes, and yet beyond the thin layer of skin he sensed red, warm light. He put his whole will into it, trying to raise his eyelid but it was as if it were sewn shut. Time, he thought. I have time to wait. And he relaxed, letting the waves of lassitude sweep over him, going deeper below the surface.

Dimly, he felt probings against his flesh, deeper soundings of his organs, a thin whirring and prickles of cold metal on his skin.

There was a pressure on his eyeball and his eyelid was gently raised. Brocassie could not focus but he could see several figures standing over him. A pinpoint of light came closer, dazzling his pupil.

"Cut back on the intravenous feed. He's got too much dilation in his pupils and no motor control," a voice said clinically. "Very poor, Alex. You want to kill him?"

The eyelid was released and allowed to drop, shutting off the light. "Give him another hour," said the faraway voice of a woman. There was a shuffling of feet and the dim red light became black and a door shut, followed by silence.

Brocassie floated closer to the surface. He could begin to distinguish smells now, and sounds. Drip of a leaky faucet. A hum somewhere—perhaps an elevator or ventilating machinery.

Without light and with no muscle control, he could only listen. The drops of water fell into a metal basin, creating a counterpoint to his heartbeat—less than once a second. He tried to time it. "One thousand one, one thousand two, one thousand three . . ." Less than that. Much less than that. Slow. Heart slow. Or was it a distortion of time? He tried to ignore the beat now, but he couldn't. Faces flickered through his mind and he tried to retain them but they were elusive as shadows. He tried to picture his father and could not. Alicia, Porto, Hagger, Luis . . . none of them. Just words that were part of some existence—something he could recall and yet couldn't. The tap of waterdrops slowed and with it, his heart. Brocassie gave up and let himself drift back into suspension.

"Bring him around," the man in the white coat said. He sat down on the edge of a desk, watching his patient begin the slow climb to consciousness. He glanced down at the patient's chart. EKG all right but still—EEG erratic as was to be expected, as was to be desired. Dependence, submissiveness, disorientation.

Dr. Daniil L. Lunts, an overweight man in his fifties, was normally a resident of the Serbsky Institute of Forensic Psychiatry in Moscow. While at the institute, Dr. Lunts wore the cloth of his profession: a white smock and patent leather shoes, polished to a dazzling gloss. But before he left for his apartment on Nizhegorodskaya Street in his chauffeured Volga sedan, Lunts drew on the mustard twill of a colonel of the

KGB, a logical adjunct to his higher calling of freeing men's minds of distasteful ideologies.

Lunts glanced at the EKG and snapped at the woman attendant, "Slow down your BPH-21 feed, Kitsloff! You're pushing him too fast."

Kitsloff quickly adjusted the drip by turning down a feed regulation screw. The oscilloscope monitor bleeped more slowly; Brocassie's heartbeat gradually returned to a stable condition. Lunts returned to the desk, seating himself, waiting. Fifteen more minutes would do it. He picked up the telephone and tapped in five digits.

"Roychenko here," a voice answered.

"It's Lunts," the doctor said. "He'll be surfaced in another ten minutes or so. You will probably want to be present. Bring the Cuban with you. Álvarez may be helpful." He didn't wait for a reply, dropping the phone into its cradle.

The whole process of conditioning had been rushed and Lunts was furious at Roychenko's insistence that the patient be pushed even faster. Emotional receptibility conditioning really needed weeks of preparation. Hunger, humiliation, isolation.

Moscow Center had flown him out to this cesspool of a place, disrupting his valuable research schedule at the institute. Lunts felt that he was on the threshold of a breakthrough in behavioral control. By surgical implantation in a "patient's" skull of a combined ultrahigh-frequency receiver, battery pack and a probe, all packaged together into a capsule no larger than a pencil eraser, Lunts, from a distance of over a hundred meters, could induce an instant blinding migraine headache. Electroencephalographs showed the shock to the central nervous system was beyond toleration if maintained for more than a few milliseconds. Half a second of the transmitter-induced pain would drive a "patient" totally mad—to the extent that one of the earlier subjects had killed himself, battering his head against a concrete wall.

Lunts specialized in the rehabilitation of dissidents. One demonstration was generally all that was required to ensure cooperation. Lunts had brought two of the units with him without consulting with Moscow Center or with Roychenko. It was possible that, if all else failed, Brocassie would be subject number seven in the series—the first where a practical application could be measured in a real-world environment.

The door opened, Roychenko and Álvarez arguing about something, both intent, Roychenko slamming his fist into the palm of his other hand.

"Quiet," Lunts demanded. Preemptively, he waved them toward a pair of seats, shielded by a curtain, beyond the field of vision of his patient. "Beyond those," he nodded toward the examination room doors, "you are in command. In here, I call the shots." He intentionally sharpened his voice with the hard cutting edge of authority.

Roychenko nodded, seemingly surprised at the outburst. Chastised, he moved toward the seats with Álvarez following.

"You'll find that this will take very little time. Make yourself comfortable." Lunts forced a clinical smile.

The two men nodded like dummies and Lunts smiled within himself.

It was, he thought, a continuum of the oldest game. Call me warlock, magician, sorcerer or doctor—all one and the same, only separated by centuries, semantics and technique. Men feared another man's power over the mind and Lunts used this fear to manipulate behavior.

Freud had been nothing more than an old ragpicker, scavenging frayed threads from the rich fabric of the mind. But Pavlov had understood the significance of the whole cloth and Lunts was a Pavlovian to the core.

"The patient, George Brocassie, is surfacing. I have induced a much deeper coma than would normally be necessary, but the preconditioning has been minimal, almost ineffective. That is the offsetting factor." He turned to Roychenko. "For that, Colonel, you will take the responsibility." Roychenko's lips started to form a denial of responsibility, but Lunts pushed on, spreading his hands in a gesture of impatience. "I have the list of questions you want pursued. He will be listening to me only. He will not hear you. If you wish to pursue any particular line of questioning, lift your hand and I will step aside to consult with you. But only I control the interrogation. Is there anything you want to add to the interrogation before I start?"

"Nothing new," Roychenko said, the tone of his voice regaining confidence. "We want to know—to know positively—how much he has found out about the complex and to what extent he has communicated it."

Nodding, Lunts made amendments to the list of interrogation questions. "All right," he said, settling himself into a chair beside Brocassie, "we start." He motioned the two attendants out of the room with a nod of his head and turned to the electroencephalograph, watching the slow, measured pace of the dot across the video screen. He opened the tap on the IV bottle, checking the flow, then keyed a switch on a console. The reaction was immediate. Brocassie's body jarred, his muscles contracting in spasms, then easing as the current was shut off. Lunts proceeded in the sequence twice more, monitoring the EEG. Brocassie's eyes fluttered, a thin drool of saliva dribbled from the corner of his mouth.

"You can hear me," Lunts demanded.

The mouth moved but nothing coherent came out. Lunts eased the IV drip and waited. The EKG bar was stronger, a little more rapid. Lunts bent forward, opened Brocassie's lid, then tested his pulse.

"Can you hear me now?" he asked.

The man on the table fluttered his eyelids. "Porto?"

"Not Porto. But a friend." He wiped the drool from the man's mouth with a gauze pad and bent down. "You've had a bad time of it, Brocassie," Lunts said softly. "But you're in good hands now. How do you feel?"

Nothing for a moment and then Brocassie moved his lips, the attempt obviously taking a great deal of effort. "Floating. Feel like—just like floating. Nice."

"It's just a sedative," Lunts reassured him. "You're all right now. You feel calm. Don't struggle against it ... relax and concentrate on your breathing." He reached over and touched Brocassie's forehead, stroking the wet skin as if he were gentling an animal. "You've had a very bad time," he repeated. "Tell me what you have found out about the complex."

"Tell Hagger ..." His muscles went rigid, his face suddenly bathed in sweat, a tic twitching the skin beneath his cheekbone. An involuntary shudder ran through his body. "Cold."

"Yes, it's cold," Lunts reassured him. "But now it's warming up. I've turned on the heater and the warmth is spreading out, warming you. Feel the heat in your skin—like the sun. It must feel good, doesn't it?"

"Yes . . . good. Warm."

"Fine. We're here to help you, to make you well." Lunts studied the list of questions. "Porto . . . ?" he questioned, letting the word frame itself into a question. "Who is Porto?"

"Porto. He's waiting for me . . . then get message to Hagger."

"Tell Hagger what?" Lunts's voice was calming.

"Complex is big. Bigger than . . ." His face contorted. "Lot of surface-to-air missiles. But something important. Very important. Got to tell him."

"What's important?" Lunts coaxed.

"The missiles. Not what we thought. Not just short-range missiles like the Frogs. Much bigger. Same as the drawings Hagger showed us. Remember them. Sandals, saw one unloaded from a flatcar by crane. Russians moving them underground."

EKG was rapid but regular. Excellent, Lunts thought.

"Luis will take a message back to Porto. How do you send it—a letter, perhaps?"

"Tape recorder. Put it all on tape recorder. Luis to take tape and film I shot. Porto can play back on his own machine, then send to Hagger."

"Is there any special code word that you use to tell Porto that everything is all right, a validation code to prove that the tape hasn't been made under—ah—pressure, that everything is going according to plan?"

"Nothing, nothing like that. No special word. Just my signature."

Lunts raised his eyebrows and whispered to Roychenko. "Were there any containers for the tapes in his possession?"

"Just the boxes that the tapes came in. They're the sort of thing that you can mail with the tape inside," Roychenko answered softly.

Lunts turned back, checked the monitors and resumed.

"You put your signature on the box. Is there anything special about the signature?"

Brocassie wrinkled his forehead. "Box?"

"The box the tape came in, Brocassie." Lunts had hardened his voice, impatient. "What about the signature?"

"Signature written with a toothpick in urine. Porto would dab chemical Hagger supplied over the signature. Turns the writing from invisible to dark red."

Beautiful, Lunts thought. Very clever in a primitive sort of way. Moscow Center would undoubtedly know about that one but it was still worth reporting. "And then Porto will encode the message and transmit it back to Hagger, correct?"

Brocassie slowly shook his head from side to side. "Problem. Radio I brought in was smashed and Maroto's is too weak to get out past the jamming. Have to send tapes and film to Hagger in Jamaica by boat—one of Maroto's men."

"But that would take a long time, wouldn't it? Why not through Guantánamo Bay?"

"Too risky. Too many Cuban troops patrolling area and minefields. Luis couldn't get through. Maybe get killed."

"But there is *someone* at Guantánamo who could receive the tapes from Luis and forward them on to Hagger?"

"Yes—Navy Commander Hall. Works for the CIA. Hagger told us to use him if no radio contact possible."

"This man Hall, he could definitely get the tapes to Hagger?"

"Yes. By aircraft to Jamaica. Hagger's there, waiting."

Lunts nodded, satisfied. He turned to Roychenko and Álvarez. "Anything else?"

Roychenko nodded. "Ask him whether Luis was suspected of being a traitor."

Lunts repeated the question to Brocassie.

"No—Enrico," he said. "Maroto thinks it's Enrico."

Lunts glanced back to Roychenko. Roychenko shook his head. "Nothing else. It's enough."

Smiling, Lunts eased up on the IV drip, timing it with a stopwatch, monitoring both the EKG and the EEG. He shook his head briefly and sat back in his chair. Slowly but perceptibly, both monitors eased back toward normalcy.

Lunts laid a hand on Brocassie's chest, stroking it with his fingernails. Lunts smiled. "That's enough, Brocassie. It's all we needed." He had the syringe already prepared. He swabbed Brocassie's arm and slid the needle in.

Lunts sat back in his chair, his feet crossed, stirring his tea. He moved the spoon circularly, precisely, not touching the wall of the cup, watching the wedge of lemon swim like a captive yellow fish through the dark, transparent liquid. "I need," he said almost petulantly, "a minimum of three weeks. Brocassie has to be established in a dependency mode. His body has to be conditioned. You are expecting instant results, Roychenko. It won't work. If I attempt to push him again as hard as I did today, you could be dealing with massive shock to the heart or significant deterioration of his mental capacity."

Roychenko doodled on a pad, drawing arrows, striking from one barb to the next in bold strokes. Deep purple sacks had formed under his eyes from loss of sleep. He looked up at Lunts. "I have to have Brocassie make that tape and I need it in two days. Moscow Center has demanded that in five days that tape be in Hagger's hands. Hagger will forward it to his superiors and then on to Kennedy. The timing has been moved up for reasons that we need not go into. Can you do it?"

"Given three weeks of conditioning, I could have him say anything, but it would take at least that long to ensure that his voice, his phrasing, the inflections and mannerisms are completely natural. The inflections of speech are the most sensitive factor. Drugs alone, without conditioning and repeated practice sessions, produce a mechanical response. This man Hagger would immediately be able to note the difference." He finished off his tea and set the cup down firmly. "There are limits to the manipulation of the mind, Colonel Roychenko, and your demands are unreasonable within the time period you require."

Roychenko turned to Álvarez. "Can you convince Brocassie to make that tape voluntarily?"

"It's possible. I would need the widest possible discretion as to how I do it. Brocassie is tough. I can't force him to do it. It has to be done carefully."

"I can use the woman if I have to," Roychenko said almost inaudibly.

Julio flushed, blood rushing to his face. "We've already been over that. If I can't persuade him, then that's a last resort. Give me some goddamn latitude. I can handle it if you let me do it my own way!"

Roychenko tapped his teeth with the pen, then smiled blandly. "You have two days."

He came awake slowly, surfacing through layers of wobbling dreams. His head, his whole body, was thudding with pain. For a second, he thought he was going to vomit and at some primitive level of understanding, he knew that if he did, he would drown in his own gorge. For he couldn't move. Felt the lead-weight pressure of his back against the mattress, his head immobile, mouth agape, raw air sucked by his lungs in short, rapid gasps, drying the tissues of his throat. Have to move, he thought. Roll over, get the old head to the edge of the mattress, like a kid on his first drunk. In his mind, he tried to form messages for nerve and muscle and tendon but there was no one on the job. Couldn't blame the poor bastards. Had a bad time of it.

Funny as hell. A laugh started in his solar plexus and bubbled up. He felt his stomach contract, heave twice. Fluid rushed uncontrolled through his plumbing, flooding him, drowning him. Mouth suddenly full and he panicked, trying to suck in air and instead, inhaling thick acid mush.

Heaved again, choking, pain from the contraction, and then pressure on his body. Hands. Rolling him over, pounding his back. He heaved again but this time his mouth was clear. The spasms subsided. A wet towel touched him, almost gently, wiping away the vomit from his lips and then he slid under, like a slippery seal, diving down through turbulence of the surface waters, swimming deeper to the cool quiet depths and safety.

Long time gone, he knew. Drifting in and out of consciousness. Found himself standing on a vast plain of desert sand, a soft wind blowing. There was the smell of sage, intense, like just after a rain. Quiet, until the faintest of vibrations worked upward through the soles of his boots, and then he could hear it, building in intensity. Like the stampede of a million cattle. It was suddenly in front of him, the light of the locomotive blinding him as it swept by him like a long snake, slithering across the plain. He heard it roaring, rails pounding in rhythm, bogies clacking over the cracks, the blur of black shapes screaming by in the blacker night. And then it was gone. He watched, suddenly at peace, as the dim red light of the caboose faded into the distance. And from far away, he heard the train's whistle blow. And then realized that the train had been time or death or both. The thought jarred him into full consciousness.

He slowly opened his eyes. No lights on but he sensed a presence. Started to say something and then choked off the sound because he desperately had to remember what had happened. Nothing he could remember except vivid colors, images whirling as if he were the center of the universe and the planets and suns and stars were wheeling around him in a kaleidoscope. He drifted back into semiconsciousness and surfaced again. He flexed his fingers, moved his toes. Better now. Not good but better. Listened and heard nothing except slow breathing, and then realized with a shock that the breathing was not his own. Smelled cigarette smoke.

Fear flooded him, knotting his stomach. They're waiting for me to come to. Remembered the prodding and the needles, the slow drip of the IV, the calm-insistent voice probing his mind, telling him to reveal things he couldn't hold back. But he couldn't remember what he had told them.

"A buck says that I can beat you down to Market Street and back." The voice, a voice he hadn't heard in years. But the taunt, the inflection, the challenge which they had thrown at each other when they were still kids was unmistakably Julio's.

"Two bucks says you can't now and never could," he replied slowly, the words thick as mashed potatoes on his tongue.

"Take it easy, Brocassie," Julio said. "The good doctor filled you up with high-test. It takes time to come down." A cigarette glowed in the darkness and Brocassie smelled with unimaginable sensitivity each individual component—sulfur, tobacco and even the faint sugary flavor of the paper wrapper. They had used a hallucinogenic, he guessed. He composed his mind, trying to fit things which had shaken loose back into their proper compartments, quieting his raw nerves, drawing down into himself. Sleep. Let the shit they pumped into my veins wear off. Take the full count before you try to get up. But before he slipped further into unconsciousness he said softly, "Fuck you, Álvarez. You always lost the race." He giggled ". . . a born loser."

He awoke to the smell of food. Again, the sensation was intense. He could tell exactly what it was: ham, squash, broccoli, smothered under lumps of butter. He began to salivate, the moisture filling his mouth.

"Lunts tells me that the stuff he used on you enhances the senses. Told me that with some men, the mere smell of perfume would induce a mile-high hard-on. Good thing I didn't wear shaving lotion." Snap of a light clicking on. "Come on, buddy, sit up. I brought you some goodies."

Brocassie slowly pulled himself upright. The room was swimming, things wheeling in double vision. He concentrated, trying to bring them together, fighting back the nausea. Two figures in olive fatigues swirled around each other, duplicate images of Julio Álvarez. The images slowly merged and became one. He closed his eyes, breathed deeply and then reopened them, his mind clearing. He suddenly realized that he felt more rested than he had ever been in his life, his body weak but alive and screaming for nourishment, every sense tingling.

"Eat up, Brocassie. The stuff's getting cold." Álvarez pushed a collapsible card table in front of the cot and handed him a fork and a spoon. "No knife, I'm afraid, for obvious reasons. But the meat's tender."

Brocassie ignored the utensils and picked up the slab of red meat with his fingers, tearing off chunks with his teeth. He wolfed down the ham and started in on the squash.

Julio picked up a bottle of beer from the floor, popped the cap off with an opener and set it in front of Brocassie. "Crystal Polar. Best beer south of Coors country. The medical people tell me that you're starved for sugar." He smiled, showing his strong teeth. The creases in his face were a little deeper than Brocassie remembered, and there were traces of silver in his black hair.

He shoveled down the food in silence but from the corner

of his eye he watched Álvarez. Still just on the edge of foppishness, the overattention to grooming, the fatigues tailored and starched in a razor's edge along the creases. Overtly self-assured, casual, but there was something else there—tension. It showed in his eyes.

Brocassie wiped his mouth with the back of his hand, forced a belch and leaned back, light-headed, supporting himself against the wall of the cell. Curious feeling—to be so completely alive and yet so weak, as if his mind were detached from his body. Floating free. He felt as if he could talk all night, into the dawn, for days, for months, forever. Drug aftereffect he knew. So do it carefully. Cautiously, he phrased the words in his mind and then said them. "So what's a nice boy like you doing in a shit heap like this, Julio?"

"It's a living," Álvarez smiled and then bent down and picked up a second bottle, Haig Dimple. He twisted off the cork and passed it across the table. "It won't do you any good but then again, it probably won't kill you."

Brocassie smelled it and took a very small sip. Christ, he thought, I can just about taste the peat smoke in this stuff. He took a longer pull and slid the bottle back toward Álvarez. "You have any cigarettes, *Comandante*? Isn't that the routine?"

"I wouldn't push it too hard, Brocassie. I'm here to help. There are other people who would like to do this a little differently, so cut the act." Álvarez's eyes were hard, watching for reaction. Brocassie felt anger welling up, ready to spill over, but he forced it back. Save it for when I can use it, he thought.

"What do you want, Julio?"

"Small talk," Álvarez countered. "Like before, when we were younger. Sit up all night and swap lies over a jug of hard cider. Except we're older and we drink Scotch."

"Spare me the bonhomie bullshit, Julio. How is Alicia?"

"Well. She doesn't know you're here if that's what you're digging for. I'm sure that if she did, she'd send her regards."

"I bet. By book code, Julio? That was a neat trick."

Álvarez shook his head. "Not of her doing, if that's of any consolation. It's a long story—one that I won't bore you with—but the bare bones of it is that we knew from Piedra

345

that you had gotten out of Cuba and were planning to come back in again. She was afraid that if you tried it, you'd get killed. She agreed to encode a message that I was to transmit to you, warning you off. Instead, I used the stuff she gave me and the book which she used to encode it to send the phony message to Hagger, setting up the Solario landing site as the drop point. Unfortunately, Hagger seems to have seen through it. I wonder why?"

She hadn't betrayed him! The identifier had been her way of ensuring that any message other than her original one would show up as an obvious fake. So even then she hadn't trusted Julio! But to tell him this would expose her. And there was one, simple explanation that Álvarez would buy.

Brocassie picked up the Scotch and sipped, putting it together in his mind. He set the bottle down and recorked it. "Everything about the code was fine," he answered carefully, "including the coding, the format, the identifier-verifier. You blew it because you selected the Solario strip. You figured that we were going to parachute in, right?"

Nodding, Álvarez said, "Correct."

"But you didn't know that we were flying gliders. Solario would have been too difficult, too exposed, too well known. Hagger made a gut decision to stick with the original plan. Sorry, Julio. You must have had a very red face when you realized that we didn't fall for it."

Álvarez drew his fingers back through his hair, a gesture more of frustration than of casual grooming. "It was a good try, Brocassie. It might have worked, but then again, it didn't." He leaned back in his chair. "Suppose you tell me what Hagger *thought* was going on in this complex."

"I imagine that my recent psychedelic trip would have revealed all."

"Maybe in your next life, Brocassie. But I have the power to save your present one, depending on how you cooperate."

Which was a pile of crap, he thought. I'm dead. Knew when I saw Piedra that I was dead. He hated Álvarez for even raising the expectation.

"You're bullshitting me, Álvarez! What guarantees could you ever offer that I could get out of this alive, or if alive, with a mentality exceeding a carrot."

"What a bad temper you have. I would have thought you would have mellowed a bit by now." He jiggled his glass, appraising the amber whiskey against the light. "Fine stuff, Brocassie. Not that easy to get." He paused, thinking, half-smiling. "What guarantees? None—just pure logic. And the logic will be perfectly evident even to you. Your release is not just something we're bargaining with—it's been part of the plan all along because it benefits us."

"*Us*, Julio? Who's '*US*'?"

"Cubans, Brocassie. Just Cubans, but admittedly with some side benefits to our Soviet friends."

Brocassie watched his brother's eyes. Nothing—neither honesty nor deceit—was there. Just bland amusement.

"Tell me the grand logic," he said finally.

Refilling his glass, Álvarez moved forward in his chair, his face closer. "Cuba," he started, "is a client state of the Soviets because we have no other choice. Fidel is not all that hot to be controlled by the Soviets, but he needs four things to make the Revolution a success. Technical assistance, military assistance, economic aid and, perhaps most important, a Cuba completely safe from American interference." He raised his eyebrows. "Make sense thus far?"

"It makes magnificent sense, Julio. What's the price tag?"

Julio rubbed his index finger against his thumb. "Quality goods are expensive. Fidel is willing to pay the price. In return for their aid, the Soviets will gain their first foothold in the Western Hemisphere—be able to expand Soviet influence into Central and South America. And perhaps equally important, gain logistical support for Soviet military activities: Cienfuegos as a base for reprovisioning submarines and airfields that they can use jointly with the Cuban Air Force. And as far as this complex is concerned, a terrific little communications facility with all the bells and whistles so that they can chat with their subs in the South Atlantic and Eastern Pacific, monitor American missile launches from the Cape, and have an electronic conduit for their satellites which are positioned over the North American continent."

"So Cuba plays the whore and climbs in bed with the Russians."

Álvarez stroked the glass, smiling. "Like the English and

Italians and Germans and Greeks and Spanish play whore to the Americans for exactly the same kind of fee. Jesus H. Christ, Brocassie! Where's your sense of proportion? What's good for the American goose is even better for the Soviet gander and what's the objection? Morality? Morality died with the nineteenth century, as far as international politics go. Nations do things out of self-interest. Like people do. And there are two people in this room. Let's talk about their self-interests."

He knew that Julio had a point, and he was too damn burned out to argue. "Spare me a dissertation on international politics or personal objectives, Julio. Both of us are sitting here for very different reasons. We're just slobs in the trenches with a mined wasteland in between us. I made up my mind a long time ago. Politics I don't give a shit about. Principles, I do."

"Ah—the ultimate personal truth!" Álvarez had a sardonic grin on his face.

"No ultimate truths, Julio. We're too old, too tired to believe in any kind of ultimates."

"There's a place for you here, Brocassie. You know these people, this land. We're going to do something with it—something big."

"Like what, Julio? Hold free elections, let the people determine their own future? Kick the Russians out?"

"In time," Álvarez answered. "All in good time."

It's the drugs, he thought. Have the compulsion to talk. "Come on, Julio. Get to the point and spare the razzle-dazzle. Your law degree's showing."

Álvarez glanced at his watch and then nodded. "OK—what did Hagger think you'd find here?"

"He wasn't sure. He sent us in to sniff it out."

"You can do better than that! He sent you and Porto in because of the films that you got out of Cuba. What did they show?"

Brocassie kept silent.

"You want another interview with the good doctor? One more of those, Brocassie, and you *will* have scrambled eggs for brains. I can arrange it in minutes if you really insist."

"I wouldn't expect anything less, Julio." There was no point in holding it back. It was something that they would already know. "Hagger realizes that there's an underground complex. Plus silos, Julio. Silos are a big deal with him."

"And what did he think were in those silos?"

"That's why I came, Julio. To find out."

"You can do better!"

Coastal defense missiles, Brocassie thought. That's what Hagger had expected, but if he said that, then Álvarez would know that the Americans were zeroing in on the Santiago area as a possible invasion landing area. "Some kind of air-defense system. Something new, he thought. Long-range stuff, maybe capable of shooting down missiles that they launch out of the Cape."

"Which is comic-book crap," Álvarez shot back. "You expect me to be stupid enough to buy that? Hagger expected to find offensive weapons here, didn't he?"

"Some people think any weapon is offensive, Julio."

Álvarez hunched forward, his elbows on the table. "We can get it out of you, Brocassie. Really, we can. Hagger undoubtedly knows that any American invasion will be on the south coast—probably Santiago. We've reached the same conclusion because it's obvious. Geography, topology and logistics rule out any other area in Cuba for a really large-scale invasion. Sure, we have short-range missiles here in this complex for coastal defense against an invasion, and we have the finest surface-to-air missiles in the Soviet inventory but there are not any—I repeat—any offensive weapons on this site, not by Kennedy's definition. Nothing with enough range to hit the U.S. coast, and not armed with nuclear weapons."

"I know differently."

"You know *shit,* buddy boy! If there were offensive long-range weapons here and the Americans found out, it would be an invitation for a very heavy-duty air strike—possibly nuclear. It's a no-win situation for both sides because there'd be American bombers killing Soviet military personnel and that upsets a very delicately balanced applecart. The Soviets would be forced to retaliate in order to square the tab." He blossomed his fingers into a flower burst. "Kablooey—World War Three."

"You're telling me that there are no long-range nuclear

missiles in Cuba? What do you think I've been doing for the last three days, Julio? I've photographed one of the damn things. I knew what it was because Hagger gave us a complete briefing on *every* type of missile the Red Army have in their current inventory. The length, profile, warhead shape, external accessories—the whole thing matches the SS-4 Sandal exactly!"

"Tomorrow, Brocassie, I'll prove to you that there are no SS-4s in Cuba and never were. What you saw—what you *think* you saw—was about as lethal as an overstuffed pillow." He settled back in his chair, arms crossed. "You ever wonder *why* we went to the trouble of trying to suck you back into Cuba?"

Get him angry, Brocassie thought. Because when he's angry, he spills out his guts. Brocassie shook his head. "I suppose you needed to justify your existence."

"You stupid asshole! We don't want mercenaries in Cuba. They tie up hundreds of our troops, screw up security and eventually some poor slobs on both sides get killed and for nothing, because a few hack mercenaries can't stop a revolution. But we have a special situation—something that puzzles the American intelligence community. It was inevitable that somehow, the CIA or the DIA or the U.S. military would learn of this communications complex. If the Americans *knew* it was only that, they'd leave it alone because they have the same kind of setups in Turkey, Iran, Japan, Indonesia, West Germany, all over the damn world, and they don't want to upset the status quo. Yeah—they may not like Soviets sitting in Cuba, monitoring American radio traffic and checking out the characteristics of missiles launched from the Cape, but it isn't threatening, understand? Just a nuisance."

He reached over and picked up the Haig, twisted off the stopper and took a drink.

"So how do we convince them?" Álvarez asked.

"Invite them in, serve tacos and beer, then give them the tour and tell them to come back anytime they're in town."

"I thought maybe we fried your brains too much," Álvarez answered. There were spots of color in his cheeks and the vein in his temple throbbed but he kept himself under control. "No, the only way that the Americans would be satisfied would be for one of their own people to report back that the complex was simply a Russian-manned communications facility with a coastal and air defense capability. Nothing long-range, nothing nuclear. *That,* they'd believe—*if* it was from one of their own agents. The horse's mouth syndrome, Brocassie."

"And the horse's mouth is me?"

"That's the idea," Álvarez replied.

"And for the sake of going along with your little joke, how do you think I'd get this report back to Hagger?"

"By tape and a blurred roll of film to Commander Hall in Guantánamo, Luis as courier."

"*LUIS!*"

"You're surprised? Piedra has been controlling Luis for over a year. Luis was the one who reported that you were leaving the Sierra. Luis was the one who pinpointed Fabricio's route between camps, and Luis was the one who suckered you down to the mines. Luis's father was an NCO in Batista's army. Not very bright—but not really guilty of anything excessive. Just your normal slob who was on the losing side. But Piedra trumped up charges against him and he's held in El Condado Prison for crimes against the state. I think you know what that means. Luis keeps him alive by supplying us with information."

The conversation that Luis had initiated about his own father, about Brocassie's father. In a way, it had been a warning and he had been too preoccupied to give it any thought. Now he understood. Too late—much too late.

"It's not going to work, Julio. *If* Luis gets the tape to Guantánamo, *if* it gets to Hall, *if* Hall gets the tape to Hagger—it still doesn't make a damn bit of difference. Porto expects me to pull out when the six days are over. If I don't show, Porto will come looking and if he can't find me, he'll assume that I've been captured. End of deception."

"That's been thought of. You'll tell Hagger on the tape that the militia patrols are too dense to retrace your route back over the Sierra and that instead you're going inland first to Bayamo and then to the coast by bus. Tell him to set up a boat to pick up you and Porto on the coast. Have him relay that information to Maroto by radio."

351

"The jamming . . ."

"The jamming isn't going to stop but it's going to get weaker—enough for Hagger with his big, powerful transmitter to get through but not enough for Maroto to answer back. Your buddy Porto isn't going to come down here looking when Hagger's just told him to bug out. Savvy?"

Brocassie listened, hearing echoes of the old Julio—the wheeler-dealer; the master con artist. "So tell me, Julio, what is the deal you're offering?"

Álvarez bent over the table and drew a large square on the worn plastic surface with his finger. "Package deal, Brocassie. Make the tape with our coaching but make it natural. No funny little phrases which would tip off Hagger. We know about your verifying the tape with a signature written in piss." He lifted his eyebrows, smiling. "How cheap of the agency, Brocassie. You'd think that they'd be a bit more sophisticated than that." He leaned back, lit a cigarette and exhaled. "Luis takes it to Guantánamo to Hall and Hall gets it to Hagger. In the tape, you've asked Hagger to get you and Porto back out of Cuba by boat. He'll go for that because he'll be anxious to debrief both of you. Set up the boat for Cabo de La Cruz on the twentieth. If you don't show, Porto will have no choice but to leave without you and we won't stop him. He gets away, Brocassie, scot-free."

"But the eventuality will be that I've been caught or killed."

"Exactly. We'll leak it to the press that you were picked up in a routine roadblock near the coast. Nothing incriminating on you, no tapes, no films. You speak Spanish, know the Cuban idiom, the customs of the people. In a civil court, you'll break down, admit that you're an American of Cuban extraction. You hired some crazy man to bring you into Cuba from Florida. You were looking for a friend you had before the Revolution but you found that he or she had been killed during the liberation of Santa Cruz. I'll ensure that the DGI takes no interest in the case and in a year you'll be swapped back to the States for some low-grade people the CIA is holding in Miami. End of it, Brocassie. One year in a cell, lousy food, but you'll live."

"And if I don't make the tape?"

"You damn well better. I've stuck my neck out a mile to get the Soviets to go along with it. So let's not even explore that avenue."

"I think we should, Julio. I want to hear it from your own, sweet lips."

Álvarez sighed, stood up and paced the length of the cell. "You'd be given a little time to reconsider, and if you failed to do what we demand, Lunts would do a surgical alteration on your skull. He has a technique that he's dying to try. And if that fails, we'd go after Porto as the secondary target. Luis knows where he is. We can get him." He swung back, facing Brocassie. "But there's another alternative—something that I didn't dream up. Roychenko knows that you were . . . involved with Alicia. He'll use her as a lever. He's told me that if you refuse, she goes first and very painfully—with you as a spectator. You know Piedra."

"*YOU FUCKHEAD!*" He was springing forward, his hands going for Álvarez's throat. The table overturned, the bottle of Haig splintering on the concrete floor, the plate and glasses shattering. He got no more than three feet and he faltered, his body unable to support him. Álvarez stiff-armed him and Brocassie landed heavily on his chest, his breath gone out of him. He felt the cold steel of a gun muzzle against his neck.

"*Don't blow it, Brocassie!*" Álvarez hissed. "It isn't something within my control. Roychenko sprang it on me. He must have planned it a long time ago when he knew it was you coming back into Cuba. That woman means more to me than she ever did to you. I love her, Brocassie. More than I ever did before, and if you cause her harm by your own stupidity, then Piedra will have to fight me for the honor of taking you apart." He jammed the muzzle harder against Brocassie's neck, the pain searing into Brocassie's spine. "Play ball with me, brother, because if you screw it up, she'll die and you with her."

Within the limits of his vision, he watched Álvarez's feet back away toward the cell door. There was a muffled sound of a man's voice from the other side and then the bolt slid open. Álvarez paused in the cell's doorway. "I have just thirty-six more hours to get that tape out of you. I'm coming back tomorrow morning. Let's do it the easy way."

The door slammed and the bolt rattled home. Seconds later, the overhead light died, but for a long while, he lay on the floor, his mind and body exhausted, stupidly seeking a way out when he knew there was none.

CHAPTER

15

Sierra Maestra, October 24, 1962

He squinted, his eyes against the binoculars, sweeping the instrument in slow increments from east to west, scanning the complex below him. He could see no movement. As if nothing existed down there, he thought, except sand and lizards and a chain link fence enclosing barren ground. If Hagger's so-called silos were there within the perimeter of the chain link fence, they were better hidden than the holes burrowed into the dirt by field mice. Possible, as Hagger had briefed him, that the silo covers had been mounded over with dirt but it was hard to believe, looking at the desolate, featureless plain of sand and grass.

Porto leaned back, covered the lenses with a rubber cap and rolled over onto his back. He shut his eyes, letting the pale light of early morning slowly warm his stiff body but he couldn't relax. The apprehension kept nibbling in the corners of his mind. Too long, he thought. Something was wrong—very wrong.

Four days—no, five, counting today—since Brocassie had headed down into the valley with Luis. No Brocassie, no Luis. The kid was supposed to come back up midweek with Brocassie's status report on tape. No report of activity other than the normal. Helicopter activity about the same—cursory patrols as always along the ridge.

Damn it, he thought. It had been like pulling teeth, arguing with Maroto to send men down to check out the mine, find out what in hell was wrong. But Maroto had finally caved in, sent two of the more experienced men who had actually been down there before. They had left at sundown and were due back sometime this morning.

The infected foot had healed without complications. He had started exercising it now, taking short walks, working the muscles, toughening the skin with potassium permanganate. Another day or two and it would be completely normal.

He hadn't heard a movement behind him until the man hawked and spit. He slowly rolled over, keeping his hand away from the Colt.

"You're growing deaf, Porto," the man said softly, squatting down next to him. He wiped his face with a rag, then leaned back on his buttocks, arms wrapped around his legs, rocking a little. "What do you see with that fine instrument?"

"Nothing." He pulled himself up into a sitting position and turned. Maroto was like a fat cow that had been cut out from the herd and had grown hard and thin on saw grass and isolation. There were still traces of good living in his face—the florid veins spanning his cheek from too much drink, the sag of flesh around his neck, for he had once been excessively fat. Now, he was all bones and he had grown a beard that obscured his mouth in a bristle of hair. It made it difficult to read his expression. "There is coffee and some beans. I have two personal eggs saved for such a fine morning. You may have one of them."

"I'll be up in a while, *Jefe*. The men: are they back yet?"

"They are. Fulgencio and Ramón got back forty minutes ago. They are now asleep, exhausted. Seventeen miles down and back in ten hours. Like mountain goats."

"For Christ's sake, is Brocassie with them?"

"You knew the answer to that before you asked it, didn't

you? Nor is Luis. There was not a trace of them. The mine was empty, no equipment, no notes, no sign of struggle and yet they had used the mine."

"How . . . ?"

"Tin cans of food that they took with them were scattered around. The smell of shit in the back of the mine, a few cigarette butts."

"They shifted to another mine, maybe lower down?"

"Ramón doesn't think so. Outside of the mine entrance, there were many footprints, all with heavy lug soles." He lifted up his leg, showing Porto the sole of his boot. "Boots with soles like these—issued to the FAR and DGI by the Soviets. These are a pair that I liberated from a FAR corporal half a year ago as he had no further use for them."

"We knew that patrols passed near there. You yourself said that the mine was a safe place, almost undetectable."

"I still believe that. You would have to know exactly where it was to see it. And yet the footprints came in a straight path directly to the mine, then headed back down into the valley. The soldiers that came there knew what they were looking for."

"Enrico . . ."

"Enrico has not been out of my sight for a week. It could not possibly be his doing. I think I have been a fool. I refused to suspect Luis because he is younger, because his father was tortured and killed by the DGI. But I have a bad feeling in my guts that it was Luis who betrayed Brocassie. The boy and I share common blood but I think I have been a stupid old man. There is nothing to be done now."

"What do you mean?"

The old man lifted his shoulders marginally then relaxed them, the gesture almost unnoticeable except that Porto was watching him carefully. "If Luis has betrayed Brocassie, he will betray us as well. He knows roughly where this camp is. I will have to move immediately, perhaps pull back toward the coast. And you will leave Cuba. Nothing more can be done. Your work here is finished."

"Like hell! Brocassie's down there. I can't leave him!"

"And what would you do? Repeat his mistake or worse still, try to free him?"

"Give me five men, ammunition and supplies for ten days. They may have him down there but they won't keep him there. Eventually, they'll move him."

Maroto looked down at his boots, swiped with his hands at a smear of mud. "Nothing can be done, pilot. This is not an army of soldiers at my command. These are guerrillas, Porto. They joined me of their own free will because they wanted to fight against Fidel—not because I could offer them money or glory. I lead by their consent. I cannot order them to do foolish things." He lifted the rag of his handkerchief and spat into it, folded the cloth over twice and tucked it carefully into his fatigue breast pocket. He heaved a long sigh as if he had made a decision. "However, I might ask for volunteers."

"*ASK* for volunteers? What in hell are you people doing up here anyway?"

"I will ignore that," Maroto answered. "You know as well as I do that our requests for supplies and munitions are ignored by your government. What we have is what we have taken in combat. Half of what we have is of Soviet manufacture. Perhaps after all, we picked the wrong patron." He bent forward, rubbing his forearms, swatting at a mosquito. "You, perhaps, should talk to your president about the fight to free Cuba. We hear the speeches on the Miami radio promising help to the gallant freedom fighters but we have not yet seen the results. In the meanwhile, we are trying just to stay alive." He edged himself up into a crouch, looking down over the valley. "You would really, truly try to free him, wouldn't you?"

"Yes."

"He is dead, you know."

"*Bullshit! He's alive!*"

Maroto nodded, turning his face upward. The sun was low in the east, the light hard. It cast the creases of his tanned flesh into deep relief, making his face look as if it had been carved from fractured rock.

"I think you are playing with yourself, pilot. It is time for you to go back to Miami and hot showers and hot food and hot-blooded women. Cuba is not a playground—it is a killing ground for the innocent, the unwary and the ill-advised."

"I'll go down there without your goddamned help!"

Maroto smiled—a long slow smile. "Yes, I believe you would. As would I, because Brocassie is one of the few foreigners who gave to our cause without asking for anything in return. But I wanted to be sure."

"Sure of what?"

"Sure that you would be willing to attempt his rescue with me." He leaned back, rocking on his buttocks, grinning, displaying tobacco-stained teeth.

"You old bastard!"

"It has been said that I am, however inaccurately. My father would have taken great objection to your insinuations." Maroto put a hand on his shoulder. "I still have a few young ones who are eager. I, myself, will consent to lead the effort but the rest have had enough glory to last ten lifetimes." He stood up. "Let us get coffee, Porto. And two wonderful eggs."

They climbed slowly up through the rock outcroppings, Maroto moving slowly, painfully, Porto hobbling behind him. They passed one guard lounging in the brush, his automatic weapon slung negligently over his shoulder. He had an iguana skewered on a stick, roasting over a bed of coals. The guard gave Maroto a thumbs-up but Maroto ignored him.

When they were higher up the hillside, Maroto turned aside to Porto, motioning him to stop. The old man held his position, leaning forward, his hands on his thighs, panting. ". . . a minute . . . not . . ." He didn't finish the sentence. He sank down on his haunches, staring out over the valley. From far away, there was the flat beat of a chopper but Maroto didn't seem to care. He sat for a few minutes, blew his nose with the rag. "I can't even feed my men, Porto," he finally said, his breathing under control. "Iguanas. Iguanas and beans. Rice. We've had rats even, pilot. It shames me that I can't provide even the minimum supplies. We need food and ammunition and your government won't give it to us. Is that something that you can explain, when we carry your fight?"

"I thought it was your fight."

"Our fight is your fight. If it wasn't, you wouldn't be sitting here on this hillside, listening to an old man whine about supply problems. But it becomes difficult when the only support we have are words on the Miami radio stations. Eating promises is like eating air. It gives us gas without the satisfaction of farting."

Porto snorted in amusement. He pulled out a cigar and lit it, enjoying the company of the old man, wanting to prolong it. The fog was burning away quickly on the valley floor. It would be a hot day and the choppers would be up pretty soon and they would have to get under cover until sundown. He pulled himself upright and gave a hand to Maroto. "Let's get moving. I'll try my best to keep up with you."

Maroto laughed. "You're a whore's son, my friend. But she was a good whore." He pulled the cigar from Porto's mouth and puffed on it, making a face, then gave it back. "I know she was good," he added, "from intimate contact."

Porto took a swipe at him, laughing, and with surprising agility, Maroto ducked away.

"Take care!" Maroto rasped, clenching his hand. "My fist is still hard, even if my manhood isn't."

Together, they slowly climbed toward the cliff. Maroto stopped once they were under the cover of a cluster of pine, sweet and thick with resinous scent. His chest was heaving and it took him a long time to regain his breath.

"I didn't come down just to insult your country and your origins, Porto. We have an interesting visitor. He came in last night. I think you should try to talk to him."

"Who?"

"That is the question. Who? A boy." Maroto combed his fingers through his beard, looking absently toward the network of caves in the cliff. He turned back. "He contacted a woman in Santiago who works for us—Fabricio's sister. She's trustworthy even though her tongue is sharp and her brain is dull. It appears that the boy was very persuasive—said that if she would not arrange to bring him to me that he would seek the help of the police. She sent him with her husband to a courier in our group who lives on the south slope of the Sierra in the village of Pico Cobre. The courier brought the boy the rest of the way. It's taken them three days of climbing from Santiago and the boy is worn out. He's sleeping."

"What concern is it . . ."

Maroto shook his head. "The concern is that the boy carries a packet which was addressed to me. Much of it is in

English, which I have no facility with. I think it best you assess its worth."

"It could be a setup—some kind of a plant by the DGI!"

Maroto shook his head. "No, I think not. His letter of introduction to the Fabricio woman is signed with a signature that I know—Alicia Helvia."

The boy was still sleeping, a dirty blanket pulled over his body. In his dreams, he moved spasmodically, lips working. His breathing was hoarse and irregular.

Back in the depths of the cave, there was no light except a small kerosene lantern which burned feebly, its wick lowered to a smoldering spark, the chimney blackened with soot. Porto bent over and turned up the wick. The boy came suddenly awake, sitting bolt upright.

Porto stared into the boy's face, not believing what he saw. The kid was filthy, hair matted, welts of red streaked across his skin from climbing through the brush, but it was the same face, transformed by time and pain, but still, the same face.

"Miguel?" he whispered, his heart pounding.

The boy was frowning and then his expression transformed to disbelief, then to joy. He scrambled upright, his arms out and fell against Porto. "Tío Porto!" He was laughing and, at the same time, crying, his face streaking with tears. "You came! I knew you would come back!"

Porto crushed the boy against him, hugging him, ruffling his hand through the boy's hair. He felt his throat constrict, unable to say anything, knowing that if he tried, his voice would break. He tightened his grip on the boy, nodding his head.

For a long time, he just held Miguel, rocking him in his arms, not fully understanding how the link between two people could be this strong. Finally he whispered, "Yes, I came back for you, *Monomín*. I truly did." He lifted Miguel to his feet, realizing only now how the boy had grown. He was taller by at least four inches and his muscle structure was mature and hard. Not a boy any longer, he thought. He threw his arm around Miguel's shoulder, moving toward the cave's entrance. They stood for a moment and in the sunlight, overlooking the valley. The day was clear and fine, the sunlight brilliant on the mountain slopes. If you believed in omens, he thought, it was a good one.

"I know a man," he said, "who has two eggs. I think that he will part with both of them in a good cause."

Miguel licked his fork, mopped at the yellow yolk with a piece of bread and drank the remainder of his coffee. The sun was high, casting hard shadows down through the pine. The shadows shifted with the wind as the branches stirred. Porto wanted to avoid asking but he had to. "How did it happen—your mother?"

The boy was stone-faced, expressionless. "It was a neighbor, the García man. My mother always said that he drank a lot and was of no account. García must have seen you leave our house because he turned us in only a few hours after you left for the airstrip. The DGI came and took my mother away in a van. I was taken in a separate car to a convent the Fidelistas had taken over. I was given a roll, a plate of beans and a glass of milk. The guard was young, not much older than myself. He told me not to worry, that there was probably some mistake and that it happened all the time. My mother and I would be back together by the next night.

"He apologized but said that regulations demanded that I be locked up overnight. He put me in a cell which had belonged to a nun."

"Your mother—what happened?" His fingernails were biting into his palms, his throat dry.

Miguel shook his head, ignoring the question. It was as if he had been turned on and the mechanism had to run down before he could stop.

"In the morning, a different guard opened the door and let a woman in. She was very fat but she was nice—you understand? She asked me how I had spent the night and what school I went to. I kept asking her about my mother but she would only say that she was 'assisting the State in an inquiry.' Finally, she pulled a yellow pad of paper from her purse and started asking me questions that a policeman would ask—who are you, where do you live, what friends come to your mother's house, what politics does your mother believe in, has she ever spoken against the Revolution? I told her nothing, nothing, nothing, and finally she lost patience and began to slap me. I spit in her face, a big one, and then she went crazy and started shrieking at me, hitting me with her fist. She pulled me up by my hair and told me to think and think hard because she would see me the next day and then the next day and for as many days as it took until I told the truth. I told her to do something dirty with her finger and she kicked me in the stomach. She started to leave but before she did, she took a photo from her bag and dropped it on the floor next to me. She leaned down and said, 'That is what happens to traitors, *chico*.' The photograph was of my mother. She was dead."

Porto turned away, staring across the valley toward the far mountains, trying to hide the tears, struggling desperately to span the years between how a child showed grief and how a man contained it. He turned back, trying to keep the hate and anger from his voice. "It was not your fault, you understand? She did it for me, to give me time to get out of Cuba. It was my fault, Miguel. She didn't—"

The boy shook his head. "*NO!* It was not your fault! It was not your hand that beat her, it was not your cigar that burned holes in her skin. The people that took her were DGI. I want them killed—all of them!" He turned away, his body wracked in convulsions.

Porto could find nothing within him to say that would relieve the boy's pain. He nodded. "I understand, Miguel."

Miguel turned back, slashing his palm across his face, smearing away the tears with a force which must have been painful. "She came again the next day and then the next. She threatened me and slapped me, but then, you see, I couldn't speak. I couldn't say anything, couldn't even cry out. I could feel something inside of me tighten, like my chest had a hard band around it, and every time I tried to speak, the band would crush me. At first, she thought I was acting but then on the third morning a man came with her. He was a doctor, I think, but he didn't carry a bag. He looked at my throat and into my eyes with a flashlight. He talked with her and finally she left. I never saw her again, except in nightmares."

"How did you get out?"

Miguel ignored the question. "They took me away to a youth camp on the coast, east of Santiago. There were classes in the morning and then work in the fields until sundown. But because I couldn't talk, they used me to work in the kitchen."

Miguel's face and voice were now expressionless, but he was working his hands together, as if he were washing them, over and over.

"I was there nine months. To my face, they called my mother a whore and traitor. They painted an American flag on the concrete in front of the dining hall and made me get down and lick it every morning before I could eat. Some of the older boys kicked me in the ass when I did but I never fought back. I just worked and slept and when they talked to me, I stared right through them like I had something wrong with my brain. And finally, they gave up trying to talk to me, gave up hurting me."

"How did you get away, Miguel?"

"They were talking about transferring a lot of the students to the Isle of Pines. I knew I would never get away from there. I worked in the kitchen. I had to load the garbage truck each night. They would drive it out to a compost pile in the fields next to the camp where they dumped it in with the shit from the latrines. On a Sunday night, when everyone who wasn't on restrictions was allowed to watch television, I loaded the truck and then I crawled in and pulled the slops over me. I thought I would suffocate but eventually one of the student guards came and drove the truck to the compost area and dumped it. By dawn, I was ten miles away. In four days, I had traveled over eighty miles, eating what I found in gardens and garbage pits. I kept heading east because I heard in Santiago that the *jefe* of the DGI lived on a very large farm east of Santiago near Berraco. It took me two days to get there, but in Berraco I heard two women talking near the town water pump about a big *finca* where the *comandante* lived. One of the women was bragging that she sold Comandante Álvarez's cook eggs at twice the price others would pay and the two of them split the profit. She was very proud of this, cackling like one of her hens."

"*Álvarez?*"

Miguel nodded. "The man who is in charge of the DGI

for Oriente Province. I wanted to see that man, to kill him for what the DGI had done to my mother. I stole a piece of steel pipe and I spent all day grinding it down on a rock into a stabbing knife, and I went there to kill him but he was gone— somewhere overseas. I was going to go and then I thought, what if I stay and ask for work? Sooner or later, he will come back and when he comes back, I will kill him. But it turned out differently because there was this woman. I don't know whether she was his wife or what. The guards called her a *puta* behind her back but she was not that, I know. She was kind to me like my own mother and she helped me. I would die for her, *Tío*, gladly."

"Alicia Helvia?"

"Alicia," he nodded. "That is her name. She allowed me to help her steal secret papers from the *comandante's* safe. She said it was very important that they be sent to Señor Maroto and so I brought them all the way myself and I want to stay and help fight against this *Álvarez*."

Porto nodded. Full circle, he thought. That's what it's come to. He reached down and wrapped his arms around the boy. "You're here, Miguel. That's what counts."

Porto studied the code sheets for the last time and slid them across the table to Maroto. The old man ignored them, sipping on a glass of brandy.

"She was trying to save Brocassie," Maroto said gently. "It is not a unique sentiment." He rolled his empty glass between his palms. "So now we must plan, pilot."

"If Brocassie is in that complex, we've got to penetrate the fence, get past God knows how many KGB guards, get underground, find out where they're keeping him, break him out and then reverse the whole process. It's not very promising."

"But Miguel said that Álvarez had moved to the coffee plantation bordering the complex and that he took Alicia with him?"

Porto nodded wearily. "I don't see what that has to do with getting Brocassie out."

"But it does. Álvarez is the key, isn't he? He obviously would know where Brocassie is held, the security setup, everything."

"You're saying that we snatch Álvarez!"

Maroto refilled his glass and poured one for Porto. He took a long time doing it, almost as if he were performing a ceremony.

"I will be straight with you, pilot," he said, his voice flat. "If Brocassie is alive, he may be underground in that rat's nest down below us, or he may have already been transferred. We cannot be sure of where he is and therefore I cannot gamble the life of even one of my men in attempting to free him. That's why Álvarez has to be our primary objective."

"And how do you plan to get to him?"

"We must contact Alicia Helvia—let her know that a few of us can penetrate the fence and get into the housing area. It is lightly guarded—certainly not as formidable as getting belowground into the complex. If she can arrange to have Álvarez there at a certain time, we can find out from him where Brocassie is. Better yet, if she can have both Brocassie and Álvarez there together, we will take all three of them and pull back into the Sierra."

"How in hell could she ever persuade Álvarez to bring Brocassie home with him?"

"I did not say it would be easy. It is up to her to devise a way. After all, she and Álvarez and Brocassie were all friends once." He lifted his hand and tapped his forehead with a bony finger. "I don't know, pilot, what she can accomplish, but she is intelligent and resourceful. And if she cannot arrange it, at least we will have Álvarez."

Maroto leaned back, dropping his worn hands on the table, carefully folding one over the other. He looked no more dangerous than a tired schoolmaster at the end of a term. But his voice had a new confidence—a certain vitality.

"What the boy did was courageous," he continued, "the opening of Álvarez's safe in the middle of the night. You questioned him about this?"

"Only about the papers that you've already showed me—the codes."

Maroto smiled and pulled out a folded sheet of paper from his breast pocket and spread it open, flattening the creases with his hands, still withholding it from Porto. "There was one document that Alicia Helvia told him to copy besides

366

the code sheets—a certain page that she had seen briefly in a highly classified manual."

The old man passed the sheet of foolscap across the table. It was painstakingly copied with a sharp pencil. Unmistakably, it was a drawing of a missile. Long cylinder shape, pointed nose cone, fins, rocket engine. Dotted lines along the body of the missile showed some type of interior tanks, two of them, roughly the same size, and at various places on the missile were small arrows, pointing to fittings with a number written in alongside each of the arrows. Porto knew—thought he knew—but he wanted Maroto's confirmation. "What do you think it represents?"

Maroto lifted his eyebrows. "Not obvious to you? It's a loading diagram for a weapon—a missile. If there are things like this in the complex, Álvarez would probably have some part in their transshipment from a Cuban port to the complex."

Porto studied the drawing again. "All right, Maroto. It's probably a coastal defense rocket with a range of about eighty miles. Hagger thought the silos would be used for the Frog Type Two or Three. It's not a big deal."

"Not a Frog, Porto. You yourself gave me Hagger's briefing sheets on the dimensions and weights of the Frog series. The largest of them weighs twenty-two *hundred* kilograms." He shook his head for emphasis. "No, Porto, I've done a rough calculation on the weight, using the figures that Miguel wrote down. They are consistent with my calculations. He made no mistake in his copying."

"What kind of weight?"

"Seventeen *thousand* kilograms, not including fuel. Eight times the empty weight of a Frog Three. You are looking at the load transfer diagram for a very long-range ballistic missile, my friend."

"*Christ!*" Porto grabbed at the paper, trying to make sense of the many cables and numbers. "I don't believe it!"

"I do," Maroto said calmly. "And if Hagger has this evidence—if we can prove its authenticity—then the Americans will be forced into a massive strike against this complex, and that will pull the trigger on a general invasion of Cuba. And *that* is the support that I seek—nothing less."

"What kind of proof could we get that would convince Hagger? A piece of paper isn't enough." His throat was suddenly dry.

"Álvarez's warm body. Brocassie's as well, if possible."

Porto stared at the old man, astonished. "What do you mean, if possible? What about that long song and dance you gave me about rescuing Brocassie? All you really care about is the proof of the missiles."

Maroto shrugged. "I do want to rescue him, pilot. There is a possibility that we may and it is for that reason that you'll come with me and my men. But Álvarez is the man I want and when I get him, my men and I will pull back out into the Sierra, whether we have Brocassie or not. It is up to you to convince Alicia Helvia that she must get Brocassie to her cottage along with Álvarez. If she cannot, then you must understand that Álvarez is our consolation prize."

The old man had the bit between his teeth now, Porto realized. His one last chance to involve the Americans in an invasion. There was no point in arguing, Porto realized.

"How do we get through the perimeter fence?" Already, Porto knew that he had made the transition between indecision and commitment.

"There are fifteen to twenty militia trucks coming over the Sierra road from Santiago each day. Some of them carry troops but the bulk of them carry supplies. We need only hijack one of the supply trucks, then force the driver to take us through the outer checkpoint and into the coffee plantation. From there, you would get to Álvarez's cottage. Plan to be there no more than thirty minutes. Take Alicia, Álvarez and Brocassie back out with you in the truck you came in. My men and I will swim the river and give you covering fire from the riverbank if necessary to cover your withdrawal. If they pursue you, we'll have an ambush set up on the Sierra road to delay them."

"The hijacked truck will be missed."

Nodding, Maroto answered, "Eventually. But how quickly? The trucks don't come in convoys. They seem to be independently scheduled. It's a chance we would have to take but if it's done smoothly and quickly, we might have as much as a four-hour head start. Enough to get out of the valley, and once we're clear, we've got thousands of square miles of the Sierra to hide us."

"Let's say I go along with it, *Jefe*. How do we communicate with the Helvia woman? She has to know what we're trying to do and we have to have some means of getting a confirmation back, assuming that she thinks that she can pull if off."

The old man nodded toward the far chamber of the cave where Miguel was now sleeping. "The boy will have to do it. He's the only link we have with the woman. And if he's caught, he will play the harmless, retarded mute that Álvarez knew him to be. It would be assumed that he simply wanted to be with Alicia Helvia because she had shown him kindness at the *finca*."

"Oh, no, you old bastard, not that!" Porto exploded. "The kid is on the raw edge. You know what he's been through!" He realized that he was shouting but he also realized that Maroto's expression hadn't altered—still calm, controlled, as if the idea had petrified into some unalterable form.

The old man finally inclined his head in a slow nod. "I know what he's been through," Maroto said, almost inaudibly. "He and thousands of others like him have lost their parents. I've lost friends, brothers, cousins. The men I lead are the same. Most of them have lost everyone and everything they had and to fight on is the only response left to them. There is no other way, Porto. He's all we have."

The words struck Porto like a sledgehammer. "I came to Cuba to get that kid out," he shot back in a hoarse whisper. "He's more to me than just an obligation. He's all I've got."

"It's your decision," Maroto prompted gently, his voice quiet but with great intensity. "Brocassie is your friend—perhaps more than that. You have to examine your loyalty to him and how far you must go to save him. This is the only chance we'll have. I will not force the boy to go. It must be your decision, your persuasion."

Was it really worth it? Porto asked himself. To risk one for two and perhaps lose both. Or to save both. He sat for minutes, torn in his decision, but he knew what the reply had to be. "I'll ask the boy," he said finally.

Maroto nodded. "It's necessary," he said evenly. "Risk is a precondition of reward."

Walking to the cave, his hands wet, his back clammy, Porto absently wondered in what leadership manual Maroto had read that little gem.

Álvarez closed the cell door behind him. He dumped a set of freshly starched fatigues on the bunk and placed a battery-powered razor on the card table.

"Let's get going, Brocassie. Ham and eggs coming in ten minutes." He glanced down at his watch. "Then the grand tour at eight."

Brocassie rolled over, watching him, keeping silent.

Julio smiled easily, no hint of the conflict from the previous evening. "Come on, Brocassie. This is a mutual back-scratching job. I need that tape and you want to live. You're not going to have to lie about what this complex is all about. It's a simple deal."

Watching him go through his little act, Brocassie thought that Julio had all the conviction of a carny pitchman. Still, he thought, a chance. And a chance was better than no chance, despite the odds. He put a neutral expression on his face and stood up, slipping into the fatigues.

Álvarez dropped a package of Lucky Strikes on the table, along with a box of matches. "If you still have the habit." He turned and paused at the door. "Let's forget about last night, Brocassie. Nothing will happen to her if you have any sense at all. Just take what I say at face value."

He wanted to tell Álvarez to jam it but he forced a smile. "I think, Julio, that we may discuss this matter again someday, under very different circumstances."

Álvarez beamed back. "Not likely. *Bon appétit.*"

He was back again in less than an hour. He pulled a plastic badge from his pocket and clipped it to Brocassie's fatigues. "Visitor's pass. Ready?"

"Why not, Julio? It's your show."

Álvarez grinned back, the retort immediate. "So true, but then again, you paid the admission price, didn't you?"

Outside the cell, a DGI lieutenant with a carbine, the safety catch off. Down the corridor, past one security checkpoint, this one KGB. Brocassie examined the guard's face. Thin, almost delicate. The guard gave a regulation smile that guards reserve for officers—no teeth and just the faintest up-turning of the lips. He said something in Russian to Álvarez. They both laughed and then the guard saluted sloppily, as if he were flicking a fly from his brow.

Down the corridor, now passing rooms that were obviously dormitories for the nonofficer ranks, a small mess hall, a reading room.

"What did the pretty boy say?"

"He asked me whether we were having American shish kebab in the mess tonight."

"How droll, Julio."

Álvarez nodded, smiling. "I thought so."

Final checkpoint in the corridor, another KGB type, this one a hard case with sagging bulldog cheeks but eyes like black marbles. He glanced at Brocassie without smiling and finally nodded them through with only the slimmest suggestion of a salute.

The corridor T-ed into a central tunnel. There, Álvarez paused, allowing Brocassie to take in the magnitude of the construction. He guessed that the tunnel was over thirty feet high and three times as wide, with walkways on either side and the central section reserved for rail and truck traffic. There was an overhead track for a moving crane and on either side of that were suspended huge pipes, each color-coded, along with a spaghetti factory of cables and wires, all running from the entrance to the far interior of the tunnel with branches into each of the cross-connecting corridors.

Far to his left, Brocassie saw an electric tug enter the tunnel, an empty flatcar behind it. It ground down the shallow grade and accelerated past them, the noise deafening in the confined tunnel. As the tug moved deeper, its headlight illuminated successive connecting corridors, similar to the one that he had just come from. "How big is this complex?" he asked Álvarez.

"Three-quarters of a mile along the central tunnel with sixteen corridors branching off the main tunnel. Each corridor is an eighth of a mile long. Fifteen hundred men and over one hundred thirty officers. There are two underground power generation stations, each putting out enough power to light a small city."

"Everyone lives underground?"

"Except for top-ranked officers like myself. The enlisted men are rotated back to the Soviet Union every six months for a month of leave and the duty pulls extra pay. We have no complaints."

I'd guess that you wouldn't, Brocassie speculated. No chaplain here to get your ticket punched if you have second thoughts about living like a mole in a concrete pit.

"What next?" he asked.

"Command Post," Álvarez answered. He reached for a telephone which was set into the concrete and three minutes later a small electric cart equipped with bench seats pulled up, driven by a KGB sergeant. Once they were loaded into it, the cart accelerated with a thin whine, going deeper into the complex. Past corridors and workshops, storage areas and armories, deeper and deeper underground.

Finally, the cart pulled to a stop. Álvarez led the way past a security checkpoint, down a carpeted corridor, through a second security checkpoint and into a massive control room. On the far wall was a Plexiglas map of the Caribbean and South Atlantic, framed on either side by the continents of Africa and South America. Tracks of different-colored lights spanned the oceans, some glowing with pulsed light and some fixed. Arranged beneath the massive board were row upon row of manned consoles, each with a switchboard and radar-scope. Cigarette smoke was stratified in the air above the operators, reflecting back the gray-green glow of the screens. A subdued buzz of voices overlaid the background hush of air conditioners. Álvarez tapped Brocassie on the arm and then led the way up a set of stairs, into an enclosed balcony which overlooked the control room.

"Soviet Western Hemispheric Situation Room—the Command Post," Álvarez said quietly, gesturing to the theater below them. "Communications, electronic surveillance, missile tracking, radar plotting, code encryption, decryption and breaking, the entire lot. This is the reason for being of the Calvario Complex. What we have here rivals the U.S.'s Defense Intelligence Agency. We keep track of all U.S. fleet movements, military aircraft tracks and even civilian freighters that are used by the Department of Defense. We can communicate with Soviet fleet submarines and surface ships. And whenever a U.S. space shot is fired from Canaveral, we can determine exactly what the purpose of the shot was and how well it did, including its exact location at splashdown. On one of their recent Atlas SM-65E shots, we knew before the controllers in Florida knew that the hydraulic system failed less than a hundred and eight seconds after lift-off."

The facility was stunning in its size and complexity. Brocassie turned to Álvarez. "This was the price tag for Soviet help."

Álvarez shrugged. "It's their money. So we gave them a couple of acres in a remote area of Cuba that isn't even good to raise goats on. What they do with it is their business. But the whole point, chum, is that this complex is a communications facility with only defensive armament. You've already seen some of the surface-to-air missiles we've got parked in the mahogany groves. Eventually, we'll move all of them underground for emplacement in silos. In the event of an air attack by the Americans, the missiles can be raised to the surface, fired and the launchers lowered again for reloading. Same for the defensive coastal missiles; Frog Threes, you thought, according to the stuff you babbled about in the interrogation. Almost right. Frog Three, Mod Three. Range—one hundred and twenty miles with infrared homing. No American invasion force could attempt a landing between the east tip of Cuba at Cabo Maysí, all the way west to Cabo de La Cruz. This complex is self-contained and guaranteed to withstand an attack from either land, sea or air. But again note the important aspect, Brocassie—it's defensive in nature. Nothing more or less than the kind of thing that the Americans have placed in Turkey or Iran. Perhaps more sophisticated but no different in concept." His face was indirectly lit from the glow of electronics in the room below, casting his features into distorted bas-relief. Like one of the witches in Macbeth, Brocassie thought. Álvarez sank down into one of the upholstered chairs and lit a cigarette. "You're not satisfied, are you?"

"You know I'm not. I saw that missile off-loaded from the flatcars onto an overhead crane which I believe would move it underground. And if there's one, there must be more."

"I believe that we should show him, shouldn't we, Julio." The voice was older, more resonant. Brocassie turned. The speaker was sitting in the back row, completely in darkness, just the profile of his face highlighted by the light of the main operations room. Brocassie saw him rise and move down the aisle to the bottom row where he and Julio were seated.

The man didn't offer his hand but sat down next to Brocassie. "Roychenko," he said. "Colonel, KGB, temporarily assigned to liaison with our Cuban allies. I suppose that I should welcome you. After all, you went through a great deal of trouble to get here." He yawned, as if bored with the entire situation. "So what do you think of our operations here in the Sierra Maestra?"

"What do you want me to say? Impressed? Overwhelmed? Dying to blow the fucking place up? Take your choice."

Roychenko made a polite laugh. "You're obviously feeling much better." He leaned forward, addressing Álvarez who was on Brocassie's other side. "What have you shown him, Julio?"

"Just the main tunnel as far as here."

"But I take it that he's interested in the SS-4s," Roychenko added. He leaned back in the leather seat, drawing one leg up over the other. "I had planned lunch for the three of us in my office. Suppose that we show him the missile maintenance bay first and then we can eat and discuss his future." He stood up. "Lead on, Julio. It's your tour."

They were five now in the electric cart, whirring deeper and deeper into the complex. Álvarez was next to him, reciting an inventory of corridors which spanned off on either side. Food storage room, electronic repair shops, diesel fuel storage bays for the power generators, vehicle repair shops.

Julio stopped once more, gesturing toward a set of locked doors. "My shop, Brocassie. Security Control. I'm showing you this place for the simple reason that I want you to be convinced that this complex is impregnable. Nothing short of several U.S. Marine divisions could take it." He cocked his head toward Brocassie. "And I want you to get this across to Hagger in the tape, understand?" He led the way through the armored doors. It was similar in concept to the Command Post but smaller. There was a central room with six men on consoles and overlooking it, a glassed-in balcony for the officer in charge. Banks of status boards wrapped the walls.

Álvarez paced slowly around the room, pausing behind each console. "We monitor everything here. TV cameras on the access gates aboveground, TVs on the perimeter fences, TVs in all the major underground areas. We have direct radio contact with all the patrolling guards and security checkpoints, both above- and belowground. In the event of a ground attack, we can throw damn near every man we have here against the attackers and call in support from regular Cuban FAR troops and militia."

He turned toward the panels. "We monitor for fires, smoke, overheating conditions in the generators, failures of the air-conditioning and cooling systems—anything that has the potential of danger to the security of the complex."

His finger pointed to an illuminated flow chart. "Diesel fuel to the generators from tank cars that we bring in at night. It's pumped from aboveground to underground storage tanks. While it's being pumped, we monitor the whole operation, control the fire doors and, if necessary, activate carbon dioxide or fire-fighting systems. Same for gasoline that we bring in for the aircraft."

Julio, caught up in his own importance, rambled on, pointing out the defenses of the complex. From the corner of his eye, Brocassie noted two men at the far end of the room, leaning negligently over their consoles. He edged sideways, trying to see what they were monitoring. The consoles had only three indicator gauges, each unmarked except for a single symbol printed above them, each different, each unfamiliar and yet still vaguely reminiscent of something he had seen before . . . from a college textbook, perhaps? He racked his mind, trying to dredge up some faded memory.

"What do you think?"

Brocassie turned back to Julio. "What am I supposed to say, Julio? Neat? Nifty?"

"It is—neat and nifty and also damned expensive. Most

375

of the gear came from Germany but some came out of the United States via a nice little import-export firm in Switzerland. I know this complex better than the back of my ass."

He clamped his hand on Brocassie's shoulder and steered him out of the room. They purred deeper into the complex on the electric cart. The doors at the end of the tunnel were solid steel, more than a foot thick. The last checkpoint, this one guarded by a KGB lieutenant and two NCOs. Roychenko discharged the electric cart and driver as well as the guard that Álvarez had brought with him. The doors rumbled back into concrete recesses, admitting them to the chamber. It was much larger than any room Brocassie had seen, a full eighty or ninety feet high and hundreds of feet across. Overhead was a continuation of the hoist mechanism which spanned the entire length of the tunnel along with a crane operator's cage. The walls were lined with electronic, pneumatic and hydraulic test equipment, all on dollies. On the far left was a maintenance bay with dozens of Frog Three missiles, each of them on a small transporter. Technicians were working on them, access panels unbuttoned, cables leading from test equipment into the guts of the missiles.

In the shop section, the glare of an arc welder sputtered and a shower of metal cascaded from beneath the welding torch. But this was not what captured Brocassie's attention. At the far end of the bay were row after row of SS-4 Sandal missiles, perhaps as many as thirty, each housed on metal cradles. Just looking at the weapons, dull black, almost elegant in their simple but lethal geometry, he felt a shiver sweep his body. The missiles were monstrous, eighty feet or so in length. They were smooth cylinders, terminating in a streamlined nose cone. How many megatons of death were in this room? he wondered. How many American cities would die in a flash of heat and light because of the existence of those things? He turned to Roychenko. "These are what the silos were constructed for! Defensive, my ass!"

Roychenko looked amused. "Not at all," he answered. "You remember the inside diameter of the steel rings used to build the silos, don't you?"

"The CIA's photoanalysis people said something like fifty-five inches, inside diameter."

The Russian nodded. "Fifty-three inches to be exact and what would you guess the diameter of one of these weapons to be?"

"About that."

Roychenko shook his head. "More—almost a foot more, Brocassie. Sixty-five inches. You may measure one if you doubt me. There's an American saying isn't there, that you can't stuff two pounds of shit into a one-pound bag? I think the same principle applies here." He dug into his tunic pocket and withdrew a tape measure. "Come along and see for yourself." He led the way toward the far end of the bay, finally stopping in front of a row of the deadly shapes.

"Pick a missile, any one," Roychenko offered.

Brocassie pointed to the third one in the row.

Roychenko threw the tape over the top of the missile and Álvarez caught the end, passing it back under the belly. Roychenko handed the tape to Brocassie. "How many inches?"

Squinting, he answered, "Two hundred and four plus a fraction."

Smiling patiently, like a teacher prompting his student, Roychenko nodded. "Excellent. You can work a slide rule, I assume?" He withdrew a small plastic slide rule from his jacket pocket and handed it over. Brocassie moved the center slide, aligning 204 with 3.1416. The answer was 65.

"So you see," Roychenko said patiently, as if he were gearing his dissertation to the dullest student in his class, "sixty-five inches does not fit in a fifty-three-inch opening. I'm sure that Hagger also discussed the fact that these missiles do not fit into a silo like a bullet in a barrel. There must be additional clearance on either side so that when the missile is fired the skin of the missile does not contact the walls of the silo. The SS-4 would require a silo diameter of over ninety inches to avoid damage to the missile's skin, but then again I'm sure that you're aware that the SS-4 has *never* been launched from silos. It's *always* launched from an open-framework launcher-erection mechanism because it has projecting aerodynamic fins." He walked toward the tail of the missile, pointing at a slot on the side of the missile. "This attachment point here, you see, identical to the other three. They're controlled from the internal guidance system and aerodynamically guide the

377

missile until the rocket engine shuts down. Once the engine shuts down, the warhead separates and from there on in until it impacts on target, the nose cone is purely in ballistic flight."

Brocassie reached up, touching the smooth skin of the missile. He knew that Roychenko was right. The silos were too small in diameter to accommodate the SS-4s and he cursed himself for not reasoning the thing through before now. He turned to Álvarez, ignoring the amused look on Roychenko's face.

"Then what in blazes are these things doing here?"

"Temporary storage. The building in western Cuba that they were originally going to be stored in had a structural failure. We had to move them down here and keep them under wraps until the launch emplacements for them are finished." He raised his eyebrows, looking at Roychenko. "How soon?"

"Three days for the Guanajay and Remedios sites. The San Cristóbal site is complete. We'll be fully operational on the twenty-eighth of October."

"You're not actually stupid enough to install these things on the northwestern coast of Cuba."

Álvarez nodded. "The whole works—missile transporters, oxidizer trailers, propellant trailers. We've built revetments, installed surface-to-air missiles, soup to nuts, Brocassie. And when John Kennedy sees the first U-2 photographs of those installations, he's going to have a gastric attack which will rattle all the windows in Washington. I'd give up a lot to see his face when someone shoves those prints under his nose."

Sweet Jesus, he thought. They were joking about nuclear war-making capability as if it were some kind of afternoon picnic they were planning. Unconsciously, he grabbed the front of Julio's jacket, twisting the material with his fist. *"You dumb bastard! The first thing that Kennedy is going to do is to call in an airstrike on those missiles. If that happens, then Soviet crews are going to get killed and unless the fighter-bombers knock off every single missile, some of them will be launched! The bloody thing will escalate into a full-blown nuclear war!"*

Roychenko took his hand gently, prying it away. Almost like a mother straightening her son's tie, he rearranged Álvarez's uniform, patting down the wrinkles.

"Julio warned me that you were emotional and I would

caution you to restrain yourself," he said carefully. "You are here to be instructed, not to instruct." He turned away, motioning an NCO toward him. The man approached, stomped his boots together and saluted.

"Comrade Colonel!"

Roychenko returned the salute. "I will want you to lift the access cover off one of these weapons." He turned to Brocassie. "You would, of course, like to have the privilege of seeing the inner workings of one of the Soviet Union's most awesome terror weapons, would you not? Which one?"

Brocassie numbly pointed to the seventh in the row. Roychenko nodded. "That one, then."

The sergeant saluted once more, did a precise about-face and motioned to a crew of technicians to follow him. Roychenko turned back to Brocassie. "This will take a few minutes. Let's be comfortable." He led them to a small alcove where there was a tea samovar and benches. He poured some tea into a glass and offered it to Brocassie. Then one for Álvarez and finally one for himself. "Odd, isn't it? The three of us standing here in a place which is critically important to the Soviet Union, having tea. What would the director of the CIA give to be standing here with us—a million, two million? Perhaps much more, I think." He raised his cup in salute and drank from it.

"No, Brocassie. Kennedy will not attack those missile sites. That would be the act of a madman and Kennedy is not mad. He's a politician, and politicians act rationally in their own self-interest. Compromise is the game of politicians, not action." He smiled and then shook his head. "Give us backward Soviets some credit. Remember that we play very good chess and it is part of classical chess to compromise—to sacrifice if necessary, in order to win. Everything that we have read of Kennedy's work, his speeches, his personal habits, has been carefully analyzed. And also the makeup of his major advisers. When Kennedy finds out that there are Soviet long-range nuclear missiles in Cuba, he will *react*, not *act*. And his reaction will be to negotiate the withdrawal of those missiles."

The tea was bitter and Brocassie wondered how anyone could drink the stuff. But he grimly held onto the cup, giving his hands something to do. No, he thought. John Kennedy would attack those missiles before they were fully operational. Because of the Monroe Doctrine, because of Kennedy's own declaration against the expansion of Soviet imperialism, to say nothing of the overpowering political considerations.

He shook his head. "You're wrong, Roychenko. When you place those missiles on their launchers, you've just pulled the trigger on a nuclear war."

"And I think you're wrong, Brocassie. Very wrong. Because, unlike our country where decisions are made by a very small group of men, Kennedy must face his electorate and beyond that, world opinion. It's well known that the Americans have over one hundred intermediate-range nuclear missiles stationed in Europe, all targeted against the Soviet Union. What's so different about those weapons than the ones here in Cuba? Is it because ours have the insignia of the hammer and sickle and that makes them evil whereas the American weapons in Europe represent God's blessing to the peoples of the world?" He slammed his cup down, slopping tea across the table. "Kennedy must remove those weapons from Europe. We will never again allow the placement of American missiles on European soil. Europe is within the Soviet Union's sphere of influence, not America's. Europe is ours, if we choose and when we choose!"

His voice was intense, every word picked out and underlined.

"So that's the trade—SS-4s out of Cuba for the Thors and Jupiters in Europe?"

Roychenko smiled indulgently. "That is just part of the shopping list. There are other concessions that we seek, namely that squalid little town the Germans called Berlin. It is a splinter in our sides and it has to be removed."

"That's another thing Kennedy will never cave in on."

The Russian pursed his lips. "Oh, I wonder about that, my friend—I truly wonder. Kennedy has picked Berlin as a symbol of Western Determination—capitalized—the lone outpost of civilization that must be defended at all cost, but the American people don't give a damn. Your Gallup poll shows it. Americans think of Berlin as a town of jackbooted Nazis and gaudy whorehouses. Fifteen years after the Second World War, they see their government still pouring dollars into that sinkhole, just to keep their former enemies cozy and secure." He held up his palm, cutting off any response. "Kennedy will be forced to sign a private protocol with our Ambassador Gromyko that will guarantee the Americans will do nothing when we make our move."

"You'd invade Berlin?"

"Hardly. The Soviet Union will simply sign a separate peace with East Germany. By doing that, the DDR will have sovereign nation status. Berlin will be an island in the sea of the Warsaw Pact. Any attempt by the Western powers to bring in supplies or troops would entail penetration of the DDR's sovereign territory and *that* would require the Soviet Union to come to the aid of a Warsaw Pact member nation. Until now, such a risk has been impossible. But with the focus on—what shall we call it?—the Caribbean Crisis, we can quietly take Berlin for the price of a pen and a piece of paper. Believe me, Brocassie, Kennedy will sign it."

Brocassie slowly began to realize that Roychenko's analogy had been precise: a game of chess with the Soviets initiating the opening gambit. Their pawns were their missiles in Cuba and as they were advanced, American missiles in Europe would be traded off against them, Berlin isolated and finally lost in a remote corner of the board, almost unnoticed. It was brilliant; he had to admit it. Except one piece was still unaccounted for.

"What's in it for Cuba?" he asked, looking at Álvarez. "Once the SS-4s are out of Cuba, what makes you think that Jack Kennedy won't pulverize this island?"

"He won't," Álvarez replied. "Kennedy dictated—I mean *dictated*—that no offensive weapons could be emplaced in Cuba, but what are these?" he asked, gesturing toward the SS-4s. "A deterrent force, exactly what Kennedy claims his intercontinental ballistic missiles are. These missiles are for the *defense* of Cuba against an aggressor. The logic of it stands up. The old quid pro quo, Brocassie. The final condition of withdrawal of these missiles from Cuba will be the pledge of the American president not to invade Cuba and to respect this island as a sovereign power whose borders are inviolate. We both understand that Americans are real big on honor, right? Once Kennedy gives his word, every administration after him will be bound to respect it." He flicked a match and lit a cigarette, exhaling the smoke in a thin stream. "That's what's in it for Cuba. We're a bastard country that Kennedy is going to legitimize."

Above the SS-4s, an overhead crane was moving. Webbing snaked down and the technicians grabbed at the end fittings and attached them to hooks which had been screwed into recessed fittings on the missile.

Brocassie watched, mesmerized. So well planned out. Roychenko had his shopping list and Álvarez his. But it wouldn't work, he knew. Not only knew but knew positively. The missiles in Cuba would be the ignition to a conflagration that would sear the face of the globe.

"You're both wrong," he finally said. "Tragically wrong. You've misjudged him. Kennedy will never buy it."

"But he will," Roychenko answered, his voice absolutely confident, as if the outcome had already been determined. "He will, because the forces acting on him and his advisers will allow no other course. We will build the tension slowly and with extreme caution. Khrushchev will deny that missiles are in Cuba. The Americans will produce photos snapped by their U-2 spy planes showing the details of the missile emplacements. Khrushchev will then bluster, warning of all-out nuclear war. Kennedy will escalate, probably throwing up a blockade around Cuba." He paused. "The American people will suddenly realize that nuclear war is no longer an abstraction but a reality. Sixty of their cities will be at risk, for each SS-4 carries a one-megaton weapon." He ran his tongue along the edge of his lip. "And then, when it suddenly seems that the world is going to go up in flames, Khrushchev will present Kennedy with a final 'compromise'—a means of averting the catastrophe that Kennedy himself has helped to create. The simple conditions: the SS-4s out of Cuba for removal of the American missiles in Europe, a pledge never to invade Cuba and finally, by separate private protocol, the acceptance of a separate peace between the Soviet Union and the DDR. If these conditions are agreed to, Kennedy will be assured through private channels that Khrushchev will capitulate. Not only capitulate but grovel before the entire world. Imagine the banner headlines, Brocassie. 'Kennedy stands firm and

Khrushchev cowers.'" He pressed his lips together momentarily and it was impossible to guess whether he was suppressing a smile or hiding his distaste. "Kennedy will have seemingly averted a war and at the same time, mined the mother lode of political fortune. We have gone to considerable effort to be absolutely sure of his reaction. With Eisenhower or Truman, it might have been different, but with Kennedy ..." He left the sentence unfinished.

"What if you've miscalculated? Suppose that Kennedy attacks the missile launch sites?"

Roychenko leaned back in his chair. He finally answered, his voice flat. "What would be our only option? Cuba, the Soviet Union, the entire Warsaw Pact have a mutual defense pact. An attack on one of these countries constitutes an attack on all of them. There would be war. We are prepared to take that risk, because if we were not, the whole exercise would be pointless."

"You'd fire these missiles?"

Roychenko's eyes shifted to the SS-4s and then back to Brocassie. "Any preemptive attack by the United States against ·Cuba would be a challenge that the Soviet Union could not ignore. We would immediately employ every missile in our arsenal because future wars will go to those who act swiftly and with total commitment. That conflict will eventually happen. Perhaps better now than later."

"The Soviet Union doesn't have the capability!"

"That is debatable," Roychenko shot back. He seemed on the verge of saying something else and then suddenly relaxed his body, as if he were forcing his emotions under control. He briefly smiled, the brevity of it no longer than the flicker of winter sunlight through passing clouds. "But we both know that it will not come to that," he added.

The NCO was standing at attention, ten paces away, waiting, his body rigid.

Roychenko threw him a salute and stood up. "Let us see what John Kennedy has to contend with," he said.

The NCO nodded and Roychenko made a fist with his thumb extended upward. The crane operator engaged the clutch, and slowly, the upper half of the missile separated from the lower half. Roychenko motioned Brocassie closer, until they could both see into the guts of the missile. Except for fiberglass reinforcing ribs which protruded a few inches from the interior surface, it was an empty shell.

Brocassie dumbly felt the interior of the missile's skin, testing the smooth surface, speechless.

Álvarez came and stood beside him. "It's a phony, Brocassie," he said, "just like all the rest of them—a hollow fiberglass replica of an SS-4, the ultimate scarecrow."

"But for God's sake, why?"

"Why?" Álvarez was laughing now, pounding Brocassie's back, as he always had when he was about to give the punch line of a joke. "*Why* would we risk transporting sixty SS-4s from the Soviet Union to Cuba and then back again when the only reason for their being here was to negotiate their removal? The beauty of it, the fucking irony of it—Kennedy negotiating away over forty percent of his missile strike force, handing Berlin over to the Soviets on a platter and then guaranteeing the sovereignty of Cuba—all for these sixty gigantic plastic trash cans!" He was out of control, howling, his words choked off by laughter. Roychenko had joined in and the infectiousness of laughter had brought embarrassed smiles to the faces of the technicians. Álvarez brought his laughter under control for a moment. He squeezed Brocassie's arm hard. "There's more to the joke—a final twist. Can you guess, old buddy?"

Brocassie couldn't answer. He just stood there fingering the interior of the fiberglass replica, dumbstruck. Almost unconsciously, he shook his head.

Álvarez erupted into another fit of laughter, stamping his foot repeatedly on the concrete. "You klutz—you're our icing on the cake. A year from now when all the dust is settled, we'll ship you off to Miami and two days after that, you're going to be telling Kennedy exactly what happened and he won't be able to do a goddamned thing because if he did, the American people would run both him and the CIA out of Washington for falling into a sucker trap. But he'll know, Brocassie. He'll know that he was taken for a chump in the most gigantic shell game of all time."

CHAPTER

16

She stood in the front doorway of the cottage, the lights switched off in the room behind her. It was raining in a fine mist and the wind had died. Tree frogs chirped like a demented string section plucking a two-note pizzicato.

She stepped forward onto the path, her face upturned. The rain was warm, bathing her face with wetness although she could not feel the touch of the individual droplets. She inhaled, breathing it in, tasting it, trying to imagine that this rain had come from clouds which had sailed from the Antilles across the Caribbean Sea, bringing with it the tang of salt and the hint of spice. But it was really the essence of freedom she was trying to taste and could not.

The shaft of a flashlight pinioned her in its beam.

"What's the problem?" It was one of the guards, Sánchez. His voice was thick, the words blurred together.

A little drunk, she thought. "Nothing," she said, stepping back into the doorway. The beam of light still glared in her eyes and then, insolently, moved lower to her thighs. She turned and slammed the door, resting against it, shame and revulsion flooding her body. The *bastard,* she thought. The rotten, drunken bastard.

She was breathing heavily. Gradually, her heart slowed and in the dark, she found her way to the couch and sat down, weary beyond comprehension. Deep inside her, she felt or imagined a small fluttering thing beating softly against the walls of her body. Her future seemed to be narrowing in on her, the options flickering out, one by one.

She sighed, reached up and switched on a light, then looked at her watch. Eleven thirty-two. Julio had not called and she was unsure whether she should prepare his dinner or go to bed. His hours in the complex were erratic. Sometimes, he would not come back to the cottage in the evening, then show up, unannounced in the early morning hours, demanding food, even if it was four A.M. And after food, washed down with beer or rum, he sometimes demanded sex. She had become skilled in feigning headaches, soreness, anything. But she knew that she couldn't hold him off forever. In the last four days, she had begun to think a great deal about her little automatic—had spent hours holding it gently in her hand like a small pet animal, then resting the muzzle against her forehead, wondering at the ability of it to transform her misery into—what? Release, reward, remorse or simply nothing? She had never believed the Church or the nuns or the priests. It seemed all too slick a proposition—something like a cartoon, with golden gates, archangels and heavenly peace—a place where cats and mice coexisted in pastel harmony, halos ringing their heads. But she finally concluded that at the very bitter end of options, she would gladly settle for a death of blank nothingness. It was the uncertainty that kept her from squeezing the trigger.

She got up and walked slowly into the kitchen. The cottage was a prison to her, much smaller than the *finca* and stinking of mold and mildew, away from the sea and the constant flow of the trade winds. Crammed into the tiny interior was a jumble of furniture, ersatz-Scandinavian contemporary, marked with labels from Rumania and East Germany. Predictably, Julio loved it, and for that reason, she loathed it.

She drew water from the tap and set the electric kettle to boil, leaning against the kitchen counter top, her hands holding her face. So tired. So burned out. Miguel gone. Had he gotten to Maroto in time? It seemed impossible. The boy had not been missed; no one had asked her about him. Where was he now? she wondered. Safe, she prayed. What God there was, protect him.

She dug her nails into her palms, wanting to scream. She had to get out of this house, out of this valley, out of Cuba. And away from Julio. There were only a few casual patrols within the compound and she was sure that she could evade the two sodden clods who guarded the house. Getting through the security checkpoint at the perimeter fence would be the hardest. Perhaps they could be bribed. She still had friends in Havana and if she was able to get that far, she would somehow get out of the country. If she was stopped, she knew that it would be finished, because she had no papers. They wouldn't know what to do with her at first but then there were her fingerprints on file and . . . Her subconscious wouldn't allow her to accept it, even to think about it. And she would have the gun and that would be, if necessary, her final passport.

At first she thought it was rain dripping from the eaves, spattering against the floor of the back stoop, but then she realized that the pattern was more regular, more insistent. She snapped off the electric kettle, listening intently. Still the noise—a quiet tapping on the glass of the window. The first thing that rushed to her mind was that one of the guards wanted in, and the thought terrified her. They had tried before, particularly when they knew that the *comandante* was going to be absent for some time. They generally asked for coffee or a glass of water or food but she knew that they wanted her; she could read it in their eyes. To them, she was just a whore, kept for the *comandante*'s pleasure. Once, the younger of the two had even waved a bundle of pesos at her from beyond the locked screen door, his mouth half-open, his tongue slowly moving along the edge of his teeth.

She reached down to the cutlery drawer and withdrew a butcher's knife, her hands shaking.

The back door was locked. She made sure of that first. "Go away," she demanded. *"NOW!"*

The voice from beyond the door was soft, but there was an edge of desperation in it.

"Miguel. It's me—Miguel."

In shock, she started to reach for the light switch and then realized that she would be a fool to turn it on, flooding the stoop outside, attracting the guards. Hurriedly, she flung the knife into the sink, unlatched the door and opened it. The boy must have been pressing against it because he stumbled in, looked back into the blackness and quickly pushed it shut. For a second they both looked at each other in the semidarkness, transfixed, and then he threw his arms around her, clutching her against his body.

He was clothed in the same castoffs she had last seen him in but he had a black rubber rain slicker over him. His boots were clumped with mud, and water dribbled from him, pooling on the tile floor.

"I found you," he said, his face buried against her chest. "They were afraid that I couldn't do it but I did because I had to get to you."

Nothing he said registered in her mind, only that he was here. "Oh, sweet Lord Jesus," she whispered, her arms around him, hugging him. "Thank God you're safe. How did you get through the fence?"

"I didn't. I swam the river and came through where there isn't any fence."

Her heart almost stopped. There was an open area near the river, bordering the motor pool, but the strip between was heavily mined. There were no fences because the riverbank was set aside as a sunning and swimming area for off-duty officers but the access to it was through a complicated path that was known only to a few of them. Julio had taken her there twice, always insisting that she follow his footsteps exactly. Miguel must have come directly through the minefield! She reached down, grabbing him by the shoulders. "You saw the warning signs, didn't you?"

"We saw them through binoculars from the other side of the river. They showed me how to get through the minefields with a sharpened stick. I had to crawl slowly, pushing the rod into the ground ahead of me. If it struck something, I would try again to the side. It took two hours to come through the minefield but it will take me only a minute to go back. I left a string across the field, held down by rocks. I'll follow that back."

"Oh, my God! You could have been killed!"

He laughed. "But I wasn't."

"The patrols . . ."

"It was raining. There's a lot of heavy ground fog down near the river. They don't look carefully. I'm small and I have this black raincoat on. They never even glanced my way, never noticed my tracks."

What a chance he had taken, she thought. An unbelievable chance. "But how did you find—"

"—where you were? I didn't, right away. I stayed down near where they pump the fuel until eleven o'clock. There are a lot of men drinking coffee, sleeping, just waiting around until they can off-load their fuel trucks at the pumping station. It's easy to mix with them. The guards think that everyone there came in on trucks and had to be cleared through the main gate. They don't check papers. And all the time, I was watching the cottages and finally I saw one of the guards that the *comandante* had at the *finca* and I knew that this had to be the one." He shucked off his raincoat and stooped down to remove his boots. He paused, looking up at her. "When does he come home?"

"I don't know—I never know. An hour, ten. A day from now. He doesn't work on a fixed schedule."

"Then we may not have much time, and besides, I have to be out of the compound before three A.M. They're waiting for me across the river."

"Who?"

"Maroto and some of his men. And Porto—the man that I told you about. The one my mother saved. He and Brocassie flew into Cuba more than a week ago."

"Brocassie's here—in Cuba?"

"Yes, but the worst has happened. He was captured. Maroto thinks he's being held here, underground in the complex, and we've come to get him out. There's no time to explain now. We have to clean up this mess that I've tracked on

389

your floor in case the *comandante* comes home. Then you show me where to hide if he does. And then there will be time to talk."

Together, they mopped up the mud and water from the tiled floor, then put his boots and raincoat in the fruit cellar. Twice, she heard the growl of a jeep but each time the vehicle passed. It was after midnight. She shut off the light in the living room, ran upstairs and snapped on a light in her bedroom and then came back down the stairs, feeling her way with her fingertips.

She made him coffee in the darkness of the kitchen while he explained: the ride that he had thumbed into Santiago, two nights of hiding in the back lot of a concrete mixing plant and then the meeting with the Fabricio woman. Three days of climbing and finally Maroto. He told her about Porto as well, and in the darkness, she could sense that Miguel's voice was straining, his emotions keyed almost to breaking. What he had risked for her, twice, now three times.

She was afraid to ask him but she had to know. "How are they sure that Brocassie's alive?" She had to hold one hand with the other to keep them from trembling.

He was quiet for a few moments, sipping at the coffee. She could almost guess the answer.

"They're not," he said quietly, apologetically. She could hear him swallow, trying to form words that he must have known would wound her. "They have no way of knowing. But Porto thinks that they wouldn't execute him because he's too valuable. They think that, most likely, the DGI would move him to a maximum-security prison, probably El Condado. Porto thinks that the DGI has had time to learn everything they need to know and that he'll be moved soon. That's when they intend to rescue him. Maroto wants the *comandante* as well. And if they can't get Brocassie, then they'll still try for Álvarez."

It was too much to absorb. And there was no time. "Why are you here? If they find anyone in the compound without a pass, they shoot to kill."

"Maroto and Porto made the plan. I am to tell you that without your help, they can do nothing." He reached under his shirt and pulled out an envelope wrapped in plastic and sealed with waterproof tape. "These are the instructions they sent. I'm to wait only long enough for you to write your reply." He stood up slowly, gently placing the cup in the sink. "There is one other thing that Porto said. He wanted you to know that he thinks the chance of doing this is very small. He wants you to understand the danger of it, both to them and to you."

She stood up, groping for his hand in the darkness. "Tell him that regardless of what he asks, I will do it. I would walk through fire, Miguel. You tell him that."

The boy nodded. "Read the letter. I will get my boots on." He hesitated. "Do you have anything to eat—something that I could take with me. We have very little food."

"In the refrigerator. And there are canned goods above the stove. Give me a few minutes to read this and write a reply." She felt her way out of the kitchen and up the stairs. In her bedroom she sat down with her back braced against the wall and read the penciled note, scratched on the moldy paper of a child's notebook:

By now, Miguel will have explained who we are, where we are and what we hope to attempt. The time that we have is very short. DGI patrols are very thick here and Maroto thinks we don't dare risk exposure beyond 72 hours from now. We think that Brocassie has probably been interrogated and will soon be transferred to another prison, probably El Condado near Trinidad, and if that happens, it will be impossible to free him.

We will need your help. I emphasize that the risk will be great, not only to us but to you.

We want to be able to take you, Brocassie and Álvarez, all at the same time. We are going to steal a militia supply truck and with this, enter the housing area of the compound. I will come to your cottage, probably through the back entrance. Miguel can brief me on how best to do this.

If only Álvarez and Brocassie are there, I can overpower Álvarez, but if there are additional guards, I will have to kill them. You may have to help me in doing this.

If we get away, we will use the truck, run the front gate and then get back into the Sierra before the DGI can organize a force to follow us. From there, we will have additional men to support our escape. Eventually, we'll be able to get out of Cuba by boat.

We need you to convince Álvarez to bring Brocassie to your cottage. Failing this, we still need Álvarez and would take you at the same time.

I will not risk sending Miguel again. Somehow, you must communicate to us when and if the attempt can be made.

Maroto tells me that you can send Morse code. Use a flashlight but tape a cardboard tube over the lens so that the beam is very narrow. Aim it from your open window toward the foothills where the old nickel mines are and send a series of Vs. If we can see the light, we will transmit only one V. If you see no response, try again slightly to the left or right. Do this between the hours of four and five in the morning and seven and eight in the evening, starting tonight. We will have two men always watching for your signal. You realize that we cannot risk sending back a message by flashlight as it would give away our position. If it is to work at all, it must be your plan and your timing.

If you think you can do it, then send us your reply by Miguel and we will wait for your detailed plan by signal for the next three nights.

There was a scrawled signature beneath the letter and printed beneath that was the name PORTO.

She reread the letter twice, then found some writing paper in the desk and wrote:

Porto—
Somehow, I'll get Brocassie here but I first must do a great deal of planning. Watch for my signal. I understand about the flashlight. I have seen Maroto do this before and I will be sure that the light cannot be seen from the street. My love to that rancid old man who pretends to be a mountain fighter. I ask that you tell him to wash his underwear more often.

She signed it with a flourish, "Alicia Helvia."

She was halfway down the stairs when she heard the jeep slow and then stop.

Miguel was waiting in the kitchen, his boots pulled on. She shoved the letter into his hand.

"No time," she whispered, desperate. "He's here." Opening the door to the fruit cellar, she shoved him down the stairs and dropped the trapdoor. Ten seconds later, the front door opened and slammed closed.

She met Julio as he was slouching down onto the couch, heedless of the rainwater which saturated his jacket. He tore it off and threw it on the floor, leaned back, his eyes closed, and said, "Christ, I'm beat. Bring me a drink. A double rum."

She picked up his jacket and went to the kitchen. She opened the back door slightly, leaving his jacket on the outside knob. She was making the drink when she suddenly realized that he was standing behind her. She turned and handed it to him, avoiding his touch.

"It was a bad day for you?" she asked casually.

"No." He swallowed twice. "No—a very good day, but a very long one." He looked down at the smeared wet tracks on the floor. "What's all that damned mess?"

There were still traces of mud and slurs of water on the tiles. She motioned toward the door. "Some from your jacket but I was out in the backyard before. Cats fighting or something. I threw a stone." It sounded weak but he seemed to accept it.

He picked up the bottle and added more rum to his glass. "Something to eat. Just a couple of eggs, fried. And some toast." He retreated to the living room and she heard him squash down into the leather chair, belching.

She pulled two eggs from the refrigerator, dropped butter in a pan and waited for it to melt. Two slices of bread into the toaster, utensils on a tray along with a folded napkin. Salt and pepper and some stale jam from the pantry. Habit moved her body through the cooking routine, her mind separate and detached, racing.

She tiptoed toward the living room and paused, listening. Sound of ice clinking in his glass. She bent over, peeking around the doorframe. He was resting the glass on the arm of the chair, his legs stretched out on the coffee table, his head thrown back, eyes closed.

She withdrew to the kitchen and edged open the trapdoor and whispered down into the damp blackness, "Miguel—the back door is open. Wait until I take the food in to him and then leave."

His head appeared in the crack of light which fell from the single lamp over the stove. Without saying a word, he winked and drew the trapdoor closed over his head.

She cracked the eggs and dropped them in, still thinking. Seventy-two hours. Three days. It seemed like an eternity, yet she knew that it wasn't nearly enough. Time—lots of time—was what she needed. Time to think and time to plan and time to devise a way of manipulating Álvarez to what she had to do. But how? In God's name, *how*?

She slid the eggs onto a plate, added the toast and carried the tray into the living room, pulling the kitchen door firmly closed behind her.

He had already finished off the glass of rum. His face was flushed, his eyes were dulling. He took the tray and wolfed the food down, scraping the egg-smeared fork back through his teeth. It was a habit she detested and he knew it.

She watched him, giving nothing away, not even a hint of her distaste. But her mind was beginning to work coherently, turning the possibilities over, rejecting one, holding another to be tested. It was quiet in the room, only the sound of his clicking fork to disturb the silence. In her mind the idea began to build, a whisper at first, growing to an insistent declaration. He grunted his pleasure and pushed the tray aside.

"Some more rum, babe—just a small one and then we'll head up to bed. I'm damned tired." He handed her his glass, intentionally keeping hold of it in his lap so that she had to stoop for it. She took hold of it carefully, feeling his breath on her neck, avoiding his hands.

In the kitchen, she poured him half a glass. There were faint smudges of wetness on the tiles. She grabbed a dish towel and buffed them dry. Safe passage, Miguel, she prayed.

She returned to the living room and handed him the drink. The idea was beginning to have shape, building on itself, sprouting out in many directions but always with the solid central core. It was a demanding thing, and it whispered and wailed, then roared with such an overpowering sound that she had to restrain herself from clapping her hands over her ears. Then it was complete, unalterable, because it had been there within her all along. What she knew she must do and for that reason, she believed in it and he would too.

"I'll have some wine," she said. "Then bed." She managed a shy smile which would be taken as a promise.

He looked up at her, his eyes focused, a smile coming to his lips. "Why not?"

She poured herself some wine and brought back the half-empty bottle of rum and filled his glass. She lifted her glass. "To the future, Julio."

He sighed and drank, then motioned for her to come closer, patting the cushion beside him. "You're unhappy here, aren't you?"

She shook her head. "Not really. But leaving the *finca* upset me. This place is so small. It takes time to get used to it and there's no one to talk to." She curled up beside him, sipping her wine, still avoiding contact with him. "And you're gone so much. Your work and all . . ." She left the sentence unfinished.

He laughed a little. "It's hard. Roychenko never seems to sleep and he expects me to be there when he snaps his fingers." There was a note of bitterness in his voice and she knew that the rum was getting to him.

She could smell him now—a combination of molasses-sweet alcohol and sweat and damp clothing. She cocked her head. "Your work, Julio. What's it like?"

"Security. Oriente Province but most important, the complex. It's just becoming operational and there have been problems."

"Like what?"

He hesitated, glancing sideways toward her. "Why ask? You know that I can't talk about it."

She shrugged her shoulders. "I just want to understand the difficulties. It's normal for me to want to know what kind of stress you have to put up with."

He settled back, his neck against the edge of the couch, his face upturned toward the ceiling.

"What are the difficulties? Men drunk on duty, fights, obvious but stupid violations in security. Friction between Cubans and Russians that has to be smoothed over. Timetables that have to be met. Shit like that."

"What about spies? That's really what the DGI is all about—I mean, counterintelligence. Is that a problem?"

His expression froze for a few moments. "Why ask that?"

"You catch them occasionally, don't you?" she said evenly. She didn't trust herself to say any more.

He laughed but the delay was long enough that she knew he was disguising what he really felt. "There are no spies—American, Cuban or Eskimo. We pick up someone once in a while wandering around the Sierra. We interrogate them and then let them go. Mostly old men looking for a lost goat or a kid who doesn't know what a restricted area means. If you're talking about Maroto and the Segundo Frente, forget it. They're finished, because they're afraid to fight. We know they're there but why risk the lives of my men trying to root them out? It's like flies, Alicia. You can spend a lot of energy trying to kill them in the summer but you can never get them all. And then the first frost comes, and they die anyway."

She drew in her breath, held it and let it out slowly. "Brocassie is your brother, Julio. We both knew him, loved him. I know you're holding him prisoner. How could you keep that from me?"

She had expected him either to laugh at her or to react violently but he did neither—just sat there quietly, sipping his drink. "Who told you that little fairy tale?" he finally asked.

She swallowed. "It doesn't really matter, does it?"

His face flared with anger. He grabbed her wrist, twisting it. *"Tell me, bitch!"*

The pain was excruciating but she had learned what she had to. Julio had captured him! He was twisting harder now, her arm up behind her back, her nerves shrieking with agony.

"WHO TOLD YOU?"

"Today—in the commissary," she said between clenched teeth, tears flooding her eyes. "Two men, both young DGI officers. They were in the next aisle, talking about the American spy. I heard Brocassie's name."

He pushed her away abruptly. "What were their names?" His voice was dangerous.

She stood on the other side of the living room, rubbing her wrist. "I don't know their names, Julio. I've seen one in a car with Piedra but I don't know who he is." That had been pure innovation but she saw in his eyes that it had hit home with brutal impact.

"*Shit!*" he swore. "The bastard couldn't keep his mouth shut, could he?" He turned to her, the anger in his face suddenly melting into defeat. He lowered his head, hair falling in a shock over his forehead. He sat like that for a long time, lips pressed together, and then finally nodded. "OK, you're right—we caught Brocassie four days ago. I didn't want him to come into Cuba—you know that. I risked everything to send your cable to him but he had to play it cute."

Liar, her mind screamed. You used me to trap him and then you sit there waiting for a benediction of my thankfulness. But she kept her expression blank. It took a great deal of effort to form the words and only then could she speak in a raw whisper. "Is he alive?"

He looked at her puzzled as if he hadn't heard her right.

Her voice rose against her will. "IS HE ALIVE?"

"Of course," he finally said, his lips barely moving. "What do you think? Alive and well. We don't torture people, Alicia. We use drugs now."

It was as if she were in a great hall, his words echoing back, repeating themselves over and over. "What do you do with him now?"

"The El Condado prison for a while. Then a closed-door trial. He'll be given a five-year sentence but that will be commuted to a lesser term. Eight months to a year in prison and then we'll ship him back to Miami in trade for a few of our people that the Americans have. That's the way it will be, I promise."

She didn't believe him because his eyes lied, even now when he was half-drunk.

"I want to see him, Julio. I want to know that he's all right, that he hasn't been . . . been hurt. I want to be sure that you're not lying to me."

397

Julio lay the glass alongside his face, studying her, bemused. "I don't think that would be possible. You have my word . . ."

"And what in hell is that worth?"

He slammed his glass down on the coffee table, sloshing the rum over the polished wood. "So Piedra bragged and somehow you heard. What's that to me, Alicia? Brocassie came in here of his own free will. He took his chances. He lost. He isn't harmed and he won't be. That's my word and you'll have to be satisfied with it."

"Then it's all over," she replied, her voice flat. "I couldn't live with you, always wondering whether you lied to me, whether Brocassie was maimed or even executed. I'm dead, Julio. Officially. There are old papers in some file that list Alicia Ruth Helvia as having been executed. I have no papers that prove otherwise. What if I walk out of here someday while you're gone? And keep walking. Somewhere, I'll be stopped and they'll find that I'm illegal. They'll put me in prison and they'll use the exquisite means that they have to pump me and then they'll really know who I am."

"You slut! I saved you because I loved you. The only thing you'd accomplish would be your own execution. I can double the guards on this house and you'll never leave this compound, not while I live."

She nodded violently. "I owe you my life, Julio, but I'm dead inside anyway. I don't believe in the Church but I do believe in God and I know to kill myself would be a mortal sin. But whether it's someone else pulling the trigger or my own hand, I'll do it. And I'll welcome it, and our son will die with me."

"Our son?"

"My period was due three days ago. I'm very regular. Your son is here, inside me." She lay her hand against her abdomen.

He swallowed twice, noisily. "It's too early for you to know, and you haven't been to see a doctor."

"But *I* know, Julio." She gave it all the emphasis that she could because she was sure that it was the truth. "He's there, Julio, already beginning to grow within me."

He stared at her, and then by some gigantic force of will,

he composed himself, lowering his voice so that it was almost inaudible. "I want you to live, Alicia. I want you with me, and I want our son. Don't make impossible demands on me. I could bring you his photograph, a tape recording of his voice, but I can't take you into the complex and I can't bring him here."

"I can't, I won't accept that, Julio. A photograph could be faked or taken a long time ago. The same with a tape recording. Your people are clever at that sort of thing. I told you my conditions. Bring him here. What harm would there be? We were all friends once, all together. I promise that we won't talk politics or anything else, just about old times. I'll make a dinner and we can laugh together if that's still possible. I just want to see him, to be sure that he's well; I want your word that he'll be traded back to the Americans."

He expelled a long breath, shaking his head. "Brocassie is scheduled to be transferred late tomorrow night. There's no time left, even if I wanted to."

"Then find a way!"

"I can't, for God's sake. You think I run this show but I don't—not where something like this is concerned. Roychenko calls the shots."

"He doesn't have to know. You're the senior Cuban officer. If you escort Brocassie, who among your men is going to question your authorization?"

Álvarez shook his head. "If either Roychenko or Piedra found out, I'd be finished. I can't risk it."

He was on the borderline, she thought. It could go either way and she gave it everything. "What I said before, Julio, I meant. If you don't bring him here, then you can forget that I ever existed because in a week, I won't."

"And if I do bring him here—if he's all right—then what kind of a life will I have with you?"

"I'll stay with you, Julio, for as long as fate allows us to be together."

He stared at her for a long time and she returned his gaze, willing him to capitulate first. Finally he did, lowering his stare. She could see it in his dulled eyes, the droop of his shoulders. "You still love him, don't you?"

She avoided his eyes, her hands over her face. "I don't

know anymore. It was a long time ago. Such a different time, and all of us were different then, weren't we?"

He didn't answer. He shuffled to his feet and climbed the stairs like an old man, pulling one foot up after the other. He stopped at the landing and looked down. "Tomorrow night, then. Nine. I'll keep my end of the bargain and you keep yours."

"I will," she answered. She listened as he moved into the bedroom, heard the running of water in the sink and then the creak of the bed as he lay down. She sat for a long while afterward, watching the clock's hands crawl around the yellowed face. Finally, she heard him begin to snore like a pig rutting.

She got up and went to the kitchen. From the top shelf of the cleaning locker she pulled out a flashlight and switched it on to make sure the batteries were fresh.

I'll keep my bargain, Julio, she promised silently.

CHAPTER

17

His cell door groaned open and he turned on his side, still half-asleep. Roychenko stood there, hands in pockets, a half-smile on his face, looking for all the world like a collector of rare species, inspecting his latest acquisition. "Good morning," he said, almost cordially.

"Is it?"

The Russian walked into the cell, an armed KGB corporal just behind him. "Yes, very much so," he answered. "A beautiful day. After all the rain, it's pleasant to have clear skies and hot sunshine—about the only worthwhile thing that Cuba produces in any quantity. It's a shame they can't export it to my country. Nevertheless, it makes one glad to be alive—which is the topic of our discussion this morning."

"I gave Álvarez no promises about making the tape."

The Russian hunched his shoulders. "So I understand. Suppose we discuss it over breakfast. Say in thirty minutes." He wrinkled his nose, delicately sniffing. "You probably could use a shower first. The guard will take you there." He turned and left without waiting for a response.

Breakfast had been set up in the alcove adjacent to Roychenko's office. Four chromed chairs backed with vinyl supposed to look like pigskin, a table of plastic teak, a couch covered in orange synthetic velvet and a bed. It could have been a room from a third-rate international hotel chain, transported intact from Des Moines, Frankfurt or Hong Kong. The only thing of real interest was one wall, blocked off with drapes drawn across it. Brocassie suddenly realized that Roychenko's office was located in the same branch-off from the main tunnel as the Command Post and that in all likelihood there was a window behind the velvet which overlooked the main floor, the consoles and the status boards.

They ate the meal in silence, Roychenko just picking at his food. He reached across the table and shoved three more strips of bacon onto Brocassie's plate. "Go ahead. Finish it." He offered the plate of muffins and Brocassie waved it away. Roychenko looked genuinely offended. "They're blueberry. Álvarez said they were your favorite. Not that easy to obtain in these austere times."

Brocassie took one, wrapped it in a napkin and stuffed it in his pocket. He felt ridiculous but his stomach had shrunk and although he couldn't eat much at one sitting, he found that he was constantly hungry. "For later," he said.

"That's really the subject under discussion, isn't it? Whether you'll be around 'later.' " He leaned back, rubbing his neck muscles, his voice relaxed. "I don't want to make things difficult, Brocassie. Short, sweet and simple. Are you willing to make that tape?"

Brocassie forked up the last piece of bacon and placed it in his mouth, chewing on it slowly, savoring the flavor. He glanced up, studying Roychenko. The calm eyes, the face expressionless as if cast from plaster, and the hands. Those hands could kill, he thought. No, this is one sonofabitch that I don't mess with. "What do you want on the tape and what do I get in return for making it?"

"What I want is the *truth*. That this complex is a Soviet communications facility. The only weapons that you've observed here are for the site's self-defense. You've seen that with your own eyes. The logical result is your report to Hagger. You will make a tape recording according to our draft outline, sign the container box with urine and Luis will carry it to Guantánamo Bay and within a few hours after that, your Mr. Hagger will be threading it into a CIA tape recorder."

"How would you want the tape done?" The words almost caught in his throat.

"Just a final report, exactly as if you were still up in the mine workings. The normal jerks and pauses in speech that one makes in such a recording. It must sound entirely natural. In addition, Captain Piedra has shot another roll of film with your camera and lens from the mine entrance, showing some of the coastal defense missiles being off-loaded and moved underground by the overhead crane. It will be entirely convincing. When Luis delivers the recording and film, he will corroborate your story."

"Just the kid to run your errands. He's got ice water for blood and about as much honor as a cockroach."

Roychenko gave a marginal shake of his head. "No, you really can't blame him. He was under a great deal of pressure to keep his father alive. I don't care for Piedra's methods but in this case, I can't fault the results." He constructed a little temple with his hands, fingertips touching, and pondered the architecture for a moment.

"And what happens to me if I agree to make this tape?"

"We would move you tomorrow night to El Condado Prison. Political prisoner with special status. You're under my protection. No interference by the DGI, the militia, the police or even Fidel. And in a year, perhaps less, as Álvarez promised you, you will be exchanged for two of our men the CIA is holding in Florida."

"What guarantees that it will work that way?"

"None that you'd believe—so it would be pointless to make any." Roychenko was flat-faced, expressionless. And then he smiled. "But you understand that we want Kennedy to know, say a year from now, that he was made a fool of and that the CIA bungled again. We don't care if you tell *The New York Times*. In fact, that would be quite desirable. Full exposure would rock the entire American government and it'd be

403

the laughingstock of the Western Powers. But we think that you'll be prevented from doing that by the CIA." He took off his glasses and polished them, then held them up to the light, assessing their clarity. He fit them on again, the gesture practiced, precise, overly fussy. "No," he said softly, "I think that the extent of the dissemination of your tale will be limited to double-locked safes and whispered conversations." He smiled once more. "You must understand, Brocassie, that we've written the script for this scenario very carefully and the play isn't over until you make your final appearance. We think that it's a fitting ending, a devastating twist of plot. And that, if you will, is your guarantee."

He felt cold all over. His hands had minute tremors which he couldn't control—fear or anger or some kind of delayed stress. He put them in his lap, gripping them together. Something was wrong, very wrong, like a puzzle that seems obvious and yet defies solution. Everything that Roychenko was saying made sense, but somewhere there was a flaw and it infuriated him that he couldn't detect it. He realized that he could only play for time. Because time was what he needed to find that flaw. Roychenko was as impenetrable as armor-plated steel. But there was Álvarez and there were fissures in Julio's personality and he needed one last chance, alone with Julio, to probe those weaknesses. "How much time do I have?" he asked.

"I want your decision now!"

"And I want more time, including a final talk with Álvarez. Five this evening. I'll give you a decision then."

Anger was burning in Roychenko's eyes but he kept his expression immobile. "You think you're going to negotiate when there is nothing to negotiate with." He sighed and then gave back a thin smile. "All right but beyond this, I make no further concessions. Five, then. I'll see that Álvarez is informed."

"Roychenko's out of patience, Brocassie. He's pissed and he wants results." Álvarez paused, touching Brocassie's arm. "Forget about playing with him. He's dangerous. Don't think about the old honor, duty, country crap. It's your life and hers that you're playing with now."

404

They walked down the main tunnel toward sunlight. "He knows that you'll make the tape one way or the other. He's holding the cards."

They passed through a section where there were steel doors, well over three feet thick, recessed back into the walls of the tunnel.

"What are those things for?"

"Blast protection in the event of an air raid or internal fire. They're all over the complex but I'm no engineer. There's probably some goddamn factory in Minsk which cranks them out like Christmas cookies, and Soviet design engineers undoubtedly have to use up the quota."

Brocassie forced a laugh, and Álvarez, probably pleased with the response, slapped Brocassie on the back.

"I thought you might like some sunshine. A walk along the river. How about it?"

"It appeals," he replied. Sunlight and air. God how it appealed.

At the end of the tunnel, they started up a shallow incline roofed over and walled by camouflage netting, past two more checkpoints and finally out into the open sunlight. Álvarez led the way, crossing over the doubled pair of railroad tracks which led down into the tunnel, heading out through a grove of mahogany toward an open field and the river beyond.

At first Brocassie couldn't see any sign of life, but as his eyes adjusted to the sunlight, he saw men in dark, sweat-stained fatigues, weapons slung over their backs, lounging beneath trees. And set back in the shadows of the trees, netting thrown over them, were antiaircraft batteries, surface-to-air missiles, exactly what he had seen from the mine only now he could see that there were more—many more. My God, he thought. The place bristled with firepower.

"Forget it," Álvarez said casually, glancing over at him. "You can't see anything from the air. Even from a chopper fifty feet off the deck, it's invisible. Everything we bring into the tunnel by train or truck comes at night. Until then, we keep it under the trees in the plantation. Quit thinking, Brocassie. You're out of the game now."

Julio led the way toward the river past a clump of trees. Beneath the branches were a series of pipes, coiled hoses and brass gate valves. He paused for a second. "We bring in the fuel at night and off-load it here. Avgas and diesel are pumped by underground pipes to storage tanks set in the hillside for the aircraft and the diesel is pumped in the same manner belowground for the generators."

"Why not take the fuel tankers directly into the tunnel and off-load underground?"

Álvarez grimaced. "Couldn't risk it. Fire hazard." He turned, heading toward a grassy knoll which overlooked the river. "Come on, we don't have that much time." He took the lead, walking through calf-high grass for a few minutes and then stopped abruptly.

"Follow me exactly now," he said. He turned back toward Brocassie. "I mean exactly."

"Why?"

"Minefield. There's an access path through it." He pointed to a clump of low trees with a squat concrete structure beneath them. "Pumping station for water from the river to feed the fire-fighting system. We have to send guys down occasionally to clean out the intake pipe in the river. Real shortcut but watch your step." He led on, walking carefully in a zigzag until they were on the muddy banks of the river.

The river was shallow but wide and stained rust brown with the runoff of the previous night's rain. Beyond its far banks were fields of brush, slowly thickening into dense undergrowth, spreading up into the foothills of the Sierra. So near, Brocassie thought, he could taste the wildness of the mountains and he inhaled deeply, scenting the freedom so near and yet so unobtainable.

Álvarez was saying something and he only caught the last few words.

". . . so it's begun. Kennedy made a speech last night."

"What's begun?"

"Kennedy's U-2s have photographed the missile sites up on the west coast of Cuba—probably the stuff in San Cristóbal. That's where we sent the first shells of the SS-4s. Kennedy reacted pretty much as Roychenko expected. He's calling in the UN and the Organization of American States. And he's instituting a shipping quarantine." He dug into his pocket and pulled out a yellow telex sheet. "We got this off of Reuters this morning." He handed it to Brocassie. The last few lines of print were underlined with a red marker pen. Kennedy's words were blunt, direct, and yet faintly compromising:

> . . . Our goal is not the victory of might, but the vindication of right; not peace at the expense of freedom, but both peace and freedom, here in this hemisphere, and we hope around the world. God willing, that goal will be achieved.

Álvarez took the sheet back and pocketed it. He grinned cynically. "Does that sound like a man about to negotiate or doesn't it? He's dickering already. He wants to make a deal, not fight."

"What else was in the speech?"

"The usual tripe. Maybe the only important thing was that he considered an attack by Cuba on the United States to be the same as an attack by the Soviets, to be met with a counterstrike."

"He may not be willing to sit in his rocking chair, passively waiting for Cuban missiles to blow up his country, Julio. There are probably a lot of Pentagon hacks beating the war drums. He can't flub this like the Bay of Pigs if he wants to win the next election. That's something the Politburo has to consider."

Álvarez shook his head. "You're wrong, dead wrong. He's going to try to bargain his way out of this. His first reaction was crucial. He wants the UN and the OAS to pat him on the back and tell him that they're all in this thing together. And by instituting a blockade, he's tipped his hand that he's gambling on a peaceful solution."

They had come to the edge of the river and Álvarez sat down on a patch of grass, turning his face up to the sun. He leaned back, eyes closed, obviously enjoying the heat. "No," he finally said, "Kennedy is as predictable as a trained dog whose teeth have been pulled. He'll yap and yap and yap but he's got no bite."

Brocassie sank down beside him, silent. He picked up a

rock and skipped it out across the flooding river, watching it ricochet, the splashes fracturing reflected sunlight until the stone sank.

"Remember," Brocassie said, "that carny show we went to in Dillon back when we were in tenth grade?"

Julio flashed a brilliant smile. "Yeah, I remember. We didn't get back until three or four and my old man gave us hell. Switched our asses."

"Remember the game? The steel ball suspended by a wire from the roof of the hut? You were supposed to swing it so that you could knock down a wooden bowling pin. I remember the old crock who ran the game let you have a practice swing for a warmup and it was a piece of cake, knocking the pin down. The ultimate come-on."

Laughing, Álvarez turned to him, his face genuinely animated. "Shit, yes, I remember him. He told us that he hadn't had enough winners and that the company gave him what for unless he gave away so many panda bears a night." He made a hook with his thumb and stuck it in his mouth, pulling. "Fishes. That's what we were, buddy. And we bit."

Brocassie picked up a blade of grass, placed it between his thumbs and blew, the sound a soft reminder of youth and open fields, fishing with bent pins from stream banks such as these. "You finally caught on to it. Figured out that the bowling pin was machined off-center. But we had already gone through three bucks by then and the guy just laughed at us. Told us we were suckers because there was always a gimmick when a deal looked too sweet." He tugged another grass blade from the earth, balling it in his fingers, letting the pungent smell escape, feeling the moisture between his fingertips. "So what's the gimmick, Julio?"

For a moment, there was only the chuckling of the river along the rocks of the bank and the sound of wind ruffling through the grass.

"There is no *gimmick*," Álvarez finally replied, scowling. "What you see is what you get. It's a ticket to continued good health. Don't cancel it out on some dumb kind of speculation." The muscles in his jaw hardened into flat planes. "It's Alicia's life as well. I know you blame me for it but that wasn't my idea. I damn well can't change history."

Brocassie hunched over, staring at the ground. It's that too, Julio, he thought. That, more than anything else, was the cruncher. "What about her?" he asked. "Does she know about me being here?"

"She does now."

"You told her?"

"She found out by accident. If Roychenko knew, she'd be in real trouble. Take my word for it."

Brocassie picked up another fistful of grass. God, it smelled good, of growing and earth and sun. Alicia and he had lain on grass beside streams like this but that time was no more than a vague dream. He found that he had difficulty even remembering her face exactly. "Don't worry, I wouldn't say anything to Roychenko." He paused. "She's OK for now?"

"She's fine, Brocassie. I'm taking you to see her tonight."

His words went through Brocassie like an electric current. "Why . . . if it's so dangerous?"

"Old home week, buddy. It was her idea and she made me a proposition that I couldn't refuse. If Roychenko or Piedra finds out about our little visit it's all over for both you and her and maybe me as well." He wiped his nose with the cuff of his fatigues—a gesture Brocassie knew Álvarez used when he was agitated and unsure of himself.

"If you take me up to the cottage we're going to pass through four or five security checkpoints. How do you cover that?"

"I don't have to. Most of them are my own men. I shifted the duty rosters around this morning. They'll cover for me if they have to." He turned to face Brocassie, unconsciously lowering his voice. "I got Roychenko's permission to bring you up to the surface this morning, just to condition the guards to the idea that you're cooperating with us, a collaborator with a certain degree of freedom. I'll get you out of your slammer about eight-thirty this evening. We'll take one of the electric carts to the tunnel entrance and pick up my jeep. From there, we'll go straight to my cottage. As long as you're with me, the guards won't raise an eyebrow. We'll have drinks and some food. Nothing personal, no question-and-answer sessions. You're there to convince her that you're still in one chunk and that your brain isn't fried. So keep it simple. Nothing about why you came back into Cuba and nothing of what's happened or going to happen. Sometime around eleven, I'll bring you back." He glanced at his watch, wound the stem of the watch and then listened. "Damn thing. Supposed to be Swiss but it's Russian copy. Keeps worse time than some Mickey Mouse watches I've seen." He turned back to Brocassie. "We split then, Brocassie. Probably permanently. Sergio Piedra will take you to El Condado Prison. You'll be going in handcuffs and leg shackles. High-priority cargo and Roychenko doesn't want any last-minute impulsiveness on your part."

He motioned with his head toward the tunnel entrance. "Time to go soon. All of this happens if you cooperate. I've got the draft for the tape. You read it, phrase it the way you'd say it and then we have a go at recording. You told Roychenko that you'd give us a decision by five P.M. That's in an hour, Brocassie."

"If I do the tape, I want it done my own way. No one hanging over my shoulder. It's not going to sound natural with you standing there, conducting the score. Just give me an hour alone in my cell and I'll have it finished."

"No tricks?"

"Lunts interrogated me with you present. You know that there aren't any, don't you? Just the signature written in piss on the container box."

"You'll do it, then?" Álvarez's eyes were hard, questioning.

He took a long breath, held it and then blew it out. This is what it came down to, the crunch. He hoped that Hagger had the balls to carry it through. "Why not?" he answered.

Roychenko rewound the tape and played it back again. He listened intently, comparing Brocassie's words to the penciled draft. He finally snapped off the tape, leaned back and lit his pipe. "You're satisfied?" he asked, his eyes glacial.

Álvarez nodded. "It sounds all right. Natural enough."

Roychenko shook his head. "I'm not a fool, Álvarez. It sounds 'all right' as you say. But do you think that there was any prearranged code to indicate that the tape was made under duress?"

Slumping down on the desk, Álvarez looked Roychenko in the eyes. "No. I don't think so. Luís says that he never heard any discussion which would indicate that they took such measures. He personally asked Brocassie about it when they were down at the mine. Besides, he knows that if he crossed us, there would be unpleasant repercussions."

"I've let you run most of this, Álvarez, because you know Brocassie. If it goes wrong, you're responsible."

"Nothing will go wrong. We have the tape. Tonight, he's being transferred to El Condado."

Roychenko thumbed a button on his desk. A motor whirred and slowly, the heavy curtain moved back, exposing the plate-glass window. He swiveled 180 degrees, looking at the status board in the control room below. A matrix of lights was illuminated, a few red, some amber, the remainder green. As he watched, one amber light flickered to green. He swiveled back.

"One hundred thirteen silos ready—seven more to go. Three of those that are not operational are undergoing final servicing and checkout. The other four have electrical faults. These Long Range Rocket Force prima donnas have promised me that the entire one hundred and twenty will be ready by dawn. I believe that like I believe in Immaculate Conception."

Standing up, Álvarez moved to the plate-glass window. It was a bit like looking down from an aircraft on a city at night—the formless maze of lights—some blinking, some static. It was mesmerizing. He turned back, facing Roychenko. "What does it matter? The Americans will cave in on the negotiations."

Roychenko rolled a pencil between his palms, saying nothing. Pinpoints of red, amber and green reflected back from his glasses.

"Well, does it matter?"

"It matters," Roychenko said quietly. "It matters a great deal, Álvarez. Ambassador Gromyko met with Kennedy less than four hours ago. Privately, Kennedy's taking a hard line, demanding that we remove the Sandals immediately. His military advisers must be pushing for a preemptive strike against Cuba. Our COSMOS-17 reconnaissance satellite shows massive troop buildups in southern Florida, including tactical fighter-bomber support wings. A naval invasion force is beginning to assemble in the Straits of Florida. Moscow estimates that in thirty-six hours, the Americans will be prepared to land over five divisions in Cuba."

"But we're not talking about a nuclear war!"

"Aren't we? Aren't we, *Comandante*? Kennedy's Strategic Air Command has gone on full alert—*DEFCON One-M*—which means that the B-52s and B-47s are now almost continuously aloft and that the land-based intercontinental missiles are being loaded with liquid oxygen and fuel. His nuclear-armed submarines have put to sea—every last one of them. Kennedy has gone on a war footing—a nuclear war footing.

"*You mean that you might get orders to launch these goddamned things?*"

Roychenko poured a glass of water from a carafe and drank it slowly, his eyes wandering over the status board in the Command Post below him. He set the glass down carefully and turned back to Álvarez. "You should know. The Americans invented the game of poker and when you play for high stakes, you have to be willing to gamble because otherwise, you can be bluffed out of the game." He gestured toward the control room. "Those are our chips—one hundred twenty of them. And the Soviet Union has almost one hundred more missiles east of the Urals targeted against the United States. The balance is not unfavorable if it were to come to war." The room was icy cold as the air conditioner droned in a mechanical monotone. And yet Álvarez felt the sweat drenching his neck and back, his armpits saturated.

"Under what conditions would you launch?"

Roychenko laughed, but it was hollow, lacking conviction. "That, in all but the most extraordinary circumstances, is not my decision. Such orders would come from Moscow."

Álvarez looked out at the status boards again: 120 missiles—120 megatons, none of them more than twelve minutes away from their targets.

"Where are they targeted?"

"Does it really matter?" Roychenko asked, and answering his own question, added, "I suppose it does." He reached down to a safe alongside his desk, moved the handle and extracted a computer printout. "Twenty into the Cheyenne and

Denver area, to take out the missiles that the Strategic Air Command has based there. The missiles are vulnerable—not hardened in silos—and they're exposed because they're now erected with full loads of propellants." His finger ran down the page, pausing at each line. "Three each to every SAC bomber base—Loring, March, Plattsburgh, Homestead, Omaha, Wichita, Presque Isle . . ." He droned on.

There was a dryness in the back of Álvarez's throat, almost a constriction. He interrupted Roychenko. "You think it could come to that?" He realized that his voice was not much more than a dry whisper.

Roychenko looked up, irritated, and then dropped the list on his desk. He considered for a while and then said, "It's considerably more complicated than you imagine, Julio. There is a major contest of wills and philosophies going on in the Soviet Union at this very moment—whether we assert ourselves internationally through military force projection, or whether we simply allow ourselves to slide back into political oblivion under Khrushchev's leadership. This complex, this project in Cuba, is the pivotal point. We plan to achieve our objectives peacefully, but we must be, we *are,* prepared to fight. If the Americans break off negotiations and attack Cuba in strength—this valley in particular—it would constitute an attack on the Soviet Union. With Khrushchev still in control, I think he would be too frightened to respond but if Brezhnev is able to gain control of the Politburo in such a crisis situation, I'm sure that he'll launch an all-out war. The Red Army stands ready behind Brezhnev and with these missiles' ability to rapidly strike into the American heartland without warning, we would win." His body was tense but then he slowly relaxed. "But I don't think it will come to that. Not yet," he added.

Álvarez leaned back, the fake leather sticking to his shirt. He listened to Roychenko's breathing, the air conditioner, the sound of his own teeth working against each other. As he looked out through the plate-glass window, another amber light winked green.

CHAPTER

18

Oriente Province, Cuba,
October 27, 1962

Through the twin barrels of the binoculars, the few lights in the mahogany grove were blurred dazzles of brilliance, set against carbon-soot blackness. He cursed, wiped the thin film of condensation from the lenses with a rag and looked again. Better, he thought, studying the grove. He could begin to pick up the details of trucks parked bumper to bumper in a long line, two freight cars backed onto a siding and the occasional flashlight of guards patrolling the perimeter fence. But these were of secondary importance. He swept the binoculars through small increments of arc, studying the officer housing area.

He counted the seven cottages, east to west, then traced back through three groupings of light. His binoculars finally rested on the one cottage.

"You have it?" Maroto breathed in his ear.

Porto shook his head in the darkness. "I have it but

414

there's nothing except lights on the lower floor." He lifted his head from the eyepieces. "What time now, old man?"

Maroto shielded the luminous dial with a cupped hand. "Eight-seventeen."

"She's two minutes late. If she was able to arrange it, she should have switched on the light in her bedroom at eight-fifteen and switched off at eight twenty-five. That's the schedule, right?"

Maroto sighed wearily like an old dog disturbed in its sleep. "You copied her coded message by flashlight as well as I did," he answered, disappointment heavy in his voice. "That was the arrangement."

Porto bent down to the binoculars again. "Nothing. Dammit to hell—nothing."

Maroto's hand touched his arm. "Check again—the cottages on either side. You could have the wrong one."

He shifted the instrument and there was the light on the second story, one house to the left. He scanned quickly again, cursed himself under his breath and counted from right to left. ". . . two, three, four, five." He rolled over on his side and Maroto kneeled down beside him.

"My mistake, old man. The first cottage had no light on at all and I skipped over it."

Maroto grunted in the darkness, neither praise nor condemnation. He drew back his sleeve again, carefully exposing his watch—a cheap imitation of a Rolex with a peeling gold case that he had picked up from a sidewalk stall in Havana before the Revolution. The old man was extraordinarily proud of it, constantly checking the rusting hands behind the glazed crystal. Porto had been reluctant to tell him that it was a fake, because to his knowledge it was the only possession of value that the old man had besides his honor—the rarest commodity of all, he thought. Porto bent down to the eyepieces, focusing on the lights, unconsciously grinding his teeth. Let this be it, he thought. Now or never, Alicia.

"Eight twenty-three," Maroto said softly. His raspy breathing was audible in the stillness of the night and Porto wondered how this old man could even wade, let alone swim, across the river.

"Twenty-four . . ."

Porto stared into the eyepieces of the binoculars, straining. He saw the movement of a curtain—a figure silhouetted against the light from behind. The figure moved away from the brightness of the window.

"Twenty-five," sighed Maroto next to him.

And then Porto saw the light flick off.

"She's done it!" he hissed to Maroto and he was suddenly grinning, elated. The impact of what would follow hit him and just for a second there was a hard dart of pain in his gut and his scalp prickled, some vague premonition of death, but he forced himself to ignore it. He squeezed Maroto's arm fiercely, exaltation overriding fear. "I don't know how the hell she's pulled it off but she has!" He stood up, casing the binoculars and then brushing damp earth from his fatigues. "Enrico's gotten the truck?"

"Trucks," Maroto replied. "You weren't listening when I told you this afternoon . . . two trucks."

"*Two!*"

"There was no other choice. Hernando and Enrico had militia armbands and AK-47s. They watched the Sierra road all through the afternoon. Finally a large number of aviation gas tankers came through—ten of them in a convoy. Enrico flagged them down and demanded to examine their trip tickets and transit papers. How is that for balls?" The old man rumbled soft laughter in the darkness.

"Isn't that unusual for a two-man patrol?"

Maroto hunched his shoulders. "Who knows? But they did it. No truck driver or accompanying militia guard is going to question that sort of action by a couple of wild-eyed *barbudos.*"

"You mean Enrico held up the whole convoy?"

"No. You don't listen, do you, pilot? Just two. There were ten tanker trucks in the convoy. For once, Enrico used what few brains the good God gave him. He checked *all* of them for their trip tickets and papers and then held back the second one and the last two for some imagined irregularity. Told them that he would have to check by radio with Santiago. About dark, he told the last tanker in line to go ahead—that he had been cleared and to pass word to the complex that the remaining two would probably be allowed to proceed by late evening if the fuel depot in Santiago could work out the problem with the mismatch in trip ticket numbers."

"But why *two* tankers?"

"He had to. The tanker truck cab holds only three people. If you're successful and get Brocassie, Álvarez and the woman out, that makes three plus you and Enrico. Too many for one truck."

Porto glanced at his watch. "So what are the arrangements?"

"You will take the place of the militia guard in truck number two and Enrico will do likewise in number nine. You'll use the original drivers. They're old men, frightened witless. Once you get past the security guards at the gate, you'll be directed to park in the motor pool. Normally, the trucks have a two- to four-hour wait before they can proceed to the pumping transfer station. According to Enrico's interrogation of the drivers, the drivers and guards sleep under their trucks until called to off-load their gasoline. How you take care of the drivers is immaterial but I would suggest that you kill them and roll them under the tanker with a blanket over them. It will appear that they're sleeping, *¿me entiendes?*"

"Negative. If we have to kill, we will, but not some defenseless old *cabrón* who's shitting his pants."

Maroto grunted. "That is your decision but I remind you that this is not a game that we're playing. If you have a distaste for killing, then use Seconal."

I'll let that one pass, Porto thought. "What about getting through the security checkpoint?"

"When the truck is loaded at the docks in Santiago, both driver and guard roll their thumbprints onto the waybill. Once they arrive at the complex perimeter gate, one guard covers them with a weapon while the other guard inspects the waybill. If the paperwork looks all right, the guard passes the driver an ink pad and a blank paper on a clipboard. The driver and the guard ink their thumbs and roll their thumbprints onto the blank paper. These are compared with the thumbprints on the waybill and if they match, the truck is waved through."

"Then we're screwed! The driver's thumbprint will match but neither mine nor Enrico's will."

Maroto snorted—a contemptuous dismissal of a small detail. "That would seem obvious, but as I say, Enrico was using his head." He reached into his shoulder bag, withdrew a bulky envelope and handed it to Porto.

"This will take care of the problem. Enrico has the other."

In the darkness, Porto opened the flap and felt the object. It was cool and yielding, like a small dead hairless rodent.

"What's this?"

Maroto ignored the question, took him by the elbow and started walking down the pathway toward the road. They passed five of Maroto's men who were hunched down, cigarettes shielded behind cupped hands—men frightened and yet impatient like all soldiers about to go into combat. They were talking softly but their voices were thin and high-pitched. Porto could smell their fear, almost touch their own fragile sense of mortality like he could his own.

"It is a simple procedure at the gate," Maroto said easily. "The system has been in effect for some time and most of the drivers are known on sight. The identity of the guards less so, because they are drawn from a large rotating duty roster. Enrico says that the procedure is that the ink pad is passed up to the driver, along with the clipboard and then to the guard. It takes but a few seconds for each of the men in the cab to touch his right thumb to the ink pad and then to roll his thumb onto the appropriate corner of the pass. Practice it several times using your own saliva until you get a clean impression the first time."

"You want both Enrico and me to smear the print and hope that they let us through without further checking?"

"No—they would simply instruct you to do it again." He stopped for a second, turning to Porto. "The object in the envelope is the right thumb of the guard who was riding in number two tanker. Enrico has assured me that the man has no further use of it." He squeezed Porto's shoulder. "Go with God, pilot. He owes us a great victory."

Porto couldn't decide whether to gag or laugh so he did neither. But he couldn't resist it. "It's a fine thing that we do, old man—finer than we have ever done before."

Maroto stood stock-still in the darkness, staring at Porto,

some invisible barrier sliding down between them. "Don't mock either God or great men, pilot."

Eight forty-nine by the clock on the desk of the security guard at the entrance of the tunnel. The DGI man bent down to his log, laboriously recorded Álvarez's badge number, name and time. Then looked up first at Brocassie, then at the *comandante*.

"He has authorization?" he asked, nodding toward Brocassie.

Álvarez shook his head. "I am solely responsible for him. I want no mention of this in the log. It's a matter of security, Lieutenant García."

The man smiled, closed the log and saluted with an offhand flick of his wrist.

"As the *comandante* wishes."

Not even looking at the man's face, Álvarez returned the salute and accelerated the jeep up the ramp and into the night. As they cleared the overhang of the tunnel, he flicked on hooded driving lights.

Neither of them speaking, they drove through the damp night. Here and there, men lounged beneath the mahogany trees, cigarettes or cigars glowing. They passed a ZSU half-track with quad-23mm guns mounted in the back, the crew clustered near the hood, drinking from thermos flasks. Past the motor pool area—tanker trucks sheltered under the trees, engines silent or just idling over, waiting to be called for fuel offloading.

Brocassie was hunched forward, his wrists handcuffed to the grab bar on the dash. The steel cuffs chafed at his flesh. "Pull over for a second, Julio."

Álvarez slowed down. "What's the problem?"

"Take these handcuffs off. I don't want to meet Alicia this way."

"I hate to say it but I can't trust you."

"It's a mutual feeling," Brocassie replied. "Pull over anyway. For a minute, Julio. I want to talk to you before we get there." He softened the tone of his voice. "You owe me, buddy, at least this much."

Álvarez drove on for a few more minutes and then pulled into a grove of trees. He flicked off the headlights, leaned back and lit a cigarette. "Better here, off the road, but make it quick because she's waiting."

He began carefully, not goading his brother. "Roychenko."

"What's that supposed to mean?"

"He's used you up, Julio, and he's about to trade you in for a new model. You don't understand that?"

"Don't misinterpret things, Brocassie. I've put the security for this complex together like a Swiss watch and I'm ten times smarter than Piedra. Roychenko's not going to make any changes in management."

"But if he wants to, he can, correct?"

Álvarez hesitated for just the span of a second but it was telling. "Yes—if he wants to."

Brocassie bent forward and leaned on the dash, taking the pressure off his back. He looked sideways at Álvarez but could see only his profile highlighted by the glow of the cigarette.

"It was a big sales job, Julio, wasn't it? The carny pitch with the ball on the wire. I think—am damn near positive— that there's something here that you're hiding. Everything you've said makes sense and that's the problem, isn't it? It's so neat that I don't believe it."

"Then why did you make the tape?"

"Call it self-preservation. Lunts would have dragged it out of me but there was a much greater reason—Alicia."

"No one would have ever touched her," Álvarez said quietly. "That was just part of the leverage," he said but his voice lacked conviction.

"You know you're talking bullshit. Roychenko would have done anything that he wanted with her to get me to make that tape and if you had objected, he would have made it over your conveniently dead body." He paused, letting it sink in. "One other thing, Julio. You really believe that Roychenko's going to let me live to talk. All that crap about letting me go back to confront the CIA with your version of what's in this complex. It doesn't make sense, any way that you look at it. Once Hagger gets the tape from me, I'm used merchandise. He'll write me off without another thought. You know that,

Roychenko knows that. Why should the Soviets blow the security of the operation on an ego trip? It's not necessary, not even very desirable. But it was a carrot that Roychenko hoped that I'd swallow. Now comes the stick."

"I . . ." Álvarez left the sentence unfinished.

"That says it all, doesn't it?" Like a door slamming shut and locking, he thought.

"It's not something that I can control. You know that. You weren't born in a cabbage patch, Brocassie."

"But I may die in one. With Piedra pulling the trigger." He swallowed, lowered his voice and asked, "Did Roychenko sign the order for Piedra to kill me? Or did you?"

"You're talking shit, Brocassie. Pure shit. Nothing like that has happened—nothing that I know of."

"And why should they tell you anyway? It will be neat and simple. Something like *prisoner died in an attempted escape* and Piedra will pull the trigger and Roychenko will sign the papers and they'll shoot a little memo up to your office with the bare details and a short note of condolence."

Álvarez turned to him. "They're not going to blow you away. I got Roychenko's personal word on that. I've done everything that I can to save your hide."

"But Piedra's personally taking me to El Condado, right?"

In the half-light, Álvarez nodded slowly, his eyes averted.

"Strange, don't you think, Julio? A captain delivering a prisoner by truck, a round trip of three hundred miles through guerrilla territory? My guess is that he'll be back in two hours."

Álvarez sighed. "I asked to take you, Brocassie. Roychenko turned me down. That's all I know."

"*Cuando se acaba la cosa, se acaba la cosa*—when it's finished, it's finished. I understand your dilemma, Julio, and I don't blame you for trying to cover your ass, but there's one thing that you have to promise me. I saved your butt once and I'm calling in that debt. I want your word on it."

"What?"

"That you'll get Alicia out of this valley tomorrow morning. Send her back to the *finca*. Make arrangements to get her out of Cuba quick if things go wrong."

"Why, for Christ's sake?"

"We're not debating, Comandante Álvarez. We're talking about a debt that has to be paid. No conditions, brother—just give me an answer. Will you get her out of here or not?"

"The *finca* is closed down—just the cook there. It would be damn difficult to explain ..." His voice trailed off. He turned to Brocassie. "What's going to happen—you bastard, you know something."

He shook his head. "No, Julio, I don't know a damn thing, but I want her out of here by tomorrow because you're playing with fire. There *is* something here, isn't there, Julio? Something hidden and because of that, everything has to eventually be tidied up if non-Soviets are involved. Roychenko isn't the kind of person to leave loose ends hanging out and those loose ends include me. And you. And Alicia." He paused. "I don't have any illusions, Julio. Piedra's not taking me to El Condado. He's giving me a one-way ride to dreamland. Maybe the only good that will come of this will be that Roychenko has to get rid of Piedra as well, but neither of us will be around to cheer."

Álvarez flicked the cigarette into the night. He turned on the dashlights, turned the key in the ignition and hit the starter. The engine coughed into life. "What are you suggesting?"

"You're on the hit list, Julio. I don't give a shit whether you believe me or not, but for Christ's sake get her out of this valley while there's still time because if Roychenko decides to replace you, she'll go too."

Álvarez squashed down on the accelerator. The machine bucked and then took up the power, rapidly gaining speed.

"Your brief recorded and noted," Álvarez said, not looking toward Brocassie.

He drove in silence for another two minutes then pulled into an overgrown driveway. He leaned over and unlocked the cuffs.

"I've thought about it a lot before you even mentioned it, Brocassie. But sometimes you get in so deep that you can't get out. Things don't always go exactly as planned." He hesitated and then nodded. "OK—you have my word. I'll send her back to the *finca* tomorrow afternoon but making any kind of arrangements to get her out of Cuba would be impossible. If something goes wrong here, if something happened to me, she could fend for herself—we both know that. I can't promise more." He slid out of the jeep and stood up, stretching. "Let's go."

Brocassie remained slumped in his seat, working circulation back into his wrists. "Julio," he finally said, "when I first flew back into Cuba, I understood the risks. We both play the game understanding what the rules are and I don't hold you responsible for what may happen to me. I love you still, despite the fact that you're a shit."

Álvarez was turned toward him but Brocassie couldn't read his expression in the darkness. When Álvarez spoke, his voice was tired. "Strange, but I feel very much the same way toward you. Love, brotherhood, and all of that crap but neither of us can change things, can we? We both always knew that the deep end of the pool is where all the action is." He motioned toward the house. "Let's go in and see her. She's eager to see at least one of us."

Nine-nineteen. Porto checked his watch for the third time in the last five minutes. He leaned back against the ripped leather seat, watching the blacktop road in front of the truck float smoothly under the headlights. He held the AK-47 loosely across his lap, the muzzle pointing toward the driver. In his breast pocket, he felt the obscene object in the envelope pressing against his skin. His stomach turned a half-gainer and he ground his teeth, trying to divert his mind from the bloodless, severed thumb.

"How much longer?" he asked.

"Two more kilometers. Then we turn right, across the bridge and then another kilometer." The man's palms were soaking with sweat and his hands kept slipping on the steering wheel. "Please . . ."

"What's your problem, Guillermo?"

"I have a family, *Jefe*." The man swallowed noisily. He was mid-fifties, balding and his gut hung out over his belt, bouncing as the truck rumbled over the rough surface. The stench of his sweat and his cheap after-shave lotion fought for predominance, the mixture nauseating. Porto rolled the window down another turn.

"So you've reminded me four times in the last thirty minutes. Doesn't your Maximum Leader pay the families of dead revolutionary heroes well?"

Guillermo downshifted, grinding gears. "I am no hero," he answered, his voice sick with fear. "I have bad nerves, an ulcer and too many children. I am not part of the stinking Revolution." He mumbled on, almost incoherent in his rambling confession of terror.

Porto ignored Guillermo's rantings. He was trying to build walls in his mind against the fear that was percolating through his nerves. He wanted to be at the gate, *now,* to get the goddamn thing over with because somehow the gate was more than just a physical barrier—it was mental as well—and he knew that he would have to broach it before he could regain faith in his own courage. He concentrated on his breathing, willing it to slow. For just an instant, in the corner of his eye, he caught the lights of Enrico's truck reflected in the rearview mirror. Good enough, he thought. He knew that if he got through the security check at the gate, the second truck would receive only a cursory examination. Two trucks together, same loading point, same destination. Porto didn't trust Enrico to pull it off on his own. Enrico was psychologically glued to the trigger of his gun and that was his solution to any sort of confrontation. If Enrico screwed it up, the escape door would be slammed shut. He didn't trust Enrico either and he could sense that the feeling was mutual.

Guillermo downshifted again, braked and spun the wheel to the right. "Please," he pleaded, his voice breaking. "I cannot go through with this. They will know and we will both be shot!"

Porto propped the AK up next to him on the seat, withdrew the envelope from his pocket and unholstered his Colt revolver. He flicked open the cylinder, checked the shells and snapped it closed. He thumbed back the hammer and laid it in his lap. Over the Colt, he spread a copy of the newspaper *Granma* which had been stuffed in the glove compartment.

Guillermo watched him from the corner of his eye, like a chicken mesmerized by a bright shard of glass.

"No . . ." he said weakly.

"Yes," Porto answered. "Do it right, and you'll live to father five more little bread-snapping bastards. Do it wrong and your ulcer will get perforated with this." He touched the shape under the newspaper with his fingertips. "You've been through this checkpoint ten or fifteen times before. Keep it simple. No talk unless it's necessary."

They were across the bridge now, the planks rumbling under the tanker, and then through the last turn. Guillermo took a deep breath and switched off his headlights, leaving only the parking lamps illuminated.

From the side of the road a masked flashlight oscillated, its beam zigzagging in the dirt. Guillermo braked slowly, stopping with a hiss of air brakes. In the dim illumination of the parking lights, Porto could see the lowered log barrier just beyond the grill and a dark figure holding a machine pistol trained on the windshield.

There was a crunch in the gravel. The tanker shook slightly as a man stepped up on the running board. His flashlight glared in Porto's face, blinding him.

"You're six hours late. What was the problem?"

"The wrong numbers, the lack of a signature, a stamp that didn't have enough ink on it. Who knows?" He forced an insipid grin. Inside, he felt as if he would explode with tension. Involuntarily, his finger tightened on the trigger of the Colt.

The flashlight played on Guillermo's face. The man was perspiring, trickles of moisture beading his upper lip.

"You look sick, Guillermo. Your ulcer again?"

The old man belched. He wiped his face with a dirty handkerchief. "It was the remains of a fish. A bonito we had two nights ago and my wife used the leftovers to make a sandwich." He manufactured a death's head grimace and belched again.

The guard shook his head. "You look like cold shit warmed over. Give me your papers."

Porto took the cardboard sheath from Guillermo's trembling fingertips and handed it down. The pink loading manifest protruded from the folder like a flaccid tongue. It fluttered briefly in the wind.

The flashlight played over the document, then the next.

"These are in order. Ninety-two hundred gallons of high-test aviation fuel. You'll be number five in line to off-load. Sergeant Duarte has told me personally to convey to you that he'll have your *entre pan y pan* for breakfast unless that fuel is dumped and the tanker is out of here before dawn. You understand?"

The relief on Guillermo's face was transparent. He gunned the engine, starting to put it in gear. "I understand. Dawn."

"*WAIT!*" The guard shoved a clipboard through the passenger side of the window into Porto's face. "The prints. You know the procedure." Impatiently, he stood on the running board, his flashlight playing on the blank form.

Porto handed it to Guillermo. The old man rolled his thumb across the inked pad, then rocked it across the paper. He stared back at Porto, hesitating.

"You!" The guard flashed the light in Porto's face and then flicked it down to the clipboard. "Right beside Guillermo's print."

Taking the pad, he rolled his thumb in the ink. Shiver up his spine, sweat plastering his back to the seat. He pressed down hard, not rocking his thumb and then, pivoting his wrist slightly, he smeared the thumbprint. He handed the clipboard back through the window, knowing that it wasn't going to work. Dumb shit, he cursed himself. But there had been no option with the flashlight on the clipboard. The severed thumb burned against his thigh. He glanced back to the guard. He was bent over, examining the prints on the blank form, comparing them with the prints on the waybill. The guard suddenly looked up.

"No good. I'll have my prick pulled out by its roots if I pass this off to the sergeant as positive identification."

Porto managed a toothy grin and then shrugged. "First time on this duty. *Lo siento mucho.* Show me how you want it done."

The man ground the muscles in his jaws. "You did it in

Santiago at the loading station, *come mierda*! Less ink on your thumb and roll it gently. You're not squashing an insect!"

Porto had the severed thumb in his hand now, pressing it against the ink pad. It felt cold and it was going putrid. He had an almost uncontrollable compulsion to vomit but he swallowed.

He caught a flash of headlights in the rearview mirror. The guard was already handing back the clipboard. Porto took it with his left hand. Come on, Enrico! Damn you, faster!

"The thumbprint, man." The guard was plainly agitated, a hairline away from suspicion.

"Ah," Porto said, craning his neck, looking back over his shoulder through the window. "The other tanker. I was worried that they had transmission trouble."

The guard's reflex was automatic. He turned his head, gazing behind Guillermo's tanker toward the oncoming lights. In that brief second, Porto rolled the severed thumb across the page. He dropped the thumb to the floorboards and then poked the guard in the chest with the clipboard. "That is satisfactory?"

The guard squatted down, supporting the clipboard on his knees, playing the shielded beam of his flashlight on the form. He studied the prints for over a minute and then looked up. "It's still bad but it will pass. Wash your hands the next time. There's grease or something on your fingers." He waved his fist at the other guard who raised his weapon and moved out of the headlights. In another second, the barrier raised.

"Move it," the guard snapped. "Take the left lane and hold it there. No lights and no smoking. Sergeant Duarte will call you half an hour before off-loading which should be about three in the morning. Whether you're finished off-loading or not, you're to be back out of this gate by dawn. You understand?"

Guillermo raised his hand hesitantly, something between acknowledgment and a salute. He ground the shift lever into first and then engaged the clutch. The tanker lurched and then lumbered slowly forward.

Porto's right hand was trembling, as if by some consciousness of its own, it had almost betrayed him. The rest of his body felt at peace, almost detached. He clamped his traitorous hand under his thigh and leaned back, closing his eyes for just a second, taking long breaths. "You did well, Guillermo," he said softly. "You will live to fornicate with whores yet unborn." He found himself suddenly laughing but his laugh had a high, thin quality—near the border of hysteria. Adrenaline was still pumping through him like boiling water, burning his nerves. Pull it together, his brain screamed. That was the worst part—the barrier. And he was through it.

The driver made a strangled noise in his throat. "They will kill me for this deception!"

"Not when they find you." He took the two tablets from his shirt pocket. "Chew these and then swallow. In fifteen minutes you'll be asleep and no one will be able to wake you for half a day. I'll tape your mouth and hands and leave you on the ground under the truck."

"I can't—"

Porto slammed the man hard on the shoulder muscle with his fist. "No *can'ts*. You live if you do what I say. *Eat them!*"

Guillermo gulped the pills, jawed on them and swallowed noisily.

In the dash lights, Porto could see the man shivering. You poor sucker, he thought. Not your day—nor mine. He glanced over, checking the side mirror. Figures moving through the glow of Enrico's parking lights, the flicker of a flashlight, dangerous seconds ticking away, the exit behind him now closed. And then the silhouette of the barrier lifting. He breathed deeply, sucking in air to the extent of his capacity, getting the staleness of fear out of his lungs. The night was damp and crisp, just the hint of autumn since the rains were finished. His nerves were stretched taut but now his brain was alive, planning, looking at a future which, only minutes ago, did not seem to exist.

The truck behind him was catching up, the parking lights growing brighter as it drew closer. He caught just the faint sound of singing and he realized that it was that crazy bastard, Enrico. More guts than brains.

In the darkness, someone swore and then barked out to keep it quiet. Effusive apologies from Enrico with a suggestion that the man's mother had indulged in an intimate relationship with her dog. Nervous laughter from several throats, immune in the blackness from the retaliation of their sergeant.

Porto didn't catch all of the reply but he recognized the self-important intonation of authority, a sharp challenge and then the threat of retribution in the form of a hard boot, strategically placed.

Enrico again, contrite, humbled, but still with the hint of a smirk in his voice.

Guillermo swung off the main track, into a grove of trees. He braked gently to a stop behind another tanker and killed the lights and engine. Seconds later, Enrico's tanker pulled into the opposite lane, paralleling them.

Enrico climbed down from the cab, urinated noisily in the grass between the tankers, then slowly walked over to Porto's side of the tanker.

"You understand why I am fighting the Fidelistas now, *Yanqui?*"

"No, not really."

"Cubans have no sense of humor left. It's been sucked out of them by collective thinking, dialectic materialism and rum rationing." He cackled, punching the side of the cab with his fist.

"Keep it quiet! That was a dumb chance to take."

"I think not. Does a thief advertise his presence?" Enrico laughed softly. "We're here. That is what matters. And now . . . ?"

Now, thought Porto. The adrenaline was wearing off. His body felt like lead but he forced himself to open the door. "Both drivers under the trucks. Tape their mouths, hands and ankles and throw some blankets over them. Then stay here. Keep a watch and stay out of trouble. If I can pull this off, it won't take more than an hour. If you hear any shooting, get both engines started."

He turned and stared toward the cottages on the far side of the roadway, counting left to right. Miguel had said that there were two guards, one always on duty, the other asleep in a shed maintained for the compound guards off duty. He tucked the .38 in his belt and took a guitar string from his hip pocket, carefully uncoiling it.

429

He breathed deeply twice and started toward the lights on the far side of the compound.

From behind him, Enrico stage-whispered, "It's an E-string that Hernando kept as a spare. Wash it off before you return it, *maestro*." The laughter followed him.

CHAPTER

19

She heard the crunch of gravel in the drive as the jeep braked
to a stop, heard the engine die finally, after long minutes,
heard the doors slam shut.

Alicia ran to the window of the darkened dining room
and drew the curtain back only inches, watching as two men
slowly walked up the pathway. They were speaking in low,
agitated tones. She recognized Julio's voice then Brocassie's.
Almost unconsciously, she crossed herself. Until now, she
hadn't believed that Julio would actually bring him here. If
what Julio had said was true, he was taking an enormous risk
and she had already prepared herself emotionally for the
crushing blow of the excuse that he would manufacture. But it
was Brocassie. As her eyes adjusted to the dim light, she saw
his slightly stooped frame, the loping gait of his walk. She
wanted to shout the joy of seeing him again.

She discreetly brushed the curtains back into position and
hurried back into the kitchen, reduced the flame of the oven,

and, pausing to check her hair in the reflection of a window, ran to the front door.

Both of them were already in the tiny hallway. Álvarez was leading, his wrist handcuffed to Brocassie's. He gave her a smile but it was brittle and dangerous.

"I believe that you know each other," he said sarcastically. He pulled a key from his pocket, unlocked the cuff from his own wrist and clamped it on Brocassie's free wrist. "He's a very special guest and I don't want to lose track of him."

She wasn't listening to Julio. She was transfixed, her eyes locked to Brocassie's.

"Hello, Alicia," he said softly. He looked down at the handcuffs. "Sorry about these. Julio doesn't think that I'm trustworthy." Awkwardly, like a small boy, he grinned.

Unaware of what she was doing, she crushed her body against him and threw her arms around his neck, burying her face against his chest. She was crying, weeping, laughing. "Oh, my God," she whispered. "My God, my God, my God. You're safe!" She turned her face up to him and kissed him hard, smelling his smell, tasting his flesh. He kissed her back, awkwardly, his manacled hands useless.

"*Bitch!*" Álvarez yanked her away, spinning her against the wall of the foyer. "You think I'm going to be made a fool of in my own house?" He slammed his fist into the wall just above her head, cracking the plaster, and wheeled back on her.

"That's the fucking end of it. I'm taking him back now." He yanked Brocassie's arm, shoving him at her. "Look hard, Alicia!" He jerked his thumb toward Brocassie. "Two hands, two feet, a stiff cock and bulging balls. Ask him to count from one to ten. His brain, whatever he had, is still in one piece." He was furious, his face splotched with red, his eyes hard and black like onyx.

Terror overtook her, sapping her of strength. How insane to have lost control. The ultimate stupidity. Álvarez was already unlocking Brocassie's handcuffs, about to snap one cuff to his own wrist.

"*Wait!*" she cried. She grabbed Julio's elbow, clutching it hard in her grip, not allowing him to move. "Julio—oh, I'm so sorry. It was a shock seeing him again. You have to understand."

The muscles in his jaw were jumping, the veins of his neck corded and pulsing. He was dangerously near striking her.

She relaxed her grip, letting her hand slip down along his forearm, taking his hand in hers. "Julio—please. It was stupid of me. But we all shared so much. I couldn't help myself. If it had been you, I would have done the same." She paused, raising her eyes to his. "Please forgive me. You've kept your part of the contract, just as you promised. Now I'll keep mine if only you'll have some patience with me." For a second his face was immobile but then she saw his expression soften.

For a second their eyes locked, his squinting as if trying to gauge her compliance, and then he snorted in some kind of acceptance and the fear in her evaporated, leaving her light and giddy. Now he was laughing but it was a humorless kind of laugh with a cutting edge. He turned away from her, unlocking Brocassie's cuffs. "I'll leave them off if you give me your word."

Brocassie nodded. "Scout's honor."

Álvarez shot him a look of distrust. "I said your word, Brocassie." He paused, the key not fully turned.

"You have my word, Julio."

Álvarez nodded. "All right, no hassles." He looked down at his watch. "Nine-fifty. We've got an hour or so. You want something to drink?"

"Whatever you're having." Brocassie sat down in one of the leather chairs, crossing his legs. She caught his eye for just a second, touched her heart and then turned, retreating to the kitchen. A tray of liquor, glasses and a bowl of ice was already laid out. She brought it back into the living room and poured all three of them Scotch and soda.

"To all of us," she toasted, ". . . to the old days."

Álvarez looked at her with a twisted smile on his face and then shrugged. "Why not?" He mimicked her gesture and they drank.

The silence in the room was like the humidity after an early morning rain, oppressive, almost smothering. Brocassie started to say something but held his silence. The clock in the hallway ticked, the ice in their glasses clinked, but there were no words and Alicia realized that in some ways it had always been like this with the three of them together: the equation of one plus two which equaled nothing.

She left most of her drink unfinished and stood up, smoothing her skirt. "The meal will be ready soon. *Matambre* and squash. And I made some ice cream." There was no response from either man. She smiled faintly and went to the kitchen.

She heard Julio ask Brocassie a question and then the mutter of his reply and a conversation started—just scraps of words, nothing recognizable. She listened for a few more seconds then went to the back door. She unlocked the latch and cracked the door open, wedging it with a folded newspaper to keep it from swinging inward. In the window over the sink, she drew the curtains fully open and hung a faded green dish towel over the rod, then drew the curtains closed enough to overlap the towel. Seen from the backyard, it would shield the light from the kitchen as well as provide a green cast which was the signal to Porto that both Brocassie and Álvarez were here.

She removed the *matambre* from the oven, letting it cool while she mashed the squash. Everything normal. Just keep going through the motions, but her mind was racing ahead. She had a pair of fatigues, balled up in the corner of the kitchen pantry. Matches in the pockets, with strings of dried meat and a package of sugar cubes. A knife, a flashlight. Next to the fatigues were a pair of tennis shoes, already blackened with shoe polish. Maroto had taught her that.

She edged to the door connecting into the hallway. Low conversation, long pauses, sounds that men make when they're ill at ease with each other. The sound of liquid splashing into a glass, followed by the chunk of ice cubes being dropped into the liquor. The scratch of a match and then the faint acrid smell of harsh tobacco.

A glance at the clock: 10:05. She lit a low flame under the coffeepot and then carried the *matambre* in on an asbestos pad, placing it on the table, and followed it with the dishes of squash and *frijoles negros.* From the refrigerator, she withdrew a bottle of dry Hungarian red, decanted it into a carafe and placed it on the table, next to Julio's seat.

The three of them sat down, Julio at the head of the table, Alicia and Brocassie on either side, facing each other. It had all the joy of the Last Supper, she thought grimly.

They ate in silence, mechanically, withdrawn in their own thoughts.

She glanced at the hall clock again. Ten-thirteen. It had to be now, because there wasn't any time left. She arched her foot out of her pump, kicking it aside, and moved her stockinged toes forward. She contacted hard boots which did not move. Álvarez was digging down into the squash with his fork and shoveling the food in, hardly pausing between mouthfuls. She chanced a look at Brocassie and found his eyes already on hers. She pressed down on the toe of his boot and he flickered a smile.

She tapped again, agonizingly, slowly, spacing out the Morse code with her foot, keeping the words simple.

Do you understand me?

He wrinkled his forehead, a question on his face.

She tapped the message again, more slowly, spacing out the dots and dashes.

This time he nodded marginally and forked up some *frijoles,* keeping his eyes on his plate.

She tried again. *Porto coming here. Escape set up.*

He frowned slightly. It took three beats of her heart for him to comprehend but then he nodded again and picked up the wineglass. "Great," he said, raising his glass. "Anything is better than what Julio and buddies provide but this is excellent."

Álvarez paused, looking at them both and nodded. "I agree. Damned good, Alicia. Better than the *matambre* that we used to get in Dimo's restaurant in Camagüey—remember? The old Argentine guy." Julio bent down again, spearing the beans on his fork.

Brocassie toasted her silently. "How did you do this?" he asked, touching his fork to the *matambre.*

"It's hard to get something like this together on short no-

435

tice, but I think it's a success." She touched his boot again, tapping it out carefully. *Between now and eleven. Does he have gun?*

Brocassie hesitated, then touched his left breast.

She glanced at Álvarez, understanding. A shoulder holster under his jacket, something she hadn't planned on because within the compound, he seldom was armed. Involuntarily, she shuddered, knowing that Porto could never be able to get through the kitchen door and into the dining room before Julio would draw his weapon.

Time was running out. Ten twenty-two. If Porto had made it this far . . . if. But it was something she couldn't even think to question. He had to make it and he would be prepared to enter the house on her final signal: a candle lit in the window of the downstairs bathroom. Damn, she swore to herself. I did this wrong, all wrong. So clever and yet it was the most vital part that I didn't anticipate.

Julio pushed his plate back, checked his watch and looked at her. "We don't have much longer. You said that you made ice cream?"

She nodded, picking up her unfinished plate. Half an hour left, perhaps less. It had to be done now. She pushed her chair away and stood up. "Ice cream, *fresas* and a *cafecito* in just a minute." She stacked their plates and took them to the kitchen, turned the fire up under the coffee and then slipped through the connecting door to the downstairs bathroom.

She slowly slid up the window and stood there, listening. Nothing except the normal night sounds: creaks and chirps and wind rustling in the trees. She picked up the book of matches and struck one. It flared, almost smothered and finally burned with a strong flame. She lit the candle and moved it to the windowsill. Only two minutes now and Porto would enter. Somehow, she had to distract Julio, to immobilize him for the seconds that it would take Porto to enter the house. She was still holding the spent match in her fingers and she looked down at it, knowing that there was a way.

From the stove, she took the boiling coffeepot, removing the lid and basket which held the grounds. Using a hot pad, she carried it into the dining room.

Álvarez was droning on about how Fidel was upping the

cane crop, keeping the conversation in neutral territory. Occasionally, he would glance at his watch. It was obvious that he was nervous, anxious to get Brocassie back to the complex.

Taking the cups and saucers from the sideboard, she put one in front of each place setting. A minute gone, perhaps more.

The two candles on the table flickered. She felt the draft, her skin sensitized—heard just the barest creak of the kitchen door hinges.

Álvarez noticed the change in some subliminal way: he was distracted, but not able to pinpoint why.

"Hand me your cup, Julio," she said, just a shade overly loud. "And mind—the coffee's scalding hot."

Without looking, he held out the cup, picking up the conversation where he had left off.

She stood there, the coffeepot in her hand, waiting, her heart pounding.

Álvarez turned his face toward her, lifting the cup. "You serving me some coffee or not?" he asked impatiently.

She nodded, hearing the scuff of a boot on the kitchen floor. "Yes. Of course. I was daydreaming." She started to pour and then upended the pot, cascading scalding coffee over his hand.

He screamed and jumped up, shaking his hand. "*DAMN YOU!*" he shouted. She snatched up a napkin, wrapped his fist in it and poured ice water over it. Álvarez was whipping his hand, groaning and swearing at the same time. "Stupid bitch! You don't have the brains of a . . ."

Porto stood relaxed in the kitchen doorway, a revolver pointed at Álvarez's stomach. "Move away from him, lady. Brocassie—move back away from the table."

Brocassie nodded. "He has a gun in a shoulder holster."

"With your left hand, *Comandante*," Porto warned. "Two fingers only. Take it out slowly and drop it on the floor."

Álvarez's face was ashen. Without protest, he withdrew the semi-automatic and dropped it.

Waving his .38, Porto motioned Álvarez into the living room. "On the couch. Facedown, hands behind your back."

"You're Porto—the other half of the act?" Álvarez grunted.

"Come on, Álvarez. Move it."

"She set this up, didn't she?"

Porto gave Álvarez a shove, propelling him forward. "Brocassie—check the front of the house. See if you can spot Álvarez's guard. Maroto wanted me to take him out, but I never saw the bastard so I just slipped around through the backyard." He turned to her. "How bad is his hand?"

Álvarez was facedown on the couch, his face turned to the side, blowing on the red-blotched skin of his wrist. She examined his skin, touching the puffy swelling. Álvarez winced and snatched his hand away.

"Superficial. I'll get some ice on it immediately."

Nodding, Porto switched out two of the lights, leaving just a dim desk lamp on. "Just as well. He has to do some traveling tonight and Maroto has bugger-all for medical supplies." He glanced out between the curtains and turned back to her. "Lock the back door first. You have any old clothes—preferably something dark—hiking shoes?"

She nodded.

"OK—then get them on and be ready to move in ten minutes." He picked up a cigar from the humidor, bit off the end and then lit it, inhaling with pleasure. "You have the very best, *Comandante*. These were worth the trip." He scooped up the remainder and stuffed them into his fatigue pocket. "What's going on out there, 'Cassie?"

Dropping the curtain aside, Brocassie turned away from the window. "The guard's two cottages down, talking to some militia guy in a jeep." He turned to her. "Short and heavy with a forage cap and dressed in fatigues—carbine slung over his back, overly long hair?"

She nodded, not speaking, and then walked slowly over to him, never taking her eyes from his face. More lines now around his mouth, and wrinkles radiating out from the corners of his eyes. Still the same lopsided twist of his mouth. Thinner now, with gray in his hair around the temples. Eyes deeper set and two separate scars, one barely healed. Oh, God, she thought, how much I owe You if you can see us safely through this night.

He was smiling at her in the same way that had haunted her for the last three years. She reached up and kissed him, her mouth open, felt herself molding into the warmth and pressure of his body. She held him, moving her hands over his back, along the side of his neck, across his cheeks. She opened her eyes. "Did they hurt you?"

"Nothing that shows." He held her for a long time, working his hands over her back, stroking her spine, and then pulled back. "There isn't time now. There will be later. But now, you have to get ready." He said it to her very quietly, very privately, just a whisper.

She took the collars of his fatigues and gripped them, pulling his face down to hers. She kissed him once more on the neck and then rushed for the kitchen.

Brocassie hunched down on the arm of the couch. "How you doing, Julio?"

Álvarez twisted his neck around, looking up. "You idiot. You're not going to get out of here in one piece, you realize that? You just signed your own death certificate and hers as well."

"That's a possibility, isn't it? But never reaching El Condado was a very real probability. Roychenko had already ordered Piedra to blow me away, hadn't he? The crap that you and Roychenko concocted about me being traded off for guys held by the CIA. You're a perennial con artist, Julio."

"I didn't know anything about—"

"Because you didn't want to know. And you would have somehow talked yourself into believing it when Roychenko told you in a couple of days that I was unfortunately killed while trying to escape. It was so damned obvious."

"Really, Brocassie? And if it was that obvious, why did you make the tape?" Turning his head away, Álvarez pressed his face down against the cushions.

"I made *a* tape, Julio, but not the one you planned on."

"You bullshitter!" Álvarez rasped, turning over, facing Brocassie. "I ran that tape through a machine a dozen times. And the best people Roychenko has analyzed it and they found nothing other than what we scripted. I was present when Lunts interrogated you under drugs and you told him that there was no pre-agreed-upon coded wording to indicate that you were making it under duress—just the signature in urine on the tape container."

"Almost right—not quite," Brocassie answered. "Lunts didn't push my scrambled brains quite hard enough. He automatically assumed that the signature would be on the container box for the tape. But that wasn't the way we worked it. Any tape going back to Porto or on to Guantánamo was to have my signature on the back of the magnetic tape, written with a toothpick or pen dipped in urine. Hagger was right about one thing—simplicity of operations is the best security because anyone looking at the tape for some kind of secret message is going to analyze the content, not the actual tape itself. True?"

"Maybe so, but running the tape through the machine a dozen times would smear your urine, even if it was completely dried. Hagger might find that there was nothing more than a tape that stinks."

"Uh-uh, Julio. The Italians used such a system during World War II. The CIA technical division checked it out. Enough uric acid is left imbedded in the ferrous oxide of the tape backing, even if the tape is washed in an alkaline solution. Hagger will run that thing through a chemical wash and know all the details of your operation ten minutes after he's gotten his hands on the reel."

"What . . . what else did you put on that tape?"

"Reams, Julio. First off, to hold Luis as the mole who blew me. Then a rough description of the interior layout of the complex. Some idea of the pattern and spacing of how the FROG missile silos are laid out. The fact that they're actually FROG Three-A's."

Álvarez's face relaxed slightly and he managed a weak smile. "So no big deal. We lose Luis but he's served his purpose. It's actually better this way, Brocassie, in fact ideal, because you've independently confirmed what the site is. He'll have what he wanted."

"That wasn't all of it, Julio. Those monitoring consoles down at the end of your shop—the ones that the strong, silent KGB types hovered over. What's their purpose?"

"You know damn well what they're for!" Álvarez had rolled over on his side, his face flushed. "Those consoles monitor the entire complex. They're there to alert us to any one of several types of dangerous conditions—explosive fumes, over-concentrations of carbon monoxide—stuff like that."

"But there's something else you check for, Julio—some other potentially hazardous condition. I saw the consoles. Three meters along the top of the backplate of the console, like all the rest, which could be switched to any one of hundreds of sensors. The meters were individually marked with the stylized letters that looked like *a, b* and a weird symbol which resembled a fish standing on its head. Familiar and yet not familiar." He pulled a pen from Álvarez's breast pocket and drew three symbols on the plastered wall of the living room:

$$\alpha \qquad b \qquad \gamma$$

He tapped them with the pen. "What do they stand for, Julio?"

"Those meters check for the quality of the air out of the air-conditioning system."

"Such as?"

"Shit—I don't keep up on that stuff. Technicians handle that end of things."

Brocassie flicked his finger against the burned area of Álvarez's skin, as if he were snapping a dead fly off a table.

Álvarez started to scream and Brocassie quickly shoved Julio's face into the cushions, muffling his voice. "Like—what—do—they—monitor, Julio?" He pulled Álvarez upward by his hair.

"*Christ's sake!*" Álvarez hissed. "How in hell do I know? Oxygen, carbon dioxide, methane, carbon monoxide—stuff like that!"

He let Álvarez's head back down gently. "It doesn't really matter, Julio. I know now." He bent down again. "I thought about those three letters for a long time, Julio. Something not quite right about them. Russian equipment, right? So I first figured those letters were Cyrillic. Then I realized that they could be from some other language, Roman maybe. And it finally dawned on me. They were Greek. Greek letters, Julio. That's right, isn't it?"

Álvarez shook his head.

Brocassie put his lips next to Álvarez's ear. "But you do know, don't you, Julio? Those letters stand for alpha, beta and gamma." He grabbed Álvarez's hair and twisted the strands, pulling up on it as he shoved down on his neck with his other hand, keeping Álvarez's mouth buried in the cushions. "You're the *bullshitter*. The sensors are in little boxes up on the walls, all over the complex, probably in every silo. And they're there to monitor for alpha, beta and gamma radiation in the event of a leakage from a nuclear warhead! That's what those FROGs are armed with!" He jammed Álvarez's head deeper into the cushions and Álvarez was now thrashing his body, suffocating.

"Back off," Porto hissed abruptly.

He dimly realized that he was losing control, sliding past that point of rationality.

Alicia ran across the room and pulled him away. "No," she whispered. "Not like this."

He hesitated, the pressure of her hands drawing him away, and then he stood up slowly, looking down on Álvarez, gradually regaining control. His heart was still thudding, the heat of anger still burning in his body, his chest heaving, but gradually he calmed under her touch. For a moment, he leaned against the wall, trying to shut everything out of his brain. He inhaled deeply, filling his lungs and letting it out slowly in a sigh. "It doesn't matter," he finally said, turning back. "Hagger is going to listen to that tape and then read the back of it. From there on out, it's in Kennedy's hands."

"And what do you think Kennedy would do about them?" Álvarez had turned his head sideways, his face drawn.

"What he has to do. It's a direct threat. He laid it out months ago—no nuclear weapons imported into the Western Hemisphere by a foreign power. He's going to invade Cuba, Julio, and the nuclear weapons in this complex are his moral justification to do so. He's got to get rid of them first before the invasion force is within range of the coast."

"How would he eliminate them? The complex is damn near invulnerable."

"He'll have to take losses but he'll blow the bejesus out of this valley. My guess is that he'll use saturation bombing with a wing of B-52s."

Álvarez struggled into a sitting position. "Can you contact Hagger?" There was an intensity that Brocassie had never heard before in his brother's voice.

"Not for days. Not unless—until, we get out of here—out of Cuba."

"You've got to somehow get word to Hagger, because he or whoever it is that pulls Kennedy's chain has to convince him that if he decides to launch a bombing raid against this valley, it'll trigger the next and last war."

"That's garbage, Julio. The Soviets didn't leave him any option. Kennedy's going to take out this whole complex to get rid of those nuclear warheads and the Soviets aren't going to war over it. They gambled and they lost but they're not going to blow the planet apart to protect Cuba and a bunch of short-range coastal defense missiles."

"*NO, DAMMIT!*" Julio spat. "You're wrong, dead wrong. Those silos are filled with one hundred and twenty long-range nuclear missiles, and if Kennedy bombs this valley, a good hunk of the United States is going to go up in radioactive smoke."

All three of them froze, staring at Álvarez.

"What do you mean?" Brocassie got down on the floor, his face at the level of Álvarez's. "You showed me those goddamn Sandals. I picked one at random and I saw with my own eyes that they were fiberglass shells."

"They are. Those SS-4s, all sixty of them, are fiberglass. Exact replicas of the SS-4 intermediate-range Sandal missile and they're sitting on their launchers right now on the west coast of Cuba."

"*Then what in the hell are you babbling about?*"

"When those fiberglass shells were shipped into Cuba, each held two SSN-5 Serb missiles—the missile that Soviet Delta and Hotel Class subs use. The replicas of the Sandals were used as shipping containers for the Serbs. Once they arrived in Cuba, they were freighted down here by rail and the SSN-5s were removed, checked out and installed in silos. Then the Sandal shells were reshipped back up to the west coast. See the logic—Kennedy and his CIA goons will be concentrating on the Sandals when the real threat is hidden down here."

"The Serb SSN-5s—what kind of capability?"

"A lot smaller than the SS-4s but they're state of the art: solid-fuel propellant, inertial guidance. The nuclear warheads came in separately so that two Serbs could be packed in each Sandal's shell. But now the warheads are mated to the Serbs and they're operationally ready. They can nuke anything south of Minneapolis and east of L.A. at one megaton a shot."

Brocassie grabbed Álvarez by the collar and twisted. *"WHY?"*

Álvarez was choking, his eyes bulging out. Brocassie shook him like a rag doll. *"WHY, YOU FUCKER, DID THEY DO IT?"*

Álvarez jerked away. His eyes were wild, his breath coming in gasps. "There's some kind of power struggle going on in the Politburo. The Red Army and the KGB are behind it and they're trashing Khrushchev and installing Brezhnev. Andropov, the head of the KGB, worked out all the details and selected a general by the name of Lazarev to put this thing into effect. Roychenko answers directly to Lazarev." He coughed twice, violently, the spasm shaking his entire body. "Eventually, the Soviet military figure that they're going to have a war with the States—a nuclear war. They know that the United States is responding to it by setting up early-warning radar chains across the Arctic Circle, watching for incoming missiles and bombers. If the Pentagon spots an attack coming in over the pole on radar, it's got maybe twenty to thirty minutes at least to launch the bombers and start fueling the missiles. But the United States doesn't have any radar systems aimed south. If the Soviets launched these one hundred and twenty Serbs, those damn things would be impacting on American silos and the airfields before anyone in the Pentagon knew what was happening because their flight time is less than ten minutes and there's no radar coverage facing south to warn of an attack. If the plan goes right, with the U.S. missiles removed from Europe, the Soviets would be able literally to decapitate your nuclear forces with just the Serbs and still have their entire bomber, missile and submarine forces still in reserve. The United States would have to surrender with nothing left to fight with."

"When were they planning to do this?"

Shaking his head, Álvarez whispered, "Brocassie—I don't know, I don't know. They're not going to tell some little pissant like me their plans. Roychenko alluded to a timetable of twenty years but he's also intimated that it could be sooner—much sooner."

"And if Kennedy carpet-bombed the shit out of this valley?"

Álvarez inched himself into a sitting position, his face blotched, his eyes squinting. "Roychenko talked to me this morning about the power struggle that's going on inside the Politburo. He didn't say it in so many words but I think that there's a radical faction on Brezhnev's side that wants to use these missiles now, before the United States deploys all the new stuff that Kennedy has in the pipeline. The force levels of the Soviets and Americans are pretty equal, not counting these Serbs, but in a year, it will be heavily weighted on the American side. If Kennedy attacks, the radical faction would use that as an excuse to fire these missiles and launch a total nuclear war." He looked up at Brocassie. "You've got to get through to Hagger to stop any bomber attack because if you don't, it's the end of everything."

CHAPTER

20

"What time now?" he asked.

Porto checked his watch with the light from a match. "Eleven fifteen." He whipped the match out and dropped it. He was highly agitated, fiddling with his hands, scratching his neck, smoking cigar after cigar until the atmosphere of the darkened dining room was stratified with layers of stale tobacco smoke.

They had left Álvarez handcuffed in the living room with Alicia watching over him while they sorted through their options. A neat word, Brocassie thought. "Options," like alternatives, like different ways of approaching the same problem but with selectively unique parameters. Also a nifty word, "parameters." A Hagger word, to be spoken in sterile, air-conditioned offices while tapping a pointer against a briefing board, but that was a world away. The subject here was escape and evasion and ultimately, survival. But survival for how many people—that was the real question.

"It's the only way," Porto demanded, interrupting his train of thought. "Maroto and I've worked it out. Two trucks: me and Alicia in one and Enrico, you and Álvarez in the other. We just pull out of line and drive back to the gate. If they try to stop us, we zap the guards with a couple of clips from the AK-47s; then full steam ahead and crash the barrier. Maroto will give us covering fire from this side of the river if it's necessary. When we're over the bridge, I'll blow the supports with some of the C-4 explosive and that will give us at least an hour's head start. When we've climbed the Sierra road to the kilometer forty-one post, we ditch the vehicles and blow them up. Four or five of Maroto's column will be there waiting for us to cover our escape and if there aren't any problems, we'll hook up with Maroto by dawn at his number eight camp—one that Luis doesn't know about."

Brocassie could sense Porto's tension in the tone of his voice. He's already mortgaged his ass to save me, he thought, and now I'm going to have to tell him that there isn't an easy way out. Brocassie had made up his mind. "Those tankers are carrying gasoline. How much?"

"Between eight and nine thousand gallons each."

"And gasoline is somewhere about seven pounds a gallon. You're lugging about sixty thousand pounds of fuel. Those trucks will have to be kept in low gear the whole time they're climbing up through five thousand feet of elevation. Too damn slow, Porto. Plus the other obvious drawback. One bullet into either of those tanks and we'll go up like a firecracker."

"Shit—if we have to we'll wait until the trucks are ordered to off-load the fuel. The trucks will be empty a couple of hours before dawn. We'll go then."

"Can't do it that way. Álvarez has to have me back by one A.M. Sergio Piedra is coming to pick me up then. If I'm not in that cell, all hell would break loose. And that leaves us just one choice."

"Like what?"

"There's an access path through the minefield which leads to the river. It's only a couple of feet wide and it zigzags but the grass is beaten down and you can feel it if you're careful. It starts next to the concrete pump house and leads down to the shore. It's a safe passage, provided that you know exactly where it is. *If* we can get past Álvarez's personal guards and the other regular patrols on the perimeter, we could get Alicia to the edge of the river and link up with Maroto. She knows the whole story about the missiles. Maroto would be able to get her and Miguel out of Cuba if anything happened to us."

Porto choked, coughing. He stomped out the cigar on the floor and hunched forward, keeping his voice low but it was ragged. "What in hell do you think the two of us are going to do? Stay here?"

"Yes. Those missiles have to be destroyed because if they're not—"

"Shit on that, Brocassie!" he hissed. "Hagger gave us a commission to come in here and do surveillance. It's up to Hagger now. Even if we could walk right into that complex, we couldn't destroy those things. One hundred twenty silos, spaced out over two square miles, all capable of being sealed off from each other by blast doors a couple of feet thick. You were telling me less than five minutes ago about the security underground. We'd be doing great even to get into the main tunnel entrance before we got smeared."

Broccassie could feel the tension between them, feel Porto's anger and fear, recognize his own. No sound except their breathing and the beginning tattoo of a light rain drumming on the roof.

"Porto, we gave Hagger a lot more than he could have expected out of us, and we both have what we personally came for—Miguel and Alicia. But I have a responsibility beyond that. I can't duck it and I can't do it alone. Porto—I need your help; together, we could pull it off."

A rain squall hit the cottage, rattling the windows and causing the corrugated roof panels to groan. Both of them listened for a minute, knowing that rain would make an escape all the more difficult.

There was something more than just anger in Porto's voice: the first rumbling of rebellion. "You just don't understand, do you, Brocassie," Porto spat back, "that a lot of people laid it on the line to get you and this woman out of here? There's nothing more we can do here except get ourselves killed in some kind of a half-assed attempt to destroy the complex. To me, it's plain and simple; get out and get to Hagger. In two or three days' maximum, we could be out of this country." He hammered his fist down on the table. "Screw it! We've done all we can do so let's get out of here." He shoved his chair back and started to stand up.

Not moving, not looking up, Brocassie said softly, "We can't leave it that long. We have to assume that Hagger has that tape right now. He's going to kick it into Steen's lap and then Steen is going to be bellowing in the ear of the director of the CIA, and you'd better believe that they'll be all over Kennedy to get a preemptive air strike launched without delay. We can't afford to wait two or three days, Porto. You understand that? We can't even wait a day. That tape is all the information that Hagger needs to convince Steen and Steen has a pipeline directly to the head of the CIA. From there on in, it'll have a momentum all its own and it's my guess that a raid will come no later than tomorrow night, perhaps even sooner."

He felt the catch in his throat, the dryness of his tongue, and tried not to visualize the image that was already burned into his brain. "If that raid comes off and the Soviets launch, then I'm the bastard that's responsible for millions of deaths. It's always been academic, hasn't it? Numbers of warheads, megatonnage, range, accuracy—all the crap about mutually assured destruction, credible deterrence—but now we're looking at the end result and that's a thermonuclear war. And we've got to do whatever it takes to stop it. Because if we don't, there's nothing left to go back to."

Sighing, Porto hunched forward in his chair, his face in his hands. He sat like that for a long time, not moving, not saying anything, and then he looked up. Brocassie could see nothing of his expression, only the glint of light in his eyes reflected from the dim living-room lamp.

"Tell me your plan and it better be damn good."

The first assault of the cold front had swept through the valley, driving pelting curtains of rain before it, but now the violence was gone out of it, leaving only a persistent drizzle and patchy ground fog. Lightning from the retreating front staggered in flashes along the *cordillera,* scorching the black horizon.

Alicia pulled the raincoat over her shoulders and opened the front door. The smells of the night rushed at her: wet earth and vegetation, the faintly sick-sweet taint of tropical mold and the musky scent of hibiscus. She breathed deeply, clearing her lungs of the cottage's staleness.

Leaving the door ajar, she walked down the path toward the gate.

Sánchez was lounging under a tree, a poncho pulled over his head, carbine slung easily across his chest. She stopped four or five paces from him.

He was smoking a cigarette and as she approached, he flicked it away into the darkness. *"Señorita?"* It was more of a leer than a greeting.

"The *comandante* wishes you to come inside for a moment."

He pushed himself upright from the support of the tree, not even acknowledging the request, and started toward her.

She let him pass and then followed. For just a second, she hesitated, turning to scan up and down the roadway. There were a few shielded lamps in the motor pool area and the jinking movement of a flashlight near the fuel off-loading standpipes but nothing else.

He was already in the partially opened doorway, stamping his boots on the flagstones and shaking his poncho like a wet dog. She came up behind him. He was slightly off balance, one boot cocked up in front of his other knee, knocking mud off the sole with the butt of his carbine. She glanced back again toward the street to be sure it was clear and then joyfully rammed her foot into his spine. He tumbled forward into the foyer, landing heavily on his shoulder, a half-strangled shriek already forming on his lips. Porto smashed him across the forehead with the butt of his pistol and dragged him inside.

It had taken less than two seconds. She closed the door quickly and stood looking down at the limp figure sprawled on the floor. She was not violent, had always hated violence, but now, standing over the animal lying unconscious on the foyer floor, she tingled with the sweet sense of revenge. There was a thin trickle of blood weeping from the gash on his forehead and his tongue lolled from the side of his mouth like a flattened yellow caterpillar.

Brocassie was already stripping the man of his equipment: the carbine, ammunition pouch. Under the man's poncho, he found a small radio clipped to his belt. A red pilot light glowed and there was the hiss of background static. Damn, he swore to himself. What if the bastard had called in? He was already turning to ask her but she shook her head.

"No—he never touched it."

He held the unit up, examining it, found the power switch and snapped it off. "Who would he communicate with?"

She motioned with her head toward Álvarez. "*His* people—Central Security. They keep in contact with all the aboveground perimeter guards by radio and all the underground checkpoints by telephone."

He turned the unit over in his hand, examining it, wondering. He stood up and took the radio to where Álvarez was lying. Brocassie stripped the surgical tape from Julio's mouth.

"This thing," he asked. "How far does it transmit, how many channels?"

Álvarez eyed him warily. "Two miles maximum. There are twelve channels, each one for a specific purpose, plus one emergency channel."

"And this can be heard underground?"

Álvarez nodded. "Yes—in Central Security. The channel that my own personal guards use is number two. The rest of them are allocated for perimeter fence mobile patrols, compound patrols, complex gate guards, fire fighting—that sort of thing." He paused, looking at Brocassie. "I don't know what dumb trick you think you're up to but I could hear you and Porto arguing. I'd follow his advice and get out of here."

Brocassie drew his hand over his face, feeling the fatigue already swamping him. So little time, so fragile a plan.

"Tell me about the underground fire-fighting system, Julio."

Álvarez's reply was sharp, insolent. "Look, Brocassie, I signed up with Roychenko for the duration. I'm not about to switch sides but I don't want to see a war start. Stop Hagger and no one's going to get hurt. This complex would just become one more thing for the bastards in Washington and Moscow to dicker about. It's a sideshow, *provided* that you can get word to Hagger in time. If you can't ..."

451

"You know that I can't," he replied. "Not for days. So I have to consider other ways, Julio." He took Álvarez's lapels in one hand and drew them together and squeezed gently, the fabric tightening around his brother's throat. "The layout of the fire-fighting system, Julio. From start to finish." He momentarily tightened his grip, compressing the flesh around Álvarez's neck. Almost immediately, Álvarez's face reddened and he started to try to roll out of Brocassie's grip but only managed to tighten the hold. Brocassie released it suddenly and Álvarez fell back against the cushions, panting more from fright than from suffocation.

He bent down over Álvarez, keeping his voice very low. "I'm going to destroy that goddamned complex and you're the only one that can supply the information I need to know. If I have to kill you, I will. If I die or Porto dies, that's part of the risk. The way I look at it, the better your answers, the more likely that a lot of people are going to remain living, so I don't have any qualms about how I get the information out of you. Understood?"

Álvarez nodded.

"The fire-fighting system, Julio . . ." Brocassie prompted.

He sighed. "It starts at the river. There's a four-foot-diameter pipe laid on the bed of the river. That leads underground beneath the minefield, into the concrete well, twenty feet in diameter, all gravity flow. In the pump house are three high-capacity submersible water pumps which are designed, once they're started, to pump ten thousand gallons of water a minute under very high pressure to the complex. You've seen the consoles in Security Control. If we get any remote sensor's indication of spilled fuel, smoke, fire or abnormal heat, the indicator lamp that designates that compartment illuminates on the board and the television monitors automatically switch to that area so that we can visually check it out. Immediately, the blast doors leading to that compartment slam shut. By this time, the pumps have started up and the lines have pressure in them. Remotely, we can control the valves so that the water is only directed to the affected area. The water goes to that compartment and fogs the whole area as long as the pumps are sucking water."

452

"What compartments of the complex are connected to this system?"

"All of them. Main tunnel, power generation stations, workshops . . ."

"The missile silos?"

"Yeah, especially the silos!" A look of realization swept his face. He shook his head. "Oh, you dumb bastard. You think you could drown those things, don't you? Wet them down like you'd put out a trash fire?" He gave a ragged laugh. "Don't waste your time. The Serbs are absolutely waterproof because they were designed to be fired from a sub cruising eighty feet under the sea."

Brocassie ignored the interruption. "Get back to the fogging down of the silos. Is the system automatic or can it *only* be actuated from Security Control?"

Álvarez hesitated, taken off guard. "It's not automatic. Only the sensors. We control the whole thing from there—starting the pumps and shutting them down."

Porto hovered in the background, tapping his watch. "Ten to midnight. We've got to shove off."

Nodding, Brocassie turned back to Álvarez.

"Important question, Julio. What happens if you have more than one silo on fire? Could you activate the valves to fog thirty or forty silos at once?"

Álvarez frowned, thinking. "More than that. It could pump fast enough for about half of the total number of silos. If there were many more, the water pressure would start falling off."

"But if the valves were activated, would you still be able to fog all one hundred twenty silos, even at reduced pressure?"

Chewing his lip, Álvarez studied the rug and then shook his head. "Nothing could ever . . ." He stopped in midsentence, puzzled. "Why are you asking me about this crap?"

"One hundred and twenty silos?" Brocassie repeated impatiently.

He inhaled deeply, held it and blew it out through his nose, like a man who had just learned the bank had called his note. He shook his head. "We could open all the valves at the same time but it would be marginal. There wouldn't be nearly enough pressure. The water from the fogging nozzles would just be pissing out—not enough to do any good. We'd go to carbon dioxide for as long as that would last, but a fire would never spread that far—not with the blast doors. You saw them, Brocassie. They're over two feet thick of armor-plated steel and they're placed at both ends of each tunnel which connects a silo to the main corridor."

Brocassie glanced to Porto, nodded, and splayed out five fingers for the number of minutes that he needed.

"Tell me, Julio," Brocassie asked, "the line that leads from the pump house well to the river. Can that be shut off?"

"That well is always kept closed to the river by a steel sluice gate. It's four tons of steel bedded in watertight seals. Maroto could never get past it."

Brocassie lifted his eyebrows and then glanced at Porto who was already smiling. "Explain, Julio. When you need water, how does the valve open?"

It was almost as if Álvarez had forgotten the situation he was in. He explained the system as if he were a proud father, prattling about his drooling child's Tinker-Toy construction.

"The sluice gate is like a window in a sash. When it's down, it blocks the water intake. If we need water, we start a remote electrical motor which winches the gate up and unblocks the flow. It's the same principle as the kind of gate used in an irrigation canal."

Glancing toward Porto, Brocassie raised his eyebrows again but Porto shook his head, his lips set tight. Brocassie studied his friend for a moment. If that's enough for you, man, it's enough for me, he thought. He nodded toward Álvarez. "You get him ready, Porto," he said quietly. He found Alicia in the kitchen, filling a canteen with water.

She had changed into dark green fatigues, a black sweater pulled over the top. Her hair was drawn back severely, tied with string, and she looked exceptionally beautiful and now, particularly vulnerable.

They stood in front of each other for a long time and he wanted to reach down and hold her but he kept his hands at his sides. He felt powerless and alone, unable to offer her anything except the risk of death.

She put her hands against his chest, sliding them upward around his neck, pulling him down to her, placing her mouth in the hollow of his shoulder. "Hold me," she said.

He lifted his hands and put them around her, moving them up until he held her head.

"You understand what you have to do?" he asked.

She shook her head, working against the pressure of his hands. "You . . . can't go back . . . in there," she whispered, her voice broken.

"There isn't a choice. It won't take more than an hour. Tell Maroto not to wait later than two-thirty and if I'm not out of there, then I want him to pull back across the river. That still gives him three hours until dawn. By then, at least, you'll all be clear of the foothills." He hesitated for a moment, turning her chin up. "You know the whole of it now. It will be your job to tell whoever will listen if something . . ." He found himself swallowing. "I'll be back before then. There's nothing to worry about."

Her fingers suddenly clutched at his shoulder blades, her nails biting deep into his flesh.

"I won't leave without you," she whispered fiercely. "I've waited for you all these years and I'll wait longer but I'm not going to . . ."

He gently put his hand over her mouth. She resisted at first but then calmed. He removed his hand. "Do as I say, Alicia. I'm coming back. But if anything does happen, have Maroto get you out of the country as quickly as possible. Head for Jamaica and then, if you can, for South America. North America might be very dangerous for a long time but regardless, you have to be able to tell what happened." He kissed her forehead lightly. "Your word on it?"

She hesitated and then nodded.

He kissed her more deeply, and reluctantly released her. "We have to go now," he said.

Álvarez was standing in the living room, his hands shackled together with the chain of the handcuffs hooked over a light fixture on the wall. He was stripped to the waist. His eyes wild, Álvarez watched as Porto molded plastic explosive into a small wad no larger than a marble and inserted a contact detonator with a finely braided fishing line attached to it. Porto then pressed the C-4 into a flattened lump on Álvarez's spine, just above the belt line. Over this, he strapped lapping layers of surgical adhesive tape.

Porto was humming, doing the work with precision, obviously enjoying himself. Finally, he led the fishing line diagonally across Álvarez's back and down the sleeve of his own jacket, the line exiting near the left cuff. He glanced up as Brocassie entered the room.

"All set," he said.

"Brocassie! What's this prick bastard doing?"

"Ensuring your good behavior. Obviously, I can't keep a gun on you when we go back into the complex. We'll be linked by handcuffs but that little fishing line will be woven through the links of the handcuffs, up my sleeve and across my back to my free hand. One jerk, Julio, and the detonator goes, as does your spine."

For a moment, Álvarez's mouth hung open and then he recovered, showing teeth and a slow smile. "You stupid bugger. You can't do shit to that complex. It's like a flea trying to fuck an elephant. Leave me here, tied up, and bug out. You'll have five hours head start by the time the sun's up."

"But I need your help, Julio. You want to stop the raid, don't you? It was your suggestion, after all."

"Yes—*shit, yes!*—I want to stop the raid. But I've told you—there's no way possible that you can destroy the Serbs. It can't be done."

Brocassie shook his head. "We think otherwise." He picked up the transceiver which lay on the couch, snapped it on and waited as the radio warmed up. "What channel, Julio, for the officer in charge of the gasoline tanker off-loading operations?"

"Six."

He unhooked the handcuffs from the light fixture and handed the transceiver to Álvarez. "Call him. Tell him that you're coming around to check on how the fuel off-loading is going. Nothing more than that."

"I . . ."

Taking the fishing line, Brocassie took up the slack. *"Do it, Julio!"*

Álvarez's face speckled with sweat. Hesitantly, he keyed the mike.

"Com-fuel, this is Security One on channel six."

A rush of static filled the receiver. Álvarez repeated the call. Again static. He was about to repeat when the speaker crackled.

Security One, this is com-fuel. Duarte here.

"How is the gasoline off-loading going, Sergeant?"

A pause, the mike open, someone talking in the background.

Very well, Comandante. Five more tankers to off-load.

"I'm coming out to check up on some things."

The sound of the mike open, the man breathing into it, probably puzzled, unsure as to how he should respond.

Very well, Comandante.

Álvarez snapped the unit off.

Patting Álvarez on the shoulder, Brocassie said, "Good work, Julio. Now repeat after me exactly what you're going to say to Duarte." Brocassie coached him, keeping it simple, one phrase at a time. In five minutes, he was satisfied. Porto helped Álvarez slide into his shirt, threading the fish line carefully. He unsnapped one of the cuffs and then resnapped it on Brocassie's right wrist, handing Brocassie the keys.

They went to the front door, opened it an inch and stared out into the mist. Nothing. Porto led the way to the jeep.

"Let's go," he said softly.

Porto drove the jeep, Alicia beside him with a fatigue cap pulled well over her hair and face, the guard's poncho wrapped around her. Álvarez and Brocassie sat in the back, the fishline carefully cushioned against the lurching motion by Brocassie's fingertips.

The jeep crossed the wide track which bordered the string of overseers' cottages from the tree-sheltered expanse of the motor pool and freight yards.

Like gigantic aluminum slugs, the tanker trucks were lined up, nose to tail in two parallel columns on the far side of the marshaling yard, sandwiched between the rolling stock and the River Yara. Porto swung from the main track, toward the tankers, bumping over the buried railroad tracks. As they went over the rails, Brocassie sensed that beside him, Álvarez was frozen in terror, believing that even the slightest jerk on the fishing line would blow his spinal column.

Smiling, Brocassie patted Álvarez on the knee. "Relax, Julio. You'll make it."

Enrico drifted out of the shadows of the tanker. Porto got out and talked to him for a few minutes, then returned to the jeep.

"No problems. Only two guards wandering around the tankers. Both of them do a thirty-minute circuit through the motor pool and along the inland edge of the minefield. It's better than I hoped for."

Brocassie bent forward, whispering in Alicia's ear.

"You'll stay here with Enrico until Porto gets back. Then he'll guide you down to the pump house and through the minefield. Maroto's beyond there, on the riverbank. Will you be OK?"

"I can do it."

He kissed her neck gently. "I know you can. Keep well and don't worry. Porto will keep the transceiver and listen for me on the channel that it's set to. I'll call when we're coming out."

She turned, brushed his lips and got out of the jeep. "Come back," she said, her lips almost silently forming the words.

He nodded back to her, "I will."

With Porto at the wheel, Brocassie and Álvarez still wedded by the fishing line, the jeep pulled away, slowly rolling toward the head of the tanker column. Brocassie looked back just once. She lifted her hand to him, tentatively, then crawled up into the tanker's cab.

Sergeant Duarte was a compact little man, all neck and shoulders with a mustache which had wilted in the soft rain. He and the driver of the tanker at the head of the line were wrestling with a fuel hose, trying to detach it from a bronze fill pipe. Duarte was cursing under his breath when Porto pulled the jeep up beside him. Immediately, Duarte and the driver snapped to attention.

Brocassie shoved his elbow into Álvarez's ribs and

Álvarez, like a robot which had just been activated, launched into his act.

"Duarte?"

The sergeant stiffened. "Comandante Álvarez. What is the problem?"

"The problem is fuel contamination. The filters in the complex are blocked with sediment from this damn fuel you're off-loading. Cease pumping immediately."

Duarte about-faced and shut down the pump on the truck. Duarte opened a sump tap on the tank and withdrew a fuel sample, holding a flashlight up to the glass cylinder.

"It is clear, *Comandante!* I check each truck three times. There has been no problem tonight."

"And I'm telling you that there has been! The gasoline is useless—worse than that because the filters must be replaced."

"I don't understand . . ."

"You don't have to understand, Duarte. I want the rest of the crap in this tanker plus the fuel from all the remaining tankers pumped into the river. How many other tankers yet unloaded?"

"Five, sir." Duarte was sloshing the glass cylinder around, his face wrinkled in puzzlement. Finally, he spilled the gasoline onto the grass. *"Comandante,"* Duarte argued, "the fuel hoses are not long enough to reach the river and besides, the danger—"

"Dammit, Duarte, once the gasoline is in the river, it'll be carried downstream. We don't have time to fool around."

"But, *Comandante,* why not send the fuel back to Santiago?"

Álvarez hesitated, unable to counter the argument.

"Because, Duarte," Porto inserted acidly, "we're still short of enough fuel for tomorrow's aircraft operations. By the time those tankers got back to Santiago with full loads, had their fuel off-loaded and took on fresh fuel, they couldn't make it back here to the complex before we ran out."

Duarte stood in the grass, his face blank, waiting for some kind of inspiration.

"Well, Duarte?" Álvarez rasped.

"I could pump it out on the grass."

"Idiot!" Álvarez snapped back. "One spark and the whole

459

lot would blow up. How can you pump it into the river safely? You're in charge here. Earn your damn pay, Sergeant."

Duarte's expression was strained. *"Comandante*—I have no idea how it . . ." His voice trailed in a thin protest.

Easing out of the driver's seat, Porto stood up. *"Comandante*—I think there is a way. Dump the fuel into the pump-house well. That connects by a pipe to the river. The fuel would flow out into the river by gravity flow."

"But that's the firefighting water intake," Duarte objected. He drew himself up rigidly. *"Comandante*—if there was a fire . . ."

Brocassie jammed Álvarez in the ribs. "Tell him to do it," he hissed.

Álvarez turned to Porto. "Excellent idea." Then back to the sergeant. "Duarte, move the trucks over to the pump house and start dumping the gasoline. I'll return to the complex and open the gate valve."

"But, but . . ." Duarte protested, spluttering like a defective outboard motor.

"Duarte," Álvarez snapped, "I want the fuel dumped. *Now!* Lieutenant Porto can oversee the dumping but I want you to return with this driver to Santiago. If you have to, get those sods at the fuel depot out of bed and check each tank for contamination. As each tanker here is finished dumping fuel, I'll have it sent back to Santiago for reloading and I want all of them plus four more tankers back here as soon as possible. You *personally* will monitor the on-loading and if there's any contamination, I'll turn you over to a court-martial for appropriate disciplinary action. Is that *understood?"*

Duarte drew himself up to his full height, smashing the heels of boots together. *"Understood, Comandante!"*

Duarte and the driver rapidly reeled in the fuel hose, capped the fuel feed pipe and rolled the tanker forward another fifty yards toward the shadowy profile of the pump house. Porto remained behind, resting on the hood of the jeep. He turned to Brocassie.

"Five tankers. That's over forty thousand gallons of high octane. Enough?"

"More than enough. Just take care. One spark, Porto, and it's all over. When all the tankers are off-loaded, give me a call on the radio. If no contact, then clear out anyway. And don't wait for me. Just get Maroto back across the river—no excuses. I'll make up the distance. And if I can get to a radio, I'll stay on this channel." He handed Porto the transceiver.

There was a silence between them now. They both knew that Brocassie had not yet figured out how he'd get out in time.

"I'll get Maroto moving but I'll wait on this side of the river until you show," Porto said finally.

"We agreed—"

"We agreed on nothing! It's my ass. I'll wipe it any damn way that I want." He snorted in the darkness. "Don't waste your time, Brocassie. I've decided."

In the darkness, Brocassie shook his head slowly, half-moved, half-irritated, but there was nothing he could do and there wasn't the time to waste.

"Just one thing," he added. "Make sure she gets out with Maroto. I want your word on that."

"You got it, Tonto."

Brocassie got up, pulling Álvarez along with him, and shifted into the front seat, Álvarez on the driver's side. He stuck his free hand toward the silhouette of Porto. Porto wrapped his hand around Brocassie's and they shook.

"See you around, Brocassie," Porto said softly and then, turning, disappeared into the blackness toward the pump house.

461

CHAPTER

21

Álvarez drove down the long ramp, moving slowly under the sodium-vapor lamps which cast a sickly yellow glow on the wet concrete. Rain dripped in a golden chain of pinpoints from the overhang, splattering off the hood. Now under the overhang, the sound of the vehicle's engine reverberated on the concrete walls and ceiling in a hollow, echoing grumble.

First checkpoint. The DGI lieutenant looked up, saluted. No words exchanged, just a slight smile on his face. He glanced at the badges and logged them, saluted again, waving them through.

Álvarez hesitated. "Where's Lieutenant Silva?"

The lieutenant looked up from the logbook. He raised an eyebrow, glanced again at Brocassie and said, "Sick. I was next on the roster, *Comandante.*"

"How about Captain Piedra. Has he made any inquiries about my whereabouts?"

The suggestion of a smile passed across the lieutenant's face before he scanned the pages of the log. "Nothing here." He came erect and snapped a salute. "Have a *very pleasant* evening, *Comandante.*"

Álvarez pulled the jeep twenty yards up the tunnel into a recess off to the side where a dozen or more electric carts were parked.

"Silva was supposed to be on," Álvarez said, almost to himself. "That bastard is one of Piedra's crowd. He wasn't on the replacement roster. What in hell is he doing here?"

"We're past him and that's all that matters. Get out, Julio. Carefully." Brocassie glanced back toward the lieutenant who was casually watching them. Awkwardly, linked together by the handcuffs, they moved to an electric cart. "OK, now head for the cells." With a thin whine, the electric cart started. Julio wheeled back into the tunnel, heading deeper down the long shaft.

"What time is it?" Brocassie asked.

Álvarez was sweating. Under the fluorescent lights, his skin was a ghastly greenish-white color sheened with tiny beads of moisture. He glanced down at his watch. "Ten of one. Piedra might be there already and if he is, he'll have an armed guard with him. And what will you do then, kid?"

Brocassie shook his head, not answering. Piedra would die if it came to the crunch—the consolation prize.

In the main tunnel were two flat cars being off-loaded, the crates lifted by fork trucks and dispatched down to various branching corridors off the main tunnel. The men of the off-loading details were stripped to the waist, grunting and sweating under the arc lights in the high heat and stifling humidity. Three KGB noncom supervisors rapped out commands and two KGB captains stood off to the side, overseeing but distracted, joking with each other. None of them gave any notice to the cart as it passed them.

Second checkpoint. The same man as the previous day— KGB, chunky body, black ball-bearing eyes which seemed to be constantly moving, inspecting them both. He looked at Brocassie, at the handcuffs, and then insolently nodded to Álvarez, ignoring the difference in rank.

"I had a note here that the prisoner was leaving tonight with Captain Piedra," the Russian said. It was more question than statement.

"He's not scheduled to pick up the prisoner for another ten minutes. I'll be in the prisoner's cell. When he gets here, send him down."

The guard didn't even salute, only stamping the logbook and then waving them through the checkpoint.

Álvarez wheeled into the corridor leading to the cells, accelerated down the long hallway and parked the cart at the sliding steel gate which led to the confinement area.

Once inside the cell, Brocassie withdrew the automatic from Álvarez's holster, then rammed home the clip of cartridges that he had kept in his own fatigue pockets, working the action back and chambering a cartridge. Only then did he release the fishing line from his grasp. Motioning Álvarez to sit down on the mattress, he moved the chair to the foot of the cot, straddled it backward and sat down, the automatic cocked and tucked carefully under his belt in the small of his back. From here, he could cover the door of the cell and Julio but Piedra would not be able to see that he was armed.

"Just sit there, relaxed, Julio. Natural last-minute conversation between brothers. Piedra will assume that you're armed and he'll be at ease, off his guard. When he enters the cell, order the guard to come in with him, and to pull the door closed." He leaned over and picked up the tail end of the fishing line, giving it a gentle tug. "Just for once, behave yourself and do what you're told to."

"For God's sake, take this thing off me!"

"Can't, Julio. Keeps you honest." He paused, half-smiling. "And I'd suggest that you not lean back against the wall. Those detonators are touchy."

Álvarez lurched upright, his back ramrod straight. "You shit! You're on some kind of freaking death kick. I know what you're trying to do with the gasoline."

"Tell me, Julio."

Biting down, his jaw rigid, muscles in his cheeks jumping, Álvarez glared at his brother. "You're going to activate the fire-fighting pumps once the pit is filled with gasoline and pump high octane into the silos."

Shaking his head, Brocassie answered, "Not *just* the silos, Julio. The whole complex. And then, when the pumps start to run dry they'll cavitate, overheat and flash off the gasoline in the lines. That flame front will carry to every silo and compartment in this complex."

"You . . ." Álvarez stared at him. "You can't . . ."

"Can, Julio. Not only can but will. I want to be sure that there's nothing left."

"There are close to a thousand men underground!"

"Ninety percent of them Soviets, Julio. Tough, isn't it?" In his mind, he revolted at the thought, knowing that he couldn't pump gasoline into the living areas, but he wanted Álvarez to accept the premise that he would stop at nothing, no quarter given. And besides, he thought, the bomber raid, if Kennedy had the guts to order it, would pound what was left into rubble. There would be nothing remaining underground except shattered, fire-blackened caverns of concrete, poisoned for a century by the plutonium of 120 fractured warheads.

"What about Piedra?" Álvarez asked. "How you going to handle him?"

"What I told you before. Convince him that Roychenko has switched the orders—that you're holding me another couple of days for additional questioning."

"Piedra's not going to buy it!"

"If he doesn't, then both our chances of survival are zip. Piedra has to believe that orders have been changed. You're his superior. Make it stick."

Álvarez bent down, slowly wagging his head like a jerky puppet. "Brocassie—you think you've got this all worked out but there's too much stacked against you. Piedra I can handle maybe, maybe not. He already has his instructions and the first thing that he'll do is call Roychenko for confirmation. Piedra has been trying to discredit me for over a year because he wants my job. Roychenko loves to pit the two of us against each other because that way he gets better results." He clenched his lips and then looked up. "No way he'll believe me, Brocassie. He'll check with Roychenko for sure."

He rubbed his chin with his hand. "And even if Piedra buys it, Security Control is going to be impossible, Brocassie. Standing orders dictate that six men are to be on duty at any given time—an NCO on the communications switchboard, four technicians monitoring the remote sensors and a duty officer to keep them from fucking up. They're all armed. You can't just waltz in there, dump a bunch of valves and fly away like Peter Pan. The best thing, the only thing, is to disarm the explosive and give me that gun right now. No one knows what's transpired. Alicia's probably safe with Maroto by now and that only leaves Porto on the surface. If the pumps don't start, then he'll have to pull out. Maybe he makes it and maybe he doesn't but the risk that you're running is ten times greater. Give it up, man." He watched Brocassie's face expectantly, obviously growing more sure of his ground.

"You were always," Brocassie said slowly, "a prime bastard. Opportunist, cheat, liar. But the thing that I give you credit for is that you're consistent, Julio; you're a survivor first and foremost."

"We both are, brother." Álvarez managed a lopsided grin. "We've both risked our asses but there's a time to quit pushing the odds. Pack it in and hand over my Lastoy. Why die when you can live?"

"Dying and living are relative terms, aren't they?" he answered. "You can live and still die inside and that's what I'm facing if I don't try to do what I know that I have to do. Those bombers are going to be launched. I've got to blow this complex and I need help to do it. So I'm offering you two choices—one or the other, not negotiable." Mentally, he was clocking what Porto would be doing on the surface. Another thirty minutes at least to fill the pit. So many things could go wrong; he didn't want even to consider the possibilities.

"Choice one, Julio. You go with me to Security Control so I can get by the checkpoints. I've got seven cartridges in this Lastoy. You get me inside, then lock the door. At that point, I've got only a few minutes to persuade them to start up the pumps and throw the right switches. As I see it, my probability of doing the job is fifty-fifty and of getting out of there alive is probably closer to zilch. You, of course, share my prospects of early demise with the remaining cartridge."

Álvarez's face was stone blank, betraying no emotion.

Brocassie flicked his finger into a V. "Choice two, Julio.

You help me. You know how the systems work, how to do exactly what I'm trying to accomplish in the fastest way. You help me, play it straight, and I'll let you walk out of there alive. This complex has half a dozen choppers. It'll be sheer chaos, everything ad hoc. Every command will be spur of the moment, just like Korea was when things got out of hand. You've got the rank to commandeer a chopper or a light aircraft with one snap of your fingers. Where you go from there is not my concern. I'm not minimizing the risk but if you don't cooperate or if I see one twitch the wrong way, you're dead meat."

Álvarez smiled grimly. "But there's a third option, isn't there? I can sit on my ass and do nothing and you'll fail. Are you going to drag me out of here against my will or blow my spine off? I don't think you have the balls to do either."

Brocassie drew the Lastoy, cocking the hammer, leveling it on Álvarez's chest. "The detonator in that C-4 is a dud, Julio. There's enough plastic explosive strapped to your back to pulverize anything within a ten-foot radius which would have included me. It just seemed like a good idea at the time to keep you on your best behavior. But this Lastoy's real and it fires real bullets, so try me, Julio." He cupped his hand, palm upward, flexing his fingers. "Come on, Julio. Try it."

"You wouldn't pull that trigger!" Álvarez hunched forward on the cot.

"Move one more inch and you'll find out. Believe me, I can pull this trigger because if you force me to, it's *my* only option." His fist tightened on the grip.

The two of them faced each other, suspended in time. Álvarez was still on the cot, frozen, but his body was coiled, on the verge of springing.

Involuntarily, Brocassie took up the slack of the trigger. He backed up two steps as Álvarez slowly stood up, all in very slow motion, like a puppet unfolding, leaning forward, back tensing, feet spaced well apart.

Brocassie tightened the trigger further, sensing the hammer was on the edge of falling. Hate and anger, frustration, but also pain and love were boiling up in him. *"Back off, Julio! Don't force me to kill you!"*

The sound of boots in the corridor, muffled voices, a pause, the grating of a sole on the concrete. The lock of the door rattled, a key turning. Indecision on Álvarez's face. He hesitated for a second and then stood straighter, his body relaxing, his hand out. "Give me the gun, Brocassie," he said softly. "It's all over."

"Like hell it is," he hissed.

His face flushing, Álvarez hesitated and then took one step backward. He opened his mouth, starting to say something, then closed it, his body sagging onto the cot.

The door swung inward. Piedra paused in the doorframe. "Good evening, *Comandante*. I've been looking for you. Where is the prisoner?"

Álvarez motioned with his head toward Brocassie, who was beyond Piedra's view, off to the side of the cell. "He's here, ready to go." His voice was dead.

Beyond Piedra's view, Brocassie lowered the Lastoy and rammed it under his belt behind his back. He moved forward, toward the center of the cell, trying to keep both Álvarez and Piedra in his line of sight.

Piedra moved into the cell, Petrov, the KGB corridor guard right behind him, his automatic drawn but held negligently, the muzzle pointed at the cell's floor. Piedra glanced at Brocassie, then back at Álvarez.

"It has been difficult finding you, *Comandante*," Piedra said calmly. He settled back on his heels, relaxed, in control, glancing again at Brocassie. "Colonel Roychenko has put the complex on the highest state of alert based on the personal instructions of General Lazarev. I have just given his orders to close all access points. The main tunnel blast doors are to be sealed. The situation is critical. Roychenko's been trying to contact you now for two hours."

"As you can see, I'm here."

"That's obvious, isn't it, but where were you?"

"There was some further interrogation required," Álvarez replied steadily. "Which, as my subordinate officer, is not your concern, *Captain*."

"But it is, *Comandante*," Piedra shot back. "For when does a senior officer interrogate a prisoner outside the holding cells? And when does a senior officer instruct checkpoint secucity personnel not to log the movements of a prisoner? It's obvious that you took the prisoner up to your quarters. How strange, *Comandante*. And there is one other thing that bothers me greatly. In attempting to find you, I ordered that one of the mobile patrols check your quarters. Less than three minutes ago, they reported back that your private guard is absent from duty and no one will come to the door. They're still there, awaiting my orders to break in. Perhaps you can enlighten me on what's happening."

"Get stuffed, Piedra. Those are my private quarters. You're exceeding your authority and I'll have your ass for it. Call those men in."

"I can't do that and still be faithful to my responsibilities as an officer," Piedra replied, as if he were delivering lines he had already rehearsed. "I have specific orders from Colonel Roychenko to find you and to bring you to the Command Post. I interpret that to mean by any method. I'm taking you into custody. It is a reasonable precaution, perhaps unfounded, but I believe that Colonel Roychenko will agree with me on this matter. I'm sure"—he paused and smiled—"that it can all be explained very simply." He nodded to Petrov who raised his automatic to cover Álvarez.

"Stand up," Piedra commanded. He then turned to Brocassie. "I had looked forward to our trip to El Condado but there are other things more pressing. Kneel down, facing away from me, and link your hands behind your neck." The flap on his holster was already unsnapped, his hand closing around the grip.

Brocassie didn't have time to draw the Lastoy. On impulse, he hunched down and lunged at Piedra, smashing into his side, knocking Piedra into Petrov, all three of them tumbling into a sprawling heap.

Petrov's Lastoy cracked once, the jacketed slug ricocheting off the concrete walls. Brocassie fumbled the automatic from his belt but Piedra was suddenly on top of him, slashing with his fist, knocking the Lastoy aside. For seconds they wrestled, and Brocassie knew that he was in trouble—felt the tightness in his stomach, and ache in his chest, knowing that once Petrov had a free field of fire, he was dead.

Piedra broke free, reeling off to one side, his fingers fran-

tically flailing at the flap on his holster, then finally pulling hi.
own automatic free.

Adrenaline surged through Brocassie. He launched him
self against the Cuban, throwing him off balance, both of them
falling heavily against the concrete wall. Instinctively, he knew
that he had to to keep Piedra between him and Petrov. He
lurched sideways, trying to clear his own Lastoy, desperate to
get a shot in, but Piedra was on him again, his left hand gouging at Brocassie's face. Too close to bring the Lastoy to bear
he flailed it sideways like a club against Piedra's throat and
face. Piedra's nose shattered under the impact of the barrel

The Cuban was grunting like a wounded animal, eyes
bulging, blood gushing from his nostrils. He jerked backward
frantically trying to chamber a round with his free hand. I
gave Brocassie only a split second, not even enough time to get
his finger back onto the trigger. He stretched his arm to its full
extent and slammed the weapon down against Piedra's forehead.

The Cuban's jaw worked like a beached fish, gasping for
air. The Lastoy fell from his fingertips and then his hands
scraped at the crushed opening in his skull.

Too late, Brocassie turned. Petrov had risen to a crouch
holding his automatic in a two-handed grip. Staring down the
barrel of the Lastoy, Brocassie realized that he was a hammer's
fall away from death.

Álvarez was a blur, standing behind the guard, swinging
his arm like a club. His forearm connected with the guard's
throat and then he jumped on the Russian, knuckles hammering at the man's face. The guard staggered and fell against
Álvarez, strangling, coughing up blood. Then both of them fell
to the concrete floor of the cell. Álvarez landed first, under the
crushing weight of Petrov, and the Russian twice raised his
Lastoy, pounding it into Álvarez's back. A high-pitched
scream, almost beyond the range of hearing, came from his
mouth.

The Lastoy was in Brocassie's hand. He rammed the barrel into the Russian's back and started to tighten on the trigger
but realized that the bullet would pass through the man's body
into Álvarez's. He hesitated for just an instant, then leaped to
his feet and kicked with his full force against the man's spine.

470

just at the neck level. The toe of his boot hammered squarely into the Russian's collar and the man crumpled forward. His body shuddered violently, then twitched, arching into an impossible shape and slowly, as if deflating, settling against the concrete.

Brocassie scrambled to the entrance of the cell, cracked the door open, listened and then carefully shut it. For seconds, for minutes, there was only the sound of his own panting and Álvarez moaning softly.

Petrov was dead. Brocassie felt for a pulse and could find none. He rolled the Russian off Álvarez and pried the Lastoy from the Russian's hand, dropping it on the floor. Then he turned to examine Piedra.

Piedra was still alive but gray tapioca slime was oozing from the skull opening and his eyes were fully dilated. He suddenly coughed a couple of times—flaccid little eruptions of his lungs—and then delicately curled forward in slow motion until his head touched his thighs. He hacked twice more, shuddered and then his head fell sideways, his mouth open, panting rapidly like a dog in heat.

Turning, Brocassie stared at Álvarez. Bright arterial blood streamed from his nostrils, dripping from his chin. Brocassie found himself immobile, unable to speak or to react.

Álvarez looked up, his hand tentatively reaching out to pick up Petrov's Lastoy which lay between them on the concrete.

Brocassie brought his own weapon up, aiming it at Álvarez. "Huh-uh. Keep your mitts off it."

Withdrawing his hand slowly, Álvarez looked up. "I just saved your worthless hide." He wiped the blood from his nose with the back of his hand and then drew a handkerchief from his jacket pocket, holding it against his face. He nodded to Piedra. "Is that sonofabitch dead?"

Bending down, Brocassie felt for a pulse and found none. He nodded.

"Which makes it all worthwhile," Álvarez breathed.

"Why did you . . . ?" He couldn't even put a name to it.

Álvarez gave a deep, long-winded sigh. He wiped the blood from his nose with the handkerchief, inspected it distastefully and then dabbed again at his nostrils, trying to stanch

471

the flow. Finally he looked up, his face pinched. "I don'
know, Brocassie. I damn well don't know, because if Petro
had shot you, I would have shot him and my slate would be
clean. All questions answered. I may have done the dumbes'
thing that I ever did in my life. You figure it out."

Brocassie's nerves sizzled, yet he felt somehow light
headed, his brain unable to function rationally. *Why?* Wha
Álvarez had said was logical and yet he had acted illogically
Why? He shook his head. "No, Julio, you tell me."

"You're asking me to explain something that I don't understand myself. What the hell—here we are, bastards of the
Revolution, in love with the same woman. Brothers, rivals
enemies, coconspirators, whatever. And now we're both under
the gun." He held up his hand. "Give me the Lastoy. I'm
going with you. We're doing it together or not at all."

"But *why,* Julio?"

Álvarez jerked his head sideways like a boy, balking at his
parents' demands. A trickle of blood had smeared his face at
the corner of his mouth. He wiped at it with his wrist and then
slowly stood up, almost compulsively brushing off the dus'
from his uniform. *"Because!"* he shot back, his face squinched
in anger, in frustration, in almost-sorrow. *"Because* I made a
massive mistake. I bet on the wrong team because I thought I
could stack the odds in my favor. I didn't stop to evaluate the
cost. And now I understand how well they used me. This
wasn't just some cute little ploy that the Soviets were dicking
around with. Not just power politics or the odd sideshow in
some kind of global strategy but the real thing—the cruncher
Cuba is expendable as far as they're concerned, as are millions
of other people who still believe that tomorrow is forever.
Roychenko and Lazarev and the rest of those pricks are going
to blow it, Brocassie. The whole damn ball of wax, the goddamn globe. And I would have been one of the bastards who
helped to pull the trigger!" He held his hand out. "The gun,'
he demanded. "You trust me now, totally, or you kill me right
now. It frankly doesn't make a shit to me because, once those
bombers launch, we're both dead anyway."

The cell stank of death. Piedra's bowels had let go and the
stench permeated the confined concrete room. Brocassie fel'
like retching but he somehow found the strength to hold i'

472

down. "I think," he said carefully, examining Álvarez's eyes, looking for any hint of betrayal and finding nothing except wariness, "that I don't have much choice, Julio." Carefully, he lifted the back of Álvarez's jacket and started to strip away the surgical tape.

Down the corridor in the cart, past the vacant security checkpoint. It was 1:20 A.M. and only a few enlisted men were scuffing down the corridor on the way to the mess hall for an end-of-shift snack. At the vacated security checkpoint, Álvarez braked to a stop and, reaching over, grabbed the telephone.

Brocassie tensed. "What are you doing?"

Holding the handset switch down, Álvarez returned a warped grin. "Two birds with one stone," he answered and then, without pausing, punched in five digits.

"Security—Comandante Álvarez here at number seventeen. Petrov is sick. I've sent him to the infirmary and I want someone down here on the double."

A pause, a tinny voice replying and then Álvarez:

"Who's on duty?"

Álvarez scratched down names on the log with a pen.

"Send Santino." He hesitated for a second. "No—better yet, wait until I get there. Santino can use the electric cart to get back down here. It'll be faster."

Álvarez checked his watch, listening, drumming his fingers against the grip of the handset.

"*Shit, NO*, Sergeant Mesa!" Álvarez shouted into the mouthpiece. "I don't want García called out as Santino's replacement. Tell Santino to get his gear together and be ready. I'll be there in three minutes and by then I want a complete status check on the whole complex." He slammed down the handset and accelerated toward the central tunnel.

"One out of six which leaves five," Álvarez said.

"This Santino—will he check the cells?"

"No reason to." Álvarez pulled a pack of cigarettes from his jacket and passed one to Brocassie. "Santino will hold down the checkpoint and that's all, unless I give him other instructions."

Deeper into the complex, Álvarez ran the machine flat

473

out down the main tunnel, past three branching corridors, past the diesel fuel transfer room, past the Command Post. He decelerated and turned right into a corridor, braking to a halt in front of the double doors of Security Control.

Santino was already there, standing just outside the doorway. A thick-necked, bearded man, his hair overly long, he stiffened as Álvarez pulled up.

Álvarez swung out of the cart.

"Get down to checkpoint seventeen. You hold it until oh four hundred and by then I'll have a replacement."

"*Comandante*—I . . ."

Álvarez gave him a withering look. "Seventeen, Santino!" He gestured toward the cart. "Plug it in on recharge when you get there. Give me call for a status report in ten minutes. If Colonel Roychenko learns that checkpoint seventeen is not manned, he'll fry my ass and I can damn well assure you that I'll fry yours in turn. One other thing—no one is to go to the cells without my express permission."

Santino stiffened and turned his eyes toward Brocassie in an unspoken question.

"He's under my control. Colonel Roychenko's orders," Álvarez snapped.

Santino clicked his heels, arched his hand to his forehead and held it.

Álvarez glared into Santino's face, then returned the salute with a sloppy flip of his wrist. "Get *with it*, Santino."

Security Control was much larger than Brocassie had previously realized. Before, when Álvarez had shown him the room, sliding doors which he thought were a wall had been closed, but now they were open, revealing a mass of TV screens and a lighted status board, showing the entire workings of the complex. Lights winked on and off around the electronic representation of the perimeter fence, showing where patrols were. Two of the three generators had green lights illuminated, indicating that they were in operation while the third displayed an orange light with a STANDBY/READY sign.

Nudging Brocassie, Álvarez guided him up the short flight of stairs into the officer's control booth. Álvarez slid smoothly into the chair behind the central console, motioning Brocassie to take the chair to the left.

Below them, beyond the plate-glass window, four men sat at consoles, monitoring the site's security. On the television screens, Brocassie could see a vast number of different compartments within the complex—some screens monitoring checkpoints, others, the flatcar movements in the main tunnel, still others slowly scanning the interiors of the silos. For the first time he saw the Serbs—tall, lean, featureless and threatening. One camera panned upward along a Serb's airframe, gradually slowing and then stopping, zooming in. A hydraulically positioned work platform had been elevated to the level of the nose cone. Three mechanics were reattaching an inspection plate. At the bottom of the television screen was a superimposed subtitle—Silo #81, tunnel 16, Lt. Samerkov Cmdr., telephone 38814.

Álvarez was suddenly tense. "Oh, shit! Four men down there. There should be five!" He thumbed a switch and then picked up a handset. "Sergeant Mesa—where is Lieutenant Herrera?"

Below them, a man turned away from his console, looking back up toward the control booth and then turning back, picking up his telephone handset.

"*Comandante,* the lieutenant is in the Command Post."

"What the hell for?"

"Sir, Colonel Roychenko ordered that he report there. There's been some trouble with silo eighty-one—a hydraulic leak—and also, something's wrong with the aviation gasoline transfer." He pointed to the display board. "Pipeline three shows no fuel being transferred and we can't raise Sergeant Duarte. Also," he added, "there has been very heavy telex and radio traffic in from the Soviet Union. I don't . . ." Mesa left the sentence unfinished.

Álvarez expelled his breath slowly, glanced at Brocassie and then keyed his mike.

"Call Herrera on the intercom. I want him back here immediately." He flipped the switch off, not waiting for a reply. "This could mean plenty trouble."

"Why?"

"Why—because the officer in charge is not allowed to leave Security Control unless there's an emergency. Any kind of a problem could be handled by telephone, so why in hell did Roychenko need to talk to him personally? Something's screwed up badly."

God, Brocassie thought, it's coming apart. Somehow it had seemed possible, just possible, but now he realized that just possible might be impossible.

"You've got to get Porto on the radio," Brocassie demanded.

Hesitating, Álvarez glanced at his watch. "Very likely bad news if we try," he replied. "He still has ten to fifteen minutes to complete dumping the avgas. If we try to get him now and he doesn't reply, it's sure to raise eyebrows. Sergeant Mesa's one savvy motherfucker. I handpicked him and he's had the best training. If Porto doesn't reply, Mesa is automatically going to want the perimeter guards to check out the operation, maybe already has. We've got to tough it out for at least ten more minutes."

"What then?"

Pointing to the status board, Álvarez traced down an unlighted gray line. "The fire-fighting system. The schematic shows the pump status and the valves. If we have to fight a fire, the senior duty sergeant and the officer in charge agree on the sequence of what's to be done. Then they each individually have to turn keys and actuate switches to start the pumps and open the valves to the area affected. It has to be done simultaneously—from this console up here and from Mesa's console down below—a kind of fail-safe system so that the fire-fighting system isn't started accidentally."

"What happens when the system *is* actuated?"

"All hell breaks loose! Ughha-horns start honking, bells ringing. The blast doors to the affected area close three-quarters of the way, delay for ten seconds and slam shut. Once we start, Brocassie, it'll be a four-alarm bedlam."

"How do we get out of the complex?" He didn't want to know the answer, fearing what it might be, yet knowing that without that hope, there was nothing except sure death.

"We can't get out the main tunnel. It'll be blocked off." He pointed to a door in the control room below. "That's a side

476

corridor which connects Security Control to the Command Post. We've got to get down that, past the control room and then to another door beyond. That leads into a dead-end compartment where there's a freight elevator and a stairway to the hangar revetment buried in the hillside. But understand that once the sensors smell smoke or detect heat, all the blast doors in this complex are going to automatically slam closed. If we delay too long, we'll be trapped."

"What about the men on this level?"

"There are some escape exits—mainly stairwells from the living quarters to concealed openings on the surface. Some of the lucky ones will get out that way, but most of the bastards on duty will fry." He hesitated. "A thousand-odd people, Brocassie. Mostly borscht eaters which is no loss." He paused, his eyes averted. "Then again," he added, "it's a shitty way to go, isn't it?"

Brocassie nodded. A shitty way to go. Forty thousand gallons of gasoline, voraciously sucking up oxygen, roaring down tunnels in walls of superheated gas, vaporizing men and metal with godlike indifference. A shitty way to go, and it might be the way he went.

The escape route Álvarez had laid out seemed like a journey to eternity but it was a way—the slimmest of chances but still, a chance. He glanced down into the control room. The door to the tunnel was just opening and a tall, thin, clean-shaven officer with lieutenant's pips entered, a clipboard in his hand. He went directly to Mesa's console and bent over, talking. Once Mesa started to turn and it was obvious that Herrera immediately cautioned Mesa not to. The motion of the sergeant's neck suddenly ceased and, carefully, almost too casually, he turned back to his console.

Brocassie felt his stomach turn to stone.

Álvarez nudged him with his knee. "You have any bright ideas?"

"We've got to stall until we can get through to Porto—either that or just give it ten more minutes and then start the pumps and hope that there's enough gasoline to do the job."

Nodding, Álvarez leaned back in his chair, giving the appearance of relaxing. "OK, that's the way we'll play it." Below the level of the plate glass, his hand withdrew the Lastoy. He flicked off the safety.

"Herrera is heading up here. If it falls apart for any reason, you cover him and I'll go down below. I've got a full clip and I can take them out. I'll throw all the switches down there and when I yell, you turn this key and, within five seconds, flip this switch." His finger tapped the right-hand corner of the console which was covered by a hinged Plexiglas plate with a key and guarded toggle switch beneath, painted in Day-Glo orange. "You understand?"

He barely had time to nod before Herrera swung open the door. He stood in the frame, highlighted by a fluorescent stairwell lamp, obviously unsure.

"*Comandante,* I've just talked to Colonel Roychenko. He wants to talk to you immediately." Herrera swallowed noisily, waiting for an answer.

Leaning back, the swivel chair creaking against its restraining spring, Álvarez took his time, fishing a cigarette from his pocket and lighting it, casually flicking the still-smoldering match into an ashtray.

"What's he want?" Álvarez exhaled, blowing smoke through the shielded light of the desk lamp, creating a layered gray-blue haze.

Herrera stood straighter, hesitated and said, "*Comandante*—I don't know. He's been trying to reach you for the last hour or so. He ordered both Captain Piedra and me to find you. The telephone in your quarters didn't answer and I sent two of the perimeter guards there on Captain Piedra's instructions. I had no idea you were here. Sergeant Mesa just informed me that you had arrived." Herrera was in a state somewhere between relief and anxiety. "He wants you, I mean Colonel Roychenko . . ." Herrera hesitated a split second, ". . . orders, that you get in touch with him as soon as possible."

We've had it, Brocassie thought. They've captured Porto or worse, Alicia. He gripped the Lastoy, the butt slippery in his hand. His finger curled on the trigger.

Álvarez sat up straighter in the chair, turning slightly toward Herrera.

"Lieutenant, my standing orders are that the officer in

charge of Security Control is never to leave except in the event of an emergency. Tell me why you deserted your post?" He said it unemotionally, but with implied threat.

Herrera was literally twitching. *"Comandante*—I *didn't* leave my post. The colonel ordered that I meet him in the Command Post." He squinted, trying to penetrate the dim light. "Sir, is this man with you cleared?"

"Of course, you twit! Up to and including R level. What the hell are you trying to say?"

Swallowing again, Herrera hesitated. He handed Álvarez the clipboard. "None of the enlisted men knows yet, not even the Russians. Only myself, Sergeant Mesa and the Russian officers in the Command Post that Colonel Roychenko has personally briefed. This teletype came in one hour and fifteen minutes ago from AW-4, signed by General Lazarev. Colonel Roychenko has already asked for and received confirmation of its authenticity."

Álvarez scanned down the yellow sheet, frowned, bit his lip and then reread it more carefully. He looked up.

"This is a joke, Herrera, or some kind of a goddamned test of operational capability."

"Sir—I assure you that it isn't. It was transmitted in the Soviet 55A emergency war order code and the format was properly authenticated. It's the 'standby to launch' order. The Serb warheads are being armed and readiness is increased to condition Bravo. Negotiations between the United States and the Soviets were suddenly broken off. Colonel Roychenko has received relayed satellite intelligence that the Strategic Air Command has launched the entire 23d Bomb Wing from their base in Fort Worth. Forty-five B-52s have cleared the Texas coast and they're heading southeast, out over the Gulf of Mexico, toward Cuba."

"Oh, sweet Jesus! What's the status on the Serbs?" Álvarez's voice was demanding. He quickly glanced down at the status boards and then back to Herrera.

"All but three are ready." Herrera shifted his gaze toward the bank of television monitors in the control room below and then turned back. "Number eighty-one is giving them hydraulic problems but maintenance estimates that the missile will be operationally ready in another half an hour. Numbers twenty-two and fifty-six have electrical faults which can't be isolated. The rest are ready."

Slumping back in the chair, Álvarez closed his eyes. "So this is what Lazarev had planned for, hoped for, all along," he murmured. He pulled himself upright. "OK, Lieutenant, I understand the status. I'm relieving you."

"But, sir . . ."

"But nothing, Herrera. I'm fresh so I'm taking over. I want you to personally get your ass up to the main tunnel and make sure that those two flatcars are out of the complex in ten minutes flat. Tell the work crews to clear the tunnel and secure the storage areas. And then I want you back here in no more than thirty minutes. I'm counting on you." He snapped a salute, not even waiting for Herrera to respond.

Herrera double-timed down the stairs and ducked through the doors of Security Control.

"Down to four now," Álvarez said. Reaching down, he flipped the intercom switch.

"Sergeant Mesa—call Duarte right now. We've got to stop any further refueling efforts because of the fire hazard."

"Sir—I called him just ten minutes ago. No answer. His radio must be inoperative. I've called one of the perimeter mobile patrols to check—"

"Dammit, Mesa. Switch me into the radio circuit. I'll call him myself."

Shrugging like all frustrated NCOs do when confronted by the irrationality of their officers, Mesa angrily threw two switches on his console and then got up, moving over to the coffee machine, his face rigid, suppressing what must have been rage.

Álvarez picked up the mike but Brocassie grabbed it.

"You out of your frigging mind?" Álvarez whispered.

"He's not going to answer you, Julio. But he'll recognize my voice and the call sign that we used. We've got to chance it."

Álvarez handed him the mike reluctantly. "I hope you know what you're doing. Mesa's going to go bullshit."

Brocassie ignored him, keying the switch. "Com-fuel, this is Ebb Tide Two. Do you copy?"

Mesa halted in midstride. He looked up toward the control booth, a frown on his face.

Rush of static, a click, hissing and then another click. *I read you.*

Brocassie keyed the mike. "Duarte, we've got some problems up here. How long to finish your operation?"

I'm pumping the last four thousand gallons. Give me five more minutes.

Glancing down at his watch, Álvarez rotated it so that Brocassie could see. Thirty-eight after. Brocassie shook his head. He couldn't spare the time.

"Duarte, cease pumping and pull out as per your orders. We're going to commence operations in two minutes."

No reply. Hissing of the open circuit. Mesa, down below in the control room, turned to one of the console operators who, in turn, swiveled around in the chair, staring toward the booth.

"Duarte—you understand?" Brocassie shouted into the mike.

Just the raw rush of static, punctuated by snaps of interference, then, finally: *Damn problems . . . four guys in a truck . . . can't . . .*

"Your transmission is breaking up, Duarte!"

Álvarez leaned forward. He tapped Brocassie on the knee. "Don't look now but it's all over." Mesa had checked the status board and picked up a telephone. "Ten to one he's calling Roychenko."

Clenching his fist, Brocassie swore under his breath. Roughly thirty-six thousand gallons already pumped. It was enough but he had to get through to Porto one more time, to make sure that he understood that he should pull out. He picked up the mike. "Duarte, this is . . . oh, hell with it. Get out of there, now—I *mean right now!* Something's wrong with your transmitter. If you read me, key your mike twice, and terminate operations—I repeat—terminate operations."

Álvarez turned up the volume. It was a torrent of noise, the hash of static filling the room and then, distinctly, two clicks. Then silence, the contact severed. Down below, Mesa was at his console, flipping switches.

481

"That's it, Brocassie. Mesa's cut us off." Álvarez was already out of his chair. He motioned to Brocassie, nodding toward the control room below. Mesa had a sidearm drawn and he was at the door which connected Security Control to the Command Post, anxiously looking down the corridor.

All of the console operators had turned around, staring toward the control booth, not understanding what was happening but knowing that something was seriously wrong. Mesa was at the door, shouting something, but his words were blocked by the thick glass.

Álvarez was on his feet, three strides to the stairwell. He looked back. "I'll take care of the bastards down there." He stabbed his finger toward the console. "You throw the toggle switch and when I wave, turn the key." His face was flushed with sweat and his nose had started to bleed again. He stared at Brocassie, eyes wild. *"You understand?"*

He nodded. "I get it, Julio." He glanced down into the control room again. Mesa was beyond the door, in the corridor. "One thing, Julio," he shouted at Álvarez who was already at the top of the stairwell. "Whatever happens, thanks . . ." He hesitated, his throat constricted, unable to finish it.

Hesitating for a second, Álvarez dug into his pocket and withdrew a length of rawhide, looped through a gold ring. He tossed it to Brocassie.

"This is her ring, isn't it?"

Brocassie nodded.

Álvarez flashed him a wan smile, looked down the stairwell and then glanced back. *"De nada,* brother." His voice was almost unnaturally calm. Then he vaulted down the stairs, three steps at a time.

CHAPTER

22

Brocassie broke the wire seal, flipped the Plexiglas cover up, and threw the toggle switch. His fingers grasped the key ready to turn it. His throat was dry, his heart thudding, adrenaline pumping through his veins. He realized fully now that he could never have done this alone, that without Julio, he would already be dead. Just five more minutes, he prayed. Give us that much time.

Below him, Julio had burst into Security Control, the Lastoy drawn. Sergeant Mesa, already at the door to the corridor which connected the Command Post with Security Control, took one look, alarm mirrored in his face, and bolted. Álvarez snapped off a round but Mesa was already through the door, slamming it behind him. Álvarez ran to the door and then, dropping the locking bar into place, wheeled back to the three console operators, the weapon leveled.

The men stared up at him, their expressions frozen.

Álvarez shifted rapidly sideways in front of the status

boards, waving the Lastoy. His face brittle with tension, he was hammering out staccato commands that Brocassie could not hear. Two of the men glanced at each other, one starting to edge his hand toward his holster and, without hesitation, Álvarez shot him through the chest. The impact of the bullet tumbled the man backward out of his chair. A dark red stain smeared the front of his tunic. Slowly, the other two console operators rose from their seats, unbuckled the web belts which held their holsters and raised their hands. Waving the Lastoy, Álvarez herded them toward the main entrance door and ordered them to lie facedown. Keeping them covered, Álvarez edged back to the communications console and threw two switches.

"You hear me?" His voice, electronically amplified, rattled the speaker in the control booth.

Brocassie didn't know which switch to throw. He threw four of them without effect, then smashed down a cluster of toggles with his hand. One lit.

He picked up the mike and tried it. "I hear you OK."

Nodding satisfaction, then reaching down for an adjacent console, Álvarez threw a series of switches. The status board beyond him came alive. The electronic schematic of the fire-fighting system suddenly lit, each individual valve illuminated in red indicating that it was shut. Then rapidly, valve after valve turned green as Álvarez's fingers flashed down rows of switches.

At first Brocassie didn't notice the heavy pounding but Álvarez obviously did. He paused, looking toward the door leading to the connecting tunnel and then yelled into the mike, "Mesa's trying to get in. He's probably got four or five security guards from the Command Post. There's no time left, Brocassie. We've got to start the pumps now." He rotated a key and then stabbed his finger at Brocassie. *"TURN IT!"*

A delay of seconds—and then, finally, green lights winked on beneath the schematic representation of the pumps. Slowly, the pipelines from the pump house illuminated, the pale yellow light slowly radiating outward, passing through valves, rushing on to individual silos.

Almost immediately, the control consoles started to scream in a shrieking vibrato and red emergency lights pulsed on. From beyond the Security Control, Brocassie could hear the howl of emergency Klaxon horns.

He was frozen by the enormity of what was happening. His mind was unable to comprehend the idea of men burning and missiles exploding as waves of superheated gas roared through the complex.

"Down here!" Álvarez screamed into the mike.

Startled, Brocassie looked to the control room floor below. Álvarez was whipping the Lastoy, gesturing him to come down. "Forget the fucking key—it doesn't have to be held once the pumps are running."

He was just to the stairwell when the door to the connecting tunnel blew in. The blast swept Security Control, shattering some of the status boards, pulverizing the radiation console nearest to the door, imploding the plate-glass window to the control booth. Razor-sharp shards sprayed above him, bare inches from where Brocassie stood in the stairwell.

Seconds after the explosion, four men charged into the control room, scattering out in a fan, taking cover behind the consoles. Bursts of machine-gun fire swept the ceiling of the room. All of the fluorescent lights were gone and a spray of sparks from an electrical switchbox showered down into the control room, illuminating it with blue-white strobe flashes as molten metal arced. The emergency lighting flickered on, off and on again.

Smoke and the dust of debris obscured his vision. Brocassie slammed the stairwell door closed and then, on hands and knees, crawled to the console, keeping his head low, yet trying to look down into Security Control. It was chaos below, fire and arcing electrical contacts, smoke from the explosive charge, from gunfire and burning wiring. The lights which remained on the panels were flickering, and then began to wink out. He shifted his gaze to the generator status and saw that both were flashing red. All of the fire-fighting panel had gone blank which had to mean that somehow the power production plants had shut down, stopping the pumps. Because they had blown or because someone, perhaps Roychenko, had shut them down? Too late to worry. He was in a box with no way out.

"ÁLVAREZ!" he screamed.

Machine-gun slugs hammered into the wall above him, chipping plaster, splattering him with a cloud of white dust. He screamed to Álvarez again but there was still no response.

Three shots blasted out from the far corner of the room and then, as if a switch had been pulled, the firing ceased. The only sounds were the erratic sputtering of electrical contacts fusing, the hiss of insulation burning, the choking of men inhaling fumes and dust.

Holding the Lastoy in both hands, barrel resting on the desk, Brocassie fired, blowing out one of the two emergency lamps.

In the confined space of the control booth, the sound was deafening. He shifted his aim to the other but before he could fire, a burst of slugs ripped into the control booth, this time only inches above his head. Chips of hot metal and plaster showered him. Another burst, this time higher and then again, silence.

He was panting, eyes burning from the smoke, ears partially deafened, knees grating on fragments of plaster.

From the corridor, he heard the sound of boots pounding down the concrete, drawing nearer.

He pulled the C-4 plastic from his shirt pocket, inserted the contact fuse and waited. The hammering of boots drew nearer, the sound of men grunting and shouting to each other, the clank of weapons. From farther down the tunnel he could hear commands shouted in Russian—Roychenko's voice, he was positive. Four or five men down below and at least that many on the way. This is the end of it, he thought. They wouldn't give quarter and he knew that he wouldn't ask for it. Álvarez was surely dead or dying. Perhaps, he prayed, she was already with Maroto now, safe, he hoped. And Porto? Had he quit pumping and pulled out? Christ, he hoped so.

No smell of gasoline, no distant rumble of explosions. Just before the door had blown, the status board had shown that the pipes were not totally filled. With the generators shut down, there would be no power to run the pumps. Consequently, gasoline had not yet reached any of the silos. It had been a damn good try.

He shifted his position and got ready to throw. Edging

higher, keeping his head from being exposed, he could still see much of the status board. The elaborate jumble of lights was dead, the glass overlay badly fractured. The communications console still crackled but there was nothing coherent, only sporadic snaps of static and undecipherable voices. Beyond the door to the main corridor, the pulsing wail of the Klaxon horns still hooted their warning. They would undoubtedly be evacuating the complex except for the absolute minimum of crucial personnel.

He felt wasted, his body unresponsive, as if the connections to the circuits had snapped. It was not the totality of dying that he couldn't accept but rather, the surety of death without fulfillment that was unbearable.

He edged his body higher, peering over the top of the desk, past the shattered pane of glass: every sound below him was now audible, as if he were high in an amphitheater, the trick of acoustics amplifying every sound.

Hidden behind the consoles, men called and cursed to the troops in the corridor. He could hear them in the tunnel, slowing, grouping for the rush. Concussion grenades first probably, followed by tear gas. That's the way he would have planned it.

It was a three-second fuse. He bit the detonator, counted to two, stood up and threw it. The ball of plastic cleared the framework of the door, skidded into the tunnel entrance and blew.

The blast was devastating—a white-hot flash and then the blast wave, the concussion literally lifting one of the men below high into the air. Another man was screaming, cursing, crying and finally silent.

Brocassie leaped up, the Lastoy now in his hand. From near the door connecting to the tunnel, he saw a slight movement—the tip of the barrel of an AK-47 lifting from behind a console, then the foregrip with a hand clamped around it, then the crown of the man's head. He aimed just inches above the skull, anticipating, and as the man stood up to fire, Brocassie hammered three shots into his chest. The impact drove the man back against the wall, and then he slowly slid down to the concrete, streaking the wall behind him with blood and tattered bits of tissue.

487

No movement below him now except for the twitching o the man draped over the console, his AK-47 still tightl clenched.

No sound from the connecting tunnel either. He had n idea whether or not men were still alive in there.

Move, his mind kept repeating. *Get out if you can.* Thre rounds left but there would be an AK-47 down below wit spare clips. He edged to the stairwell, moving his feet carefull to avoid the chips of concrete which would grate and giv away his position. Down the seven steps: at the bottom now He pushed carefully against the door. It swung open onl inches and then met resistance. He pushed harder.

The body blocking the door was one of the console opera tors. He was showered with concrete dust, his body was un marked, but rivulets of blood oozed from his ears and mouth

"Brocassie!" It was Álvarez's whisper, barely audible "Keep your head down. One of the bastards is left and he' under the radiation monitoring console."

"I . . ." He was unable to finish the sentence, unable t believe that Álvarez had lived. He lowered himself onto hi hands and knees, using the dead man as a shield, and the slowly turned, inching his head around. Behind him, eight fee away, crouched down behind an overturned file cabinet wa Álvarez, grinning back at him, his whole body whitened wit the dust of pulverized concrete.

Something down deep in him awakened, flooding hi body with a sense of power and hope.

Álvarez grinned again, his face crazy, lifting the third fin ger of his bloody right hand in a salute. "Come on, bonehead,' he whispered. "We can still pull this off. We've got to get those pumps running again. I'll shift to the left and you go to the right—give him two targets. When he shows, we nail him.' Without waiting for a response, Álvarez levered himself up exposing his body from the waist up. He snapped off two shots from his Lastoy, shouting in Russian, then shifted away from the file cabinet, exposing his entire body, still screaming in a gut-wrenching shrill. He aimed and then pulled the trigger again but it snapped on an empty chamber.

The KGB guard scrambled to his feet almost immediately

488

and in a crouch, danced sideways, the AK-47 spewing lead, stitching a chain of craters in the concrete wall, hosing in a continuous phosphorus stream toward Álvarez. It was like time-lapse photography, seconds seemingly cut in halves, then quarters, then eighths. In his peripheral vision, Brocassie saw Álvarez double up under the impact but now Brocassie was firing without aiming, watching as the bullets from the Lastoy impacted on the throat, chest and gut of the Russian. The man's body heaved backward, doubling over. His head crashed against the floor and he jerked twice spasmodically, then fell back lifeless.

Brocassie scrambled over the dead console operator on all fours, getting to Álvarez's crumpled body. Álvarez was alive, pain burning deep furrows in his face. He was biting his lip, his teeth puncturing the flesh, and he was swearing, alternately, in three languages. The wound was almost shoulder high on the arm near the joint, fragments probing out through the seared flesh.

"Julio—you hear me?"

"Jesus Christ—of course I hear you!" Álvarez opened his eyes, squinted and then focused. He grimaced insanely, biting his teeth down again, his face an agony.

Bending down in the dim light, Brocassie unbuckled his belt, stripped it from the loops and wound it around Álvarez's shoulder, cinching it tight. He pulled the empty clip from Álvarez's Lastoy and, using it as a lever, tightened the belt with a Spanish windlass. The pulsing flow of blood slowed and then stopped. "Get up, Julio. Lean on me. I'm getting you out of here."

Álvarez's eyes clenched shut, then opened. He squinted, trying to focus, and then he nodded. "Think you got a damn fine idea." He tried to pull his legs up underneath him, but then he frowned, puzzled. He reached down with his good arm, his fingers digging through the cloth into the flesh of his leg. Suddenly, he hammered with his fist against his thigh, striking it so hard that his whole body shuddered. Then he fell back against the cabinet. For long seconds, he stared at nothing, his eyes unfocused. He turned, facing Brocassie.

"I don't . . . don't think I'm going after all, pal. Not now, not ever. I stay—you go." He tried to smile and failed, the expression a grimace. He pointed down to his legs. "Can't feel them. Can't move them."

The fabric of his pants just beneath the beltline was saturated. Gently, Brocassie rolled him over, lifting the layers of cloth.

The wound wasn't large—just a furrow of ruptured flesh across the top of the buttocks, but the bullet had fractured the spinal cord. He looked at it, knowing that Álvarez was right—that he would never move from the waist down again. He rolled Álvarez back over and lowered his head to the floor.

"I can carry you, gimp," he said softly. "Carry you forever—to the Mountains of the Moon if I have to." He bent down to lift him but Álvarez grabbed his arm, pressing his fingers into Brocassie's flesh like steel pincers.

"I've seen wounds like this in Korea. There's nothing you can do and no time to waste. You've got to go and I've got to stay because someone has to be here to finish it off." He suddenly hawked up in his throat and spat phlegm to the side.

"I can—"

"You can do shit!" Álvarez screamed back at him. "All our lives, you've fucked up because you didn't do what I told you to do and you're not going to bust this one." He twisted his mouth, looking up, his eyes going in and out of focus. "Not this one, Brocassie. This one is *mine*."

"Julio, I . . ."

Álvarez reached up with his right hand, clutching Brocassie's shoulder, the nails clawing into flesh. "Do me a favor," he screamed in a cracked voice, spittle flecking Brocassie's face. "Do it *my* way because I'm the only one who knows how to do it. Your job is to get the hell out of here because someone has to be able to tell Kennedy how I saved his worthless ass and you damn well better make sure that I get the Congressional Medal of Honor with all the fucking tutti-frutti clusters and a five-hundred-gun salute. Drag me down to the firefighting console and then get the hell out of here—down the tunnel to the elevator. You'll have only a minute or so to get out before this place blows."

"What in hell can you do here?"

Álvarez glared at him. *"Listen*—nothing—not a damn

thing has happened, understand? The whole place should be rocking with explosions by now. Roychenko somehow put it together and pulled the plug on the generators. It's an impasse right now. He doesn't have power to launch but we don't have power to run the pumps. Big difference is that he can wait it out, blow us away at leisure and have power restored within thirty minutes."

"Then we're screwed!"

"Not yet. Roychenko can start or shut down the two main generators but I've got sole control over the standby generator. It doesn't put out much but I can put it on line and spoon out the power carefully. I'll open the blast doors first and then start the pumps. One spark, one match, anywhere and the whole complex will go."

Oh, goddammit, Brocassie thought. Not this way. He shook his head. "I'm staying."

Álvarez softened his voice. "No, you've got to go, savvy? Give me some protection. Keep that corridor clear just long enough to let me finish my act. Then you get up the elevator. If that's out of commission, there's a stairwell next to it. The door's locked but you can blow it apart if you have to. Two stories and you're on the surface."

"I . . ."

"I know," Álvarez said softly. "I know. But we can't change things, can we? Just get me down to the fucking console and bug out."

Brocassie put his hands under Julio's armpits, dragging his dead weight. Álvarez didn't make a sound, but blood was streaming from his lips as he bit down, trying to counter the pain. Brocassie picked up a chair and lifted Álvarez into it, rolling it in front of the console. Some of the lights were still burning—others shattered.

Experimentally, Álvarez flicked a few switches and lights winked on. He grinned, wolflike, and rubbed his good hand across his face, brushing the grit away. "It'll work, I think. The battery banks are still holding and if I can get the standby generator running, I'm in business." He turned, looking up. "Three minutes, Brocassie. Hold 'em for three minutes and I'll give a Fourth of July display like you've never seen."

Both of them heard the pounding of boots, the echoes

magnified by the corridor. They were still at a distance but getting louder. Sixty seconds, no more than that.

"Sounds like Roychenko is sending in the third team. You better be good, 'Cassie. They'll be more careful this time."

Brocassie bent down. He felt his eyes burning, blurring his vision, but there was nothing he could say.

Álvarez, eyes wild and uncoordinated, blood trickling from his lips, looked up. "No regrets. It was fun, buddy. How much fun I could never tell you but it was worth every second and a whole pack more." He hesitated as if he were afraid to speak and then he said softly, hesitantly, almost as if he were embarrassed. "Bro—I honestly loved you but I could never say it and I was always afraid that you'd be better than me and that's why I gave you all that shit. So make this the way real brothers part, just this once. Give me your hand, you stupid bugger, and then get the hell out."

Brocassie took Julio's hand, squeezing, then bent down and held his brother's head against his. He couldn't hold back the uncontrollable convulsions in his chest that rumbled up into his throat. His heart was exploding, his lungs racking up guttural sounds and half-formed words, drawn from images and feelings he had forgotten or had never even been able to acknowledge.

Álvarez pushed him away roughly. *"Go, motherfucker— get out. NOW!"*

He didn't, couldn't look back. Scrambling, slipping on the spawls of fractured concrete, he hesitated only long enough to pry the AK-47 from the dead fingers of the KGB security guard, slip in a fresh clip and jam two others into his fatigue pockets. As he ran, he jammed back the loading lever, chambered a round and dove into the tunnel. Over debris, slipping, ricocheting off the walls of the tunnel, tripping and falling, he stumbled over the bodies of the dead assault team. He landed heavily on his shoulder and then rolled, soaking up the impact.

A couple of feet in front of him a man crawled on his hands and knees, his face down, grunting with pain. He was dragging a leg, wincing with each move as he tried to propel himself with the other leg and his hands.

Brocassie was raising the butt of the AK-47 when he realized, even in the dim emergency lighting, that the man's face was blown away and that he was blind and probably deaf because he gave no indication that he had heard any movement behind him. The man was angling in, crawling closer and closer to the tunnel wall, then brushing it with his shoulder. He stopped for a second and felt the damp concrete with his fingers, then started edging along the rough surface with his shoulder, letting it guide him.

Brocassie couldn't bring himself to kill him. Then he saw that the man's combat harness was studded with grenades. He slung the AK-47 across his back, picked two grenades off, filling his hands like a greedy schoolboy stealing apples from an orchard.

Much closer now—men running, the clank of gear, the beat of hard leather boots against the tunnel floor. Fifteen—twenty seconds, maximum.

The wounded man hadn't even reacted, as if his senses had retreated to some lower, primitive level of consciousness. Brocassie shoved down hard on the man's back, sending him sprawling forward onto his face, then plucked a pin from the first grenade and cocked his arm.

Just as he hurled the grenade, he could see the dim shapes of men in dark green uniforms lumbering toward him, weapons held in the assault position. He heard the clang as the grenade hit the surface of the tunnel, a burst of automatic fire and then a scream of warning. He threw himself flat, covering his head with his arms.

The concussion was tremendous, cascading in shock waves down the tunnel. Microseconds later, shrapnel whistled overhead, followed by the rattle of falling debris.

Still facedown, panting, he took the second grenade, pulled the pin and then waited, the firing handle held down tight in his fist. It had been a four-second fuse, maybe five. Rolling over onto his left elbow, he threw the grenade sidearm. He heard it grate on the side of the tunnel and land, bouncing twice with metallic clangs, then the thud of bodies throwing themselves at full run onto concrete.

A shriek, someone down the tunnel screaming an order.

One banana, he counted.

Two bananas . . .

Three bananas . . . and he realized in a sickening flash that he had thrown too soon, too far, and should have released the bloody handle two seconds before throwing it because the survivors of the first grenade were now that much closer and someone—boots scuffling frantically against concrete—someone with more guts than brains was scrambling to pick up the grenade and hurl it back.

He waited for the impact. Grinding his face down into the concrete, arms covering his head, he could already feel the white-hot fragments tearing into his exposed flesh. Unconsciously, he was still counting.

Four ba . . .

The blast hit him like a massive bludgeon, hammering at his body, lifting him for what seemed like a wheeling eternity and then slamming him back down again. He lay there, a continuous roar in his ears, his muscles jumping involuntarily as if he were being probed with electric shocks. He couldn't get his breath, his lungs sucked but nothing came, as if he were trying to inhale in a vacuum.

He lay there for what seemed to be a long time, waiting for some dumb reason that he couldn't really comprehend—only that it was very good, very desirable, *wonderful* (he giggled) just to lie still and to lie still and to lie still and the words were like a scratched record, scraping the same grooves over and over in his brain. Forever, he waited, feeling nothing and wanting nothing, and then he was shot through with a prickling like needles. The real pain swept through his body in pulsing waves. He was afraid to move and afraid not to. He pulled himself to his knees, fell forward, heaving up his stomach and yet nothing came up. He swallowed and tried again, on all fours, then twos, stumbling to his feet. He staggered a little, fell down and got up again. He was choking now, the air thick with dust and cordite. He gagged again.

All the emergency lights were shattered except two, far down in the tunnel. He started to shamble toward them, only dimly understanding that there was no time left, yet knowing that there was something that he must do. Something about the tunnel. But he couldn't organize the fragmented images into coherent thought. The only thing he understood was the compulsion to keep moving down the tunnel, toward the flickering lights.

He was drunk with shock, stumbling, off balance. Inadvertently, he crossed his feet, one in front of the other, which caused him to stagger and fall sideways. He hit heavily against the tunnel's side and rebounded, regaining his balance. Something he had to do but he couldn't put it together. Trying to clear his mind, he started lurching toward the lights. Gradually, like an old man, he picked up his stride into a pathetic shuffle.

In the dim light, he could see three men in a jumbled pile, thrown together into a final heap of blasted flesh by some freak effect of the confined detonation. Farther down the tunnel yet another man, still moving.

He was already by the fourth man when he heard the squawk of a radio—a voice in Russian, repeating the same phrase over and over again. Brocassie stopped, hesitated and went back to the man. Like a butterfly pinned to a specimen board, the Russian was fluttering on the edge of life, his movements growing weaker. He was whimpering something unintelligible. Clipped to his belt was a still functioning radio. Brocassie snapped it up, clipped it to his own belt and turned again, heading down the tunnel.

His mind was clearing rapidly now—everything almost crystallized in form and intensity. Every part of his body was screaming with pain. He knew that there might be internal damage to his organs but he realized that at least he was a functioning whole again—not just individual, uncoordinated jerking parts, working against each other.

He picked up his pace, now trotting stiff-legged. Something like a machine that had been overstressed but still functioned. Amused, he managed a self-congratulatory smile and found that even that hurt.

He remembered now that Álvarez had said he had to keep the tunnel secure for three minutes. How long had it really been? It had seemed forever, but it had likely been only a minute or less. He inhaled deeply, increasing his gait, breathing more easily. He had a screaming headache and he realized that his hearing was shot, but he was alive and he didn't give a shit about anything except giving Julio the time that he needed to complete the destruction of the complex. Maybe a minute and a half, possibly less. He found his body growing lighter, as if he were floating. Pain diminishing, vanishing—adrenaline flooding into his veins. Involuntarily, he yelled a cry of triumph and it echoed down the tunnel and back again, amplified.

Settling back against the chair, Álvarez smiled, almost euphoric. His shoulder throbbed with every pulse of his heart but even that was growing less painful. He felt light-headed, as if he had had a couple of drinks. His mind was racing ahead, the plan and sequence burned into his brain.

Know this damn system because I dictated its capabilities, he thought, and now he was manipulating it like a virtuoso.

The status board was incomplete, some of the lights inoperative. He threw a switch and held it. The light flickered from red to amber to red again. He tried it again and the red flickered through amber to green. The standby generator was running. So I have power, he thought. Not to squander it. Very easy, very gently. Just a little at a time, feeding juice to each tunnel in sequence.

He selected a section of switches labeled BLAST DOORS and started throwing them, one at a time. Some lights turned from red to green, indicating that the blast doors were opening. Other lights were shattered, giving no indication, but he treated them with equal care, watching the power meter of the standby generator intently to make sure that he did not overload it.

He was enjoying himself immensely now and sang, off-tune, half-aloud, "I'm Popeye the sailor man, I live in a garbage can . . ."

More lights winked green. Green like spinach.

Too bad no more Olive Oil, no Alicia. The thought sobered him and he steadied down.

Thirty—forty seconds he estimated had elapsed and by now, he had three-quarters of the lights changed from red to green. Others remained stubbornly red and the remainder had blown bulbs. The status board twinkled as he manipulated the console. Like a Christmas tree, he thought. Jesus, could really use a smoke. He patted his breast pocket but the package of

Luckies was lost. Shit, he swore. No succor for the weary. No juice left. Just lazy languor and the desire to drift off into sleep. Felt nothing from the waist down and now sensation was fading from his chest and back, his arms numbing, his fingertips dull. Not to worry. Still operational from the neck up and that was what mattered. It's the head that counts, he thought.

Abruptly, he heard a concussion and seconds later another from far down the tunnel. Brocassie!

His mind came fully awake now. Euphoria gone. How many seconds left?

He scanned the board. All blast doors open that were going to open.

Hesitant at first, he flipped one switch, carefully watching the generator load factor, and saw the fire-fighting system come alive. Running just under a 45 percent load factor. He started the second pump. The load factor meter flickered into the red overload arc as the pump started, then fell back to the green sector. The lines radiating out from the pumps were illuminating now, and he knew that they were filled with 135 octane aviation gasoline. The lights in the lines kept lengthening, finally reaching the silos—one and then five and then fifty and finally, almost all of them.

He leaned back, immensely satisfied, knowing that he had done what he could. The seconds remaining were running out, the pumps still ramming raw gasoline into the lines. Once the pumps sucked dry, they would overspeed, building up revolutions until they self-destructed. By then, the lines to the silos would be filled with a mixture of raw fuel and air, and as the pumps cavitated in their last agony, a flame front would race in a roaring flash to the silos.

He glanced at the clock on the wall—probably less than a minute before the pumps ran dry. God, what he wouldn't do for a cigarette. Had wanted to quit smoking all his life and found it funny that now he would, if he could just have one more cigarette.

He leaned back, letting the chair support his neck, listening. Still the Klaxons hooting but nothing from the tunnel. Somehow, Brocassie had held them for more than two minutes. Only one to go.

He was having trouble seeing now. He levered himself forward again, having to squint to see the console. One switch still left to throw. He found it and curled his finger over it, waiting for the first indication on the status board that the pumps were beginning to cavitate.

Behind him, he heard the main door to the corridor rattle against the lock. The intercom squawked.

"Let me in, Álvarez!" It was Roychenko, out of breath, panic in his voice.

"Why not come through the connecting tunnel, Colonel?"

A pause and then a mirthless laugh. "I'm told that it's quite crowded in there."

Álvarez glanced up to the second hand. Forty seconds, maybe less. It would be cutting it fine.

He thumbed down the intercom bar. "Only you. No one else. I have a gun, you understand?"

"I agree. I just want to talk."

He picked up the empty Lastoy and pressed the switch which unlatched the main door.

Roychenko pushed the door open a hair, looked in and then swung it fully open. He was unarmed, but three KGB types stood behind him with automatic weapons.

"Close it," Álvarez demanded, keeping the Lastoy centered on Roychenko's chest.

Roychenko eased the door shut with his elbow, listening for it to latch. He had his hands at half-mast.

"Far enough," Álvarez said.

Halting in midstride, Roychenko stood still. Álvarez waved the automatic toward an overturned chair. "Use that. Put your hands in front of you where I can see them."

Roychenko manufactured an expression of mild disapproval but complied. "You've made quite a mess of it, Julio."

His vision was fading out. He had thought that the batteries were failing in the emergency lighting but he now realized that he was dying from loss of blood. It took a monumental effort but he nodded, gently lowering the Lastoy to the desk, the muzzle still pointed toward the Russian.

"Depends on your viewpoint," he answered.

Roychenko glanced at his watch. "You must realize that I

have orders from General Lazarev to carry out. I need your cooperation."

Álvarez motioned toward Roychenko's tunic pocket. "You have a cigarette?"

Roychenko nodded.

"Then light me one and throw it to me." He rotated his wrist, bringing the Lastoy up, butt still resting on the console, the barrel wavering in the general direction of the Russian.

With exaggerated care, Roychenko slowly dipped his hand into his tunic, extracted the pack and inserted two cigarettes into his mouth. With the same hand, he fished out a lighter from his pocket and lit them both, finally tossing one to Álvarez.

The pump was still running, the line still filled. Porto must have been able to get in the final four thousand gallons. So much the better. Álvarez sucked the smoke into his lungs and exhaled.

He glanced once more at the status board and then at the second hand. He drew in on the cigarette, luxuriating in its dulling effect on his pain. "So here I am—on the job, just as I should be. What's your problem, Colonel?"

"Absolute loyalty, Julio. You must remember your vows of loyalty." He glanced at the bodies littering the floor. "Apparently they did." His hands played with the cigarette, turning it one way and then the other, his eyes averted. "You understand," he said, "that the Serbs are in Condition Bravo. A SAC bomber wing is headed for Cuba. I can't allow the Serbs to be lost."

"Put it another way—you're going to launch them if you can."

Roychenko shrugged. "I am simply preparing for a contingency, just as the Americans are doing. If it comes to war, then we will dance to whatever tune Moscow plays." He sighed, lolling back in his chair, relaxed as if time or circumstance had no meaning to him. "Soldiers are not political animals, Julio. We follow the commands of the politicians." He tapped the ash delicately with his index finger. "I think, my friend, it is time for you to quit and go home."

"This is what Lazarev and Andropov had planned on all the time, wasn't it—the missiles here, a first strike, a war, a gigantic gamble?"

The Russian shrugged. "It was not *the* plan—only an option. Brezhnev did not favor it but he went along with the contingency planning to secure the support of the military and the KGB in his struggle for power." He sighed. "Don't try to change history, Julio. The conflict will be trying but the outcome was never in doubt. It is something that we both knew was necessary, something that served each of our own desires for power. Shut down the pumps, Julio. There's still time to drain the silos and to make the Serbs ready."

"Ready for launch," Álvarez said quietly. He held up the cigarette, fumbled, and the cigarette fell to the floor.

Roychenko's voice was fading in and out, the light slowly going into tunnel vision, becoming faint. He knew that it had to be now. "Clumsy, aren't I? Light me another, Colonel."

Smiling, Roychenko went through the same elaborate measures, plucking the pack from his breast pocket, fishing out his lighter. He flicked the flint wheel twice and then the flame caught. He inserted a cigarette between his lips.

Álvarez tried to pull the switch and found the effort inconceivably difficult. In slow motion, he stared down at his hand and willed everything he had left into the effort. His fingertip almost slipped away from the switch but the toggle finally snapped to the on position and within seconds, he dimly sensed the overpowering, pungent stench as a high-pressure fog of gasoline sprayed into the room. He inhaled once, a full breath, wanting it to be painless. In one last nanosecond of white-hot incandescence, an entire sun expanding into nova, he knew that he had won.

CHAPTER

23

Brocassie was nearly up to the second level of the stairwell when the tunnel blew behind him. He felt the shock wave first and then heard the sound: not just one explosion but more like a ragged artillery volley, hammering in a rolling barrage. The concrete wobbled and then heaved under his feet, cracks radiating out in a spider's web until whole chunks of the stairwell fell away. Seconds later, the bulbs of the overhead emergency lights burst.

He was in absolute darkness now, stumbling, leaping desperately, taking two and three treads at a time, for he had smelled the stench of raw gasoline and immediately realized what was about to happen. He sucked in a lungful of air, holding it, trying to move even faster. Almost immediately, there was a tremendous *whump* from far below him and then a hard yellow flare of light. He was suddenly enveloped in a greasy column of black smoke roiling up the stairwell, faster

501

than he could climb. Waves of heat swallowed him, his hair frizzling, his exposed skin burning.

The superheated gas and flames enveloped him, then flashed past him with a hollow roaring. He was slammed forward against the stairs by the force of the blast. He picked himself up, beating out the flames which smoldered in patches on his fatigues, then scrambled up the last three risers onto a concrete landing.

His eyes were burning, tears rolling down his cheeks. He dropped to his hands and knees and started to crawl. Overhead, a Klaxon suddenly howled, but he only dimly registered its warning.

The sound of rumbling, metal grinding over metal, startled him. It was close and getting closer, and for a second, he thought the whole stairwell was about to collapse. Frantically, he moved faster, but his breath was giving out, lungs screaming for oxygen, red streaks of light flaming in the retinas of his eyes.

Scuttling forward like an animal under attack from behind, he bashed into a wall with his head and shoulder—then reached up and felt it with his hands. Metal! Oh, God, his mind screamed in rebellion, a blast door!

He stood up, hammering insanely against it but it wouldn't give. He realized with a flash of hope that the door was still partially open but rapidly moving closed. He desperately reached out, feeling for the narrowing gap and found it, rammed his body into the opening. He fell forward, twisting his leg, his right boot wedging in the depression of the floor which guided the blast door.

He lay there, sucking in great lungfuls of air, his chest heaving, heart pounding, his mind beaten down into some primitive level by lack of oxygen, unable to comprehend anything except that he had survived.

He was only dimly aware that men were shouting, boots thudding past him, only feet from where he lay. He started to twist into an upright position, trying to extract his boot which was still wedged in the depression at the bottom of the sliding blast door and then he was slammed roughly onto his belly. He felt rough hands forcing his boot out of the track, while his own muscles and tendons stretched to the point where he screamed in agony. The boot tore loose just as the blast door slammed shut—tons of metal ramming through the last ten inches, sealing off the fire and explosions below.

Brocassie looked up in time to glimpse the man's face and then the man turned away, fighting against the stampede of complex personnel who streamed toward the stairwell, all heading for the surface. Some were naked, some in fatigues, some just in underwear; all were fleeing in panic.

He felt pain, intense then unbearable, like a growling animal, gnawing down through his flesh. Arching forward, he looked down and saw that his fatigues were charred, the fabric carbonized and smoldering around his waist and the pant legs of his fatigues. Frantic, he started to flail at his fatigues with his bare hands, trying to extinguish the burning patches of fabric. And then the same man was back with a portable extinguisher in his hands, spewing a fog of carbon dioxide gas over his body, extinguishing the burning fabric, chilling the skin. He rolled Brocassie over and worked over the back of the fatigues and finally, the nozzle coughed and gave out.

The man—but he was really no more than a teenager—stood over him grinning, the extinguisher still dangling in his hand. He was no more than seventeen, maybe less, dressed only in fatigue pants and an olive-drab undershirt. His features were a broad mixture of Spanish and Indian. *Cuban,* Brocassie knew; not Russian.

"You can move, *compañero*?" The kid flicked his eyes back to the stairwell, obviously anxious to get moving. "We have to evacuate!"

The stream of men was thinning when Brocassie felt the first detonation, then another, and then a whole cluster of shock waves pummeling through the complex. Concussions of successive explosions fed on each other, building in intensity like the drum roll of a gigantic timpani. My God, he thought, Álvarez had pulled it off! The silos were blowing, one after another. Damn bloody sweet ridiculous bugger. All his life, playing games, scrambling against odds, defying or trying to manipulate the systems that he had chosen or which were imposed on him by his own damn stupidity, and finally, only in death, beating them all. Sleep well, brother, he prayed.

He pushed himself into a sitting position and the boy

helped him to his feet. Half-pulling, half-dragging, the kid assisted Brocassie up the final chain of stairs.

At the top was a steel blast door, still open. Beyond the door was a hangar and maintenance shops neatly built into the overhanging rock ledge which skirted the valley. He was oriented now—knew the river was to the north although he could not see it in the glare of emergency lighting.

The hangar was chaotic, floodlit with the headlights of trucks, jeeps and jerking flashlights as men jostled each other, frantic, all semblance of discipline gone. The blare of Klaxon horns was deafening but overlaying that were the screams, curses and orders shouted by men desperate to save what was salvageable. Mechanics were frantically tearing down maintenance stands which surrounded a helicopter, then pushing the dolly which supported the aircraft toward the opening of the revetment. Even before the chopper cleared the hangar door, the engine coughed into life, spitting blue flame from the exhausts. The blades started to turn, building up speed, throwing clouds of dirt and debris back into the hangar, suddenly reducing visibility to zero. A jeep filled with men roared past the hangar door and collided with the tail section, shattering the rotor blades. Bodies and parts of bodies, fractured blades and torn aluminum spewed outward, and almost immediately, flames burst from the fuel tanks, pouring liquid fire across the floor. It was a scene straight out of hell.

In the distance, Brocassie heard the metallic rattle of small-arms fire and the thump of mortars, then a series of short hiccup bursts of automatic weapons. Either men were firing at phantom shadows or more likely Maroto was fighting his way back across the river. He had to get there—to the river.

He and the kid broke into a loose run, clearing the burning gasoline and wreckage, when suddenly the beam of a powerful flashlight pinned them.

"WHERE DO YOU SONS OF WHORES THINK YOU'RE HEADED?"

The kid skidded to a stop, Brocassie beside him. The AK-47 was still slung across his back and it was too late to make a move to unsling it. He stood at attention, mimicking the kid, panting. No documents, no orders, no dog tags. Somehow, he had to bluff his way out of it.

The flashlight spotlighted their faces, and behind that light, Brocassie was positive, there would be a gun with a finger on the trigger.

As the light came closer, only a couple of feet away now, he could begin to make out a frizzle-headed, gray-haired noncom, the burned-out butt of a cigarette stuck in his face. The light from his flashlight glinted off the barrel of an automatic.

"Hold it right there," he barked. He had a clipboard and he waved it. "Give me your name, rank and serial number."

The kid snapped to. "Alberto Chibás, private." He rattled off a string of numbers.

The NCO scanned down the list. "OK, Chibás. You're from perimeter motor patrol, right?"

The kid nodded nervously.

"How many men left down there in the quarters?"

The kid wavered, indecision on his face. "Sergeant—I don't know. I was one of the first out but this man needed help. I had to go back for an extinguisher and . . ."

Pivoting back, the sergeant stared at Brocassie, sweeping the flashlight over his smoke-blackened face. "What fuckin' furnace did you crawl out of?"

Brocassie had already anticipated what was going to happen. "I was with Comandante Álvarez . . . courier from his headquarters in Santiago. Captain Piedra had just taken me to the *comandante* when there was an explosion in Security Control. The *comandante* ordered us to clear out."

"How many men still down there?"

Brocassie stiffened. "Ten—fifteen—thirty—maybe as many as fifty. Shit, Sergeant, I don't know, but they're all fried meat." He raised his voice, the thin edge of hysteria in it. "Security Control, the Command Post—all of it gone. Explosions in the connecting tunnel. I got out with an officer, five or six others behind us and then the fire. He was a lieutenant I think—a Russian. We got to the elevator at level three and then the power failed. I blew the lock on the door to the stairwell, and then we were in flames and smoke. I made it to the blast door on the second level just in time. Chibás pulled me through just as it was closing and then he got an extinguisher . . ." He let the sentence hang.

The NCO had watched his face through all of the explanation, keeping the flashlight in his eyes. He lowered it, inhaled, and let his breath out in a long sigh. "What's your name?"

"Gómez," Brocassie said mechanically. "Carlos Gómez —squad leader of the fourth division, DGI, barracks three, Oriente."

"The lieutenant . . ."

Brocassie shrugged. "I don't know. He was behind me when we were on the stairs."

"You're sure about the rest of them down there? I've got orders to keep the blast doors open if there's a chance."

Brocassie shook his head. "No one, Sergeant. It's finished down there." Álvarez had said it exactly—a shitty way to go.

The NCO slowly lowered the flashlight, then flicked it off.

"You understand what's happening, Gómez?"

"No. An accident?"

"No *fucking* accident, Gómez." He gestured with his head toward the river. "You hear that, don't you? We're under attack. American paras and counterrevolutionaries, probably. I don't know anything except that we've got a firefight near the river, we're taking heavy losses and we've got damn few men to fight back with. Most of our combat troops were trapped down below on the third level and the stupid bastards that got out from their barracks on level two were so involved with saving their asses that they didn't stop to bring their weapons. On top of everything, the command channels from Havana are screaming reports about an incoming bomber raid on this complex and in the meanwhile, this place is going up in smoke and that's *my* immediate concern."

"I fought with Fidel's Second Brigade in the Bay of Pigs. You tell me what you want and I'll do it." Brocassie straightened his back, smashing the heels of his boots together with what he hoped would pass as mindless patriotic fervor.

For the first time, the sergeant grinned. "You know how to work quad-fifties?"

His mind somersaulted eleven years back to a frozen trench in Korea. He knew how to use fifty-caliber machine guns and quad-fifties were just four of them bolted to a single frame.

SHELL GAME

"I can handle them but I'll need someone to feed the belts."

"So take"—he glanced down at the clipboard—"Chibás here." He forked his thumb toward a set of headlights. "It's a ZIL half-track mounted with surplus quad-fifties left over from the Batista days and it's all I got left. The driver's a Russian . . . name like Markoff. Understands Spanish if you keep it simple." He turned, pointing toward the river. "Take the ZIL due south to the minefield markers which parallel the river and then start west along the fence. Hold up at marker nine and cover that sector against any attempt by the enemy to come through the minefields and scale the fence. The action is farther west right now but that might be just a diversion from the main thrust of their assault. No lights, understand, Gómez, and no firing until you're under attack. Just hold that position and if they try to penetrate the minefield, cut loose with the quad-fifties. I'll be on your flank with another dozen men, two hundred yards to the west. We'll have reinforcements in from Santiago and Trinidad de Cuba by dawn. Now get with it!"

Broccassie grinned insanely back at the sergeant. "Count on me, Sergeant. They shall not pass!" He saluted, grabbed Chibás by the arm and headed toward the ZIL.

"Chibás! In the back of the half-track." He heaved himself up over the armor plating into the gun pit and pounded on the top of the cab. A steel flap on the back of the cab slammed open and a beefy-red face filled it.

"Where is the sergeant?" the Russian demanded.

"I'm in command. Get this pile of junk moving south to the minefield and then turn west. I'll tell you when to stop—and *no* lights until I tell you." He slammed the flat of his hand on the roof of the cab again. "Come on, Markoff, move it!"

Chibás had vaulted into the gun pit. With a flashlight held between his teeth, he was frantically feeding belts of cartridges into the quad-fifties, hammering back the loading levers to chamber the cartridges and then moving to the next gun.

The ZIL lurched forward and then on one track, straightened out and ground forward toward the river. Men in the path of the ZIL scattered as the machine accelerated.

507

Well away from the hangar into clear open fields, Brocassie looked east toward the silos. It was a holocaust of flames and smoke, missiles exploding in a raging inferno. Concussions rocked the earth and even from this distance, he could feel the intense heat. In just the span of a second, a whole sequence of silos blew, spraying out flaming debris in a fiery fountain, burning junk cartwheeling as it fell to earth again.

Chibás was beside him, his mouth open, his face lit by the glow of the fires.

"Mother of Christ," he swore. "How did it happen?"

Shaking his head, Brocassie couldn't answer. Álvarez had always said that he wanted to be cremated, regardless of what the Church dictated, and this was the fulfillment of that wish. Spears of flames lanced skyward, illuminating the night so radiantly that men and physical features were thrown into bold relief. It was a spectacular funeral pyre. Álvarez would have approved of it. He turned to Chibás finally.

"I didn't thank you, Chibás. I do now, and I'll pay you back before this night is finished."

The kid stuck out his hand and Brocassie took it. Chibás opened his mouth, moved his lips, trying to express something but unable to, finally smiled, squeezed harder and then, embarrassed, dropped his hand and turned away.

The ZIL was more than halfway to the minefield. Tracers arched through the sky to the west. The rattle of automatic weapons was almost continuous. Three flashes of exploding mortar rounds or grenades flared along the bank of the river, followed by the hollow *crump* of the detonations. Maroto should have pulled out by now, he thought. What was the old bastard trying to accomplish? And then it struck him—Maroto was probably pinned down. With the quad-fifties and the armor plate, he could equalize the firepower, if—if he could get to the river. The question was, would Markoff follow his commands, regardless?

"Chibás—you understand what we're doing?"

"No—I mean, yes. We're defending—"

"Not defending, Chibás. We're counterattacking. I'm in command of this machine and I want you to do exactly as I tell you—no time for questions. You understand?"

"Of course, but—"

"You *understand*?" he screamed.

Chibás shrank back, more astonished than hurt. Brocassie grabbed him by his shoulder. "Chibás—understand—you do what I tell you to do if you want to stay alive." He pushed roughly against the kid, propelling him toward the front of the gun pit. "Climb down over the cab on the right side and get in with Markoff. When we come to the minefield, have him turn west and run up the line until you get to marker nine."

Chibás glared back at Brocassie, and then nodded. He scrambled over the top of the cab, then vaulted lightly down to the right-hand running board and seconds later, the passenger side door slammed shut.

Brocassie pulled the transceiver from his waist pocket, switched to channel six and squeezed the transmit button.

"Ebb Tide One, this is Two." He repeated the call three times. Nothing—not even the hiss of static. Damn, damn, damn. He smashed down the transmit button again and called but received nothing.

He hammered on the radio with his fist and suddenly it came alive with a rush of static and then, just as suddenly, went dead again.

He felt a rush of hope. Bad electrical contact, he realized; the damn thing could work if he could isolate the problem. He felt the unit, moving his hands over the metal surface, probing gently without effect and then, frustrated, squeezing it with both hands. Nothing, and then his hand was at the top of the unit and the metal whip antenna, fractured at its base, came away in his fingers. He jammed the whip back into its receptacle and held it, then listened. The frequency came alive, spitting out background hash. He tried it again. "Porto— Brocassie! Do you read?"

The reply came back, almost laconic, *Where you been, shithead? We've been waiting for you.*

The ZIL wheeled to the right. In the glow of the fires, Brocassie could see that Markoff was now paralleling the fence, heading west, much slower now.

He lost his grip on the antenna for a second, the metal slipping in his sweating hand and then, with great care, he pressed the ragged metal stump on the antenna down, making contact. The unit hissed and crackled intermittently. He pressed down with more pressure, trying to offset the jarring, lumbering motion of the ZIL as it traversed the rough terrain. He squeezed the mike button.

"No time to bullshit, Porto. What's the situation?"

Not good. We've lost five, another two wounded. Firefight at the fuel tank just about the time we were finished off-loading. We had to pull back to the river. We're on the near bank but we're pinned down by mortars.

"Alicia . . . is she . . ." He couldn't finish the sentence.

Porto came back immediately. *She's fine, tough as old boots, right next to me, loading clips for my BAR . . . What?— then . . . She says that you owe her a bottle of champagne and she's not leaving this place until you're back in one piece.*

"Tell her it's on ice." He swallowed hard, squinting toward the river. "Can all of you move downstream—to the east?"

We can try. The bank of the river on this side gives us some protection but some bastard has a mortar and flares. Even if we can link up with you, we'll never make it across the river without getting cut to shreds.

The ZIL shuddered to a halt, the engine still loping over, the chassis shuddering. Marker nine, he thought. Chibás had pinpointed it, even in the dark.

He keyed the mike again. "Watch for tracers, angled up at forty-five degrees—three separate bursts—and take a bearing. Move downstream toward them and don't stop regardless of what else happens. Without waiting for a response, Brocassie angled the quad-fifties up through half their elevation and squeezed off three short bursts. The quads bucked under his hands, the tracers floating up in a fiery arch, then curving over and falling toward the far side of the river.

I got it!

"Three minutes—no more. I'm in an amphibious half-track and I think we can ford the river with it. It's our only shot, Porto. Make it good."

Just the rasp of static, then, *Brocassie*—Porto's voice, on the edge of desperation. *We'll try it. I . . .* Porto's transmission cut off suddenly. To the west, four bursts of light flashed along the riverbank, moving east to west, followed by a trail of sparks and the flowering brilliance of a parachute flare, petals of green-white light blossoming over the river. A second flare followed the first and both slowly descended, swaying from their risers, bathing the river with brilliance.

He must have been shouting in the mike, his voice badly distorted. *TAKEN HITS. TWO ROUNDS RIGHT NEXT TO ... WE'RE MOVING.*

He knew that there was no more time and hammered on the cab. "Chibás!" he screamed into the port. "Get your ass up here right now—I mean RIGHT NOW!"

The kid tumbled out of the cab, running before he hit the ground. He was scrambling up into the gun pit when Brocassie grabbed him by the shoulder.

"We got orders on the radio to pull back. Run west along the fence. The sergeant has a bunch of men with him. Tell him to pull back to the marshaling yard and have him pass the word up the line. Everybody—everyone without exception—pull back to the marshaling yard."

In the firelight and the glare of the flares, the kid's face was gaunt, the eye sockets sunken in blackness, his cheekbones highlighted. He worked his mouth, words forming but nothing coming out.

Stabbing his finger toward the exploding silos, Brocassie screamed at him. "You see that! The wind's shifted this way and it's blowing fallout downwind and we're right in the path. *Bug out, Chibás!*"

Chibás never looked back. He stumbled twice, legs driving, flailing through the tall grass and back over the rough ground.

Markoff's face was framed in the opening to the cab, his expression uncomprehending. Brocassie ducked down to the same level.

"Does this thing ... shit, forget it. Turn left and roll through the fence and head straight for the river. You understand?"

"The minefield!"

"You drive and I'll worry about that. Get this sonofabitch moving!"

"But ..."

Brocassie unslung the Kalashnikov AK-47 and rammed the barrel into the slot. "Get this thing going! Keep it straight for the river once you're through the fence; I'll blast out a path through the minefield with the quad-fifties. We're attacking by order of Colonel Roychenko."

The use of Roychenko's name was inspired, the name galvanizing Markoff. He nodded fiercely, turned back to his controls and seconds later, he was wheeling the ZIL away from the fence in a teardrop turn, both treads alternately spewing geysers of dirt and then swinging back, full throttle, taking the fence head-on, the engine howling.

The chain link fence buckled under the onslaught of the half-track, sparks arcing as the hood of the vehicle tore through electrified strands. Brocassie already had the quad-fifties depressed to their stops at the lowest elevation, swiveling the guns around to fire directly ahead.

He depressed the triggers and the four barrels exploded in a thundering roar. He swept the bucking quads through small arcs, hosing the ground in front of him with torrents of copper-jacketed shells. One mine, almost too close in front of the half-track, blew, a geyser of earth erupting, shrapnel pinging off the armor plate. He raised the elevation, reached out with the guns, working ahead of the ZIL like a man playing a hose, blowing autumn leaves from the path before him. Two more mines blew thirty feet ahead. They were more than halfway through. The river glinted under the sparkle of the flares.

Brocassie hammered on the armor plated sides of the half-track with the heel of his hand, urging it on, willing it through the final yards. He screamed a guttural war cry, rising to a shrill, carried across the river, reverberated back, echoing off the hillsides beyond, a ragged mocking cry, overlaying itself, one echo merging with the next until it was a continuous, hideous shriek of death.

They were beside him now, other men, switching the flanks of their ponies, lances jabbing upright at the night sky, foam flying from the mouths of the animals, all of them one. Together, as a body, they screamed the cry again and their lances came down, reflecting back the sparkle of the starlight.

One final mine blew in a brilliant flash, metal fragments spattering the ZIL, throwing off showers of sparks and molten metal. Suddenly the ZIL was bouncing over the edge of an embankment, the steel treads grating as they ground over rocks, and then, nose down, it ground to a shuddering halt in the river.

Back across the minefield, a stream of tracers laced above him, and before he heard the blast, he felt the snap of shock waves as the projectiles whined past him. He swung the quads through 180 degrees and squeezed off short bursts, traversing a wide arc, eating up the fence line from west to east.

A flare bloomed in a shower of light, this time fired from the east. He had seen the sparks trail as the rocket was launched and he rotated the quads to the sector, sweeping a line of trees once, then traversing back again. No second flare but the first was brilliant, bathing him in a hard, greenish-white light. He elevated the barrels, aiming higher than the flare, and fired. The flare jerked and, like a falling star, spiraled downward in a lazy corkscrew path, finally plunging into the river with a hiss.

Markoff was shouting at him through the trap, obviously screaming obscenities in Russian. Ignoring him, Brocassie scythed back across the minefield behind him with the gun, watching fascinated as the tracers stitched quadruple lines of gold thread along the perimeter fence. Then one gun hammered on an empty chamber, the other three shuddering dead only a heartbeat later.

Markoff was clambering over the top of the gun pit, screaming, something in his hand. Brocassie swung once, missing, and then Markoff reared up, preparing to lunge.

The AK was on the floor of the gun pit, underwater, and Brocassie grappled for it, the ribbed barrel of the weapon first tantalizing in his hand, then slipping away from his grasp as Markoff dove on top of him, smashing him down into the water which slopped on the bed of the gun pit.

Brocassie scrambled on all fours, then stabbed back-handed with a left jab, but his fist whistled through air, banging against the gun mount. A flash of pain roared through his nerves, paralyzing his hand—the whole of his arm shocked and tingling.

The Russian, enraged, leaped, his knees straddling Brocassie's body, then lifted his arms over his head, hands clasped together and slammed down with a sledgehammer blow onto Brocassie's chest.

513

The first impact was brutal, exploding the breath out of him. Like the sound of kindling being broken, Brocassie heard a crunching, felt the excruciating pain in his chest, knew that ribs were broken. His eyes flooded with tears and he felt the salty taste of blood filling his mouth. On the edge of panic, he twisted, trying to get away from the crushing pressure of the Russian's bulk but he was pinned against the side of the gun pit. Desperate now, he struck back with his right fist, his knuckles grazing Markoff's cheek. The Russian howled in rage, screaming invectives, and lifted his hands once more, together, as if he were chopping wood. Almost in a dream, exhausted, Brocassie watched the Russian's silhouette rise up against the reddened sky.

With everything that he had left, Brocassie rammed his knee up into Markoff's crotch.

The Russian bellowed, propelled forward by Brocassie's kick, his face slamming against the side of the gun pit. Somehow, he staggered to his feet, clutching his genitals with both hands, bent double, stomping from one boot to the other in agony. Brocassie pulled himself up, one hand at a time, sucking in what little air he could get, the tearing pain stabbing at his chest. It was as if there were a roaring fire in his lungs, beginning to burn through the skin. No time, no strength, almost nothing left.

Markoff was staggering around the gun pit like a rabid animal, banging off the sides, seemingly impervious to additional pain. And then, by sheer strength of will, he slowly straightened up. He was mammoth, Brocassie realized, a full head taller than he with shoulders half again as wide. The red glow of the silo fires backlit him, as if he were something stepping out of the fires of creation. Very slowly, distinctly, he said, "I kill you now, *dourak.*"

He lumbered toward Brocassie, his hands spanned out like a Sumo wrestler's.

Backing away, Brocassie felt the edge of the gun pit in his back—too late to throw himself over the ledge into the river. Markoff paused, only a foot or so away, inhaled, preparing to strike, then lunged again, his head low.

With everything that he had left in him, Brocassie

grabbed the gun harness with both hands and heaved. The four barrels of the quads scythed clockwise on their greased swivel, smashing into Markoff's spine. The Russian reared, his back bowing under the impact, roaring in pain, and then he crashed forward, knees buckling, hands gouging at air for support. His body impacted against the edge of the gun pit and his forehead smashed against the armor plate.

Brocassie sank down on his knees, panting, pain lancing through him. He slowly eased down to the floor of the gun pit, stretching out in the warm water, wanting only peace. He closed his eyes and it seemed as if he were sliding down an infinitely long tube, constellations wheeling past him, individual stars of blue-white and vermilion streaking through his vision. Pain, hard in his chest, pulsed with his heartbeat and then gradually diminished to black nothing.

He came to, his mind fluttering on the edge of consciousness, the pounding beat of the diesel vibrating the floor of the gun pit beneath him. He tried to move and found that something was holding him, his body restrained.

"Don't try to move," she said. "Not yet. It's all right. We're safe for now."

He opened his eyes, squinting, looking up into her face. Her hair was matted and damp, her face bruised, dried mud and white dust clotting the pores of her face. She was framed against a steel-gray dawn.

She bent down, putting her lips on his, and kissed him, holding his face gently in her hands, cradling his head between her thighs.

"I thought you were dead," she whispered. "When the explosions started . . ." Twin tracks of tears ran down her cheeks. "You crazy, lovely man. How could you have done it? Maroto told me that both you and Julio were finished, but I knew that you had to get out, knew you would get out, and I told him that even if he and his men left, I would stay because I knew you would come." Her voice was tight and thin yet curiously rich. She kissed him again, her lips holding against his, softly and then fiercely, her hands combing back his hair like a strong spring wind raking aspen leaves.

"He did it, you understand?"

"Julio?"

Brocassie nodded. "He stayed so I could get out. He knew how to destroy them and he did. I lived because of him—*only* because of him."

She looked away for a second, toward the valley, then said, "I thank him for giving you back to me." She put her head down against him, rocking his body, sobbing. They didn't speak for a long time.

Gray turned to cream. Brocassie held her, his eyes focused at infinity, watching the sky framed by the square edges of the gun pit. Branches of pine whipped by and, for a while, he saw the crumbling face of a cliff and a flock of morning doves flushed from a ledge of rock by the howl of the diesel.

The ZIL was climbing like a goat through the lower foothills, the engine straining as the grade became steeper. At times the ZIL would angle up as it scaled an embankment and seconds later would cant crazily downward as it traversed the bottom of a culvert.

Brocassie didn't care anymore, pain and fatigue pressing down on him. She fed him a chocolate bar and water from a canteen, stroking the scar on his forehead, telling him to sleep and, incredibly, he did.

The sun was hard in his face when he awoke. There was something different, and he realized that the ZIL was dead, the engine silent.

The tailgate clanged down. Porto was standing there, his hands on his hips, grinning triumphantly. He was saturated with sweat, filthy with mud. "You want to see what thou hast wrought?" He reached up and he and Alicia helped Brocassie up into a sitting position.

They were halfway up the slopes of the Sierra, just on the tree line. Somehow, in three hours, even though he was unfamiliar with the ZIL and its eccentricities, Porto had brought them up terrain which they couldn't have climbed on foot in six.

Porto slowly scanned the valley floor with binoculars, then handed the glasses to Brocassie.

A thick, rolling carpet of greasy black smoke covered the valley floor, bright splotches of orange glowing through. As he watched, an explosion vomited cartwheeling chunks of debris from a silo. There was a second detonation from the same silo, this time more violent. Meteors of white-hot metal looped up and fell back to earth.

He kept the binoculars to his eyes, fascinated with the destruction. "How many silos went?" he whispered. He handed the glasses back to Porto.

"I don't know. There's no telling. But a lot of them. All of them, I hope."

"Julio . . ."

"Yes—she told me." Porto reached up, holding out his hand. "Come on down—you're the walking wounded now."

Brocassie slid across the gun pit, edged over the gate and dropped to the ground. His brain spun, eyes unable to grab onto something to fix his focus, shapes whirled past him as if he were on a carousel. Porto was holding him by both shoulders. He refocused and the world gradually slowed and then stopped.

"Two ribs, Injun. She's strapped them up with a belt to keep them from moving around too much. You'll need some quack to tape them up properly before too long. Maroto's going to get you down to Trinidad de Cuba. You'll lay up there for a week and then he'll arrange a fishing boat. It's the best he can promise but it's good enough, I think."

"Where in hell are you going?" He examined Porto's face, looking at deep ravines of fatigue spanning out from the corners of his eyes. "We came together, we've got what we wanted and we all go out together!"

Motioning down toward the valley floor, he handed Brocassie the binoculars again. "Down to the left a little, near the outcroppings where two ravines converge."

There was a column of men more than a mile below them, just motes of dust, drifting in slow motion across the rocky sunlit landscape. He counted, squinting. Fifty, he guessed—maybe sixty. He handed the glasses back, his body chilled.

"We've got to get moving again—higher! We can set up

snipers and hold them off until sundown. By tomorrow morning, we'll have lost them."

Porto shook his head adamantly. "We have to split for a while, Brocassie—real soon. I've got an inventory. There are only seven of us left and of that total, four wounded, including yourself." He nodded toward the cab. "Miguel's in there, conked out on morphine. He caught a hunk of metal in his leg and Enrico's going to carry him. Maroto's got a metal splinter in his eye and the other kid—Ruiz—lost a lot of blood and three fingers. Alicia stays with you and that leaves me to volunteer—ace half-track pilot, bullshit artist and mountain goat."

He leaped up into the gun pit and started pulling ammo cans out of the locker, feeding the belts into the loading mechanisms. Finally, he loaded and locked. The brass cartridges gleamed in the morning sun like fingers of burnished gold. He dropped back to the ground.

"The ZIL has a quarter tank left. I can't get her higher on this slope but I can run east along the contours—five, six miles maybe. She's an old, cantankerous bitch but she'll do. You can be damn sure that they'll follow the ZIL's track and when she runs out of fuel, I'll jump ship and head higher and we'll meet up again tomorrow night on the far slope of the Sierra."

"We'll stay with you!"

"And if you did, what would that gain us? If all of you start moving directly upslope, I'll be able to draw them off and still have a good three mile lead on them."

Pulling a cigar from his pocket, Porto bit off the end, spat it out and then lit it. "Fucking piece of cake, Brocassie. They slog up a hot mountainside while I ride in style. They'll follow the tracks of the ZIL but I'll be making six miles an hour to their three. This goddamn thing even has air conditioning— you believe that? Socialist comfort cooling for the armpits of the working masses."

He stepped closer, gently put his arms around Brocassie. "Take care of Miguel, OK?"

Brocassie nodded dumbly.

Porto dropped his hands, not moving, just standing there, smiling. "We had one hell of a good run, didn't we?" He turned to Alicia, kissed her and turned to pull himself up into the cab. The engine ground over twice and then grumbled into life, blue smoky exhaust hazing the slanting sunlight.

He stuck his head back out of the cab, shouting to make himself heard over the noise of the engine.

"Brocassie—if you ever decide to fly again—buy a ticket on Eastern." He showed a mouthful of teeth, cigar canted, laughing.

The machine lurched, tracks grinding, the steel gouging into the rocky ground. The ZIL accelerated, heading east along the contour.

They climbed slowly but steadily, staying hidden in the ravines. The pace was painfully slow but they kept going, not even stopping for rest.

Sometime after eleven, they had breasted an overhanging rock ledge which gave them a broad view of the slopes below.

Twice, in the last hour, Brocassie had heard the distant thumping of the quad-fifties and the answering fire of lighter field weapons. Lying on the edge of the rock, he could no longer see the snaking line of men. All of the firing was well to the east. Porto had given them four, five, maybe six hours of lead time. Enough, he thought, because Maroto was within half a mile of linking up with the rest of his force and they would cover the retreat if it came to that.

She lay down beside him, her hand lightly on his back.

"Can you see him?"

He shook his head. "No."

"Any helicopters yet?"

He turned to her. "I don't think they'd try it. The quad-fifties are antiaircraft weapons. A chopper couldn't get within a mile if he heard them coming. He'll make it." He dropped the binoculars and then reached over, squeezing her arm to reassure her.

The sound at first was masked by the whine of wind in the piñon pines—just a high whistle, very faint, but it grew.

Oh, God, no, he swore. Not now.

He scanned to the east, squinting against the sun, and picked up the wink of light on metal, two specks, very high. The specks grew and now he could hear the hollow roaring howl of their engines.

They were MIGs, the distinctive swept-back wings and shark-fin tails. The fighters split-essed, one following the other only seconds later, diving for the ground.

They dished out below the level of the ridge, flattening their approach, now no more than a few miles away, vectoring east. As they thundered past, he could distinctly see the tanks slung under their bellies, could imagine the pilots leaning forward, centering their target in the reticule of the sights. Both planes jinked in their flight path, making last-minute corrections.

A stream of tracers arced skyward, slinging armor-piercing shells into their flight path, and it was then that the leader jettisoned his tank, his wingman dropping only a split second later.

The tanks tumbled end over end, turning like whirligigs, sparkling in the sunlight, and then Brocassie could see them no longer. There was the lapse of seconds and he was screaming at Porto in his mind to ditch the ZIL, to put distance between himself and the drop zone, and then he caught the wink of the flash and then another, then saw the boiling orange and black cloud of smoke from the napalm.

The fighters pulled up steeply into a chandelle, arced over the top again and started their second run.

The filthy black cloud had mushroomed, billowing up vertically over two thousand feet and blowing off in an anvil trail as the winds caught it.

The fighters came in even lower this time, cannons spraying the terrain in front of them. It was over in seconds and they pulled up, both of them executing a victory roll as they clawed for altitude.

He lowered his head into the cradle of his arms, his lips touching the rock, and wept.

CHAPTER

24

Montana, December 22, 1962

The Chevy pickup barely made it up the final grade, the tires spinning, the chassis slewing from side to side on the frozen crusted snow. Brocassie rode the clutch, willing the damn thing to make it. They crowned the rise of the knoll and slowly drove the last hundred yards. He pulled off the road beside the snow-drifted iron gate of the cemetery.

He left the engine running and the heater on to fight the bitter cold which penetrated the cab. The wind buffeted the truck, rocking it, and snow granules, picked up by the driving wind, whipped past the pickup, through the stakes of the cast-iron fence and danced around the headstones. White dust devils mocking the dead, he thought.

He turned, looking back through the rear window. Behind them, a desolate expanse of plain, achingly white, marked only by a rusted wire fence and the rutted tracks of their own passage. To the west, a range of mountains prodded the bleak skyline, their worn crests hidden in the overcast. But to the south, the plain rolled to infinity with just the haze of a distant mountain range suggesting a horizon.

Turning to the boy, he tried to lift himself from his depression. "In the spring . . ." he said, ". . . after the snow melts in the chinook winds, when the streams run again and when the sun comes north, there are wild flowers as far as you can see, all the way to Mexico." He took his hand and ran it through the boy's hair. Miguel looked up at him, his face bright in anticipation.

"We'll do it this spring? I mean, get horses and ride . . ."

The pale disk of a sun broke through briefly, its light tearing after shadow across the snow-covered plains, and then it was swallowed again by the clouds.

"No, not this spring. Not yet. Another spring," Brocassie answered softly, carefully. "But we'll do it—all of us together—someday. My word."

Miguel accepted it. "I never thought that it would be this big, this empty—empty like the sky—vast and beautiful." He stared for a second toward the south. "Utah's south of here, isn't it? That's where you and your father lived. Will we stop there?"

A cottonwood overlooked the stream where his father rested, finally in peace, Brocassie thought. Our land now, out of their hands. Hagger, at least, had made good on that. "Yes," he answered, "we'll go there. We'll surely go there, Miguel."

Alicia reached over the head of the boy between them and touched Brocassie's neck, stroking it. "And he'll tell you the names of the stars"—her eyes caught Brocassie's—"like he once told me."

He reached back with his hand, taking hers, holding it and then squeezing. "I'll tell Miguel about them. And someday, your child—our child—as well."

She was looking at him, tears suddenly brimming in her eyes. "It is. Ours. I want it to be *ours.*"

In his mind, he knew that it was. Ours. He looked back at her. "A girl."

She shook her head. "No, it will be a boy. Brave like you."

"Braver," he answered, his heart full of love and sorrow. As brave as his father.

He stood next to the pickup's cab, surveying with the binoculars the white vortex of snow which trailed behind the gray car.

It was nondescript Dodge, no markings, a government issue. Two men in the front seat. As it crested the far knoll, it suddenly braked and slewed to a stop. For a few minutes the two men talked and then they got out and walked around to the trunk. The lid opened and one of the men extracted a leather case, opened it and withdrew a rifle. Both of the men looked toward the cemetery on the knoll where Brocassie stood and then they separated, the one left behind resting the rifle on the roof of the vehicle, a telescopic sight winking with reflected light.

Brocassie opened the door of the pickup and gave her the binoculars.

"It's him," he said.

"You're sure it's safe?"

"Yes, it's all right," but he knew that it wasn't. "We have to be finished with them. We can't run forever."

She reached into the glove compartment and removed the Beretta.

He shook his head. "It won't come to that. I can't handle it that way anymore. It's either clean or . . ."

Miguel reached out, taking Brocassie's arm. "I can come with you. I want to be there."

Brocassie shook his head. "No, you'll stay here. Another time when we're here by choice, just us alone." He looked toward the far knoll, then back to Miguel. "If anything happens, *anything*, understand, you and Alicia start south along this road. Keep going and don't look back."

"NO!"

Brocassie took the boy's hand, a strong hand, and folded it in his. "There are things that we all have to do. Sometimes, even when we don't want to. Porto would have told you the same. Do as I ask." He squeezed hard and after hesitating, the boy squeezed back.

"Be careful," she said.

He nodded and closed the truck door, waiting for Hagger.

Hagger labored up the final grade, his white breath ripped away in vaporous balloons by the wind. His skin was wind-blasted scarlet and he wore a fur hat with flaps pulled down over his ears. He looked back once toward his car and then, frowning, covered the final few yards between them.

He reached out and they tentatively touched gloves.

"Long time," Hagger said.

Brocassie nodded. "Not long enough," he answered. Hagger's head was shrouded in a hood lined with wolf's hair. The parka was shabby, a cheap imitation of Air Force winter issue. Brocassie had on snow-white leather mukluks with beaded piping, and canvas trousers which fluttered in the gusting wind. He stared back at Hagger, defiant, unblinking.

"So I'm here," Hagger finally said. "As requested."

Brocassie ducked his head in agreement. "I thought it was finally time we talked."

Together, as if by mutual tacit consent, they turned and headed toward the iron-fenced graveyard.

"You brought it?" Brocassie asked, pushing the gate open.

"I brought it," Hagger acknowledged. He hesitated, stopped. "I'm not going to bullshit you, Brocassie. I want you to know right now that they didn't go for it. Steen fought like hell and paid for his stubbornness with dismissal without pension."

"They fired you too?" Brocassie wasn't even looking at him. He kicked at a rock, half-exposed above the snow but frozen in solid, immovable.

"They're sending me to a place called the Plain of Jars. In Laos. Some kind of a job called 'forward liaison.' The deputy director told me that if I don't catch a bullet or die of malaria, I'll shit myself to death." He tried to smile but the intense cold had cracked his lips.

Brocassie was looking at him intently. "Then how did you get it?"

"In a pawnshop. Some guy who fought in the Second World War. His stepson hocked it for the price of a bottle of wine. It cost me fifteen bucks. I had the original inscription buffed off and Álvarez's name engraved on it. The total was twenty-four fifty. The bastards . . ."

The injustice of it locked up in his mind, constricting his throat. Brocassie swallowed. "They could have taken it out of the coffee fund."

Hagger didn't say anything, just looked down at the snow, mechanically stamping his feet.

Brocassie kept his face impassive. He put out his glove.

Hagger pulled the box from his pocket and Brocassie took it, fumbling open the catch. It was lined with mildewed velvet. The medal rested in a fitted depression. He nodded and turned away, treading tiredly through the stubble, past rows of marble tombstones dulled and eroded by the gritty wind.

There were four markers spaced out in a row, two of them a dull bronze-green, the inscriptions already obscured with verdigris.

"His father and mother—in a way, mine too," Brocassie said, nodding toward the older markers. "A mine cave-in got him and she died a few months later—a disease they couldn't be bothered to identify but I think it's called heartbreak." The other two markers were foundry bright.

In front of one was a shallow hole, no more than a foot square, pickaxed out of the frozen ground, the tools lying in the snow. "I got the markers cast in Dillon and came up yesterday." Brocassie took one final look at the medal, snapped the box shut and placed it carefully into the hole.

He shoveled the frozen clods of dirt into the depression, then hammered the pile down with the back of the shovel, gently at first and then harder and harder, then violently, the steel of the tool ringing like a dull bell.

Hagger hesitated and then took Brocassie's arm, restraining him, slowing him, finally stopping him. Not even looking aside, Brocassie nodded slowly. "I'll come back," he said. "Some spring, when I can do it right. He'd understand."

Hagger awkwardly wrapped his glove around Brocassie's arm. Together, they walked back through the stubble of the cemetery. "The other marker was for Porto. Why? They weren't rela . . ." He stumbled on the word, unable to complete it.

"... related," Brocassie finished for him. "No, they weren't related, Max. If anything, they were enemies but they were still brothers. All of us were brothers in some kind of fucked-up way. *Hermanos,* understand? It's only if you really know the Spanish idiom that you understand what the word means." He paused and looked back at the markers for Porto and Álvarez. The stores in Dillon were broadcasting Christmas carols over street speakers, canned, commercial and impersonal. But one replayed itself again and again in his mind. God rest ye merry, gentlemen, he prayed.

They stopped downwind in the lee of the pickup, stamping their feet, the numbing cold invading their bodies. The cab's windows were misted over but Hagger caught the white oval face of a woman, a hand smearing the condensation, and, beside the woman, the face of a boy.

Brocassie spoke first, his voice flat. "So it turned out right and it turned out wrong. What finally happened, Max?"

Hagger sniffed through his generous nose. He buffed it thoughtfully with a gloved hand.

"After I went through the tape and spelled it out to him, Steen carried it directly to Kennedy, stepped on a lot of people's toes doing that. You might write him a postcard someday and tell him that you appreciated his trying."

"I suppose. And Kennedy ..."

"... did nothing. You understand the way that it works, don't you? Decision by consensus. Committees, contingency planning, State versus Defense, Intelligence versus Pentagon; all of them simultaneously waving their hands and covering their asses. Kennedy chose not to bomb the complex because it was the difference between being morally justified and being politically adept. He didn't give a shit if there were missiles hidden in Cuba as long as the ones that were visible, even if they were phony, were removed. The slopes call it 'saving face.' Other people that I know call it political expediency which rhymes with bullshit."

"But there was a SAC bomber raid inbound on Cuba. Soviet satellites picked it up and relayed their track to the complex."

Hagger nodded his head. "Thirty minutes after Kennedy got the tape, he launched an entire wing. His gut reaction, I suppose, but who in hell knows? They were recalled fifty miles short of Cuba. No explanation. Whether Kennedy got cold feet or whether he was talked out of it by the chicken-shit advisers, no one's going to tell—not in our lifetimes."

"So what's the final score?"

Hagger shrugged, banging his gloved hands together. "You read the papers, don't you?—or do you?" He scuffed at the dribble of his nostrils. "All the U.S. missiles out of Turkey with the rest of the ones in England and Italy to be dismantled next year and promise, cross your heart, never to allow Cuban nationals to invade Cuba from U.S. soil."

"He said he wanted on-site inspection as a final condition."

"He 'said' which is a lot different from he 'demanded.' Castro claims that the Soviets and the Americans made a deal without his consent and he won't let anyone tread on his sovereign soil. It's a dead issue and no one commented on its passing, least of all John Kennedy. In return, the Russians shipped out the SS-4 Sandals on freighters. The fiberglass shells were exposed, their canvas covers thrown back so that we could photograph them for the Sunday edition of *The New York Times.* My guess is that the SS-4s will be sunk in backyards of the party faithfuls' dachas and used as swimming pools for their grandchildren. That's it." He paused. "Oh—just one more small detail. Kennedy pledged never to invade Cuba with U.S. troops but he made a big deal of telling the Russians to keep their hands off Berlin." He stiffened, saluting an imaginary flag. "Land of the free and the home of bravado."

Brocassie edged back and sat down on the bumper of the pickup. "It doesn't matter—not to me, Hagger. Julio took out those silos. Whether or not Kennedy bombed didn't make a difference in the end. They were rubble."

"Eighty-seven of them," Hagger responded, straightfaced. "Key West Naval Air Station picked up low-level radioactive dust two days after your fireworks display and called the Pentagon. The Pentagon called the DIA. The DIA called the CIA and the CIA got a U-2 up over Cuba. Very high levels of radioactivity in that valley with infrared photos confirming only eighty-seven silos blown."

He stomped a two-step on the snow, puffing out his

breath in cadence, and looked hard into Brocassie's eyes. "Which leaves thirty-three untouched. Two weeks after the complex blew, the Soviets flew in decontamination crews, Russian supervisors in hermetically sealed units with self-contained breathing apparatus. And for the last six weeks, they've had round-the-clock shifts of five-hundred-odd Cubans excavating the contaminated topsoil from the silo fields with hand tools, none of them with even the most rudimentary protection. They're all political prisoners, Brocassie, mainly from El Condado Prison and the Isle of Pines. We estimate that the contamination down in that valley is ninety rems—hot enough to give a healthy man a lethal dose of radiation in less than four days. So the Soviets are working them until they drop and then they bring in a fresh batch of five hundred more. It will take months, but they're cleaning it up and we can't stop it because as far as the administration is concerned, the Calvario Complex never existed. The Soviets are probably going to reconstruct the launch facility and there's not a goddamned thing that we can do."

The silence between them was a fissure, then a chasm. Brocassie turned to the cab of the pickup without looking back, his hand on the door.

"I have a message," Hagger shouted after him, competing with the wind.

Brocassie paused, turning, his glove shoved into his parka.

"They want to debrief you. They knew that you and the woman and that kid made Jamaica and then they lost you—picked you back up in the Caymans—lost you again and finally spotted you in Tampico. They let you through the border because they wanted you in U.S. territory. I've got orders to take all of you back."

Brocassie shook his head slowly, almost sadly. "You people never learn, do you?" He rammed his finger against the fabric of the inside of his jacket pocket. "Don't be stupid. I have binoculars. I saw the man with you and his blue-barreled toy with the big scope. Wave him back inside your car and be damn careful how you do it." He nudged the fabric harder, producing a bulge. "Now, Hagger!"

"I don't—"

"Now, Hagger!"

Keeping his hands low, Hagger chopped his wrist sideways. Light glinted from the the rifle's scope and then the figure trudged to the trunk and put the rifle in its case. Ten seconds later, the man disappeared into the fogged interior of the gray car.

Brocassie spoke, carefully, slowly. "They never planned to debrief me and you know damn well why. What they *do* want is another three markers in that row of graves because if it ever came out what really happened in Cuba, there would be a political upheaval in this country unmatched by anything in history. The great unwashed masses of the American people are a good deal more savvy than anyone in Washington ever gives them credit for. Forget it, Hagger. I've got eighty-five double-spaced pages of details on this episode and I duplicated those pages in Mexico and mailed them to six different individuals, to be opened unless they get a postcard from me once every six months for the rest of my slightly unnatural life. Tell them that in Washington, Hagger. It should keep at least half of the agency busy for the next ten years."

"I can still pull you in, Brocassie! Anytime, anyplace."

Brocassie smiled, cracking open the door, then pausing, his foot on the running board. "But you won't, will you? You'll tell them what I just told you and they won't move a finger because they'll be scared shitless." He smiled. "Let the history books tell their lies, Max. It won't be the first time."

"BULLSHIT TO THAT!" Hagger flung back against the wind. "It's my ass on the line."

Brocassie shook his head slowly. "Where's the real moral indignation, Max? Deep down in that fat gut of yours, you realize that you're as guilty of incompetence as the rest of them. All of you, like me, have to learn that freedom doesn't come easily. There's always a price to be paid and sometimes it's painful." He slammed the door.

The pickup, instead of turning back, started south across the track, whorls of dusty snow swirling in its wake.

In his rearview mirror, he saw Hagger raise his fist and for the first time in a very long time, he felt free of the past.

"They'll let us go?" she asked.

"In a manner of speaking," he answered.

The pickup rumbled through frozen ruts, heading south, chasing the sun.

"Where are we going?" she asked.

"Where it's warm and the sea sparkles and the people speak a civilized language. Where it's safe."

She slid her arm across the back of the seat, touching his cheek with her hand, the filigreed ring brushing the stubble of his chin.

Like the warmth of a Mexican sun, he felt its heat.